Senseless

A NOVEL

Paul Golding lives in London.
This is his second novel.

Also by Paul Golding

THE ABOMINATION

Paul Golding

Senseless

A NOVEL

PICADOR

First published 2004 by Picador

First published in paperback 2005 by Picador
an imprint of Pan Macmillan Ltd
Pan Macmillan, 20 New Wharf Road, London N1 9RR
Basingstoke and Oxford
Associated companies throughout the world
www.panmacmillan.com

ISBN 0 330 42721 0

9 8 7 6 5 4 3 2 1

A CIP catalogue record for this book is available from
the British Library.

Typeset by SetSystems Ltd, Saffron Walden, Essex
Printed and bound in Great Britain by
Mackays of Chatham plc, Chatham, Kent

This book is dedicated to Meredith Daneman,
with love

Acknowledgements

The author would like to thank Gillon Aitken, Stephen de Kerdrel, Richard Fowler, Barry Goodman, Daniel Ivens, Karen King, Nigella Lawson, Hugh Lawson-Tancred, Julia Macmillan, Josephine Marchment, Susan Moncur, Jane Reid, Sarah Spankie, Jeremy Wayne, Donald Woodford and, especially, Malcom Todd.

Touch

sense /sɛns/> *noun* **1** any of the five main faculties used by an animal to obtain information about its external or internal environment, namely sight, hearing, smell, taste and touch.

By the time I found myself resorting to the dictionary, I knew that I was running out of words to define my plight, which was overcast. The revelation that I was sailing close to **despair** ('the state of having lost hope') offered me no more guidance than it can have offered comfort to the handful of people whom I then considered my intimates, but whom, despite the pentangle of their affection, despite the glittering asterisk of their assurances, I suspected of moaning in undertones of exasperation about my general impossibleness. It was as if those five disparate digits — falsely extended, varnished, bitten, buffed, filed-down — were, in fact, conjoined, like extensions of the same black glove, a glove which, from the place where I lay floundering, seemed resigned to wave with quiet regret and mourn the loss of me, even before the rocks of disaster had properly been dashed. But, to be fair to those people, to be faithful after my fashion, I *was* a troublesome anchor, rusty with disuse, misuse perhaps. Too heavy to drag.

And yet, those stalwarts of mine, so patient, so forbearing, so full of bounty: how they, for their part, dragged my spirits down. On the advice, I think, of the most outspoken, who happened also to be the loudest, face-to-face encounters with my tricky self were deemed inadvisable — the polite excuse being that I kept peculiar sleeping hours. But the truth, as we all knew, was not so much that I seldom bothered with the telephone during my season of slump, as that I couldn't guarantee any member of my circle, civil as each member was, even the semblance of a civil welcome, any more than they could guarantee that their fruitful kindliness, which I, in my despondency, found the more crushing, would prove beneficial to what they regarded as my tiresome state of mind. For their animated anecdotes about their lives and loves struck me as animated stabs.

And so, instead of calling on me personally, those well-intentioned guardians of my sanity would, with sinister regularity, dispatch to my address – by special delivery, so as to force me to get up, or by courier, if the contents of some cushiony bag seemed, to the relevant sender, to palpitate with vital urgency: scraps of psychobabble about roads less travelled, or pamphlets about SAD, or mystical spookery by Teresa of Avila, or packets of melatonin smuggled from America, or (when I could scarcely drag myself to the lavatory, never mind to the music-system in the study) 'restorative' CDs which amounted to choral nightmares, or even, Christ above, carefully selected nuggets of Literature – in other words, material claiming to pick at the scab of the human condition, a condition with which, try as I might (and to begin with I tried hard), I could not begin to identify.

In my sulky self-absorption, I seldom troubled to acknowledge the receipt of those unsolicited packages; and rather, after a cursory glance at the title of whatever had been sent (and always sent with fondest love), or beyond a sneak at the author's or conductor's or philosopher's close-up, which, to me, was about as inspiring as milk that had soured, I would dump the contents of such heartfelt gestures beneath myself, beneath the bed which once, incredibly, had been like a breathtaking pagan island, yet now remained unmade and grimy and moribund and, of course, lopsided. And then I would consign the postcards which generally accompanied those tributes in the name of (onerous) friendship – lugubrious reproductions of hallowed canvases from the great galleries, depicting, for instance, a shaded tramp with an arty cap of some musty velvet flavour, squatted in a garret which, despite its obvious lack of height, the description of the picture termed a Lofty Alcove, that kind of gag – to the murk beneath the dormant springs of my remembrance. And further weighted into lassitude by the tidal wave of my thesaurus, by its frothy great verbiage, by its sea of wishy-washy, many-shaded, adjectival lies, I would drop that former source of linguistic colour which, in my youth, had seemed more magical to me than any paint-box, into the depths of my squalor, leaving it to gather dust in the gloom that engulfed me, and to mingle – in the company of rotting cartons delivered from Vietnamese restaurants – with floaty, downy balls of apathetic fluff, and the promise of rodents. But what seemed to gnaw hardest at my innards was the fact that neither my feral instinct to survive, nor the reams of information which I'd digested in the past, held me in any kind of stead once I found myself abased to my nadir.

Thus my routine became that when I slept, I merely slept, and when I woke, I swallowed sleeping pills. As a lifestyle this seemed practical to me, unsentimental, businesslike. And sometimes, while I waited for the drowse to take effect, I would hazily revisit my last resort, which, as I say, had become the dictionary – returning, at one point, to its very beginning, opening at the preface in the hope of gleaning something original. Yet what I gleaned was this: that where 'derivative words are obvious, they may also be left undefined (e.g. **bitterness**)'. Bitterness: undefined. Imagine. And then, I looked up **love**, that reddest, hottest of nouns, merely to find myself fobbed off with tepid instances such as 'brotherly love', and 'love of chocolate', and even, I ask you, 'love of the outdoor life'. So in the end, I cast the volume aside, and quietened down, no longer daring to risk a search for that most perfect word of all, which is, in any language, **paradise**, *paradis, paradiso, paradisum* – in case of further disappointment. In case it turned out be a club forbidding entry.

The entryphone buzzed; but finding itself ignored for too prolonged a sequence of dots ...... it buzzed once more, harshly now, as if affronted. What *is* it? (Pause of surprise.) Diliv'ring flowers, rose the reply. To what flat? Yours, mate. (My turn to pause, then groan): Third floor, come up. Because my real thought was: Thanks a bunch for forcing me to root around in search of a vase, *mate.* And yet my friends, those friends whom I had doubted: I sometimes suspect that I didn't do them justice during those delicate, terrible months in the mire, for the truth of the matter is that — for all my sourness and my bile — they were, in their way, wise, and careful, and generous with their time, just as it is true that, despite the sting in the nettles which I'd allowed to entangle me, all of them managed, with their varied interpretations, which were like differing species of the same essential plant, to read me like a text-book palm, like an open, upturned hand: with skill and yet with honour, intelligently, and always — it is true — with fondest love.

Indeed, the incident of the florist's boy, who was their arrow, their envoy, their Mercury in disguise, serves as an instance. For, as if to refute my surly preconception of a hassle, what, in the event, materialised was not some heavy floral imposition, demanding that stems be docked and leaves be plucked, and warning, on a bossy complimentary card attached to a sachet full of salts, that fresh water be provided without fail on Monday-Tuesday-Wednesday-Thursday while capricious Mother Nature took her course. Far from it; shamingly not. (I was so often wrong; I so often wronged my people.) Instead, what was conveyed to my door was a small, white cardboard box with a hole on top, its fragile lid and body held together by a yellow satin ribbon, a box which might, in another context, have housed an Easter egg for a bachelor, or a newly-hatched chick, some fledgling full of dreams. Yet when I took possession of that trembling mystery, I did so less gingerly than crudely, half-cursing that what the world owed me was not dreams, but a life. A tip for Mercury? You must be joking.

Tucked beneath the bow, and almost obscured from view, I found her note, composed in advance – in advance, that is, of her walk to the florist's; because, knowing her as I did, a walk it would have been, a bracing one in lace-up shoes. When, once, I had tried, whining down the telephone from my bed of apathy, to explain that I couldn't go for supper because there was a Tube strike and I'd never find a cab – A cab? she had rebuked me; why on earth should I need such a thing? I had a working pair of legs, didn't I? Well, then; I was to move them, did I hear; no good lazing about. See you at eight fifteen.

I regretted that she, however fondly, should consider me lazy – as opposed to, say, languorous, which, not least adjectivally, I would have found less damning; but even when my life became a fallen pack of cards – got out of hand – she was never, despite her vigorous principles, so frank as to call me a slob; not, at any rate, within my earshot. Her opinion (and, being a seasoned analyst, she was probably the most qualified among my friends to formulate such a thing) had been that my spirit, and not my stamina, was what had weakened; it had been my heart, and not my legs, which needed airing; it was not with my ingrowing misery, but with my dark reclusion, that she took issue.

But you see: in my late teens, when she and I had first been introduced, I'd been the kind of boy who inspired high hopes. There'd been a brittle brilliance about me, for I was reckless, and stylish, and on occasion witty. People could tell that soon enough I'd vault into the future like a gleaming javelin. Yet as the years began to creep, and still I showed no signs of pulling off that trick known as achievement, my mouth grew pinched, and the faces of the people round me assumed expressions of uncertainty, disappointment even, as if, having earlier taken it as read that I was bound to impress the world with some great feat, now, though they regretted it, really they'd been left no

prudent option but to harbour second thoughts in advance of
– as it were – publication.

Anyway, she, the analyst, had never (ironically enough, you
may think) indicated that I seek psychological treatment – an
arrangement which she could have made in a matter of
minutes, seeing to it that I went to one of her more 'intuitive'
colleagues. Rather, her view was that I simply needed redirect-
ing – like that javelin which, though feared to have gone
missing, had merely strayed a little melodramatically. And
the redirection of my self could best be achieved, she once
explained, not by years of intensive therapy, nor, indeed, by my
constant popping of pills, which she openly criticised as cava-
lier, but, more simply, by what she called decent (meaning
honest) guidance. Loving guidance from my friends; guidance
from my loving friends. Take your pick. In retrospect, I think
that despite her seniority, she may also, of my group, have been
the most naïve. Without doubt she was the most spiritual.

The florist's where she had gone, would, a year before, have
been her local, a mere few yards from the place where she then
lived; but now that she was married, and she had married late,
it lay some greater distance from the house where she held
intercourse with her distinguished husband, a white-haired
physicist who, though newly risen toward rich, had already
begun to droop, like some contradictory graph, toward dreari-
ness. Yet that greater new distance, that extra wedded mile,
wouldn't have concerned my friend at all – not a whit, not a
jot. (Such, despite her philosophical claims to classlessness, were
the old-fashioned glints, the flashes from a privileged upbringing, which sometimes escaped to betray her otherwise neutral
vocabulary. 'Dashed' was another.) Anyhow: the florist's shop.
This, you could tell from the lettering that crawled, caterpillar-
like, along the narrow yellow ribbon securing the box which
I was still holding, was a staple establishment in Knightsbridge,
quirkily traditional, and possibly boasting a royal warrant – not
that such trivia would have impressed my friend. Petty social

accents left her cold. It was simply the type of place to which, in her girlhood, she would have been dragged by her mother during some shopping jaunt, and to which, year in, year out, she now returned from comfortable habit rather than out of snob-bishness. The interior was almost shambolic, like an English country house during the holidays, and the floor, as well as being littered with foliage, was often rowdy with dogs. But more relevant, from my friend's point of view, was the fact that it sold the most resilient flowers to be found in town, grown on the estate belonging to the woman, or should I say Lady, who ran the shop – as a hobby of sorts, one half-suspected, as a means of seeing her London friends more often than if she were permanently ensconced in the provinces. For, on the occasions when I was driven to those premises (literally, I'm afraid to say), the air seemed filled, despite the grimness of the street, with the chirrups and the trills and the thrillings of a cocktail party swelling into blossom on some summer lawn in Gloucestershire.

I presumed the note to have been written beforehand – first, because my friend was a thoughtful woman rather than impul-sive: I couldn't see her leaning on a soggy marble counter to concoct some message off the cuff. And my second reason con-cerned the envelope itself, which, in deliberate contravention of what is perceived as smart, meaning the smart sort of stationery customarily found at florists' shops, my friend had used an en-velope which was remarkable for its very ordinariness – though, in deference to her claims to classlessness, one might refrain from describing it as infra dig. Yet it remains the case that, if only in social terms, her chosen envelope was inverted, verging, as inverts often can, on the indiscretion of transparency, and erring, in odd places, on the side of shabby. But I knew her well enough to rein back my critical horses, for she belonged to the type of sensibility that values the high seas and mountain peaks and tropical rainforests above the slickness of the city. It would never have occurred to her, as it sometimes did to me, that among the purposes of nature's splendours was surely the provision of worldly luxury. I suspect that she found sophistication vulgar, and sybarites, by and large, dreary (unlike physicists), because, on several occasions in the past, occasions which, when I think back, seem to have grown in frequency as her rhythms towards matrimony grew, she chided me for what she viewed as my suspect fondness for the superficial – social niceties, as she dismissed them. Never mind that she should treat her father's exquisite fountain-pen with such uncommon ardour: the implication seemed to be that, had the vintage implement been a humble twig which once upon a time he'd used to amuse himself playing noughts and crosses in the sand, she would have prized it just as highly. I doubt that she really understood how my affection for what she – fondly but sardonically – described as Matters Isthetic, had little to do with my insecurities in the face of the public, with my panic in the teeth of society. The reverse was true: if I valued objects of quality and beauty to a degree which she considered exceeding, it was because they assuaged my private anxieties, my inner – but waking – demons, which were proportionately exaggerated, and ugly. She, however, would have none of this, or, at any rate, feigned not to comprehend such superfluous attachments to what she termed the Inanimate – as if seas and rocks and skies had hearts.

Her script, to which the envelope bore witness, was loosely (yet safely) italic, and, like the books which she insisted on sending me, insisted on being taken seriously. But it did so subtly, for, in scale if not in content, it was smaller than an academic's. Were one to be feeling mean-spirited, one would say that it hoped to be regarded as scholarly, for those minuscule words of hers were almost immodest in their smallness, inflated despite their diminution: they taxed your eyes, and seemed to suggest that if you were a worthy reader of her wisdom, the least that you could do was jolly well pick up your magnifying glass, which she called a loupe. It got on my nerves rather; but, admittedly, it didn't take much to enervate me in those days; so I pushed the note aside, opting, first, to go for the box. And yet

– was there no justice? – even the ribbon proved irksome, for, beneath its fetching little bow, there lurked a tight, obnoxious knot. But I don't suppose that she could reasonably be blamed for this. Scissors.

What lurked within the crinkling folds of tissue was a single, monstrous thing: its complexion, bilious green, as if diseased; its petals, stricken with flesh-coloured frills, like puckered scarring; its body, splattered with a spray of blood which seemed to deepen as it rushed toward the focal orifice. And since the flower (as you've already guessed) happened to be an orchid, the whole thing struck me as, well, not exactly apposite for a twitchy queer, which is why, in my spikiness, I chose to inter-pret my friend's gesture not as a token of amity but as a tissue-veiled (yet blatantly homophobic) insult – less botanical than anatomical, like a sexual slight from a siren to some impotent. But I felt relieved rather than peeved that her vulvar snub should possess no distinctive scent – not just because I reviled, no matter how fresh, the stench of fish, but because, in my days of absorbing useless data, I had learned that certain members of the orchid family come imbued with canny under-smells designed to attract libidinous insects, smells such as that of rotting meat, and that of chocolate (like the **love** in the dictionary). So while I extracted the repugnant floral specimen from its cardboard carapace, I tried to temper my spleen with the hope that, if nothing else, her botanical conceit had cost my friend a pretty penny. Which reminds me.

Her name was Cara, and, despite the envenomed swamp through which I was then wading – even then – it befitted her; she wore it well. People in her midst, myself included, held her dear, though, on occasion, one couldn't help but hear, tagged to her appellation, the (perhaps less unconditional) attribute Formidable. But it nevertheless shames me to recount how, during one of my final forays before recoiling into chronic anti-sociability, I foolishly unhooked the sturdy coupling of our former friendship, the shining bond which for years had linked us, and set the wheels of my own wagon, which, though the younger, felt more loaded, into reverse motion, allowing myself to roll and roll away until, by the time that I had come to a crashing standstill, a painful chasm had opened between us.

It happened during a dinner held at her old flat in honour of the white-haired physicist, to whom she'd already become engaged and whom she wanted me to meet; but I doubt that anyone's approval came into it, for the dynamics between the newly betrothed bore all the signs of a fait accompli. At any rate, shortly after we'd been seated, my friend began, perhaps out of nervy timidity, to tease me about my weakness for bath-oils blended by monks in Fiesole, and bed-linen embroidered by nuns in Seville, and about my rampant materialism, and about what a sucker I was for beauty and all the rest of that shit – but she made these observations not conspiratorially, not like some affectionate in-joke just between us; oh no, she did so most publicly. It was all offered up, or so it seemed to me, like a tray of extra titbits for the delectation of the company, as if my pleasures, or my failings, were dainty sweetmeats eventually to be gobbled with coffee, delicious; and suddenly, too entrapped to think, I heard my mealy mouth, loud and fast and clear, snipe and ask whether the assemblage took the name of our hostess to mean that truly she was cherished, or – now glaring at the newly rich physicist – plain expensive. It all went askew: the table chilled in an instant, the air fell silent, glasses were set down swiftly. Freeze. But it served her right, I recall telling my-self: the radiantly happy should watch their radiant repartee, to say nothing of their menus. I mean, producing oysters, the nerve of the woman. Yet within seconds I was sorry, and later, sorrier still, for I never forgot how her features crumpled at my viciousness, a viciousness which, for once, had vaulted round the room like a superlatively directed javelin, bouncing from corner to corner to corner, eventually to return with a glitter-ing summersault, and pierce her. And ever since that dreadful evening, I had feared that the pastoral landscape of our earlier intimacy had been marred beyond the possibility of a second view – especially once she had ceased to be single. All of which perhaps explains why, now, I felt apprehensive about what might yet be awaiting me, tucked within the gummy flap of that remarkably ordinary envelope, which was self-sealing. But in the event, what I was about to read, conveyed on paper torn out of an exercise book (and I'll skip the opening endearment) was this:

I hope you won't treat the enclosed as an excuse to laugh about my taste having sunk to the level of a floozie, because I'm sending it for a better reason. I won't deny that for myself I might have preferred some rarer member of the species, such as a Lady's-slipper, which still crops up very occasionally in Yorkshire of all places. But for you I've chosen, & with some care, what I wd like you to take as a sign of my basic respect for yr love of artifice & luxury. What you have here, or rather there, is a prize-winning Asiatic hybrid, specifically bred for the increase of beauty, known as a Clair – not Claire, please note – de Lune. This particular flower is described in horticultural circles as a masculine type on account of its heavy texture & chunky appearance, which if I'm not mistaken is how you used to like your men before you decided to descend into your well of loneliness (joke). Anyway, it's a butch flower, so please let's have no talk of yoni (!). I miss you. My life isn't always as good as it seems. Yours isn't always as bad as it feels.

Fondest love,
C.

P.S. We're all going to be fine. Touch wood. xx

I took her at her word: I did touch wood, and touched it almost instantly, because tears from her masculine flower were dropping, like medicinable gumme, onto the gleaming face that was the surface of my table, tears which I quashed with a finger, and licked. I should explain that during the months of my descent into the well of loneliness about which my friend had joked (months which – even if one weren't a lesbian – were actually no joke at all), only that table, of all the valuable but futile props which then shored up my solitude, vied with the four-poster for my wasting reminiscence; and yet, even as I lurched, half-stoned, from bed-pillar to postal knocks and, past the table, back to rot, it seems to me that I must have shrunk, must have shrivelled from a proper noun into a superfluous adverb. In lesbian terms, you could say that I'd become the embodiment of that ultimately pointless Just in the song where the white Sapphic beehive with the soul of a black girl cries, in a voice of such wrenching futility as to make you want to gash your arteries, that she Just don't know what to do with herself – only to change her tune, a few bars on, and wail, instead, that she don't know Just what to do with herself. The switch in emphasis may seem hair-splitting to you, teasing; and fine, call me a pedant, but let's not call it quits, because it didn't feel like quits to me, not during that irritable era. Even lyrical inconsistencies bothered me; they niggled. Remember: I was still at the stage of mere furniture, of objects inanimate, like the seas and the rocks and the skies which my friend, the thoughtful analyst, whose life wasn't always as good as it seemed, regardless admired.

I returned to bed, dragging in my wake disordered recollections of the table. We went back years, it and I. We shared a history. Let's rewind. By the time I'd finished school and moved to London, I was already involved with someone whose reflection I had met, by sexy accident, along a shop-glass on some high street in town. From the point of impact, by which I mean our first encounter during one of my half-term exeats,

I'd been struck by two main things about him: his blond and blue-eyed charm, which seemed to smile almost to distraction, and the fact that, unlike most of my earlier pick-ups, this one seemed classy, spoke not with the dreary nasal whine of some naked civil servant, but like a gentleman. He, however, had, in priceless contrast, been impressed not by my voice, nor by my youth, nor even by my starving eyes, but by my jumper, which (mistakenly) he diagnosed as Punky. It made you think of a man remarking on a girl's smart frock when in point of fact she's wearing a pinafore; yet, to me, such lack of fashion-savvy seemed endearing, sort of masculine. Perhaps, however, I should have paid closer attention to his polo-neck, which would, very likely, have been of black lambswool. But because he was rushing off on some appointment and couldn't stop for a drink and a chin wag on the genius of Hockney – the sort of topic which, in those days, queers employed by way of investigative overture – I scribbled down his number, told him I was going back to boarding school in the morning, but added that I would phone. Promise! he shouted as he raced away to the Underground; and I remember waving in a daze, as if my promise went without saying. And as I turned and returned to wherever I should have been, I knew with sudden certainty that I was smitten. Because not once, during the rush of blood from my brain to my heart, had I given a thought to his penis. This was different.

We dated during my escapades from school on odd weekends, and once or twice indulged in variegations of MM (mutual masturbation); and even though the grail of simultaneous climax seemed to elude us, I was unconcerned. It would all resolve itself, I felt convinced, once he'd asked me to move in. Which, in the fullness of time, he did. And thus I came to live, in a cul-de-sac considered smartish, with this man, who, being both circumspect and personable, had accoutred his bedroom with twin beds, as if he had a brother – yet whom (even as he gave a wide berth to the pornographic outlets of Earls Court, with their shelves of cellophaned grot and fridges full of poppers) I soon discovered liked, by way of bedtime sport, to conjure from beneath his single mattress: a leather collar, safely tan, conventionally studded, and purchased from the pet shop at Harrods – a restraint which, thinking back, I wore with most revolting acquiescence, and to which, with a creak and a click, he used to link a matching, top-stitched, everlasting lead: lead-kindly-light-among-the-encircling-gloom-lead-thou-me-on.

Religiously minded was this man to the degree that, after I lost my faith in him, and lapsed, and buggered off with some much grander find who carried my bags but didn't offer to house me, and I began, from the principality of Bedsitland, to hit the hardening discos where, just before the initial tide of rectally-begotten hepatitis, I found myself, predictably enough, treating hopeful men like hopeless mongrels, I learnt from a chatty **sheitel***-basher (homo-Yiddish for a hairdresser, until the global homo opted for the Belsen cut) that my former Chum, with whom this crimper had seen me out shopping, though not at Harrods, was well on the way to becoming a bride of Christ – a *via crucis* which he was to complete, it later transpired, with the full-pelt fervour of a charity marathon, in record-breaking time. But I'm rushing.

Mr Respectable was, during the weekdays of our unholy alliance, a not very able barrister who called people Sunshine, misused words like *Simpatico*, and occasionally was heard to whisper, in relation to some colleague – always male, and always (purportedly) handsome – the quaintly predatory initialisms favoured by pooves of the era, initialisms such as TBH (To Be Had). But at weekends – on Sundays, to be precise – he was in the habit, after an ecumenical apéritif at some camp Victorian shrine embedded in the folds of London's *shmatta* quarter, of jumping into a cab and rushing, full of ardour, back to the flat, where, once he'd yanked down the blinds and scrubbed his

---

***sheitel** (pron. shytl): wig worn by Jewish orthodox married woman (Yiddish).

lollipop with soap that stank of carnation, we would celebrate our regular, conjugal, bestial mass, which, to me, was a bestial travesty, for I was in search of stallions in my youth, not spaniels, or poodles, or pugs. But, you see, the bribe which I chose to pay for the balm of feeling wanted seemed, to me, not ruinous at the time, for I knew boys who, so frenetic were they to show off the safety-pin of Loving Coupledom, that they assented to being swaddled in nappies, in which they had to wee-wee, the better to provide Best Uncle, or Kindergartenmeister, or Baden bloody Powell with a 'good' reason for spanking. Naughty Baby; Baby Naughty (whack). And after their drooling initiators had wheeled out, from unobtrusive cupboards, assorted components of cot, which could be assembled in a trice, those boys, those babies who were only babies emotionally, would further accede to wearing bonnets of frilly *broderie*, and – foetally curled on plastic sheets which resembled dead stretches of skin – to being snapshot with Polaroids while sucking a thumb, or chewing on an ivory teething-ring, or milking some overscaled dummy, of pastel infant blue, but always, always trying to be natural, coyly to smile, like consenting adults. Their feet stuck out beyond the white bars. I'd seen the photographs. One such boy was my brother. But he can wait, no reason why he shouldn't; not now. It's the story of the table that can't.

While I lived with the man who was destined, in time, to apply a dog-collar to his own straining neck and, with stupendous irony, transubstantiate the object of a fetish into a symbol of piety, I was forbidden from answering the telephone. It would have been a transgression; I must be strictly outgoing; I was on my honour to observe this small commandment, which, by hushing it, he tried to dress down to a request, like a low-mass chasuble rather than some high-flung vestment. And though times have certainly changed – insofar as now I couldn't be more inward if you paid me – his little rule used to make me feel like a houseboy who couldn't be trusted not to blurt out that Sir was having his siesta; but my landlord's point was that you never knew who might ring, any more than you could tell what they might think if their calls to a confirmed whatsit were to be answered by some unknown quantity (meaning Dizzy Queen – and underage to boot, which older fairies called Chicken, even if what they really meant was chickenfeed). I told him to get those people whose unreadable imaginings inspired such enigmas to ring him in Chambers. He told me to grow up and be reasonable. But the (unconfessed, uncomfortable) truth is that reason had less to do with our connection than the fact that, despite the gap of fifteen years which yawned and blushed between us, and despite his amateurish claims to dominance, the man was feebler, and feebler-minded than I – and heaven knows there's nothing more infuriating than a smart-arsed teenaged fruit. Dear God Preserve Us was one of his more frequent invocations, and I presume that in the end God did. But during my period of bondage to Mr Respectable, as he then was, he devoted his working day to fouling his legal briefs, and to keeping the shame concealed in the company of his great other professional secret, of which, then, I was living proof, while I mooched about the flat, musing over the bore that was the noun **career** (as opposed to the verb, which seemed less dreary) and binding bits of legalistic tape – described as Red (like love), but actually, and perhaps more fittingly, Hot Pink (like lipstick) – around my genitals.

I was expected (for the sake of decency – which, from him, in contrast to my friend the analyst, never once meant honesty) to pay good honest rent, like a good honest paying guest, PG – a service which I used to render by cheque. But from the outset I was asked to leave a blank in the place of a payee, as if I were amnesiac, in case he should 'forget' to draw lolly from his smart bank in the City, and unexpectedly need to cash, at the local all-night supermarket, my weekly contributions to what he called the Kitty. Discreeter, really, than having some unrelated name crop up with suspect regularity on your statements. You get the creepy gist.

If he took me to *Simpatico* restaurants, which occasionally he did – generally in basements stapled with hessian, and generally when he was feeling miz after some (undisclosed but transparent) litigious defeat – it wasn't because he was liberated when he was in civvies: it was because he feared to be seen associated with me in the less straightforward, less forgiving Het arena. He thought, and often said, that I gave myself away, dressing like That, by which he meant: like a **mincer** (not defined, derivative word obvious); and I would try to explain that the only person I was giving away was him, because I had sweet FA to fear – but such, I suppose, is the false courage of youth. Yet what lay beyond dispute was his other reason for dragging me to those subterranean pits where the food was worse than uneatable and the service better suited to a folding escort agency, down on its knees. And the reason, you see, was that he felt allured to the uncomplicated charms of yummy little waiters who didn't speak English but smiled like a dream, and who, as a matter of course, seemed to park their yummy little crutches on his corner of the table, treating me, while grinning at him, with the specific sort of scorn more customarily reserved for the Other Woman. Meanwhile I, in my adolescent desperation, could be heard to protest that waiters so distracted by the art of being coquettish that they couldn't distinguish between their left and their right, between a fork and a knife, weren't really of much use for the purposes of waiting. He would make a point, while persisting with his treacherous flirtations, of ignoring that which later he would criticise as my petulant behaviour; so I, as if equally oblivious to his antics with those waiters, would move on to the subjects of the tacky paper tablecloths, and the crappy flower arrangements, and the nasty salmon candles stuck into cheap bottles of rosé, and on and on I would go, inwardly weeping tears of candlewax, while the man-cunts on nearby tables muttered among themselves, arching well-plucked brows, about how, OK, so I was a Dish and TBH and practically jailbait, but really, poor Mr Respectable, what a penance to have to pay for the sweet crime of my proximity. Rather him than them, sort of thing. Hideous, the very memory.

When his parents came for supper (which he called Dins), I was always requested, with elaborate and slightly nervy courtesy, to make myself scarce for the evening, could I possibly, and to clear the bathroom of incriminating evidence. His jittery index would quiver over my moisturizer by way of instance, as if the offending tube were a tube of lubricant. So I, rebuffed but obedient, would take myself in exceedingly constricting jeans to pubs where I got pissed on the kindness of strangers whom, after I'd stood on a basin and smashed the light-bulb on the cottage ceiling, I would encourage to go ahead and suck on me, though not in the cubicles. I wanted parties. There was something refreshingly vengeful about those high-speed orgiastic scenes, starry almost; but they were also, I've realised since, counterproductive, for they bred a confusion: I was, in effect, misusing men whom I might perhaps have liked yet had no chance of liking while my feelings remained chained, like a dog to its kennel, to the rotten wood of the future priest – an offence more grave than answering a forbidden telephone. An offence for which, ultimately, there *is* a price to pay, and not by cheque to some bank in the City.

Those parents of his were, he said, nice – which didn't ring entirely true, rather like the expression Straight-Acting. They lived in Hampstead, a district which, though unknown to me, he managed to portray as tantamount to a social knife-edge, for my beloved (and it horrifies me to admit that I loved that man with a passion more blinding and more potent than bleach) liked to emphasize how, despite the location of their homestead, his Ma and Pa were – Look, put it this way – emphatically Goy. His sister, the *shiksa*, whom he called Siss and I had heard wore spectacles, was training to become a bookbinder, a circumstance which seemed to worry the rest of the family: this was no way to find a husband. I was never to merit an introduction to my common-law in-laws, those 'nice' people; but their only son, whose (Christian) name was David, used, when away on holiday – which he always took 'solo', and always at give-away Sitges – Easy, he called it – to sign his illiterate letters to me (which I treasured, and kept, and to this day retain – come and have a disbelief some time: talk about evidence) with the pseudonym Daddy. Perhaps this was in a bid to protect his legal purity; perhaps it resulted from some less pure instinct; but, whatever the reason, he needn't have worried, not really, because his writing alone, taught to him by some army-buffer at a prep school for thickos, betrayed him with ease – like Sitges. And yet, notwithstanding the ignominy of that revealing scribble, he, in keeping with the class of his parents, the Goys of Hampstead, would have regarded it, basically, as Pukka. Pukka my arse. But I'm steering too close to **bitterness**.

As the wastage of my feelings for my fatherly landlord began to dawn on me (and it's surprising how long it can take to stir from the obstinate sleep of enthralment), so another wastage – perhaps less harsh to confront, but no less vivid for that – began to spread, like a **rash** ('an outbreak of red spots'), over my mirror-image. It involved an unattractive change of tack (the mental equivalent of scraping gunk from one's eyes); and yet, after the first few hesitant blinks of disbelief, this reflective shift, this alteration, seemed to stare back at my blotchy features and refuse to budge until I'd accepted the facts, which lay beyond financial, or even legal, dispute. Here was I, I suddenly realized, shelling out good honest rent, by the week and blithely upfront, to a man who, though he was never officially to declare either my payments or my (im)proper status in his inner chamber, treated me less like a rightful tenant than as a cornered servant, a servant who, whilst forbidden from answering the telephone, and forbidden from engaging with his master's social circle, was nevertheless encouraged, under implicit penalty of emotional death, to submit to that same master's strictly personal and confidential pleasures – his assertive am*use*ments, as it were. Firm but fair, you might say; or Suit yourself; or even – had you been he – It's a free country, Sunshine, take it or leave it. But when the farcical injustice of my domestic set-up finally struck me, which it did like a fist crashing through glass, it was my pride, and not my face, which was left bloodied; for, though my heart had become enslaved by stupid mishap, my spirit had never been servile. I may even, when at last I saw the miserable light, have smirked at myself in that bathroom. Certainly I hope that I moisturized. And thus began the discontented worm to turn. I decided to do nothing **rash** ('reckless', this time), but rather to prepare, with cuntish guile, to reclaim my freedom before I died; I would start to make provision for an afterlife, like a disenchanted girl who, even as she spreads her legs to welcome her man, is already making plans for his successor. Survival. Cheap at the price. That was the truth of the matter.

Which is when I began to lie. As if to test the strength of his Christian charity over the strength of his less admirable impulses, I pleaded, on an evening like any other, a sudden, painful attack of poverty. My parents' infantile allowance, I cringed, no longer stretched to meet the needs of my grown-up life. I had fallen on hard times (like the prodigal son with his parabolic tail tucked up his arse). Mr Respectable had been right, I flattered him: I must learn to stand on my own two feet (like a dog performing tricks). And then, as he summoned a grimace of concentration, I wondered whether he'd react like a flustered landlord trying to mask his outraged avarice, or whether he might put a nicer complexion on the issue, like his parents, or nicer still, sort of nice with a twist of *Simpatico*.

He did, initially, look taken aback, though less like a landlord than like a penitent whose confessor had doled him too harsh a penance; but then, he turned reflective, contemplative, until, in the end, he buckled under the pressure, like a believer who's been good-and-properly had. The best that he could offer, he announced with protracted gravitas, was to waive my rent for what he called the Duration, as if my life were a war, on the understanding that I promise, as from tomorrow, to make a concerted (not effort, but) resolution to find some (not job, but) gainful employment. I could not have been more grateful, nor, in my own deceitful turn, nicer about his (not response, but) answer. And later that night, after a stiff covert whisky, made covert by a glug of mouthwash, I whimpered with great gratitude as he lashed my hide with his strap – a touching performance, you might say, since I was, after all, touching my punter for the money, touching him for the knockdown price of my ill-but-hard-earned liberty. Fake your way out of it, I told my yowling spirit; feign commitment to this agonizing imbecility; pointless to growl, never mind bite, at the hand which doesn't even know that from now on, slowly but assuredly, it will be feeding you the succulent bone of your exit. Heel, Achilles.

I heeled all right; heeled until he, patting about his person for spectacles-testicles-wallet-'n-watch, as was his matutinal tradition, had left for The Temple. And then I headed out, dolled up like That, in a beret and a pair of navy pumps, smoothly past the supermarket, to the Post Office a few doors down, where I opened a savings account. And for quite some weeks – months, in fact – as Mr Respectable and I, his impoverished lodger (whom he, without a trace of irony, described as 'strapped'), persisted with the pantomime of our mismatch, I paid myself, with dogged, faithful regularity, my unpaid rent, the spoils of my emotional handicap, spoils which, at first, I merely accepted as my dishonest justice, but later, as the stash began to mount, I grew to regard as a glinting two-edged weapon, rather like Hampstead.

On the nights when he was – sorry, Sunshine – working late, or attending an ecumenical charade followed by some similarly garnished repast, or paying a call on his bookbinding Siss (who, after all the worry, had put her specs to efficient use and found herself a man – though not, it was sincerely hoped, a prospective husband, for the family was of the opinion that her Chap, as they called him, some seedy librarian from South London, didn't altogether cut the mustard, but anyway, who gave a damn), I would make out that I was meeting friends of my own age, survivors from my school, a hyper-religious asylum which, though notably more rigorous and infinitely more snotty than the dump which had taught Mr Respectable his pukka but risible hand, he nevertheless saw fit to criticize for having failed in its essential function; for we, he said, (by which he meant the few contemporaries whom I, in my rose-tinted folly, had introduced to him at the start of the mirage which was to blur into a sadomasochistic farce) had all turned out to be a bunch of screaming nances. I put him right. We had turned out to be nothing of the kind. We had turned into symbols of promise, pearls within oysters. For we considered ourselves to be silver-tongued, and sharp as all get out, and cynical as undertakers, and surely destined for the stratospheric heights, which we didn't imagine encompassed either the law or sanctimony. Watch this space, we used to tell ourselves. Only takes one break, one lucky photograph. Matter of time. That kind of guff.

When we Chickens got together, which was generally in pairs, but sometimes in more colourful nosegays, at bistros in Chelsea, it was neither for discussions on the meaning of life nor for tips about the stock-market, although one of us – not a schoolfriend, as it happened – did make a point of wearing (folded, never rolled) the pink financial paper under his arm. No: when we convened, it was for more subversive meetings on how to screw the system, which, often as not, boiled down to Parents: What was the use of money to Crinklies, for God's sake? It was the young who needed readies to make headway in the world. But anyway, at these sessions of ours, where a single glass of wine, ever diluted, could be made to last a lifetime, the sole noun to be outlawed was, needless to say, Career (unless that noun should happen to be preceded by the adjective Modelling); but everything else, including composite cards and casting couches and the myth of a perfect sixty-nine, to say nothing of **feltching***, was on the agenda. And thus we would sit, in attitudes of smoky ennui better suited to the cafés of Montparnasse, swapping intelligence of our latest discoveries – the marvel of henna, for instance, marvellous for its impermanence, or the madness of a perm, which turned you straight into Colette, or the tacky appeal of a good cap sleeve, which transfigured you into a *matelot* from Marseilles – and arguing about whether folkloric dress could ever be stylish, which, with the exception of the sari, I strongly doubted. I mean to say: lederhosen, too incredible.

But we all concurred on two things: the irksome supremacy of black queens when it came to disco-spins, and the utter fabularity of the wedge-cut, always flicked to best advantage in ultraviolet nightclubs where they blasted you with tracks about being In The Navy, and about being More Than A Woman, and about Family (which my brother and I had refined to a grinding, incestuous classic), and even – the irony of it – about Doing or Dying; clubs where, if any of us happened to meet, the deal was to see who could get bought drinks quickest, which often meant trying to predict what the benefactor whom you had picked would want to hear: that you were butch, or, (less often) bitch. Drinks: one for yourself and (this was the tricky bit) another for your friend over there, who, as you pointed toward a bleary distance, was nowhere to be seen, for he was always round the corner, making up to some other possibility. And

***feltching** (sexual slang): the custom of sucking one's ejaculate out of one's partner's anus and introducing it to his/her mouth. (No longer considered smart.)

yet we, we greedy chickenfeed, seemed never, either sober or pissed, to discuss the question of love. I think that we found it embarrassing. But the embarrassing truth is that on the evenings when I pretended to Mr Respectable that I'd arranged to meet those screaming nances of whom he held so dim a view, I'd made no plans whatever, because, in my frenzy to find some new redemptive love, I always sallied forth alone, believing that such arduous, ardent searches aren't assisted by the sight of your friends catching sight of you across the bar and laughing, or catching you with your favourite pair of jeans, the colour of clay, rucked about your ankles.

It was on one of my solitary excursions that I met the much grander Find who was eventually to come to my rescue – an eye-surgeon with an hereditary title. This honour he wore ambivalently, with an awkward sort of pride, as if he were sporting an eye-patch; and yet, for all his honorific bashfulness, there could be no doubting his regard for his well-earned house, which overlooked the river and was spectacular – though not, I was to discover, too spectacular for unattributable skidmarks, but let's not be unattractive – floor upon floor of Georgian brick emblazoned with historical plaques and, at the back, a garden designed by Gertrude Jekyll – pronounced Jeakle-as-in-Treacle, he was quick to apprise me. It was here in this garden that, a few weeks later, at a drinks party, I was to meet the woman who, in time, would become my good friend Cara. I can't remember the nature of her connection with the Find – perhaps it was professional, perhaps it was neighbourly. Either way, it hardly matters now.

On a Sunday afternoon when, strictly, I should have been communing with Mr Respectable, the Find invited me up to his gondola-bed but declined to let me fuck him, because, he said, it just wasn't him, lovey, he couldn't abide the smell of amyl – as if amyl had ever been snorted in ancient Athens. Pre-

dictably enough, we hit an erotic reef; and so, over an intercourse ciggy, which he forced me to inhale in the kitchen,
shivering in a T-shirt while he made a pot of jasmine tea, he
began to stroke my hair, and to try to read my scowl, and to tell
me how he could tell that beneath my hard-nosed façade there
lay a sweet, soft centre – the sort of rubbish which, too often,
the young have to hear from older shags. I suddenly found
myself inspired to fabricate a sweet, soft-centred lie about how
my (not lover, but) landlord had given me notice, because he
wanted to install some (not dogsbody, but) woman in his pad,
and how this was all a bit of a (not drag, but) bind which left
me somewhat up a gum-tree, bla-dee-bla. The Find, who,
though selfish in the sack, was generous in real life, tilted his
head this way and that until he remembered that he had a friend
– not a friend in the Naughty sense, he emphasized; married to
a very smart woman – a lesbian, actually (as if such status were
proof of something, but anyhow): actors both. This acting
couple, who lived, but didn't sleep, together in Belgravia, happened also to own, just off King's Road, a further house which
they'd converted into bedsitters, to provide them with contin-
gency funds when they were out of work and a bit hard up,
and well, one never knew, it wasn't impossible that help might
be forthcoming. Worth a try. The Find would enquire. And
enquire, to my surprise, he did. Found out.

A few evenings later, while Mr Respectable was at the flat,
involved in what he liked to term 'unwinding', I rang the Find
from a coin-box outside the supermarket, ostensibly to arrange
a further tryst, but in essence to determine whether he'd managed to make contact with his friend, the actor. Once we had
established that he had, and that a room would be up for grabs
at the end of the month, and that the end of the month meant
not the 31st but its final Saturday, and that no deposit would be
required – friends of friends and all of that – he invited me over,
in order to take me to meet Mr Not-In-The-Naughty-Sense
and his Sapphic spouse, both of whom – stiff gins in hand, tonic

at room temperature – performed much in the manner of the larger-than-life kaftans that one would imagine, but described me as quite the little madam. After all, declaimed the actor, I was getting the best room in the house, on the First Floor – the *pearnoh nohbilay*, piped up the lezzer – so why on earth should I need to inspect the premises beforehand? And anyhow, what did I expect for thirty quid a week, dearie, the Palazzo Gritti? I mustn't be so, so touchy; besides, the room was still occupied, one couldn't just barge in for a snooparound; so look, I was just to take their word for it, all right? And thus, rather than upset the dramatic apple cart, I did as asked: took their word for it and held my tongue. But I remember thinking that this favour-business was a minefield. And when we left, the Find and I, the couple wagged at him how they could see that his little friend was a bundle of (not fluff, but) trouble, and, at me, they wagged that I wasn't to run rings round the Find, whom they described as an absolute sweetie, good enough to eat.

And so, back to his house for a quick bite, served in the Jeakle garden, because (said the Find) wasn't the evening just lovely. We kicked off, I recall, with his latest Greek passion, taramasalata (divvy, he called it – nothing like amyl). Next: breast of chicken Kiev, whose juicy surprise I managed to splatter all over my shirt-front. But the Find told me not to worry, didn't matter in the slightest – as if he'd been the victim of my mishap; and then he proceeded to wipe me down with the solicitous yet slightly squeamish ceremony that people sometimes adopt for the removal of other people's cum. And after a bowl of yoghurt, roughed up with honey, we progressed, skipping coffee and oblivious of garlic, to a drawn-out slobber and a superfluous mutual wank – the sort of superfluous second pudding which, a few years on, would come to be described, in picky personal adverts, as Strictly Vanilla (meaning: no weirdo kinky stuff). The Find looked a bit alarmed when he discovered the trellis of welts which of late had been embossed upon my back, but he exercised the tact not to mention what, to him, must have betrayed my sinister depravity.

When I prepared to leave, it was not so much because he had to be in Harley Street at what he called the Crack, which sounded like the name of a club, as because (unbeknown to him, unlike my apparent penchant for punishment) I had to get back to Mr Respectable that night. But as I lolled on the step of the Find's historical threshold, he suggested – for which I shall always be thankful – that, since I had too much junk to fit into a cab, and didn't own a car, and couldn't drive a rental van, he should pick me up in his spanking new Range Rover – 'sinfully black' – at 10 a.m. on Saturday, and rescue me from the dreary barrister who was chucking me out in favour of some woe-man – as he styled the non-existent concubine. But just as, in truth, Mr Respectable had never given me notice to depart, so I, being as bilious as I was broken-hearted, omitted to inform him of my plan to quit the painful confines of his cul-de-sac. And while my landlord presumably continued to make messes, if not masses, in the courthouse, I crept into the spare room of his flat, where my clothes were hung like That, and where the rest of my clutter was stashed ('out of harm's way', as had been advised), and I proceeded, in apprehensive silence, to gather and pack my life. On that final evening, which I spent alone, staring at the sky as if it held not stars but answers, I kept the door to the spare room firmly shut; and when, long after midnight, Mr Respectable swaggered back, his drunken blood running high, I submitted to a summary thrashing in order to tire him out.

By ten the next morning, I had bathed, picked out an outfit, cleared the bathroom of incriminating evidence, and lit up. The doorbell rang. I had hoped that Mr Respectable would have snored on, undisturbed, in his circumspectly accoutred chamber; but no: just as I was heaving a load of suitcases onto the landing, and the Find, supreme in cashmere, stepped inside to lend a hand with my few remaining bags, out popped Mr Respectable, wrapped in a grimy towelling-robe through which he was scratching a buttock. Next, he scratched his hair, as if that hair whose blondness I had once considered blonder than the very sun, were not just greasy, but baffled. And yet the Find, rising above such antics, conducted himself with superlative disdain, like a prize-winning giraffe. Not a word was traded between our icy triangle – other than, perhaps, a frost-bitten goodbye, which I've amputated from recollection. But after my chaperon had led me out, and I had clambered into his sinfully black motor, witnessed through a cloudy window from on high by my former landlord, the Find prodded a tape into action and sped away into the distance, telling me, at a set of traffic lights, that it was weird, you know, but he could swear that he recognized that barrister-bloke from some gay watering-hole somewhere. (Gulp.) And yet, as if attuned to the song blasting out, I was no longer afraid, no longer petrified; no longer thought that I could never live without my former landlord by my side. I would survive. And thus: welcome to the principality of Bedsitland.

The room, miraculously for that era, was practically unfurnished: a marble fireplace, painted purple, which I stripped to its bare, essential grey; a great sash window – handy, I predicted, for summer sunbathing; a single bed, no worse than the bed which I'd just fled; a chair; a built-in wardrobe; no fridge as yet, but the Find promised to get me one, by way, he said, of house-warming prezzie; and a dilapidated desk in formica teakette, which, after a bit of pestering, the actor-châtelain allowed me to drag – crash, bang, wallop – to the basement. And thus we come to the table. Love is like good furniture. Worth the wait.

Partly in order not to blight my rich romantic aspirations by dint of an interior which smacked too hard of penury, and partly in order to avenge, at a single stroke, my living death with Mr Respectable, I decided that the legacy of his unpaid rent, the lot, must be blown on the one specific item for which the room most loudly cried out: a focus on which to feed myself, and sign enormous cheques one day – the day my break, or prince, had come – a prop on which to lean and yak if I had visitors, or, if I had none, hunch and wail and tear my hair out to the strains of No Regrets, no tears goodbye. Smaller requirements, such as lamps and cutlery and rugs – coffee machines, even – were, then, simple to 'acquire'.

I should say that when it came to the business of shoplifting, the friends of my youth proved dar(l)ing in their complicity; but it is possible that such alacrity was fostered by the fact that, since several of them were still shackled to their families, my premises could be shared by all of us, as a sort of communal boudoir in which to tart up before venturing forth to ravish the night – in separate directions, depending on our predilections, which, like our faces and our cruising garb, varied widely. And frequently shared it was – until, that is, some of the gaggle began to suggest that I should avail them, once in a while, of what they called my place, which was my palace, for a quick disgrace with some anonymoid. They promised to take my sheets to the launderette 'should the need arise', but I wasn't buying any of that crap. Go to the Heath, I told them. And when, even as they bitched about my double standards, they did troll off to the wilds of northern London, in order to partake, unhampered and weather regardless, of a spot of F&F (Flora and Fauna), I would stay at home to labour with inexpert strokes over my walls, which I glazed in muted, overlapping pastel tones, touches of Whistler. And when at last the job was done and I stood back and looked around, I witnessed that my shell, lit by a neighbouring streetlamp, glowed nacreous; and I was able to shimmer like a lone pearl within, in solitary splendour, in splendid solitariness. Mixed blessing, you might say; and you would, of course, be entitled; but better, I'd reply, than a knife-edge such as Hampstead, for which my friends – among others – were better cut out.

(Although, in time, it would become imbued with a whole

geology of reminiscences, like layer upon layer of ancient beeswax), when I first unearthed the table from a neighbouring emporium, it felt, weirdly, less nostalgic than predictive; seemed, in some manner, to reflect the way ahead for me, to point not at the sort of queen which I then was – bohemian without a scrap of the requisite ease – but toward the type of queer whom I hoped one day to be: mature and straightened out, though never in my life straight-acting, and never again to be had; classical yet unconventional, like unspeakable love; strong without being solid – neither chunky as some naval chest nor dainty as a Sheraton writing-cabinet; elegant, confident, stylish, versatile; witty, now and then; well-preserved, with a bit of luck, and – as should be clear by now – expensive. It cost me an arm and a leg, that table; and later, by way of elbow-grease, a virtual dislocation; but I minded none of these damages, even if, since, I've had occasion to regret that I never quite lived up to, never quite grew into, its potential. Failed it.

I found it on a Saturday afternoon like countless others, after an abortive visit to the type of twinko-regimental pub likely to have furnished the Find (to whom, by this stage, I'm afraid I had given his marching orders) with his earlier recognition of Mr Respectable (who never had the brutal frankness to give me mine). I remember the day because, since the Post Office closed at lunchtime, I was later prevented, when I needed it, from getting my mitts on the money. But the dealer-queen who dealt with me – pewter pageboy-cut, gaucho moustache, lurex bowtie, Aztec jumper with a reflective badge designed to wink the fashionable fallacy AC/DC – pretended, despite his shifty signals, to trust me, and said that he'd reserve what he called the Piece until next week, dear.

Two days later I returned, looking like death in shredded denim after a night squandered on a foreign duvet, and feeling like a pearl which, having rolled out of its oyster, had merely grown sullied. Yet, despite my outward shabbiness, I came well-groomed, came interlined in pristine cash: six hundred well-earned pounds, three-score tenners precisely, which I remember spreading like the scalloped wing of a period fan upon the patina of my hopeful future, the result of my hopeless past. But in humbling point of fact, I was next required to pay some unexpected surcharge – excavated from a grimy pocket at my buttock – in order for the Piece to be delivered to my palace. Still, I suppose that the dealer-queen – credit where it's due – did spare me the backlash of value added tax.

The first thing that I did was carefully to remove, with nail-scissors, the tag bearing the vital statistics of the Piece – its price and its description: circular drop-leaf dining table, padfoot, mahogany, early C18 – 48" diam., 27" high; and, on the verso, like a work of surrealist art, the coded amount L/009 (meticulously quilled in black), with the motto, diagonally across and passionately overstamped: SOLD (in blood). Next, I set off in search of the best available polish, the most exorbitant around. I could easily have nicked the cylindrical tin which (silverish, like our youthful tongues) at length I found, and which, as fate would have it, was labelled Renaissance; but something told me to watch my step, to show respect, to thank the lucky stars which, at last, seemed to be falling from the bewildering sky. So I coughed up, willingly and without a hint of a scowl. Oh, I paid with a smile far broader than the smile of any yummy little waiter. Because maybe this time, for the first time, something was bound to begin.

My table, unlike the dealer's winking badge, turned out to be no mere pathetic fallacy. (**pathetic fallacy** > noun in literature: the transference of human feelings to inanimate things, as in *a frowning landscape*.) No; this was the genuine article. It frowned at me, and later learnt to sigh and beam; and later still, well, it practically learned to tell my story for me – burns, cuts, lacerations, the whole forensic bit. So perhaps Cara, the analyst, had not been wrong. Maybe the skies and peaks and forests so beloved of her did have souls, did have hearts. The things which bred mahogany.

Mahogany tree. Slumped on my bed, I returned to the dictionary of my woozy vagaries, idly to review the unlikely world of its possibilities; but though my gaze hovered for direction, and my fingers, half-insensate, fumbled for the semblance of a forward cue, my faculties remained too dulled to taste the tarnished tang of **umbrage** (sense **1**, annoyance, offence). Yet next, as if I'd tripped, I stumbled on the fact that **umbrage** (sense **2**, the shadow cast by a tree) lends a cool green shade, a couple of branches down the page, to the **umbrella bird**: a creature of black plumage, native to the rainforests of South America, with a crest of raised feathers on its crown, which, when opened during courtship, does credit to its name. Umbrella bird. No oxymoron he. Rather, an ironic miracle. A perfect definition. A lover of the outdoor life, at freedom to sleep by moonlight in the arms of his tropical lumber, the answer to your prayers, the god of your innermost anthems.

The Central and South American Mahogany is a tree with a canopy (like a bed). It has a straight trunk (like a man), huge buttress roots at its base (like a fortress) and reaches an average height of 100 feet (like a javelin). In contrast with such trees as the fig (the love of woman) and the cocoa (the love of chocolate), it doesn't yield a fleshy fruit (even in its teens). Because its wood is so keenly sought for the production of fine furniture (Isthetics), the Mahogany is currently threatened with extinction (like queens). Noted for its combination of hardness, strength, and beauty (like the truth), it assumes a high degree of polish (like poetry), has an attractive grain (like a hazy memory), and is ideal for carving (peculiar works of art, such as coffins and caskets – shuttered niches, contradictions, hapless non-sequiturs).

Love; touch; wood. I resolved, after centuries, to act. I exhumed a tin of wax – still, after all this time, Renaissance; I found a duster, the colour of fire; I set to polish, prepared to buff. And as I worked my way around, sliding from chair to chair as I advanced, I reflected on other woods, and other loves; mused on how the former could define the latter; on how the queens who had stolen the best disco-spins were akin to the West African Sapele, which, in woods, is said to win the beauty pageant; on how the Find, with whom I'd stupidly lost touch, had, in his way, been akin to the Walnut, which is judged to be the noblest of the hardwoods; on how Mr Respectable, despite his pretensions to toughness, had amounted to Pine, the most common softwood; on how the Chicken of my youth had been like Birch, easy to steam, pliable, good for bending back and, better still, for thrashing; on how Teak, even though a wood which stands for durability, for lasting love, had seemed fated to grow beyond my chart; yet I possessed within my grasp Mahogany, not the winner of any category, but handsome notwithstanding, and dependable, and trustworthy.

And I told myself that when-when-when he came, the lover of my life, yes, he would be like that, my canopy, my trunk, my buttress. And if I closed my eyes, I could almost feel his skin as I ran the softness of my cloth over his muscular arm, around his contours, along his highs and his declines, his hollows and his juts. And if I looked with care, scrutinized, as if, at last, I'd picked up Cara's magnifying glass, I could even discern the grain of his pores and his smoothened patches, could acquaint myself beforehand with the texture of the man, whom I could rub and polish hard for richer nourishment, or more lightly, for quick results, to add an easy pleasing shine, say, to his cleavage or his inner thigh. And the closer I came to his surface, which smelt of nothing less than the outdoor life, the better I could sense the prospect of my future lover's scars from other loves, scars which through my ministrations I would heal and make vanish, along with his bruises, and his tears, both shed and held back; and I could almost hear the laughter of the wind in his eyes once he was mine, and see the heat of his smile in my hands once he had caught my heart, and claimed it, ever to sleep in the embrace of his safe, strong branches, au Clair de Lune, by moonlight. It took me back.

The Moonlight was a club when I was young. It must have seemed anomalous in the London of the era, not so much because it boasted a silver-service restaurant with an ornamental pianist, togged-out beneath a palm in an alcove, nor even because it had existed, in a state of quiet prosperity, for absolute aeons, but because, while a host of new nightspots, trendier and brasher and bigger and louder, were springing up all over town and competing for the custom of the pink avalanche, the Moonlight made a point of standing apart, serenely, and of peering, a little snottily, like some marvellous old actress, towards a higher, if retrospective, galaxy. Its precise location tended to be kept an imprecise mystery, at once shady and élitist, for the club preferred to swathe the allure of its identity in the chiffons of secrecy, like a woman who would rather not divulge her scent lest she thereby lose some essential ingredient of her mystique.

The Moonlight could not have been less moved by such tawdry considerations as packing in the punters or following the current fashion. Exclusivity was its *raison-d'être*; Discretion, its maiden name. Pop stars of the minute, for instance, were never made welcome, less on account of their creepy shades and proletarian eating habits than due to their sachets of cocaine; because the Moonlight, you see, was too old and too wise and too damn grand to get itself busted for the sake of some jumped-up one-hit wonder. That seemed to be the inference. The star, whom the management would always address as Sir despite the discomfort of retching its own genteel bile, amounted, alas, to unaffordable luxury. Greatest apologies. And then, the door would close with a dignified absence of sound, unless, that is, the rejected party happened to slam it. Slam.

The lowest that I ever knew the club to stoop was to the

level of (exquisite) air-stewards, all of whom seemed to wear a duty-free lotion which they pronounced Ekwy-Parjy, but was spelt Equipage, and all of whom preferred to pretend that they simply 'travelled', as if their passports averred: Occupation . . . Gentleman. These curious denizens were not, as far as I recall, yet known as Trolley Dollies: they were known as Cart Tarts. And when, with the miraculous advent of Concorde, the cream of those well-travelled boys graduated to the most prestigious cabin crew of all, so their honorific rose to that of A La Carte Tarts. I think that their counterparts in Cape Town were called, more simply, Corphy Morphies, but I no longer know anyone who could confirm, never mind spell, this fact.

Anyhow, prospective members of the Moonlight were always vigorously vetted (if not frisked); hefty black balls, dropped with impunity (if only metaphorically); and (not just one, but two) well-heeled sponsors required by anyone seeking admission. The most pleasing of these sponsors, pleasing because they were happy to oblige the young – whom they never called Chicken, they called us charming – and whose intervention could spare one the annoyance of having to wait a month to receive a pass-card, included the looser change of royalty, who, though we referred to them as half-crowns, seemed always to refer to themselves as Tony, or Patrick, or Michael, unassuming names like that. You get the picture. I'm afraid that I loved it. My prince was bound to come.

But one of the problems of being young is that you're always in such a rush that, while you're rushing, you take your strokes of luck for granted, with the result that when, long after the event, you try to search for someone who deserves to be thanked, that person, by some mocking twist of chance, is nowhere around. The Find, for example: I was often to wonder about him. And about lots of others. And this is why I cannot tell you who the people were that sponsored me to join the Moonlight, or how they came about – probably through introductions at the restaurant, where guests were allowed. But what

I can, however, tell you is that my friends, those friends of whom Mr Respectable had taken so dim a view, took, when invited to the Moonlight, a proportionately dim view of my new club, simply could not comprehend, they said, how I could have gone and blown that minor fortune on some campy shrine full of prisses, a shrine, furthermore, where you ran the gauntlet of being clocked by someone embarrassing, such as your (married) bank manager. It made no sense to them, not when you could go to anonymous great orgies in the under-skirts of town, and without risk of detection – because those orgies (once you'd negotiated the rack of lorry-tyres which tended to be placed like an assault course at the entrance, to discourage speedy exits by pickpockets) were always held in the dark – and when, what's more, you could, if you were young and even half-attractive, get in gratis. Oldies with proper salaries were expected to contribute lager, as if to justify them; but on the occasions when I attended these events, I too carried alco-hol – in a flask which (because the contents of your jeans were up for grabs), I kept tucked in a sock – so that, occasionally, between snorts of unknown poppers and phantom breakages of heart, I could crouch for an illicit glug, to infuse my ventricles with courage.

The answer to my friends' objections – had I dared to voice it, but perhaps I hadn't yet managed to formulate one – should, of course, have been that I found safety in small numbers. That's why I liked the Moonlight. And also because those snobby queens whom they, my friends, so grandly despised were always polite, never pushed too far, just let you go downstairs and dance all night and didn't call you a fucking cock-tease if you happened not to fancy a fuck, and bought you cocktails with-out invisible strings being attached to the stem of the glass, and gave you advice, some of it as contentious as it has proved invaluable, advice such as: Don't forget that a shared predilec-tion doesn't mean that we all share the same class. Some of these old queens had been friends of Radclyffe Hall, for God's sake, and of Gerald Berners and Norman Douglas and Harold Acton and Brian Howard, my **Uranian*** forerunners. No wonder I liked the senior members of the Moonlight, those mentors in my dark hours: they made me feel privileged, as if, in some strange way, I were being granted, through their auspices, licence to ride on the coat-tails, to join at the tail-end, of our history. Little did I realize that I hadn't even arrived at the proper beginning, at our second coming. Renaissance indeed. Very funny.

The funniest thing about the Moonlight (apart from its entrance, which I recall as an overblown homage to Beethoven – walls overpapered with scores of the Sonata, niches decked with *Wilhelmine* candlesticks of flaking silver, busts of the composer amid heavy swathes of drapery) was probably Hans, its elderly patron, to whom, when his blouzy back was turned, we referred as *Die Baronin*. Every evening, at precisely the same hour, nine o'clock by the cuckoo call, he would descend with great slow grace from his brocaded eyrie (which hung above the premises, and which I only knew him once to have shared – disastrously – with an unusually comely bartender, but this was long before my time) to dine at the restaurant, called Ludwig's, and ensure, as he sipped the contents of a solitary bottle of claret from a heavily cut glass, that we were all happy: all, that is, except for the staff, whose happiness no longer mattered to Hans. Efficiency alone concerned him now. And it has to be said that both the food and the service at the Moonlight left the rest of London's poovy dives, those hessian dumps so favoured by the likes of Mr Respectable, out of the running.

***Uranian** (adj.): sense **2**: homosexual. Term first coined by Austrian writer Karl Heinrich Ulrichs (1825–95). Derived from Greek Uranos (Heaven) in the belief that such love was of a higher order than ordinary love, and referred to in Plato's *Symposium*.

If Hans could have found enough straight waiters to go round, he would have had us all attended, with fantastic irony, by fiercely regimented heterosexuals; but, in the absence of such a possibility within the food and beverage trade, we were served by men so perfectly trained that only their insubordinate eyes, very occasionally, gave them away. Their every other move seemed to have been professionally curtailed; even their hands had been edited of superfluous gestures and accessories. And, as if in revenge, any jewels worthy of note were firmly placed on Hans' own, refined and polished, frame, which, as often occurs with the delicately inclined, was paradoxically large.

People were sometimes heard to whisper that Hans had started life as a Weimar tart, and later made a bomb out of some sugared duke in London; but, to me, he just looked resigned, like a foreign actor who made up for his defective English by means of a dazzling, and dazzlingly well-capped, smile. Yet beyond that smile, or above it, if you looked through his tinted lashes and pale fish eyes, you could almost see the soul of a woman rebuffed, of a woman who should never have been a courtesan, who had been jilted far too often and far too hard, and now lay abandoned in the gutter of her perished prime. Hans should have kept cats. But life must have hardened him, because, instead, he kept buying diamonds, which he sported in socking profusion, night after night, as if those eye-catching jewels were his morganatic progeny, whom one could never, quite, politely admire. And yet we felt oddly protective of his dodgy, slightly ludicrous flamboyance, perhaps because, in return, he – also every night (bar *Montag*) – protected us, and indeed because, after a couple of enormous kümmels at the bar furthest from where we used to dance, he would call us, without regard for age or aspect, his *Liebling*-darlings. The thing about Hans was that you could have taken your mother to his club and not been embarrassed, for there was a bleak, almost mystic purity to the man. Yet it was rumoured that, once a year, he descended from his quarters bedecked in full drag, which was probably the night when you would rather not have taken your mother.

Observed even in his dotage, when his spine was beginning to break ranks, he still remained too tall ever to have been a hussar; and yet you could envisage him, despite the womanish aura to which, late in life, he'd run for refuge (the magnificently blonded coiffe, the virtual lack of stubble, the broadening hips, the elongated manicure, the warm creamy handshake, the cigarette holder, the crêpe-de-chine foulards, the copious pendants and chains and medallions), despite all these things you could envisage him as a young guardsman of very serious Aryan beauty. And because, through the richly scented cloud of his current, lavendered life, you could still glimpse the wonder which he must have been in his past, so you admired him, looked up. No fucking about, not even when he swished into the restaurant wearing a smoking jacket with (whoops) a jabot. I think that he was just too bizarre, and too melancholy, to be sent up. And his club, whatever the sorority may like to claim now, was unquestionably the best in town. Ask Tony or Patrick or Michael.

The one true Michael in my life was not, in fact, a prince. He was my brother, whom we called Kelly (a title raped and pillaged from the Italian *Michele*). All of us seemed to wear nicknames in those days – as if to acknowledge, I suppose, our comings-out, our homosexual natures, which we preferred to regard as gifts of special value, talents from the heavens rather than a leprous sign of evil. To us, the mark of the beast had nothing to do with liking penises: it referred to holding your knife like a pencil; but still. Unlike most of our fellow queens, who had, historically speaking, been more correct by properly crossing, as opposed to merely bending, the gender of their sobriquets, Kelly and I had elected carefully androgynous ones

– less because we couldn't think of ourselves as wholly Fem (though we probably lacked, at that stage, the requisite self-irony), than because, had an honest-to-goodness girlie-word, like a poisonous bloom in a verdant idyll, inadvertently sprung from our lips while we were camping around the house which our parents imagined was home, such an indiscretion, venial as it might now seem, would, then, have incurred a hefty penalty, and been deemed to call for radical pruning, if not actual hacking, by our begetters, who, though luckily transplanted to a remote and backward distance, were firm believers in convention. The pair of them, who were considered paragons in their little Eden, lived entangled in the complicated branches of morality and religion, like a couple of fine monkeys, trapped but closely entwined somewhere up there, near the clouds, and would, without a doubt, have sought to protect their ideological habitat by crapping on our allowances, the condition of which we guarded with greater care than any monkey ever guarded the palette of its arse. Kelly and I, when liberated from our dreadful family and its equally dreadful entourage, could be seen, in our giddy relief, to grow manifestly (almost defiantly) Queer – a term which though, back then, sounded less trendy than punitive, we'd adopted for two reasons: first, because it smacked of dirty, wartime, vicious, gorgeous, clean-cut Nazi youths (a kink which would have made our parents fall, in conjugal unison, from their endangered tree), but largely, and more seriously, because Bender and Fairy, and Nancy and Nellie, and Pansy and Mary, and Cissy and Gay, and Pouffter and Homo, and Bugger and Faggot, and all the rest of the sodomitic repertoire, didn't do the trick for us. I was personally quite partial to the classification Deviant, but Kelly considered it too pathological by half. As for Invert, we were both in full accord that it sounded excessively social, almost bourgeois, made you think of Hurlingham Club. No question: Queer was sexier. That's why we chose it.

Not long after my admission to the Moonlight, Kelly was

weaned off the nappy thing. His emotions became potty-trained for good. Of this I remain certain. For he pitched up at my door one night, late and without notice, having been evicted by the fool who'd attempted to initiate him, the creep who'd dared to trade my brother's open smiling childish love for a plastic dummy and a couple of smacks. I recall how, when the bell rang, I'd been lying on the floor, trying to imagine how it would feel to be on the brink of dying, an illusion which wasn't too distressing, more romantic, because it seemed about as likely as going down on the Titanic. But, my musings having been cut short, I pushed an ablative-absolute glower through the window, to find Kelly standing on the pavement, looking up, and looking, perhaps, a trifle wanner than was his habit. This, I remember thinking, must mean that he wanted to borrow something, probably to go dancing, such as my new best cowboy boots, deep purple – which had hailed from a witty little shop called R. Soles, but which I had stolen (my joke). I concluded that Kelly must be trying to look pleading, puppyish, too adorable for possible denial. Old trick of his. I wasn't his (slightly younger) brother for nothing. Wrong. He told me to let him in, you stupid idiot. So I pulled myself together, grabbed my keys, and threw them down to him; but no sooner had he charged up to my room – and just as I was about to make a bemused enquiry as to What, and Owe, and Pleasure – than I saw that he was crying, which made me sick, so I turned off No Regrets, put on a recent hit, and we got sloshed on *Campari-arancia*, which was our grown-up tipple in the fleeting interval before we were forced to grow up.

It turned out that, in a fit of pique over some other, younger, up-and-coming baby-diddums, Kelly had hurled a well-aimed sewing machine across the 'nursery' at Kindergartenmeister, a couple of whose pathetic ribs had been shattered in the fracas. Naughty Baby; Baby Naughty (whack). I quickly stepped into the part of confidant and started asking loads of stuff; yet Kelly, who must have felt uncomfortable, wouldn't dish any of the real muck, the crucial details for which my prurience lusted, such as what a sewing machine had been doing there in the first place, and whether it had been a Singer or a Brother. I now suspect that someone must have been toiling over the *broderie*. The things we do for love. But I told him, quite firmly, that my bed was strictly mine and he had to sleep on the floor if he wanted to be Put Up.

A couple of days later, when we knew that Kindergarten-meister was out, we let ourselves into the peachy-pastel flat on the wrong side of the river which had amounted to Kelly's equivalent of my torture with Mr Respectable, and packed up all his junk. After ransacking the premises, we finally found, and nicked, the sole remaining evidence of that hapless, childless marriage – the pervy Polaroids – which we unearthed from a pile of (fascinating) correspondence from other nappy enthusiasts. But after a ceremonial incineration of Kinder-gartenmeister's touching little snaps in the grate of my stony hearth, I decided to come clean, and proceeded to inform my brother (not so much on account of the dreadful smell of burn-ing laminate, as because I couldn't stand another minute of his dossing about) that there wasn't enough room for both of us at my palace, which he kept calling my poncy boudoir. Kelly was mad for modernity, you see, so taking the piss out of my old-fashioned penchant came as a cinch to him, all too naturally; but I think that the divorce, his break-out through the cot-bars, must have rendered him overexcited, because suddenly he was ringing all these people, and inviting them over, as if no longer concerned about the décor which, but recently, he'd claimed to find so laughable. And before I knew it – wouldn't you know – he was hoping to borrow my bed for a tumble. Sorry, I said, I'd help him find a place of his own if he liked, talk to the landlord if necessary, but we just weren't cut out to cohabit, least of all in such restricted confines. He called me pathetic, but I decided not to retaliate: you couldn't be too careful with words intended to convey annoyance, such as Rattle. Yet he, oblivious of my self-restraint, went on to explain that what he needed was not some patronising lecture, still less a boring **vada*** through the To Let ads, which he could scour without my assistance any time he desired; no, what he *required*, he said, was my moral support at the clap-clinic. Crabs, he summarized – which freaked me out, because, to me, crabs could only mean one thing: cancer. And so, by taxi, to the local hospital. What a dump. We had overdressed by miles.

Dr McManus was a right one, but also, in his chirpy Grampian way, quite funny, and did, whatever else, awaken us to the benefits of a double-act. We always jumped the queue when he was around, because, as he invariably explained to the disgruntled nurse at reception, he could deal with the toothsome twosome in double-quick time. But the truth, I think, is not so much that McManus could be trusted to be expeditious with us, as that he fancied the idea of being squashed inside a sibling sandwich. Kelly and I, however, were, from the outset, intransigent about the curtain round the examination couch, primly insistent that it be drawn at all times – a demand which I suspect must have miffed McManus, whom (obviously) we called McAnus. But Kelly and I came from such a pent-up background that (incredible as it mày sound) we'd never clocked each other in the buff, and nor were we about to start now – not I, at any rate, not for all the alternative medicine in China. Yet we got our comeuppance soon enough, because whenever, thereafter, we attended that venereal establishment (and briefly I decided to spare myself the expense of a private doctor for the routine indignity of grubby check-ups, just as McManus, equally briefly and no less grubbily, doubtless hoped for a reversal in my prudish attitude), the good physician would welcome Kelly, who always led the way, as if he were some

*vada (pron. varda) – (noun, infinitive, imperative): a look, to look, look (Polari/Parlare).

enormous piece of class – Monegasque, for instance; and me, with the following – exceedingly shrill – salutation: Ooch, heer comms Muss Clara Bow-Lips! Goes without saying that he wasn't referring to my cupid's-whatsit. What he was doing was announcing to the whole omnium-waiting-bloody-gatherum that I was up-tight. Tight-arsed. He may have had a point. Certainly he had a finger. But I wonder where Dr McManus is now.

For as long as I could remember I had hated my official name. But given that I was born less than a year after Kelly, who was obviously still, at that stage, Michael the little archangel, it seems fair to surmise that the airborne monkeys of our engendering, our paragonic parents, had, between syncopated shrieks of expectation and binges of mouth-to-mouth *cacahouettes*, been busily beating their chests in anticipation of the arrival of a baby girl. In our teens, Kelly, who by then had fluttered down from the ranks of the angelic to those of the plain irritating, was, from the comfort of his closet, which he proved slow to throw open, to joke: What the hell did they *think* that they'd produced, second time around, but a total girlie? – as if he'd been bred (not first, but) butch as Trajan. Anyway, perhaps because my disappointing gender had caught the monkeys off-guard – on the hop, so to speak, between their complicated branches – or because someone had unwittingly wished to chastise me for daring to materialize equipped with the wrong parts, it was decreed that I be named after (not some great emperor, but) the month when I was dumped by the proverbial stork over the confusion of our genetic foliage. And this is how I came to be christened Quintus – a choice which strikes me as the nastiest to be made without actually dubbing an untimely son May. So, as soon as I had learned to voice my loathing of this titular absurdity, I began to accuse our parents of having been idiotic in their selection, because Quintus, far from conjuring a springtime page on some classical almanac from Rome, simply suggested that I was fifth in line to their leafy throne, whereas, of course, I was second — and, furthermore, their (simian) terminus. And besides (I would bang on), the daft initial which they'd inflicted on my ego, that accursed Q, was fine-and-dandy for some boring theatre-prompt, or a bouncer at some seedy club in Soho, or the son of a snooker hoodlum, but quite unfit for the likes of me, by which, in my muddled dreams, I meant someone predestined by the fates to wed a prince and vault into the future like a gleaming javelin.

Once I'd got away, dishevelled but unbowed, from the imprisonment of school, and resolved to liberate myself from that other great enslavement, the straitjacket of parental discipline (only to be landed in the slavery of Mr Respectable, but that's all history), I decided to take proper action in respect of my hideous proper adjective — it hardly amounted to a noun — the shaming entry which defined, and yet defaced, my birth certificate. Pointless, I reasoned, to tip-toe through the minefield of my days burdened at the shoulder (a joint which tends to chip) with the inflammatory weight that is the threat of ridicule, a threat which can ignite and explode in one's face without warning, any minute, and ad infinitum. I would craft myself anew, transform my old identity, design myself a safer, future set of wings, sounder and lighter and better-fitting than the waxy wings of Icarus. After all, since actors and writers and monarchs did it, just as cities and kingdoms and whole empires did, who the hell was to say that I — an historically entitled deviant — wasn't too to take the liberty? So I put my mind to the business, and was, eventually, rewarded with a solution — a double one, in fact, because Kelly and I, as it turned out, were to be relabelled in unison.

It happened directly after our reciprocal unmasking, our mutual coming out, the kind of confessional two-way mirror which tends to present itself to queers whom life has bound by blood. And yet the occasion did not turn out (not even warmly blurred by the Vaselined and tinted lens of memory) to be a cameo of heightened mutual avowal shared by unnatural brothers. The reality couldn't have been further from that romantic fraternal pastoral, because our critical landmark cropped up (not by providential candlelight, but) by tacky accident. This is how. Halfway between the painful confines of the cul-de-sac and the historical brickwork of the Find, there was a pub, an equidistant spot, known as The Queen & Garter – which didn't leave much room for doubt. But even if one had, at one's hesitant start, suffered some niggling anxiety about the specialised nature of the beverage served inside, which was not in every case the milk of human kindness, any such fears would have been dispelled, creamed-off in one, by the gaggles of walrus-queens in aviator shades who habitually colonized the cobblestones beyond the kerbside, waving their puzzle-rings in the sun, and manhandling, as they rolled their eyeballs at one another's juicy tittle-tattle, their excruciated packets, which were ever oppressed to one side. I would linger alone, as a matter of stand-offish custom, deep within the bowels of such establishments, as if reduced to killing time on some foreign railway platform while waiting for the train of love to ferry me to the hardest place of all, the place called Paradise. That's the look which, irrespective of the climate of my flies, I used to harbour – desperately detached, frantically absent – but I don't suppose that it fooled anyone, least of all: him, the most unexpected person, oddly the most surprising, as he made his breezy entrance through the swing-doors, cool as a model-cucumber swanning down the catwalk of life, and smiling to left and to right at absolute strangers who cut their yabbering the better to admire him – my brother. For, whatever my shock at the time, and whatever the people who subsequently came to know him, biblically or otherwise, may like to claim now, assuming that they're still around to perpetrate some lie, my brother, in that blossoming and sunny period of his life, more than merited the flattery of speechless wonder. Even swaddled in the passing horror of *broderie*, he would succeed, somehow, in looking lovely.

He had moved to London an academic year ahead of me, but this lead was not, any more than the lead deployed by Mr Respectable, to be put to academic furtherance. Rather it was employed for the semblance of seeking employment, while, in effect, seeking emotional rescue, seeking it with such unwavering avidity, yet sexually so cheaply, as to obfuscate the heavy eventual cost of such pursuits to his light-hearted spirit. Nevertheless, my brother did, in the brief interim before I came to join him in town, enjoy the advantage of a new, fluorescent urbanity over my opaque and provincial public-school ignorance, which brought up the rear. He had already learnt — as I've already told — openly to ravish the faces of strangers, specifically male ones, male marauders even, even down-the-Dilly; learnt to be nice about things, to seem amenable rather than suspicious, willing rather than wilful — a skill which, in my personal instance, has never ceased to elude me.

After the revelation of our double-queerdom (a condition which, when some time later it was learnt at the family tree — by means of a single letter adorned with two very florid signatures — was interpreted as the darkest of sins, warranting the darkest social secrecy, a secrecy which laid my mother prostrate on her couch for three long weeks, and culminated, with her eventual recovery and my father's complicity, in our joint banishment, for years on end, to the smog of genealogical Coventry), we were effectively disowned, left to survive on our meagre wits, like crabs in a genital wilderness. Anyway, the people whom, in our bizarre trajectory toward premature maturity, we were to meet — to meet, that is, in a context where dialogue was permissible — seemed often to think that we were sexily identical, swappable even, of kinky interest. McManus, for instance, just to point the finger. But such an outlook was as myopic as it was silly. You only had to see us together to realise. My brother was the taller and the darker and the swarthier of the two of us; I was thinner, more sallow-skinned and jagged – in profile most markedly. His mouth was sensual; mine, slim-to-mealy. His eyes were opened wide; mine, narrowed in perpetuity. His hands were beautiful; mine, merely bony. And yet there did, I admit, exist vague similarities in our vocabulary and demeanour, as well as in the emotional air that we struggled to breathe, which, on account of the suffocating moral and religious temperature of our rearing, was not wholly balanced, pointed toward difficulty, felt wheezy, and was hampered by the thoracic pressure of guilt. But such resemblances, such hapless coincidences, owed more to our unhealthy conditioning than ever they did, I still believe, to weirdo-genetic predisposition. Within the homosexual spectrum, viewed through its prism, my brother and I could not have been more different. If he was bright orange (scarlet and yellow), I was bright green (yellow and blue). Take it from me – even as I loitered by the cottage at the Queen & Garter, thinking not of him but of the train which I had yet to catch, and which, just for a change, was overdue.

He sported, on that least expected of occasions, a fearlessly beautiful shirt, voluminously white, Shakespearean, with enough deep pleats along the yoke to render its pressing a grievance. Sleeves rolled up over the elbows; buttons undone to the cleavage. That great show-stopper of his, pre-empting the vogue which, not long thereafter, would be christened New Romantic – a fever for sashes and bandeaux and frills – he had purchased, I recall, in Athens en route to Hydra, whither he had been invited by some enigmatic, upwardly-mobile cicerone, some socially-downcast sodomite – Kindergarten-meister in his guise as landlord, I'm now inclined to hazard. And I would doubtless have been wearing, when he peered toward my shadow across the yeasty fug, the pallid safety of overwashed jeans, a denim jacket, and a white cotton T-shirt proclaiming, at first glance, the letters **o w d y**, which people presumed to be part of some American welcome, but which, whenever the jacket came off, professed me to be a **C o w d y k e**. At any rate, he half-smiled at me, but with the vague neutrality which one accords to a presence devoid of precise context, to a memory which one can't quite pin down. And then he was offered a voddy by some blazered moustache. And next, after checking the pickings, which were slim, he got a grip, and came across to where I was slouching, and he looked at once relieved and peeved, as if to imply that, since I was here, I was welcome to join in the hoolie – on condition that I not block his light, which was vital. And finally, just before closing time, he introduced me to a few of the gathered, a James and a Neil and an Adam, (a Jane and a Nell and an Ada). And that's how it all began. The cat of our parents' catastrophe, even before it had leapt by airmail to their branches, was out.

Outing ourselves to the monkeys would take time – time to muster the requisite courage, which would need to be considerable, since the monkeys were considerably less partial to fruit than they were to peanuts – but alighting on the nickname Kelly happened almost automatically, like a pleasurable landing. I think that before our chance encounter at the Queen & Garter, my brother had been resisting the force to wear a sobriquet, a force exerted by his acquaintances in London, all of whom had already 'gone over' to Camp; and I suspect this resistance to have stemmed from the fact that, secretly, he found the notion of femmy pseudonyms a bit trashy, rather like drag. But then he, unlike me, didn't have much to dislike in his own name, Michael – besides which, its most obvious flip-side, Michelle, would – let's face it – have been a bit damn naff. Yet he would never, at that time, have admitted fostering snobby reservations about any aspect of the homosexual panorama, because people in the ghetto had always, thus far, treated him kindly – apart, that is, from Kindergartenmeister, about whom, as you know, I yet knew nothing.

When I first moved to town, my brother and I had simply told each other that we were renting rooms in flats and kept it as vague as that. In retrospect, of course, neither of us can have been too keen to elaborate beyond the sketchiest of outlines. But after our meeting at the Queen & Garter, everything became open, other. Yet I, unlike him, with all his hesitancy, could not have been more pleased by the sudden prospect of shedding the Q of my lifelong discomfiture, the bane of my biographical alphabet; and so, as soon as I gleaned my chance – what with Jane and Nell and Ada – I confessed to this pressing desire. Truth to tell, I became a complete pest about it, would not let the matter pass, until, in the end, worn down, my brother agreed to keep me moral company. We would dive from the same high plank at the same time, vaulting swallows in unison, siblings in a truce of future solidarity – so long, he insisted, as I was prepared to be subtle about it, *subtle*, and not (as he put it) go the whole tranny distance – because it was crucial that the monkeys not get wind of our racket, even from their giddy great altitude: otherwise, remember, they'd consti-pate our wallets.

And so off we took, whooshing over Michael, bypassing Michelle, and gliding towards Shelley, which struck me as poetic but he claimed to hate – cheap stilettos, was his take. Obliged, therefore, to turn on our airborne heels, we headed back to England, briefly to refuel at the name of origin; yet next, probably because we were perched at some pizza parlour, pecking at garlic bread while knocking back *Campari-arancia*, we decided on a wider, wilder route for our second trajectory, which seemed to point us Italywards, and thus we came, guided by the arrow of some quivering inner compass, to the name *Michele*, which despite its lingering echoes of Shelley, we short-ened to Kelly, and there, in a diminutive peanutshell, you have it. **Bona*** (not boner). *Fatto*; done. Kelly had arrived.

Yet the task awaiting me wasn't so breezy. Linguistically, it

---

*bona (key adjective/adverb): good, attractive, beautiful, well done (Polari/Parlare).

felt more arduous, tiresomely uphill – not only because there was little, in the realm of comedy or irony or any of that, to be done with a dead-loss name like Quintus (which was a joke in its own right, though a very bad one), but because, deep down, I wanted shot of the idiocy outright, and shot of it far more urgently than ever I wanted to rack my brain about some clever variant or deviant or what have you. So together we changed tack, and tried, instead, to think of names for girls which didn't sound completely girlie when applied to a man.

Bisexuals, we agreed, would have to be scrapped: Hilary and Lindsay and Jocelyn and Robin and Evelyn and Vivian and Claude and Carol – all too dated and, frankly, too WAAF. Next we circled over names of boys not strictly meant for girls, but which girls sometimes affected to be larky, sort of pony-ridy, yet none of these seemed to suit either, names like Bobbie (too policewoman), and Ali (too Baba), and Nicky (too shoplifty), and Ducky (too cowardly), and Jackie (too wanky), and Ronnie (Veronica? Sorry, darling, I didn't have plans to mop anyone's brow). What about Johnnie? Too rubbery, I ejaculated. Too dykie, he out-ejaculated me. Charlie, then? Vile scent; not on your life. Freddie? Possible . . . but, on second thoughts: too mercurial, too goofy-pop-star. Binkie? Too fat. Bunny? Too Hefner. Sasha? Too cummerbund. On and on we went, round and round and round, until, once the booze had started to cloud our marbles, we began to fear that we might need to postpone our travels for the night, resign ourselves to the headache of a spinning question-mark. Make a list, Kelly prescribed. But as I grabbed a paper napkin on which to write, the solution sprang to mind. I hope that the name which I elected had nothing to do with our mother, who, in our childhood, as we hobby-horsed on the high branches, was sometimes heard to sing some song from a Sixties film about swinging down the street so fancy free, because – oh, I don't know, it's all so long ago – it just felt right, that name, right and liberating, both girlish and boyish, gentle but energetic, modern but classic, sort of custom-made but better built than the wings of Icarus, the perfect cut-and-fit for a promising javelin. And the name was this: Georgie. It suits me still, even decades after that baptismal evening, and even if those who came to embrace me with it are – well, no more. Gone beyond recall. Now I'm simply George.

But to return to the days that I'm trying to describe. My brother and I swiftly became known, by all and scenic sundry, as Kelly and Georgie, recognizable accomplices to a common crime, nature's double-joke. I think that although senior, more experienced queens considered us colourful, and although they found us kinda sexy in our counterbalanced acts (me, surly in general denim; Kelly, sunny in pleated white), nevertheless they viewed us as spoilt and unpredictable, tricky to handle. *Prenez garde*, you sometimes heard some sozzled fart emit as we stepped into the Queen & Garter. And perhaps such people were, at least in my volatile regard, right, right to watch out; because when, for example, anyone enquired, perfectly politely, and merely by way of innocent conversation-starter, whether my elected name was Georgie after the film or the song or whatever, I would snipe, forgetful both of my manners and of our mother, so frenetic was I to conceal the Quintus which still lurked, obscured, within the covers of my passport, that it certainly was not. *My* George, I'd reply (as if the ensuing differential rendered me legally entitled), ended in '*ie*' and not '*y*', whereas the emotional weakling in that film, a film which I'd never even seen ('before my time', was my charmless sideswipe – though I was all too aware of the lyrics about how nobody you meet could ever see the loneliness there, and the question about why do all the boys just pass you by, could it be you just don't try, and the lecture about the clothes you wear, and the shit about not being so scared of changing and re-arranging yourself, and about how it's time to jump down from the shelf), she, that other George, had spelt herself Geor*gy*, as in Cor*gi* and Por*gy*, get it? I became ugly in the face of such enquiries, enquiries that, at worst, only ever amounted to harmless chat-up. But, at some uncomfortable depth, they made me feel as if people were trying to catch me out, prying too profoundly, digging beneath safe ground. And if I resented their accidental excavations, this was probably because I needed to keep buried the evidence that not only was Georgie a novelty in my life, but a novelty which, far from symbolizing my wholesale purchase of the gender-bending homosexual lifestyle, had merely provided me with a convenient means of divorcing myself from my oppressive past. I had, in effect, abused the privilege of a noble historical tradition for ignoble personal reasons, and I preferred to spare myself the blush of being found out. That is why, I think, unsolicited attention on this front felt like attack, and caused, to some extent, my symptomatic, anti-social pedantry. But, in the event, even such defences were destined not to last. They were soon to be dismantled and scrapped; for, a matter of months into my journey through the sexual mire of London, I was to meet (alone, which aggravated matters) a fantastically handsome man, perhaps even – who could tell? – the prince of my desperate imaginings, who, having heard some extraneous queen greet me across some equally extraneous bar as Hey There Georgie Girl, asked after my (by now exceedingly tedious) mythology. I spun him the line about corgis and Porgys and the rest of my smart-arsed way out, whereupon he – robbing me of a riposte, and robbing me for life – explained, very calmly, that my rule about g i e being soft, as in gee, and g y being hard, as in gyno, didn't hold water. Wasn't logical. How otherwise, he said, nailing me to the stake of my own ignorance, would I suggest that one pronounce a word such as: Orgy? And then he set aside his drink and walked out of the pub and evaporated from my life. I don't know how Kelly dealt with the ripples of his own re-christening. Probably openly, honestly, with a smile. That was his charm; just as, in a way, it was to prove his tragedy.

When I pause to consider those times, I think of us less as a spoilt, unpredictable pair of faggot-brats, than as a couple of brothers hindered by circumstance, by which I do not so much mean our parents, against whose choking strictures we were, and would remain, indissolubly united; no: what I mean is the constant comparisons to which, despite our manifold differences (physical, aesthetic, intellectual; moral come to that), the curse of our shared blood constantly gave rise, comparisons which, I now understand, were bound, sooner or later, to hamper our passage through the bogus but broadening landscape which served as cyclorama to our early adult lives, a landscape which, beneath the glare of its increasing voltage, and despite the stepped-up heat of its erotic climate, was to grow harsher, less kind, and, from my narrow vantage, unbearable to admire, until the collective bulb of our culture, which was the culture of an imaginary, never-ending bacchanal, fused the circuit of our ghetto, and blew itself, as indeed it blew us all, out, plunging us back into the darkness which marked our second coming.

But one thing was certain: either you were partial to Kelly, modern and grateful and gullible, or you were partial to the other, spikier customer. Never to both of us; not equally; not possible. Perhaps that is why, in the end, we had to grow apart: perhaps we sensed that we were bad for one another, destructive in some unspoken manner. And yet there's no doubt in my mind that, had it been possible to weld and merge and alchemise our many contrasts into one single substance, the result would have been without match and above damage, beyond the flaming blend of green and orange, beyond the most sacred, cleansing, iridescent fire. Perfect and enviable. Yet envy was, I also think, at the core of relations between the two of us. And this particularly toxic product of hatred and love did concern, did touch upon, the subject of our parents, the high-handed monkeys.

Sibling Rivalry: a bittering chestnut. This is how it came about, how it went awry. Kelly was born, and – to judge by all the aerial photographs – born lovely, gurgling and grinning straight into the sun. But before our mother had enjoyed a chance to sit down, or turn around, or whatever it is that a convalescent woman does, I seem to have materialized – sporting a uric erection and a head like a zeppelin. And it must have been then, at that precise natal juncture, that some miserable part of her decided to attach me to her disappointment, for she had failed to provide her simian mate with a simian daughter to swing around their matrimonial jungle. Which explains why, before I'd even grown the teeth with which to bite her, I seem to have been turned into her (unequal) partner, her inner emotional rock against outward conjugal disaster; and thus she and I became interchangeable, and mutual (though mutually non-suckling) comfort-rags. Meanwhile Kelly, who, even before my unsettling advent, had earned the rank of firstborn, now, with my untoward arrival, grew into the chubby apple of our father's beady yellow eye, into the great seminal hope for his vainglorious continuance. But boy were our parents, in their separate ways, to be humbled. And girl were we, for our separate sins, to be punished. Yet, from the start, and despite our ironically parallel sexual orientations, which pointed, with parallel hardness, away from reproduction, Kelly and I had fallen into opposite camps, and been pitted, before we could even sound a word of objection, against each other, till death or dementia do us part. I see that now. Boo-hoo. Yeah, yeah.

Of course, it was never made to seem like that. If while out, hunting for coconuts or dates or bananas, we ever got into a sibling scrap, and one of us clambered back to the family tree bedraggled and blubbing, the other would always be reprimanded. When the fault was perceived to be mine, it was invariably our father who delivered my chastisement – to my rump. But if, on the other hand, the blame appeared to lie with Kelly, then our mother would perform the honours, by means of a hefty slap across his snout, which I suspect to have been the more offensive punishment. Yet the monkeys were, whatever else, consistent in the exaction of our discipline, and shared their corrective duties with unwavering symmetry – a symmetry which was, however, by its very design, divisive. And although, with our transition from childhood into adolescence, Kelly and I were to pit ourselves against our parents just as often as we did against each other, really the pattern, which was shaped like an X, remained a (not kiss, but) corrosive constant, a costly multiplication. The monkeys always stuck together, but split the unpleasantness; we, meanwhile, kept apart, but pretended to be pleasant about it. And by the time that we had been packed off to school (where we saw neither hide not hair of one another, or, if ever we did, made out that we hadn't), the damage had been done, mutual envy had been contracted. Later, in London, even if we made an effort to appear united, we must both have known that any such unity was circumstantial, *faute de mieux*, for our parents were absent from the picture, and we, for better or worse, had no-one else to whom to apply. But it was a sham, ours, the sort of sham that one sees performed by animals behind bars. A show – not a bond – of solidarity. Peace in our time. For now.

Now that Kelly's crabs had been burned, or drowned, or whatever the lotion was meant to have done, and he had removed to a nearby attic, which, for all of his moans about neverending stairs, was a proper flat with its own bathroom, he seemed to relax, breathe easier. He was nearly twenty-one. He would soon be coming into a bit of money, left in trust by one of our grand-monkeys. He had plans. He would travel. He would meet the perfect someone. He would return, ever smiling, and settle down with this discovered answer, who would absolutely have to have blue eyes and measure Kelly's exact height. They would both get jobs and, after work, go dancing. Together they would wow the town. They would buy some place completely fab; decorate it in the latest style, sort of Bauhausy. Any minute now. Kelly was on the brink of real life. I knew the feeling. The feeling felt hard. The hard thing was waiting. And waiting and waiting. In the nacreous shadows of Bedsitland. But what good was sitting alone in your room? Exactly. You had to get out. I was off to the Moonlight. And, on this exceptional occasion, because Kelly owed me a bundle of favours – what with the sewing-machine fandango, and the trip to McManus, and the removal to the attic – he said that he would come, which filled me with gratitude, and hold my hand, which narked me. But . . . (*God* how he loved a proviso) on condition that I pay for dinner – sign on account. Forget it, I told him: Go Dutch – proper attic-style – or nothing. And although he called me a cunt, he also grinned half-wryly, perhaps because he recognized my falling crest, the droop in my tiara. He would pick me up at nine. There was a kindness to Kelly. Even if I say so myself – I, a cunt.

I'm glad, and grateful that, despite the gallons which we went on to down (and down on account, since, in the end, I softened – for I, no less than he, did [then] have my soft side), I can still recollect that once-in-a-lifetime-night-to-end-all-nights. I suspect that sometimes one gets a hunch, a premonition of pluperfect magic, an otherworldly intuition that seems to sharpen all one's senses, all at once, into a lather of awareness which not even an ocean of drink can dull. Kelly, as agreed, picked me up at nine – although (surprise) in a taxi; but then again, he knew my little weaknesses; called them my *faiblesses*. In fact, he sometimes used to say that he was (obviously) a queen, but that I, my dear, was a total bloody regina, broke out in a rash if I so much as clapped eyes on man-made fabric. This (he claimed) was why I rarely slept out, preferred to drag my trade back to Bedsitland. (He was mistaken, as it happens. I preferred, while waiting for my train to come, to get off in public lavatories, but I didn't need to volunteer this fact.) Anyhow; we had decided, in advance, what we should wear, and I was relieved to note that, for once, Kelly hadn't played a fast one. We had opted, after a telephonic confab (he, from the comfortable privacy of his attic; I, shoving money into the coin-box on my landing), for a fashion-story in blue and white, or white and blue, depending on which of us you were admiring, for we were convinced that, with style such as ours, admire you could not but. We settled for a cannily concocted mix of ritzy-glitz and casual, so as not to seem, either way, too desperate; and we also settled for light colours, to beat those treacherous disco-lights, which, if ever you wore dark, afflicted you with the semblance of out-of-control dandruff and completely scuppered your chances. Kelly wore a brand new cotton T-shirt, of mouth-watering aquamarine — exceedingly baggy, as was, that season, obligatory. But, because it was so long, he'd had (he told me in the taxi) to chop six inches off the bottom. Why? I asked. To get into *these*, he said, breathing in and nodding towards his middle. In my self-absorption, I'd completely forgotten that he'd decided to don (which I took to be something of an honour) his absolute faves for our outing, ivory satin disco-drainpipes — then the *crème de la crème pour le soir* — into which, I could quite see, there was no question of shoving a load of spare T-shirt. Your backside, hugged by such marvels, had to look absolutely smooth, perfectly rounded and covetable. And your lunch-box — but let's not get into that, not when we're describing my brother.

I, meanwhile, stuck to washed-out jeans, though to my tightest pair, which could only be done up by jumping pogo-style. Once encased in these, it became well-nigh impossible to bend your knees for the first half-hour, until the cloth had stretched a fraction; but anyway, to finish regaling you with my ensemble: in order to compensate for the low-key character of my jeans, I wore, in combination with them, my pride and joy, a polo-neck from Benares, the colour of clotted cream, which, as well as being spun from wild silk, had gold-thread embroi-dery and semi-precious stones and god-knows-what-else thrown at the cuffs and collar-band. This was precisely the sort of creation which Mr Respectable would, in his wisdom, have deemed mincy (not meaty), but Kelly (who, thankfully, was never to meet him) did not agree. For he, like me, could appreciate its exotic (not so much Indian, as) Cossack appeal. And thus, lost in gasps of mutual admiration, and amazed by the success of our telephonic styling, which had come to such felicitous fruition without so much as a dress-rehearsal, we drew up to the door of the Moonlight.

Kelly paid for the taxi – telling our driver to keep the fiver, because he didn't want any coinage wrecking his satin – and into the club we sashayed, absorbed in each other while muttering stage-rubbish, with me, for once, at the head of the charade. The doorman could not have been more charming; half-doffed his cap, and I, being not indifferent to doffs at that time – even half ones – was suitably gratified; but I behaved as if such courtesies were usual in my magnificent life, entirely habitual. The queen at reception was a very skinny queen indeed, who, as a matter of custom, sported a scaly silver bangle in the guise of an asp, Cleopatran in spirit, along with a corresponding ring which slithered round his fuck-finger. Very Berlin before the Blitz. He tended toward the dry (both locutively and cosmetically), but tonight, as he patted his back-hair, which looked a trifle out-of-curl to me, he astoundingly beamed, particularly at Kelly, who did that to people. Next, the queen requested that my guest, after I had finished, please sign the book; and I couldn't help but notice how Kelly entered himself not in our simian surname, but, instead, as K. Grace, claiming Monte Carlo as his address. Still, the lie must have worked, because, as we set off toward the restaurant, I got the distinct impression that the doorman, who, by now, was hovering more inside his post than out, took my guest to be some very special kind of catch. Why else, otherwise, should he have winked at me, and next, as if I were engaged to it, winked at Kelly's eye-catching arse?

Down the dark green corridor we went, breezily through the array of candles, and into Ludwig's restaurant. Silver service.

Ornamental pianist. *Guten Abend*. Actually, the place could, in my honest view, have done with a few more diners – i.e. admirers – but Kelly reckoned that too many gathered heads-of-state just stole one's thunder. Still, before we'd even had a chance to clock the competition, we were greeted, with elaborate cordiality, by the maître d', who must, by this stage, have recognized me as one of the regulars. He led us to a good table. Our faultless outfits floated, in faultless choreographic unison, down to the buttoned moiré beneath us, our descent light as the gusset-feathers of some fabled Bavarian gander. We leaned back a fraction to behold the pinkness of our damask napkins being raised aloft, and thrown open with a great flourish, and released to the skies like a flutter of doves at Faringdon. And next, our countenances, without so much as a blink, countenanced those napkins to be placed upon, and almost stroke, our laps. Thank you so much. Now, what would the young gentlemen like to drink – glass of champagne perhaps? Champagne would be lovely. Kelly looked a bit alarmed, for, if I sinned of being tight-arsed, he, I'm afraid, sinned of being a bit tight-fisted. But it was all going so swimmingly that I wasn't going to let a little thing like stinginess jeopardize the delirium. So I laid his anxiety to rest by telling him – confidentially, because I didn't want anyone imagining that I was trying to impress my catch – that tonight was destined to be (as used to be said) my shout, or, at any rate, the shout of my account. *Danke* dear, he replied. I told him not to be such a Heidi.

I forget what food we ordered, not so much because it wasn't what the Find used to call Divvy – I'm sure it was – as because we were too consumed by other issues, such as who was who, who was what, and marks for their respective outfits. Hans was already leaving, which, for him, seemed on the early side; but still: he smiled across at us, and, after steering a slow turn, embarked on his departure, stately as a Teutonic galleon. Then our drinks arrived. Toasting was always tricky for us: I couldn't bear to echo Kelly's Cheers, which reminded me of yobs and beer, and Kelly couldn't stand my To Your Health, which made him think of gonorrhoea. This is why, in the end, we generally found ourselves reduced to exchanging sarky Chin-Chins – simultaneously biting and grinning, as if cast in an advert for toothpaste, to promote the ring of confidence, ding; because, though we found the expression Chin-Chin silly, at least we were agreed on one thing: that its semantic root had less to do with the ales of Newcastle than with Cinzano and Capri – Capri being, as I'd learned from the Find (along with the tip about Jeakle-as-in-Treacle) the legendary home of capers – capers in every sense, not just young flower-buds pickled in vinegar.

But I felt awkward that, once we had ensconced ourselves, and been reduced to what used to be described as Restaurant Line (one's upper half), Kelly, in his plain cotton T-shirt, looked – next to my silken Cossack splendour – a trifle humble-mumble. I said as much; yet he, being confident of his élan, even in what he called the Nuddy, said not to worry. But anyway, to compensate for what I felt had been my oversight, I signalled to the sommelier, who (quite out of character) stumbled into a leg of the piano and nearly wrecked a schmaltzy version of What I Did For Love. Kelly sniggered; I slayed him with my nostrils; and then I asked the sommelier for help with more champagne. He gave it with pleasure. Probably thought it was the boys' anniversary. But I was beyond caring now, suspended from my own disbelief, steeped in the method of remembering my own memories, swimming in my autobiographical formaldehyde. Couldn't even hear the muffled, rhythmic thuds which occasionally filtered up from the dance-floor.

Kelly was growing impatient. I could tell because his leg was jiggling about. He blamed it on the heat from all those flaming candles, but I knew him well enough to know that he was simply hotting up for a boogie-wonderland. No coffee, thanks. Next, while I signed on account – a bill that turned out to be not so much a shout as a scream to curdle the blood – Kelly slipped away to the upstairs lavatory. Yet, when he came back, he wore (not a look of relief, but) the very eyeballs of outrage, and, seating himself to tell the scandal, told me that he'd found some buffer wiping his dick with lav paper, presumably to stem the driblets of prostatic urine. Kelly called it Gross, because he liked Americans; I called it Disheartening, because I didn't know what I liked; but then, as if I were certitude incarnate, I proposed that we go down for *eine kleine tanz*. And as Kelly glided out – inspiring the assemblage of bifocals to goggle at his bi-orbital glory – the sommelier told me that we'd find the rest of our fizz in a bucket at the bar where Hans normally sat.

Downstairs was packed, so it must have been a Friday. To your left, at the base of a flight of carpeted steps which, if you possessed any self-regard, you descended at the greatest of leisures, was the low-lit bar where Hans, though absent tonight, as a rule presided: intimately dark, of indigo lacquer, shaped like a horseshoe, and, with luck, *romantisch*. Then, to your right, as you engineered a narrow ramp where strangers had a habit of taking harmless accidental liberties with occasional bits of your anatomy, there was an open counter. This was the bar from which waiters (clad not in the peppermint petal-pants which, elsewhere, had become the wanky fashion, but fitted into proper uniforms which seemed to ensure that members, however drunken, remained respectful throughout the night) served the bulk of the punters, who, if they were feeling up-beat, jiggled about the shadows and observed very hard, or, if still waiting to be mobilised, clustered round the banquettes of buttoned velvet which bordered the dream of the disco. I recall those waiters as fabulously slim and fast, much more fabulous than Cart Tarts, experts not just at lip-reading and taking orders in sign-language, but also at weaving through the throng with huge silver platters which, once relieved of glasses, they held up, like gigantic discuses, to shimmer and glint beneath the throbbing lights. You rarely see, these days, the magical globes of faceted mirror which then, like an omniscient eye, used to hang above, watch over, dance-floors. I rather miss them.

I cannot speak for Kelly, who was never, as I've said, less than the model cucumber; but I, for my part, used, after the ordeal of making an entrance, to feel too fraught within, too bonkers inside to slide myself back to serenity and pretend that nothing was happening. My progress towards the dance-floor thus became automatic, an instinctual gravitation, as if I'd crossed the length of the universe to reach this vital place before the tragedy of closing-time. And so, tonight, I led the way, while Kelly followed my false calm, but he must have been holding back, like a greater calm behind me, because it took a while for the reality of his shadow to loom over – and eclipse – my own reality. The crucial square of floor was on the small side, and tended quickly to become packed, yet people were always happy, as they proved right now, to make way like retreating clouds for the blessed arrival of late but phosphorescent stars. It was natural. Youth; false courage; all of that. Vanitas Vanitatum. *Mit Humor*, mind.

The disc-jockey stood effaced behind a fantabulosa vase – a great frosted still-life of chilly roses, dead white; but despite his vanishment from sight, which was his trademark, it always seemed to me, in my humourless young vanitas, that he was glad to have me about; because, whenever I stepped onto that floor, which I preferred to approach as if by accident, sometimes even backwards, his choice of music from that moment onward-onward-onward seemed to suggest (not Christian soldiers, but) to hell with the rest of the crowd. For he would raise – more than the heat of his sound and the speed of his lights – the pace of my pulse; and all that I recall from my nights at the Moonlight are songs which, since, have come to haunt me in other clubs, because I'm starved of them now, songs which loosened my limbs and suited my style and struck, beneath my heat and my speed and my late-adolescent charm (for I see no modesty in pretending otherwise), at my late-adolescent, latent, heart.

Love Is in the Air. Send in the Clowns. Don't Stop the Train. Believe in Dreams. Knock on Wood. Light my Fire. Do or Die. *Do or Die.*

It may, of course, merely have been a coincidence; or, perhaps, a sign that, despite the traits which I've described as contrasts between myself and Kelly, there endured resemblances, genetic *faux-amis*, which still conspired to betray our siblinghood; because, either way, I remember attributing to our joint appearance on that tiny beautiful dance-floor, in the manner that we all attribute to ourselves certain songs and claim them for tiny beautiful eternity, the song which next spun onto the turntable and spun the whole room round, a song which was nothing if not right, right and fitting, titled: We Are Family – our most especial number, our big one, our refined but grinding, sexy but incestuous classic. The clouds retired; the stars came out. And yet, that bloody brother of mine. Rather than perform a charade of forbidden fraternal love for the benefit of the titillated public, he seemed, weirdly, to prefer a tacit contest between the two of us. That is why, now, he treated me less as his fellow-jiver than like some trashy piece of rent from some public lavatory – I, a glittering young Cossack who would not be let, would not let himself go, to less than a prince of the blood. And because Kelly was the taller, so he appeared to be the stronger, while I, in my determination to remain calm, could only field his bully-spins and grin – until I was driven, in a snatch between breaths, to tell him to Cool It – to which he, after yet another vicious double-spin, replied from somewhere beneath his armpit: As a Cucumber, darling – this delivered with a Chin-Chin grin. And yet, oh bugger the Chin-Chins. Because sometimes I miss Kelly more than the very Moonlight. But let's not get drippy at this late hour.

Finished by our Family fiasco even before the song was done – and faintly nauseated by the drivel about life being fun, and about how we've just begun to get our share of the world's delights, and about high hopes for the future, and our goal being in sight, and how NO we don't get depressed, and the golden rule about having faith in You and the things you do — I decided, at the first hint of a fade-out, to take a brief sabbatical. I set off in search of our ice-bucket. Kelly eventually caught up with me at the horseshoe bar, but he took his time about it, because apparently people had kept stopping him, to shout (through the smoke and the great noise, which they abused as an excuse to get too close) what a marvellous dancer he was. Stunning, I seem to recall, was the adjective which, as he mounted his velvet stool, he proudly cited; it wouldn't have been Staggering, that's for sure; but still, now that his satin buttocks were safely out of the limelight, I began to feel restored to my former humour. And so, bottoms up, lots more bubbles, until suddenly — disaster — our bottle was over. But no sooner had we awoken to this catastrophe, which, at the time, felt global, than some globally-renowned pianist (the gobbledygook of whose name naturally meant nothing to us — Shura Something) told the barman to freshen us up. And it's just as well that Kelly resisted the strumpet's gag about being fresh enough already thanks, because, here in this vaulted cellar, the currency to be tendered was not shouts, but fresh cash — a sea in which we weren't exactly swimming. So, together, we raised our flutes to good old Shura, and flashed our rings of confidence at him, double-ding, after which, we rose — not to take our bows, but to avoid the risk of encores. For though we both agreed that our patron must be a sugar-at-heart, we were also agreed that he looked less like a concert anything than a penniless immigrant. That's youth for you. But as we began to retreat, I heard the noted pianist tell the barman that we were a couple of lovely **Boychiks★**, weren't we, which, considering my problems with metaphorical poultry, sounded suspiciously like an insult. But an insult diluted by fizz. Follow me.

Back to the action. By now the place was jumping: the

★Boychik (noun): young boy/bit of a lad (Yiddish).

narrow ramp, impossible to navigate without a permissive attitude; revellers, dancing in the aisles; strangers, necking in the alcoves; the cottage, full to bursting; waiters, rushed off their platters . . . all of which, for me, was, would ever be, the Moonlight at its brightest. Because everyone, absurd and sentimental as it now sounds, did, at that moment, strike me as wonderful: old and young; slim and fat; denim and satin; lounge-suit and leather; wedge-cut and flat-top and short-back-and-sides; prince-of-the-blood, Cart Tart. I can't explain. The drink, the swelter, the late hour; the smoke, the dry ice, the demented rainbow lights. The best of times. The highest of highs. And swept into this whole elation, Kelly and I found ourselves pushing ourselves back toward the front, back onto the dance-floor. To get stuck in. To get on down. Stars among stars, whirling and glittering good and hard, until, just at the point when I could have exploded into a thousand tiny euphoric shards, a calmer song came on, as if to ground me. It was one of those great good-nighters, growled from the gut by a pop-sensation of the time, a woman who behaved like a man and looked like a panther, whose cover-version of this period classic I then loved, but loved too badly to perform with my brother. *Too romantisch.* For I write of a place where, and a time when, men could still, if they so desired, dance enraptured in each other's arms, and do so without censure from those chippy queens who, though as yet fermenting in the prepuce of our history, would soon enough materialize, bacterialize, come crawling, in their macho-political legions, out of the pink, to pronounce, with dreary whining unity, the verdict: Prissy. Fuck Prissy, you right-on, rat-faced creeps. It was fantastic. And nothing to do with pseudo-hetero anything. Just beautiful. You should have been there; you should have been so lucky. And then the lucky people took each other in each other's arms while the rest of us watched and admired and (I) tried not to feel left out.

But next, something weird began. Shoulders near me started turning round, to face away from the dancers, and to point and gawp and marvel − quite at what, I couldn't tell, because the place was so packed, and many of the shoulders too high, or, by now, on tip-toe, craning for a vada. I told Kelly to peel his eyes on my behalf, which pissed him off because, at that sacrosanct instant, some horny piss-pot had begun to touch him up. The groper leered at me while he was at it − into the bargain? Sorry, darling, no second-fiddle stuff tonight. And then, for the first and only time in my love affair with all the loveliness of the Moonlight, it happened. The waves of people seemed to part in collective deference, and to stand back for some newly-arrived actress or diva or crown-empress or something, and then everyone began to clap and shout and cat-call as she strode most tall and blonde and Amazonian toward the dance-floor; and now the clapping grew louder and devouring and ravenous and engulfing until . . . bugger my umlaut if the goddess wasn't: Hans. Hans in the most incredible Dietrich drag. Even your mother would have passed it.

And the cover-version which, a moment earlier, had suffused the room, seemed, in a manner that I was never to understand, for it's a manner known as magic, somehow to merge with, and rewind to, and become, the song itself, the original − though without words, for Hans would never (*Gott in Himmel*, no), ever have mimed. And as Marlene, in her third transfiguration (not Weimar tart, nor popular pin-up, but) Historical Cabaret Star, made her progress through the multitude and took to the stage, the floor grew dark and was reduced to a single, unforgettable waterfall of light; and the crowd came surging over, pushing and shoving to where I was standing, half-blocking my sight; but I managed, thanks to my elbows, to stick to my front-row guns. And for a few precious moments, I became an impossible thing: a child again, wide-eyed.

But Marlene was no dummy. She knew better than to try to schmooze us in her native tongue − too obvious, too easy, and perhaps undiplomatic. As for English, it would have been, well, unimaginative; plus, remember, *das* was *nicht* so *gooot* the language of our star. And so she sang, or rather, talked – fabled *diseuse* that she was – in the language of romance, a song which she claimed to have discovered after the war, in Paris, but which (we weren't dummies either, *Liebling*-darling) she had simply stolen from a sparrow, a collaborative one from Pigalle, but – big deal. The important thing is that Marlene managed, as with all well-stolen things, including hearts, to make of her theft a triumph. And the words which she gave us, although you know them well, allow me, nevertheless, the pleasure of quoting:

> *Des yeux qui font baisser les miens,*
> *Un rire qui se perd sur sa bouche,*
> *Voilà le portrait sans retouches*
> *De l'homme auquel j'appartiens.*
>
> *Quand il me prend dans ses bras*
> *Il me parle tout bas:*
> *Je vois la vie en rose.*
> *Il me dit des mots d'amour,*
> *Des mots de tous les jours,*
> *Et ça m'fait quelque chose.*
> *Il est entré dans mon coeur,*
> *Une part de bonheur*
> *Dont je connais la cause.*
> *C'est lui pour moi, moi pour lui, dans la vie*
> *Il me l'a dit, l'a juré, pour la vie*
> *Et dès que je l'apperçois*
> *Alors je sens en moi,*
> *Mon cœur qui bat.*

And as Marlene serenaded us with her untouched, untouchable portrait of a man to whom, of course, she never did belong, I remember being surprised by how much more seductive the French language sounds transposed to a German accent than the other way round. But when I turned discreetly to confer this cultured pearl upon the ear of Kelly, he told me, in no uncertain terms, to shut my trap: *Ta gueule* is what he said, in fact. Because, even on my own beat, and even inadvertently, I was pissing on his parade, blocking his vital light. Groper O'Leery, you see, had managed, by the second verse of the proceedings, to introduce his paw to the rear of Kelly's satin – to its interior. Tacky. *Ta main.*

Not so Marlene. Nothing tacky about her; not in any shape or idiom. She looked entirely amazing, transcendental, and wore (not some little black dress from Paris after the war, but) a shimmering sheath, a miracle of silken mesh and bugle-beads and watery sequins which hinted at nudity yet remained, in essence, ethereal; a second skin whose flesh-coloured base, depending on the lights, altered hue from palest pink, to peach, to silver, to frosted crystal, and which, thanks to some transformative basque, rendered her slim as a phial of elixir, chic as any woman from France. The inadmissible pride of Weimar. There was something at once fragile and defiant about her stance. Her mannish hands were poised upon her hip, so that her thumbs alone – impeccably manicured – ever met your eye. Didn't do to show too much in this business. Marlene knew. No dummy she, even as dummylike she stood, impassive and beguiling in her honey-coloured wig, which rose at the side and paused, before swooping down across one cheek. Her eyes, while she performed, remained half-closed, as if preferring to look back, back through the lashes of make-believe, into an imaginary past rather than toward an unimaginable future, a future of unimaginable gloom. But her beautiful opalescent lips – regardless – sufficed. Her melancholy pout said it all: *Mon cœur qui bat.* Who could ask for more? Well, Kelly apparently. For by the time that Marlene had drawled to her closing line, my shaming brother had vanished. To the cottage. Too bad, as they say in America; *tant pis*, as they say in the language of romance, because Kelly, in his eagerness to be taken to the top, had missed the single climax worthy of note. And as our star took her bow, and the crowd erupted, and everyone went mad, Bravo-Bravissima-Brava, a torrent of roses was suddenly rained upon the floor (by the disc-jockey, whose face at last you saw), and Marlene, greatest rehearser of them all, bent down in a teetering half-curtsey, and claimed a single of her many trophies and smiled with the modesty which results from a meticulous choreography, and, before the spell could be broken, was allowed to fade into the mists like the goddess that she was. And then I stepped forward, just before the final disco-spin which was meant to coil us back into the mortal world, and, without a thought, I snatched another of those roses, and took it home, and let it dry, and have it still, in a box from a shop called Nostalgia; and although, like so much in the realm of memory, my commemorative flower has shrunk and gone to sepia, whenever I happen to catch a glimpse of it while rooting around for some other old memento, say a letter, or a card, or just a pack of lies, that Moonlight Rose still looks to me, in the manner of magic, to be of the purest white. And ever since that night – do you know – I have found myself to be more tolerant of lederhosen. Honestly.

But the honest truth, I now believe, is that Marlene's evening marked a point of rift, a soundless (but chronic) fissure between Kelly and me. For, even though, back in our heated youth, we'd stood too close to the beat of immediacy to read or realize anything with any degree of accuracy, later, in morbid retrospect, I would come to recognize our visit to the Moonlight as punctuating the loss of hope for us as siblings. We had little to recommend our lives, I grant you; but we did have choices, and these we had in abundance – choices such as the use, or misuse, of: the colon. Yet the divergence in the choices which Kelly and I were to make would eventually direct us on such opposite paths, propel us in search of such antithetical solutions, that any further contact between us – in shops, in clubs, in seedy cinemas – was to prove less fortuitous than accidental, and, later still, to amount to gestures of goodwill, designed to assuage the malingering ache of guilt.

Marlene had, like a contentious revelation, brought us to a peculiar schism: I was in raptures about the whole incredible drag experience, which struck me as almost spiritual, full of complicated beauty and complicated dreams; Kelly was in raptures about O'Leery, whose appeal, though Kelly described it as cathartic, was simple. This is not to say that I was averse to promiscuity. I wasn't. I went with it, with its anonymity, its ephemerality, its diffusive benefits, its quick efficacy, the whole bang shoot. But it *is* to say that, as a vehicle, Kelly deployed this sexual perk, which, a silver jubilee back, a universe ago, felt so particularly ours, so singularly male and so freewheeling, for aims that didn't tally with my ideals. If earlier I'd been narked by his quip about coming to hold my hand at the Moonlight, now – a mere day later, at the Queen & Garter, while his sights darted about in search of fresh meat at the same old abattoir – I was more than merely narked. I was taken aback and wounded and angry, because next Kelly told me that he felt (not grateful, but) sad. Sad and sorry for me. That I was doing it all wrong. That I should follow his example. That the Moonlight stank. That it was for failures and has-beens and jumped-up trash. That I was messing up my life. That there was a proper way to go about things. That I'd learnt zilcho from my time in London. I told him, to get my own back, that he was like that girl in *Looking for Mr Goodbar*, and that, just like her, he was headed for disaster. He told me that I drove him mad. And then he stormed out, wearing shoulder-pads.

There were two types of men for me at that time, neither of which I could properly handle: those with whom I could fall in love, to whom I would look up, and those with whom I screwed around, on whom I could look down. I seemed unable to reconcile these two types. I was too frightened of disappointing the first and being dumped, and too frightened of being plagued by the second – the embarrassing pick-ups, however well-hung. With the princes, I could focus on everything except their genitals; with the tricks, I could focus on nothing but. I could talk with the former, but no sooner had I opened my mouth than I became convinced that I'd blown my erotic chances; and I refused to talk to the latter because I hated their stories as much as I loved their cocks and balls and arses. This dichotomy, which came from fear, was nearly to cost me my balance, but it would ultimately prove valuable, because, in the absence of my rightful Tony or Patrick or Michael, I, ever stubborn and intransigent, wouldn't let anyone – Tom, Dick, or Harry – stick it up my arse. Fucked-up, perhaps; but fucking lucky.

Kelly's attitude to men was different. His take on them was purely linear. You met someone you fancied, tall and blue-eyed. You went to bed with them and were reciprocal. No holds were barred. You kissed them the morning after. You exchanged opinions about everything, including Bauhaus. You were open from the start. You told them about your homo-brother. You might well bitch about him. And then you would embark on a (monogamous) marriage. This marriage could last a month, a week, a weekend, or a matter of hours. Its lifespan was irrelevant, because, every time, you went into the business entirely; you embraced the potential of each new such affair with the same smiling honour, over and over. And if it went wrong – oh well – plenty more fish in the sea. In the sea? Where man cannot survive?

Where Kelly went to survive was an amorphous thing known as the Scene: plummeting dives where the way you looked and moved and danced was all that counted. And these looks and moves and dances changed, as did your partners, with a frenetic regularity. But either you followed the flow and rhythm of such dictates, whose instigators were a mystery to me, and an irritant, or your sexual credibility floundered. Difference spelt arrogance; homogeneity, solidarity. Yet Kelly, and jillions of others like him, called this lifestyle Gay. I called it galling. His people holidayed in Mykonos, Fire Island, Key West, or, at a penniless pinch, in Gran Canaria. But how could I seriously consider such resorts, such queerly aggressive locations, I who couldn't even come to terms with the soft option of being a Village Person? I longed, instead, to be taken back, back to the Deauville of the Twenties. Or to Petersburg before the Bolsheviks. Or to Beirut when it was fanfared as the Paris of the Orient. Or to Buenos Aires when it was hailed as the Paris of South America. To landscapes of delusion, to impossible colour schemes – given the denial of which, I preferred to stay put, here in Limbo, Wishin' and Hopin'. Never really thinking.

I think, however, that I must have taken Kelly's critical concern, his concerned critique, to heart, because, for a while, I did persuade myself (for my own good, as he had put it) to do the rounds of the suitable, promising, vibrant clubs that he had advised, details of which he had taken the trouble to post to me – jotted on the back of a card, featuring Carmen Miranda in a single, strategic banana. Those clubs, miles away from anywhere comforting, were underground miasmas, roughly modelled on some rank American prototype; and though – on account of my youth, or my denim – I seemed, at their respective entrances, to pass muster, yet I couldn't ever feel, once within, more than left out, like a wet blanket or damp squib or failure. It was in places of this nature that, as I mentioned earlier, I was to find myself treating hopeless men like hopeless mongrels, usually in the back-rooms, where anonymity was everybody's right, but anonymous overtures to people in my fucked-up category were not always wise. I would stand around, peering at the fluctuations of copulative scrums, generally flabby leather-queens in the most absurd ensembles imaginable, and, as they panted and grunted and slavered and yeah-manned and exchanged all manner of unearthly everything – save orgasm – I would try to pluck lyrics from the darkened, throbbing skies, and wonder whether the appointment of a central chandelier would have been such a crime. I preferred, you see, men in black tie with their flies undone to pallid lumps of simulated masculinity smeared in slime. That was my problem, my hang-up.

When, thanks to the muscle-relaxant of amyl nitrite, the fashion for fist-fucking was brought to town – demurely, to begin with, which is why this gestural practice was initially labelled a Kit-Kat (four fingers max.) as opposed to a Head-bang, which denoted the pitch to which sexual modernity had apparently escalated in the Big Apple, I began to feel trapped, or redundant. At any rate: out of the running. And outnumbered. For, not only would I have preferred to shove, sooner than any part of my frigid self, some foreign item up a stranger's extraverted arse (a cabriole leg, for instance, not that such strangers would necessarily have told the difference), but I also found, by weird reversal, the attempted insertion even of a wriggling pinkie up my pent-up jacksie to be more forward than flattering, like the attentions of McManus. Plus (oh what a stupid fucking nance) I couldn't stand the fumes of other peoples' leaky crap, never mind risk, when those dungeons grew too crowded, the warm but questionable compliment of an unsolicited golden shower down my front, or a smeary fae-cal hand imprinted on my back. So let me just reveal my own hand now, and open myself to the scorn of the likes of my brother: I simply happened to prefer the Moonlight – all right? – where I could dress as I liked, and dress beyond the nines, and enjoy dinner beforehand rather than posthumous fish-'n-chips in some grubby back alley, and dance without being shoved around, and star without malice, and mix with people who made it not a threat, nor a profession, to be homosexual. Who made it feel special. Which is why, in the end, I flunked out of my further sexual education, and elected to flounce back into the lazy safety of my childish, old, romantic club.

It must have been a good, but not very great, while later (certainly closer to my purchase of the mahogany table than to the present day) that I next ran into love. I remember how, by this stage, Kelly had reached his majority and, with it, come into his money. Almost on a reflex, he had given up his attic, which, though he now seemed to despise it, he offered me the option to colonize. (What, quit my palace and remove to nether-Fulham? Thanks but no thanks, darling; not for all the bathrooms in that soulless borough.) In the event, Kelly bought himself a studio-flat in Holland Park, a district which, though not, back then, as desirable as it is now, was certainly desirable for such healthy pursuits as Flora & Fauna – plus the Underground. For, no sooner had Kelly gained the deeds of his new property than he also managed, by some amazing fluke, to gain employment with one of those straight-laced firms in the City – proffered by some closet-case who'd taken a blatant shine to Kelly, and whom we may therefore presume amounted to the Fluke. But since Kelly, as well as smiling to perfection, spoke perfect Spanish, he may have impressed his employers more for his interpretative skills than for his straight-lacedness; because suddenly, quicker than you could say Bauhaus, he was overtaken by the wheels of chance and despatched on an eighteen-month secondment to some enormous banking high-rise in Los Angeles – a prospect which, despite the annoyance of not being able to enjoy his first proper taste of ownership, he welcomed. For aside from the fact that he still hadn't chanced upon his blue-eyed answer, who might well, in the circs, turn out to be some drop-dead Californian, the money was beyond resistance; top dollar. Furthermore, Kelly was sure that he'd enjoy the faggy American lifestyle, its oceanic air, so cool and so laid-back – from the beach-boys and the dream-boats, all the way down to the winking versatilities of the adjective Gross. And so I, who, let's face it, had nothing if not leisure on my hands, was left entrusted with the ironic task of supervising Kelly's workmen, and trying to ensure that, by the time they'd been paid off, a finish of such hypermodernistic excellence had been realized that I couldn't myself afford to rent the result. The plan, instead, was that the studio should be let to a friend of Kelly's, a boy called Matthew, whom I didn't know. Kelly had, in point of fact, been forced to arrange it all beforehand, because I'd refused to pimp, beyond completion of the job, for a suitable tenant, by which Kelly had meant homosexual. At any rate, this unknown Matthew (Kelly filled me in) had recently split from some creature with a roving willy, and decided, despite the hassle of having to commute, to move back into his parents' house in Kingston, because he wanted to lie low for a while, and besides, his parents were at ease with honorifics such as Queen; so that all I had to do, once the studio had been completed, was to tele-phone this Matthew, fix a meeting, and hand over a set of keys. The rent, needless to say, was to be paid straight to Kelly – by direct debit, thereby neatly circumventing my itchy fingers; but I can think of more sensitive, more delicately indelicate, prudences.

On the day of his departure, I accompanied Kelly to Gatwick, and though I tried to appear grown-up and respon-sible, I also attempted to bring a touch of levity to the proceedings. I made Kelly promise that, even if he should happen to cross the border into Mexico, and even if, as seemed equally likely, he should happen to dabble in recreational weed, he would never, under any circumstances – whether high as a kite, or down in the dumps – be tempted into a poncho. And I remember offending the snot-faced officials at passport control by kissing my brother's cheek for the first time in all the years that we had been brothers; and then, oblivious to their sneers, I further remember watching his smiling loveliness stroll away towards that unexpected new blossoming which the gods had suddenly awarded him, and watching him stroll so full of hope and promise and young life, and transformed, for all the world to see, into an adorable Preppy before he'd even reached his goal. And as I waved, a little gauchely, stiffly, I recollect being seized by an unexpected pang of the oddest thing, a sort of homesickness – not for the monkeys, you fool – a sickness for him, for Kelly, for his former company, which I'd taken as given, and had undervalued, and was now on the brink of losing, and for his proximity, however crabby, of which I'd never contemplated being cheated. Because now, whatever I may have earlier feared, I really was alone, on my own without devices. I may even have blubbed in the taxi back to town – but, Christ, pull yourself together: Kelly said that he planned to come back for Christmas, to hold your stupid hand. So get a grip, get into your glad-rags, get into a cab, get yourself back to the Moonlight, and knock 'em dead on your way down to the bar. Buy yourself a great *Campari-arancia*, make it extra-strong and extra-scarlet, and, raising your tall glass high, make a silent toast, as he flies across the firmament, to your brother's new life. Grin a Chin-Chin if you like, but don't, whatever else you do, close your eyes. Be vigilant. Don't miss a trick. He might be round the corner: your princely knight, your shining stallion. The love of your life.

I get muddled now. It was either at the end of that same night, or of another very like it; but it was certainly in the darkest early-morning hours, outside the Moonlight, and shortly before closing time: I used to make a point of getting out ahead of the rush. The street was glittering from some earlier shower. The air was brisk; it steamed about your mouth. Absolute soundlessness as you wrapped up. I decided to head down, downstream to the confluence of traffic. Then I stopped at a corner, in the hope of hailing (not Mary, but) a cab. And, while waiting, I remember vaguely thinking about the day to come, about its thankless tasks – sorting out my place, polishing my palace – about the impossible chore of meeting my own unmeetable standards. And then there was a screech of brakes nearabout. A taxi. I awoke to my chance. Someone was getting out, some man. But

I didn't run. You just would not have done. You would have walked much as I did, very slowly, very calmly. We have all the time in the world.

I think that he was drunk. Heaven knows that I was – perfectly. I stopped in my tracks. I dug my fists into my pockets. I turned toward my right, by forty-five degrees, by forty-five precisely, rotating in the most self-conscious quarter-revolution known to man. And now, I did that ancient thing: I stared at a shop-glass. He passed beneath the streetlamp behind my shadow; but as his shirt, which was checked in red-and-black, and large, and broad of shoulder, and worn outside, like the shirt of a forester, went by, ignoring my worsted back, I could tell that his eyes were set on my reflected image, which looked ashen. There was a pause, and then, he did that obvious other thing: he equally stared at the shop-glass. We uttered nought. No smiles were swapped, not even of enquiry. But next, there happened this: he slowly took my hand, took it out from my pocket and placed it, held it, kept it in his large, black-gloved one; and then, as if following some torrential upset, as if wishing to comfort a disconsolate child, he led me away, away from the echoes of the Moonlight – to which I suspect that he'd been bound – and into a whole blood-orange sunrise of enchantment. I have to tell you: I had absolutely no doubts. I had the most absolute certainty. It was just as you had always avowed. It was just as it must be when you meet the man you're meant to marry. Prince, stallion, canopy, trunk, buttress. Whatever. Whatever the stars have planned.

We strolled for longer than, alone, I might have done, round a couple of needless squares of Georgian silence. His strides were slower, but more empowered, than mine: I walked from the brittle ankle; he, from his muscular thigh. He wore, I can't forget, corduroys at that genesis, very baggy mustard-brown, and heavy brogues, or boots perhaps. Inevitably he brought to mind a woodcutter. That is what I could not but imagine as I watched his trousered legs proceed, progress below us, all that way down, making headway through another land. But I also thought that he had the touch, the feel, the spirit of a monarch. An authority about him, a virile force, a confident refinement. He smelt, just faintly, of lemon-groves – or perhaps it was I. Unimportant. Immaterial. Mine was his and his was mine. Another taxi passed. I hailed it on an impulse, and directed it to Bedsitland, mumblingly embarrassed. The driver forced me to repeat my whereabouts. I need not have worried. My guest, my everlasting love-without-a-doubt, could not have cared a copper tuppence. He was already inside, installed, but holding the door ajar. Sitting on the left, ceding me the right, like a gentleman. See what I mean? Bingo, jackpot, bull's-eye. Still not a word had passed between us. He pulled off his gloves. And then – forget the driver for once – he took my frozen face in his burning hands and kissed me upon the brow. Twice. It never gets better than that. You can close your eyes now.

In Bedsitland, my nacreous shell glowed (not quite pristine, but) presentable. I had a habit: when invisible, I doubled as my valet. You never knew; you lived in hope; you could afford (not slaves, but) order. For, if, after a night abroad on slip'ry tiles, you rolled back home, relieved of sperm but resigned at heart, resigned to the fact that tonight was not the night, not it either, not the thousandth-and-first, nor second, nor sixty-ninth, then you were grateful to your secret self for the comforts of a warming light, a record in place – some fugue, some unaccompanied toccata – and a bed (of sorts), neatly turned down. Over the mantle, I recall a vase of veily froth, gypsophila. Its whole cheap innocence: I loathe it now. But then, in my twentieth idiot year, it made me conjure clouds and dreams of triumph.

By the time we had sat down, I had begun to fear that something might be up – an uncommon language, perhaps, or dumbness; because, though he replied – with a m'hm – that he wouldn't mind a drink, this announcement issued from his chin and not his mouth. I suspected that we might have been attracted, drawn to closeness, not by any urgent need of dialogue, nor by the wish for immediate sexual respite, but by some mutual sense of loss or sadness. That is how it felt to me, melancholy – a sea in which, unlike the sea of cash, I had routinely swum. Kelly would have laughed. Or, at worst, he would have said: And if it all goes wrong – so what? – plenty more fish, etcetera.

My lover, for lover he already was, was older than I; rising, I would surmise, toward the cusp of forty; conceivably just gently over it. I couldn't have given a damn. He was a man, a grown one, and mine. I held up two bottles, one in each hand: vodka and wine. He nodded toward the latter. His name – once (to my relief) he answered – was: Thomas. Low and dark though it came out, I harboured not a doubt. And yet, that first and sacred name of his, was, on that first of our sacred séances, all that I learned about him. He didn't ask if I was George, not straightaway, not in return. He knew about tact; he was at ease with silent calm. He drained his wine in one, without a sound; looked around the room, as if to drink it up; and next, stood up. He turned towards the place where, at that congress, I remember that I sat, near the edges of the table, near my own glass; and, from all his way up, from his mammoth great height, he unbelted his trousers. Now he knelt between my thighs, and fiddled with my buckle. He won. I was, was being, had been undone – until . . . he took a pause in mid-action. I neither minded nor worried. What was, what is, what could ever be the hurry? We have all the time in the world. He laid his head upon my lap, as if our roles had been reversed and now it was I who had become the trusted beloved. He even stroked the tail of my belt against the back of his neck, or his neck for the solace of my leather; and the fairness of his neck, I saw, was burnished by the sun, like the neck of a true traveller, a lover of the outdoor life, a man who worshipped not only the elements, but every element of my own nature – inner, outer, (pending), future, past. I kissed his hair. I could not but. A lemon-grove. Exactly that. Already, I swear to you, it was enough. It would have done.

I could have died without a qualm. If my friends could see me now – with Thomas, *Tomás*, Tommaso, *Tomasz*. Anywhere and anyhow. An easy name to carry – even in your wildest, most unbridled fancies; even to Los Angeles. I looked out of the window, far and away, up into the bruised thereafter.

Then I looked down. He was slapping his profile with my strap, as if in self-mocking chastisement, with an irony that I couldn't altogether fathom – too profound, too private. I think that he was blushing as he gathered himself back. He apologized in a manner which amounted, well, to manna. He said that this was all too good to start now, so late at night. Would I be cross if we postponed it for another day, an afternoon perhaps, then go for dinner somewhere? (Would I be cross? I was flipping ecstatic. I could wait till kingdom come. He could do whatever he liked. But I,) I would like, I said, to drive him back to wherever he wanted. (I wanted to do something. I wanted, of course, to have him by my side for as long as the fates would have it.)

Kelly's reward to me, in return for the business of the studio, had been the loan of his car, which, though nothing very special, did, nonetheless, avail me of a freedom which, before that time, I had never imagined. And never was such freedom imagined with more gratitude than it was now. We got in, Thomas and I. I switched on my headlights. We could have been off to wheresoever you liked, on honeymoon, or simply away, or away for the rest of our lives. He told me, with his hand, re-gloved, to drive straight on along the Embankment, and turn, once I'd reached the second set of traffic lights, sharply to the left; then, to head up and follow the curve of the road towards the park. I didn't know where I was going. I was going mad. I was thinking about whether he mightn't have some lover. It made my breast start up, begin to thump. What rubbish. Grow up. First set of lights: a gorgeous emerald. I drove on, wizzed past. Next set: bright red. I slowed to a halt. Rain was starting. Windscreen wipers. I geared myself down; then, depressed the clutch. Suddenly he grabbed my hand-break, and yanked it up, like a driving instructor, or examiner, or guardian. As if he were Something. I went into neutral, to show that I'd got the message. He looked at me. No smiling. But next, in a perfect sort of symmetry, as a perfect echo of our first beginning, he went and blessed my soul, erased its turmoil with a kiss upon my brow. Red, by now, had wedded amber. I sped ahead into the night, and swung sinistrally, as was required. And then – but seconds down the adventure – it happened, right up my backside: police-lights, followed by some hysterical siren. A vanload of the mothers. I felt so ashamed. I told him please to go. I told him I was sorry. I felt (not sick, but) sickened. I said that it was easier if I dealt with this alone. He said that he understood. We both got out. And as the uniforms bore down, he said, across the icy chill, a most bewildering thing, probably to protect the precious secret which, whatever else, must be preserved, concealed in safety from those pigs. And what he said, very nearly with conviction, was this: Bad luck, old boy, give my regards to your father when you speak. And then, he was no more, was gone by some quick turn into the murk of some dark side-street. And now the questions from officialdom began. And well-worn notepads were produced from dark-blue rumps. And that was when I realized that I had no greater means of reaching him than I possessed the means of rewinding. The law had seen the 'snog'.

But, needless to say, the police – at least, the pair of constables who did for me, while their law-abiding cronies cackled in the snug immunity of their elevated vehicle, alarm-lights (still) all-of-a-spin, as in a flashing disco – admitted to no such thing. They said I had a flat (not top, but) tyre. I said I was surprised to hear this, because the car had only recently been serviced (on Kelly's instructions, but for my benefit – a detail which was neither of, nor in, their interest). They asked if I'd been drinking. I said that I'd been out to dinner. To *dinner*, Sir, at three in the morning? And then the breathalyser appeared, with a sinister sort of efficacy. I was shaking. I didn't know how to breathe. I was a queen. Thrice I failed to register, like Wallis Simpson – or was it St Peter? They said: Sod this. I thought that they were going to tell me to watch what I did in public, and send me off with a flea in my ear. Not a bit of it. They bundled me into their van, which stank of curried farts and constabulary armpits, and before I'd finished hearing all about the previous evening's football semi-whatsit on the telly . . . *cor*, we'd arrived at the local nick. Despite its moralistic reek, the place was deceptively attractive: old-fashioned, not unlike a well-regarded ale-house, garnished with healthy-looking hanging-baskets and similiar niceties, and set in a most respectable street. I seem to recall a flurry of campy little fuschias about the doorway. I also recall that this particular station was located exactly four doors away from a studio once owned by (not Kelly) but Noël, the sadly lamented Coward, late of Kingston (not on Thames, but) Jamaica. I know because, these days – oh the serendipity – I practically *live* in that bloody studio. Call me Gertie; call me frigging Ermintrude; I couldn't give a flying finger. Not any longer, not now that the pig-hole has been ripped to pieces; has had to be rebuilt; because no-one, as justice would have it, wanted to inhabit those filthy bricks, which, despite their facile and deceptive floral cutesiness, were like the bricks of a hospital-wing weighed down by too many bad memories ever to have stood a change of use.

Memories: I remember this, and I'll be quick because it's dreary. I was received by a black – yes, black (for, along with my late-adolescent charm, I see no point in pretending otherwise) – sergeant, who was flicking through the previous evening's news. As I ventured into the glare of his strip-lights, trying to pretend that the denim beneath my coat was a full (not give-away, but) ermine lining, he coolly glanced up, then loudly asked, as if I were deaf, whether I'd got aids yet. My hearing nearly failed me. The irony almost escaped me. Then, I was stunned. I bit my lip, clamped it. And next, they gave me a blood test, jab. And thus it came to pass that, when the limit came, I was soaring high above it, surprise-surprise. And then I went to court. And, for my appearance, I wore a brilliant tie, whiter-than-white with a load of black dots dancing the fucking mambo. And I was given a crappy barrister, who got bollocked by the magistrate, because His Worship was keener on hookers and vagrants and stabbers and muggers and credit-card sharps than some silly defendant who – there but for the grace – could have been his nellie grandson. Kindly let's not waste more time. Next case, please; hammerbang. And thus I lost my licence for a disgrace of months, with the additional, not very special fine of £100. I didn't tell Kelly; I didn't dare; not until his place had been done up. Later, Matthew would inherit the use of that car, because someone had to keep the engine alive. But that was yet to come.

First, I had the problem of Thomas to sort out, his whole enigma, that haunting dream of paradise which, thanks to the law's irruption, I couldn't seem to summon back. And for some while – some weeks, in fact – it propelled me, wishin' and hopin' and thinkin' and prayin' and plannin' and dreamin' each night of his charms, all over wretched town, from sauna-bath to pub to club to pub to sauna-bath and round and round, until, in the end, in the full stop of time, it drove me, weepy with exhaustion, and with tyres of sleeplessness under my eyes, back to my doctor's side. It was a Monday. I couldn't bear to start another week, never mind another life.

By 'my doctor', I do not mean McManus. Now that Kelly was gone, the thought of the chirpy Scott at the public clap-clinic had become as appealing as sibling sandwiches. No, my real physician, my true and trusted one, who, for a foolish, penny-pinching while, I'd thought that I would bypass, was emphatically Private. That's why his identity must remain emphatically that; but he was, in any event, quite simply known as Dr John – by all of us, by anyone who (not had a heart, but) happened to coincide at his practice, which was neo-classical. And Dr John, I have to say, was the only queer ever truly to confound me. For although – with the merciful exception of feltching – he couldn't have been at greater verbal ease with sexual gerunds such as rimming and sucking and fisting and fucking and bleeding and cumming (nor – apparently – a more successful champion of the hulky rowing type), yet he couldn't, to my eyes, have seemed more straight or more correct in his handsome chalkstripes, less salacious or less shabby. He never touched you other than respectably, with a respectful sort of detachment, as if you were a chipped, or cracked – but always reparable – work of art, rather than a lump of meat flung onto a slab. No softish erring fingers; no underhand massage-stuff. Not once. He was like an old-school diplomat.

Dr John took care of patients whom one could describe as arty – largely male and largely deviant, generally attached to the higher ranks of theatre and film and ballet, plus the occasional, exceedingly superior, dreadfully overqualified, A La Carte Tart. How I, a complete, unpromising nothing, ever managed to land upon his bandwagon is almost a matter of melodrama, entirely thanks to the kindness of one of the gaggle so reviled by Mr Respectable – the boy who used to wear the financial paper folded under his arm – but I don't want digress into that anecdote now. Anyway, I hesitate to use about Dr John's practice the élitist letter Alpha, in case, by this, you should infer a happy-clappy Evangelical quill in my cap. For if ever I frothed about the mouth and rolled about the aisles and babbled in unspeakable tongues, it was never in real life. It was only ever here, only to you, all over the squirming parchment. But my point is this: the quality of patient to whom Dr John attended, whose welfare he supervised, was – regardless of preferred erotic posture, and elected brand of lubricant, and size and cut of member, and orchidal pendency, and national identity, and income bracket and all the rest of that rubbish – high. Classy. No porno stuff. No escorts. No model-boys. No riff-raff.

When I was shown into Dr John's consulting room, there was a shaft of dusty, old-fashioned light warming the space between us. We were both wearing suits, I remember – he, as always, with his Corpus Christi tie; I, with an open-necked shirt, white button-down: any constriction about my neck would, at that time, have made me gag. As ever, we shook hands; and then we walked around the gulf of his Persian rug to our designated islands. He sat behind his desk; I attempted to settle in front. He said that he was glad to see me, and sounded as if he meant this formality – a formality which I, however, suddenly found myself unable to volley back. Not one of my syllables would rise to the challenge. I was starting to retch. He tried to help. How was I keeping?

I slid my gaze along the leather of his desk, but couldn't summon the strength even to meet the contour of his mandible, which, though square, was finely sculpted. The peace of his sanctum, this sudden unexpected calm, was filling me with tears from another land. I looked, for relief, beyond my knees, toward my feet; but everything down there, in that realm of frozen life which reminded me of Georgian squares by moonlight, was starting to swim before my eyes. And then, as I began to raise my speechless hands by way of substitute, my head seemed to float away and forward, as if turning in deep waters, and to alight, very slowly, forehead onto wooden ledge, upon the shore of his prescriptions. And then the surface of his table became flooded, in a manner which it shames me to recount, with my maudlin tears, which would not cease. I couldn't come to an end, nor yet could I begin. I could not breathe – in or out; out or in. Thus seized, thus paralysed midstream, I was incapable to the last degree. Not a quarter, but a total revolution. I remained in this position, on the blurry verge of faintness, for a century, just wanting to go to sleep. And that, in the dreadful end, is what I told him. I just needed some sleep.

Dr John said that we all did. Nor was he being facetious. He was almost solemn in his reaction to my predicament, which, even though, as yet, unknown to him, he somehow made me sense that he could feel. And then he asked why it should be that I couldn't sleep: any reason in particular, anyone responsible? The man was a gentle genius. He made it seem so easy. He led me back, as if by the hand, to the core of my childish misery. And so, while my hand attempted to control the pulsing throb along my jugular, I told him that a man had, perhaps, been close to the cause initially, or rather, the loss of him; but then I added that since the person was no longer around, thanks to the intervention of the police (a circumstance which I did not explain, just too humiliating, and which Dr John probably took to mean some cottaging incident), now, in the aftermath, I found myself dragging, as if it were a leaden carcass, a load of residual symptoms: anxiety and insomnia and lassitude. And it was with the mess of all this, I said, that I sought his opinion. Did he think I was ill?

I was not ill. He was sure of it. But perhaps a little bit depressed? Was there a possibility? The possibility had never really occurred to me. I had never heard my state of statelessness so clearly, or kindly, put. Might I, he asked, be stressed? Stressed, to me, was a novel adjective (more novel than Strained by far); it almost sounded as if he were asking whether I ever wore an accent; took me back to Latin class – to scansion and spondees and dactyls. Stressed how? Under pressure, he replied. I wasn't under pressure. (I was just submerged and lonely. But, in order to dissimulate my plight) I said that my brother had recently left for Los Angeles. The doctor ignored my flight into irrelevancy, and asked what I was doing with my own life. My own life? Professionally, he elaborated. Well, I replied, I wasn't a prostitute (nor yet was I). He laughed. I wiped my eyes, and blew my nose, and tried to laugh back. Already I felt lighter. Dear boy, he said – which made me fall a tiny bit in love with him – and then he suggested: did I need a break, ought I to go travelling, when did I last have a holiday? I didn't know. Beyond the previous month I remembered next to nothing. I was vacant, yet I was also stuck. I said I'd go away when I was twenty-one, once I'd come into some money. I would vanish from this godforsaken town. That's more like it, he encouraged.

But more like it is the fact that Dr John did, in the end, though with a heavy, most conservative reluctance – which made me fall straight out of love again – provide me with a script for sleeping tablets. I still remember the name of those pills, because it was so brilliant: Tranxene. Made you think of some Country & Western songstress with huge hair and a micro-mini, belting it out to her lousy cheating prick. Dr John made me promise to stick to the right dosage (a single tablet, one hour before going to sleep) and to watch my intake of drink. I should ring him in a week. But by the time I'd left his surgery, I knew that I was fixed. The pills were just a reward for my melancholy, like sweeteners. And when, after a trip to the chemist's, I opened the little brown bottle for an introductory peep – guess what? – I saw that Tranxene and her many sisters were all, to a woman, pink.

And then I flung myself upon my couch, which I regret to say was (not turned-down, but) all messed up. Oh do relax: what's the good of privacy if not to afford one the occasional slip into slatternliness? So I reclined in the swathes of my palatial informality, and settled to ponder my advancement; because, thanks to Dr John's diagnostic wizardry, the future seemed, despite its recent clouds, suddenly to glitter sunnily. And yet, in order to get that bloody sun up and running, I decided, on the spur of the moment, to settle a couple of minor issues – the first being this: I was whacked, and, after my many nocturnal manoeuvres, in dire need of a siesta – a need against which the traffic, like some artillery batallion, seemed determined to conspire. So, in order to beat the annoyance, I adopted the most sensible strategy, the most cunning, which was a catalyst. In short: I popped one of those little pink pills. Bless you, Tranxene. You went down like a dream.

And now for the second issue, to which I could attend while the soporific kicked in. I strutted down to the landing, and picked up the payphone, of which I was completely sick. I may not have been privy to the joys of a high attic, but I had lofty concerns to deal with, such as a low tolerance of the strictly outgoing, and a dislike of clanking coinage. So I dialled the operator, and asked some woman to put me through to the engineers, which she, having told me to hang on a tick, did. And then I informed one of her male colleagues, who sounded thirteen and not exactly Euripides, that I'd like to install a telephone in my new premises. And when he demanded the subscriber's name, I flicked through my address-book and informed him that I was (not George Anything, but) my landlord, and confirmed that Bedsitland was indeed where the new line was to go, and further, that all bills should be sent to this same address, *not* my house in Belgrave Road (so that I could intercept and settle these accounts independently); and then I italicized the fact that I *absolutely* needed the new line to be installed at the first opportunity: it was a matter of (not life and death, but) something more critical. Which is when I dredged up, from the well of my muddied loneliness, the clean-forgotten, spectral fantasy: career. He fixed me an appointment for later in the week. And satisfied at last, I stomped back up, slammed the door shut, and took a glug of vodka: because now that Kelly had gone American, I realized that *Campari* was the bevvy (not of the young, but) of spaghetti-*puttane*. And while involved in such philosophies, I must have dozed off. And when I awoke, around sunset, it was to the distinct, premonitory ring of my forthcoming telephone. Bugger the car, which, even in the days when I had driven it, had only been a token. This, a phone, was my first proper step towards freedom. And tomorrow, I'd take my second: go and find myself the latest gimmick, a funky answering machine. But tonight? Tonight would be plain sailing. In breezy seagull denim.

I took myself back to the grimiest pub in the vicinity, the one where the handsome clever-dick had taught me about the softened hardness, or the hardened softness, of an oral 'g'. For it seemed to me, revisiting my recent biography, that all my present difficulties stemmed from that single rude awakening, and I thought that if I returned to the scene of my original (phonetic) sin, I might set everything to rights and manage to resume my search for Thomas – whom, even if his personal kingdom remained unknown to me, and even if our courtship had been hampered by a herd of pigs, I still knew to be my rightful prince. My prospects remained on track; marriage, strangely within view; I could see our matrimonial carpet, long and parallel and serpentine, strewn with the carmine petals of that reddest of nouns. Something told me that – in perfect symmetry – he would at this moment be thinking, and doing, exactly the same thing, racing around the city in search of our reunion, galloping towards it. Telepathy: it's not very difficult. Not when you're fated to meet and to keep.

At the pub, I started with a(nother) vodka, plus a half-tab of Tranxene, to steady my shaky innards – an objective which the pink half-moon soon achieved, like a misty calm brought over a sea. And then I floated about the arena, glancing here and there and everywhere for checks in red-and-black and trousers of *corde du roy*. And leathered people seemed to stop to make enquiries, as if conscious of my search, as if wishing to be of assistance. They could see that since I was working the room with such determined industry (which, to me, meant such determined heart) the matter must be a grave one, or a hard one, or just sad. Who was Wanted? Had I been stood up? Smile, they said (looking glum): it can't be that bad. No (I told those well-intentioned tankards), I'm just looking for someone, thanks. And then I fetched myself another vodka, double. And as was bound to happen, I got drunker and drunker. Yet, by closing time, I still hadn't managed to chance upon my prince – neither in the cottage nor outside it. So I dawdled on the pavement for a while, as was then the cruisy custom – until I saw a man. Not quite Thomas, yet oddly like him. A prince apparent. Similar look, similar build, similar non-committal hunger. I was bored with standing back, bored with being so passive about my life. I decided to change strategy. I would grab the initiative. Assume the whip-hand. Brave my luck.

The man in question saw me, but pretended not to have done. He moved along the block, and then, hung back. He was giving me the (not runaround, but) walkabout. I could understand; I'd done it myself a thousand times. But I felt stronger now, more resolute, more like my own master. So I went and stood beside him; leaned against a wall; may even have propped a foot under my rump, stuck a knee out. I must have stared at him then, with glaring intent, meaning Let's Not Waste More Time, for the crowd was beginning to disband. My hopes were running dry. And then, the man, who – to be adulterously frank – looked just as handsome as Thomas by this juncture, came across, and said: Don't wanna seem unfriendly, man, but can't ya kinda take a hint? Hint? I echoed back, as if the word meant blandishment. Sorry, guy, he stabbed; you're not my type. And then he turned, and walked away into a more typically pleasing distance. I honestly don't think that a rejection so frankly delivered, a rebuff so blunt, had ever, before that moment, befallen my vanity. But he was American, you see. And Americans don't mince their words, or their hips, or any other anything. No shit. That's why Kelly liked them. I lurched halfway round the block, counterclockwise, and there, again, he was, busy posing hand-on-cock for the benefit of someone who seemed no more sold on him than earlier he'd been sold on me. It was deranged, deranging. Who the hell was this fucker anyhow, who the hell did he think that he was: Brando, Burton, the Prince of bloody Darkness? And then I did the most disgraceful thing that you will read in this whole chronicle. (Never mind not finding people who deserve to be thanked. When I think of the ones who deserve an apology, it freezes my horrified pulse.) Because what I did was walk up to the Native New Yorker, and tell him that I most certainly could take a hint, and that the hint lay with his accent, and that I didn't fuck with fucking Yanks, 'cos Yanks, as we all knew, were spreading a mortal disease. He winced; was winded; looked about, as if frantic for a witness. And then I returned, inhaling his defeat, gobbling the helium of victory, to Bedsitland, where, in my sleep, I was forced to wade through Hades. On my own. It was all wrong. I was on a hiding to nothing.

I tried to pull myself together. I told myself to concentrate on Kelly's builders, who constituted my most tiresome difficulty, not just because they couldn't have cared less about the bleatings of some stupid honky-tonk, or dipstick, or sausage-jockey, or shirt-lifter, or whatever else – between their munches of bacon sarney – they chose to call me, hee-hee, but because, now that I'd been banned from driving, the job of keeping up with their antics had become an aggravated penalty. Sometimes I would spend a tortuous hour squashed in some stale old bus, only to be greeted, when I reached Holland Park, by a blank canvas, an abstract joke: the arty irony of general non-attendance. Or I might discover, for instance, that Kelly's men had got entirely the wrong tiles for the bathroom – white, not ivory; sheeny, not matt – yet gone ahead and slapped them up regardless. A tile-was-a-tile-was-a-tile, mite. I couldn't understand. After all, queens come programmed with a whole glossary of nesting terms, such as stop-cock, and piston, and fuse-box, and plug-hole, and skirting, and pile, and grate, and finish. Was it a question of sexuality? I mean, they had even managed to foul up the grouting in the kitchen: not bothered with grey, as Kelly had specified, but done the job in black. It looked so tacky. My brother would go mad. How (I asked the foreman) could they expect to get paid for stuff that the client didn't want? Didn't they realize that I had to report back to Los Angeles? What was the bleeding difference? he replied. Weren't the place a rent-job anyhow?

Kelly sent a card of some enormous desert-cactus with a lizard disporting itself around the trunk, lounging about in sun-shades and smoking cannabis. Hi, babe! he began. (Obviously on drugs.) He was having a great time. Work wasn't too bad. Night-life was wild! Tons of knock-out guys. Parties every night. Brill apartment. Weather fab. How was I getting on with the studio? Had I been in touch with Matthew? I must visit California sometime – so, tone up! He sent Much Love. By the time I bothered to reply, I was the owner of a telephone, and, thanks to it, of a magical number – the sort of numerical sequence which need never be written down, because people just learn it in one, absorb it like a mantra. Of all the regrets which I took with me when, eventually, I moved away from Bedsitland, the greatest, I would say, was having to part with that number. But anyhow, with the pretext of telling Kelly how Alexander Graham Bell had finally visited my palace, I wrote and explained, towards the end of the second side, that the builders were being a bit of a handful, and that I thought the job might take longer than at first had been imagined. The men just wouldn't take orders. Hated faggots. Couldn't mitre a tile. Attention to detail not exactly a priority. He should visit some-time. I sent him (toned-down) love.

Kelly didn't take long to attack the (office) dial. He said that he was browned-off, a very monkey adjective, whereas, in fact, he was Fulminating, a mood emphatically the colour of arson. I'd *committed* myself to getting the studio done (he hissed down the line), so why for Chrissakes couldn't I pull my finger out? I was so damn-goddamn unreliable. How could he possibly be expected to deal with the (no longer mere studio, but) *apartment* from all that way-away, huh? What the hell was my problem? Why couldn't I just grab the car, drive up to Holland Park, and kick *ass*? And to cap it all (he ranted), Matthew'd rung him in the middle of the night wanting to know if the deal was still on, because apparently he hadn't heard a dicky-bird from sodding Georgie. (Kelly obviously thought that restoring a property was a quick cinch, closer to repairing a sewing machine than fixing a rib.) I said nothing. He said: Well? So I said that I was doing my level best. Well, my level best obviously wasn't good enough, was it, you stupid twerp. And then he hung up. Marvellous manners, my brother.

One lunchtime, on my way back to Bedsitland after a skirmish with Kelly's louts ('trouble with you gay-boys is yer fuss too much'), the oddest thing happened. Someone seemed to be dawdling on the steps of the house, as if unsure of which bell they were after. The caller, male, looked, though official, famil-iar. Peculiar. But as I drew nearer to the front door, I realized — bang — that it was Thomas. He was wearing (not checks of red-and-black, but) the darkened trappings of a pilot. He carried a cap under his arm, which for some odd reason brought The Night Porter to mind. But I was too deranged, too undone, to say very much. I simply led him up. The palace looked tidy — thank Allah for that valet. Thomas didn't allude to the car; just said he was sorry he hadn't dropped round earlier; been on some long-haul something-or-other and taken ten days off on the homeward lap. I think he said Majorca. I think that he said hill-climbing. For all I cared, he could have said Up the Khy-ber, or Tiber, or Liber. He was fantastically tanned. From his briefcase he produced a bottle of wine, which he plonked on the mantle. Claret. He did not smile — but did possess (I could not but admire) the sort of mouth which, even in repose, curls upward at the sides and lends its subject an expression of docil-ity — of gentle, confident, princely charm. I handed him a corkscrew and a couple of glasses. I chose some music. (Barber's *Adagio*, unless memory lies.) His hair had been cut. It was the pigment of sand; but his lashes were dark – the sort of colour-clash for which ordinary mortals would dye. I said I wanted to take a shower. He said: Go Ahead, which I loved. I gave him, while I remembered, my new telephone number. He repeated it once, only once. It was carved upon his heart. I pointed to my answering device. I went out, carrying a clean pair of jeans and a T-shirt (not 'Cowdyke' – not on your life; plain white). I raced through the quickest shower in the history of that appliance, and, by the time of my return, the pilot had taken charge, poured some wine and placed our glasses side by side. His own, however, was already half-drunk. He was browsing through my books, which felt embarrassing. *Men in Love*: who needs to be caught with that? He'd taken the trouble to (come on baby) light my fire. He shrugged off his jacket. Thomas was the only man I ever knew to manage – to pull off – the tricky combin-ation of short sleeves worn with a tie. He freed his belt, and left it on the table like a placid snake released into some woodland. He had lowered the blinds. The sun bathed our room in gilded dust. The air became, it seemed to me, forever stilled. We had all the time in the world. The flames were high. I remember light-ing up. Thomas didn't smoke, thanks. But next he grabbed my cigarette and devoured the profoundest cloud you ever imag-ined. Mine was his, his was mine. I watched. The whites of his eyes looked shot with fine branches of blood, as if he'd been walking against the wind, or crying. It moved me; it thrilled the hell out of my lower half. He asked for a towel. I gave him one – white. He ripped off his trousers and pants – in one, like a heterosexual. Loosely now he wound the length of cloth around his abdomen, in the manner of some tropical garment – a kakoi or sarong or pareo. Next he unbuttoned his shirt (also white), but kept it on his back, as if to shield him from the blaz-ing midday sun. I could swear that I smelt brine. And as he walked toward the bathroom, it felt as if, already, we were gone, gone to some sultry distant place full of unknown habits where everything was different and what anyone did was any body's business. And just before he vanished, he told me to take a look inside his briefcase. He must have brought me a trophy from his travels. I resisted for as long as I could stand it, because I wanted to savour, to roll in, to somersault, to dive, to splash, to revel in, the moment.

I found a pair of ear-plugs – which I didn't know that pilots still employed, not since the war – and a curious leather object, shaped like a spatula but known as a paddle. I wasn't so green as not to comprehend its dark (corrective) function, but nor did I have a clue as to how this cobra's head, which glinted with steely studs on one side, would be handled. I was stumped. If my friends could see me now. I decided lots of things at once: that I'd ignore it, that my lover would be my guide, that, in any case, it was time I became conversant with these customs, that with Thomas – as opposed to Mr Respectable – it would feel (not squalid, but) romantic, that there is pleasure in pain, ecstasy in agony. Ask Teresa of Avila. I lowered the lid. Sat down. Hung about. Looked around. Went blank. He was back. He opened the briefcase. Left it ajar. And now, he took me by surprise. Those plugs of yellow sponge went into his ears, not mine. He placed the paddle next to the belt. He threw off his shirt and towel. A pewter epaulette caught my eye, flash. He went towards the mantle and downed the dregs of his glass. He poured another, and drained it as if parched. He brought my own empty glass to where I – nervously erect, half-hardened – sat. I stood up. He sat me down. In a virtual reconstruction of his movements on our first unfinished night, he knelt between my thighs, undid my front and took me out. He laid his head upon my lap, and, once again, he stroked my belt along his neck; then slapped his profile as he slurped about me. His face was redder than the noun. It all felt faintly formulaic, but I was ready to countenance anything, any formula, because repetition with your lover feels like ritual. He held my empty glass to my full penis. He meant me to piss in it. I did. It was one of my party tricks. He drank me like a chalice. He wanted a reprise.

Again I pissed. Now he raised my glass up to my lips. My turn to drink. My turn was easy. My rivers were warm and sweet. We were floating somewhere in India, where the practice of imbibing urine is habitual, medicinal, and where white is the colour of mourning. Oh I could do anything – give up the ghost for him. And then, too loud, on account of the ear-plugs, he delivered a trinity: One: No bruises that last longer than a week. Two: Blood's off limits. Three: My boyfriend gets back on the 5th. (I was dead. It was easy.) And then he dug his teeth into my penis. I leapt to my feet on an outraged reflex. But I wanted him to think that I was equal to this, not reeling. I took Barber back to his beginning. His strings were weeping. I tried to think. Now the pilot took away the briefcase and moved it out of the picture. He positioned himself on, laid his chest upon, the mahogany, head to one side, pelvis on the wooden edge, genitals hanging free. I couldn't see them; but his legs, the backs of his thighs, were widespread. Viewed from the rear, he looked massive. I stripped with frantic urgency: chuck, chuck, chuck. His rump was large, and muscled, and covered with fair down. He was tanned entirely. He had bathed without trunks. Majorca. The sun. Hill-climbing. Who gave a fuck. I was finished. I picked up the belt, folded it in half, wrapped the buckle round my wrist, but could only bring myself to tap at his buttock, tap, like a novice, like some stupid nun. Not a flinch, not a sound. I tried harder, then twice, then followed the twice with a thwack. Still no reaction. It made me feel inadequate, below sadistic par, not up to the loving task. I went for the shoulder-line. Only the merest of writhes. I struck him yet harder. Nothing. The pilot was stronger than suffering, not human. He grunted – grunted because I'd let up. A drop of sweat fell from my brow. It trickled down his flank, the left one. Without need of a backward glance, he picked up the paddle and shoved it at me. I struck him with the plain side. He grabbed my wrist and turned the cobra round. I struck him with the studs. He flinched from his thighs. I aimed for them –

but then, my grip seemed to baulk at the punishment. His studs went crashing onto the mahogany. I could show you the scars. I began to beat him rhythmically, regularly – though with syncopations, to surprise him. He was like a work of art crying out to be damaged. He was prize-winning meat upon a slab, beyond the slaughterhouse. I wanted to get at his inner thighs, his tenderest parts. I told him to get up; I wanted him lying down. He didn't hear; was deaf, was deafly absent. Dead but alive. I did not have the touch. When at last he rose, it was because I'd ceased (not from Mental Fight, but) thrashing. His neck and back and arse were lacerated. His flesh was mortified at last. I turned the melancholy music louder, lest the neighbours imagined trouble. My trouble was inner. My insides were howling. The pilot's were soundless and calm, as if he were flying through the night. He ignored the bed, went to the heart of the carpet, dropped to the floor and just lay there on his back, moribund, face-up, head slanted, slack; but his thorax, now, was breathing hard and fast. His feet were splayed out. His eyeballs had rolled back. His lids were flickering with involuntary rapture. His genitals were fabulous, but flaccid. I couldn't bear for him to see my shadow. I blindfolded him with his own tie. Tighter, he grunted. It came out as a command. The tie bit into his temples. He chewed at the tail while I walloped his hide. He loved it. I loved him. The sweat was pouring off me. Blood was racing to my eyes. I stepped against his sac, which was frozen but hard. He pushed against my foot, as if to incite me. I suddenly found, as I struck at his breast and traumatized his crotch, that I was crying. Isn't that the most pathetic? Blame it on the music. Blame it on the emotion. Put it down to the confusion. And then, through the confusion of my tears, I saw his fleshy, flaccid penis, without any sense that I could see, come. We were done. It had taken twenty minutes. We have all the time in the world. My prince got up, smeared his spunk against my towel, stepped calmly back into his garb, removed his ear-plugs, and smiled; but it was a strange, unfathomable grimace from some strange, unfathomable land, somewhere between the realms of vengeance and of gratitude. Never mind the appointment of a chandelier. Would a kiss have been a crime? He left his paddle behind. No tears goodbye.

A rough week later – when the bite-marks round my penis were beginning to subside – I received a message on my answerphone, a message which, at first, I took to be a dud. Novel gadgets. Errors happened the whole time. Caller sounded like a stranger in a call-box: 'Hi, it's Tom, Tom Bland.' And then, a pause; and in that pause I understood that Tom, Tom Bland, was Thomas. The pilot. I can't, despite what I have told you, pretend not to've been glad. I was excitedly surprised. I was hooked to the sound of his vowels. I waited for him to go on; waited for him to say that he wanted to come round. And then at last I heard him say Um-Look, thing was, while he was in Majorca, he'd sorta fooled around with some local guy and hadn't been feeling too hot since he got back, sore throat, glands up, so he'd been to the doctor, who told him to notify his Contacts (*plural*) that they should be tested for gonorrhoea. Probably just a scare, but best be on the safe side. I should go for a check-up. Course of antibiotics should do it. Any problems, I could ring him, so long as I was, you know, discreet – and then he left a number, which pointed towards (not a park, but) an airport. And he ended with a Sorry that sounded like a See Ya. And slowly he replaced the receiver. Bland. I looked him up in the directory. His address, to me, meant nothing. Somewhere vaguely around Chiswick. I was blushing. I felt feverish. I was a walking burning fear. I couldn't pee. My rivers had grown bitter. Hell hath no idea.

I rang Dr John, and rushed – in no mood for a suit – to see him. I told him that I was sleeping like a dream. I told him that the man who'd vanished from my life had made a surprise appearance, plus, most likely, given me VD. I repeated the message which had been left on my machine. Dr John said to relax a minute. He seemed to be more displeased by the manner in which the news had been transmitted than in the possible transmission of the disease, which he called of no real gravity. We just needed to take a quick look at me, here and now, there and then, check me over, see about treatment. He patted my shoulder. He sent me to the lav to produce a (not party trick, but) sample of urine. I returned with the warm glass beaker. Next, Dr John pressed a depressor on my tongue, took a swab, and made me gag (the pilot hadn't kissed me); he stuck a glassy rod into my scandalized urethra (the pilot hadn't sucked me); he shoved some cream, and then some light, up my wincing arse (the pilot hadn't fucked me). The pilot had done nothing – except bite. But Dr John was taking no chances. He took some blood. And when it came to names, he wondered, for the purposes of the lab, what I fancied by way of alias. I zipped up. I said: Carmen Miranda. He smiled, but told me that I'd better be a man. So we agreed on George. I dithered over Sand, then settled for Eliot – which was, from that day on, to remain my sexually-medical monicker. Confidentiality is everything. Trust me. Dr John now trusted that I'd simmer down, go home, and take some tablets which he described as a safeguard. He'd be in touch as soon as the results were back. Four days at the outside. It was a Friday. (Isn't it always?) And then he told me to stop being silly, and to start behaving like an adult.

I did. When he rang to announce the all-clear, I was less relieved than rabid. I told him to send me the bill. He said that he would – at the end of the month as usual. I told him I needed it sooner. Really? Really, I insisted. Reason in particular? I told him. He sighed. Wasn't I making a bit of a song and dance about this? Hardly song-'n-dance, Dr John: Grand Opera's more like it. Again he sighed. But then, despite his implicit disapproval, he indulged me with a most dramatic word: Touché. Next day, the bill arrived: fifty-five dramatic pounds. I settled it at once, but acted as if I hadn't; because what I also did was forward it to Capt. Thomas Bland, along with the following message: You might stump up for this abortion. Within forty-eight hours, he had – in crinkled anonymous cash plopped through the battered letterbox. Grimy brown envelope. Backward writing. And I was left to dread the prospect of ever clapping eyes on that (not prince, not impostor, just) punter. I had become a prostitute at last. Persona Non Gratis.

Sight

When I next clapped eyes on him, the pilot was no pilot. He was next to nothing, hardly recognizable, a reddish speck in a bad atmosphere who, bloodshot and askance, half-nodded as I passed. Yet I, though passing, could not but blank him, for the mere glancing blur of the man had arrested my arteries. This accident, this non-encounter, occurred, of all unlikely places, at an eye-clinic which I happened to be visiting with Matthew. But I seem to be hurtling over events, racing over hurdles, referring to a time that still lies obfuscated in the fogs of an unfathomable future. Beyond sight.

For in truth (back in proper time), Matthew only meant, as yet, a name to me, an entry at the back of my diary, a stranger whom I should contact once the studio was ready to be occupied; but, after my recent earful from Kelly, I confess that the thought of this unknown character was beginning to worry me. I mean, supposing he got tired of waiting? Say he went and opted for alternative accommodation? It would become my additional burden, additional to the whole headache of refurbishment, to find a 'suitable' new tenant for Kelly. I'd be up Shit Creek – without even the assistance of the pilot's paddle, which I had flung out. And so, one jittery wintry eve, I braced myself and rang the number in Kingston, to test the waters of this Matthew – cool him down, warm him up, whatever was required. But his gentle neutral tone, when it came on, was calm, becalming almost. He didn't seem concerned on his own account; said that he was happy to move in whenever; no desperate rush; just wondered how things were going, whether I was coping, because he knew that with Kelly's snap-departure I'd got landed with the whole hassle. I told him it had all been a bit hairy: the builders were lousy, but since Kelly was the one who'd hired them, I didn't have the guts to fire them. Still, the worst was over, so hopefully he shouldn't have to wait much longer. That's great, he said. (Then, nothing.) It made me feel trite. But next, as if to compensate for my reduction, he wondered whether I needed a hand. Hand how? (It transpired – which Kelly might have told me – that Matthew worked on some architectural journal, and was more than conversant with plans and sections and elevations and plumbing and wiring and heating and lighting and all the rest of the techno-decorative palaver. Plus he was used to dealing with bolshy underlings every day of his life.) In which case, I admitted, never mind a helping hand: I could do with a fistful. He laughed. It was a laugh which, in the unforeseeable fullness of time, I would come to recognize anywhere, anywhere at all. All over my heart. At all hours of the day and night. In clubs and dungeons and cathedrals. Ribald, ironic, swooping, generous. Mischievously large. I would learn, in years to come, to wear it like a (secret) amulet. Like an amulet stuck in my gut. But let me take you back before I get angry.

We agreed to make a date, so that I could show him the progress of the studio. Luckily he didn't suggest coming to Bedsitland: I preferred not to publicize the fact that, for all of my pearlescence, I couldn't even claim possession of a proper bathroom. Besides, he was bound to be another of those neo-Bauhaus maniacs: it fitted the current architectural likelihood. In the event, we arranged to meet, after he'd finished work one evening, at the Ripe Banana, a homo-pub near Holland Park which – like it or loathe it – all of us knew because it was so superbly ghastly, full of the fumbling toothless. But it was handy for the studio, and that's what mattered. Next, however, I found myself obliged to moot the squirmy question about how we'd recognize each other. Matthew volunteered, in a sassy Yankee-profundo, that he would be the one wearing the (not buttonhole, but) butt-plug. Where? I enquired – in his mouth? No, honey, stickin'-outa-ma-flaaahs. I told him that he sounded like a most fantastic lesbian; and he can't have been put out, because next he demanded, quick as a flash, that I call him Billy-Jean and light his cigar. Let's face it, he added, we'll be the only two people in the place without a pension. And thus was the mystery of our respective identities left to gather moisture in the unlikely lap of Sappho.

I got there early, to spare myself the trial of a paranoid arrival. He, meanwhile, appeared bang on time, and came straight over, smiling as if he'd caught me out. We shook hands – with the left, which, among queers of our type, was then regarded as a social halfway between straight-acting and going the full mwah-mwah. I offered him a drink. He asked what *I* wanted. I had, in fact, just bought myself a vodka, a move which suddenly felt ill-mannered, like attacking your grub ahead of your dining partner. I produced the offending glass, which had been cowering on the shelf behind me. He said: Don't hang about, do you? then added: Won't take me long to catch up. Off he strode to the bar. Several things, as I watched him order, surprised me. Matthew was older than I'd imagined, thirty or thereabouts, and wore a moustache, dark brown. Though not quite my height, he was broader of build than I, sort of ruggery, particularly around the thighs and arse. Briefly I sizzled with an odd erotic undercurrent; but my voltage was soon tempered by suspicion, the suspicion that he might, in some discreetly omit-ted past, have been a conquest of my brother's, or the other way around.

He returned and eased himself toward a swig, then grinned. His open, honest face was perhaps not as chiselled as mine, but it boasted, in revenge, both of my great envies: a deeply cleft chin, and the dimples of all time. It made you want to take his head in your hands and sculpt like a blind man. His hair, cropped short at the sides, was quiffy above, and glossy. Voguishly hard. His brows were thick and dark and horizontal, like confident brushstrokes. No arches, as was my handicap. His eyes were of a speckled tawny green, and immoderately wide, almost unmanly, more like the eyes of Hedy Lamar. I asked how he had recognized me. By Kelly's purple boots, of course. I crossed my ankles: *these*, it so happened, were mine, even if Kelly *had* seemed to reckon that it was he who'd been made to walk in them. Fancy Nancy, grinned Matthew. I downed my drink and, emboldened, decided to come out with my (not Something Stupid, but) forefront worry. Had he ever slept with my brother? His pupils went up. Well, I persisted, *had* he? Hardly. Why hardly? Because, for starters, Matthew'd been involved with oh – some creep until quite recently. (Roving Willy, of course. Bygones: all of us had them.) And for seconds? Well, Kelly wasn't really his type. (Nor was he mine.) I admit: I was delighted. We left it at that.

Outside was growing dark. We ambled along the avenue, down towards the studio. Matthew walked from the neck, very erect, and had the habit of looking up to admire rooftops and skylines and all of that. Visually inclined. We climbed to the second floor. I unlocked the door, but it was he who found the light-switch. It took him, despite occasional pauses to comment ('What, no dimmer?'), under five minutes to inspect the premises. He scribbled on some pad – or sketched perhaps, I didn't ask – then shoved his notes back into his jacket, and next, as I was trying to lock up, suggested that we go on for a bite. Once we had sat down, and ordered a bottle of house-white at some *frou-frou* joint nearby – chez Didier, later closed in a great hurry, re-named, and heterosexualized – he said that he was taking a day off next week (dentist, haircut, have a look around the shops, do the things he never seemed to get done) and could, if I liked, meet me at the studio when the builders were on site. Sure, I said; if he could spare the time. Of course he could; the place just needed pulling together slightly, especially that bathroom. Did he mean the tiles? He told me to stop worrying: between us, he foresaw, we would do Kelly proud. Matthew had an authority about him, a quietly stubborn power, so it must have been he who decided that next we should talk of (not tongue-and-groove, but) life. He was eight years my senior, a queer generation wiser – and blither – than mine.

It seems hard, as I look back, to believe that despite the litany of disparities which crackled between us, disparities which, given my volatile character, could so easily have proved incendiary, we should have been fated, in the end, to become so tightly bound, bound tighter by far than by the bind of siblinghood. His background, unlike mine, was solid and humble. He was rooted in, and bolstered by, a great normality: unremarkable but devoted parentage; called his father Dad, not Father; his mother made marmalade and shepherd's pie and went to the shops with a basket; there was some much older step-sister, long since married and removed to Canada; but basically, Matthew's story was an easy one. Happy enough childhood; grammar school in the outskirts; sandals in the summer; football in the garden; Scrabble on Sundays; untroubled, untroublesome start. While at art school (his first departure from the straight and narrow), he had grown his hair down to his clavicle and given himself a centre-parting. He dated girls, shacked up with one, and, for a while, the two had lived as lovers. Yet by the time of his diploma, he had in the simplest way decided that he simply preferred those of his own sex for sexual company. He and the girl, whose name, was Anna, duly broke up, but they made a point, a pact, of not losing touch, and continued to send each other birthday cards, changes of address – mild but mutual tokens of affection – for years thereafter. Matthew hated combat. Just as he hated goodbyes.

So he cut his hair, went home, and told his parents, whom

he trusted, that he was homosexual. They hadn't, apparently, batted an eyelid; didn't blink once; merely replied along the lines of his orientation having no bearing upon their love. It made my jaw go slack. They'd wanted for him nothing more (and nothing less) than happiness. And so he moved, his conscience light, to town, shared flats, got jobs, went out, met boys, made friends with the likes of my brother, drank in clubs, slept around, found his feet, kept his balance, took his boyfriends home sometimes. But he didn't, at his parents' house, share a bed with these bedfellows: courtesy mattered more to Matthew than the militant infliction of socio-political attitudes. Plus he preferred, he told me, to sleep alone in the room where he'd grown up, which remained stacked with flags and comic-books and trophy-cups and model-boats and forty-fives and assorted biographical memorabilia. Part of me envied the fact that, in his late teens, he should have known women intimately, for it appeared to furnish him with a muted confidence, a physical ease which rendered him tranquil. He could afford to embrace his queerdom in a way that I never could – philosophically – didn't need to be defensive about it, or aggressive, or squeamish. If I was soft about being hard, he was hard about being soft, for his face (and indeed his arse) matched his personality: open, honest, friendly. Come-hithery. This endeared him to the world, drew people to him, and had, in the past, covered him with benefits. By the time of our first meeting, he had bedded, or been bedded by, more men than there are days in the calendar, and been, by a number of these, loved richly. But he didn't brag about such feats – as if statistics, like achievement, were meaningless. And yet there was, I later learned, an impressive tale about him, set in a beach-taverna on Santorini, where, surrounded by a gaggle of other queens, he'd got pissed and leapt onto a table and pulled down his Speedos and squatted in full view, and, without even the need of spittle, proceeded, in what used to be called a dry run, to impale himself upon a towering bottle of (gently does it) Galliano. The company had apparently

been lost for words, but clapped; yet, these days, Matthew preferred to keep such over-spirited juvenilia under tactful wraps.
People said that he resembled a roxy pop-star of the time, who
dated equine Texan model-girls but was glamorous as fuck.
I never saw it, to be quite frank. To me, he resembled no-one.

I think that his working life had begun at some printing
press, from where, by the law of averages (for he was never
burdened with ambition), he had drifted into the realm of
architectural journalism. He sometimes said that he supposed he
ought to be moving on, moving up the ladder of a formal career,
but he was accustomed to the set-up at the office, where his
team was bright good company, the job itself not too demanding, and the money satisfactory, so that escalation on this front
felt more like risk than benefit. Really he preferred a placid,
pleasing life to notions of promotion and the dubious price of a
glitzy salary. It wasn't, he said, as if he needed to keep a family.
What he needed to keep was his freedom. And his sense of
humour, which had no price.

His choice of dress, at the outset of our acquaintance, was
Glam. Mine, like my moods, varied wildly, could swing from the
bespoke to the bedraggled; but his, like his nature, was constant.
Because he was kind, he called me versatile; because I was not,
I called myself erratic. Matthew tended away from the clonish
toward the shiny, from the sexy toward the stylish, which, give
or take a jacket, could carry him with steady smoothness
through the soft professional day into the harder amateur night.
Like Kelly, he fussed over the cut of his underpants, whereas I,
too often, preferred to venture without. But, by contrast, he was
lax about the quality of his socks, too sporty, too casual for my
liking. I insisted on knee-length lisle, which he dismissed as
unsexy hetty drag. And yet, one fashion-look on which we did
coincide, and which, with the growth of our alliance, was to
mature into a speciality, was Country & Western. For, aside from
our brief obsession with the hysterical ballads of the genre
('They Ain't Makin' Jews Like Jesus Anymore'), both of us

adored the ornate accessories which then abounded: metal clips which you could screw onto the wings of your collar, and plaited horsehair tassels which could be worn as ties (but were lost in darkened clubs if you necked with too many men at once), and steely points for the tips of your toe-caps, and straps with spur-like attachments, and elaborately stitched belts with buckles crafted as harps, or hearts, or heads of rams, and scarves knotted at the back, peaks slipped to the front, rodeo-style, and even leather chaps – in saddle brown, not bugger-black. But the truth is that this ranchy apparel, this raunchy man-drag, suited Matthew better far than ever it suited me, for he had the legs for the business and mine were too skinny. Yet I would never in those days – not even to myself – have admitted such a thing, because the costume seemed to decant confidence into me. Now, of course, I realize that any such confidence flowed not from what I wore, but from the fact that I had the great gift of Matthew about me.

His 'other' name, I discovered during the course of that first supper, was Blanche. I made the usual gaffe of presuming its provenance to lie with Baby Jane, whereas, he clarified, it derived from *A Streetcar Named Desire*. Miss DuBois, he reminded me, had been a fading but aristocratic Southern belle who'd lost her ancestral home, Belle Reve (Hang on, I inter-rupted; how can Reve be feminine, surely it should it be Beau? Belt up and let me finish, would you?) who'd lost her ancestral home, as well as her teaching job, as a result of a slack morality. The virile wings of his moustache flew up toward his eyes, which fluttered Southern belle-style. It was a gorgeous mixture. He resumed his earlier 'gravity' and, with it, his seminar: Ten-nessee Williams, who'd created Blanche Dubois, had referred to her as delicate and moth-like, but Matthew had his doubts about the aptness of such an analogy, because moths aren't waterproof, and Miss DuBois, in the absence of a man, liked nothing more than hydrotherapy to simmer down. And indeed, it was on account of hydrotherapy that Matthew had earned himself the nickname Blanche, for he, too, was enamoured of his baths; would spend forever lolling in watery dreams and soap-suds – a quirk which, at one of the flats that he'd shared when he first came to town, had annoyed the rest of the gang, who were constantly banging on the door, and threatening to have a slash in the kitchen sink if he didn't come out *now*. I was myself, in fact, only to call him Blanche at the start, and then, when I meant to be sarcastic, for, as a pseudonym, it struck me as wrong for him, ill-fitting, pallid and washed out, too insipid for such a vivid personality. It made more sense to me that he should be called, for instance, Tammy, which rang properly Country & Western and had an air of Matty about it, but he quickly vetoed this idea: he wasn't a whiner, still less a wynette, plus Tammy sounded like a sanitary whatsit; so if I didn't cut it out, he'd start calling me that word with a Q which he'd somehow discovered – from Kelly, no doubt. He won. I cut it out. But with hindsight I suspect that if I grew to avoid the nickname Blanche, such avoidance probably had less to do with my desire to cover my nominal arse than with the fact that his sobriquet was retrospective, referred to a period in which I hadn't played a part, and I think that I felt envious of Matthew's easy past, his smooth head-start. His great advantage.

The next time that we met was back at Kelly's studio. As on the evening of our introduction, I arrived before the appointed hour; and Matthew, when he pitched up, proved again to be punctual, reliable. But I'd decided, rather than confront the workmen unaccompanied, to wait for him outside, hang around the avenue, park myself on a bench, light up. I was so strung out, you see, so tense and so entangled, because if earlier I'd been worried about letting Kelly down, and worried by the prospect of his sniggering louts, now, to add to those worries, I further worried about earning the ridicule of Matthew, whom I wanted to like me. But it seemed logical, almost automatic to me, that, in his eyes, I must look foolish, for I had failed to correct, never mind avert, the blunders which he was about to want rectified, the jottings which he had made on that pad. I was wrong, as it happens. Matthew, when he came, came loaded with (not superiority, but) surprises.

The first, most visible surprise was the erasure of his moustache, a feature which, I later learnt, had been but an ephemerality, a brief facial whim conceived in the aftermath of Roving Willy. New face, new life, sort of thing. And yet, notwithstanding the brevity of this whim, Matthew was the first homosexual I knew to rid himself of what, back then, in our skeltering heyday, was a dominant fad among queers. Nowadays you hardly ever see such things, just as you hardly ever see the globes of faceted mirror which, as you know, I still miss. The world keeps turning. But anyway, clean-shaven, Matthew suddenly looked ten years younger, more like my junior; and I suspect that this rejuvenation is what put paid to any weird erotic hankerings which I might, up till that point, have been nurturing. His face seemed to have softened, to have grown more innocent, more dimpled, more feminine, with the paradoxical effect that his body seemed to have grown hunkier. But from my perspective, he resembled, after this transformation, a potential friend rather than a potential fuck. And yet, even if I no longer wanted him to be my arrow of desire, I still hoped that he might be my bow of burning gold, my spear, my cloud unfolded, my chariot of fire.

The second surprise was subtler: he was dressed as he had been at the Ripe Banana – and yet he wasn't: that is to say that while he observed the exact same formula as at our initial encounter (denim shirt, blue jeans, dark jacket), each of these articles was marginally other, had altered. Confidence, you see. Matthew had it in magnums. He couldn't have cared a tinker's toss if tossers chose to imagine that he wore the same old garb day-in day-out, whereas little, in my youth, filled me with greater horror than the thought of being spied repeating outfits.

Even my surly denim ran a broad tonal gamut – from dry-ice to dirty white, via ash and dove and pearl and aqua, all the way down to indigo. I drew the line at black. Black isn't a colour. Black is black. (I want my baby back.)

And my third surprise did not become apparent until we'd gone up to the studio – which, having (not shaken with the left, but) kissed twice, we did now. What ensued, from my point of view, was a good strong lesson in good strong manners, a lesson in not being cowed, in meeting hetties in the eye. Matthew, who seemed to have placed himself in front, knocked on the door (a courtesy which hadn't ever crossed my mind), shook hands with all four builders (ditto), and simply took charge. He wasn't flirty; he wasn't funny; he wasn't chippy; he wasn't sarky; he was polite but frank, and absolutely calm. Full of authority. Free of petulance, which was my pouting personal attribute. And presently he'd subjugated the quartet of recalcitrant louts, who nodded and grunted and conceded to his remarks – for even they could tell that Matthew's were the views of an interested, knowledgeable party, rather than those of an ignorant, uninterested, middle-man. The pack of them, I saw, were eating out of his hand. So, into his hand, as we left the house, I commended the key to (not Kelly's profit, but) Matthew's new chapter. He was infinitely better at this business than I. He didn't bother to deny it. False modesty wasn't his style. Instead, he offered to supervise the remainder of the work on my behalf. He would take up my cudgels, fight the final thrusts of my inherited battle; he would be my spear, my bow of burning gold. I couldn't have been more grateful. I invited him out. He couldn't have been gamer for a night on the town. And as we sauntered off to the (not Queen & Garter, nor Ripe Banana, but) Red Heart, we agreed that he needn't pay rent until he was satisfactorily housed. I have a suspicion that he dragged a few shags up there before the place was done, but I can't say that I blame him; because, much later, laughing, he would come to describe Holland Park as the Garden of Gethsemane.

In our carefree beginning, ours were, for the most part, nocturnal meetings. Apart from odd lunches snatched near his office, events which I disliked on account of the rush that both defined and undermined them, our friendship was set, like some mysterious lunar hybrid, to flourish in the darkened hours. I find myself unable to depict those nights for you other than by rewinding and fast-forwarding at the same time, as if peering from both ends of a telescope at once – confusedly, illogically – for, looking back, yet also looking round toward a temporal middle-ground (the ground which, once our bond had been established, was to be fully shared by us), those nights return to me as one exquisite fluttering romance, sharp yet unfocused, singular yet serial, at once specific and spread out, full of motion and colour and sound, and brimming with high contemporary currency – yet frozen in history now, rather like the scalloped wing of the period fan which, long before Matthew had entered my life, I had spread, for purchase, upon the table of my hopeful future and my hopeless past, rather like the table which, long after he had melted into memory, I would revisit for peculiar, lugubrious sustenance. The initial force of our connection had been like a sudden stone which had surprised the surface of some water; but, in order for you to understand the real eventual worth of that most precious stone, you would have to survey the many floral ripples which, with the passage of the years, it wrought; for, as a friendship, ours was to grow, oh, so much greater and broader and more beautifully patterned and more complicated than its mere initial splosh, so much lovelier and sadder and colder, even after the stone had sunk and crystallized and gone, even after the laughter had been reduced to an amulet which became knotted in, and rotted by, the acids of my stomach. They call it the mourning process. Don't make me vomit.

Vomit. I liked that word in my late boyhood. I deployed it with widespread generality, bandied it about with a — dare I suggest — gay abandon. I would level it at anything that made me uncomfortable: the past imperfect, places left behind, monkeys back-turned on their branches, puzzle-rings waved in the sun, Kindergartenmeisters, even blue-eyed answers. It was only when Matthew pointed out that Vomit, being an ugly word, made me sound, by extension, unattractive, that I paused, and bothered to think twice. I suspect that whilst, before that time, I had frequently been criticized — and most often by those who claimed the most to love me — no-one, certainly none of my instructors, had ever taken the trouble to broaden my horizons by opening my eyes. Matthew proved to be that great, surprising eye-opener. He was the person whom, in retrospect, I would have to credit with having dispelled my blind-spots, with having diluted my bile, with having brought an unsuspected sweetness to my tongue. For he had learned that life should be tasted with a neutral palate, not sampled through the spices of ire. Smooth head-starts, you see; great advantages. Even my trials with the sergeant at the pigsty had made him shake his head like the-head-of-the-wise and laugh. He couldn't comprehend my abiding rancour; just thought the entire thing mad; dotty, he called it, whereas dotty, before that point, would have put me in mind of the tie which I had worn to the courthouse. My friend may not have been Socrates, nor Euripides, nor really — come to that — glamorous as fuck, but he proved to be my perfect mentor; for few of the lessons which I had yet to learn could (then) be found inside hard covers. He knew pre-Wolfenden queens who'd been sent to the slammer and survived, but who, as a matter of regal principle, only related the nightmare in Polari. He knew queens who had peddled their arses in order to drum up the requisite funds for that life-changing trip to the famous clinic in Casablanca. He knew the arts — both lowly and high —

of seduction, which we called Trapping. He knew that double-ended dildos weren't as practical as was made out, because the other party invariably tried to colonize more than its fair half. He knew that it was pointless to fret about brown breath when you woke up, because if, the morning after a tumble, your shag was still around and stirring for action, all you needed to do was suck on his cock before letting him suck at your mouth. He knew that one should never trust a man who's entirely devoid of camp – whether straight or otherwise. He knew, even, that one should never trust a man who – the subsequent irony of this half-undoes me – makes love with his eyes shut.

But back to the night at the Red Heart. He peered into my face and told me that I looked so (not glad to be gay, but) cross to be queer that it was almost comical. He told me that he wished he could make me less unhappy. No-one had ever told me anything so lovely. Few have done so since. And although I couldn't possibly answer for Matthew's feelings during the period which I've come to review as our gilded prelude, I can safely vouch for the fact that the miracle of our acquaintance was, to me, like the greatest breath of fresh air, an air which relieved the thoracic pressures of my simian history. Furthermore: despite the intimations which you may have gleaned, do not be deceived: that miracle, in its essence, never ceased to be. It was never to be cheapened. It was never to descend, like a punctured parachute, to the lowland of exploded myth. No. The scales of my enchantment were never to be dissolved in, nor tainted by, messy reality, by the real mess of my tears, toxic and fluent as those tears would one day be. Because: Body and Soul: I kept them separate. Which is why, which is how, on that second evening, the evening of the entrusted key, I fell for him. Fraternally. Like the love in the dictionary.

Words. I think it must have been our weakness for them that first drew us in. Later, once our backgrounds had enjoyed their first brief season – that gilded prelude – and, with it, the chance to mingle and entwine, our grafted vocabularies (mine, the more

florid and foreign and adjectival; his, the more colloquial, slang-
ier, but sturdily rooted in nouns) sprouted a dialect which felt
superbly ours, singular and hybrid – like the lunar flower which
was set to blossom by night. It was a language full of pollinated
idioms and thorny tricks and honeysuckle rhymes and spiky
puns, and descriptions which, though they perfectly matched, in
our eyes, to our minds, the requisite meaning of whatever we
liked, sounded, to the world, like gibberish, senseless. Words like
Fraucht – as in: the vicar is a total *fraucht* (part-Frau, part-fright).
But, once brought alive, such words, such buds, could open like
botanical marvels and expand and change their tone and texture
and spread out, to cover anything – people's décor, for instance,
or their hair-don'ts, or even the strappy platforms of Princess
Margaret Rose. Matthew was sharper than a (scarlet) stiletto; and
his wit, like a bouquet of bloodied rapiers; which is why it
wounds and shames me to confess that, since those days, I've
forgotten half our lexicon. Yet it swells me with a convex pride
to tell you that, since then, I haven't met a soul with whom to
speak that lost but sacred language, with whom to resurrect
those buried words which once were ours. Because, as used to
be said in Mesopotamia: one hand alone does not clap.

If Matthew and I lacked anything at the start, I would have
to say that it was reverence. There was little then, including men,
out of which we couldn't get a rise. I think that, let out of school
(for want of a better metaphor), we must have made an irksome
couple, nettlesome to handle, for we frequently found ourselves
flung out of bars – bars which no-one in their right mind
should be reduced to patronizing, but whose staff were sometimes reduced to yelling Oy! at us and telling us that we were
barred – for meddling with the objects of other men's desire, or
aping people in the cottage and turning their porno into panto,
or asking the security man whether he fancied a quick snort of
amyl. That kind of prank. But then, almost without fail, we
would hear, as we staggered convulsed into the night, some

official voice acquit us: Not barred for good, mind. (Why?) Because we were good for those dumps. I'm sorry to sound smug, but people drank us with their eyes; for, apart from being attractive, we were bright and lively, and our bright liveliness rendered them parched.

A few weeks into our pairing, we had a pair of T-shirts printed up: mine, announcing Slap; the other, Tickle. But such jokes pall quickly when you live in dread of repeating outfits. So we bought ourselves a second pair – this time: Hit and Miss. I chose the one saying Hit, less because I wanted to be read as a success than because I didn't want people 'having me for bitch'. Besides, Matthew was cool about being Miss: he didn't give a flying *fraucht* about being seen to wink with his arse, even if he didn't – not quite yet, at any rate – need some new-found Roving Willy targeting his bull's-eye. I suspect that with our ingrowing friendship, my friend saw respite from the grown-up pressures of monogamy, while I saw respite from the puerile pressures of polygamy. Of course, we still kept sidelong lookouts for both of the gammies, Polly and her sexy antithesis, but really, with the progress of our alliance, the whole business of Trapping seemed somehow to fade in attraction. Together we preferred to hang (not loose, but) out; get drunk; go dancing. Night after night we used to say: Let's get (not laid, but) clubbed.

My friend turned out to be the kind of dancer that I loved, better than Kelly by miles. His style was sinewy and luminous and quiet. He moved, I should have known, just as he walked: from the neck, with distinction. His energy seemed to rise through the column of his spine to the capital of his jugular, to the veins which ferry lifeblood to the head, and, thence, down to the heart. His feet scarcely shifted at all, like the feet of those funky blackmen who sway to the plaint of jazz. Meanwhile, my feet, well, they too danced as they walked – from the brittle ankle, the affectations of my youth having tended more to the balletic than jazzward. And yet, perhaps, in some manner, we complemented one another. Don't know; not sure; doesn't even matter; because what I know for sure is that never before that whoosh of good fortune, that love at second sight, had I felt so comfortable on a dance-floor. It was as if I were alone, yet were accounted for. I could do my own thing, but I was never lonely. I was free to fly, but I was also free to fall, for I was grounded in loyalty. I could dream and dream until the hearts came home. I could become the lyrics of the song, its lachrymose verse, its euphoric chorus, the singer's very voice, her open welcome, or the sad farewell to the whole damned lot. And I never thought I'd feel this way, but as far as I'm concerned I'm glad I got the chance to say I loved him. So just close your eyes and try to feel the way I did, and then: Keep smiling, keep shining. Know that you can always count on me. In good times, bad times, I'll be on your side. That's what friends are for. He came and opened me, and now there's so much more I see. And I thank him. So just close your eyes and know: these words are coming from my heart: Keep smiling, keep shining. You can always count on me. Keep smiling, keep shining, keep smiling, keep shining. Keep on going.

Despite his japes and former hi-jinks, there was something weirdly adult about Matthew, staunch and measured and moral. Virtually puritanical. He was the type who believed (not in seas and rocks and skies, but) that life could be straightforward so long as you were prudent in its management. If, for instance, you couldn't afford to have something, you simply weren't to have it. Obvious, he called it – glaringly. Better hand-on-cock than stuck in hock, was one of his dictums. Didn't I have a telly? Nope. Couldn't I read a book? Not from choice. Then go to a museum, for heaven's sake, or get a job. I told him not to be common. Well, get a snobby hobby then, or window-shop, but do *something* with your life, for God's sake. He even disapproved of shoplifting – which struck me as pretty damn hoity-toity – and told me to get a sense of glamour, not a criminal record.

Seriously: did I really need to mess with the law? Didn't I think that queers had enough problems with the police as it was? I paused; I thought. That must have been when I told him about my meeting with the pilot. That's when he would have laughed at my rancour over the sergeant. The bottom line, he said, was that I had driven a car while drunk, right? So the sooner I faced facts the better. Rules were rules, and rules were simple. I found this whole discussion tiresome; but it was also, I admit, good for me. In his position, I certainly wouldn't have bothered risking my animosity, because — as you scarcely need to be told — aggro speaks louder than words. But his criticisms were a sort of compliment. Even then, that much was obvious to me — glaringly. So I tried, despite itching for a tantrum, to make myself sound grown-up, and, gritting my teeth, invited him to (not sod off, but) visit my *piano ignobile*. And when, a couple of days later, he paid me the first of his countless calls, he appeared with a bottle of (not immoderate Galliano, but) Prosecco. That was Matthew all over.

All over; wine gone. We raced to the shop; I paid for a sequel; I was ready to squander: Matthew had been kind about my room. I could tell that he understood it. He'd referred to Whistler. His approval had thrilled me. I wasn't yet familiar with his own aesthetic leanings, but he reckoned that décor was the best thing about Trapping. He said that someone should produce a coffee-table book with loads of fly-on-the wall photographs, taken with the nifty sort of cameras that spies secreted in their watches, titled 'Sex and Décor: A Marriage Made in Hell' — with candid shots of macho hulks sprawled against knicker-blinds and pink pagoda lampshades, or heavy-duty rubber-queens featured on Edwardian love-seats quilted in the waxen posies of dowager-chintz. Patterned duvet-covers, I discovered, were his absolute bête-noir, especially those trendy new *trompe-l'œil* ones. I admitted that I'd never managed to divorce myself from linen sheets — a reluctance which he found hilariously trad — practically Sapphic. And then he told me to call him (not Billie-Jean) but Una Troubridge. So, you see, even at that dicey beginning, there *were* things on which we could agree. There was scope for (not malice, but) manoeuvre, (not cant, but) candour.

Yet the candid truth is that I can't imagine how, during our season of late nights, Matthew managed, at the office, to get any work done. We were young, I suppose; we had vigour; or maybe he just kept his droopy head below the bureaucratic parapet and delegated. Meanwhile I, as far as I recall, devoted my waking hours to mental embroidery, to fictionalizing. I would pretend that I got up earlier than I did, so as to avert his irritation; would pretend to be reading books that I'd already read, because, as well as being short of moolah, I was short on concentration; would pretend to apply for jobs that hadn't even been invented; would pretend to write to people long since scrapped from my agenda. Busy-busy-busy, I made myself out to be. In reality, however, I was only busy in the sense that a dog left at home ever is, a dog unleashed but circling on the spot without cease, chasing its own tail until the blessing of evening rewards it with the solace of companionship. Sometimes, because of the midweek hassle of his last train back to Kingston, Matthew spent the night with me – though, in a direct reversal of my arrangement with Kelly, it was I who slept on the floor while Matthew slid between the sheets; the point being, I used to insist, that he was the one who needed a decent night's kip. More to the point, however, is the fact that my deferral felt not like subjugation, but like the most natural thing in the world, closer to gratitude, almost pleasurable – because love had looked at the two of us, strangers in many ways. We had a lifetime to share, so much to say, and, as we went from day to day, I felt him close to me. But time alone would tell.

By the time that I next thought of Kelly, Matthew had moved into the studio. It turned out that he'd been keeping an eye on the builders without me, having wisely, kindly, decided to spare me reports of their finishing touches, their concluding thrusts; yet my exclusion, when I learned of it, felt not like betrayal, but like blessed relief. In any case (said Matthew), it had only been a matter of sorting out a few last-minute details – dimmers, heated towel-rail, waste disposal, that kind of thing. The bulk of the credit he attributed to me. Genuine modesty his, you see. And when he finally asked me round, I saw that the final result emanated a genuine charm. The studio was clean, and clear, and warmly lit, yet it was decorated not at all as I'd envisaged. Though sparsely appointed, the place was gentle; though modern in flavour, it was eclectic, for Matthew's taste echoed, more than any British architectural anything, the taste of quiet, but chic, Parisians. His eye was less taken with frivolity than finish; he preferred a perfect corner than ever a perfect corner-cabinet; and his choice of furniture was accordingly streamlined, utilitarian: double-bed of steel, wicker coffee-table in the middle, a couple of canvas chairs, chest-of-drawers in pale veneer. Yet any risk of visual stiffness was softened by occasional artefacts, careful touches of ethnicity: a rug from Turkey; an African carving, full of curves and sensual sheen; a faded Colombian wall-hanging; a vast silver anklet, fit for a Sudanese chieftain; a single massive ancient candlestick with flaking, peeling pigments, medieval in spirit. Zero memorabilia. Plain duvet. Plain pillows. No hint of *broderie*. No fuss to speak of – except, of course, in the bathroom, which attested to his lifelong susceptibility, and boasted the vastest, creamiest towels that ever you did see: big enough to involve a couple in a lingering kiss, so warm and velvety as to elevate the bore of bathing into a spiritual routine. Move over, Tennessee. No moth-eaten delicacy here. Matthew's towels were the business. No tenement shit.

Kelly, as it happened, didn't make it back for Christmas. Instead, he sent a greetings card with a crib-load of genuflecting, hairy-chested trannies in plunging Nativity outfits meant to whisper silk-brocade but screaming of herpes-acetate. These queens, though visibly weighed down by a glut of shopping bags from the flashiest boutiques in Beverly Hills, nevertheless looked replete with goodwill to (not just men, but) all-and-sundry – but perhaps this resulted, more simply, from the glittery caption which they were enacting: Jesus Loves Drag. Anyhow, inside this card, Kelly enclosed a photograph of himself – looking, I have to say, half-nakedly dreamy, like a swimmer between swims. Yet he was sharing his vital light with a (not blue-eyed answer, but) pumpy-stumpy Latino, gospel-named Zaqueo. Zac, as he apparently preferred to be known, seemed to be sitting on some planty wall while Kelly stood alongside, all of a cheese and beaming at a moon beyond us; yet, if you looked closer, if you homed in on their portraits, the posers appeared to be not what they were – of irreconcilably different statures – but harmoniously shoulder-to-shoulder. Although Matthew and I laughed our heads off, we didn't call Zac a dwarf: we called him the Cyclops, because Matthew's beady eye detected that the questionable answer to Kelly's multiple-choice sported a glassy left orb. Yet, regardless, Kelly said that things were great, that Zac had taught him bedroom-stuff which you would not believe – Far Out! was the exclamation. Oh yes, Kelly had mastered positions of which ballerinos may only dream. But I wasn't to worry, he reassured me. He hadn't gone all married, dear; no; he and Zac enjoyed an Open Relationship – which made me wonder which of the two had opened it. By way of reply, I sent a post-card of a pair of ancient bull's horns, and informed Kelly that the studio was done, that Matthew was more or less installed, and that the first lot of rent should reach LA by 1st Jan. And, in the interim, I wished him a (not Happy Holiday, but) Merry Christmas, signing myself, I'm ashamed to admit, not with the honest truth, nor even with my customary pseudonym, but with the chapter-and-verse alias: Sycamore, Lady Jericho (née St Luke). I can't imagine that Zac saw the joke, but Kelly would have done, no question.

He rang – though not to give me a bollocking. He rang to give me the lowdown: Zac was history, *finito*. Why? Because apparently, at some scuzzy downtown club, he'd got his rocks off with some pimply rubberite – and, what was more, right under Kelly's nose. Could I imagine? All too clearly: fags were like that. Kelly didn't know what fags were like, but he said that Zac was garbage, total trash – plus, he added (after a slight yet audible waver), his mother was a char. I asked what they called chars in America. He told me to cut the crap. I said: Anyway, Zac had been challenged in the height department, hadn't he? Kelly told me that there was no need to be unkind. I apologized, but not because I was sorry. I apologized because I was delighted.

Our exchange now strikes me as puzzling: why should I have welcomed the dismissal from my brother's life of someone who signified nothing in mine? Was it because I was gratified to discover that the Open Marriage racket was, deep down, as unpalatable to Kelly as I myself had always found it? Was it because Kelly's ultimate refusal to stomach a set-up which hovered unsettlingly between monogamy and polygamy rendered me, in some unspoken manner, closer to him, in greater harmony? Was it because, in the final analysis, it is preferable to be forever auditioning than accepting the crummy part of understudy? Actually, it was none of these things: it was plain envy; for, just as earlier I'd felt envious of Matthew's easy past, more recently I'd felt envious of Kelly's gorgeous, sunny, smiling, laid-back here-and-now. And so, to spur him toward recovery, I fed him a taste of his own medicine, and prescribed: Plenty more fish. To which he replied: You betcha, darlin'. But before Kelly had the chance to dazzle me with the wonder of some other, taller, better, richer, sexier paramour, I interrupted to ask how Zac's meat-'n-two-veg had fared on the Richter scale. Kelly laughed a little coyly, but wouldn't co-operate, so I knew that any envy was wasted there, because Kelly was like those people who forswear that their latest beau is just the Best – the cock of Priapus, the bod of Charles Atlas, the face of Adonis, the voice of Barry White, the stamina of a Titan, the kisser of France, the bulldog's bollocks, the whole shebang – but who, no sooner has the swain absconded, or been told to get stuffed, begin to whine about the sexual lot which the departed had *actually* left to be desired – wouldn't go down, couldn't get it up, sloppy about hygiene, retracting nuts, hair on the back. Kelly was very like that. So for him to have yielded not one drop of vengeance-juice about this Zac must mean that the latter was (not just stunted and glass-eyed, but) an abysmal fuck, and, furthermore, that if any erotic positions were ever dreamed up, they were dreamed up by Kelly, and not at the ballet.

But I got off the subject, and boomeranged back to London. I told him I had an admission to make. What admission? Well, a confession more-like. He told me to spit it out. I could picture him gazing out at the ocean, narrowing his eyes. I told him I'd been done for drunken driving. He said: You stupid prat. I thanked him for his understanding. Well how else did I expect him to react, and, more to the point, what had happened to his car? Nothing. *Nothing?* Exactly; that's why I was wondering whether the policy mightn't be changed to cover Matthew: Matthew and I saw quite a lot of one another, and the car may as well be driven by someone; so, what did Kelly reckon? Kelly reckoned that Matthew and I must be shagging. I said: Rubbish. In which case, why was I being so Lady bloody Bountiful? I wasn't being so Lady bloody Anything; it just seemed like a practical solution in the circumstances. Kelly said that *he* would give me a practical solution in the circumstances, you pompous ass. Fine, I shrugged; then leave the car to rot till you get back. Kelly went spookily quiet, but eventually capitulated: What a pain, OK, he'd organize the ruddy transfer. And next, by way of postscript, he called me, with a perfect donnish accent, a stupid cunt. Yet the pejorative felt, this time round, like an easy insult, cheap at the price, because when I told Matthew about the plan, he yelped with excitement, and I, though not a yelper by nature, was naturally excited to know that Matthew, as well as already being my champion spear, and my bow of burning gold, was about to become my chariot of fire. The cloud, of course, had yet to unfold.

Once the insurance paperwork had been effected, and Kelly had given the go-ahead, Matthew and I sped off like a couple of maniacs to (not the horizon, but) Tango class. I can't quite remember why, or how, we got into this particular racket, but I do recall that, much as we liked the trappings of Country & Western, I was against joining that particular crowd, because their class was too popular, always packed, and involved line-dancing and group interaction, and, to be quite frank, collective efforts weren't my cuppa. Anyhow, the tango is a fiendish dance to master – all about precision, co-ordination, and pretending not to count – yet its technical demands appealed to us, for, after our travels through discorama, we considered ourselves advantaged in the kingdom of choreography. As it happened, Matthew was, of the two of us, by far the more instinctive dancer. But, in my teenaged years, I'd become smitten by the lyrics of the whole tango genre, and I think that he, after I'd translated some of my favourite lines, may have contracted my malady. In any case, lyrics aside, I nurtured a vain little fantasy that, should I ever find myself re-called to Monkeyland in the season when societal balls were happening, I'd be able, instead of loitering in the shadows like some piteous wall-pansy, to grab one of the débutantes (who were traditionally forced to learn this dance in advance of being launched into society), escort her onto the floor, assume a mask of Argentine dourness, and sock it to the crowd. None of the younger men in that self-satisfied land ever bothered to learn anything – except, perhaps, how to throw their confidence about – so there was a vindictive thrill inherent in the idea of being regarded, for once, as a desirably masculine flower – one who, though not a proper cunniphile, could properly perform this most heterosexy of dances. That was one of my reasons.

The second is trickier to work out, and I can only surmise it, for Matthew and I were never to speak of the matter, perhaps because, at our start, we didn't quite understand, or care about, what was going on between us. Later – let's just say that by then there were more pressing issues to discuss. But my sense, looking back, is that our romance, though unorthodox insofar as it never trespassed into the sexual miasma, nevertheless called for outward manifestations which conveyed to the world that what we shared was somehow exceptional, went beyond even friendship, that ours was a bond which, though not erotic, nonetheless possessed, as well as emotion, a certain physical charge. I would say that this is accurate. And that's why the tango, being so intimate a dance, provided us with the perfect means publicly to display the intimacy of our alliance. Besides – ¿Quién sabe? – one day, when we'd got our nerve up and had practised to impeccability both in Bedsitland and at Holland Park, we might dare to perform a sultry impromptu at the Moonlight. Yet, in order to scale this campest of heights, we would need to be tutored at an academy where the prospect of two males encoupled was (not accursed, but) countenanced. And it was this aberrant requirement that led us in the direction of a not madly attractive Gay & Lesbian Centre on the underbelly of town.

The lessons were held on Sunday afternoons, and given by a very skinny, tightly-trousered couple of professional queens without too many professional commitments; but whatever they may have lacked in fame and riches, they more than made up for in jangly limp-wristedness, which, from our point of view, was just the ticket. The pair of them belonged to the same old-fashioned school of preciosity as the doorman at the Moonlight, the one with the Cleopatran ring on his fuck-finger, so you get the rough picture. Anyhow, along we went, one Sunday close to Easter, to this peculiar institution (which provided, as well as dancing classes, counselling to battered lesbian mothers, alcoholic vegans, epileptic strippers – that kind of thing) and enrolled on the tango course for beginners. Just as Matthew, during the phase of our printed T-shirts, could not have been less troubled about wearing the one proclaiming Miss, so, now, he proved unperturbed by the idea of following my dancing lead – a prerogative on which I had insisted. For I was **bent** (sense **4**: intent) on the role of *Hombríssimo* – not only in case I ever found myself dragged to some poncy monkey-festivity, but also because reversing made me horribly giddy. Yet, when the pair of tango-teachers started clapping their varnished finger-tips, and squealing Class! Class! Can we please have a little order now, let's separate you people, leaders over here, followers over there – everything went a bit haywire. For I, an aspirant to leadership, suddenly found myself flanked by a line of threatening-looking diesel-dykes in biker jackets and combat pants, while, opposite, Matthew stood amid a row of elderly trannies – of the housewivey variety: mumsy heels, suburban specs, acrylic cardigans. Matthew's eyes were popping out of his skull, but you weren't allowed to laugh, not on your life, not even before the initials PC had been worthified – by which stage, in any case, my understanding of those capitals had been narrowed to the business of (not police constables, but) personal computers, which I found equally problematic.

There were all these mad steps to be learnt – Closed Promenade, Progressive Link, Rock Turn, Open Reverse – which the teachers (slow, slow, quick-quick, slow), demonstrated by way of introduction, at lavish length and long before any of us had the foggiest inkling as to how such feats might be accomplished; but it was a glamorous affair, theirs, no doubt about it. I couldn't claim with certainty that the leader was necessarily the butchier of the couple, but I can safely confirm that his follower, Nigel, looked not so much severe as severely miffed not to have a rose clamped between his canines. Both men wore character-shoes, I recall, which wasn't in itself remarkable – it was meant, I suppose, to look 'professional' – so if my memory of this detail endures, it probably owes less to those teachers, Len and Nigel, than to the fact that, before we had even set off for our first lesson, Matthew and I were already at ideological loggerheads – over footwear.

When he pitched up to collect me, he was wearing cowboy boots – which was wrong, pure and simple. We weren't going to Country & Western, I (as self-appointed stylist) felt it necessary to elucidate. Bugger *where* we were going, Matthew replied; the tango *called* for a bit of a heel – especially if you were the woman in the affair. But I didn't give a damn. I was the man. So I refused to change out of my loafers, which seemed to me the furthest that a novice, without incurring the scorn of fellow novices, could safely venture in acknowledging the proper, patent dancing shoes which were customarily sported by monkeys in tuxedos. But Matthew said that the tango, Georgie, was a street dance, invented by the people for the people in the bars of Buenos Aires. Nothing grand about it. Besides, we weren't exactly headed for some glitzy ballroom; we were off to Ghetto-land. And he was proved right, for when I found myself embroiled in a pile-up of dykie Dr Martens and trannie court-frights, I did, I admit, feel a bit of a prat.

However, it was the second lesson that really flummoxed us, for although I stuck to my precedent of loafers, and though Matthew stuck, much as I'd imagined that he would, to his cowboy boots, little else turned out as we might have imagined. We should have seen catastrophe coming, but we couldn't see beyond impromptus at the Moonlight – with the result that, even once Len and Nigel had taken us through the basic steps, and even once it appeared that those steps had been mastered, we remained too blinkered to foresee the obvious, which came as the damnedest surprise: the tape was abruptly switched off, rewound in a great flurry, and we were suddenly forced to swap partners. This provoked a virtual mutiny in the class, because it transpired that neither the dykes nor the trannies wanted to dance with a man. They got all vocal about it. But Len would not be shifted from what he called a professional attitude, and, thanks to that attitude, I found myself condemned to a vicious older switch-bitch who, irritatingly, boasted a better grasp of the tango than I did – an advantage which led her, as soon as she sniffed the chance, to complain about me to Nigel on the grounds of my (not gender, but) lack of aptitude. Her feet were outsize; and her hands, as well as being larger than mine, in graver need of electrolysis. The back of her brassiere felt too tight. I didn't dare to look at her face, any more than I dared to look across to check how Matthew was faring in the arms of Sappho . . . But once we had got out, I spiralled into a diatribe about how the trouble with dykes was that they were so bloody short on humour, and how the problem with trannies was that they were just so fucked-up – not so much between the legs as in their skulls. I mean, to think of the years which they spent saving up for the snip – only to discover, thousands of pounds down the line, and quite aside from the post-op agony – that nothing had really improved in their lives, apart, perhaps, from the size of their bra cups. Little wonder they were always resorting to suicide. Matthew thought that I was being unfair, because he'd heard of trannies who'd had their bits chopped off in Morocco and flourished. Flourished how, with Arabs? Flourished in relationships, he replied. I said I'd need to think about that one, but, meanwhile, would he kindly take us for a well-earned drink and a spot of practice back at the studio in Holland Park – which we came to know, during those roseate dancing days, as Hernando's Hideaway.

We rolled up the carpet, pulled down the blinds, switched on a tape, and got started. Even if, looking back, I view those private rehearsals sentimentally, the less-than-sentimental truth is that, while we were getting to grips with the tango, it was largely I who tripped up. But, as I've already explained, Matthew was, of the two of us, the more able dancer – indeed, he seemed, in addition to his own steps, to have mastered mine – so he was always able to put us back on track. And thus we would rewind and resume our positions and begin for the hundredth time. And it was all such a release from the dictates of the external homosexual lifestyle, that sometimes we preferred, rather than bother with Clubland, to stay indoors and tango. And laugh. And imagine. And we would imagine, for instance, that we were aboard some sumptuous liner which, though departed from Capri forty years beforehand, remained ever-bound for Buenos Aires; and I would become, say, some lezzer out of Compton Mackenzie, such as hispid-chinned Aurora (Rory) Freemantle, who famously bred bulldogs and trained female boxers; and the spectacle of a mannish woman in black tie dancing with another lady-passenger, would, of course, both scandalize the (immaterial) diners and consternate the captain. Or, otherwise, I might decide to impersonate the captain, who must always be darkly taciturn, in order that, while Matthew became the loveliest girl upon the ocean, the captain could conceive darkly amorous designs in the leg of his trouser, and thus the studio would become the enormous ballroom of that fabled liner, and every time that we approached the centre of the floor, my partner, the prettiest gal of all, could, while adjusting some invisible corsage of velvetish, African violets, be heard to remonstrate: Oh Captain, very well, if you absolutely insist, but really this must be the last, you have me quite exhausted, you naughty man. And then we would play *Olé Guapa*.

As the weeks slid by, some of the gang inevitably fell by the choreographic wayside. But those who persevered with their instruction, grew, as well as in aptitude (for a dyke can prove surprisingly light on her Dr Martens), in truculence. Indeed, it was this very mounting truculence which, in the end, I think persuaded Len and Nigel, who were never in greater favour of anything than they were of an easy life, to substitute for their professional attitude a more permissive one. And so it came to pass that, after a squabbly group-rendition of *Adiós Amigos*, our teachers decided to change tack, and decreed that, beyond that first contentious term at the Gay & Lesbian Centre, our pairings could be uni-gendral, which meant that the dykes and trannies were left to consort and Close-Promenade with one another, while Matthew fell to Len, and I fell to Nigel. Easier all round – at least for a while. And I say 'for a while' because it didn't take long for those trucker-voiced trannies, who, of our company, were the less tolerant incumbents, to begin to mutter grudges about injustice. Matthew and I, they claimed, were benefiting from special tutelage, practically one-to-one, and improving in leaps and bounds. This may not have been inaccurate, but nor was it less accurate than the fact that injustice is a much-bandied noun among people who've (intolerably) been born with the wrong tackle.

Once we'd tackled all the basics, Len announced that it was time to go for Fancier Stuff. Matthew seemed, in principle, up for this; and our teachers proved, in practice, all too up for a demonstration of fanciness: nifty syncopations, asymmetric sways, trixy little leg-wraps, refinements of that type. But at this point (which was the point of touch-and-go), I became sneakingly sceptical – not because I didn't want to get fancy with Matthew at the Moonlight (I could think of nothing more fabulous) – but because, conflictingly, I doubted being able to get too damn *fantástico* with some taffeta débutante back at the Bamboo Club. Complicated choreography required concerted practice, whereas I, in my vain simian fantasy, sought a spontaneous perfection – instant and basic, like the perfection of love. Nevertheless, I behaved myself; I did go through the motions; I did take the trouble to simulate those supplementary embellishments, which had no real substance, but were like the punctuating commas and colons and accents and dashes of the dance. Indeed, in the heat of a heated Rock Turn, Nigel, with an adulterous little gasp, marvelled at how (not fluid, but) fluent I had become.

Until, that is, the following Sunday. We gathered for the lesson. We paired up as we liked. We went through the previous week's fantabularity – which I (having grown a bit blasé by now) had confidently absorbed, digested, and passed aboard that marvellous old liner ever-headed for Buenos Aires. Back in class, however, the company was presently instructed to perform a general swaparound; so I found myself partnered, as had become the custom, by Nigel. We went for a little glide-about. Fine. But when we were told to step back, Class, and make room, and observe (which meant admire) our finest exemplars, my gullet began to play up. Len took Nigel in his slinky arms and slinky thighs, and though the effect resembled the very start, lesson one, it no longer seemed baffling or defying: rather, by this stage, it felt demystified, easy to grasp and break down, like a garish spread of food upon a package cruise-boat for the rabble. Did I suppress a bloated yawn? Did I want to get back to Holland Park, which was Capri before Gracie Fields went and crapped on it? Did I buggery. What I did was draw the line – because, to my sudden consternation, I saw Len, in all his tutorial mastery, introduce the final vulgar *coup de grâce*, which felt like the final stab; and what he did, before the entire gathering, and before the very gods of dance, and before anyone who might have cared to attend the Gay & Lesbian Centre, and before even Freddie Ashton could have averted the catastrophe, was this: he *knelt* before Nigel. Like some greasy Casanova in the slums of Buenos Aires. Well, *mucho* sorry; I wasn't about to kneel in front of anything or anyone (or so I imagined). And thus, at the end of that session, I told Matthew that we'd learnt quite enough, that Len and Nigel had gone too tango-far, that this wasn't *Come Dancing*, that I was sick of all those weirdos anyhow, and that I was never going back. Matthew looked a bit nonplussed; said he didn't get what I was getting so het-up about: a move was only a move, not some mortal crime. And then he told me to stop being such a (not Heidi, but) Concha. I told him that I could never be that, because a *concha*, back in Buenos Aires, meant a cunt. How apt, he muttered as he dumped me back in Bedsitland. But, with my defection, the Len-'n-Nigel farce was over, and over for both of us; because, as you know – and as Matthew was forced to grant – one hand, even after Mesopotamia became Iraq, alone does not tango. Not in my book it doesn't.

When I came of age, the monkey-bank released my grand-money. I couldn't quite ignore the fact that Kelly, on reaching his own majority, had received a fatter cheque than the slip-of-a-one which now sat propped on my table, but I wasn't about to bemoan the discrepancy between Kelly's legacy and mine, because, ever since our foliaceous infancy, my appeals for more (not peanuts, but) pounds had invariably fallen on deaf ears, so – whatever else I may have failed to learn in those early years – at least I'd come to learn the sterling difference between wasting time for no good reason and wasting it for a properly bad one. Comparisons were otiose; primogeniture, unavoidable; injustice, a gripe for tango-trannies. And besides, as words went, gifts and horses and mouths struck me more interestingly than interest, inflation, and converted currencies; which is why I simply interpreted this family trust – happily broken, for once – as my personally unfair equivalent of Matthew's easy past, my version of his great advantage. And even if my belated econom-ical leg-up didn't feel as valuable as his emotionally secure head-start, I told myself that it was, well, something. I felt my stroke of luck, and I was thankful.

But thankfully, I didn't go mad. Matthew saw to that. He sat me down and told me to do nothing. I went to the (not Post Office but) bank, wearing a suitably unsuitable ensemble, and told the manager, Mr Chortle-Buffer, who must have been the most boring commuter for leagues around, to stuff my cheque (not up his recreational argyle jumper, but) in a high-yielding deposit account. I added that, much as I thrilled to letters from people claiming to be my most obedient servants, I sincerely hoped – now that my prospects had chirped up – that it would be a creditable while before I was next reduced to looking down and choking on the typed expletive: Overdraft. He went har-har, and creaked himself up. We shook hands, but I twisted mine slightly sidewise, as if now it was I, not Matthew, who was wearing the violet corsage on a boat ever-bound for Buenos Aires, and desired – as well one might – to verify that my erstwhile usurer possessed the grace to bow. He did not. He looked completely baffled. But I rose above his frown with a beaming Chin-Chin smile, and then, while the lackey held ajar the door of his stuffy sanctum the better to expedite my departure, I flounced out, like That, my head whistling in a cloud more elevated than the cloud of any back-turned monkey. I would live to regret the luxury.

But anyway, the bulk of that money was, as it happened, to languish quietly, quietly gaining bulk, in deposit for some time. I left it in dusty abeyance – a decision both uncharacteristic of me and, contradictorily, in character. Ostensibly, no-one would have fainted at the news that I had gone and squandered the whole nest-egg in a single, deep-fried starburst – on a painting, for example. But nor would you, who know me better than the merely ostensible, be surprised to learn that, because Monkey-land didn't feel like a safe branch, and because I knew myself unlikely to receive a second stash in the near future, and because Kelly had already opted for the bulwark of bricks and mortar, I resolved to follow his sensible suit and channel my windfall into the whirlwind of property. Yet the thought of entering into negotiations with masonic spivs, who postured as estate agents and detested queers, somehow felt too onerous, too adult for a quivery-quavery javelin. I would wait for Kelly to come back. He was into the housing market. His foot was already secured on the first rung. He was into money: his fist was even tighter than my arse. He would help me to be (not a Cyclops, but) wise. Besides, the eye is a great deceiver, and mine, being idle into the bargain, had grown accustomed to the false parameters of Bedsitland, to the security of its narrow horizons, to the cosy limitations of its muted palette, to the comfort of its high, hopeful window, gazing forever out. And all of these things, I suspect, conspired to make me view myself as temporarily comfortable. In no immediate hurry.

More profoundly, however, I think that my reluctance to stake an instant claim in the market was linked to my uncertain status in the world, which remained a question-mark. Yes, I could have gone and bought some temporary little *garçonnière*, and dolled it up in a quick-'n-sexy, non-literary vein; for, though unpersuaded by buttony chairs and ink-stained curtains and dusty vases of dead hydrangeas, I wasn't entirely devoid of imagination. And yet, the very image of builders bursting back into my life was beyond imagining. I would say that if, earlier, at the Respectable cul-de-sac, I'd behaved like a girl spreading her legs to welcome her man while making, instead of love, cuntish plans for his successor; now, in Bedsitland, I conducted myself more in the manner of a promiscuous virgin, always putting out, often getting laid, but never going the whole honest way, hanging back for the unreal reality of matrimony. And it was this false romanticism which, at base, must have prompted me to stall, to refrain from taking action. For, though I wished to see myself committed, and committed wholeheartedly, I could see no-one to whom I wished wholeheartedly to commit. Where, for God's sake, was my prince? Where was that basic but instant bliss which not even the tango could bequeath? Precisely.

And then, there was the imprecise alternative of Matthew. Just as we had never discussed whether our friendship amounted to an alternative romance, nor whether, if that were the case, our romance possessed the physical charge which I now suggest propelled us toward dancing class, so I didn't suggest to him the option of setting up home together. Not yet; not quite. Kelly would return soon enough, whereupon Matthew would be compelled to seek new pastures. That would be the moment for me to surrender my silly sentimental obstinacies and moot the more realistic question of sharing a pad. And in this way, the money which, if not having freed me from my private gloom, should at least have furnished me with a private bathroom, was left to fester behind the bars of a Mayfair banking-house. I didn't even take the trip that Dr John had encouraged. I went to bars. I went to clubs. I got plastered. I fucked about – from misplaced pride, not from proud love. I danced with Matthew. I continued my dalliance with sleeping tablets. Between a couple, I told the niggle of my guilt to buck up. I applied for a very menial post in publishing. They turned me down. They found me underendowed, but called it overqualified. I felt like an A La Carte Tarte. I applied for a job with a classy perfumerer, recently arrived in town. Süskind's book had just come out. I'd inhaled it profoundly, though not in its original package, which was the language of Hans. The perfumerer was Parisian. Hers was the language of romance. It would all be fine. Madame required an apprentice. She couldn't afford to pay one. I poo-pooed this commercial cedilla, called it of no real gravity, like Dr John discussing the clap. She liked the adjective Vocational. I liked the noun Musk. She was bound to admire my nasal channels. I deployed them like a double-barrelled gun. It all made sudden sense. Essences, not perfect love, would be my passion. I mentioned Süskind to the quilted handbag. She thought the man was – how you say – Rhöbish; but I don't suppose that Grenouille, the name of his protagonist, can exactly have enhanced her critical faculties. From her maple desk – and not her *sac à main* – she offered me a manly Gauloise. I accepted it like a man, and rammed it into the cleavage of my index and its *voisin*. She clicked me a flaring light. I thanked her; I sat back; I began to expand. And then, she pronounced that a Nose couldn't smoke. *Desolée*, Monsieur, she lied. I stood up, said absolutely *rien*, shook her superfluous hand, massacred my stub in her pristine cut-glass ashtray, and *au revoir*ed her in the eye. Puff the Magic Dragon. (I've since discovered that with this myth, and not the creator of *Perfume*, lies the real rubbish; for I have it on professional authority that Noses smoke with greater alacrity than the chimneys of de Maupassant. It's just that the confidence is kept quiet, discreetly in-house. Same goes for gurgly-spitty oenophiles: tobacco doesn't spell the automatic desecration of their sybaritic tastebuds. As for snuff and snuffing it – I'll pass on that. But people – as I had yet to discover – do like to talk crap. Or rather, **ordure** [14c: French, from *ord*, meaning filthy or foul]. *Excusez-moi*.)

Harder to excuse, when I first learnt the news (courtesy of the answer-phone, if you don't much mind), was the fact that Kelly decided to come home three weeks before time, thereby forcing Matthew to clear out within forty-eight frantic hours. But there was, to be fair, a mitigating reason for the sudden change of plan, and it was the following, exceedingly queer one: with all his devotional gym-bunnying and determined pumping up and all the rest of the narcissistic beach-boy dream-boat funk, Kelly had gone and earned himself a (not blue-eyed answer, but) hernia. And because he didn't have medical insurance in America, and his stint out there was all but done, it was decided – through the intercession of the susceptible City Fluke – that the poor blighter, as he referred to my brother, should be exonerated from completing the tail-end of his Californian contract and be allowed to fly back to London, hobbling a little heroically, like a soldierboy after a brush with shrapnel, in order to be speedily and privately hospitalized. And yet, despite the injury, I don't remember Kelly ever having looked so fantastic as he did on arrival. Even if his humours (and his tissues) were on the frayed side, his general aspect was – well, the loveliest that it would ever be, at its absolute zenith. It made me feel so wan and weedy that I was reduced to pretending to be sniffily chic. His hair was much shorter now, virile, with boxy sideburns attached. His skin was caramel, and shiny. His teeth had been capped – not in the style of classic Hollywood tombstones, but capped with a naughty cosmetic irregularity, mischievously designed to promote a conquering smile. His outline was finer even than in the shot which he had shared with Zac – tauter, more muscled; cut. His shoulders were bulbous, like a sculpted great clothes-hanger, no need for shoulder-pads; and the clothes – tight across the trunk but easy across the rump – in which he ignored the men at customs, were triumphal. I can't deny it. He looked like a star. I leaned up to kiss him. He told me to act like a man. I pushed the luggage trolley to the taxi rank. He bore himself high on a wave of admiring glances. Call me a tango-trannie, but it did feel a bit like rough justice.

Meanwhile Matthew, who wasn't the type to cause a rumpus, parked our fiery chariot for the last time, skived off work on some pretext or other, and got packing. I wanted him to come to Bedsitland, where, between dances and mad nights, we might discuss the next impending facet, the possibility of sharing a rented flat, or applying for a joint mortgage – that kind of stuff. For the pleasure of his company I would have slept in the communal bath. But he decided to return to Kingston – to think (he said) about things. His father had apparently developed a dicky heart. My tricky one developed fears that Matthew might be thinking about some shady secret close to his come-hithery arse. These fears proved, as it happens, to be founded. There was, or had been, some passing someone, encountered after dark in the gethsemanic gardens of Holland Park, but years would have to elapse before that revelation came to light – by which stage, I had myself been round so many fraught and throttled sexual corners that I no longer knew what was wrong and what was right, what was mortal folly and what was vital love.

The thing, said Kelly, was to get him to a consultant fast: his groin was bloody killing him. And so, as in the days of McManus, I found myself enlisted to keep my brother company: first, at the surgery of his GP (not Dr John – some stiff-collared medic in a basement near the studio); then, at a snazzy set of rooms in Harley Street, which, though it evoked the type of haven where brides-to-be place wedding lists, turned out to be where the surgeon flicked through Kelly's notes and prodded at the borders of his (not Swiss lingerie, but) Kleinian briefs; and finally, at a fragrant private clinic, full of lilies and marbling and grown-ups in cashmere, all very warm and serene. I won't tell you the name of the place, because I want to tell you the story without inhibition.

Kelly was admitted like a dream. The people at reception couldn't have been sweeter. His beautiful new teeth were plainly doing the trick. The nurse who took us to his room might have been conveying us to the honeymoon suite. Strangely, I can't remember what we were wearing. Yet something in Kelly had changed, something which, in turn, seemed to have changed the balance between us. It was as if, although he (obviously) remained my older brother, and the more experienced, and certainly the more striking, America had wrought a subtle alteration in him, an alteration subtler than his switch from the words darling to honey, or sexy to horny, or queer to faggot, or vest to singlet, or chest to pecs, or stomach to abs, never mind the switch from kissing your cheek to telling you to act like a man. I would say that whatever California may have done for the enhancement of my brother's musculature, it also did, in proportional contrast, for the reduction of his inner power. His stint by the laid-back ocean had taught him to (not speak American, but) hold back, to be (not up-front, but) hesitantly polite. And on account of this passive, taciturn new reluctance, which made me impatient, I found myself compelled to take control on his behalf, to play the mediator, to tackle awkward subjects – such as the Nuddy. But wishing to spare myself embarrassment, I inflicted my embarrassment on the staff. I told them, for instance, that it was *their* responsibility, not mine, to help my brother with his bath. Why else did they think that people took out medical insurance? I sounded like the pompous son of some pompous monkey. I found myself behaving like a counterproductive mother. It made me angry. It made me ghastly.

During the week that Kelly remained hospitalized, I was never able to stand the strain of him for longer than two hours. I used to keep a surreptitious check upon the time. If I tried to get us off the topic of scalpels, and asked him, for instance, about clubs in Los Angeles, he would tell me not to be fatuous. If I tried to be serious, and asked what I should do with my money, he would tell me that he wasn't my sodding bank manager: he had better things to worry about, in case I hadn't noticed, such as a Hernia. I tried to be funny; said that surely a man had a Hisnia. The gag – if you could call it that – misfired. Kelly erupted. Bawled me out. I felt dreadful, not because he'd been in the right, but because I'd got it all so wrong, had gauged the moment so badly. I went downstairs, and bought some flowers, parrot-tulips burnished to the glow of an expensive sunset. I took the lift back up, herded myself in among a tribe of djellabas, prepared my discourse of contrition as I drifted along the fitted carpet. I knocked at the door; I didn't wait; I stepped inside. I found him pretending that he hadn't been crying. I pretended that I'd noticed nothing. I think that he was frightened. I forgot to apologize. I vanished for a vase; came back; faffed about like a wife; told him that the sooner we were through with this fandango the better. Too damn right, he snapped; and then he told me to go over to the studio and get it ready for when he came out. It wasn't much to ask. Not in the circumstances. I said that I'd be back at five.

And was. Some nurse of the male variety, garrulously camp, freckle-armed, and delighted to be familiarizing himself with such *bona*-chicken company, was sitting on Kelly's bed, patting at the blankets and brandishing a grin the size of the Ripe Banana. Kelly was being typically adorable about things, but admitted that he was getting a bit sick of (not pricks, but) jabs, for it transpired that, in my absence, he'd been subjected to a battery of blood tests. What, for a hernia? Yes dear, the nurse replied; routine procedure. But the grin had sort of dwindled. I looked at Kelly. I looked at Nursey. I gathered myself to my full, mediocre height. I assumed the (not initiative, but) first person plural. And then I said, very slowly and quietly, because I was starting to feel panicky: so there's nothing else we need to worry about, right? But my rhetorical non-sequitur must have seemed so banal, or sounded so muffled, that it failed to elicit a reply. I tapped the nurse's freckled arm, and stared at him hard, yet my words, as they came out, sounded more like a threat or rebuke or command: In which case (I began), I presume that tests for anything other than This Particular Condition will remain your own private business, because we're not up to dealing with other issues at the minute; by all means take whatever precautions you see fit, but keep your routine voodoo strictly to yourselves; confidential; understood? The collared tunic was blushing at the ears. The grin had been wiped clean. His mouth was antiseptically neutral. But I don't think that the patient can have been entirely with it, because, after the nurse had tottered away, like some busy manicurist with a rack of ruby-lacquer test-tubes, Kelly asked what I'd been on about – hepatitis? No, I replied: hysteria. And then he said that the thing which drove him really hysterical was the thought of convalescence. All his hard work at the gym would be up the shoot.

Soon thereafter, the consultant arrived. Knock-knock. Come in. Hello chaps. He remembered us from Harley Street. Luck was on our side. I stood up. He sat down. Be operating in the morning, he announced. Surgery scheduled for ten forty-five. Kelly was second in line. Fine, I said; no point hanging about. Quite so, agreed the consultant. He fiddled with his stethoscopic rubber. He leaned to glance at Kelly's charts. Like the room? he asked. Kelly said that it seemed fine, thank you. Good – well, I'll be off then; try to get some sleep; see you before theatre, and, of course, should you feel restless in the night, by all means ask for a sleeping tablet. Again Kelly thanked him. The consultant departed. I told Kelly I was going to get some coffee. I shot after the pinstriped Knife. I found him at a corner. He looked surprised. I was panting. I told him what I'd told the nurse. He told me that the nurse had told him. I don't know where I found the word Consent, but he said: What about it? I replied that we wanted to withhold it, that it couldn't be granted. The consultant looked yonder, beyond me, as if rising above a tiresome child. He wanked his tie. I said that my brother was too jumpy to handle other matters. The hernia was enough. He quite understood, old chap; nothing to get worked up about. And I took him at his word. I didn't get worked up. I skipped coffee, fetched Kelly the paper, told him to watch the box for a while, and said that if he wanted me to bring anything in the morning, to give me a buzz. He told me to come here. He kissed me like a man. He kissed me like a brother. I was shattered. I raced back to Bedsitland; had a bite; had a bath. And then I rang Matthew.

So (he began), what news of Arnie? The op's tomorrow, I said, around eleven. How long were they keeping him in for? I presumed a few more days, till he could walk on his own, or perhaps till the stitches had come out; I didn't really know. And then? Then back to Holland Park, most likely; though there were those stairs to contend with. Matthew told me to throw a (not tantrum, but) party. A party? Here in Bedsitland? Was he mad? Sanely enough, he said that Bedsitland was where I lived, wasn't it? Where I lived At Present. Well, what better place to have it then? Easy and central, he called it; handy to get to. I wasn't so certain. It wasn't so simple. He told me not to be so bloody chippy; you could fit twenty people in there easily. I digressed. What was this party meant to be in aid of, anyhow? To Matthew, my twenty-first seemed like a pretty good reason. On the other hand, if I was going to be trixy about having hit adulthood, I could always turn it into a hero's welcome, to cheer Kelly up, give him something to look forward to; but no, not a surprise – Kelly was bound to want some of his own crowd invited. And next, Matthew said that I should also ask those friends of mine whom he had never met, so that everyone could get pissed and have a good gossip about the brothers (not Grimm, but) Twink. And then he told me to stop being such a downer. Be fun.

I said that I'd mention it to Kelly – assuming that after surgery he was less grumpy. But then Matthew suggested that perhaps, in any case, I should simply treat the party as marking the end of a chapter: wasn't it time I started looking for my own flat? Funny he should mention that. Funny why? Because seeing as we were both in the same boat – looking for places to live – I'd been wondering how he felt about joining forces with me. We could rent somewhere with a couple of bedrooms, more space for both of us; a garden-flat might be an idea; or we could apply for a mortgage if he liked. Matthew went quiet; took longer than I would have liked to say that my suggestion wasn't a realistic one. My unrealistic heart shrank. (He didn't like me enough. It wasn't a romance.) But my self-protective mouth managed, after a minor gulp, to reply that perhaps he was right. He said that queens shacking up like spinsters was sort of dodgy – bit like the long-hair thing. You know, if you grew it while you were young, it might be considered stylish (as indeed it was during the New Romantic era); if you grew it when you were old and silver, people might reckon it to be distinguished. But, in the middle years, it seemed a bit pathetic, a cop-out really. I knew what he meant; but copping out, to me, felt better than not coping.

He laughed. I asked what was so funny. He said Christ, the thought of it. I'd be hell to live with, always banging on about the tube of toothpaste, and the lid on the loo-seat, and the nail-brush having to be bristles-down, and about a special spoon for the marmalade, and all the rest of the spinstery crap. Well, I answered, I'd rather worry about that crap than be the type of crappy queen who only worries about her douche-bag. He hit back: Who says spinsters don't like enemas? Or dykes? Or tarts? Or nuns, come to that? For all we knew (according to Matthew), nuns used holy water to flush out. How hilarious, I replied. And then, in mock horror, he gasped: Oh my God, sister, have I sinned? So I said: Yes you have, you filthy-minded heathen; you've probably blasphemed; get on your knees and say your creed. But Matthew said that he'd rather smell it – creed being his favourite poof-juice. And then we moved onto other stuff, such as how he'd sooner come and stay with me than be my flatmate, because, as a guest, you always had the upper hand. And briefly we talked about his father, whose dicky heart – funnily enough – was back on track, and about his mother, who was going in for some scan, but none of it really registered, because thoughts of Kelly were cluttering my mind. Matthew said to speak tomorrow, Friday. Was I game for getting clubbed? I said: Is the Pope a Catheter? He assured me that he'd never been so shocked in all his life. I said: Better shocked than shafted. And on this lame alliterative note we parted telephonic company. But by the time I realized that Kelly might have been trying to get through while I'd been yabbering, it was late, too late to call and say goodnight. I might have woken him up. I took a tab. I slept badly; fretted; sweated in the linens of my spinstery shroud; woke up too early; felt a bit fuggy.

I got to the clinic an hour before surgery, but my knock at Kelly's door earned no reaction. I went in. He was out. The bed was made – by him, I could tell, because it lay flipped back, the top sheet at an angle, like a sail drawn by a child. A vestige of our infancy. It reminded me of our nannies, who, eternities back, had performed the task on our behalf. Kelly's room seemed creepy without him, airless, hollowed-out. His slippers, at the foot of the bed, under the clip-board of spidery graphs, appeared shrunken. The tulips looked hung-over. Fresh water. Perk up. The nurse with freckled arms made a flustering arrival, clutching a pair of Kelly's underpants. He tut-tutted as he shoved them in the drawer of the cot-side cabinet. It made me want to slap him, or sack him, or something – grubby slut. I asked where my brother had got to. Ooh, you must of missed him, lovey; he's already been taken to Pre-op; wicked boy shouldn't of been wearing knicks, though – *told* him it were bad for circulation. I asked if I could sit with Kelly while he waited for the surgeon to get started. Shouldn't bother, dear, he's already pretty zonked. And then the nurse looked at his bosom-watch and advised me to go home. I was to ring after (not lunch, but) dinner, meaning (not dinner, but) lunch, by which stage the patient should be coming round.

I didn't go home, as it happened. I went — because it was closer — to Kelly's studio, which still felt strange without Matthew's artefacts. Kelly hadn't had a chance to do his Bauhaus number. But I tried to make myself at home, playing twelve-inch singles and expelling smoke-rings and snooping around. I picked up an album of photographs from our childhood (photographs that I wouldn't myself have wanted, though I do sometimes wonder where they ended up), of our heads in sailor-hats, frozen against streaks of blurry turquoise, and of our bottoms, crawling over lunar sandcastles on some beach of glittering black, mementos of outings which now meant nothing. Next, a snap, pre-dating those, of Kelly waving through the wooden banisters of a high balcony, and trying, with his other hand, to rock my pram — this, sprouting a white parasol of ironical *broderie*. Then, a further shot, taken against a torrential flurry of bougainvillea on the steps of an old hotel — the Quisisana, since demolished to provide apartments for luxurious newly-weds — showing the pair of us, aged, I would say, four and five, leaving, or arriving at, some children's fancy-dress party. Streamers and balloons abound, obscuring the face of a nanny. Kelly wears folkloric costume (from Zamora, I think), while I, his peasant-girl accomplice, sport a massive frilly harvest-skirt, a shawl (knotted at the front), a headscarf (knotted at the back), and a furious scowl — like the monkey-girl whom our parents never had, cast in the sort of travesty that used to amuse adults of their amusing caste. Then, a formal, studio portrait of us boys — taken in the softened black-and-white which remained the stubborn fashion among indigenes of that remote society. We're dressed identically, as was also fashionable, in piqué summer-shirts and striped bermuda-shorts, though the colours of those stripes elude the observer in the retrospective aftermath. We must have been a little older by this time. Kelly stands behind me, forcing a grin for the benefit of some coercive (invisible yet envisaged) grown-up; I, the while, sit limp-legged and fat-thighed on a swing which swing it mustn't. Sulking hard. There are pictures of the monkeys, naturally, wreathed in exemplary simian smiles: our mother at a *cóctel*, wearing a midnight velvet trench-coat with a buckle of rhinestones which seems to twinkle at me from the past. She's flanked by the turning back of some broad consort who seems to be pouring himself a hefty drink from a hefty tantalus. In another shot, a couple of pages on, she sports a vast pink hat of Andalusian flavour with a dark organza flower – implanted underside, in the shadows of her powdered profile. Her encroaching, unavoidable husband is trussed into morning coat and spats. Topper at a jaunty cock; gloves, gripped in one hand. I wonder. Wedding on the Peninsula? Races at Ascot? Can it matter? Did it ever? But before I know, before I knew, it was time to get back. I took a bus to Kelly's bedside. No great hurry. I'd forgotten to ring in advance.

When I jumped off the bus, I was humming along the lines of an anthem. I was glad. Unto Me. Let us go. My temples were pulsing; my spirits, jubilant. The worst was over. You know when you know. The girls at reception waved as I breezed along. I waved back, and rushed past the flower-stall, driven by a sense of importance – not of my own, but of the occasion. And on this occasion I can tell you precisely what I wore, because it would become – indeed it was – historical: hacking jacket of a pinkness so corrupted, so flecked with grey and sage and lilac, as to verge on dullness; baggy pleated flannels, of the sort that decades earlier had been worn by flapper-boys at Oxford; soft suede brogues; plain silk shirt, slubbily raw and unbuttoned at the collar. I must have looked like some pansy from before the war. Backwardly forward; or forwardly backward. Perfectly wrong. But I felt perky. On form. It was, after all, my (not prerogative, but) point.

During the lift-ride up to the fifth floor, which involved a load of stop-offs for people in dark shades or pale clogs (never both), I made a mental note of topics to be broached: how Kelly should avoid going back to work for as long as possible; the half-forgotten albums which I'd found at the studio; whether the monkeys should be informed about his stint in hospital; the brill new songs which he'd brought back from California; the knickers which the nurse had stuffed into the bedside drawer; how Kelly had felt while he was stoned; what he'd been forced to don for the op – paper bonnet? Baby-doll smock? – whether he'd talked gibberish under the influence; whether I could admire his stitches; whether he was hungry, whether he was thirsty, whether he fancied a drop. Even – grumpiness permitting – whether he wanted the party of which Matthew and I had talked. It wasn't a bad list. It just required commitment. To memory.

Events were to thwart me. Kelly, I discovered, had been moved – over there, by the fire doors, last room down the corridor. The first thing which, as I approached, I saw, was a low large momma's bottom, straining in a bright blue overall as it heaved itself up from the floor. Must have been scrubbing the linoleum. Kelly's door was practically closed. Darkened interior. The momma seemed to be mumbling, or perhaps grumbling, through a protective mask, like a muzzle – histrionic. Back on her feet, she adjusted her specs, fiddled with the mask, and shut the door. As she turned to go, I noticed that she was gloved beyond the elbows. She looked awkward. Then I saw the door. Splattered with notices. Isolation. Highly infectious. On no account. On your own head. At your peril. Alarm bells. Panic stations. No entry. Historical.

I stole within, trying to minimize my noise, and nearly tripped over a tray that had been dumped by the skirting-board. Kelly was awake. He was struggling to get down from the bed to the floor. He seemed in a state unknown to me, a state beyond mere grogginess. Whisperingly I asked what the hell was going on. He yelled at me to close the effing door. He fell back on the pillows. I picked up the tray: sealed sandwich, sealed yoghurt, lidded glass of water. I felt wobbly. The tulips were gone. He asked what had happened to me this morning? I said that by the time I'd got to the hospital, he'd already been wheeled up to Pre-op. So why couldn't I have gone upstairs to where he was? Could've, I supposed, but the nurse had told me that he was already zonked; didn't really seem much point. Much *point?* Oh Kelly, come off it, aren't you making a bit of a mountain?

From a pocket in his dressing-gown he produced a packet of fags. He lit up. Sod the rules, he grunted. I was desperate to do likewise, but, typically, thought twice. I compromised by asking if I could have a drag. He said: on condition that I fetched him his tooth-mug – as an ashtray. He told me to open those filthy curtains. I did, but the window wouldn't budge. A chilly winsome light seeped into the greenish confines, which felt like a fish-tank. Kelly looked out. His eyeballs seemed to roll up in the way that they do when people are frantic to govern their lachrymal ducts. And then he gave me the soliloquy of his life. I didn't understand it.

As far as I was able to make out, this is what had happened. Long before Kelly had been due to go into theatre – while he was still brushing his teeth, hunched over the basin in the previous room – the surgeon had apparently pitched up, surrounded by a posse of interns who had gathered round the bed looking serious and all kind. The Knife had apparently said that he was a firm believer in establishing a bond of trust with all his patients – a platitude to which the disciples had nodded in sycophantic unison – and then the surgeon had added that, contrary to what Kelly might have been led to suppose, Certain Blood Tests had in Deed been carried out, purely as a matter of procedure, you understand, but that the results which some of these tests had yielded would necessitate measures of extra caution; so Kelly wasn't to be surprised or put out or anything; and if, of course, at any stage after the operation he wished to be apprised of his overall medical (not condition, but) Status, the Knife would be happy to oblige. And then the Knife and his little blades had flown out, making way for the freckled arms, which entered bearing a shiny metal tray with Kelly's pre-med jab.

Well-go-*on*, I pressed him. But Kelly went on looking out of the window. It all felt heavy to me, weighty, constricting. The sensation was back to thoracic, closer to guilt than adrenaline. He whispered, seething with sibilants, that it didn't exactly take a thesis to suss out what the stupid surgeon had been suggesting, did it? How did he mean? And then he said that he was obviously Positive. I deflated with relief, and thanked Christ that Kelly was clear. But Kelly called me a stupid idiot. Positive, you fool, meant that you *had* It. And then he started sobbing with such dereliction as I hadn't seen since we were children.

I went into action, talked reactive rubbish, blabbered, became imaginative. I told Kelly he must be (not strong, but) out of his mind. I said that the surgeon was full of crap, probably didn't like fags, just trying to put the frighteners on us. I swore that those sorts of tests were always carried out at clap clinics. Hospitals were just too busy with things like, you know, casualty. I was (not positive, but) sure of it. I asserted the position with unbrookable authority. Let's face it, I told Kelly as I gestured toward his aura with wide, arm-sweeping magnificence: he was in amazing nick, brimming with strength and well-being. He corrected me with the beginnings of a grin: Rood health, dear. (My perky lies – the point of me – were doing the trick.) I returned to the recent beginning, to his appearance at the airport, and told him that when I'd seen him swanning round the Arrivals screen I'd practically been sick. Sick? With jealousy: he'd looked as if he'd been walking off the set of some flipping movie – tall and tan and young and lovely, better than the whole of Ipanema. His health, if you asked *me*, was too damn rude: that's why he'd been punished with an injury – in case he got too big for his boots, too cocky about his looks. Anyway, the hernia was fixed. *That* was the main thing. The Knife had done his bit. The insurance would meet the bill. Our job was simply to get Kelly back on his pins, and escape from this dump – discharge ourselves if need be. And then I produced the flask which, to infuse my ventricles with courage, I had, in another life, concealed at orgies in the darkened suburbs. I told Kelly to take a good glug. He did so greedily, like an infant assaulting a nipple. Chin-Chin. Again he grinned. Those teeth. What about them? I told him that they were completely bloody brilliant. *Danke, Liebling*, he agreed. And for a moment, yes, it did feel as if I'd managed to effect the frantic miracle, as if I'd succeeded in returning us to the Moonlight, in restoring us to a time which, however contentious then, now felt, next to the current contention, like child's play. I went into the bathroom, poured away the ash, shoved the illicit filter down the plug-hole, rinsed the toothmug, and sprayed deodorant around, to atomize our veniality. Kelly told me to stop being such a Scarlet, because frankly, my dear, he couldn't give a fist-fuck.

Next, the Knife was back, but without his collection of serrated disciples. Despite my efforts to camouflage the stench of fags, it is not impossible that the surgeon might have surmised our contrary penchant – not because he did anything as unseemly as sniff around, but because there was something sly about the contours of his smiling. I myself could see scant reason to smile, though I perceived an ample scope for slyness. But notwithstanding I leapt up, sprang to the sort of knee-jerk courtesy which, too often, is expended by the young upon their mere elders. Then, almost on the rebound, I plonked myself back down and crossed the voluminous legs of my flannel bags, having suddenly remembered that I was meant to be Kelly's guardian, or mother, or wife. I swung a bony ankle in a feminine array of light. The Knife didn't seem to be put out. In fact, he looked as if he didn't have the least intention of stopping for, of stooping to, any kind of a bedside dalliance. He had graduated to a bow-tie. Quite the dandy. He buried his bloodless hands in the pockets of his dapperly-braced trousers, and, shifting from

lace-up to sheeny lace-up, trotted out the usual claptrap: operation had gone according to plan, everyone very happy, essential
to start walking now, resume an active life, expect a bit of pain
in the next forty-eight hours but, after that, the stiffness should
subside and basically everything would be back to normal. Anything Kelly'd like to ask? Yup: could he go home before the
stitches came out? So long as he took it easy, said the Knife –
then added, with a lubricated chumminess, like a grown-up trying to coax a brat into a discussion of the facts of life: Anything
else at all? Kelly turned his pillowed head toward my rigid one,
and gritted his famous caps. I turned my grinding molars
towards the Knife, but my demeanour struggled to exude an air
of absolute nonchalance, as if I were either royalty or retarded.
Such as? Well (replied the Knife), such as, well, for instance, the
reason for Kelly's room-transfer. My hand flew up. I recall the
gesture exactly, because, as my elbow went crack and my wrist
reached its uttermost outstretch and my palm assumed an
emphatic perpendicular, like a signpost meant to halt the traffic,
it made you think of Stop In The Name of Love. You won't
believe this, but Kelly sniggered. Talk about timing. Later he
would claim that the camp had been too much. But I wasn't to
remind him, because it creased him up, and the stitches were still
agony. Agony. Too much.

At the time, however, I dropped my embarrassed hand and
let it melt into the shame of some shadow; but next, the mettle
of my tongue glinted at the Knife and asked whether we might
have a chat, to which he replied: Certainly, to which I replied:
In private, to which he replied: If you like, to which I replied:
If you don't mind, to which he – damned if he wasn't going to
get the last word in – conceded: A very quick one then, I'm
expected home for dinner, we've got company – an admission
to which, admittedly, there was no possible (polite) reply.
Though stumped, I jumped up. Kelly didn't appear patronized
or babyfied by the thought of not partaking of the looming
discussion; rather, he appeared relieved that, while his stamina

flagged, I should be assuming charge. The suggestion, as he sank back, was that he was granting his younger brother temporary licence to become his older one. Afterwards, after he'd laughingly tried to apologize for having laughed at the hand that had tried to stop the surgeon in the name of love, he also said, albeit with greater gravity, that he would make this whole thing up to me. And make it up he did, by means of a platter of glass, blown clear yet smoked to the colour of ashes. I have it still; I live with it. But back then, on that singular medical evening, I meekly followed the heels of my Iscariot toward some creepy roomlet where next-of-kins were routinely counselled, or their grievances mollified with tissues and tripe. I think that Kelly thought I could be trusted. Trusted with the facts. Trusted not to lie to him. But I trusted my knowledge of my next-of-kin enough to know that lies, not facts, were the vital requirement. He was good at believing. He was keener on the hopeful delusions which to date had carried him through life than on the hopeless illusions which, for me, made any hope of progress a virtual non-starter. Kelly belonged to the faithful type, and I tried to be faithful to that.

I wish that I could tell you that my audience with the Knife proved satisfactory, or, failing satisfaction, cathartic, or, failing catharsis, trenchant and vicious and mordant and bloodied and lethal and vengeful and loud; but I regret that – of all those impassioned adjectives – it lived up to none. The unequal pair of us just bore each other for a quarter of an hour in a frustrating pseudo-professional temperature, nebulously pitched somewhere between chilliness and charmlessness. Briefly, to begin with, we hovered: he, near a window from which hung the descending dark; I, near an Impressionistic poster of a happy family sitting on the sun-drenched grasses of better times. The Knife unblocked his nasal ducts and made a brave attempt to minimize the sound of mucus bobbing to circumvent his windpipe. I, meanwhile, struggled to dredge up saliva, and blotted the dampness from my palms against my jacket. As the

Knife slid out a chair, and claimed a corner of the table, and eased himself onto a cushiony seat of pitted orange plastic which phutted at the marriage with his thighs, he exhorted me, of all the absurd imperatives, to make myself At Home, and compounded this absurdity with the ironical prescription that I not get Worked Up, when (never mind my unworked body) my head wasn't even worked out.

Returning to that horrible encounter, I think that I was just too muddled and frenzied and young, and, as an ignorant result, attempting to be too many things, too many people at once. First, I wanted to be Kelly, wanted to stick up for him, the outraged party with neither the strength to articulate his outrage nor the courage to embody Damocles. Then I needed to be (to be like) his imperious, glacially-principled mother, even though she, however scandalized by the events of the last ten hours, would, in ten seconds flat, have shifted the onus of scandal from the head of the hallowed surgeon to the head of her pervert son and thence from the head of the blood-of-her-blood to her own self-pitying bloodless one, the shaming sinful ache of which (she would have avowed) simply made her want to die, or — a comparable tragedy — withdraw from society. Next I wanted to be (to imagine being) Kelly's delusory man-wife, his elusive blue-eyed answer, who, whether miscast a million times or right at last, would, from this landmark on, henceforth-ad-infinitum, need to be told, need to have spelt out, the deadly serious reason why No, not for any amount of conjugal Bauhaus, could the freedom of full congress ever be on the cards. Stop in the name of love. And last, since my categorical request for medical (not discretion, but) silence had categorically been flouted, I wanted, selfishly and dramatically, to be the (not injured, but) insulted party. Yet ethics were never my subject; transgression was more my speciality, and, within it, the empurpled horrors of love. Oh I knew nothing then about the lurid luminescence of the term Assault, that crucial, legalistic, bisyllabic technicality which (though not having earned poor

Kelly the good fortune to turn back the clock, or granted him the option to confront his future when he so chose) could have won him enough damages to shop until he – literally – dropped. But so damn what? So damn what if I felt wronged? The Knife just needed to get it right, and get out, and get himself back to the hillock-upon-Harrow and his entertaining wife, who, thanks to her husband's superior professional acumen, was known (by Freckle-Arms, to cite but one admirer) regularly to hobnob with retards and royalty; sometimes both – rolled into one, like snot.

It all comes back as such a pointless waste of anger. I began by asking why, directly against our instructions, Kelly had been told about his blood-test results. The Knife shook his head and closed his eyes and fairly pouted, then replied that my brother hadn't actually been told, not as such. I pointed out that Kelly hadn't actually been left much room for doubt *as such*; so the Knife drew my attention to the all-important difference between an implication and an inference. I tried to draw the Knife's attention to the all-important difference between a Condition and a Status; but he, after a hairy nasal sigh, began to waffle along the lines of Difficult Decisions, and Sensitive Issues, and Lesser and Evils, and attempted to make a plea for Mutual Understanding. He may have murmured the word Mindful, and even, at a pinch, gone as far as Cognizant. But next, the river of his words flowed into a flattened sea of stubborn silence, during which I feared that if I didn't do something constructive, such as envisage him having a crap, I might cry.

I asked why my brother was having food dumped at his door as if he were a leper, and what this stuff with nurses in gloves and masks was (not in aid of, but) about. Another silence, but somehow less stubborn, more charged, morally more pungent. My inference was that the surgeon's obtumescence implied that he didn't think my leper analogy a bad one, but I couldn't stop to fret about that. Instead I fretted, and aloud, over the fact that I still hadn't been given any proper explanation as to why our refusal to grant consent had been disregarded. In the interests of General Safety, argued the Knife. But surely the medical team could have carried on in perfect safety without need of disclosure, particularly disclosure minutes before surgery and in front of a bunch of strangers? He gave me the proverbial shit about (not counselling, but) earning his patients' trust. I said: Terror more like. And then he, after some incomprehensible subordinate meander, ascribed to his superlatively condescending self the noun Justification. He sounded like he owned it. He dared to call his conscience clear. I could not, still cannot, believe it. I sat there like an atheist. He glanced at his ticking wrist with steely deliberateness. Well, I spluttered, what the hell was Kelly supposed to do now? The Knife's reply was that my brother was at liberty to inform himself whenever he so pleased about (no longer his Status, nor Condition, but) The Prognosis – as much for his own sake as (and he paused to drive the point in) for the sake of 'others'. And what (I enquired) was I supposed to advise him? *That* – reckoned the Knife – must be a matter for me to decide in conjunction with my family. And then he stood up and buttoned his fine jacket and dusted himself down and led the way out, and managed to turn off the light before I'd even had the chance to say Goodnight.

I suppose that what I'd wanted from that godlike consultant was both the moon and the stars, by which I don't mean just a silver apology and a constellation of golden retractions. I mean the properly impossible, the very thing which I never could have had: the sunny assurance that Kelly, silly old so-and-so, had got it all completely wrong and was completely all right. Very bloody likely. Nevertheless, one minor truth lay beyond argument: I had unarguably, and abruptly, grown up. Indeed, I even proved grown-up enough, as he rushed in search of more auspicious circumstances, to thank the Knife for his trouble. Name of Jackson. Still around. Look him up. Credentials: admirable. Hobbies: book collecting, reading, opera, the arts. I was never again to encounter that artful bastion. Nor, in fact, was Kelly – because, when the moment came for my brother's stitches to come out, the chore was carried out by some other (not less harrassed, but) less squeamish pair of hands. Risk of blood, remember.

Kelly, when I returned to his room, had company – in the shape, as luck would have it, of the City Fluke, who, apart from the distinction of a receding hairline, and the lesser distinction of an old school tie from one of those didactic abbeys, looked much as you'd expect: grey all over and genially resigned to it. He shook my hand with just the right amount of vigour and said: How-D'You-Do-Heard-Lots-About-You. Next, as if the obvious needed stating, he stated that he'd just popped in to check on the poor blighter, to see how he was doing. I was dreading some enquiry about the notices outside, but the Fluke made none – because, as it turned out, he'd already remarked on them before my arrival. Later I learned that Kelly, who was almost as lightning a liar as I, had apparently told him that it all referred to some other patient – malaria, typhoid, something – someone since discharged. Perhaps the Fluke was brighter, and kinder, than I then realized; perhaps he didn't want to pry deeper into the matter. At any rate, I remember feeling completely out of it, disconnected, powerless to involve myself in the current chatter, but also powerless to reconsider my exchange with Kelly's consultant. And yet nor could I vanish, not straight away, not politely. As I began to calm down, I sensed that the Fluke, though keen on handsome, gifted Latin types like my brother, of whom he couldn't have met a bundle, was really a greater fan of delicious sweet-skinned Orientals – more numerous in London at that time, and more easily To Be Had, being, as they often were, by nature attracted to the comfortable charms of the older gentleman. Queers can tell these things about each other – their respective little penchants – even through the protective bars of broking stripes. There was a blend of fear and bluster to the man, a sort of jittery joviality, particularly about the digits, which, though they wore the shrillness of a signet ring, couldn't, by dint of their upbringing, gesticulate as loquaciously as perhaps they might have wished, and instead, as if for consolation, caressed each other with a suppressed, perhaps unconscious, sensuality. The Fluke belonged to that nice, well-established but unsexy sort of bachelor (maisonette in town, oast house in the country) whom we used to describe as (not mere Rice, but) Jade Queen – jade being the superior commodity, a financial cut above rice. Jade could afford the luxury of live-in houseboys, not just an occasional aromatic massage in some time-honoured Burlington parlour. But you also felt that out of closeted propriety, or a wish not to be ostracized from some quaintly rural parish, or a dread of blackmail, he preferred, while stuck in Blighty, merely to dabble with Onan, and only played in earnest, only properly engaged in game, when safely – and exotically – away from home: 'Bali, great place, wonderful people, so friendly and welcoming, you really should try it.' I'm afraid that Bali didn't sound like my kind of thing: voodoo dolls, batiks, noodles, fish. But anyway, City queers in those days (and I don't quite know why this should have been – perhaps it was to do with the fact that their livelihoods relied to such an extreme on the Old Boy reference-system) did have to watch their backs with greater perspicacity than most other desk-bound deviants – apart, that is, from one exceptional personage, universally known as Uncle Monty: some very senior homo whom Kelly never allowed me to meet, but who was known to raise the eyebrows of the whole Square Mile by swishing about in a shameless maxi-sable, given to him by 'Darling Ivor', and, what is more, to get away with it, because – of course – he was *richissime*. Let's be honest: money makes the world (not just go round, but) sexy.

Kelly asked me, sort of between the lines, with a nervy insinuation (meant to mean: just-stick-to-the-Hernia-bit), how I'd got on with the specialist. Fine, I said, and then threw in: But what a prick. Kelly's visitor went a discernibly paler shade of pallid, probably thinking it ill-advised of me to speak in such a

way of so renowned a medic. I took no notice. I noticed that the
Fluke had brought a bottle of shampers plus a jolly Get Well card
from Kelly's pre-secondment chums, among whom, soon
enough, he would once again be numbering. I couldn't resist
having a nose at their chappy signatures and their variegated
greetings on the theme of recovery; but when I fell upon the
salutation Cheers! I decided to leave the boss and blighter to it,
and just told Kelly, as if nothing were amiss – quite the reverse,
as if I held the key to eternal peace – that I'd see him in the
morning. No cissy kissing. Cut that out. Act like a man. Outside
was the night.

   I was meant to be meeting Matthew. But before I got to
Bedsitland – before I get to that – I need a brief aside. Although
everything is wiser and more sussed and sassier now, back then,
in the dawn of Kelly's twenties, when he was scarcely more than
a grown child, and (literally) fresh out of nappies, well, one
wouldn't have believed this stuff. You denied it. You had to. We
all did. I promise you. The bliss – if bliss it could be called –
depended on the ignorance. Forget prophylaxis. Never heard of
such a thing. The thought of diagnosis was enough to contend
with. There was no magical pill. And thus, what earlier had
appeared so male and so freewheeling, so singularly ours and
plurally liberating, suddenly felt not so damn brilliant, more like
a poisoned chalice, brimming with the juices of treachery. Just
as people say that queers exist but not in *this* family, so we, I
suppose, felt that the looming crisis of which we'd vaguely
heard, however real, was not a reality that was ever going to
impinge – not on the likes of you and me. *We* were different.
And spokespeople outside the ghetto, straights who (then) felt
safe in the convention of their couplings, orthodox in their bedroom positions, called the plight of our remote but inexorable
apocalypse all sorts of things – among them: divine retribution.
Very occasionally, you saw people-who-knew-people-whom-
you-knew on television, serious people, clever people, religious
even, advocating the importance of national screening, and rec-

ommending that members of the public found infected should be interned in Special camps. I don't think anybody bothered with a more specific adjective. Too awkward. Embarrassing. For there was a shame to the face of this illness; a bleakness. A ghoulish moral complexion attached to it – not so much because, like lots of other things, it was incurable, as on account of the revolting way in which it was transmitted. I don't recall much talk back then about the dangers of sharing intravenous needles, nor about contaminated blood transfusions. That was all to ensue, along with the panic over poisoned mother's milk. At the beginning, I only recall hush-hush giggles about rubber whatsits, and, on the street, occasional curses from gypsy witches, who, if you declined to buy their heathered sprigs, wished you the malediction of the disease. But most of all I recall a lot of turning. Hands being turned to worthier medical issues. Noses being turned aloft, to rise above the encroaching stink. Blind eyes being turned; deaf ears being turned; even tacit-turning.

That night, when I got back to Bedsitland, my answering machine was flashing like mad. A rosary of hang-ups, followed by one cross message from Matthew: Where the hell *was* I at quarter to nine? He was sick of waiting; was leaving the house; would ring once he'd got into town; crap day at the office in case you were wondering. Clunk. I poured myself a drink. I ripped off my clothes – corrupted, hacked. I crouched to light the fire. A hiss of gas. I lay on my back. I did not cry. Actually, I was thinking of the monkeys.

Next time Matthew rang, he was at the Queen & Garter. Blazered laughter in the background. I said: Sorry, I'm just not up to it. What! (he shouted). He couldn't hear me – wasn't I up to getting clubbed? I tried to explain that something ghastly had happened. What about? I just repeated the word Ghastly. My throat was choking up. He said he'd be right over. Matthew was a sweetheart. (It *was* a romance. I won't hear otherwise.) I took a shower. I towelled myself dry. The doorbell rang. My friend had arrived. I went downstairs to let him in. And now – no sweat – I did cry. In the middle of the common parts, for the benefit of whomever cared to give a damn. He stroked my hair. He led me up, his arm wrapped round my back. He sat me down. He chose a song. He put it on. Do You Really Want To Hurt Me?

He poured us vodkas. I poured the tale in one – from the withdrawal of my Consent, to the Goodnight I'd never got the chance to utter. Matthew remained – guess what? – exceedingly quiet, until – guess what again? – he laughed; laughed the laughter of the prematurely wise, laughed the laughter of the dungeons and cathedrals which, one day, would become rotted in my gut. And then, at last – guess what a third time? – he denied. He called it a load of rubbish. He told me to get Kelly out of that place fast, send him back to work, and shut up. But, after all was said and done, we did go out. Out clubbing. I'm not ashamed to say that on the very day when Kelly was (il)legally assaulted by that Knife I went and danced upon a grave which hadn't even been imagined. Kelly wouldn't have minded. Queers can be like that. Matthew and I went to the Moonlight. No chance of a tango; but still, I got myself a fuck; ended up performing at a kitchenette in Putney, with a lover of distressed pine, all very rustic. Geoffrey was his name. I remember only because he was keen to make it plain that it was Geoffrey with a G. Matthew, meanwhile, took my key and spent the night in Bedsitland. I crawled back home at sunrise. I climbed into bed. He was wearing underpants. He was dreaming hard. He called me Darling. He was facing me in the dark. I turned him round. And thus we slept, front to back, like inverted commas, like a quotation without conclusion, until lunchtime.

The telephone woke us up. It was Kelly – not angry, surprisingly. Oddly revitalized. How was he feeling? Fine – and sounded it. But, talking of sounds, Matthew went and coughed on his way for a slash, which I could have done without. Kelly asked (not who the hell was that, but) when was I going round. In about half an hour – anything he wanted? An umbrella. I told him he was mental, but took along my best one: khaki canvas with a walnut handle. As I hurried to get dressed, Matthew told me not to rush him: he had a monster hangover, and wanted a leisurely bath. I didn't blanch. Not one DuBois. He said that he would let himself out.

At the hospital, the mood was of low drudgery: weekend weather; nursing at half-mast. But Kelly was bristling with life: freshly shaved and fully dressed and enjoying a smoke in the bathroom. I found him sitting on the pan, an arm propped over the basin, for the simpler disposal of ash. He grabbed the brolly from my hand, and very gin-ger-ly got up. See? He was (not unaided, but) mobile. Recovery, he called it. I would have called it shuffling – but anyway. With a suspect formality he enquired whether I would be so kind as to carry his bag. It seemed to be packed. Carry it where? *Out,* he replied. We were off, darling. Because, as it transpired, he'd already been discharged. Discharged with (not reluctance, but) ill-suppressed enthusiasm, and a meaningful (not Get Well, but) Good Luck. It would be the first of many such goodbyes. The duty nurse agreed that yes, since Kelly was able to get about, he was really better off at home now. The consultant would be in touch with his GP in the next forty-eight hours. Kelly, leaning on the umbrella, didn't give the banners of alarm outside his door a second glance. We took a taxi back to Holland Park.

He asked me about my conversation with the Knife. I said that I'd discovered nothing. I told him that there must have been some muddle, because the Knife wouldn't come clean, which otherwise he would have done – he'd obviously been trying to cover his (un)professional arse. I said that besides, all the people who'd contracted It were older than us. Kelly said that he was worried, worried by America, where it was already sort of happening. I was worried about Zac, but instead I pointed out that Kelly had always been a worrier. Look, I said,

he was safely home now; he was on the mend. Kelly sighed protractedly. I told him not to be dramatic. He told me to give him
a break. I told him what he needed was (not a break, but) a
party. A Party? . . . I could picture thought-rings bubbling from
his skull. He said that he wasn't ruling it out; but then he
resorted to facing Reality. Facing it how? Financially: he wasn't
wasting dosh on parties; he had more important things to buy
– like furniture for the studio. Wrong end of the stick, I said. I
meant that *I* would give it: I could dip into my grand-money.
He could ask some friends if he liked. We could celebrate in
Bedsitland. But twenty people maximum. I must be the twenty-
first, to symbolize the age I had become. He said: Yeah, might
be a nice idea, once I'm up and running. Whenever, I replied,
any time. Sooner the better. I wanted to get out. I wanted to get
lost. I didn't know how. Don't leave me this way; I can't survive.
I suggested lunch – two doors away, at the place where
Matthew and I had gone after the Ripe Banana. On condition,
Kelly said. On what condition *now*? Two conditions, actually:
that I gave him time to change (fine), and that lunch be on him.
I called it a deal. He dressed. He got into heavy lace-up boots,
and turned-up jeans, and a leather biker's jacket – the first in
which I'd ever seen him. Blacker than black, of a black that
hinted at many colours, like a rainbow crushed by the pressure
of dark glass. He looked a total stranger. He looked strangely
fantastic. Like no relative of mine, like no-one from our background, but fantastic. I could see that.

What I couldn't see, however, was into his mind. I asked what
he was thinking, and busied myself lighting up. He glugged some
wine, too much, too fast. His dark-brown eyes flitted about,
then settled downward. He didn't really know. He was in a
quandary. What about? Those blood-test results. I said: Christ,
we're not back to *that*. He told me to shut the fuck up. I apologized. (I apologized. Understand? Even without meaning to, I
was already conceding to the very thing which I was meant to
be denying. I may have seemed on top of things, but I was

168 ~ Paul Golding

petrified.) We parted company outside his house. He wanted to climb the stairs alone – without being gawped at. And by the way: would I take that umbrella back to Bedsitland? He could manage without poncy walnut handles, thank you.

The next few days were in their way dramatic, not least on account of the speed with which Kelly took action. The first thing which he did was search for a gym, find one, and join before he was even fit to resume exercise. The second was to visit his GP, who said that though the stitches weren't yet ready to come out – not quite dry enough – he'd been informed of the bad news by Kelly's consultant. Kelly said that he'd come back. It didn't happen. He went to the shops and, mooching around Habitat, decided that he didn't want the news to travel – not to the Fluke, not to the monkeys, not to anyone. He enlisted at another practice, with another doctor, whom he didn't even need to meet. He simply told the woman at reception that he'd been working for the past two years in (not America, but) Switzerland, and that he needed a GP. Yes, he was living locally. Yes, he was back for good. She gave him a form to complete. I know neither what it asked nor what was volunteered. I wasn't there. And then, inevitably, he decided to consult McManus. This time, I did go with him. This time: no smiling, no queue-jumping, no cheekiness, no sibling sandwiches. Nothing. We no longer amounted even to a toothsome twosome. Now we were just a couple of ordinary numbers, paper tickets quivering in our own palms, like the palms of tetchy customers at an overcrowded butcher's counter. I noticed an abundance of rough leather in the gathering. Sure, I'd made a point of dressing down, but not to the level of bar-drag. Suddenly, we'd been announced: Numbers 20 and 21, for Dr McManus. We were pointed through, in the manner of a couple. McManus didn't get up. He looked worn out. Over his desk, dozens of letters lay scattered – letters marked, I could see from where I sat,

CONFIDENTIAL

Kelly began. He told about the hernia; he told about having had to fly back; he told about the operation, and about the blood tests leading up to it; he told about how we'd asked not to be informed of the results, but how, despite this fact, heavy hints had been dropped by the consultant, and then – I butted in to tell about the food being dumped on the ground, and about the screaming notices outside, and about the masks and gloves and all of that, until – Kelly snatched back the mike and said that the consultant's hints had been confirmed, or near as dammit, at a meeting with his GP a few days after. McManus lowered his eyes and went quiet. Kelly said his stitches still needed taking out. Where should he go? What did the doctor advise? McManus' biro was clicking like the clappers. Now he put it down. Now he stood up. He told Kelly to hop on the couch, and patted it. The screen to protect our pudenda blurred into insignificance. Kelly dropped his chinos to his ankles. McManus cut the stitches out, snippety-snap, easy as that. Kelly didn't murmur. Nor, despite the tempting tan on Kelly's hairless thighs, did McManus. Somehow we, by which I mean queers generally, had progressed to another sphere, descended unto a lower plane, where the humour and the laughter which had earlier been so strong a mark of our collective character, suddenly felt too onerous to enact, too distant to summon back. McManus ripped away his gloves, chucked them out, and, while he washed his hands, remarked: OK, that deals with that; bonny wee scar. Kelly finished getting dressed, buckled up, came back to join us. So (said McManus), what was to be done about this blood-test business? Exactly. McManus, after a tell-tale gulp, said that since Kelly, rightly or wrongly – and in his opinion very wrongly – had already been led (not a merry dance, but) so far down the line, perhaps the prudent thing would be – though Kelly *must* have a think about this, it wasn't trivial matter – to have another set of blood-tests done, just to make absolutely certain that his fears were not unfounded. Forewarned (supposed McManus) was forearmed – until he explained that medical research on this new virus was as yet in its infancy. Kelly listened. He thought for a few seconds in the searing way of people too frantic to think, and then, the decision was reached. Kelly said: Let's get it over with. But McManus disagreed: Hang on; mustn't be hasty; Kelly wasn't to rush into this. Kelly said he'd had more than enough time to consider the issue, ever since the heavy hinting. And then McManus, who, for all of my bitching, wasn't a bad man, did the deed, drew dark blood from my brother's arm, blood proclaiming to be my own blood. It felt so easy, so peaceful. Plus there was a peculiar honour to the ritual, because, since none of us was safe, one may as well be tried – put to the test – by another of the great unsafe, another homosexual.

The party happened fast. I made quite sure of that. I needed to push hard: Kelly needed (not corroboration, but) distraction. Everything is more efficient now – and, I suspect, less macabre – but in those days, those early days before the flood, results for blood tests of this type, unless divulged in hospitals, were slow to come to light, slow to wing their way, like lazy vultures, from the laboratory to meet your flickering eye. Your Status, regardless of whether you were lonesome or married or a bride of Christ, was delivered on a handwritten slip the colour of bile, not unlike the slips which banks, before the universe became computerized, would sometimes pass under the counter to notify their customers of healthy balances – or heavy overdrafts. But in the courts of medical (in)justice, the process of official sentencing, even after you'd turned yourself in, even after you'd given yourself up, could take as long as a fortnight, and that fortnight wasn't funny. The hiatus rendered you speedy, feverish; it heated you with a babbling inner anxiety. You slept badly; you generated the most convincing nightmares imaginable; you induced shivering sweats and woke up drenched – to wring yourself out. And, once the hellish interim was up, you were meant to appear in person – phones, in the interest of confidentiality, having been ruled out – to discover how your future had been analysed, to face your own worst music, to be delivered the score of your life, to learn whether you'd been cast as Damocles or as Dam Lucky. Sometimes people grew so frightened, so petrified at having taken the gamble of their diagnostic plunge, that they changed their minds midstream, and chose to float along open-ended waves of ignorance rather than crawl back for a result, preferring, on dreadful balance, to abandon their fates, to leave them in vague abeyance, silently to merge with a pile of countless others in some godforsaken colony for the venereal. The safest way to think was this: I shall conduct myself as if I had It. I shall behave responsibly. And if I act responsibly, there's a chance that God will spare me, a chance that I'll get off scot-free. Maybe I'll be spared the grim reaper. Maybe I won't die of ignorance. Maybe just; just maybe. And while we racked our brains with such absurdities, Kelly (who had moved beyond the absurd into the deadly serious) walked out one midsummer morning, out into the mocking street, and bought me the platter of ashen glass – on which we served simple food, open and unsealed.

Who came? Cara, most memorably. In a private sort of way she was my special guest; for though, at that stage, she and I were only tentatively acquainted, I recall having felt, ever since our introduction at the Jeakle Garden, drawn to her quiet confidence, and having wanted, more than to befriend her, to make her my friend – my need having always felt the greater in our connection. I remember, for instance, the oddly excessive pleasure which, when I telephoned to invite her, her acceptance – instant and delighted – had caused me. Closer to triumph.

She wasn't really Kelly's type – too old, for one thing, being our senior by a decade. Kelly tended to prefer the company of closer contemporaries, perhaps because his elders, people who had trifled with his innocence, had rendered him wary. Further-more, Cara was resolutely uncool, dowdy even, certainly not hip to the fashion-rhythm, which, then, was stringently seasonal. Sure, you could opt out of the whole conspiracy, and refuse to keep up with the Trendies, and choose, for instance – as Cara did

– to appear timelessly bohemian; but you couldn't really cheat.
The swings in cuts and cloths and colour-schemes were just too
extreme. And yet, notwithstanding the anachronism of her
appearance, which Kelly would have deemed a definite defect,
there was an air to her which intrigued me, a graceful distinction, most likely to do with her spirit, which was strong, strongly
developed, and unlike anything I'd met previously. Serious (as
opposed to unfunny) women scarcely figured in my youth.

Her humour, which took me a while to appreciate, was
subtly bitter, very dry and crunchy, like the brains inside a walnut. And yet, despite the barbs that fenced the borders of her
bleakly appointed wit, there was an inherent calm to her, a
pastoral tranquillity which I wanted both to observe and learn
to inhabit. She had qualified recently; I recall mention of
Zurich; but her appeal was more abetted in my view by the fact
that she seemed a foreigner to prejudice – even regarding the
territory of pathological deviancy. Indeed, this led me for a
while to wonder whether, despite her small-boned femininity
and loosely conventional mien, she might not, even somno-
lently, be lesbian; for, as if to encourage that suspicion, her voice
was deep, and sometimes inclined toward the mannish; it grew
gruff in disagreement. But I was, as it happens, entirely mistaken
on this: for, free as Cara was of bigotry, she was also straight
beyond belief.

Her delivery was slow and measured; her cadences, elusive,
closer to running water than to music. There was an old-
fashioned turn to her speech; it carried in its wake an almost
fusty echo, like ghostly memories. She steered, you sensed, clear
of colloquialisms: the direction of her words was subtly articulate, meticulous. It pointed toward literature. Her phrases were
like carefully selected but quietly packaged treats. She was incapable of (or perhaps opposite to) small talk, with the
consequence that, in her company, you felt compelled to steady
your slang, to cool it man, and instead, to tilt your language up,
pitch it high toward that elevated realm which used to be

described as the art of conversation – a moribund place among my acquaintances then, who, for the most part, preferred to muck about unhampered in baser rhetorical climes. What appealed to us was not the courtly traffic of grave ideas, but larking around in the linguistic sandpit, building quick, if unstable, constructions with the plastic spade of syntax, and employing the handy bucket of grammar merely to lend scaffolding, then flight, to our fancy. We spoke more for effect than ever for substance. Classical purity worried us as little as structural soundness, because words, to us, just existed for the taking, for the hell of it, to be enjoyed and exploited and trashed, like monkeys, or chicken, or love. And thus we would embellish our flimsy verbal follies with disproportionate ornaments of camp, and emblazon them with the rosy plaques of Polari, and weather them with showers of expletives, and brighten them, given half a chance, with pergolas of mime. Our yabber may not have been consequential, any more than it would stand the test of time, but it felt like conversational fun. Cara was different. Cara liked to toil at dialogue, preferred to feel her intellectual way about, could not resist the lure to mull and analyse. She didn't merely try: she endeavoured. She didn't say that things were nice: she said that they were pleasing. And yet, for all of that, you would never have called her stuck-up. Because she wasn't. You would have called her fine. And once you had grown to know her – and, if lucky enough, grown to be liked by her – you would have called her loyal. And, somewhere along that temporal path, you might have called her handsome.

At first glance, the most forceful of her features was her hair, which, though destiny would later fade it, was, in the springtime of our friendship, of a dense, though never heavy, auburn. Strangely devoid of lustre. Quite matt. While lacking either the length or the luxuriance to qualify as a mane, it grew beyond her shoulder-line, and though casually swept back, would, if left to its own devices, fall into a centre-parting, then tumble over her eyes with a repetitive insistence which, as she pushed the nuisance back, seemed to incur her slight vexation. It possessed a freshly washed lightness; it floated about her. You felt that at bedtime she would have bowed her nape to brush it, and that as she brushed, her hair would have crackled and flown about, erupted in a burst of static. There was something potentially wild about it, almost wiry. Her brow was set too high. Too far back. Even in the region of her imperfections, intelligence was apparent.

When she arrived at the party, I failed, very nearly, to recognize her. She had put her hair up. There is something both enticing and disheartening about the first time that one sees a woman arrange herself thus – something lovely but dismal – for an upswept style can strike the observer both as an aesthetic refinement and as a visual admission on the part of its subject of having grown up, and, in having left youthfulness behind and accepted maturity in a manner so public, as a poignant further admission of time having passed, of time running out. The very dignity which such a hairstyle can convey, also betrays, by strange reversal, an ephemerality. Cara had dug hair-combs into this ephemerality, and coiled it up, and bared to the world the nape which I had envisaged being brushed; and I saw, as she turned to close the door at the entrance, that hers was the palest nape imaginable, a classical stranger to the sun. You sensed that the merest exposure to hot light would blotch it up. And it appeared to me that the desired formality had backfired, for the unexpected revelation of that nape made one feel prurient, almost made one blush, as if one had accidentally chanced upon her, coming naked out of the bath.

What this upswept head, this hair drawn away from the face, now unveiled was her otherwise less obvious, but truer, great asset, namely her eyes, which were large grey, steely in colour, and almost painfully shiny, as if varnished. Deeply set, they bore a slightly exotic cast, reminiscent of the eyes of Russians, with fleeting Eastern quirks at the sides. But they were underscored by permanent crescents of darkness, less residual of sleeplessness or recent illness than permanent attributes, like the rings that are sometimes to be found on the face of a sombre child. They lent her a sadness which, to my own eyes, enhanced her. I never knew Cara to wear either shadow or mascara, nor lipstick, nor scent, nor powder. She was resolutely about good soap, and well-buffed nails, and the very mildest hint of rouge, scattily applied – more for the sake of form than as a vanity. She might conceivably have employed night-cream, or splashed her face with rosewater in the morning, but you would never have quizzed her on such minutiae: it would have seemed beneath her, piffling. Cara left you wondering. I think that she encouraged this, drew satisfaction from it even, for, by remaining elusive, she succeeded in suggesting that there existed to her even greater substance than the substance which, already, she permitted to be perceived. Mystery hung suspended, like the hint of gunpowder, in the arsenal of her gifts.

She was the type who preferred to open presents privately, never unwrapped them in front of company; for she was as averse to displays of simulated gratitude as I suspect that she was partial to the exercise of an aloof – perhaps protective – formality. The result was that she left you never knowing quite what she thought, quite what she liked, quite where you stood in her regard. It was frustrating, this ruse, yet irksomely effective, for one found oneself, oddly, going along with – and hence compounding – it: no matter how dispiriting her preference for the negativity of omission over positively faked exuberance, one colluded with her choice of initiative, and thus became a party to the very evasion of which, in one's secret insecurity, she stood accused. You would never have risked saying: Open it now; let me see; do you like it? Because, in the politest fashion, she would have declined, which, for all the politeness of her denial, would have cast you down. And besides, on this occasion, it was she who came bearing a small package: a couple of books – wrapped, typically, in fresh brown paper, and secured with green twine, of the type employed by gardeners.

I led Cara from the landing in, gave her a drink, and introduced her to Kelly, who seemed to be hovering absently, half-distractedly, as if lost in that dark new distance toward which one struggled not to travel. But almost at once, I was forced to abandon them – someone else was arriving – and by the time that I managed to get back and check on everyone, Kelly was away, chatting to some glossy queen, unarguably conceited yet indisputably beautiful. Meanwhile Cara seemed to have gravitated, less as if by chance than led by instinct, toward Matthew. The two, by now, were sitting on my bed, calmly side by side – she, in a long flimsy skirt of dark silk, gazing down at the floor; he, in a pale, high-necked T-shirt, peering out of the window. Both were laughing like old friends headed backward, rewinding to a land of shared nostalgia. It made me feel uneasy, inexperienced. But Matthew had always had a way with women. Even at work they'd sought his company. They liked to pet him. Later, of course, they would come to pity him.

Various other girls, though none was destined to remain a permanency for me, came to that party: a rich girl who pretended to be poor at art school; a poor one who pretended to be rich while slaving for a famous fashion magazine – famous, besides its prestige, for its niggardly salaries; a girl of mesmerizing prettiness who, though lazy beyond belief, would never have had you believe it. Absolutely *not*, she would insist: she was fiendishly busy with her thesis. *What* thesis? *You* know: Nineteenth Century Venice and the English Romantics. Then, a further girl, more ambitious, who called herself a personal assistant and could be personally called upon to assist her boss's dick; another, who swore by all that was dear to her (her oblivious [dead] mother included), that she'd never chased any damned dragon, nor snorted any line of anything – this despite the evidence of out-of-orbit pupils and heavily descended eyelids; a plain girl, plain boring but plain sweet, who needed good styling as badly as she needed the sort of love which it was understood that boys like me could not give.

I recall these girls not because I have pictures to prompt me, nor because I ever bothered to keep a diary, but because Kelly and I had argued about them, had come to a strange sort of grief over females and their influence. My point was that even if sleeping with women wasn't our thing, I nevertheless found their proximity appealing, the lateral trains of their thought intriguing, their colours decorative, their fragrances alluring. I also derived from their company a certain safety – perhaps, I now realize, because it freed me from the pressure (however self-inflicted) to appear sexy. With women, friendly was sufficient; flamboyant, if you wished; but the burden of oozing desirability didn't enter into it, not for me. Yet Kelly, in keeping with sundry mysoginistic queens of that era, reckoned that Tuna – which is how they dubbed women – was a killer at gay festivities, socially inhibiting. I disagreed, and dug my heels in.

Despite his protestations about hettie people at the workplace being infliction enough, I could never understand – still can't – the wisdom of mixing solely with inverts outside office hours. Why go to the trouble of barring women from one's social life when such antisocial, artificial measures are so often, and so readily, provided by gay clubs? Never mind merrymaking in men's lavatories: it was poovy parties which, if anything, struck me as unnatural. All you ever heard at those stilted little gatherings was titters about who was drooling over whom, who'd already had it off with whom, who'd gone down on whom, who'd been up to what with whom and in what position(s), who'd lost whose virginity, who was currently hitched to whom, who had taken whom from whom, and who had given whom, by way of parting gift, good reason for penicillin. I may have been an oddity among the queers of my youth, but, on the occasions when I happened to be invited by them, even to quite formal dinners, seldom did a female preside among the numbers. Or, come to that, a hetty man, by which I mean a properly straight one. Sexual ditherers sometimes showed up, but who the hell wants to get stuck next to some unmade-up (not face, but) mind.

Perhaps in an attempt to avenge my insistence on mixed company, Kelly had insisted that the mixed-up Fluke be asked. Politic, Kelly had called it; and the Fluke, for his part, had called it How-sim-ply-mahv'llous. And yet, despite my submission to Kelly's demand, I can't pretend that I didn't find the prospect of his employer pitching up at my party a bit of a bind; for although, agreed, he'd been good to visit Kelly in hospital, and good to produce booze and bonhomie for the benefit of the poor blighter, I still feared that his presence would prove troublesome on the night, would compel the rest of us, as soon as his bearing upon Kelly's livelihood had become apparent, to be on our best behaviour, to mind our every gesture, a prospect ten times more inhibiting than the presence of any woman.

But I needn't have worried, for the Fluke, when he turned up, far from promoting any social astringency, seemed, rather, to grow socially moisturized. You could catch occasional glimpses of his previously cautious hands breaking from their finger-lock and fluttering unguarded, and clapping with a coquettish sort of delight, and of his throat, cravatted in some bright pattern, being thrown asunder to say Wahnderful, or the better to laugh – mostly for the sake of boys: the prettier the boy, the prettier the laughter. And though I took good care to keep his glass topped up, I took an equal care to keep my distance, for, as I said earlier: either you were partial to Kelly, or you were partial to the other, spikier customer – his brother. And it didn't take a syndicate to guess where the Fluke's creditable sympathies lay banked.

The single other boy whom I distinctly picture at that gathering was – is – Douglas, whom I, and I alone, called Dugsy during the period when I was Georgie and both of us were coursing full of hope around town. Unlike the transient girls whom I've sketched out, Douglas was to remain permanently painted on the canvas of my life, embedded yet almost embossed, and bright beyond encroaching shadows, and thickly applied with character, and rich with fleshy tones and high in facial colour and vastly alive and loud in scale and confidently blurred, as if depicted by the impassioned brushstrokes of a drunkard. The composition of my world has necessarily grown broader, if not deeper, since that time, so that Douglas seems to have shifted sideward, or to have been removed from the central ground, and now stands – gin-glass perpetually in hand – closer to the dextral margin, and further to the back than in our first summer, but, as ever, smiling distortedly at the mouth of someone whom I no longer recognize, smiling as if he'd rather be smiling into the mouth of someone other, a true lover, who is absent. Now that years and years have passed and we've grown up and grown apart, and difference, like a hard hot heavy pyramid of silence, has plonked itself between us, I find it awkward to rewind; I don't know how to start; can't fathom how to dismantle the whole wonder and build it back into the obstacle that it has become. So Douglas, wherever the present may happen find you – and I realize that whilst, spiritually, you dwell great leagues away from my current lifelessness, I could be with you, be at your beautiful house, be in your tremendous hug, within the hour – know, despite our distance, that when I think of you, I do so still (yes, it is true) with fondest love. Meetings don't matter. Not any more. Of course they don't. For crying out loud.

Douglas had originally featured – with the pink financial paper folded under his arm – among the group of teenaged fruits who once had sat at bistros wondering and wondering, a group which, as reality began to worm its way into our flimsy balsa fantasies, rotted, flaked away, and fell apart. It was nothing deliberate, this gradual collapse. Only an idleness. But you got tired of keeping up with people's quick-change whereabouts, their great new jobs and great new friends and great new flings and flats, and you no longer felt like bothering their parents (who disapproved of you) in order to keep tabs. Then, in late December, you ventured out, squelching over the slush to buy a new diary, and found yourself, once returned to Bedsitland, entering fewer names in the section for addresses at the back. You scrapped the grotty pick-ups, and you scrapped the fair-weather surnames which no longer seemed to seek your company. Neater all round. But not – not so with – Douglas. Douglas was good about contact. I'll give him that.

Ever since we'd known each other, he had been in thrall to a well-heeled man, a bridge-playing charmer who had charmed the pants off Douglas long before the ties of friendship had drawn me to my friend's essential charms, which I came to prize. About this man, whose name was Jack, I harboured, from the start, unfriendly doubts; yet if he failed to persuade me entirely, it wasn't so much because he was 'genuinely' straight-acting, nor indeed because, minutes into our introduction, he had performed a gauche advance at my tight-jeaned uptight-ness, as because, being in greater need of amusement than he was of money, he used to do charity work at a boys' reforma-tory, and later boast, with chuckles that would have chilled your blood, about the forbidden favours which, in return for forbid-den cans of lager, he habitually received from his delinquent charges. Douglas was worldly about – almost above – such ban-ter, but not in the style of a powerless courtesan, which, give or take a gender, is the sum to which he amounted; no; he was worldly in the manner of an elegant, experienced wife, firmly established and long anaesthetized to her husband's once-painful, now tasteless, philanderings. And though, when Jack was about, Douglas called the object of his adoration an absurd old braggart, he would also call him, when the braggart was out of earshot and sloshing about in the bathroom, full of crap. But the sweet affection that accompanied this insult was almost audible, like a gentle underwater harmony; because Douglas, being besotted, would not (though he could easily have done) have had it otherwise. A rake, and *that* one, in emotional italics, was what he wanted: raffish, sporty, big-bollocked, old-fashioned. And yet, to me, Jack felt — as is sometimes mumbled about dubious works of art — Not Quite Right, not entirely worthy of Douglas's trust, a trust which, though Douglas described it as realistic and adult and open-eyed, was blind.

Let me look back. What kind of boy was Douglas at the outset of that ancient, faded story of ours? I wouldn't say that he was handsome, though he was blessed with what I took — still take — to be great innate panache. He moved in marvellous strides, practically with a swagger. He wielded an umbrella like an ambassador. He gave no outward sign of being an invert — a fact which Jack would have regarded as a solid asset. Douglas simply struck the observer as a wholesome young man from some stormy castle in the Highlands — fair-skinned and ruddy-cheeked and curly-haired and well-mannered. He wore aggressively-polished shoes, with soles of heavy rubber, like tyres, and classic coats of tweed, and bobbly Aran jumpers. Being strongly set and broad of build, he enjoyed, among his bodily attributes, the perfect calves for a kilt. There was a windswept romance about him. This could be discerned with greatest clarity in his eyes, which were almost Nordic in character, narrowish, delicately coloured and pale-lashed. His brows were prematurely lush. I only saw him cry in sober-earnest once (much later, at a train station, where he'd tried to put an end to it all, but bungled); yet when he cried, Douglas would wipe away his silent sobs, which were slow to fall, with a silk handkerchief — dogtooth on that occasion. Well (I remember telling him), you can't get more stylish than *that* — to which he, grinning lop-sidedly, had replied that he'd been saving the stylish little *pochette* for a rainy day. How I loved his bitter comic edge. And then, after going the whole bitter hog and blowing his nose into the checkered style, he had burst out laughing. The laughter that issued from Douglas was, in contrast to his muted sadness, always shuddering and far too loud — to the invariable consternation of the adjoining public, which glared and tutted and was forever turning round. But, to me, it was a fanfare of adorable, almost moving, anxiety, for it never quite knew how, or when, to subside; it went on and on and on, perhaps in an attempt to please you more and more and more, but perhaps, as much, in order to enquire of the world: How much longer must I sing for my thankless supper before someone deems me good enough to go to the ball?

In those early days, Jack kept promising that, in order to clear the way for Douglas, whom he called the Cub, he was on the brink of coming clean with, and dispatching, some long-term, live-in, lover-cum-business partner – a baroque entanglement which, for unravelling, required an unpleasantly financial and ever-protracted, but (to the mind of Douglas) blessed transaction. Meanwhile, which is why the Cub and I saw such an abundance of each other during my initial months in London, Douglas lived with (not Jack, but) little option other than to hang about, for he was as vinculated to his idol as, a brief while back, I had been to Mr Respectable. First Love. It screws you up; it hits you hard. And hard as Douglas screwed around, his dreams of a gilded everafter in the golden tennis-arms of his beloved would not allow themselves to be tarnished. It was simply a question of disposing of the redundant third party, a sulky Frenchman, in as civilized a manner as could be mustered. That's how Jack, and by extension Douglas, made the situation sound. Patience: I remember much (weary, wearisome) talk of that. Seven endless years the patience would be called upon to last. But while it lasted, it was always understood that if you made a plan to meet with Douglas, this was necessarily on condition that, should the case demand it, you were also up to the trial of being stood up. For if, at the last moment, Jack should happen to find an open window in the glassy edifice of his adultery and glean a chance to summon the Cub to his side, the Cub must feel free, without fear of offending, to drop the bone of your contention, and race, tail wagging, tongue flapping, to the call of his master. If you were friends with Douglas, this sub-clause, however discreetly mooted, figured in the contract. And yet, as provisos went, it wasn't such a dreadful one, for, even if he wasn't always straightforward, Douglas was, by and large, frank.

I sometimes think that had we met a decade further down the line, when both of us were more advanced, more adept in matters of depravity, he and I might have made (not perfect lovers, but) a good couple. We had a high esteem for one another; neither of us was a dunce; surely we could have worked it out. Yet at the start, when I was nineteen and he was twenty-one, there was just too much swirling opalescent muddle about. Douglas, I now see, was a sand-boy belied by the frame of a Viking; while I − and this, even then, was plain to me − was a warrior betrayed by the shape of a weed. Such confusions were further compounded by the fact that, though physically so disparate, he and I were attracted to precisely the same type of man: the rugged sophisticate, the ruffian with class − which, ironically, almost pathetically, both of us might, in maturity, have become. Don't misunderstand me: Jack *was* sexy as buggery − big-thighed and thick-haired and deeply tanned and naturally muscular. Yet if I didn't have a bash at him, or vie for a trium-virate with Douglas, it wasn't from any noble sense that loyalty to my friend overruled my loyalty to my lust. It was from scep-ticism: I just could not believe that anyone who fancied Douglas could also fancy me. Not equally. Not when we were young. If anything, the situation worked another, more perverse, way round.

Often, when I sexed about with someone whom I feared had found me too bony-cornered, or brittle in manner, my mind would shoot across to Douglas, who would certainly have played my role more satisfactorily, for he was as tender in his touch as he was heftily constructed. Once or twice, I even furnished those pick-ups whom I sensed that I'd left wanting, with Douglas's number; and in this way my friend came to sample − perhaps, who knows, even improve upon − a few of my fucks.

But, of course, it was never really adequate, because, profoundly, Douglas was already so completely espoused to Jack that, while he waited for the benediction of a key to the conjugal glass-house, he didn't really feel inclined to waste his time on cast-offs upon whom I'd wasted mine. We were meant to be friends, not traffickers of trash. That was the inference. And he was right; for, despite his considerable (properly anonymous) interim revenge-fucks, Douglas remained, on the way toward his prime, an obdurate romantic. Later, by the stage of my collapse, he had grown vociferously cynical, grossly disenchanted, and the compromises which he was eventually to make, felt, by then, more regrettable to me than, to him, can have felt my obstinate refusal to compromise, which I know that he despised. But this was all to come, to bubble with the scum that rode the surge toward our rupture. In our youth, we were inseparable, like a pair of handcuffs, and together we got up to all sorts of stuff – orgies, for example.

At one particular such gathering, in the most opaque, most absolute of darknesses, I remember finding myself involved in an erotic overture with an unknown someone, a great hairy shield of a man; and as I felt about his chest and trunk on my way to feeling for his flies, I discovered that he came designed with not two nipples, but five – like the tentative beginnings of an animal. Those nipples seemed to be ranged in a downward parallel, reminiscent of double-breasted buttons, though the surplus glands were smaller than the regular; had yet to ripen. I wondered about warts along the abdomen; I wondered about being too smashed; I wandered away from the dark, but the stranger followed the direction of my path. And, once returned to the red-lit landing, I discovered that the sexual freak who had for an instant filled me with such freaky ardour was – none other than – Douglas. So now you know why I called him Dugsy. But the anatomical curiosity wasn't to be broadcast. These days, well,

I can think of more essential confidences, more imperative avowals.

A further detail was to engrave that orgy upon my mind, because, though Douglas seemed entirely unfazed by our mammary embarrassment, and soon enough returned to the miasma for a resumption of fun, I myself became so shamed by the fiasco, and accordingly so drunken, that, while I waited for my friend to get his satisfaction, I was compelled to weave my way toward a window, prize it open, and stick my head out in the hope of sobering up. But between my heaving ventilations and the fluctuations of my eyes, I must have craned too far and lost my balance; for, after a brief, abortive grapple with the parapet, I fell into some stony yard. Dull thud. Result: concussion. Douglas, who, on our arrival, had been clocked as my companion, was hauled out of the dark by the glare of torchlight, but proved chivalrous about the interruption, and zipped up. Next, having been led to our harnessed host's neat lounge – anaglypta painted lavender, crammed with photographs of old actresses when they were young – whither I, by that stage, had been ferried and flung like some party-pooping encumbrance, Douglas rang, despite the lateness of the hour, his doctor for advice. The latter, who practised from home and had just finished supper, told Douglas for goodness' sake to stop apologizing, jump in a taxi, and take his friend straight round. Which is how I came to land on the bandwagon of Dr John, who was a brilliant man, and would become more brilliant as my life became more dark.

But when Douglas and I first met, we made discoveries more immediate than our shared susceptibility to the same kind of prey. Among these was the mutually dispiriting subject of financial straits, for both of us were sailing close to broke – I, just about surviving on a meagre allowance from my parents; Douglas (whose parents had long ago given up on him), subsisting on social security handouts. And yet, because at that time I wore my pride in all the wrong parts, I should have preferred, rather than stoop to governmental charity, to stoop for an income to the wrong hotel foyers, by which I mean the few remaining Wildean ones. But Douglas was a gentleman, and far more of a gentleman than I, so he weathered his trips to the dole-queue with an evergreen candour – sometimes, even, in a taxi.

Although he was, and would remain, among the brightest, keenest men that one could hope to encounter, the chance of permanent employment seemed, at the start of our connection, to confound him. This obstacle, which plainly attached neither to denseness nor to idleness, was a lingering, and frustrating, repercussion of his adolescence, during which, even by his own account, he had proved a handful. Douglas had been raised an only child, and, like many a solitary infant, showed himself to be both inquisitive and imaginative. I suspect that he was always drawn to the theatre of fancy; but, once he had outgrown marionettes – yet before he had become one – he swivelled his attentions from the management of puppet-strings to the management of his strung-out, thrusting sexuality. Having taken an enquiring glance around the Highlands, but met with no encouraging answer, he came to the conclusion that nether-Caledonia wasn't really the location for a youth whose gumboots didn't feel inclined to accommodate the hind legs of a farm animal. And thus he resolved that his salvation must lie nowhere near his homeland, but rather in what, sentimentally, he must have pictured as the metropolitan Elysium of London. Yet since his parents were determined that the boy pursue some everlasting education close to home, which they insisted was The Only Bally Hope, Douglas determined that the only bally hope for him was to go AWOL – once, that is, he had garnered enough funds for the project.

He wasn't interested in newspaper rounds, which paid peanuts; nor was he interested in lending a hand at the local funeral parlour – which, even if more remunerative, would have meant waiting until the summer. Douglas wanted money now, and he wanted it in stacks. And providentially enough, having crouched before some stranger in a far-flung cottage in the wilds, a stranger who, as chance would have it, ran the single, hush-hush homo-pub for miles around, Douglas landed his first job – initially (when he claimed be revising at a friend's house) serving behind the fairy-lit bar; and, soon thereafter – when the resident performer flounced off to Glasgow – by assuming the cudgels of drag. How this extracurricular godsend ever came to official light was never properly discovered, but what remains beyond doubt is that Douglas – sporting one of his mother's old wigs, which harked back to the Queen when she still had an empire, masses of paste provided by the publican's 'pal', and the greatest of false lashes – managed, despite his hairy armpits, to entertain the cosy clan of salmon-pink tartan with a woeful rendition, three nights a week, of Whose Sari Now? But, next thing he knew, he'd been booted out of school and walloped by his father, neither of which fates seems, at the time, to have worried him. For whatever else Douglas may have been, he was, even at sixteen, a hardy lad; and, whatever else he may have failed to be, it wasn't broken-hearted at not having to sit exams. No, the thing which broke the heart of Douglas was the realization that the fountain of his income had gone phut.

As a result – in the hiatus before being pushed into some deathly local crammer – he grew sullen, played his records at full blast, drank expectorant by the gallon, chain-smoked soggy roll-ups, grunted rather than answered, and generally skulked. Yet the fates, as if wishing, despite his slovenliness, to reward his obstinate dreams of romance, did not tarry to advance a solution, a solution that enabled him to swap the financial allure of drag for the lure of a greater adventure in the company of some horny lorry-driver who, as well as promising Douglas that he wasn't married, promised to take him travelling. And so Douglas, who had bugger-all to lose, murdered his old piggy-bank, packed his overnight bag, and scarpered. But, after a squabble on the approach to Birmingham as to who, the trucker or his passenger, was paying for what and how, and a further one, at a lay-by close to Knutsford, as to which of them had been eating onions, the trucker decided to dump his plummy-voiced cocksucker on a roundabout near London. I don't recall how Douglas finally made it into town – whether he legged it all the way, or managed to hitch a ride; but I do recall being told that after a couple of nights sleeping rough, the weather turned foul and he was forced to check into some filthy doss-house where he crashed out, had his wallet pinched, and was savaged by lice. Thus began his picaresque trajectory toward the place where, by the time that we met up, he resided – a room in the flat of some cockney-queen who forced him to walk a Chihuahua in exchange for using the tumble dryer. And it turned out to be this queen, whom Douglas called The Kray Sister, who, much as a mother puts her daughter on (not the stage, but) the pill, put Douglas on supplementary benefits – reaping, for a considerable while, a chunk of the proceeds.

To break the deadlock of his penury, Douglas was constrained to labour menially: as a char for a couple of bric-à-brac dealers, until one of them caught him thumbing through their skinny-pics; in a pub near Marble Arch, known as the Elephants' Graveyard, from which he got fired for guzzling on the side; in occasional small-fry restaurants, where, because he reviled washing up, he generally bolted on the first pay-night . . . It was a hapless catalogue. But notwithstanding such reversals, Douglas struggled hard to keep his pecker up. And yet, for all the quick elation provided by his quick dalliances, he didn't always rise to the challenge; for, after repeated visits to recruitment agencies in central London, he grew disheartened by the surprising similarity between the adjectives Unqualified and Unwanted. But then he met Jack, in the very public lavatory where Gielgud once got nabbed, the cottage near the barracks where, in its heyday, the graffito had proclaimed:

THERE ARE FAIRIES
AT THE BOTTOMS OF
OUR GUARDSMEN

I never understood quite what kept Douglas, who, as I say, was a bright man, hankering with such mindless insistence after Jack – only to be forced, in the bitter end, to admit defeat and surrender his emotional towel in sodden tatters – but I suspect that Jack, during the period of incredible protractions, saw no real harm, no actual damage, in keeping the Cub dangling. Yet when Douglas (exhausted by his continuing lack of funds and apparent lack of prospects – both professional and conjugal) began to show the first signs of growing up – namely his fangs – and threatened to savage his way out of the prison of his patience, and run, for honest game, back to the Scottish jungle, Jack, to tame the danger, did what he should have done aeons back – lend the Cub a leg-up – and, in the simple way that figures of his type then could, procured for him, by means of a well-placed call and an interview which we might elect to term informal, a junior post in the world of finance, a post from which, deservedly, Douglas rose fast. This may explain why, by the time of my party, he and I were no longer as close as once. Now, he was occupied during the day, spinning around the stock market, making (not mistakes, but) yummy money, and often occupied at night, socializing with spivs who, by dint of their profession, had more in common with Kelly than ever they would have with me, slickers who wore stripes to work, and, after work, wore themselves out on company freebies at wah-wah restaurants, where, during coffee (but sequestered in the lavatory), they awarded themselves the bonus of white Colombian granules chopped to finest powder with the cutting edge of credit cards which were still, then, the preserve of the financially smart – granules which, once aligned at a sharp diagonal along the lid of the pan, were snorted up through a tightly-rolled banknote of freshly-minted £50. For a few stalwart months, Douglas struggled to make out that the balance had not altered between us, and I would also say that I connived with this inaccuracy, because there was such a quantity to him which I admired, strengths of which I didn't want to think myself deprived: his humour, his loyalty, his melancholy substance, the great safety, even, of his great size. His tremendous contact. But the truth is that despite our wish to pretend otherwise, Douglas *had* moved on, *had* gone abroad from my life. His formerly beleaguered own was, at last, and very respectably, on track: he had shifted from the dim East End to the twinkling epicentre of town; he had bought himself a flat which a decorator panelled with the masculine mahoganies of a yacht-cabin; he now sallied with connections who launched forth, like voyages of discovery, well-connected soirées to the dream of El Dorado; and, to crown his manifold triumphs, he could still rely on the lifesaving ring of Jack's telephonic laughter, full, as always, of conciliatory espousal. Thus it felt to me as if Douglas, afloat on his careerist raft, had quietly bobbed away from my small island, toward a broader continent in which I couldn't conjure, not least because its natives spoke another tongue – the high-pitched dialect of portfolios, and risks, and disasters. Yet it is similarly true that, if Douglas's alteration didn't harm me as grievously as it might otherwise have done, this was because I myself had simultaneously swum into Matthew, who, all too fast and all too powerfully, had become closer to my tough but marinating heart – as if an unwitting, but parallel, prayer had been answered.

The party, I have a feeling, marked the first occasion when my friends, although they'd heard of one another, were joined in a cohesive reality – most significantly Cara, Douglas, and Matthew. If, of the nucleus destined to survive until my slump, Cara was characterized by well-buffed nails, then Douglas was defined by bitten ones, for, in marked opposition to Cara's controlled calm, there was, despite his recent suits of faultless cut, an ancient rawness to Douglas, a bestial agitation. He sweated too much. If ever you happened to dance with him, as he and I had earlier done – sometimes even feigning to be (not partners, but) lovers – you had a job stopping your hand from slipping out of his clasp as he spun you round the The Moonlight. Unlike Cara, with whom I never got the chance to dance, but who, both in her intellect and carriage, strove toward containment at all times, Douglas strove to burst beyond the barriers of Jack's cramping *ménage*, out into an imaginary, sun-drenched, smiling panorama where the rake, ever in tennis white, would obviously still pre-side, but where not a syllable of sulky French would again need to be uttered. Cara and Douglas (as much out of consideration for my comfort as because, unlike me, neither of them was keen on combat) were always to maintain, when mutually confronted, a mutually courteous front; but, from the moment that they first shook hands and clashed in their opening gambits – he: 'Hello Cara' (smiling); she: 'How d'you do' (deadpan) – I realized that they would only, at best, ever respect one another, and, equally, only respect – never understand – the reasons why I'd been so equally drawn to their so different charms.

Douglas, during the phase when he still seemed pleased with women, preferred to deal with glamorous examples, more obviously impressive than Cara, more publicly admirable: taller-heeled, tighter-dressed, bigger-bosomed, redder-mouthed. He resembled Kelly in this particular, Kelly for whom females must by definition offer something beyond brains and humour – both of which, he reckoned, queers possessed almost by birthright – in order to merit his company. And Cara, as if sensing something unattractive, seemed, at that time, to veer towards more delicately-crafted personalities than either Kelly, the harshness of whose notions, even if unspoken, must have felt punishing, or Douglas, who, versed as he was in the poetry of punishment, seemed just so large, so loud, so unmanageable. Later, when my story went mad, I was to shoot into the vein of Cara's open judgement a cynicism of such potent concentration that, despite the cool dilutions of her rationale, she was brought, as if altered by a drug, over to my disaffected side, to accept that any claim to brains and humour on the part of faggots was – as it remains – a big fat fallacy, for the majority of fags, like the majority of the world, is blessed with neither. Yet back in the days of the (mislaid) Find and the Jeakle Garden and my sojourn through the principality of Bedsitland, I was lucky to have fallen – or to have been perceived as having done – within the slim parameters of Cara's delicately-crafted category, because, when I succumbed to pathological dullness, and turned into my own most boring, slothful shadow, she, as real friends tend to do, could not, I do not think, regard me other than as I had seemed at the start: as a promising young javelin. Even when I nose-dived and impaled myself in the manures of my self-pitying ground, she refused to resign. She didn't write away my state as terminal: We're all going to be fine, she had avowed; Clair de Lune, she had sent round. A masculine flower.

Which brings me back to Matthew, who took the party, as indeed he took the whole of life, in his comfortable stride. Of all the people who, once I stepped onto the road to adulthood, were to cross my path, Matthew emerges – more so, even, than the famous dreamboats of Los Angeles – as the one who best personified the phrase Laid Back. Only with me, and only in private, did I ever know him to sit up and act, rebuke me for this or that; but now that the whole question lies beyond an answer, and that answers, in any case, no longer matter, I like to think of such exertions, such rare exceptions to his attitude, as flattering, as symbols of his love, as proof that he was ready to make special efforts on my behalf – for the sake of my further instruction, in order to broaden the scope of my short-sighted horizons. Yet, as regarded the random public, which included Douglas, Matthew was (not uncaring, but) detached, detached as much about the affinities that appeared to bind people, as about the disparities that cast them into contrast. He was able, like a paradox, to observe the point and pointlessness of everyone, including the boss, the boys for whom the boss laughed, and the poor blighter; the pretty girls, the plain but sweet one, and the woman of profounder substance, Cara. His mental gaze could encompass the general spectrum of ages and genders and natures and backgrounds, as if our unremarkable society were a remarkable landscape. And because Matthew, being unnaturally wise, was at such easeful peace with his own mind, and so blithely indifferent to the frantic escalation of those ladders which more avid individuals viewed as vital, he was able, with the confidence of his neutrality, to enjoy the privilege of leaning back to watch and admire, or dismiss, or fondly laugh. And this objective stance, I still believe, is what – over and above the retrospective culture to which both of them had access, and from which, as I have said, I felt left out – attracted Matthew to Cara and Cara to Matthew. Another factor which drew them into affinity was, I suspect, that they came to view me as their shared shackle, almost as the object of a mutual surrogacy, for, at different points in our triangular time, both were to make me feel like their tiresome, but fortunate, child.

Tiresome, fortunate children is, I realize now, what the most part of us were when we converged that night in Bedsitland: Douglas, in a green plaid shirt and vintage 501s – but unaccompanied by Jack, who, at the unforeseen eleventh hour, had regrettably become (not held, but) tied up, apologies on his behalf – Douglas whom, now that fate had pointed him upward, one would never have suspected of feeling let down, even as he chatted to the doleful girl with druggy eyes about the niceties of opiates; the Fluke, who, though theoretically grown-up, was sexually puerile, and yet, tonight, had made sufficient strides as to shed his cardigan, roll up his sleeves, and lean against the mantle, his pelvis inclined at an obtuse angle, perhaps in an attempt to entice a boy of translucent pallor, one of my bistro chums whose hair had yesterday been coloured to blue-black and shaved along the back, and who, being an erotic Methuselah, wouldn't in a million years have compromised the hard-core of his life for a tentative erotic retard, but who, despite his sexual travels, which had led him far and wide, would, within eighteen months, return to base, signed over by the Dutch, sealed in a black body-bag, and delivered by cold-storage to the doorstep of his mother, who — as if I stood for death's accomplice, or society's most ghastly nightmare — vetoed me, in favour of more wholesome, varsity types, from the boy's funeral; then (to get back to the party), the plain sweet girl who needed styling, squiffy at last, grinning into the cleavage of another girl whose demeanour grinned encouragement; Kelly, superbly recovered from the hernia fiasco, looking superb in a muscular T-shirt and low-slung sailor-trousers, my brother, whom, as he laughed and drank and demonstrated the first symptoms of itching for a dance, few can have imagined might be paralysed inside. I know that such events are meant, for the host, to pass in a flash; and yet to me, even as I dwelt within that festive capsule, the sounds and motions of the company struck me as slurred, and slowered, and, now that I reel back, disconnected, like a documentary from somebody else's past, from the life of somebody silly and misguided, who still held, as a hand holds on to a bunch of something lovely, to dreams of sweet romance.

When the crowd began to disband, I noticed that Matthew and Cara, slumped against bolsters of grey flannel, yet comfortably side by side, were still colonizing the divan, their glasses held aloft for some distracted passer-by, somebody young, to freshen up. Other guests were drifting vaguely, and vaguely swapping round, and occasionally flirting with an able eye, or, as often happens in the dash toward the stop of such minor social paragraphs, squabbling about which song to play next, slow or fast. I remember feeling quite drunk, but not quite right: for people seemed, by this advancing hour, to be whispering amid titters which stirred my discomfort. I couldn't figure it out — not until a friend of Kelly's, the beautifully glossy one, sidled up and put his hands around my ear and whispered the plan, which epitomized the cod-diplomacy favoured by gay-boys of the time. And the plan was that (in order to get shot of the women courteously but fast) the rest of us should pretend to be going home now — gorgeous party, million thanks, talk in the morning — but instead, reconvene at such-and-such an agreed club, to shimmy under the disco lights, plus, if there were any justice, trap. I don't think that a night on the tiles could, then, be complete without a fumble in some back-room. Fine, I said, so long as the Fluke wasn't in on the scam. The whisperer rolled his eyes, and agreed: Too Right. And thus the boys and girls trundled off downstairs and kissed and scattered, until I alone, the irregular pearl, was left in my shell, rattling around. I tidied a quick minimum, ever my own valet. I gave my teeth a brush; dealt my hair a (studied) ruffle; and then, rushed out to grab a cab and join the rest of the gang. But when I found them, posing in licentious attitudes round a mirrored column in the shady basement of quite another life, called Subterrania, I noticed that Kelly hadn't pitched up. Which wrecked my night.

Three days later, amid backslaps of departmental welcome, he returned to the Square Mile. He reclaimed his former desk, and, while making out that it was great to be back, and that life was fine-and-dandy, he hung about, in mounting trepidation, for the call from McManus. During the ensuing fortnight, which proved a testing time all round, Kelly took to ringing me from work virtually hourly, but merely to relate inanities conceived by the light side of his brain in order to suppress those worries which lay throbbing deeper down. I remember how, oblivious of his open-plan environment, he would prattle on unguardedly, and laugh maniacally down the line; but though his blatherings concerned me, since they ran so counter to his usually sober professional character, and though I found them taxing, because they weighed excessively on my already sunken morale, I did not misunderstand them: I interpreted them all too accurately;

powerfully; I could read the signs between his spoken lines; I could hear between his consonants; for, while Kelly doodled skulls and hangmen on his pad, and waited for the hatchet of diagnosis to come down, a strangulated panic, a shrill precipitation, warped his vowels. Meanwhile I, flagging under the pressure of his relentless need for distraction, sometimes even cowering behind my answering-machine rather than be noosed into his anxiety, began to wonder where to turn for guidance about, or relief from, my own plight.

Predictably, I suppose, I turned to Dr John, hoping that he might put me on stronger tablets. But no sooner had I described, by way of explanation, Kelly's unexpected nightmare, than he told me that he couldn't discuss my brother's specific circumstance. This struck me neither as a feeble means of covering up for the Hippocratic Knife, nor as a cool dismissal of cases not directly linked to his own practice. It struck me as the most phenomenal relief, because, suddenly, and in a sympathetic atmosphere, I saw myself being granted the benefit of my own hearing. Although Kelly was, of course, ahead of me, ahead in the race toward sexual sentencing, the bleakness of his position didn't render my own position any the cheerier, or calmer, or simpler. My inability, given his predicament, to discuss my private terrors with my brother, didn't mean that I considered myself immune to the killer which already – at least in theory – had claimed him. I sensed its peril fiercely.

In the decades that I've drifted through the gloomy provinces of this disease, I've never felt about others' mortalities the way that I did about Kelly's. Something about the fact that my own (my only) brother, the closest blood to my own blood, was, or would in due course be, stricken, made me feel stricken too, almost as if, by sinister genetic implication, I had become infected – infected by *him* – so that he, by spreading to me his catastrophe, might succeed in halving the odds of catastrophe which seemed already to be pitted against him. The fear of which I speak was wholly illogical, I realize, and yet it was wholly real, acute to me. For, regardless of medical confirmation and anonymous little chits, regardless of whether you were a National Health number or a private-sector pseudonym, regardless of whether you'd already entered the official pool or were still loitering along its shaky springboard, wondering if you'd ever summon the valour to dive in, your brain, which is your greatest enemy, told you, kept telling you, the very thing you already knew: that yes, you could try to fool yourself, and yes, you could try to fool the world, but you couldn't fool, would never succeed in fooling, the grim reaper, who already had You★, asterisked, down on his special-guest list. And the fact that your brother – with whom you shared the most intimate consanguinity – was himself a foregone casualty, only served to increase your own vulnerability, your vulnerability to It. And as these thoughts, which, for some weeks, had been upsetting my equilibrium, assumed some sort of order, and began to voice themselves to the tranquillity of Dr John's room, I could hear myself talking in the lethargic monotone which, since, I've come to recognize as the leaden drone of melancholy. I suspect that Dr John recognized it too; because although, as I later learned, I was the first of his patients to have shared with a sibling the danger of this specific ill, he placed the greater accent not on my exposure to the workings of the malady but on my exposure to the workings of my psyche, which he described as Iffy.

Dr John suggested that we look at the problem sensibly, shall we. He stressed that there was nothing in my history which gave him cause for worry. This encouraged me. Had I ever injected heroin? I hadn't. So could we discard the intravenous side of things? We could. Blood transfusions? Never had one. Had I ever slept with a woman? All too often. He grinned, then said he presumed that we need only consider the illness from a homosexual viewpoint. I agreed. He said that this virus, though transmitted with ease, was – if you knew the rules and adhered to them – difficult to catch, for it was transmitted neither through the exchange of saliva, nor through the receipt of urine, nor through licking pre-seminal fluid, still less – as charlatans were claiming in Italy – from the seepage yielded by 'disciplined' nipples. It was contracted anally, pure and simple. It was about sperm meeting bloodied tissue. It was about lacerated sphincters. It was about the type of intercourse which, among physicians, is termed Traumatic. And it was the receiver in this transaction, not the giver, who emerged the imperilled – traumatized – party.

I had always it made clear to Dr John that I didn't take it up the **clacker***, because I hadn't done so for aeons. But there had, in my uptight beginnings, been very occasional slip-ups, odd, submissive attempts at idylls, abortive thrusts, excruciating fucks, which now, as I began to admit to them aloud, allowed for a hottening doubt to undermine my balance. He told me to cast the doubt aside. I said: Easier said than done. And yet he, even without altering his optimistic stance, must have sensed my racing pulse, my rising panic, because next he said that if I should decide to take the test and it turned out, by some infinitesimal stroke of ill-luck, that, like Kelly, I too was a viral casualty, he felt apprehensive on my behalf. He had reservations as to how – in addition to the stress of coping with my brother's adverse status – I'd be able to cope with the stress of knowing my own. He prescribed a sexually cautious attitude. He did not prescribe a cell count.

But I was in a jam. I wanted to buy a flat, and it was this, this pressing dream of a new life, that eventually brought me to crisis. The whole system, in the days of screeching alarm, was pitched – almost overnight – against single males such as I. High Risk, was the label attached to us. Bad bets; bad bachelors; bad luck. The bureaucracy was taking no chances. Yet I, because I couldn't afford to buy in cash, needed a mortgage; and I couldn't get a mortgage without life assurance; and I couldn't get life

***clacker** (slang): derived from Cloaca: excretory duct of a frog, Latin for sewer.

assurance without submitting (in my own name) to the very thing against which Dr John had advised: a 'thorough' check-up. He told me to stick to the rental market until medical research was more advanced. I told him that I couldn't do that, that I must, one way or another, sort myself out, both for my own sake and for that of my brother. Was there *no* way, I asked, that I could take the plunge and still buy a flat? Dr John looked at me hard, as if he were trying to weigh me up. He sighed, but indicated nothing. He went over to a filing cabinet, foraged about, produced a little book, opened it roughly, flicked fast, and sat down. He found what he wanted, made a note on a pad, and passed the note across to me. It wasn't a prescription for stronger tablets. It was the name of a medical colleague based in Paris. I could be tested overseas, and no-one in England would be the wiser. He was, you see, a brilliant man.

Kelly rang. He'd been to see McManus. My chest went Thump. I managed to say: And? (But nothing.) Kelly dismissed their meeting as No Great Surprise. Yet, to my surprise, Kelly sounded more relieved to have the long suspense behind him than he did resigned to a fate which, however uncertain its strain, certainly now confronted him. McManus had apparently – unlike the Knife – been gentle about it, and told Kelly that the crucial thing was to stay calm. He should avoid stress, feed himself well, take lots of vitamins, keep going to the gym, not overdo things, look after his immune system, and, obviously, use protection at all times. That was the best way to stave off infection and prevent the virus from progressing to the stage known as Full-Blown – a term too beautiful for comfort; makes the closing nightmare sound like some voluptuous, open rose.

But now that McManus had stated the obvious, and that the obvious was categorical, I could do little to alleviate Kelly's pressure beyond claiming that we were all in this together, and that I'd decided to take the test myself, but wanted it done in Paris to avoid hassles over life assurance. Kelly got all dismissive about my ploy, and said that if I tested positive abroad, I was hardly going to test negative back home. Agreed; but if I knew that I was positive beforehand, at least I could try to get round the bureaucracy, apply for an independent loan, approach my godparents, the monkeys, someone. And besides – I hazarded – matters may not have to come to that. Kelly sounded vacant, distracted, almost as if he were holding something back. To this day I can't decide on which side of the fence he hoped, deep down, that I would fall: whether he wanted me to be negative or positive, to beat him or to join him; but perhaps he hadn't given the question of my diagnosis much thought, because what concerned him most, he said, was trying to forget this whole business and getting back to his life and his friends and his job. And then, almost as an afterthought, he told me not to blab about this stuff to anyone – understood? – not to a soul. He made me promise.

Within minutes, I had blabbed to Matthew, who didn't look surprised; said that ever since the racket with the Knife, Kelly's situation had as good as been foregone. I mentioned my own visit to Dr John; I paused; I seemed to stall. Matthew told me to go on. I said that I was flying to Paris – the day after tomorrow. Why – to audition for the Cage aux Folles? To get tested, you idiot. He called me (not glamorous, but) paranoid. I said that I was being (not paranoid, but) cautious: I needed a mortgage. Briefly Matthew looked perplexed, as if one of us had lost the plot, then said: So what? (Did I *have* to spell it out?) So there might be a hitch over my life assurance. He scoffed: why couldn't I just do the same as everyone else? Meaning? Lie on the questionnaire; just put No where you mean Not Sure. But I was already too far gone, too fraught, and besides, I've always been wary of officialdom. Shameful, I know.

In the end, we went to France together, he and I; flew across, and stayed at a small hotel on the rue Jacob, chosen by Matthew because the neighbourhood, between the wars, had been popular among lezzers considered top (not hat, but) drawer: patronesses of the arts, proclaimers of blank verse, promenaders of pug dogs. If I concurred with this choice, it was less on account of Matthew's Sapphic anecdote than for the simpler reason that, according to my (not Baedeker, but) Spartacus, there was a faggot club a few yards down the cobblestones, encouragingly called: Le Trap. You never knew. You lived in hope. But first things first. We dumped our bags and took ourselves directly to the practice of the man proposed by Dr John. Matthew waited for me outside, smoking on some leafy boulevard. At reception, I produced a letter of introduction, which was conveyed to the Colleague while I paced about an empty room. When – quite soon – I was ushered through, the Colleague proved starchily polite, almost petit-bourgeois; treated me like a wayward débutante in need of something more efficacious than a knitting needle and a bottle of mother's ruin to sort me out. We exchanged the briefest of euphemisms, and then, without further anything, he did his bit: made a quick call, spoke to some nurse at some *laboratoire*, made an appointment for me to have an *examen* (this for a disease whose acronym sounded nothing like the one we feared in London), hung up, gave me the address of a haematology lab which, bafflingly, was called La Scala, warned me to expect to pay (what to me was) an absolute aria, told me that if I hurried I could have my results back by tomorrow at five, and then, by way of parting shot, he said (not Good Luck, but) give my best to Dr John.

I think it's fair to claim that, at the time of this particular trip, Paris was ahead of us in the management of It: better informed, better equipped; less embarrassed, certainly less punishing. These advantages may have been connected to the fact that its population was, then, more assorted, more intercultural than ours, and that sexually its people were, as they have always been, less stringently conservative in their penchants; but, at any rate, I remember feeling, when we walked into that blood-test centre, grateful to find myself in France. The interior had been painted (not white, but) in a brilliant palette: orange, lemon, turquoise, lime. The floor had been covered in (not linoleum, but) matting the colour of sand. Music from the tropics swirled around the background. There wasn't the weighty air of apprehension to which, back across the Channel, people of my type were having to becoming accustomed. I recall a few pregnant women about, optimistic vessels of new life; a sprightly old man, keen, perhaps, to keep his sugar-levels down; a child, dressed as I'd been dressed when I had been a child; and yes, of course, a few odd faggots – mostly in couples, their shaky knees brushing. But the brightness of the place, and the variegation of its public, rendered the ambience less unbalanced, and less ugly, than that of the squalid, segregated, underground departments where, in England, high-risk patients were told to give their arm.

Matthew must have been a more adept distractor for me than ever I was for my brother, because, of that critical jab, I recall nothing. Suddenly we were back outside, strolling along the Left Bank, gazing across the water in silence, a silence drowned by the sound of speeding cars. My head felt breezy – light rather than high. Near a bridge, he stopped for no good reason. He turned to me. He held me by the hands. He said that he was proud of me. I regret that in return I said that he should save his pride until the moment of judgement. He told me that he wasn't talking about test results: he was talking about courage. This time I said nothing. We ambled on, reached the hotel, and showered. We decided to have supper at one of those enormous old-world brasseries which, though later glitzified to the pitch of providing polyglottal menus and purchasable ash-trays, still exuded, then, a reassuring, well-worn, shabbiness. Over coffee, Matthew wondered what I wanted to do now. I wasn't really in the mood for clubbing; but, rather than admit as much, I asked the question back. And he, as if my inner workings were transparent, agreed: Nothing tonight. But then he added that tomorrow he would like to visit some museum in St Germain. Upstairs, back in our room, I closed the shutters while he fiddled with the bedside lamps. We drank a nightcap. We shared the bed. We wore T-shirts and underpants. We slept the sleep of close companions. Stainless and becalming.

After a breakfast of hot chocolate and *pain aux amandes*, we went along to the museum that Matthew had wanted to check out. What we came across looked like a (not museum at all, but) hollow ruin from ancient times; yet he, adamant that we hadn't bungled, managed to discover, round the narrow corner, a proper entrance through a well-kept inner courtyard. Mercifully, my friend belonged to the type of visualist who likes to work his way through an exhibition fast, and prefers, once the basic recce has been done, to stop and concentrate on one specific work of art. Otherwise, you just got cultured-out. And since culture wasn't exactly my speciality, it was he who decided that we pause before, and focus on, an intricate six-panel tapestry, featuring reverse perspectives and floating islands and symmetries designed to fool the eye, such as you might find upon a maddening jigsaw puzzle. The series was displayed in the round, a fact which was meant to contribute to something. From my personal point of view, it contributed to my ability to observe the uniformed attendant without appearing overly crude about it; but anyhow. This tapestry, which apparently dated back to God-knew-when, had allegedly been discovered, after centuries of obscurity in some provincial backwater, by George (not Eliot, but) Sand, and had (to judge by the heraldic banners and escutcheons aflutter in the background) originally belonged to some big spender called Le Viste – presumably a man of distinction, because historians, in these enlightened days, credit him with having been a President of the Court of Aids. That's about the only biographical snippet that I do remember.

The panels depict a mediaeval Lady, demure in a flaxen way, who, as you drag yourself round the stages of her allegory, festoons herself with ever more spectacular silks and velvets and brocades. Jewels and chains and turbans abound. Camp, I murmur to Matthew. He murmurs back: Just *look* at it, can't you. (I try.) The Lady, surrounded by animals – domestic and mythical and wild, from doggies and birdies and bunnies, through monkeys and cheetahs and lions, to a uni-whatsit with a horn which might be said to err on the immodest side – the Lady is always up to something, whether flanked by her hand-maiden (the latter, conveniently stunted), or unaccompanied. Every time, she is planted in a formally pastoral ambiance, prac-tically two-dimensional, and her vignettes are decked with deliberately appointed trees in fruitsome ornament, and foresty glades, and innocent flowers reminiscent of the papers which, occasionally, you still find along the walls of old French houses. There's invariably some symbolic accessory in evidence: a gilded hand-mirror, a miniature organ, a florid wreath, a goblet of treats: objects meant to attract your beady eye – because, of course, this is no ordinary tapestry. Aside from the genius of the draughtsman who conceived it; aside from the skill of the embroiderers who toiled upon his massive, six-part feat; aside from the fabulous pigments, which have scarcely faded with the progress of the years; aside from all these things, which are tech-nically remarkable, the sequence fascinates Matthew on other grounds. What we have before us is a visual meditation on the Senses; and, indeed, the first five panels attest to those faculties. Hence, in Sight, we observe a head reflected in a looking-glass; in Hearing, the lady plays her miniature organ; in Smell, a mon-key sniffs at a carnation; in Taste, his mistress seems about to pluck a sugared almond; in Touch, she's handling the horny uni-corn in a manner that looks – hello – a little suspect. Matthew tells me to grow up: I should be concentrating on the final scene, the enigmatic sixth, not behaving like some schoolbrat on a day-trip. OK. Let's be serious. Here, in the concluding tap-estry, the Lady stands under a tent emblazoned with the motto: A MON SEUL DESIR. Meanwhile, her maidservant holds ajar a small casket of luxury; and, on the assumption that the Lady is replacing her jewels, not extracting them, and on the further assumption that this is an act of renunciation, not of avarice, the theory is that the final panel should be interpreted as a distancing of the self from those passions which can render the senses unbridled, because only through this distancing – only through this Sole Desire – may wisdom result. That, at any rate, was Matthew's take. It would take me years to mince the notion through my skull; but I don't regret our visit to that dark, circular gallery, because, even though I should myself have been content with a flick through the catalogue, and even though you're welcome to call me a tawdry philistine, the attendant's beefy thighs made it all worthwhile.

By twenty to five, we'd pitched up for my results; but (the French being such sticklers for bureaucratic exactitude) found ourselves instructed to take a seat and (of all suitable verbs) *patienter* – wait – wait until (not *cinq*, but) *dix-sept heures*, for heaven's sake. I closed my eyes; I clenched my face. Matthew told me to relax. Do breathing exercises. We sat. We hung around – I, inhaling too hard; he, pretending to browse through a magazine while sneaking me furtive glances. Gradually I became aware of an altercation broiling at the front, a squabble between a nurse and a tall young foreign woman who seemed not to be getting what she wanted. I pointed my antennae; I eavesdropped on the action. I heard the word *Elite*, I heard the word *Agence*, I heard the words *Cabine*, *Come on*, and *Casting*. But the nurse didn't couch her indifference in politeness. Rather, she rasped the reprimand *Retard*. And next, I saw the young woman go snatch, grab her appointment-card from the nurse's hand, stalk off, and plonk herself a couple of seats away from us. She may have been American, but the language of her ire was international.

Even if her aspect was to change more often than I can recount, she seems, when I envisage her, always to return to my mind's eye as she was that afternoon, in half-profile. Her portrait is a riddle, a muddle of contradictions; doesn't add up. It's as if she'd rather have you puzzled than have herself sussed out. She has shoved, any-old-how, a peasant beret over her head; but her hair, exorbitantly sculpted into a short, straight bob, evokes, with its shiny, hard-edged blackness, the meticulous refinements of Japan. Her make-up is too thickly applied. Her face is painted out to geisha pallor, and bears, around its pulsing jaw-line, the powdered down of undernourishment. Her mouth has lost its colour, as if someone had kissed it too hard and stolen its carmine, and yet, despite this lack, the bow of her lips remains exact, sharply pouted. Her eyelids, heavily clouded with shadow, lend to her gaze a downcast sadness, as if she were mourning the loss of some stormy lover. Her lashes are so long, and so fea-thered at the sides, as to hint at fake ones. But against these overlaboured, overly cosmetic eyes, she wears, like a reflective mask, a pair of spectacles – almost comical, seemingly out of character, with naïvely rounded frames made of clear plastic. Just beneath her bob, you catch, as she cranes to rummage in her knapsack, a glint of silver shooting from a pair of gypsy hoops which quiver under cover; yet the impression that results is one of harassment, not romance. And now, in a brutal silent outburst, she whips off her coat and stands up. She's had enough.

Though she hunches like a willow by the counter, she can't but tower above it. Even in a crowd she could not hide, so you're excused for staring at her heightened, haughty elegance. Her body, you now realize, evokes two people, two genders, at once: for, while its trunk belongs to a dancer in a practice-leotard – meagre bust; neck that rises up and up; vulnerable shoulder-line; thinnest arms imaginable, covered to below the elbow in grey lycra – her waist and legs and arse, belted into sloppy khaki pants, and her feet, laced into boots both bulbous and scuffed, befit a foreman on a building site. She may be standing as a ballerina stands, but the heel of one of those boots is crushing, punishing the toe of its partner. There is a heated anger to her lower half; an airy delicacy above. She adopts, by taking off her beret and shaking her bob asunder and extending the great length of her neck into the immediate future, a posture of (pointless) defiance. It makes you want to call her back to where you are. Sit down; it isn't worth the trouble. But at that very moment, before she gets the chance to pull the trigger of her argument, I hear my name fired out. I look to Matthew. He smiles. His is the hesistant, tremulous sort of smile normally saved for goodbyes.

As I closed the door into the room of rooms, my temperature plummeted. My backbone shuddered. The haematologist, a pristine woman with a snooded chignon and a bracelet full of charms, beckoned me hither, like a no-nonsense teacher. Yet the welcome on her face contradicted that authority: her smile approached a wincy grimace. I didn't know what to think. I hadn't thought how to be. I'd forgotten, even, to sit. I put my hands behind me. There was a silence. Was she bothered? Was she embarrassed? She was neither: *Mme. le Docteur* was charitable. Considerate. Presently she switched to a competent English, full of guttural precision – as if, in advance of **coming out** (sense **2**: entering society), she'd attended some finishing school near the Swiss Alps. She enquired whether she was right to imagine that I hadn't slept with men of colour. I nodded in the affirmative – despite the query of darkrooms; but next, notwithstanding my answer, I pressed her: Why? Because (she pointed out), if at any stage over the last five years I'd been 'involved' with non-Caucasian 'contacts', a further set of tests would be required. Different strain, different factors. No, I tried to reassure the pair of us, there'd be no need for that. Very well; now; had I been offered counselling? In London (I made out). Ah yes: London: she liked London very much: Covent Garden, Royal Academy, Harrods. She spread the net of her nostalgias wider, to encompass Cambridge and York and Bath; and yet, throughout this strange, strangely protracted preamble, she refrained from lowering her sights. She was trying to be kind. She joined her kindly hands. A solitary diamond irked my eye. And now, at last, she slid the flimsy sheet, the rustle of my verdict, to my side. I didn't pick it up. Rather, I peered down – and not too very far, for suddenly there seemed no hurry. The print below was faint and full of numbers. Symbols and dates and rubbish. Coded insults: Viral something; Antibody or other. The single thing which I did make out, because it had been entered in broad black marker, was: -if. If what? She frowned and took the sheet back, inspected it, then smiled; and next, reverting to the language of romance, explained, quite unromantically: '*Mais oui, jeune homme, c'est à dire que votre résultat est négat-if* '. It seems incredible now, yet my immediate impulse was to (not kiss her twice, but) whack her one, as if she'd put me through this hell for nothing, as if she'd been the culprit of my nightmare. She folded the sheet in half, advised me to look after it, and, gesturing toward the door at my back, added that I could settle my account at the front. I can't honestly recall whether I thanked her, but I have a vivid recollection of getting the fuck out. Fast.

At reception, I found Matthew chatting to the American girl. Seeing me emerge, he cut short their conversation, excused himself, and came over to the desk where I had stopped to pay. He mooted a guarded: Well? – Yet words, words suddenly failed me. I felt breathless; fretful; just said: Yes-Fine-Negative. Without warning or concern for the outside world he grabbed me and held me there . . . and that was when I realized, as he wrapped his arms around my ribcage, that some quaking inner part of him had secretly feared the worst. He freed me from his grasp; I saw that his eyes were wet; but he pulled himself together and said: Well done – as if a mere stroke of chance deserved congratulation. I suggested that we go. In a sec, he said. Must just say goodbye to that girl.

We returned to the waiting area and hovered over her chair. Hi-there, she drawled, affording me a cursory attention. Her spectacles had been shoved onto her head in the manner of some kooky hairband. She was fiddling with a mirrored compact and putting away a lip-brush, and inspecting, slightly askance, her mouth, which, during my absence, had been repaired to an unrepentant damson. From her babble, which emerged regardless of her artwork, there escaped a dry, sardonic laugh, suggestive of drink and tobacco. So what's the story, guys? The story: I'm unsure as to the chronology of our discoveries, but it transpired that although she and I had both rolled up at the wrong hour – she, made late by some job which had run over time; I, made premature by excess (not time, but) anxiety – both of us had come propelled by a similar, similarly bleak desire: the urge to ascertain where we stood in relation to the same dread virus. She raised an open palm, as if testing out for raindrops in the atmosphere, and, without quite meeting my eye, hazarded: You OK? . . . I said: Miraculously. Matthew butted in, to inform me that so was – er – She. And She, as if this pronoun were her cue, clacked her compact shut, smiled with her eyes, and tendered an astonishing manicure: a hand of inscrutable beauty, with everlasting over-claws of Oriental ruby. I later learned that she always kept her nails – that is to say, her real ones – neutral and trimmed; yet, when I think of her hand, I do so still as it was at that beginning. As an emblem of exquisite artifice. If Cara's nails were buffed, and Douglas's were bitten, the nails of this young woman would, in my reminiscence, forever remain false and long and hard and crimson and imperial. We shook. Her grip was strong but bony. She stood, picked up her knapsack, slung it over her shoulder, and, while arranging her beret and glasses, almost timidly proposed a drink. She knew the perfect place, she said – some bar on the Ile St Louis. I worried about Matthew; but no: quick drink was fine by him. So we piled into a taxi, which sped us through the mist across a bridge, and, before we knew it, we were sitting in some fuggy den, toasting (not Cheers, nor Chin-Chin, but) the cross-shaped irony: *Santé*.

Sukie. Let's go back to that – to her (not given, but) elected name, a choice which – so reedily pitched, so Eastern in flavour – must, in some odd way, have been devised to augment the distance between the woman whom, by the time that we met, she had become – transplanted, admired, successful – and the background which she had escaped – white-collar, tight-arsed, Mid-Western. Originally Sukie had been Sue, pretty enough but not considered special. Astigmatic. Lanky. Taciturn. Yet, from the secrecy of her ordinary girlhood, she engendered fervid dreams of reaching to the ballet. She stepped out of her bed, and drifted like a vision to the landing. A glow of lamplight filtered through her night-dress. She expressed a wish to go to dancing class. Her mother refused; her father obliged. Years of sweat ensued; years of rigour at the barre; years of promise and of longing and of muscular trials; years of arching her back and stretching her calves and mashing her toes to a pulp. And then, seemingly overnight, up-up-up she sprouts, and suddenly she's towering above any man in tights. And thus, when, aged sixteen, her hopes of making it to a swan finally died, she decided, rather than bemoan the pointlessness of *gargouillades*, to transport herself to a broader canvas. She travelled to the blurry abstraction of New York, where, at a loss for clearer focus, she enrolled on a course to study philosophy. But then, one cold Manhattan morning, as she hung about a bus-stop, she found herself accosted by some handsome, sunglassed stranger claiming to be a model-scout, who, despite the dodginess of his approach, managed to produce a card which did look bona fide, announcing the particulars of an agency about which she'd read in *Glamour*. She said that she would think about it. She walked around the block, went up to a public phone, cranked up the nerve, shoved in a dime, and dialled. She was put on hold, and hold, and hold, until, in the sempiternal fullness of time, she was granted an appointment by some snotty-nosed-goddess-assistant type.

Four days down the calendar, she flicked a half-smoked cigarette into the gutter, double-checked her image on a shop-glass, hurried into a building with a blushing façade, and took the vacant elevator up. She was pointed by some secretarial biro in the vague direction of an overheated sanctum, where, having skirted round a potted jungle, she was greeted with nodding interest by the main agent – a hard-nosed, well-known harridan who suggested that the girl run home at once, steam her black-heads for a fortnight, and then – but only then – go call on a bunch of young photographers and get herself a set of test-shots for a composite. Yet everywhere she knocked, Sue (as she then still was) met with the identical, flat response: sure, she was poetic and soulful, but her look was kinda wrong. And, to be fair, this did occur during an epoch when the fashion-predilection in the States was all for amber-coloured Amazons with shoul-ders out to here and gilded undulating manes down to their coccyges; so a girl who resembled a saluki and, worse still, snooted at the mere mention of Lingerie, was barking up the wrong aesthetic tree. She gave this shit three weeks – after which, with precious little left to lose beyond her twitching dig-nity, she stalked back to that office, demanded to be seen, and told the boss to tell it like it was and stop taking the piss. And yet Eileen, the agency queen, didn't put the opinionated little bitch back on the street. Instead, she gave her a last-ditch chance to become a mannequin: a one-way ticket to Paris (not Texas, but), France – plus a packet of laxatives. And it was during this flight, between dashes to the lavatory, that Sue made up her mind: changed her self to Sukie, and that was that.

By the time of our encounter, she'd been based in Paris for a good while, a decade or thereabouts. Her life, by then, amounted to a merry-go-round of presents and parties and weekends in châteaux and rides through the *Bois* to dinners in highly starred restaurants chosen by ardent professors of love. Everywhere she went, people seemed to know her name, seemed to know her whims, seemed to recognize her from the covers of the latest magazines. But one would be mistaken to suppose that her rise to stardom had been breezy; because no-one, she once made clear to me, no-one ever helped you in this goddamn business, certainly not the other girls, so mean and insecure. You had to learn the ropes yourself. The hard way. And yet I think that, even though she proved a good hard learner, Sukie nonetheless enjoyed a special favour with the fates, because, however wrong her look might have seemed in the States, it couldn't, when she landed in Europe, have been righter for the moment or been made more welcome – its jagged sophistication, its wilting delicacy, its sexy unsexiness. Designers and photographers succumbed, open-mouthed, to her ghostly silhouette. They chased her services – designers, not just because she was so (immoderately) modest, but also because her measurements were millimetre-perfect; photographers, because she didn't moan about being tired, didn't gripe about the vagaries of hair and make-up, and took direction like the best of them. Even if, when she did the Collections, she notched up enough shows to earn, in under a week, over six months' rent, she was never much enamoured of the runway – down which, in any case, she only ever ventured unspectacled and champagned – i.e. blind drunk. What appealed to her was the intimacy of studio work, and the mystique of faraway locations, and the thrill of bringing uncommercial dreams onto the glossy page. Beyond the skill of striking a million poses – over and over, and in whatever temperature – the gift which elevated Sukie from the horde of her competitors was, I would say, her aptitude to inhabit roles. She became what she wore; embroidered mental stories round her job; could impersonate whatever mood she was told. Even in a context where, for other mannequins, such a thing would have been impossible, Sukie could summon, and exude, emotion. Sweetheart! – photographers would exhort her – Look angry! Look jealous! Look sleepy! Look snotty! Look happy! Look clever! Look devious! Look as if – hold-it-there-that's-gorgeous – as if you like to swallow. And that's what made her a Top Model.

From the outset, Sukie had intrigued me. It wasn't just the paradox of her off-duty appearance – half-lout, half-ballerina. It was also her screwy, but individual, way of thinking. For instance, that which other people would describe as Dressing Up, she, who wore the best clothes in the world and wore them season after season, dismissed as Dressing Like a Dummy. There was, for her, no pleasure in the practice: it was merely how she happened to earn her living. That is why, when her time was her own, she went around disguised as such a (ravishing) no-one. And if, despite her wish to pass unnoticed, passing strangers happened to remark upon her beauty, she weathered those plaudits with the same supreme indifference as the very rich indeed wear blandishments about their very rich indeedness.

Sukie taught me lots of things – and not just trivia like the tip that if you trim your lashes they'll grow back longer and thicker. She also taught me that the medical certificates which were then being pulled out, in sauna-clubs and discotheques and along the Tuileries gardens, were not to be taken at face value, because there was a healthy black-market out there, which, for a price, enabled people who had been contaminated to pretend that no such thing had happened, and (in an echo of yesteryear's malevolent syphilitics) spread a little happiness – get even. But, above everything, Sukie taught me about equality: the equality which, in sexual terms, can exist between men and women, the similarities which can mirror the practices of straights and queers. Although by the stage of our drinks on the Ile St Louis, her career had already peaked, she remained an active woman – if not emotionally (the pangs of love having, as yet, eluded her), certainly in the realm of her erotic dealings. Given the liberated era in which she had lived, and the sphere in which she had done that living, she had sampled a greater share of men and ease and stimulants than, for instance, the wave of models who succeeded her, who defined themselves as Super but were essentially propelled by a priggish sort of greed, preferring to devote their hours in dressing-rooms to the discussion of off-shore accounts and conflicts of interests than ever to underwater blow-jobs or the possibility of drawing fluid from a man's nipples. But Sukie, like the flower of her contemporaries, wasn't squeamish: she was perfectly au fait with the bouquet of filth which previously I had presumed to be the questionable province of queers. With the right (wrong) guys, she had writhed in the satins of deviancy: done it on Quaaludes, done it on mescaline, done it with amyl, done it with sulphate up the rear, done it with horse-whips and dildos, done it handcuffed on her knees, done it gagged, done it blindfold, done it in every (balletic) position, done it in secret, done it on the street, done it with groups, done it, done it, done it. I had always imagined the private lives of mannequins to have been conducted extra-curricularly, because such a disproportion of men in that rarefied galaxy (designers, assistants, hairdressers, bookers) are inverts; and Sukie elucidated little by observing: Well, male models, I wouldn't know, too vain to be completely straight, too vapid to be completely gay, but boring either way. Yet what she did make plain was the fact that, in her apogee, no shoot, or show, or post-show dinner, or after-dinner disco, had been complete without the tingle of some burgeoning overnight tryst – with the photographer, if you were ambitious. All of which explains why now, in the aftermath, she'd been driven to the same laboratory as I. Because both of us, however ignorantly, had taken hefty gambles with our lives. I don't recall much else about our cele-bration at that bar, except that we swapped addresses and telephone numbers, and that – in the wake of her departure – I staggered drunk to the lavatory, where, presuming H to stand for Hets, and F to stand for Fags, I walked into the ladies' hole-in-the-ground and got bawled out by some cunt-faced janitor.

Matthew and I were starving. We stopped at a (visibly) **pédé★** restaurant, where we got treated like scum, got given horse-flesh

★**pédé:** (nm abrév de **pédéraste**): queer, gay.

in lieu of hamburgers, and got overcharged. When the bill arrived, I was all for a scrap with the manager, but Matthew told me to sit down. Come off it, he said; who gives a damn; considering your test-results, extortion feels cheap at the price. I saw his point; I shut my trap; I took out some money. But he, as if to teach me a further something, wouldn't let us go halves. No, he said, tonight was Georgie's night. So he met the damage, left a tip into the bargain, and, shaking his head from side to side, said: When will you learn to stop fussing about things that don't matter? I didn't apologize: I thanked him: because the mood, its enhancement, is what counts. Not the gripes.

Walking through the streets of St Germain, and laughing at the prices of 'Tribal Art' (hairy masks and Nancy Cunard bangles), he mentioned, almost en passant, that my visit to the laboratory had encouraged him; made him feel readier to take his own plunge. In the end (he reckoned) you can't beat peace of mind. I wondered what Kelly would have reckoned about that, but I kept my distant counsel. Matthew nudged me back with: Anyway, what's the plan? He didn't suppose that I could face anything as trashy as a dance. I replied that I'd rather save my stamina for matins, but – all right, if he was absolutely desperate. We returned to the hotel; shaved, showered, and changed into faggot-drag. We grabbed a glug of courage from the mini-bar, told each other that we looked fantastic, then rushed down to Le Trap, which, as clubs went, took us slightly aback. It was really just a sleazy dive with Euro-music blaring out, porno videos aflicker over the bar, and a crush of desperados leering at the screen, or lurching about, occasionally acknowledging one another by dint of a cursory: Ço vo. We ordered vodkas; and the waiter, a hot-panted North African with an eye for fresh blood, gave us whopping great ones – continental doubles. See? said Matthew: Makes up for the restaurant. Swings and roundabouts. Tits and arse.

But from this overcrowded, smoke-filled ground, we

discovered that a wobbly, metal staircase spiralled up, as if rising through the hollows of a tower. Heads, like gargoyles round the interior of a castellated parapet, glowered down, to gauge the ascending talent, or competition, or duds – a bummer for baldies, this vantage, but there you are. Once arrived, you found yourself cast into darkness, as if you'd suddenly been struck blind; yet, as your eyes adjusted to the teasing opacity, so they began to discern a compact maze of cubicles, reminiscent of sea-side changing-huts on Scandinavian winter-nights: black floors, black walls, black doors, and, if you stepped inside, black benches at the back – presumably for the convenience of cock-suckers too grand to go right down, or perhaps too old for the part. Rubbish, said Matthew. When it came to head, toothless fairies gave it best, everybody knew that.

Figures, stooping slightly, seemed to be shuffling about, occa-sionally clicking lighters to verify what others were up to, or to check how the opposition was hung. The air was laced with amyl. Pop songs glided upward and spread their wings about; yet, throughout these, despite them, you could hear hot grunts along the narrow passageways, and slaps donated in the lock-ups, and the occasional *Ah-merde-arrête-putain-j'adore-ça.* Matthew and I decided to separate before it got too farcical. I went downstairs in search of a top-up, and he, by my return, had vanished into the folds of enigma. It's always tricky when you go to a grubby joint with someone who isn't a shag – remem-ber that orgy with Douglas – but nothing awkward reared its head between us at Le Trap. I found a tiny heaving darkroom behind a *pissoir*, and ensconced myself right at the back – as much to protect the pockets at my rump as to get a frontal prospect of the shapes advancing – while Matthew, I imagined, hopped from hut to hut.

Hours of serial rapture must have passed, because, having fallen in and out of love a dozen times, having lost myself among the mouths of men who wanted anything but my heart, I dis-covered myself standing in a sudden draft, flies still at half-mast.

The place seemed to have almost emptied out. As I wandered from the back-room – not because I'd gone and come, but because the notion of myself as a bitter-end die-hard felt just too dire – I caught sight of Matthew, clambering back from the bar. He said he'd had a total ball, and yes – since I asked – with just one man; but he agreed that enough was enough: we had an early plane to catch. I helped him get his drink down. And at that moment, as we descended the spiral, clinging to the banister and laughing like idiots and declaring it all to have been *très-très-amusant*, the closing number started up. You can always recognize the swansong of such nights, their melancholy rallentando; but if I mention this particular one, it's because, in some peculiar way, it returned me to the days of Marlene and the Moonlight and her cover-version of the hit belonging to the sparrow of Pigalle – although the song that now came on, at full tragico-medic blast, was (not La Vie En Rose, but) Non, Je Ne Regrette Rien. Not half.

Our return to London landed me in the quandary of how to tell Kelly about my result, but, later that day, he rang, and, in a roundabout manner, enquired 'about Paris'. I owned up to my Negative outcome. He reacted by replying that he supposed if nothing else this meant that when his health got really bad I'd still be around to (s)mother him. Smother him? Yeah, you know, like with a pillow over the mouth. Robbed of joviality, I said: Very funny; and he, with an unconvincing laugh, replied: I count on you to use the finest goosedown, darling. (Camp irony. Nothing like it, huh?) And then we talked about inconsequential other stuff – stuff that didn't require acting. Because the (unmasked) reality is that Kelly and I, despite the many similarities which bound us, were never, from that day forth, again to view the world through similar, sibling eyes. How could we have done?

Shortly after this landmark, I met him in Chelsea for lunch, so it must have been a Sunday, his Saturdays being by tradition saved for more rewarding pastimes, such as lolling in bed with potential blue-eyed answers, or shopping for designer-mufti. I recall that after our main course at a local *trattoria*, he did a thing which struck me as weird: signalled to the waiter and, after ordering a couple of *espressos*, wondered whether he could also have a toothpick. Perhaps this was the thing to do, rough-tradish, cool. I turned a blind eye to the business – not out of prudence, but lest he tell me to get hip. Along came the nasty cruet. Kelly grabbed a stick, forced it through its papery sheath, and began to fiddle with his teeth, sucking and grimacing. Yet once he was done, and had broken the stick in half and dumped it in an ashtray, I noticed that its tip was stained with blood – not that he can have realized, because, while licking around, he joked that someone's pube must have got stuck in his gums. And next he asked – incidentally, simply while we were on the subject – whereabouts my dentist practised. He hadn't had a chance to track one down since getting back to London.

My dentist was a woman, efficient and no fool. Her set-up, though well-managed, was smallish and new: only one other partner – some sporty-looking he-man – plus a spike-heeled hygienist whom I suspect of having been his bit on the side. I was due for a check-up shortly after that lunch; so, when the appointed day arrived, Kelly came along to suss the place out. The dentist opened the door for us, and looked a bit surprised, as if I'd sprouted an extra branch; but she proved welcoming enough, told Kelly by all means to sit in with us, and asked him, while she grappled with my mouth, to complete some form or other: Age? Maiden name? Pregnant? Heart trouble? – the usual rubbish. Yet by the time I'd had my final rinse and been divested of my tissue bib and stood back up, I saw that Kelly was staring at me freak-eyed, frozen but panicked, like a creature caught in the glare of headlights. I wised up fast. I waited hard. Kelly began. He explained that he had recently returned to England, needed a dentist, and wondered whether he might be seen here;

and then he added that . . . well . . . it was tricky to say . . . (deep breath) . . . but he was, you know, Positive. I did my glacial mother thing. The dentist did absolutely nothing. Eventually she asked whether Kelly had answered that specific question in the affirmative. He had. She thanked him for having been honest enough to've done so, and decided that she saw no reason not to treat him. (Phew). That woman, let me tell you, was a very great exception in the London of which I speak. People of her (not vocation, but) profession – a profession where blood is an occupational whatsit – were particularly jittery, particularly ignorant, and particularly bigoted. The majority of patients in Kelly's position, faced with such practitioners, merely omitted to volunteer the truth. I mean: what did the orthodontic contingent expect you to do: take the test every time you needed a filling? She entered Kelly in her book, and, smiling as we left, said that she looked forward to seeing him the following week.

Next day, however, she rang *me* – sounding distinctly ill at ease, cagey even. Needed to speak. Face-to-face would be easier. Could I pop round for five minutes, say this evening? I could and I did – to learn the following: that the he-man had got hold of Kelly's form, expressed the strongest objection to such a patient being taken on, and refused to have the rest of the practice put at risk by a victim of this disease. *Victim*? I squeaked. She winced. Her partner's choice of word, not hers; only quoting; no offence. I stared. (In slow due course, specific clinics would be established for the treatment of people with Kelly's needs; but at the time of this little hiccup, the overwhelming medical consensus was that dental problems ranked so low on the list of priorities as scarcely to amount to an issue. Just brush your teeth.) She stared back, thinking. She clearly took exception to the he-man's attitude, but this was all so tricky, so politically sensitive; what could one do? In the end – because, as well as being no fool, the woman was plain good – she agreed, amid conspiratorial whispers, that if Kelly were prepared to re-register under an alias, she would be prepared to treat him after hours, when the surgery was officially closed. But remember (she concluded): whatever his decision, mum was the word. I never properly acknowledged her brave kindness, but Kelly did: sent a bunch of ivory something, and signed the card with his chosen pseudonym, which – rather brilliantly – turned out to be our mother's maiden name: Simeon.

It seems to me that everything – not just Kelly's identity – was undergoing an alteration at that time. We were no longer considered young. A fresh new wave of influence was coming up. The disco fever of my teenaged nights was giving way to House and Garage, techno-cultures which preferred hard-headed thuds to lyrics for the soft-hearted. The resultant, endless pump-pump-pumping, which, though it wore you out, seemed never to reach a climax, led to a clamour for invigorating drugs: speed and acid, at the start; MDMA, not long thereafter, which inspired you toward the fantasy that you were ecstatic. But even if you went to some illegal rave, and sweated up a storm and got right off your face, you still retained the sense to steer well clear of the (previously covetable) air-conditioning vents. Face it: who needed to flirt with pneumonia? Indeed, our people could be heard, while ordering drinks at bars, to add (not 'nice', but) 'no ice'. And the tenders of those bars, normally so quick to quip back, would batten their traps and leave it out. For whilst the ghetto may never have been so well-informed, so finely apprised, its moral face had been dealt a resounding slap. A silencing. The wary public – in airports and in supermarkets and in high-street stores and behind company typewriters and even in corporate lavatories – was raising its brow (not at, but) about us. The world was keeping careful tabs – and not just on stock-market indices of condoms and razors and toothbrushes. So queers closed ranks, joined up, and stitched themselves together into starry, spiky patterns of pink triangles. The epidemic may not have been our mortal crime, but, in the days when the medically blind were leading the whole blind charge, and chemical giants were rubbing their hands with gleeful dreams of avarice, it was very much regarded as our specific, self-inflicted damage, as the monstrous product of our filthy mutant love.

I may be mistaken in this, but my belief is that queers, beleaguered and blighted, now ran for subconscious cover, gravitated toward a blander manner, opted to merge with the general morass rather than court embarrassment, or worse, be made redundant. Character, charisma, courage, all that glittery social coinage from our former lives had lost its currency. Strength, if strength it could be called, now lay in (not laughs, but) numbers. Queer-bashing was on the rise. Night-buses, car-parks, subways after dark: to be avoided. At all costs. Like the plague. For dear life. And because the feeling in our faction appeared to be that what was bad enough for us was bad enough for everyone, we changed the signposts of our aspect. We performed, as one, a visual turnaround. Call it mendacious camouflage, but we made it harder for the world to tell us apart, the butch from the fem, the sheep from the sheitel-bashers. Few things struck me as sillier than truly queeny queens, those erstwhile divas of eye-batting brilliance, going all gruff and virile, but then: who am I to judge? Adjectives such as Divine and Refined and Sublime deferred to straighter ones like Scared and Tired and Angry. Our very clothes became generalized, heterosexualized — because obtrusion, on any front, felt inadvisable, provocative, to be discarded. (Bandannas? Sailor-trousers? Shoulder-pads? Were you stark staring mad?) Now you covered up in mammoth bulging anoraks, to protect you from the elements outside: the hostile cold, and hostile eyes. If you were attuned to the climate, you lost your shape entirely, togged yourself out as an amorphous mass, wore baggy pants and hooded tops and clumpy trainers with loose tongues. You cropped your hair too short, like a prisoner of war, or a lunatic with lice, and hid yourself under some baseball cap. On the street, you didn't play volley-eye. Nor did you smile. You held yourself in check, right back, because even social niceties were being modified. For instance, now you only told people that they'd lost weight if you meant to (not flatter, but) alarm them. And yet, when the rains came down, and threatened to flood us, the waters of our ocean divided. It may all sound too biblical for words, but, basically, that's what happened. The darkened waters of our ghetto divided.

Take Kelly, who was in the British vanguard of that whole ghastly tide. True to form, he embraced the changing fashions with an almost manic alacrity. He took the latest drugs, and gobbled them with gusto; he danced on imaginary Ibizan sands, and waved his arms like palm-trees ever-skyward. He raced from club to club to club, as if weekends were round-the-clock treasure-hunts. He even adopted the sloppy *patois* of the time (*yeh, nah, what are you **like**?*). But he was leading a difficult, double life, which I suspect awarded him few prizes. During the working day, he went along with the motions of the Square Mile, and fulfilled his duties without trouble, for he was as industrious as he was eager to prevent his mind from straying into awkward tangents. *Don't Worry, Be Happy. Things Can Only Get Better.* Such were the slogans of the time. So, after work, he would board the tube-train back to Holland Park, change into the type of gear that I've described, and (assuming that this wasn't a gym-night) take himself to alternative classes: yoga, t'ai chi, meditation, shiatsu. Lessons in chilling out. Lessons in following the advice of McManus. And yet, while learning to get in touch with his inner calm, he teamed up with, and befriended, people whom, earlier, I doubt that he would have done: outwardly bellicose; inherently dull. People nowhere near his par. But (never mind the toothpick saga): now, when you caught Kelly off-guard, you could catch him affecting nouns such as Meal and Serviette and Toilet and Lounge – Non-U sources, once, of snobbish mirth to us. I couldn't fathom what was happening. I just couldn't see what he saw in such company. It was as if he were becoming someone else, someone else's brother. Yet, in reality, it was I who was being blind. For when, at last, I awoke to the facts of Kelly's life – at a pub where we happened to coincide; I, on my frosted own; he, modelling a quilt of allies – I verified that yes, he had indeed gone over to another faction, an alternative brotherhood. Because, when the waters of our subculture divided, he shot, like a shark, to the far right.

Not so I. I found myself shunted to the opposite side – shunted not by choice, but by Kelly and his kind. I do not doubt that my brother's new society was traumatized, distraught with worry. But adversity had rendered its members exceedingly up-there, defensive and splenetic and bilious and wild. I didn't – still don't – blame them; yet nor can I pretend that their stance was other than patronizing. If earlier Kelly had bitched about his brother to his blue-eyed answers, now he bitched about me to all-and-stricken-sundry, and did so in a more pernicious man-ner: he betrayed my Status to them – a disclosure calculated to earn him as much sympathy as it earned me snideness. My Negative diagnosis grew, or so it felt to me, into some awful shaming secret, because those foul-weather friends of his, who could never be pleased, and whom I took pains to avoid meet-ing, regarded me with ill-dissimulated ridicule. To their collective, I was (not fortunate, but) fucking pitiful. Call yourself a queer? That seemed to be the inference. The jutting sneer of their lips alone conveyed to me their verdict that I couldn't – not properly – ever have lived. At best, I could only have amounted to a cheap little prick-tease, since I had never *truly* given – offered up, immolated – my precious rear. (Even if, to the neutral onlooker, it had become trickier to distinguish straights from queers), within our ghetto, which was riddled with vigilant cynicism, two sudden factions, distinctive and inimical, had come into being. The triangle of our minority, once so equilat-eral and pink, had been split into a couple of chippy scalenes. We had become divided, segregated into unequal warring lots: the Positives and the Negatives; the Hivs and the Hiv-Nots. That was the long and the short of it. No right angles. Sorry.

I made no apology for having been saved from the hatchet of disaster, but nor did I linger in Kelly's unwell-coming company for further punishment. I retreated both from him and from his sympathizers. I adopted a peculiar other life – the life of the unbrothered, a life more akin to that of an only child. I remember, even, writing to the monkeys, which goes to show how lone I had become, and how rudderless; yet, in that closely-dated volley of letters which I airmailed to their distant altitude, I never once alluded to their elder son – an omission which, to my mind, seemed to kill two birds with one stone; for, in addition to letting me off awkward topics, it made me appear – or so it appeared to me – grown-up, as if, at last, I really *were* sailing under my own steam, flying with my own wings, vaulting like an independent javelin. And yet my reticence on the subject of their firstborn, being so unlikely, or so unlike me, must have glared through my elaborate banalities and alerted them to something, because, soon enough, they were on the blower to Kelly in Holland Park. He and I hadn't had some tiff, had we? Kelly got quite shirty, apparently, and told them: Nope, just a mild *froideur*, though, to be frank, he was Sick and Tired of my lazing around. Wasn't I able-bodied? Wasn't I able-minded? Naturally, the monkeys had replied. So why was I still loafing around doing nothing? He called me an embarrassment. (He called me an embarrassment.) The monkeys, unembarrassed but disgruntled, placed a call to Bedsitland – just as I was playing I Am What I Am. I turned down the sound. I told them: Lies: I was doing some translating for some publisher; I was researching some obscurity for some eventual article; I had applied for some interpreting post with some multinational company. (Lies.) I further made out that there hadn't really been a rift between us; it was just that Kelly and I didn't live in the same beat; London was a big city, and he was busy with his (not bullshit, but) business. Yet no, they couldn't leave it at that, had to spin me a homily about how it was a pity to grow apart, about how – precisely because London was so far-flung – Kelly and I must make extra efforts to keep in touch. We must be grateful for our link: we only had each other in England. Supposing there were some crisis? Family; kinship; they socked me the whole bit. Those people were living in oblivion. But I allowed myself to think that it was up to Kelly, not to me, to enlighten them as to his darkling secret. Up to him to get them to get real.

Meanwhile, I took myself to films, sat in underpopulated auditoria with the grannies of the parish and their aluminium walking sticks. Occasionally, I snivelled, not because I was moved by the action on screen, but because I was driven to self-pity by my dreary, maudlin, own inner movie, which no amount of celluloid could, even lightly, relieve. I tried, to a passing degree, to make friends out of tricks – to push myself beyond the basic sex thing – but the exercise proved abortive: I didn't want any body coming close to my futility. Harmless questions harmed me. I was covered in loud fears, fears from which only wordless congress ever freed me. Or pills.

Matthew didn't exactly drift away from me during this period, but he did seem less available to meet. He was still based in Kingston, and increasingly stuck with his family. (That, at any rate, was his theory; and it was, in practice, easier for me to believe that he was ensnared by filial duty than suspect that he was giving me the slip.) His mother's scan had given rise to anxieties, oblique. His father's dodgy heart was apparently back on the blink, acute. The old man, now that he had retired, was forever getting under the old girl's feet. The pair of them would hit the sherry at noon, and spend the afternoon bouncing insults at the television; so that by the time Matthew walked in, either someone was non-compos or both combatants were on non-speakers. And thus Matthew found himself forced into the role of piggy-in-the-middle. I don't think that it suited him. He mentioned getting lost, getting out; said that he was browsing through particulars – at the office.

I began to hunt for my own flat, but neither with success nor great enthusiasm. Perhaps I made the task unduly thankless for myself – as if property were love. I rejected possibilities on the basis of mere measurements, not even ground-plans. I rarely bothered with appointments to visit those alleged gems which defied photographic justice. I dreaded meeting agents, who, while waxing on about (not real estate, but) being realistic, made me feel too lowly-of-budget to warrant their real interest. What, after all, was *I* to those property whiz-kids? A poxy commission. Nor could I stand meeting vendors, who were even pricklier about selling than I was about buying, and whose places, besides, were just so grubby. You should have seen those dumps: grimy walls, rising maps of ancient damp. Either I succumbed to maroon carpets, or I succumbed to being marooned beyond the Circle Line. I gave up. I rang the monkeys, and told them I was up a gum-tree: I may as well resign myself to Bedsitland. They recommended that I count my blessings and make the best of what I had: capital. (I knew, even as I warmed to my part, that I was acting like a spoilt brat, so spare me your sancti-monies now. Because next) I said that the market had gone through the roof and my inheritance just couldn't stretch to an even vaguely decent flat, certainly not one in which I could envisage myself being happy. They told me to stop moaning and start earning a crust. I told them to shut up. They told me, in conjugal unison – from stereophonic ends of the same crackling line – not to dare to speak to them like that. I slammed the phone down. I turned the hi-fi up. I was what I was; I banged my own drum; life wasn't worth a damn. They rang straight back. They caught me out. I blubbed like a débutante without a dowry. My mother (who had enjoyed a lavish one) softened; her husband (who had devoured it) hardened. I nearly said Injustice. But instead I said that Kelly had come into a larger lump than I at twenty-one, and now, despite my putting aside and high-yielding account and the rest of the circumspect financial conduct, this was the result. My money fell short of the mark. Pure and simple. Primogeniture – just priceless. Second sons – of little value. My mother sighed lethargically, and said that they would have to think about it; see what could be done. Her spouse – prudently – said nothing.

It took a while for the business to fructify, but our parents, in the fullness of their leafy, lofty time, reached a consensus about Kelly's embarrassing brother, and came across; came up trumps. Yet it was our father, who, true to character, got all huffy and hacked-off down the line, and mixed his hackneyed metaphors and made it a condition that I keep the windfall under wraps to not upset the applecart. (Divide and rule; sibling rivalry.) I gave my word of honour, and honoured the commandment; but Kelly, despite not voicing a suspicion, wasn't a dunce: this latest withdrawal of (not money, but) trust can't exactly have thawed the fraternal chill between us. Still, the monkeys agreed to bump up the sum which I had left with Chortle-Buffer, and my prospects began to brighten. I found my chances risen by one – small but significant – rung, which meant that I could aim to buy within the postcode that I wanted. Yet, in a perverse way, my stroke of luck was counterproductive, for, whilst I wasn't broke enough to feel forced to buck up, nor was I anywhere near flush: I only had the cash to just about scrape by. Nevertheless, the plan became that – even after all was spent and done – I would still have to repay a (minor) mortgage from my (meagre) monthly income, and any ancillary expenses would, needless to say, remain my personal look-out. Look after the pennies and – yeah yeah – I'll look up your arse.

Kelly, once his (not teeth, but) gums had recovered – the matter with him having been a negligible dose of gingivitis – continued racing through the frantic schedule which he must have felt best matched his frantic circumstances. The oral inflammation subsided. His winning caps remained intact. He was free to go now, free to go on smiling. Don't worry; be happy. Already he was bandying a new term in viral parlance: the adjective Asymptomatic, whose prefix – A – must have been devised by the medical almighties to sound less disheartening than its alternative – Un. Better, after all, to be Asymmetric than Unbalanced. Kelly understood as much – just as he understood that I shouldn't be left too long unsupervised. Weekly he would call me up; yet his subtly formalized attempts at brotherly informality (designed, I'm sure, to ensure that I didn't blab to the monkeys) had a habit of backfiring. His very voice made me want to run for cover. I lived in dread of what he might announce. His opening gambit tended to be: Did I wake you up? – a bait to which I rarely bothered to rise, not only because it didn't strike me as funny, but because he often had. And if, for instance, I enquired how *he* was, he invariably answered: Good. Yet, rather than ignore this irritating usage of an adjective as adverb, I would bristle and rebuke him: Wrong – he was (not Good, but) Well. So he, having told me to sod-off-you-stupid-pedant, would replace the phone and not ring back for days. This happened often. But the intervening silence never brought me remorse; it brought me solace, because Kelly had become so strident, so finger-on-the-moral-pulse, so up-to-the-minute in the face of contemporary catastrophe, that the mere reminder of him made me feel ignorant and left behind and almost culpable – strangely tyrannized, like the victim of the victim, like his fall guy. I preferred not to dwell on the matter. That's why I liked the great uncertain silence. And yet, one thing was undoubted: gone were the days of Kelly's search for distraction. The boy who not so long ago had needed lies so badly, had, since that time, grown addicted to (not drugs, but) Reality. Now it was all about Life – lifespans, lifestyles, walks-for-life. I no longer suggested meeting up. I no longer enquired after blue-eyed answers. No news; good news. Today's news; tomorrow's trash. Tomorrow and tomorrow and tomorrow we die. But listen: Kelly was fine.

Matthew found a place which he liked, and, before I even

learned of the fact, had exchanged contracts. Within weeks, the purchase had been done. He had plumped for a two-bedroomed flat in (what sounded like) the suburban outback; but, then again, he had always painted with a broader geographical brush than I, lusher and braver and more widespread. His mother was delighted, because it got her husband out – to check on the alterations while Matthew was at work in town. Matthew told me that he would take me round once the decorators had done their stuff. He said that he would pick me up. Pick me up? Yes: his parents had dipped into their savings and bought him a car. I called him a jammy bastard. Not as jammy as it sounds, he replied: their supposed act of kindness came closer to a bribe, because now he was expected to ferry them around the whole time. So, in my hypocrisy, I recommended that he count his blessings and make the best of what he had.

What I, meanwhile, had to do was look (not on the bright side, but) about. Galvanize myself. Kelly – charged-up, encouraged, asymptomatic – was back in control of his life. Matthew was on the brink of becoming properly housed. Douglas, irrespective of Jack, was more than established. Cara was already headed for marriage. I had waited long enough. I got up; I went out, and, this time, refrained from making unrealistic demands. I inspected every option in my price-bracket, and, sooner than I had imagined, found a place which, if not exactly fabulous – a flatlet – met my requirements. Although small, it was in a quiet Chelsea side-street. Although three flights up, it had a lift. Although the kitchen was poky, and the bathroom grim, both had windows overlooking airy trees. The bedroom was drab, but I told myself that I'd known drabber – as indeed I had. The sitting room, even if tiny, was mitigated by a fire. The largest room of all, bizarrely, was the hall, a good square entrance that made you think of European apartments before the war and gave the impression of greater general spaciousness than there really was. Absolutely right for someone with all the wrong priorities. Presentation is all. Ask any homo.

I made an offer which I claimed was first and final, sweated out the interval, and, two days later, got my reward. The agent called. His vendor had acceded to a price-drop. So I went to a solicitor, and, in sluggish legal course, signed along the official dots. It felt momentous. Yet there was also a melancholy to the moment, a melancholy profounder than the surrender of a catchy phone number, and it was the realization that my condition had ceased to be one of provisional (rented) loneliness and become one of permanent (purchased) aloneness. It was a bit like Cara putting her hair up – an admission to the world. It made me feel old. But as soon as I'd announced completion to my circle, they surprised me with their all-round warmth. Cara said that she would like to give me some new stationery, whatever I chose; just to go ahead and order it. Kelly didn't ask how much the flat had cost. Instead, he offered to lend a hand with the removal. The monkeys volunteered to have some bits shipped over: Did I need a chest-of-drawers? Did I need a wardrobe? Did I need pictures to go on my walls? I didn't, but I thanked them all the same, and genuinely, since they seemed, for once, to be granting me some kind of laurel. Tenuous as was the branch which they were extending, perhaps it pointed toward potential closeness. Perhaps **coming out** to them (sense **10**: sexual) wasn't out of the question. I would have to consult Kelly. Even Douglas, from whom I hadn't heard in ages, sent me a note: 'I bumped into your brother at Monument station. He told me the news about your new flat. I'm so glad. It will make all the difference. What do you need? A mirror no doubt. Ring me.' And, long before I'd done so – never mind had moved away from Bedsitland – I sent a change-of-address card to Sukie in Paris.

Even while the flat remained unoccupied, I used to enjoy the sound of post coming through the letterbox, and the ring of the telephone coming alive. It made me feel transplanted. My neighbours, when our paths eventually crossed, treated me

gently, perhaps because I was the youngest person in the building, and single, and anxious. The couple with whom I shared a
landing put a note through my door to welcome me, telling me
where the bins lived, and whom to contact in the event of leaks,
or if my heating went on the blink. Another couple asked me in
for drinks, but didn't ask me what I did(n't). Helpful people, not
prurient. And between them, those various unexpected well-
wishers, who were hetty to a degree that didn't bristle at the
sight of queers, made the whole transition easy for me; lent me,
without knowing it, spirit; infused me with energy; inspired me
with an eagerness to get moving and get in. To dwell in their
midst.

This is naughty, but I enlisted a couple of former tricks to
help me tile the bathroom and re-fit the kitchen. DIY freaks.
Dab hands. Always handy to have. Matthew, who had paid his
men in cash – not kind – disapproved of what he called my
Services Rendered Scam; but still, once the jobs had been done,
and the jobbers been dispatched with a lascivious sort of gratitude, I painted the walls myself – in a tonal stroke of luck. I can't
recall the brand-name of the shade with which I ended up. I
only recall that I bought it by accident, imagining it to be something other; but it turned out to be the colour of bone, or
parchment, or pale stone, a colour which altered depending on
the time of day, and the plain on which it had been rolled, and
the weather and the season and – as time dragged on – the year
in which you noticed. Sometimes corners became almost two-
tone. Sometimes ceilings grew progressive; ombré. Matthew
finished off the woodwork, because he had a sharper eye than I,
and a steadier hand, and eggshell can be a bugger. Bare boards
were not allowed, so I opted for rush-matting. The kitchen and
bathroom were done in non-descript lino. Easy-wash, easy-
wipe; functional. I hung some blinds, and replaced a couple of
door-handles. An electrician came to install a ceiling lamp; and
suddenly, I was ready to quit Bedsitland. From my former palace
I threw out a pile of junk amassed during that wasteful, wasted

life – clothes I'd half-forgotten that I had, cards of lost significance, bibelots tantamount to dust-traps, books which now felt
embarrassing, towels forever tarred by the brush of the likes of
the pilot – and thus, one sunny autumn Saturday, Kelly, forego-
ing his usual blue-eyed raptures, drove me, as he had promised,
to the flat – his platter on my lap, my hi-fi in the boot of the
car, and my mahogany table, wrapped in a blanket, on the seat
behind us. The remainder I managed by taxi. It wasn't much. But
just as I had purchased that table with the unfair advantage taken
of Mr Respectable, so, with the sum saved through my prop-
erty-haggle, I decided to splash out on a bed, the bed which,
soon enough, would become the covetable four-poster of my
uncovetable account.

It was what the Serious like to dismiss as a Decorator's
Antique, in other words: an item of dodgy provenance which
happens, visually, to please. Easy on the eye, but not legitimate.
Yet, if I loved that bed – which I did on sight – I loved it
precisely because it was bastardized. It was also wildly priced,
though I didn't, when I found it, entertain a doubt. I jumped at
the chance. Jumped on it, and succumbed. The bed stood high
off the ground, which pleased my secret valet, who was sick of
bending down to tuck. It also lacked a canopy, which pleased his
master, the man of meagre circumstances, who was thereby
spared the expense of pelmets and curtains and tie-backs. But
anyway, in essence that four-poster amounted to a stylistic mish-
mash: a carved headboard with curlicues dug out, twisted
columns of varying heights, finials shaped like wilting pine-
apples, legs with the claws of tigers, a wooden dolphin flying
across the foot-panel. A mish-mash. And yet, these disparate elements had, since their garnering, been dunked together in a tank
of stripping-acid, given a light wash, and roughly limed, so that
what the assemblage of its features brought to mind was a blend
of ancient fragments, as if that dolphin had come swimming
through the seas, gathering bits of driftwood in its voyage

toward my life. I found it magical. I also found it well-sprung.
Well hard.

The next few months seem to boil down to a tranquil time, during which I settled into the beginnings of a simple, adult, life. I
no longer had to go to the launderette. I no longer had to share
a bathroom. I was sleeping in a proper bed at last. I owned a full-
length mirror, thanks to Douglas. I owned some decent stationery,
thanks to Cara. Matthew had contributed toward my sofa
– plain linen, undyed. Sukie had sent me some tea-towels –
damask, striped. Kelly had bought me a halogen lamp which he
knew that I liked. Small luxuries. Nothing grand, but nothing
tacky. The street beneath was perpetually quiet. Everything I
needed was to hand: grocer, baker, florist, the occasional restaurant – not that I ate out very much, for, gradually, I was learning
to accept my own company, even to value it. I felt organized,
composed enough to imagine that perhaps I might attempt to
do something productive.

  Mid-morningish one day, as I was browsing through the Jobs
pages, the doorbell rang. Who could I be expecting? I picked up
the entryphone. It was Matthew (skiving from work, no doubt).
I grinned to myself and buzzed. The lift came up. He had
arrived. I tried to look tut-tutty. He didn't seem to find it funny.
(Had he been sacked?) He walked straight in; no kiss, no nothing; just flopped down on the sofa, and muttered: Christ, can we
have that racket down? I lowered the sound. Did he want some
coffee? No. He wanted a brandy. What was up? (Silence.) I went
to the kitchen to pour him a glass. Bugger the time – I poured
myself one. Back at his side, I found him sitting hunched, head
buried in his hands. Again I asked. Now he looked up. His face
was flushed. His father. What about him? Heart attack. When?
Middle of the night. How'd Matthew found out? His mum;
phoned him at work just now. Where from? Hospital. Shouldn't
he be there with her? No, she was off to her sister's house. Why?

Because the old boy had kicked the bucket. Dicky Heart had given up. We got smashed. So, apparently, did his mother.

The funeral was held at Kingston a week later, but Matthew, whose parents I had never met, released me from the penance. Easier to stick to family. His mother wanted it over and done with. No fuss. Apparently his half-sister was flying in from Canada – to sniff around. Father's daughter from some wartime mismatch. Matthew called her a dreary cow. His mother had decided to stay at his aunt's for a while. Sisters together. Both widowed now. Not exactly merry, but not bad. Feeling a bit fragile. Something was up. Tummy trouble. Matthew offered to move back, or take his mother to his flat, but she said: Stop worrying. She didn't say Advanced. She didn't say Liver. She didn't say Cancer. She kept him in the dark. Very no-nonsense. Very English, that. And, with almost farcical propriety, she was declared Terminal within the month. What happened? Nothing. Spare her the chemo lark; she didn't hold with medical tampering. She wasn't going to fight. She was broken-hearted (not by the thought of dying, but) to think that the old man's ticker had packed up during an argument. She no longer even wanted to get drunk. She wanted morphine now. And, despite Matthew's after-work attempts to bring her succour – but before he could summon the un-English courage to tell her that he loved her – his mum, the woman who had told him that she wanted for him nothing more (and nothing less) than happiness, was off the planet. Matthew was remarkable. Didn't cry once. The sole thing that he asked, to brighten his sadness, was that I refrain from calling him Orphan Annie.

His half-relative with the Canadian passport, after instructing Matthew to dispose of her chattels once probate had been granted, flew back across the Atlantic buoyed by the prospect of forthcoming monies – monies which Matthew agreed to have the lawyers wire over (in *dollars*, as the beneficiary had specified). Consider it done, had been his reply, but Good Riddance, was his truer reaction; because, to be honest, anything to get shot of the woman. And yet, even after he had honoured her requirement, and dealt with the further annoyances of double fees demanded by solicitors, and death tax payable to the government, and commission taken by the local auction house and the rest of the subtractive hoopla, Matthew didn't do badly. But, rather than relinquish his flat, to which he had grown attached, he resolved to flog his parents' house – the house where he had been brought up – and did so summarily, without a sentimental qualm. Why? Because the place was meant for a family. Too much garden for a single pansy. He didn't need the hassle. So he bequeathed his childhood memorabilia – those flags and comic-books and cups and boats and forty-fives – to charity; told his widowed aunt to grab whatever she wanted before the clearance truck came round; and, once the bureaucratic dust had settled, redeemed his mortgage. Outright. He said that there wasn't a feeling quite like it. He only kept a Chinese vase which, if I remember rightly, had been his mother's mother's, and an ancient photo-album which used to make him laugh because (he said) his ancestors, despite their lacy caps and stove-pipe hats, had looked – well, so Darwinian. But, on occasion, in bars where the humourless crowd led us to unhumorous subjects, he sometimes spoke about his parents, and about the whirlwind of their (not romance, but) parting; and always – looking afar – Matthew said that the best way to get out was the way that they had done: sharpish. And yet, when he made such observations, it wasn't thoughts of myself that entered my mind. It was thoughts of my brother. Thoughts that made me uncomfortable.

I suppose it must have been the recent ghouls revealed to Matthew – the spectre of mortality, the realization that its ugly truth will always out – which led me to suggest to Kelly that perhaps the time had come to come out to the monkeys. If I liked, he replied; he wasn't really bothered; they were so far away, so out of touch, that it hardly seemed to matter; after all, it wasn't as if they encroached upon our lives. (But it *was*, I told myself, as if Kelly encroached upon mine. I had no desire to get landed, when finally his hatchet came down, with his finale. Not single-handedly. No, thank you. It may sound selfish; it may sound callous; but I'm not going to pretend otherwise. My blood ran cold at the prospect: the finest goosedown, the [s]mothering – even the camp irony.) Anyway, Kelly, unaware of my self-interested cowardice, eventually said: All right, and told me to run a draft past him. I didn't quip about pneumonia. I did as I was asked. And after a brief debate as to whether, in such documents, one should enter the word 'gay' or stick to homosexual, and whether it was right or wrong to appear apologetic, and whether to send love or make them earn it, Kelly said: That all seems fine. He suggested that I (not write, but) type the result. The finished product should look like a (not coercive, but) collaborative exercise. And once the finally final version had been drawn up, Kelly drove round to inscribe his Christian name next to my pagan, Q-shaped flourish. The upshot was the declaration which, adorned with two very florid signatures, culminated in our simultaneous banishment from the family branch. And yet this banishment couldn't, in one sense, have been more timely – that is to say: have proved less damaging – because, by this advanced chapter, both Kelly and I were free of our parents' (pecuniary) clutches. And besides (I reasoned), if, beyond this rupture, they had no desire to be kept abreast of what they would come to describe as our revolting lifestyles, no-one, later, would be able to blame anyone for having with-held facts, facts which went beyond the long overdue formality of confirming our 'bachelorhoods'. And, since Kelly didn't mention the other business, and I hadn't dared to hint at it, no reference was made, in this (first and final) stab at frankness, of his medical predicament, a predicament which, steady as it currently seemed – asymptomatic as it was decreed – neverthe-less remained, like my psyche, Iffy.

Our divorce from our (not betters, but) begetters – against whose moralizing, as I have mentioned, Kelly and I were to remain indissolubly united – had the ironic repercussion of rending us brothers more forcefully than any of the sundry wedges which had hitherto driven themselves between us. For it was Kelly, the lesser equipped to cope with the stresses of attack, who found himself subjected to the brunt of our father's sanctimonious bluster – first, in a call which Kelly truncated ('Get stuffed'); then, in a follow-up letter which, though posted to the pair of us, had in essence been conceived for the 'remedy' of the elder son. I myself was treated to a photocopy of this fantastically dreary piece of (il)literature, but it reached me a day after Kelly's, by which stage its priggish substance was already amply known to me, so I binned it. But Kelly, understandably, was none too pleased; for (despite the fact that it was I who had mooted the whole idea, and I who had stirred my personal heat into his cool indifference, and I, indeed, who had cooked up the ingredients of the missive) now, regardless of my hand in the initiative – a hand which, like that of our mother, events permitted me to keep concealed – Kelly was getting all the stick. Not only had he been the sole recipient of what he called our father's holy bloody earful, but also (since our parents' offensive was, on account of the primogeniture thing, primarily aimed at him) he felt cast as the prime villain of the epistle – that unoriginal piece of joined-up shit about sin. So – I said in an attempt to mollify him – who gives? *I* do, he screamed. Yet, despite the unhappy outcome, secretly I felt relieved: one less weight to drag around – two, actually. But Kelly, after calling me a lazy arsehole with nothing better to do than make (not love, but) trouble, distanced himself dramatically, backed right away from me, away into his world of high finance and blue-eyed answers and quarterly check-ups. For ever, most likely.

Matthew, conversely, came back into my life. For good, I trusted. For the good of both of us. Sometimes I get moods when I look back, and I see those moods in colour. And the mood which colours the time when everybody vanished from our canvas (Kelly, the monkeys, Dicky Heart, Matthew's mother, even the dreary cow from Canada) returns to me in a certain, uncertain violet – diffuse and abstract – as if the calm which succeeded that stormy recent past had unfolded behind the dusty distance of a scrim. This violet, like all violets, was a tonal marriage; and yet it was unique, unique entirely, entirely ours. Matthew's and mine. It was the union of the heightened blush which I shall never cease to associate with his sunny laugh, and the baser, saltier blue, which for years would taint my mouth and contrive to make me sound harsh. But the mixture wasn't bad; there was a harmony about it. We complemented one another. I think that we thought ourselves, on balance, happy.

The events which I attribute to that brief interlude, that parenthesis of gauzy ease, I view almost two-dimensionally, like the moves of silhouetted partners on a stage, figures set against a sky without perspective, without clouds overhead. It was as if we were engaged in an almost soundless dance – the slowest waltz imaginable – drifting through the violet climate of those nights and days where patterns and returns and turns and brief retreats and gestures of unspoken gentleness were everything, without reference to, or reflection from, the world. Perhaps, of course, my memory romanticizes. But perhaps the mind is allowed to indulge the heart.

We would meet with regularity, whether at his place or at mine. He would go to work; I would try to do something. We ate at home, or we ate out. We went to films; to the theatre; to the ballet. We took strolls around the park, and dared to amble arm-in-arm, but no-one ever bitched at us. The bitching went on in clubs. And yet, even though we still liked dancing, we no longer really hunted. If either of us happened to trap, it was almost accidental, incidental. For, just as Matthew wasn't burdened by ambition, so our friendship wasn't hampered by combat. No scores; no notches; no competitive subtext. Which is why anonymous dalliances only counted, only warranted account, if they properly amounted to anecdotes, such as the occasion when Matthew was getting fucked, and, at the priceless point of climax, the other guy spat at his mouth. Loved and loathed at the same time. Fabulous. But the majority of those encounters didn't merit subsequent discussion. Post-mortem is, I believe, the popular metaphor.

Sometimes we teamed up with Douglas, and that was always a gas, not just because he was good at checkered laughs, but because, with his brogues and plummy voice and Aran jumpers, he looked as if he'd happened upon Faggotland by accident. Sometimes too – around the closing days of Cara's flat – Matthew and I were asked for supper. Eight fifteen for eight forty-five. Bit of a stickler, madam, but I liked that about her. I also liked the fact that (in contrast with her frostiness toward Douglas) she was never less than fond with Matthew. She often sat him on her right. And even as I yabbered further down the company, I could tell that when they got together, those two discussed me. Their heads, at social gatherings, would move too close for my comfort; almost brush; and then, one of the heads would swivel a fraction and pretend not to be shooting me a glance. But I preferred to be the cause of their concern than the yawn of their indifference. She would have suggested, I suspect, that perhaps what I needed was more time, that perhaps I needed to summon more courage; but he, I have no doubt, would have said that I'd already had too much, that I ought to be pushed out. Cruel, kind, wrong, right; I really didn't mind. They were, I realize now, my seas and my rocks and my skies. They were, even before the expression had entered the vernacular, my Elective Family. Sister, brother; mother, father; mentor, ally, guardian, dancing-partner. Lucky stars. Luck; chance; hazard. I hazarded to chance my luck. I dared to hope that my life had begun. And suddenly it had.

It started with a common cold. I caught it first, and gave it to Matthew. Nothing odd there. Happens all the time. Matthew dragged it about for a while, snivelling and snuffling, but, beyond multivitamins and tissue hankies, did nothing. Eventually, when the nuisance escalated into an agony and his throat felt as if it had erupted, he sought antibiotics from some doctor in his borough. He dutifully took the tablets, and, at night, took care to wrap up tight. Whisky, honey, slice of lemon, all of that. But: still nothing. So he went back, wearing a scarf the colour of dust. He swallowed hard, and told the doctor that his glands were up. The doctor warmed his practised hands and rummaged inside the scarf. He said that there were various ways of treating such symptoms, but that in order to determine the most effective, he needed to know Matthew's status. Had the patient been tested? Bang. Sent him to some hospital nearby. Matthew took it like a Stoic from ancient times. He waited for the requisite fortnight to elapse; then returned – (im)passively – for his result. Positive. There you are. He'd always known deep down. What he didn't know – could never have imagined – was his T-cell count. You were meant, as far as I recall, to have 500 of those tell-tale corpuscles. My friend had twenty-five. He may have looked younger than his years by far, and glamorous as all get out, but already he had crossed that all-important, healthy boundary-line; had wandered into a realm which clanged with the bells of alarm. Forget asymptomatic. He drove to my flat.

He was so calm, so grand. He began with the business of the boring cold, moved on to the raging throat and useless tablets, briefly quoted his GP, skipped the eternal fortnight, and finished with the explosive punchline. I felt it in my stomach. I asked him how he felt. He said that he felt fine. He supposed, when all was said and done, that he'd been lucky in life; at least he'd managed to fulfil his three big aims: to travel, to own a place outright, and to be loved. Doesn't it sound simple when distilled to that? But he added, on reflection, that he was glad his parents weren't around: he would have hated for them to be put through this stuff. I got up. I walked to the window. I saw nothing. I saw no doubt. I sat back down. I didn't touch him. I went nowhere near the risk of patronage. I wasn't anything as obvious as sad. I wasn't really frightened. I was certain and resolute. I knew exactly what I was about to utter, even though I can't have understood quite what it signified. And then I made my solemn vow. I swore. I swore to him that, if he would have me, if he would allow it, I would husband him through whatever came up, steer him through whatever course the fates had planned; for however long, and however hard; I would espouse him. Of that, he could be certain. On that, he could rely. All the way to the final curtain? Yup. (No regrets. No tears goodbye.) He said: You're a brick, darling. But just as I knew myself to be no such thing, so I knew, so I know, that he believed me. He mentioned dignity. That's the word that keeps returning. And laughs. Laughs would see us through the nightmare. No bitter-queen shite. Promise me that.

You have to understand something. I didn't undertake this task because I was remotely good. Goodness is what you find in spinach. I assumed it simply because it was right. Right for *me*. It was a selfish decision. The job happened to suit. It gave me an identity. It made me feel real. Anybody could have done the things which I'd be called upon to do. But no-one else got to reap the specific, special benefits which I did. Selfish, see? I hope that's clear. I would never have committed myself to anyone but Matthew, not unconditionally. Kelly would have been the first to vouch for that. Nor could I ever have impersonated that misleading word Buddy, which had nothing to do with friendship, and everything to do with compassion to pariahs, plus a bit of money from the council. In point of fact, none of the words which were then being adapted seemed to apply: I wasn't a 'partner' in that Matthew and I had never been lovers. I wasn't a 'carer' in that I didn't care a bugger if people imagined that we had been. I wasn't his keeper. I wasn't his kin. If anything, I suppose that I was his kith; but try explaining that to a lispy lass, fresh out of nursing school in Grimsby. Relationship to patient?

In desperation, Matthew said: Put down Best Sister. The girl giggled.

I took my lead from him. He told me to chuck out my wooden spoons and chopping-boards and spatulas, which, he said, were crawling with bacteria, and to replace the lot with plastic – more hygienic – otherwise he'd never feel relaxed about eating at my flat. He told me: No more tap-water, only mineral. He told me: No more aspirin, only paracetamol. He told me: No more scented soap, only hypoallergenic. He told me: No more semi-skimmed, only full-fat milk. He told me: No more saccharine, only proper sugar. He also told me that he wanted to be registered at my local clinic, a flashy new one for Hivvies, because he could go there in his lunch-hour without people at the office getting ideas. He added that he wanted, for as long as it was feasible, to retain his freedom. I could completely see that. But he needed to be assessed. There wasn't time to waste. And so, next morning, along we went. You're bound to think this fatuous, but we glammed up for the occasion. We made the effort. Sometimes it helps.

They weighed him. They asked a load of questions. They took an ever bigger load of blood-tests. They gave him pills to delay the onset. And at last we drove away, as if toward my flat. But next, without warning, he pulled up. He stopped the car. I thought that he must be hungry. I thought that he wanted a bite. He told me to swap round. He wanted me to drive. I hadn't been behind a steering-wheel since my fracas with the pilot. Rusty wasn't the word for it. Suffice to say that we were forced to get a pair of learner plates, front and back – the big L; bright scarlet – because in time, said Matthew, I'd have to take over the driving. I still remember the corners which, in time, I took too fast, corners which frightened him. I try to avoid them now.

In the beginning, Matthew's visits to that clinic were routine: uncomplicated and once-weekly. The staff immediately took to him, because he was a pleasure to deal with – placid and polite and good-looking. Nurses called him Sweetheart. I always accompanied him, not only because it was part of the deal, but because I wanted to be on top of every detail of his future. For a while, I kept a notebook. We used to meet (not on the pavement outside, but) in a bookshop down the street. It seemed discreeter than dawdling in full view. Various doctors – their portraits pinned upon a board – were on offer, and, from day one, you were told to make your choice. I don't recall a picture of a female. Still: on the advice of a gossipy receptionist, Matthew opted for a youngish medic known as Willy-Nilly, whose actual name was Nilson – a decision prompted less by assurances that the man was devoid of *attichoode* than because apparently he hailed from Kingston. Matthew reckoned that, as kids, he and Willy-Nilly would have jumped on the same buses, and swum in the same baths, and kicked their heels in the same parks. Nilson, at our first encounter, confirmed this hunch. He urged us to call him Will. We never did. I was wary of chumminess. Better to keep our distance. Perhaps I lacked the inner authority to indulge in outward informality. But perhaps what I lacked was the forelock of servility so encouraged by certain physicians. Either way: meet Dr Nilson.

Nilson was a Mulierast – a lover of women – but this penchant wasn't publicized. Not here. Here, everything worked differently. Even the air flowed inward, was inverse. Hetties, being in the minority, kept their orthodoxy secret. And yet, notwithstanding such enigmas, I soon clocked the direction in which Nilson's willy nillied: for, despite his leather jacket and short-cropped hair and Ortonesque demeanour, he wore brown paisley socks with his black Levis, which – sorry – a queen would never do. Other doctors, the more popular full-on queers, some of whom were closet-Hivvies, you recognized from (not the Lancet, but) the bacchanals of yesteryear. Somehow that felt sinister. But perhaps I should explain the clinical mood of the era.

If this whole branch of medicine was anything, it was that ironic thing called Sexy. There attached to it a hip allure, a voltage more magnetic than mere vocational pull. For there sizzled round the edges of this modern scourge a seductive urgency – invigorated by ruby ribbons and eye-catching rainbows and fundraising galas and charity premieres and lashings of glittery showbiz. Anyone-who-was-anyone suddenly seemed, as if by spooky coincidence, to know someone who had danced with someone who had danced with someone who had It – Rock Hudson, for instance. And thus a new (inverted) kudos was accorded to professionals involved in Immune Deficiency Syndrome, certainly greater kudos than could ever have been found in – say – bacteriology. Yet it went beyond the strictly medical, this heightened search for a vaccine: it was also political. Indeed, you sometimes heard rumoured (not without good reason, in my opinion) that the leading institutes around the world – in Paris, London, and New York, particularly – far from working in unison, far from pooling the results of their research in an attempt collectively to combat what, by then, had become accepted as an epidemic of the direst potential magnitude, were being, if not actively deceitful, thrifty with their respective truths. They weren't mutually co-operative, those people. Sure, they all delivered recondite papers on Sustained-Release Zeropositive Thingummy-Jig, yet conflicting shades of fact betrayed their conflictive interests. This might explain why, if you sought to obtain independent information on the disease, you found yourself flummoxed by disparate pharmacological strategies and tables-upon-tables of contradictory statistics. But then – don't you see? – there were chemical fortunes riding on all this, and reputations to be gilded, and honorific scrolls and medals to be received – in Stockholm, ideally. So, in effect, the race was dual. Certainly there was a rush for the quickest cure, but there was also another, more considered rush, which perhaps worked counter to it: the rush for the glorification of the century's top medical genius. Tricky for those whose lives depended

upon scientists torn between two clashing goods: the good of
the public, and the good of the individual.

The atmosphere within our clinic, too, was sometimes tricky
– not least because, while you waited to be seen, your eye could
not ignore the presence of patients at various stages of diminution. The apparently healthy were (understandably) averse to
the spectacle of the patently stricken, who, notwithstanding
their dramatic loss of weight and shaven scalps and sunken sockets, could, on occasion, still be recognized as former pick-ups.
And the moribund, for their part, could appear vindictive in
their plight, for, without needing to spare you a glance, they
nonetheless enabled you to read their minds, which seemed
practically to broadcast: You haven't got a clue what you've got
coming. Furthermore, there was the risk of bumping into people you knew socially, such as the girl with out-of-orbit pupils
who had come to the party in Bedsitland. I once caught sight of
her – the only girl about – dragging herself through the foyer,
on crutches. We smiled as we passed. We said nothing. Would she
have assumed that Matthew and I were there for Matthew's sake,
or mine? She probably didn't give a hypodermic damn. But I
remember asking myself which I should have preferred: that she
took me to be ill (like her), or that she took me to be well (like
me). It was a discomfiting dichotomy; for, whilst I wanted to be
entirely identified with Matthew, yet I also wanted to be viewed
as safely apart – imagining that the healthier I myself remained,
the longer I'd be able to keep him alive. Mad.

But Matthew was bearing up. Occasional bouts of herpes, I
grant you; yet this, considering the stress of his parents' deaths
and the resultant hassle, was hardly surprising. Besides: herpes
was, by now, old-hat, old-fashioned; even people's aunts were
known to have it. Just slap on the cream and get on with your
life. That's what I prescribed. After all, Matthew didn't feel run
down; his weight remained high; his appetite hadn't suffered; he
never chucked up; he didn't have the runs; he wasn't getting
cramp; he didn't have rashes; he didn't feel lethargic; he wasn't

sweating at night. And his blood-count remained constant. It was, according to Nilson, just a matter of 'hanging in there'. It was also, according to me, a matter of deflecting my friend from worries about where the foe might strike: at his brain, at his gut, at his skin, at his lungs.

In point of fact, if anything was worrying Matthew, it was his age, dear. He had lately caught himself holding magazines at a distance. Road-maps, too, had become a pain to read, especially at night – all that stopping and starting against whizzing head-lights. Did one really need a prang? Exactly. So: bugger the vanity; let's get some glasses. And thus, on our next visit to Nilson, Matthew wondered – sort of by the by – whether he could have his eyes tested in the hospital, to save time. Some of us – he nudged me – had *jobs* to get back to; this was meant to be his lunch-hour. Nilson proved helpful about it. Sure, he said: good idea, main building, second floor; should be someone up there. So off we went, swanning through some massive, elec-tronically revolving doors that gave onto a magnificent atrium, reminiscent of a spanking Middle Eastern airport with glisten-ing granite floors. Perfect for cat-walking. Remember: you're a model.

We were borne up on the escalator. Rising through that vast, high space, you became amazed by all that you surveyed: palm-trees like great birds, fluorescent undulations of tropical aquaria, gigantic mobiles bobbing in mid-air, shiny cafeterias, busy people on their way. It almost made you want to wave. Presently we found Ophthalmology, and knocked on a door marked Reception. Out came a nurse. Did we have an appointment? Not as such, but we'd been sent – or rather my friend had – by Dr Nilson. She explained that the clinic hadn't started yet; ten minutes to go. I asked if we could wait. Fine by her. So Matthew went off in search of a phone, to ask some bloke at work to cover for him, and I was left to fantasize about a cigarette. Matthew returned. We settled to a debate on the relative merits of spectacle frames – steel-rimmed versus Trumans versus tortoiseshell. Next, an optician emerged. Chinese, I think. Tricky diction, but brisk and efficient. He ushered us in. You→here, he told me. You→there, he told Matthew. And then the lights were dimmed. Matthew was taken through the traditional ritual: pyramids of letters in gradual diminution, designed to make you squint; numbers without sequence; jumbled symbols in flashing chiaroscuro: circles, diamonds, crosses, crescent moons. The room was so still that it made you sleepy. Then, Matthew was put on one of those machines where the guy peers through binoculars while you just stare back at him. I remember thinking how handsome my friend looked amid all that apparatus – perspex strap across his brow; shiny hair above; cheekbones framed by aluminium bars; chin on rest; lips slightly ajar; jaw clenched hard; thick long lashes; eyes, unwavering, to the front. The optician said: We do other test with drops now; go to nurse outside, she bring you back. We were pointed to the corridor. We were told to sit in line. The gallery had become crowded. That's when I caught a glimpse of the pilot, but I didn't tell Matthew, because Nurse Pipette was busy putting some solution in his eye. Look up, she said; right up. Suddenly, Matthew was going shit-shit-shit. Christ. Agony. She said: Sorry, this your first time? That's when I panicked. I looked around. Everyone seemed (not just poor-sighted, but) viral. Too many wheelchairs for my liking. Then she went for Matthew's other eye. He was hissing like mad and clenching his fists and stamping his feet on the lino. Later he told me that he'd never known pain like it.

Vitreous surgeons are a weird bunch, not like any other strain of doctor that we were destined to encounter. Closer to astronomers, really. Dryly detached, almost devoid of personality. Not exactly versed in the diplomatic arts. But I think, to do them justice, that because their work involves observance of the eyes at such proximity, and sometimes into surfaces flooded with dyes which make the ocular globes look abstract – unearthly but beautiful, like planets afire – they tend to overlook the obvious: that the objects which they're scrutinizing belong to human subjects, with nerves and hearts and minds. A tear-duct may be one thing, but a tear is quite another. Even a run-of-the-mill optician knows that. Still, let's make this quick because it happened fast. By the time that Matthew was summoned back, his sight was blurred, his corneas numb. He kept looking down, and wanting to rub. He couldn't peer out. It seemed to affect his balance. The nurse said she would guide him, but I grabbed my boy away from her. I took him by the arm – as if his current penance were a saunter through the park. Once engulfed by shadows, I was told to help my friend sit down. I said: Gently, darling. Matthew fumbled for my palms. He had the softest hands. I steadied his warm head into those metal brackets. I retreated to the background. The specialist wriggled and faffed and muttered for a while; then, was done. The lights came up. He sighed, and suggested that we see MV. Who's MV? No, he grinned peculiarly, curving his thumb and index into a C. Very slowly he repeated: C . . . M . . . V . . . Understand? No, actually. This time he looked almost angry. It meant: Bad. It meant that the patient would go blind. CMV Retinitis, to be precise.

Back at the Hivvy clinic, Nilson commiserated with Matthew, and didn't sound too plastic about it. But then he went and fucked it all by saying: Forewarned is forearmed, so look on the bright side. Anyhow, CMV, it transpired, was an 'opportunistic' bastard, a member of the herpes clan. Its initials stand for Cytomegalovirus, which sounded paradoxically glamorous. Cyto-megalo-virus: you could roll the word about, really tongue it. But this was the first time that the nurses who regularly took Matthew's blood, and gave him pills and called him Sweetheart, patted his hand, looked a bit glum, and told him to keep his spirits up.

In the London of the time, two drugs were on offer to CMV sufferers. Both were at the initial stage of trials, both were intravenous, and both were lousy. I daresay that they served some preventative function, but, for people such as Matthew – the luckless who had passed beyond the luxury of prophylaxis –

they were of precious little comfort. And yet, as Nilson – eye-brows raised to mean: Do you want me to lie? – was honest enough to point out, those two drugs were all there was. So: which was it to be? Rock, or hard place? Devil, or deep blue sea? Up to you. Take your pick. Say your system rejects A? Switch to B. Say your system rejects B? Switch back. You can(not) but try. Do or Die. Matthew did. He didn't want to die. He chose the second drug – Ganciclovir – on the grounds that its final sylla-ble –Vir – struck him as quite manly. Flippant, yes? Well, flippant as it sounds, selection was as arbitrary as that, because both of those drugs, though innocently transparent, were equally nox-ious in substance. They eroded your veins to a mush. I remember some analogy about bleach being poured through a drinking-straw, so you get a measure of the subtlety. But let's not be sour: at least there was a way to circumvent such damage – surgery, as luck would have it. They shaved your chest, made an incision to your breast, introduced a little trinket – akin to a rubber pin-cushion – sewed you closed, and hey, you were back on your feet in no time. You could resume a normal life, hurrah. You could medicate yourself when you got up, spend the working day as if nothing were the matter, and, at sundown, enjoy the freedom of managing your own slow-motion decline. The infusion took two hours. You injected a needle into that surgical gadget, care-fully avoiding the stitches round the scar; you attached the needle to a tube known as a line; you watched telly while the liquid drip-dripped from some bag – hung from a hook behind a door, for example, like some old enema – and thus the juice flowed safely to your heart. Subsidiary veins remained intact. Quality of life. The box was called a Portacath, which made you think of lots of things – a mobile lav, a harbour somewhere, a lesbian porter in a block of flats. Anything but the future.

Before leaving Nilson's room, Matthew fixed a date to have his op. He wanted a few days' gap; needed to sort himself out. Work and stuff. As I led him out toward the encroaching night, he said: Thank Christ it's Friday. He felt half-stunned by what had happened, but – one just had to cope, didn't one? Pointless to mope. No bitter-queen shite. Unlocking his car, he gazed about and blinked a few times and reckoned that his eyes were still too dodgy to drive back. Could we go to my flat for a while? Sure. He opened the passenger door. I took over. Let's go home and have a drink, I said. And about supper – what did he fancy? Chinese, funnily enough. But, most of all, he fancied a bath. We parked and went up. He let the waters run until he'd found the perfect temperature. He lowered the blind. He lit a candle. I fetched him a glass of wine. He needed to relax. I knew that he'd be stuck in there for hours (Blanche Dubois), so, while he sloshed about, I telephoned Cara, ostensibly to chatter, but, more intentionally, to find out whether she knew what had happened to the Find, the eye-surgeon with whom I'd stupidly lost touch. Last she'd heard he'd moved to Cape Town. For good? For love.

Our exchange was brought to a sudden close – by Matthew; Matthew yelling out. I hung up, and went to find him a clean towel. I told him to give me a bloody chance. But he wouldn't; wouldn't stop; just went on shouting. I was standing, I recall, outside the bathroom, for such (then) were the prudish courtesies between us. Just come *in*, he screamed. So I turned the doorknob. And then I saw. He'd been shaving in the bath, with a mirror propped between the taps, when, suddenly, one of his eyes had packed up. In his panic, he had cut himself. Blood was running down, streaming from his face, oozing down his neck and clavicle in long loose ribbons of carmine, flowing into the steaming water and paling away to nothing. In any other context, I would have described the image as lovely. But here, there was no image. This was the context: Matthew covered his left eye, and said that everything else had gone (not red, but) black.

Hearing

You've heard of false alarms. This was almost one. I rang the place for Hivvies, to ask them to bleep Nilson, but Click: recorded answer: The clinic is now closed; please try our central switchboard. I tried. No-one replied. I phoned Enquiries. I jotted down the number for Casualty; dialled. Engaged. Engaged again. And then, in one of those brainwaves that can sometimes tempt you to believe in higher powers, I suddenly remembered the name of an eye-hospital where the Find had operated in the antediluvian past, before the floods. I bundled Matthew into the car and headed out toward the Eastern side of town. It was one of those rare, limpid nights in London when you can glimpse the lure of stars. It was also one of those nights when you have to watch your tongue. I couldn't ask Matthew to keep a look out for road-signs. Nor could I ask red herrings about Poseidon or the Dragon. I asked him to strap up. He tutted but complied – at a set of traffic lights. Drizzle began. Briefly I thought of the pilot, and of Kelly's old car. Matthew groaned about the wind-screen wipers. I thought that he meant their sound – the relentless squealing of rubber against glass – but no: it was their movement that he couldn't stand. He said it felt as if they were going (not from left to right to left, but) *at* him, attacking. We compromised: I switched them off until their use had become paramount, at which point he would close his eyes. His head lolled back and forth. I leaned across, and fiddled with the radio. Pressed On. In another of those instances that can make you wonder about higher powers, some easy-listening programme happened to be playing a number about how when you were down and they were counting and your secrets were all found out and your troubles took to mounting and the map you had led you to doubt and there was no information and the compass turned to nowhere that you knew and the doctors failed to heal you and no medicine-chest could make you well and no counsel brought you comfort and there were no more lies that you could tell . . . you should let your soul be your pilot – I pretended to be deaf. I turned to another station, which was airing some sepulchral Irish dirge, wheezing gothic melancholy from an asthmatic old melodeon. I pressed again. But Matthew said: Hang on. He liked that song. And, just as in Paris he had told me to Look at those tapestries, so now he told me to Listen to these words: Would I walk with him beyond the road's turning, where day took the valley that led into night? Would I walk with him all through his journey, or only till the light? If I would love him as he loved me, who cared how dark the night may appear? If I would love him as he loved me, he would know no fear. The signs on the road were just there to mislead him. The turn of the road – that's where he needed me: tears always blinded his eyes. But Matthew's eyes were dry. He wasn't into blubbing. Nor, much, was I. We had arrived. No problem parking.

Arm-in-arm we trod the long red stripe which, like a river of fresh blood, is painted along floorways in hospitals for the frail of sight. Not a soul about. Our steps, marking time, echoed through the sanitized galleries. Striplights shone harshly; neon from all sides; faint buzzing. Matthew's arm felt rigid in mine. I squeezed it slightly. He squeezed me back. We turned a corner, and another. At last we found a desk, behind an arch. The duty-nurse was fast and commanding: stood up; came round; made you feel in safe hands. Matthew seemed to relax and brighten. No, he wasn't in actual pain; just couldn't see out of his eye – his right one. She ushered us into a lift, and led us down to some buried department, full of chairs with padded wings and padded arms. Matthew sank into the comfort, stretched his legs, crossed his ankles, sighed. I told him I was going to the lav. I ran after the nurse, to fill her in on the MCV stuff. She said: CMV you mean? I said: That's the one. She told me not to worry; said to go keep my friend company while she called a doctor down, all right?

Not exactly. Tests again. Drops again. Pain again. But Matthew knew what to expect this time, so his response was more of resignation than alarm. After an elaborate examination, the doctor, who was young, removed his head-light and explained that Matthew's retina had become sort of semi-detached. He fumbled in a pocket, but swiftly took his hand back. He parked it on a thigh. I could tell that he was gasping for a fag. Takes one to know one. Only semi-detached? said Matthew. The guy looked baffled. Matthew admitted that, as retinas went, he would frankly have preferred a fully detached one with a swimming-pool and garage. The doctor laughed. Laughs would help us through the nightmare. But they wouldn't get the patient out of it. He was admitted at once. Supervision was vital. Super Vision. Vital.

Odd, driving back. Unsettling, unbalanced. I'd never been in that car without Matthew. And as I wended my way home through the nocturnal, unknown districts of an unknown nocturnal map, past carefree youths who were messing around outside pubs, or rushing headlong into clubs, it all felt wrong to me, weird and unreal and almost unjust, as if I'd been prematurely widowed without ever having been married. I was alert, but I was also tired. I ought to have been hungry, but I felt stuffed. It was too late to ring anyone. No message to play back. Silence. I went to bed with a tablet. I awoke before the larks. I flew into the shower. I was so wired-up that I mistook my tension for excitement. I made a cup of coffee and scribbled a list of tasks. With the former, I managed to scorch my mouth; the latter, I managed to leave behind. I drove to the hospital fast, in an attempt to beat the morning rush. Only halfway through my hurry did I realize that today was Saturday. The sun was out. The blossom was coming. Springtime at its most beguiling.

They had stuck him in a women's ward – no beds on the men's side; but still: better for the likes of us to be amid a gaggle of buttoned-up grannies than among a bunch of ancient codgers with their goolies hanging out of their pyjamas. Although Matthew's bed was curtained off, he pre-empted my arrival. He could tell my cologne anywhere. He went: *Bonjour Tristesse*. I peered inside. He put up a smile. He was sporting an eye-patch. I said: *Vada* the Pirate. He said: A little respect, thank you. I went to kiss him, but he flinched, drew back. You may kiss my hand. I obliged. I noticed a drip in his arm. I pretended that I hadn't done. He called me Captain. We were back on that old liner bound for Buenos Aires. I asked: Breakfast to your liking? Gone on a diet, he replied – the Nil by Mouth. He was wearing a cornflower gown. I said: What's this drag? He said: Off to the theatre, dear. To the theatre *now*? That's right: Hivvies go to matinées; soirées are for geriatrics. He winked with his good eye. But before I'd had the chance to wink back, everything had wound ahead, forward into a fluster: pre-med jab, chat with some consultant, visit from the anaesthetist, forms of consent to be signed, plazzy bracelet, paper bonnet, trolley, blanket, and – on your marks. I told him that he looked most stylish. He told me not to exaggerate. It was only pret-à-porter, darling; nothing grand. The wheels began.

Retinal detachments tend, in keeping with glaucoma and cataracts, to affect people past their prime, so, even in this anonymous, impersonal atmosphere, there was something special about Matthew: he was the ward's most junior incumbent, its (unsung) mascot. Yet, beyond such a distinction, a further distinction seemed to attach to the swift correction of his sight, for, in a hush-hush sort of way, it was understood that his future, unlike that of other patients, was curtailed, that he was in a critical race, that his life was doomed to go to waste. It felt strange to be walking in that (first) procession, pacing behind my friend, behind his head. Viewed from above, he looked so small, so vulnerable. He could almost have been lying in a pram. But my job was not to indulge in maudlin comparison. My job was to make him laugh, because his humour is infectious, and members of the medical profession, where leadenness can predominate, are partial to the occasional dose of levity. It makes a change. It earns you favour. And thus, thus favoured, we set off, with stewards and nurses in attendance. We drove into a lift marked Staff Use Only; ascended to the floor reserved for surgery; drifted along a sweltering corridor; passed a fire exit; crossed a notice of Emergency; and now the trolley was gently steered toward a wall. Our cortège had ground to a halt. I could hear walky-talkies, and beep-beeping noises, and bustle beyond. My cue to go. The scene had been stolen by strangers in masks and coats. I tried to underplay the moment. I told Matthew that I'd be back when he came round. He said: You better had; I'm expected at a *thé dansant*. Someone chuckled. I hesitated for a moment. I told myself to grow up. I bent down. My lips approached his brow. No chuckling now. And then I went – face twitching, eyes welling, throat in an uproar. To the shops.

Driving into the West End, I tried to memorize the list that I had left at home. I parked near a department store where, on account, they sold you the very world. The first thing which I bought was a shaver – battery-operated. The second: a toothbrush – rubber-handled, distinguishable from mine – plus a small tube of paste to last Matthew while he was hospitalized. Next, some sundries: tissues (man-sized), deodorant (non-scented), a spiky hairbrush of the brand that he liked, his usual gel, body-lotion from (not Perfumery, but) the chemist's counter. Upstairs, in the hi-fi department, I chose a stack of audiobooks to kill the boredom of recovery: television was bound to be out of bounds. I took the lift – one, two floors down. I continued on my round. I splurged on the best pyjamas to be had: white-on-white Sea-Island cotton with vermilion piping, plus a creamy dressing gown, plus – bugger sensible – a pair of velvet slippers. We shared a shoe-size. I went and bought some tuberoses, stalks of unrivalled ugliness whose heads are of scent beyond rival. I also bought a vase. Hospitals can't be relied upon. And then I ran out of hands. I loaded the boot of the car, climbed into the front, and strapped up. Matthew – he'd be out for the count by now. I'd been told to allow three hours. I had scarcely squandered one.

The hospital cafeteria was distinctive for two reasons: for the tentative, submissive way in which everybody drifted, and for its ubiquity of white sticks, which, jutting out aggressively, threatened, paradoxically, to make you trip. I joined the queue and grabbed myself a bite to eat. I poured myself a luke-brown coffee. I neared the till, paid up, and went to sit – feeling jittery, queasyish. Despite the humid heat, which put you in mind of the Palm House at Kew, there lurked around my bones a peculiar chill. Please not flu. I headed off in search of the car, managed to find it, and dragged my shopping out. I walked in past the foyer, went up to the ward, and turned sharply to the women's side. On Matthew's empty bed I dumped my spoils, and took the vase to find a tap. With my hands, I arranged the bunch. With my teeth, I bit off price-tags. I hung the dressing-gown, and looped its belt round. Slippers by the chair. Pyjamas in the cabinet. The remainder, in a drawer. Tidily. I scrunched and chucked the rubbish. Some old girl was telling some old girl: Them two seems like nice boys. Slowly I drew the curtain closed. I needed to lie down. I made me down to lie. A half-forgotten prayer, the *Memorare*, echoed through the waters of my mind; but – the flattened air, the broad monotony, the dullness of it all, I don't know – I must have nodded off.

Sounds of muffled motion. Sounds of steps approaching. Sounds of voices gaining volume. I sprang to my feet with a jolt. I put my shoes back on. I plumped up the pillow; turned it over. The curtain was ripped open. Made me feel at fault, exposed. I backed out of the picture, into the middle of the ward. Matthew had returned, but returned unconscious. He moaned most slightly. You might not have noticed. They shifted him across, over to the bed, with a tenderness that moved me. They took away the pillow; handed it to me. To have and to hold. Now they rolled him very gently round, onto his front, and placed his head in rigid profile, strictly to the left. The nurses covered him up, tucked him hard, said: There we are. I asked how it had gone. Early days, someone replied, and added: Fingers crossed. I said that I saw. Her glance was eloquent. It meant: You moron. And then they raised the sides of the bed, the metal bars, the prison of his cot. Head half-bound, eyes bandaged, he looked – oh – fabulous. Heroic. Romantic. Like the casualty of some great war. Home at last. Home and dry. My boy.

We were left alone. The swathe over his eyes lent to his cheeks a healthy sideward flush. His hair was damp and wild, as if he had passed through some tremendous storm in order to get back. The plaster on his shaving-cut made you think of a scratch from a branch in the night. His bony chin, unshaven, remained the chin of a fine young man. His earlobe, which I had never properly noticed, was small. His nostrils flared and retracted softly. His mouth was slightly ajar, as if about to utter, or break into a smile. His dimple would not subside. There was a placid beauty to his reposing countenance, a beatific something, a wisdom which, though impossible to describe, struck me. It struck me as lucky. I was perversely thankful. I wanted to be holding his hand when he woke up, but it was stowed beneath the blankets. The nurses caught me fumbling, and flung me out. I protested that I'd promised to be there when he came round, but they insisted that he'd still be groggy for hours. All through the night. Course they were sure. Done it a thousand times. Visitors had to go now. Come back first thing. And stop fussing. Just leave him to us. You look washed out. I went home, washed, and went out. Clubbing. It was to become a pattern.

Reviewing that time, I would describe the detachment of Matthew's retina as an important landmark – important for both of us. In his case, it proved beyond physical doubt that which, until now, had been open to mental denial: the premature beginning of his premature mortality. In mine, it proved something other – less brutal, less futile, and less immediate in the fathoming. Hitherto I had amounted to a ravel of contrasts, to a tangle without rhyme or rationale, to a mish-mash of advantages and handicaps. I had muddled through my changing stages guised as a figment, not a character, and existed in a state of mounting contradiction, until, far from having grown mature, I had merely grown extreme, become the personification of an oxymoron: strongly weak, politely rude, cleverly stupid. I defied straightforward definition. Little wonder that I should have seemed, and felt myself, incapable of making a straightforward living. Then came the retina thing, the watershed which was to induce a great, but gradual, alteration in my being. It infused me with adrenaline. It transformed my way of thinking. It lent focus to my feeling. It sharpened me to a pitch. And so, from a previously passive existence, devoid of initiative, I now sprang to an acute itinerary, charged with active responsibility. No room for lassitude. I had Matthew to busy me. I had a duty to fulfil, a role to inhabit; and I wanted, for once in my deficient history, to bring some credit to it – in order, whatever else, to provide my friend with the dignity that I had promised him.

For months beyond belief, I forgot to be languid. Instead, I bristled with vitality, seemed to live on tenterhooks. But what I was really doing, even as I wandered off alone to clubs, was, I realize now, spying on the crowd; keeping tabs. Sometimes I saw people whom I hardly recognized – not because they'd shrunk to shadows of their past, nor because they'd shorn their scalps down to the Belsen cut, nor even because, conversely, they had cultivated topiaries around their mouths, but because they'd opted, in desperate pursuit of muscular enhancement, to ram needles in their thighs. Those who imagined, simply because they no longer fitted into a conventional pair of trousers, that they had grown into icons, were little more than dollies trussed up as thugs, who, despite their anabolic growl, still held their mentholated cigarettes like damsels. Neckless and pneumatic, always on the brink of (not fulfilment, but) a temper tantrum, they would pose in halter-tops of camouflage, bursting at the cleavage, bloated at the gut, arms tattooed with garlands of barbed wire and jaded legends such as: All Loved Up. Too 'masculine' ever to dance, too wary of their treacherous waggle, those creatures clung together hard – biceps rubbadubbing, jaws thrust out, sights hell-bent on some phoney horizon – as if the darkened corner where they presided was (not a vain cavern without visible way out, but) some luminous, international VIP lounge.

Sometimes I met people whom I properly knew, and, on occasion, serious conversations resulted – regarding, for instance, who had just died. But when (less out of social regret than to learn how exequial productions were managed) I did attend some funeral, I also made a point of not telling Matthew – this despite the fact that, queers being what they are, those supposedly sombre gatherings were often cruisy as fuck. Throughout this time, a bizarre influence seemed to enrich my every action. Even the slightest, most banal encounter could furnish me with currency, a currency which, in some elusive manner, converted itself to energy; and this energy, in turn, I would take back to Matthew – often in the form of reported advice: The ex-boyfriend of Such-and-Such says that autogenics are a total waste of time. Or: Derek Doodah swears by jabs of megavitamin Y. More usually, however, my energy dressed itself up as anecdote. For instance: my tryst with a leather-bound (not biker, but) banker who, too sozzled to get it up, told me: Wait until you've witnessed my unruly member rise to its full majesty – and who, after an interminable half-hour, during which I contracted jaw-cramp, referred to his ejaculate as his Honourable Discharge. Or the time when I was taken back to a swishy council flat where sex-toys were displayed, with most particular exactitude, along the shelves of a mirrored cocktail-cabinet – as if to suggest that a dry Martini should only be made by hands wristed in manacles, and shaken, for best results, in a vibrating phallus. Or, come to that, the night when, in the throes of a sub-dom fandango, I found myself entangled with a doctor of Philology who kept calling his arse a cunt, and me, his arm-slave. And thus, even from the gutter of my sexual bankruptcy, there could rise, as if by magic, unexpected notes of laughter.

But my escapades weren't always funny. Once, at a staple old club, still staple despite a recent spate of drugs-busts, I was taken by surprise. The Haven was one of those massive, massively frustrating places where, if you let your attention, even for a split second, wander from a man whom you found attractive, you might lose him for the rest of your life; so while it was easy to get away from those who weren't your bag, it was harder to show interest with subtlety. You had to be up-front. Either you dared to risk rebuff, which, if delivered, sent you packing, or you yourself did the rebuffing and remained implanted. Several dance-floors were laid about this club, so if, like me, you were a solitary scavenger – disinclined to socialize – it was often awkward to decide what you most (badly) wanted: to dance near someone whom you fancied, or to dance to the music that you liked. Only seldom did the two coincide, and then, only for a brevity of tracks; which is why, for the most part, you dawdled awkwardly between two gerunds – dancing and desiring – and compromised by vacillating in the muddle of some halfway bar . . . precisely where you would have clocked me on the night which I'm describing.

From the stool where I sat slumped, I remember looking (not cool, but) up toward one of the club's high balconies, and catching sudden sight of Kelly under the glare of a skeltering light. Even from my distant vantage – my disadvantage – I could tell that he was flanked by a blue-eyed answer. It was something about the ease between them, something about their mutual, sensual understanding. They seemed to be smoking ganja; they had that woozy sway about them. Next, the spot had circled down, and round, and captured me, and, in that frozen instant, Kelly saw me back. He began to point me out. He waved a beckoning hand, as if exhorting me to climb to their plateau. His other hand he held as a visor. He looked handsome and deter-mined, poised and proud. I clambered to their height – via the lavatory, where a skinny boy was puking up. And crying about not standing it.

The couple was attired alike – black vests, black jeans, black boots, designer stubble. Together they nodded Hi. None of us embraced; no-one shook hands. Instead, a joint was trafficked round, like an emblem of some trust. I turned it down, which took some gumption, but the lovers rose above my stuffiness and beamed – at one another. They kissed with their eyes. My eyes felt embarrassed, like the eyes of a cuckold. Kelly glugged some beer from a bottle with a lime-wedge in its sphincter. He wiped his lips, and proceeded to introduce. But so noisy was the climate that, although I put my ear close to his shout, I failed to catch the name of this new paramour. I caught myself glancing at the paramour's flies. I leaned across and yelled: Your name is What? His name was: Hunter. I said that I was George. He seemed to know. He smiled. I smiled. Kelly screamed that Hunter was American. I could have told Kelly that; but anyway: his latest (lasting?) blue-eyed answer, who was ashly blond and very tanned, might perhaps have been a little older than my brother, and a little broader and a little craggier – although, among queers of Kelly's type, who, rather than exist as distinct halves, prefer to double up, it's always tricky to tell such people apart. For, once they've met and merged, they become a single item and that's that. Deed done. Don't ask. Indivisible and undoubted. Invincible for as long as it lasts. To me, it all felt discomfiting, less because I was the outsider – I was accustomed enough to that – than because Hunter was bound to have insider dirt on me. Occupational hassle. But he didn't look the vicious type. Actually, Hunter looked Germanic. Competent. Obliging. And – to do Kelly justice – yeah, dead fuckable.

I think that Kelly had, by this stage, relaxed. Certainly he seemed better grounded, more self-possessed than in the past. More grown-up. Perhaps this newest love had rendered him adult. But perhaps, too, his dalliance with the moral undercore of London's queer morass had lost, for him, its former charm; because, after his earnest cracks at friendship with that clique of viral blabbermouths who thought that Class was crap, and who called Kelly (not Pet, but) Public School Wanker, and who reckoned that Hets were naff, and that this whole affliction was a (not great wrong, but) human right, and that being on benefits was a Positive advantage, and that Limited Lifespan meant the latest lifestyle, and that Terminal pointed to (not The End, but) endless sprees on the never-never, and that Disabled discs enabled you to park on triple-yellow lines near porn-shops where they peddled Ketamine under the counter, well, Kelly must have had occasion to consider whether comfort was ultimately to be found among such company, the company of men for whom Straight Talk had nothing to do with waxing lyrical about vaginas, and everything to do with tips about cosmetics to conceal Kaposian lesions from the prurient glow of holograms. Men who, for all of their voluble anarchy, were to be found, within six months, silenced six foot under – while Kelly had the temerity to remain asymptomatic.

If earlier I had felt my Negativity to be disliked by a certain faction, now, years since his fracas with the Knife, Kelly too began to feel small darts of spite directed at him. The problem seemed to lie, of all the creepy ironies, with his very resilience, with the fact that he'd survived for longer than was (not explicable, but) polite – and further dared to do so without call for prophylaxis. What was more, by having outlived most of his peers – a blessing that appeared to weigh him with a peculiar, concomitant guilt – he seemed also to have lost any claim to continued sympathy. But how could a patient who flew, and flew so flagrantly, in the face of statistical probability *really* expect to have his questions taken seriously, particularly when, in his healthy obstinacy, he had declined to play the guinea-pig, and wouldn't – not even in the name of altruism – volunteer to pop a 'placebo'? See what I mean? We all make our choices, and Kelly's, though unsporting, had been simple: that his records be kept (not only confidential, but) clean. Free of experimental interference. The result was that the accordion of his charts, though it grew fat with repetition, would play no deadly melody. His check-ups became dreary. He could read predictability on his nurses' lips: Nothing new; see you in June. His doctors, too, seemed almost miffed; but given that Kelly had contributed to none of their research initiatives, why should this Non-Participant merit even hypothetical interest? And yet – to be fair to those clinicians – wasn't my brother being a trifle oversensitive?

You tell me. When, sexy as all get out in evening-studs and black lapels of double-breasted grosgrain, Kelly attended charity shindigs hosted by A queens – single QCs in need of a suitable fillip – he often prompted horns in men who, though plentifully homosexual, were first and foremost (not gay, but) attached to the medical profession. Yet no sooner had those men manoeuvred to shake hands with Kelly than they lived to regret it; for his talk, which was anything but small, swiftly awoke them to the fact that the figure who had at a distance seemed like pretty prey was, at closer quarters, a pitiless inquisitor. Between candle-sconces of rococo ormolu, he would pin his victims to the silken wall, until they, like helpless moths, began to flap and squirm: Don't get us wrong, but at this point asymptomatics aren't really the issue, because erm, without wishing to sound uncaring, those people have already been Exposed, quote-unquote, so they wouldn't be eligible for an eventual vaccine anyhow, which of course has always been our main goal, but because they're not – well – sick as such, they're not actually in need of our assistance, so it's sort of a tricky Catch 22 thing, but very nice to talk you, do excuse us, must just say hello to Professor Bl- *oh*, you *know* him, do you? And Kelly would bare his beautiful teeth.

I tell you: those people were something. Kudos radiated from them even in the glaring fiction of the Scene. Forget our former pin-ups – our porn-stars and our athletes and our actors and our singers. Now, no sooner had a figure allied to the common cause stepped into a club than word buzzed round the multitude. Punters-in-the-know would instantly drop everything to rush across the room like desperados at the first day of the sale-to-end-all-sales in a frenetic bid to snatch the chance to stand the hallowed guest a dram. Our queens would swarm round those messiahs like bluebottles round cowpat, eager to notch up brownie points which, with any luck, might earn them advantage – such as first-hand gen on some new drug. But the actual worth of such self-seeking gallantries only became apparent when its recipients – those doctors and nurses and health-workers and registrars – were overheard to rue, among themselves, the way in which their public profiles had come to impinge upon their private lives. Poor things couldn't even trawl the Heath without some patient crawling out of the woodwork. Oh well, no rest for the **wicked** (sense **3**: excellent or cool).

Kelly said that he was sick of all those people – full of bullshit; worse than useless. It was they, not the disease, who half the time were doing the killing. Those so-called experts were just pumping patients full of poisons which their livers couldn't take, and then, when it was all too late, making out that it had been a privilege knowing What's-his-name. Hunter, with a finely tuned diplomacy, now offered to get more drinks. Great, said Kelly; I'll roll us another spliff. He turned his back to the public and jostled me to shield him; and while he fiddled with the paper skins, I noticed, after the long estrangement between us, the long elegance of my brother's fingers. Ravers in the arena began to scream and blow their whistles: The Sign – that was the song of the season: *Was it so hard to find the key to turn your mind*? Hysteria hammered at your eardrums. Lunatics were dancing into loudspeakers. Kelly shouted: So I'm splitting. I stared at him, bewildered. He screamed that he had wangled a transfer from the City. A transfer to? The States. The States a*gain*? But not LA. He signalled me to guess. New York? Correct. Why? Lots of reasons. With his digits, he enumerated: (1) a change was as good as a rest; (2) he was cool about his health; (3) most of his London friends were ↑ (i.e. 'upstairs', meaning dead); (4) America paid better; (5) Hunter had a sub-let in TriBeCa. A sub-let *where*? Triangle Below Canal Street! he yelled, as if I were (not deaf, but) the Village idiot. He licked his spliff; now lit it. The deal was this: he and Hunter would swap studios, and Hunter would fly out to see Kelly every couple of weeks. Air-miles; bucket deals; tickets nowadays were cheap. I didn't have the nerve to enquire who would be stumping up for these – still less what Hunter did. I said: Very jet-set. Kelly said: Plain sensible. But – sensible or no – one thing is certain. When my brother told me of his intention to move away, I felt a great heavy burden remove itself from me – in part because his resolve must mean that his health remained unimpaired. Mostly, however, I felt relief because his absence would enable me to concentrate, without conflicting obligations, on my friend.

Which is where the surprise came in. Hunter was back – with beers for Kelly and him, and a rattling great vodka for me. How'd he known what I was drinking? Kinda guessed, he grinned. Kelly rubbed his bottle against the grain of his lover's bristle, took a swig, and went on talking. Hunter took a toke on the new spliff, swallowed lengthily, and leaned over the balcony. He left us to it. We retreated into a corner, away from the din. Kelly said – in a calculated tone which brought our mother to mind – that it appeared that I'd been seen at hospital appointments with Matthew. My heart began to thump, as if I'd committed some crime, but all I said was: And? And this: Kelly hoped I wasn't getting *In* too deep. Meaning? Well, come on, Matthew was only his ex-lodger; I shouldn't get things out of proportion. I didn't argue. I didn't try. I could tell where Kelly was gunning. And now he opened fire. He said that I shouldn't wear myself out. He said that I should save my stamina. He said that you never knew how things might turn out. He said that the day might come when I was called upon to look after Blood. And, at that very moment, I swore to myself that whatever bloody happened I wouldn't be *In* on Kelly's final cameo. I asked if he had told the monkeys. What about? (He obviously hadn't.) I said: The Big Apple. He ignored this tangent, reverted to Matthew, and said that he was only joking; to lighten up. But he wasn't − not entirely. I finished my drink. I had to get back. I claimed that I was tired. Kelly gave a nod − to mean: I understand. I kissed him. He kissed me back. I wished him luck. Hunter came across and gave me a sort of hug. And then I left the club.

The morning after Matthew's operation was a Sunday; but, thanks to barricades erected for some marathon, I reached him later than I should have done. Breakfast trays were already being wheeled out. A fresh team of nurses had taken its stand. The ward had been returned to the stuffy quiet of weekend apathy. In the distance could be heard a television, playing religion: Remember our brothers and sisters who have gone to their rest in the hope of rising again . . .

Matthew was lying on his front, face to the side. His eyes were still bandaged. He was wearing his new pyjamas. The drip had been taken out. The near side of the cot was down, but I couldn't tell if he was napping. I wondered whether drawing the curtain would wake him up. Suddenly, he thanked me for the flowers. His voice made me jump. I asked how he'd known about them − smelled them in the night? No, some nurse had dropped the vase. Typical, I said. He chuckled. What was so funny? He said that it was murder finding decent staff. I tuned into his wavelength and replied that this was hardly a liner bound for Buenos Aires. His thoughts entirely, Captain. And then he told me to look at a form which had been left on the chair beside him. I picked it up. Some old girl was telling some old girl: His friend is back.

Illustrated on the form was a cross-section of an eye with a baffling couple of arrows, and, alongside, an equally baffling diagram of a man snoozing at a table, shaven head reposed upon crossed arms. There was a Buddhist flavour about him. Over his tranquil outline, the title of his tale was writ large. I read aloud: INSTRUCTIONS FOR POST-OPERATIVE POSTUR-ING. *Posturing?* spluttered Matthew. Was this some modelling assignment? I told him to shush: a nurse was headed for us. She arrived – to take off his bandage. And thus, while unwinding it, she spared me the trouble of wading through the rest of the mumbo-jumbo.

Posturing was a process vital to recovery. It varied depending on the specific nature of the detachment. Its purpose was to ensure that an oil bubble, inserted during surgery into the patient's eye, exerted maximum pressure on the section of the retina which required flattening. In Matthew's case, she said, he must lie on his front, or sit forward if he liked, but always keep his face – she checked the form, then emphasized – Right Side Down. On no account should he go on his back. Matthew said: Doggie-position here we come. I said: Needs must. Matthew said: Devil drives. The nurse said: Would you keep your voices down; you're in a ladies' ward, if you don't mind.

I asked how long this posturing lark was meant to last. Procedure, she snapped, and reckoned – assuming that no com-plications cropped up at the halfway check-up – that it took three weeks on average. Matthew went: Christ. I went quiet. (Three weeks? Didn't she know about the Hivvy stuff? How was Matthew meant to get to the clinic for his infusions of Ganciclovir?) I said: Are you seriously telling us that people are expected to remain in a fixed position for three whole weeks? She told me that if I bothered to read the literature I would see that patients got ten minutes' grace per hour. And then she added that, all things considered, Matthew had got off quite lightly. I asked: Quite lightly how? She replied that some poor chaps had to posture upside down. What, like bats? That's right. Matthew supposed that he ought to thank his lucky stars. I said that I wouldn't myself have put it as strongly as that. But the nurse said: Done. She left with the bandage. The patient was left with a pad across his eye, strapped from his forehead to his mandible. It itched like mad. His other eye, he said, felt fuzzy but fine. About Posturing, his sole remark was: Can't be helped, just have to manage.

Next day, I rang his office to explain what had happened, and to let them know that Matthew had been told to rest for (not three weeks, but) a full month. (I needed extra leeway for the additional [secret] insertion of a Portacath.) The voice at the other end said that it was sorry to hear all this, and that Matthew's colleagues were bound to want to send a card. In which case, I pointed out, they shouldn't post it to his address, but to mine. And who was I? Did it really matter? The Voice went: Touchy, are we? I answered: Just in a hurry; d'you want to send that card or don't you? The Voice took down my details, but, before I'd said that Matthew would be phoning once he'd been discharged, it had hung up. I couldn't stop – or start – to worry. I telephoned Nilson, and tried to sound calm. I repeated the retinal saga. I explained about Posturing. He agreed that the installation of the Portacath would have to be put back. I added that I was worried about Matthew's Ganciclovir: couldn't a nurse be sent to inject him at my flat? Nilson thought that oral medication ought to keep him ticking for now. He would send a prescription down to Pharmacy. I could fetch the tablets any time. I said: I'll do that. Then I drove to collect Matthew. He was dressed and smiling. He had an end-of-term air about him. His belongings had been put in a yellow plastic bag – emblazoned with the scarlet motto: DANGER – DESTROY BY INCIN-ERATION. I took it from his hand. I offered him my arm. He said: Steady, Captain. I said: Won't you tango? He said: Not without a corsage. We left the flowers behind, and the vase. Don't forget those Posturing Instructions.

Matthew postured. I instructed. Neither of us much relished the parts imposed on us, but he was right: it couldn't be helped, and we did manage – managed to work it out. Patience is a (not virtue, but) bugger. You don't have to admire it: it need only be recognized. And while I recognize those long three weeks as a cycle of rhythmic sufferance, of tacit consent granted hourly, of monotonous, repetitive transfer, I also acknowledge them as a period of value, with lessons to be learned and rewards to be garnered. Though cast in sharpest contrast to our actual personalities – his, so independent; mine, so indecisive – our temporary roles were equally sharply defined. This helped. Matthew's convalescence may have been a penance, but it was never a muddle. It was simply, I later came to realize, a test on the subject of Time. It taught you the difference between making it and wasting it, between beating and killing it. It taught you about its unreality. It taught you how to fill it, how to fool it, how to profit despite it.

Our days became directed by the alarm, but we didn't let its tyranny undermine us: the fight felt worthwhile – worth the fighting chance that Matthew would recover his full sight. During those fifty-minute lulls, his job was to keep his head stilled, even as his brain kept running. Mine was to prepare for the forthcoming flurry, the 'grace' which that nurse had made sound like a carrot – so that my friend could snatch a bath, or have a shave, or clean his eyes, or grab a bite, or take his pills, or stretch his legs, or go to the lavatory. Such were the paltry awards for his endurance. But I noticed, while he endured, that the noise of my activity was counterproductive – not because he griped if I made a racket, but because, when I did, he seemed to ask, more frequently than otherwise, what was the time. And thus I learned to wander like a shadow, with slow music in the background – *molto legato, tranquillissimo, lento, largo*, the classical tempi of enforced calm – while the long hand of the clock performed its dreary round and, sluggishly but surely, approached the X on its dial. Time.

Take his baths. You just needed to be practical: run his water in advance, place his towel close to hand, remove all objects except soap and sponge, lay down a mat, leave his lotion on the basin-surround, hang a fresh pair of pyjamas on the heated rack, unbutton the jacket, and, once everything was organized, lead him from the place where he lay slumped – the four-poster bed, the mahogany table, the sofa – to the better place where, for a fleeting while, he could immerse himself and vanish in the steamy, hydrotherapeutic past of Blanche DuBois. You closed the door, and, as he rested from his tiresome rest, you did whatever needed to be done: air rooms, change sheets, plump cushions, push vacuum, re-set the alarm. Valet-stuff. Small fry. But when I went about those tasks, I would also think about Matthew; and I would think about the thought of blindness; and I would shut my eyes. And I would stumble in the shambles. I would find myself unable to get far, even in my own, familiar surroundings. I couldn't engineer a corridor without reaching out for the wall. I couldn't pick the proper key for the front door. I couldn't dial the telephone – not by touch alone. I couldn't strip a new CD of its cellophane. I couldn't light a cigarette. I couldn't set the microwave. I became useless. But I could cheat, needless to say: I could peer for an illicit second, as if peering from beneath the darkness of some sadomasochistic blindfold. Why? To glean the things that might need to be known if things went wrong.

Which they did not. At the halfway check-up, we met with the vitreous surgeon. Prognosis: So far so good. No promises, but he felt optimistic about Matthew's progress. He said that the padded gauze could come off. It was replaced by a pink plastic patch with a tiny central hole – funkily prosthetic, modern. We were led toward the exit, and told to keep on posturing. We were reminded that our next appointment would be back at the Hivvy hospital. Matthew thanked the man, grabbed my arm, and headed for the central hall. He said: My pins feel wobbly. I said: You must be wearing the wrong stockings. He stopped, parted his coat, fumbled around his trouser-pocket, and, striking a Betty Grable pose, announced: My suspender's broken. He raised his head, and wondered of the world: Anyone got an aspirin? I said: What for? He said: To fix it, of course. But no-one did. Not even here. So we drove home. Christ, Isadora, mind that corner.

Afternoons were always easier. Around two thirty, after we'd eaten, I would switch on the washing machine. There was something soporific in its distant circularity, a hypnotic comfort to its monodrone. Matthew liked to take his siestas in the bedroom. Meanwhile I would sneak a nap on the sofa, or make calls about which I didn't want him to know. But when he awoke, it was always in a brightened humour: the back of the day was broken. So I would take advantage of the moment, and try, if it was needed, to cajole him into the trickiest of our chores: hair-washing. This he loathed – because he couldn't manage on his own. And it *was*, to tell the truth, a bit of a performance. You sat him on the lav and plonked yourself on a chair opposite, with a basin of warm water on your lap and a hand-shower attached to the taps. You secured a square of clingfilm over his bad eye, to prevent shampoo from getting at it; and, once you were ready, his job was to lean forward, bend his head right over, and cover his face with his hands. But he tended to play up; liked to drama-atize; would make great weeping sounds, as if he were wailing by some tragic riverbank. So I would tell him not to be such a Mariah – an allusion to the woman of Magdala – both because her testamental sobs have earned her the word Maudlin, and because her **riah***, as everybody knows, was gorgeous.

In the evenings, we usually had company. Visits syncopated the routine, relieved its tedium. Occasionally, friends of Matthew's, strangers to me, would drop in – a couple of women from work,

*****riah** hair (Parlare backslang).

perfectly nice in an auntly way; Anna, his former (art-school) girlfriend; Tony, his first homosexual acquaintance, since turned schoolteacher and since 'turned' straight; a devoted couple of lesbians; but, for the most part, those who visited were people whom we knew mutually. Shared connections. I remember the night when Cara came – exuding, despite the tousled strain of a day with schizophrenics, her customary serenity. She brought a present: a cassette of Love Poems recited by Richard Burton. This turned out to be a felicitous selection, because Matthew, we discovered, had long since held a candle for the handsome Welshman. And Cara must, to some extent, have shared this admiration: she had specialist information: she knew, for instance, that some critic had once credited the actor with having a cathedral in his eyes. Matthew twanged the elastic of his patch, and said: Never mind the eyes, dear; what about the cathedral in his pants? Cara said: Alas, I know not *that* . . . But when, a few days later, Douglas pitched up, grinning from ear to ear and brandishing a bottle of Galliano, this token proved less of a triumph – not because it didn't get drunk, and not because we didn't have a laugh, but because, after he'd gone (to meet dull Jack), it earned me a mild reproof from Matthew. Did I really have to go repeating all that Santorini stuff? So, to make amends, I told him the story about the dugs. I think, on balance, that it balanced out.

Not long thereafter, Kelly rang – to announce his departure. Leaving when? First thing tomorrow, from Heathrow. Matthew was lying beside me, posturing on the sofa, but I told Kelly nothing. I felt both ashamed and protective. Bizarre. Anyhow, Kelly said that he had sod-all other news; just wanted to let me know. I asked how could I get hold of him. Preferably through Hunter on the London number. I told him to give Hunter mine. He already had. (Distance – Kelly wanted it, wanted it established. I went along with that.) Gotta go, he said; and hung up. As I replaced the phone, I had a recollective flash of his first trip to America, of our parting kiss at Gatwick, of the pang which, then, had struck at my hopeful heart. How altered, how adult, everything felt now. Matthew yawned and stretched and asked: Some fancy-man? Very bloody likely; just Kelly – off to the Big Apple. The town may be changed, Matthew said, but the well could not be changed. What was he talking about? Confucius, darling. Did I know nothing?

And thus, between his wisecracks and those book-tapes and our music and our friends, the Posturing eternity came to an end. The Chinese specialist who had first detected Retinitis declared the operation to have been a success, and supposed, with a shrug which defied interpretation, that Matthew could, if he wanted, have some spectacles made. In retrospect, I recognize that shrug as having meant: Don't waste your money. But at the time, I thought: Sod this for a game of chopsticks. I spoke to my own oculist and explained the position. She said: Absolutely. I was to take Matthew to see her. She would see what could be done.

I recall our appointment as magical, not because anything miraculous happened, but on account of Matthew's reaction. The oculist asked him to sit down. She slid a pair of empty frames – steel-rimmed and infinitely adjustable – up to the bridge of his nose, slipped the metal arms over his sideburns, propped them on his ears, and said: Remember, this is all about trial and error. She began to insert before his eyes, and swap around, a whole array of glassy discs, with convexities of various degrees. Matthew kept demurring, murmuring doubts; couldn't seem to make up his mind; wouldn't decide whether this latest lens was, or wasn't quite, better than the last. To me, it looked as if he were resisting any choice that might prove too rash, too final. In fact, he was merely being exact; observing his exacting standards. This, after all, was his chance to make up for lost time, to return from his retinal exile, to reclaim the state where once he had conjured, and conjured so powerfully – the state of the visually inclined. When, in due course, the perfect combination had been found, I recall how he stood up and gazed around and marvelled. Amazing, was his adjective. His smile was an enormous grateful rapture. I presumed recovered focus to lie behind such sudden excitement. But I was wrong: the sharpened image came as no surprise. He had imagined that. His wonder seemed to lie with the return of colour to his sight, with the shimmer of those reds and blues and greens and oranges and violets. He said that it was as if the last few weeks had been in black-and-white, whereas now, suddenly, the whole rainbow had come alive. He called the feeling very Dorothy. The oculist laughed. She wrote him a prescription, folded it in half, and placed it in his hand; and No, she said: no charge. Matthew didn't answer that he wouldn't hear of it. He answered: That's incredibly kind. And then, we raced away to order his new glasses, at the fastest place around. He entrusted me to choose his frames on his behalf. I trust that I chose rightly – with my heart. The specs were ready in a matter of hours. Matthew said that they were fab, surprisingly light and just the right side of designer. Yet he cannot, when he looked into the looking-glass, have failed to note how one lens magnified far harder than the other. His blighted eye seemed disproportionately large and dark, almost ugly, almost bovine. But at least, I told myself, he was looking (not inward, but) out. Look out.

I only knew my friend to lose his temper once, and it happened that same night, on the eve of the insertion of his Portacath. Fitted with his new glasses, he reclaimed the ignition of his car and drove us to his flat. He sorted through the mail, paid a few bills, and, while he enjoyed one of his baths, played Julie London. Cry Me A River. Moments Like This. They Can't Take That Away From Me. I mooched around the garden, which was wildly in flower, abundantly bedraggled. I remember old wisteria. I remember ancient vine. I remember premature nostalgia. I came inside. We tidied up, and, before dusk – to avoid the glare of twilight – headed back to town. Not much traffic.

We parked outside my house. We strolled locally for supper. We drank. Of course we drank. Wouldn't you have done? And then we went on clubbing. From lazy expediency we chose a place nearby – once called Sugar, now called Plumb.

The joint was jumping. Queers, in those days, seemed not to work much: either they had opted for voluntary redundancy, or, as often, been sacked. England was going through an unfavourable economic patch, which, favourably enough, pro-vided bosses with a blur between commercial common sense and common sexual prejudice. Belt-tightening referred to (not loss of weight, but) financial restraint. Regrettable measures; unavoidable cutbacks; terribly sorry; best of luck. But you wouldn't have believed it, not in Ghettoland, where any night was party-night and luck was up for grabs. Monday, Tuesday, Friday, Sunday; it really didn't matter. Business was doing just fine. Drinking and dancing and drugging and fucking. Little else to live for, when you thought about it – which, of course, you seldom did, because it was the working of your thoughts, and not the thought of working, which might upset your balance. What you sought was nocturnal respite from diurnal nightmares – at whatever cost, and in whatever guise. I was personally baffled by the changes which had come over the Scene: pen-sioners, marooned survivors of our flood, wearing Walkmans at the bar, as if yearning for the harmonies of another land, a land upon which Wolfenden had never chanced; under-agers, late arrivals to the viral avalanche, wielding, with rings on touch-tone thumbs and studs piercing their tongues, cell-phones in the lavatory; grown men sucking lollies in the subculture, to provide their mouths, parched by uppers, with recreational saliva; body-builders smearing VapoRub on one another's pectorals, the better to inhale the fumes of abandon; streetwise urchins, expert fiddlers of the dole, wearing trainers on the dance-floor, as if, at any moment, they might be called upon to bolt. It was all a far cry from the Moonlight, which had recently closed. Member-ship had fallen, people had moved on, and well, you know how it goes. Hans had retired – to Hove. But no-one gave a toss, because frankly, that whole other world, with its petty codes and snobberies, was Over. People now were Out & Proud. Sorted. Their love shone a light; their search was for the hero inside; their lives were guided by visionary anthems; their flights, by the stuff of silver linings. But Matthew didn't see it that way. Not tonight. Tonight he saw it as I could never have done. With twenty-twenty accuracy. With new (not eyes, but) glasses.

Our tumblers glowed a luminescent aqua. We retreated from the bar. We headed for a passageway known as the Meat Rack, where, in shadier times, our men had hung about like ravenous carnivores, but where, ever since the lights of vigilance had been turned up, they merely went to chat. It was no longer very popular, this narrow gallery. And yet, when Matthew and I arrived, we were surprised to find it packed – with Fatties. I use this term advisedly, in the same advised (but cautious) manner as one might say Bears or Chubs – labels which, though likely to inspire mirth in some, are as likely, in others, to incite an ursine disgruntlement. Nowadays, of course, you can access endless websites dedicated to this hybrid speciality where obesity is the bottom line and orgasm, it is argued, attainable by rubbing stomachs. You can crawl round subterranean chatrooms where novices are tutored on the most effective means of gaining forty pounds within a fortnight. You can learn from armchair-Sumos about poultry-hormones to broaden the buttocks. You can download underpanted flabby-snaps of bearded odalisks in drooling attitudes designed to inspire the drool of others – squatted on picnic hampers, for example, tongues lapping at jumbo-jars of honey. That is now. But at the time of which I write, Fatties were a novelty to us, a curiosity brought from America, which is the continent of fantasy-becomes-reality. I don't deny that since forever, ever since passion began, homosexual passion has admired – perhaps overmuch – the virginal aspects of manhood: its beauty and its youth and its gracile outline, its smoothness and its lightness and its fleeting loveliness.

Nor do I deny that as a physical ideal, this aesthetic, which over-looks pubertal silliness in the name of hot young blood, may have seemed tyrannical to those who (however big their brains, however big their hearts, however big their hopes and appetites and incomes) felt marginalized by the classical standard – those against whom the odds of being desired seemed mercilessly stacked, and for whom the word Slim was hopelessly shackled to the word Chance. And yet, whatever one's sympathies for those outcasts in an underworld already outcast, something should perhaps be clarified. When Fatties began, long after Stonewall – but *en masse* – to agitate for an erotic profile and kick against Adonis, who, to their collective, epitomized the constraints of the traditional physical archetype, this was not, as tends to be made out, because they were docile and cuddly and shy and, accordingly, reticent about making a public stand. It was for a subtler reason, less to do with poor self-image than with a sharp sense of timing. Hitherto, excess weight had, in the general con-sciousness, been associated with high cholesterol and heart attacks, whereas leanness had been linked to lively vigour and ebullience. But suddenly everything was otherwise. Thinness now pointed, and pointed overpoweringly, to illness, which provided fat men with the perfect opportunity to wade forth from the beaches of (postcard) ridicule into the homosexual mainstream. Unprecedentedly, the more massive your girth, the further – the safer – you seemed from the jaws of disease; the more wholesome and fortunate and privileged. And it was in the context of such privileged creatures that, as Matthew and I squeezed through their midst, some soft great arm bashed into his wrist, and vodka went flying at a pair of furry tits, whose owner, outraged, growled at my friend: Watch where you're going, you blind twat.

Matthew didn't apologize. He moved ahead, slightly unsteadily, trying to wipe his hand. He led me in the direction of a second bar, where people at that time played snooker and darts. His drink had all but vanished. I suggested another. He can't have heard. He glanced around. His damaged eye was welling up. His mouth had hardened. Listen, he said; you may not believe this, but there was a time when men stood back for me. I could have had anyone. Anyone I wanted. And now, just look around. What a load of sour-faced wankers. It really makes me angry. I mean, *I* wouldn't touch them if you paid me, but what's *their* big gripe? Don't know? Well, I'll tell you. It's this bloody Retinitis. My specs give me away. I may as well have my cell-count written up in lights. People can read the signs, and they don't like being reminded. I may have done my share of sleeping around, but those shags of mine were twenty times better-looking than this sad bunch, and funnier and kinder. And *spare* me the shit about Sisterhood. No, I won't calm down, because there *is* no bloody sisterhood. It's all a sham. It's every-one for themselves now. Every selfish faggot minding his own pathetic back. My sight may be buggered, but I'm not *blind*, and I'm not a complete retard, and one thing's for sure: in *my* day, that fat git at the Meat Rack just wouldn't have got a look-in. Wouldn't have dared open his mouth. Just goes to show how tragic this whole scene's become.

I was stunned. I should have been prepared, I realize now, for an outburst of this type, but the rant had been so sudden, and so counter to Matthew's usually easy character, that I had no ready word of comfort – except, that is, for: Vodka? Drunk enough, he replied; but then: Sod this, let's dance. We wove behind the snooker gang and through the queue for darts, toward a further, lower space from which frenetic music blasted out. Coloured lights flashed round the ceiling like euphoric astral shafts; but the floor, as we drew close, loomed lunar-dark. Matthew said: You go in front. I wanted to take his hand, but stopped myself. (Don't patronize.) I led our progress down a wobbly gangway. As we joined the revelling masses, whose spines seemed to stiffen at our passage, I felt Matthew's fingers hook onto the back of my waistband. I was glad of his (not reliance, but) trust. And yet, I would say that in our strange romance, in our strange exchange of trust, this was the night which marked the unfolding of his cloud. Matthew entered the miasma looking down; Matthew who had always held his head so high. Can you imagine? Can You Feel The Love Tonight?

The multitude was chanting: *It is where we are!* – and God help you if you thought otherwise, because those sweating zealots, however headless and undone, knew their stuff, were on the way back; they had every line off pat. I tried to push ahead, deeper into the mindlessness, but punters, as if hoping to puncture the stars, were pumping their fists into the heights, and grinning with a savage sort of jubilance, and making it hard. You should have seen them preen and grind to the rhythms of their fallacies. You should have witnessed their ecstatic hands touch whatsoever they felt like touching. You should have heard the gushy mantras that spouted from their mouths as they proclaimed that yeah, it was enough for this restless warrior just to be with me, it was enough for this wide-eyed wanderer that we got this far. But the truth is that the scorn poured on my friend that night was enough to make both kings and vagabonds believe the very worst. Enough to make you a homophobe. I came to a halt. I cleared a space. And suddenly, there we were, in the middle of hell: the two of us pitted against the rest – out of kilter, out of humour, and in bad odour.

While Matthew tried to dance, he kept turning his head away. The lights were getting on his nerves. I could tell that he was telling himself to be patient, that he needed to get used to his new specs. And then, from somewhere in the midst of the frenzy, from a splintered second in the rave, a happy shiny elbow went Bash into his ribcage. A spotted nonentity smirked a meaningless apology. But Matthew glowered at *me* – as if to say: See what I mean? I signalled: Want to split? He shook an angry index, making clear that No, he damn well didn't. He was sticking here. I persevered. I felt both flushed and chilled, torn between wanting to dance for myself and wanting to dance with him, between rising above the scummy tide and sinking with it, between screaming Matthew's difference and concealing it. He was fumbling in his jeans. He found, and produced, a handkerchief – pressed and squared and almost too pristine. He opened it with a slow flourish, and into its folds he commended his glasses, and he slipped them into his shirt, into the pocket at his breast, over the place where, this very day, fate was to cut him open. I glanced at his face, but his eyes were closed. And now he began to smile, to smile to himself and sway, sway as he had always done, with graceful calm, with slow great confidence, until – for pity's sake – he got bashed again. I myself would, at this point, have given up, have called it a (lousy) night. Yet Matthew's spirit was not to be cowed. His pride would not allow it. My own pride smarted on his behalf – until next, in the way that these things happen, we found a victorious way round, a triumphal compromise. I took hold of Matthew's wrist, and then his hand, and placed my other hand behind his back; and now, as if no-one else and nothing mattered, as if finally we had alighted at most beautiful Buenos Aires, yes, we properly danced. And although earlier, years back, long before this tale got ugly, you may have sneered at that pair of silly queens who went to learn the tango, you had better believe that no sillie queenerie ever proved more timely. Because, despite the unfolded cloud, despite the toxic climate, Matthew and I managed to dance as we deserved, absolutely as one, absolutely encoupled, my beloved friend and I, on the spot and very fast, faster by far than all those wound-up funsters who, at long bloody last, got out of the sodding way and watched out. Thanks, guys. So kind.

We left before the closing hour, but late enough. Matthew didn't bother with his glasses, not until we were outside. He put his arm around me, and, as we strolled toward my flat, said: Sorry I lost my rag. I replied that there was nothing like Catharsis. And I must have been right, because he quipped: You mean Portacatharsis. We got home. We collapsed. We both took a tablet. I clicked off the bedside lamp. Matthew warned: No funny business, Captain. His wish, I said, was my command. We floated into a soporific drowse. His breathing was constant. It dipped and rose like a summer sea by night. He didn't sound anxious. My chest was thumping.

The insertion of a Portacath, though procedurally delicate, was (Nilson assured us) neither risky nor worrisome. So long as one managed to stave off infection, all should be fine. In his experience, Portacaths had served some patients marvellously. I wondered for how long such patients had required the marvel; but Nilson, innocent of my scepticism, reiterated the wisdom behind this minor intervention: it enabled patients to manage their own medication, plus it put paid to the danger of damaging arm-veins. Veins, he explained, increased in size as they travelled toward to the heart – rather like roads on the map, which got bigger as they neared London. Matthew burst out laughing: he wished that he could say the same about the men who came to town. Nilson pretended not to be embarrassed. Instead he said: Nice one. And, after patting Matthew's back, sent us across to the main hospital.

Matthew had been allocated a single room – a surprise which, far from causing him disquiet, he welcomed. En-suite bathroom; stroke of luck. I suppose that he must have been adequately treated by the nursing staff, because I remember nothing about them. The mind tends to cling to the bad stuff. But his surgeon, whom I do recall, was a good man, dry in the right manner – honestly unsmiling – a quality far preferable to 'personality'. Characterful medics have always struck me as suspect. Think of Kelly's Knife with his natty ties and aureole of grandeur. Anyhow; the operation went without a hitch, and Matthew, after the postponement caused by his retinal detachment, appeared to be relieved to have this other, pending trial behind him. By the following morning he was walking around, spirits braced, specs in place, putting a brave face on whatever the future might be holding. Although he admitted to feeling squeamish about having to inject himself, he claimed to be delighted with the Portacath. He said that the scar, with such dinky needlework, exceeded his wildest expirations. And thus, within thirty-six hours, having mastered the long ladder of steps required to flush and sterilize a line, and inject an infusion of diluted Ganciclovir, and govern three-way taps and Sterets and needles and phials and bungs, he was back at his flat – ready to cope, ready to work, ready to drive, ready to resume a 'normal' life.

I should have found some private comfort from my return to inaction, but, oddly, the respite that resulted from the insertion of Matthew's Portacath only conspired to churn me up. It felt like waiting for a race to start, like hanging about for the inevitable shot of gunfire. During the next few weeks, when I ought perhaps to have been harnessing the stamina which Kelly, before vanishing to America, had wrongly assumed to be his right, I expended it by screwing around and worrying – worrying less about whom I was screwing than about things that I wanted for Matthew. I knew what I could bring to him: my loyalty and my love. I knew what I had promised him: dignity and laughter. But I also knew what was beyond me to provide. I suppose that what had triggered me had been his outburst at that club – about how once upon a time he could have picked up anyone he wanted. And what I wanted for him now – while there still was a chance – was, of course, sexual satisfaction. I have since had cause to consider what it was that held me back from offering myself to Matthew. Congress with my friend would not have been a crime. Indeed, certain people – hetero-sexuals among them – might have viewed such a development as (perhaps not natural, but) logical enough. So, what can have made me hesitate? My vanity? My fear that he might have turned me down? My fear that he might have regarded such attention as (not genuine, but) charitable? My fear that humour – so vital to our romance – is death to the sexual act? Pointless to conjecture. Yet what lies beyond conjecture is the fact that there exists no substitute for carnal partnership. Sublimation is a wank. If celibacy is a vow, it wasn't a vow ever taken by Matthew. Why should he have been deprived of validation on the erotic front? Because he happened to be viral? So were thousands of others. Because he was going to die? So are you and I. But the subject – so easy and yet so hard – was never broached between us. Instead, I was left to hope that, on the side, he might be getting laid by someone somewhere somehow. Roving Willy. Anyone.

Meanwhile, he, feigning to the world that nothing in the world was the matter, struggled to maintain an orderly front. And yet, at every turn, his efforts became challenged. At the garage, he kept pumping the wrong petrol into the car. At the supermarket, he kept walking off with the wrong products. At home, he kept putting washing powder in the dishwasher. At the office, he kept overlooking errors which, earlier, he would have spotted in a trice. Even at the hairdresser's he found himself con-founded. When he sat to face the mirror and, taking off his glasses, told the usual girl that his barnet looked a fright, he felt her fingers dawdle at the edges of his hairline. She paused; she scrutinized his brow; she wondered, in a whisper that betrayed the smell of trouble, whether he'd been put on medication of some kind. Why? Because his hair was falling out. She suggested – in the chirpy register espoused by those who, then, habitually cropped the heads of faggots – that perhaps the time had come for a re-style. Something fresh and radical. Matthew forbad her from dealing him the Chemo Cut: Go shorter if you like, but don't send me to Belsen, dear. I don't look good in stripes.

Which was rubbish. Matthew looked good in anything – he had that knack – but I would say that he looked best, by this stage, in his work garb. The pared-down elegance of his jackets, combined with his natural ease of carriage, lent him a distinct but low-key glamour. And yet those jackets – always Japanese and always dark – now possessed, beneath their expertly

undertailored deconstruction, a darker function: to protect the
lump over his heart. For the first time in our time, he took to
wearing breast-pocket handkerchieves – white ones – as if wishing to disguise, yet emphasize, that part of him which had
become so vulnerable: a careless knock from some passer-by
could have wreaked havoc with the needle which, taped
beneath a gauze, lay embedded in his Portacath. He began to
drive to the office – to avoid the risk of squash-ups on the
Underground. He became punctilious about his hours, so as not
to be late with his Ganciclovir. He grew more responsible, more
disciplined, tidier. Even people at the magazine remarked on it.
Matthew'd got serious, they would tease. And he, peering across
the room, over the blur of heads and desks and plants and
screens, would answer: Serious, me? Give me a break – it must
be my executive specs. But then he would look down again,
and, while checking proofs before they went to press, don a pair
of headphones. He said that he preferred partitas to inter-
departmental twitter.

Such twitter sometimes touched on the financial climate of
the day, which was precarious. Matthew's magazine had, long
ago, been taken over; so that what had started as a smart but
struggling architectural journal had grown, over the years, into a
more successful, more commercial venture. But the title now fell
under the umbrella of a massive corporation – essentially the
property of a Czech who, after the war, had emigrated to
England and shown his ingenuity (despite the patent illegality of
such activities) by publishing the work of German scientists over
here. Still: on such dicey foundations was a vast communications
empire built – an empire which, in turn, was fated to make history. You probably remember the hoo-hah, and probably better
than I do, but – to be brief – it transpired that the 'tycoon', while
schmoozing with all the right politicians, was simultaneously
engaged in a bit of a wheeze. The Bouncing Czech, as he
became known, had been siphoning cash from his public companies (whose staff, including Matthew, subscribed to in-house

pension funds) and channelling that money into a string of other, private, enterprises. And thus it was that when the gangster, pissed one night, decided to take a leak over the side of his yacht, and, losing his footing, keeled into the ocean, and disappeared into the deep, eventually to be washed up along the distant shores of where my parents lived, his legacy – a megamillion pension deficit – was revealed.

None of this would have been of the slightest interest to me, were it not for the fact that, a brief few weeks after Matthew's return to work, he found himself, along with the very colleagues who had joked about his seriousness, hauled into a meeting, delivered a sombre homily, and put on the street – needless to say without a hope of indemnity. But Matthew was sanguine about his dismissal, for, despite the misfortune implicit, I think that he was relieved to have been despatched for reasons not explicitly related to his illness. On a reflex, I suggested that he apply for another job quickly. He didn't reject the idea, not completely. But first he wanted a breather – a desire with which, given my own *C.V.*, I was hardly in a position to quibble.

Matthew called this breather his sabbatical. He said that he would give himself a month. He hadn't had a holiday. He felt entitled. The previous year had been a bummer – first his parents, then his health, and now his salary. But he still had some savings in the bank, so he wasn't going to panic. We continued with his check-ups. The results looked encouraging. His hair might have been falling out, but his weight was rising. His system was responding well to the Ganciclovir. The professionals had got the dosage right. Nilson said: Good lad. We continued with the eye-clinic, where (although actual improvement was too much to ask) we were told that the virus did appear to have been stabilized. We bought some prescription sunglasses, which helped dissimulate the imbalance of his eyes. But, off his own bat, Matthew also sought, and found, a magnifying glass, of the type used by embroiderers, gigantic, because his specs, he said, weren't always strong enough, not for really close-up stuff, not when he was tired and dealing with his medication at night – the needles and bungs and changes of line. He rearranged his kitchen to double as pharmacy. He sorted through his airing cupboard. He chucked out old records, old guidebooks, old clothes that should have gone to Oxfam ages back. He had a blitz in the garden. And, once he felt reorganized, he said that he must make a will. He had made up his mind. My own mind couldn't get to grips with the notion of life after Matthew.

Afterlives. Both of us had, by peculiar coincidence, been reared on Romish diets; but whereas mine had been dished out institutionally – in repeatedly nasty snacks – Matthew's, which was served to him at home, had apparently not been too unpalatable. Yet the pair of us had long since lapsed – he, largely out of idleness; I, from something more reactive, closer to bile. Matthew's reservations were casually theoretical: he didn't go along with the Vatican's claim to spiritual supremacy; he didn't get the point of compulsory worship; he wasn't into guilt; he wouldn't swallow transubstantiation, and he remained open to the possibility of reincarnation. My own objections were more practical: they were, in practice, sexual, for (aside from the church's ban on contraception, which I left to the consciences of my more 'rhythmic' girlfriends) I baulked at the papist pill about queers being mortal sinners and their love irredeemably evil – dictums delivered by the lips of people who had pledged themselves to an institution which, for centuries, had furnished inverts with the safest haven in the West. You only had to speak to someone who had 'failed' his vocation – some former seminarian – about the English College in Rome, to discover how novices, despite orders that they refrain from bovine, canine, feline or feminine nicknames, could not resist endearments such as Daisy, Fifi, Kitty, and Big Shirl. You only had to flick through some enquiring journal to glean how the Lord's representatives, decked in unholy denim, used to cruise the Holy City's homo-bars and parks, and sometimes suffered heart attacks in massage parlours, and, on occasion, succumbed to an enigmatic malady which didn't quite wash as cancer. And yet, regardless of those lurid paradoxes, Matthew and I concurred on one thing: that whatever the mysteries of doctrinal life, there had to be more to death than dust to dust. I was glad. It provided me with an anchor – even if, in the aftermath, that anchor was destined to grow rusty; heavy to drag.

Matthew dragged me to Mass, because (he said) you never knew: it was probably as well to err on the safe side. This prudent line of argument bit into my late-night clubbing, but I didn't make a song and dance about it: I could see that peace of mind was his entitlement; and I daresay that, had our roles been reversed, I too might have wanted to cover my spiritual arse. So, for a good few Sundays, church attendance became the pattern – a different church every Sunday. Matthew didn't have to spell it out. I understood, deep down, what he was up to. He was shopping around. For a suitable venue. Dignified. Not that our search didn't sometimes yield undignified surprises. Take a famous shrine in Knightsbridge – more famous for its Tridentine tendency than ever for its oratorical prowess – where its padres skirt round Poverty for the privilege of hundred-buttoned couture cassocks. At the entrance, as if by way of welcome, we came across a notice asking visitors to (not MIND THE, but) WATCH YOUR STEP. It was Matthew who, blinking with incredulity but managing to laugh, pointed it out. I said: Silly cunts. He said: Not now. We stepped inside. We looked around. We gave it a try.

Wherever we ventured, we sat near the front. I used to attempt to concentrate, to empty my head of bad traffic. I even tried to pray sometimes. But God, how could one? Never mind the disruption of late arrivals, and hacking coughers, and squalling brats; it was the sermons that drove me bananas, the unimaginative guff which those preachers dared to churn out. It made you want to leap up before the collection plate came round, and start heckling about (not charity, but) value for money. My best bit, on the other hand, was when some happy-clappy celebrant exhorted the convened to offer each other the sign of peace – an entreaty to which I readily submitted, for the spectacle of two men kissing made the worshipful a teensy bit jittery, morally uneasy. Matthew would mumble: No Frenching, Captain; but I – joking aside – sensed that there was something special about embracing my friend in God's house. And the music: yes, the music was often lovely. Mozart's *Lacrimosa*, Rossini's *Stabat Mater*, Verdi's *Pezzi Sacri*. If you don't know them, waste no time. Bin this book and run to buy them, because sacred music, more than any manufactured sacrament, is what feeds the mind with faith in some hereafter. The sound of heaven. The rest is drab. But Matthew, who wasn't unaware of my recalcitrance, was – to be fair to him – always fair about recompensing my indulgence. Which is why, no sooner had we heard the valediction: Go in Peace, than off we went – to get pissed. It was our Sunday treat. He took me to places which I would never normally have considered visiting, such as pukka hotels where, even at weekends, they demanded that you wore a tie. The Connaught comes to mind. But the wonderful, old-fashioned cocktails that they served, served to redeem the general stuffiness. And when our glassy chalices landed, glinting with chill, on the table between us, we would pick them up and hold them high and make a toast to – what else but – Buenos Aires.

But back to London. One morning, mid-week, Matthew rang to say that he was coming into town. He asked me to meet him in Victoria, at his bank, round the corner from the place where, until recently, he had whiled away his working hours. Yet, now that he was without work, he seemed in a great hurry: Tasks to be done. Such as? Florist. Florist why? To order a corsage. Who was the lucky damsel? Himself, strangely enough: his admirers had all gone to ground. I can't have caught the blackness of this gag, because I merely asked: What time? He said: Eleven thirty all right? Eleven thirty was fine. I reached the appointed place at the appointed hour, but he had already drawn his cash. He was sitting in an armchair, peering at some list, and twirling a silver biro in the sun. He looked untroubled, almost happy. As we strolled back out into the street, he said: Come over here; I want to show you something. We crossed the zebra arm-in-arm – I, on his right, as had become our habit, safely away from his Porta-cath. We walked past a parade of tawdry souvenir bazaars – beefeaters and bulldogs and bosomy mugs – and then, without warning, he led me down some alley: *Vada.*

Westminster Cathedral. I hadn't been near it since childhood. But I knew that Matthew, during his time in publishing, had occasionally escaped there when the going at the office had got tough. As we crossed the piazza, he told me that the red-bricked façade, with its silly industrial bell-tower, had never really been his cuppa, but that the interior was a different matter. Christian Byzantine. Very Constantinople, darling. And yet his steps, though casual, felt formal to me; thought out. An ulterior import seemed to attach to this supposedly spontaneous detour; a meas-ured gravity. Inside was quiet. No service in progress. A few small heads; a few stooped backs. Dusty noonday light. Votive candles. Vestiges of incense as you advanced. At the front, dotted about the altar, odd bursts of flower, lilies and lilies, orange and white, beginning to wilt, probably in memory of some honeymooning couple. We promenaded round – counterclockwise. It put me in mind of our progress in Paris. The circle of tapestries. The Senses renounced. My sole desire. Matthew said: This is where I think I'll have it.

Later, when all that there remained for me were phantoms of my wrecked romance, and I began to exhume bare bones of fact in an attempt to clutch at particles which were no longer mine, but scattered ash, I learned how utterly, how hysterically appo-site had been my friend's selected place for his final Mass. The cathedral stands on a former prison-site; it rises over ground of underlying hardship. It is dedicated to the Most Precious Blood

– don't ask me its group and cell-count. The foundation stone was laid exactly a century before the year of which I write; yet, to this day, the grandiose decoration remains half-done. It never lived to enjoy the fullness of its rightful finish: fate robbed it of the chance. The lower half is rife with lively extravagance – gargantuan slabs of ornamental marble, and glittering mosaics, and opulent side-chapels – whereas the vaulted upper part remains brick-clad, and, with the passage of the decades, has darkened to the cavernous vastness of a starless Eastern sky. And yet – aesthetic impurity notwithstanding – cognoscenti claim that it is in the starkness of this accidental contrast that the church's very magic lies: high camp below; simplicity above. Incompleteness: a blessing in drag.

The Stations of the Cross are remarkable – in more ways than one. Those fourteen panels of pale Hoptonwood stone, which illustrate, step by ritualistic step, the bumpy ride to Calvary, have, since their completion some eighty years back, spoken to seekers both of penance and (se)pulchritude. They were carved in bas-relief by a staunchly married convert who, though a committed Tertiary of the Third Order of St Dominic, and an habitual wearer of the girdle of Chastity, and a stickler for Matins and Compline and Benediction, turns out to have stuck it into his sister with eager frequency, stuck it into his daughters more eagerly still, dabbled in the art of cock-sucking, and personally verified how a dog will join with a man. Talk about boning, but anyhow. The Church, unsurprisingly, nowadays prefers to keep the peccadilloes of this rogue, whose talents it once lauded and rewarded, away from the respectability of its fold; but I bet that Matthew, even though he mentioned nothing, was up on the gossip. Why am I so sure? Because, in the glove compartment of his car, he had tucked a well-worn copy of the lecher's biography. Eric Gill. What a guy. Check him out. I could give you the relevant page-numbers, but I haven't got time. My friend was in a hurry.

Next stop: florist. I recall this trip with an apprehensive sort of clarity, because Matthew, while speeding along a busy triple-carriageway, suddenly announced: Shit, I'm getting cramp. I tried to be (not petrified, but) practical. I told him to flex his ankle and point his foot up. He said: It's my right one. I said: At the next set of lights. He didn't reply. I think that he was angry. Someone was hooting behind us. He kept checking the rear-view mirror. I kept my eyes to the front. He slammed a hand against the radio; killed its sound; shouted that he couldn't stand bloody Rap. Inwardly I chanted: Please don't let us have a crash, please don't let us have a crash, please don't let us – Don't look so worried, he snapped. He began to slow down. The pain, he said, was easing up. He drew closer to the lights – thankfully red, for once – and came to a standstill. He pressed the clutch, slipped into neutral, wiggled his leg, let out an exasperated sigh. I said: Bit of a close one, that. He said: Tell me about it. He also told me that he'd recently been waking up with cramp. I pretended that the same thing happened to me sometimes. He swung away from the main traffic, and headed into Mayfair. The danger had passed. The noonday streets were quiet. He said: Let's have some decent music, Captain; won't you find us something jazzy? I said: Consider it done. I twiddled with the dial, and came across a programme. Summertime. The fish were jumpin' and the cotton was high, but there wasn't no daddy and there wasn't no mamma and no baby was going to cry. And by the time we'd found a space in which to park, both of us were (after a fashion) recovered. Grab that book from the glove compartment.

Matthew had obviously researched the question of his corsage thoroughly, because he'd opted for (not a local florist, local to his flat; nor indeed the place where I, thanks to Cara, occasionally took my custom – the one with all the country blooms and barking dogs and mad Sloaney laughter – but) somewhere more fashionable, sharper in profile. It was run by a queer-about-town whose hard-edged style had, during a recent Biedermeier revival, enjoyed the raptures of interior designers – perhaps because the work doubled as sculpture. Those arrangements – those obelisks and pyramids and orbs and spirals – were, while rigorously classical in structure, outlandishly crafted, from driftwood and sea-shells and starfish and sponge and coral and pebbles and coloured shards of frosted glass. There was something fantastical about them. Mythical. Timeless. They were like living tributes to dead matter.

We went in. I recognized the guy: he practically lived in the Sunday supplements. Fake hair, fake tan. God-awful jingle-jangle, but great hands – sinewy and wide. Hands of an artist. He smiled at us with the winsome hesitancy which used, during that era of uncertain custom, to be accorded to faggots. Floral concepts had become a minefield. Matthew said: I've come to order a wreath. The queen didn't flinch. The queen merely claimed to see. Matthew flicked through his book and opened it. The corner of a page quivered. I couldn't tell what was being shown – some darkened circlet? Some ring? It was, in fact, an illustration of a wood engraving. A coronet of wheat. Com-memorative. Matthew pointed to it. The queen said: For a dining-room? For a kitchen? Matthew said: For a funeral. The queen's pout twitched. Matthew proceeded: Someone I know is on the way out and I'm not going to be around when it actually happens, so I can't be precise about the place and time, but my friend here will take care of all that. The queen said: I'd like to take a Xerox if that's all right. Matthew said: Fine. An assistant was duly despatched. Meanwhile, the design was discussed, approved, and entered in a ledger with dark covers: Funeral wreath, wheat, in overlapping scallops as per picture – diameter 18", details to be advised. Matthew rummaged in his wallet; then, forked out. The queen wrote: Paid in cash; and below: with thanks. I couldn't get out fast enough.

I said: You might have warned me. He said: What about? I said: That you were going to pull that stunt; I mean, who ever heard of someone ordering their own wreath in advance? – it's so macabre. Matthew replied: Rubbish, grow up, one day you'll understand; come to think of it you'll probably thank me. Anyhow, let's go for a quick bite; I'm starved; I also need to ask you something – once we've sat down. We went to a sandwich bar, but I could scarcely touch my grub. I could hardly open my mouth. I was too undone, for, in my selfish way, I felt that all my efforts at distracting him, at sustaining his morale, had been as if for nothing, that I'd failed him on the laughter front, that he couldn't really trust me to be dignified on his behalf, that – however unintentionally – he was slighting me. He mentioned that he'd made an appointment to see Charlotte. Charlotte came next on his list of tasks. Charlotte was a mutual acquaintance of ours, originally mine – originally Kelly's, actually – who had recently been made a partner in a firm of solicitors at Lincoln's Inn. Swanky set-up. But why should Matthew want to call on *her*? Because she specialized in Wills and Probate. Oh for God's sake, did we really have to go into this *now*? Flatly he remarked: You don't, I do. In which case, I countered, include me out. He said that he hadn't intended to ask me to accompany him. So what was it that he *had* intended to ask? He paused. He smiled a saddish smile. He wondered which of his many chattels might warm the cockles of my arse. I said: Listen, this is getting really heavy and I don't like it. None of us likes it, he replied, but it has to be done, so what's your answer? I said: Do whatever you want. Leave your stuff to the dogs' home for all I care. I'm interested in *you*, Matthew, not your fucking chattels. And then – to crown this tacky cameo – I began to cry. Matthew said: Darling, don't start.

He offered to drop me at the Underground, but I said that I'd rather take a cab. He got into his car and headed off to see Charlotte. In the event, however, I walked home through the park. I needed to digest my (not lunch, but) discomfort. I think that I was envious of Matthew's courage. His resoluteness made me feel redundant. That's the truth of the matter. My identity was being undermined. I didn't feel relied upon. I wandered through the summer grasses, and dissected, step by step, the stages which had led to this odd pass – the bank, the church, the wreath, the final testament. Then I remembered: I was forgetting my own vows. I (re)capitulated. Love Matthew's courage, honour his desires, obey his requirements. Give him dignity. Give him laughter.

He rang that night. Charlotte had apparently been fabulous, made it all a painless exercise. Even the location for his requiem had been decided, because, by stating this in writing – by making it legally binding – you could later pressurize the padres, who were never very keen on people from outside their parish – unless, of course, one happened to be a duchess. I said nothing. Matthew asked if I still had the hump. No, but I found this whole thing hard. Well, he said, you needn't any more, because it's done, so we can just forget about it. And by the way, in case you were wondering, I haven't saddled you with the job of executor: Charlotte's firm will deal with the administrative side. I said: Right. He said: One small favour, though. I said: Only like big ones. He said: Can we go to Gay Pride? *What*, on the *march*? No, just to the party. Thank Christ for that.

But I was horrified. The thought of all those homosexual multitudes, swilling lager and trading belches and puking up in some suburban outback, was not exactly my idea of a party, still less a source of pride – vicarious or otherwise. Years back – amid high bluster about emancipation and ages of consent and Section 28 and duty to one's forerunners and the rest of the right-on cant – Kelly had dragged me to one such knees-up, and I tell you: although he couldn't have got enough of those leather-clad accountants on big motorbikes, or minded less about the sight of lezzers with moustaches and prams, I've rarely felt less true to type. I'd told Kelly as much. And Kelly had told me to chill out.

Matthew said that he would drive, otherwise God knew how we'd get back. I said that I would get some drugs, otherwise God knew how I'd survive. He rang my bell mid-afternoon. I raced down to the car. Jump in. Strap up. I swallowed half a tab, and then, on second thoughts, its other half. Matthew said: Share and share alike. I said: Stick to a quarter, darling, we don't know how this stuff will mix with your Ganciclovir. He said: Have a heart, Captain. So, in the end, he got a yellow half-moon. He gobbled it and said: Down the hatch. We arrived. I said: I hope you can remember where we're parked. He said: Don't nag.

We mooched about the outskirts of the crowd, along the borders of some pasture, some vaguely verdant land. You could almost picture it as the scene of a gnarled historical romance, Elizabethan perhaps, a romance perhaps forbidden, perhaps hunted down, perhaps, even, discovered and bludgeoned – yet old and strong and beautiful for all of that. Good times. Give them back to us. Since my earlier foray onto the highlight of the faggot calendar, I was, I admit, struck by how much bigger, and better orchestrated, these events had become. Was it the drugs? Was it Matthew? Does it matter? There were tents and tents and tents, given over to a whole array of specialities – Tarot readings, dance music, gardening; incense, unguents, scented candles; bibelots and greetings cards; piercings and tattoos, and – for the doggedly avant-garde – branding; meditation, astrology, holistic massage; medical advice; organic produce; fetishistic fashion; pension information; religious guidance. You name it: it had been provided. There were bars. There were stands. There were ice-cream vans. There were barefoot sarongs. There were studded harnesses. There were checkered cowboys. There were terriers with bandannas. There were children in sunglasses. There were straights with wonky brothers. There were, even, decent lavatories. (You boys wanting to have fun? a uniformed attendant asked some horny couple. Well, you'd better find a bush, my lovebirds.) Matthew put his arm around me. A stage had been set up – miles away, beyond our horizon, which was peopled with balloons and bunting. A concert was being held later that night, at dusk, all proceeds to charity. Chrissie Hynde would stand by us. You could hear the heads of microphones being tapped, and voices testing-testing-testing. A breeze freshened the sun. It was July. We bought some bottled water. We clambered up a hillock, feeling warm and slightly buzzy. It made you smile. It made you expansive. It took away the trouble, dispelled the fear of sudden thunder. People could forget that they were fighting for their (not rights, but) lives. Today was party-time. Today was another matter. Today should last for ever. Today should be so lucky.

Sometimes I get moods when I think back, and I get those moods through sound. But the sounds which I recall from that afternoon at Pride return to me diffuse and in snatches, in passing blasts, almost beyond grasp, like echoes, like bubbles, like the hollow remnants of an anthem heard through loudspeakers from another culture, in the language of a vanished nationality. Idle handclaps. Arpeggios of laughter. A wolf-whistle of wonder. A click from a camera. A picnic admiring a kite. A helicopter passing. A dragonfly. A sigh. A syllable somewhere. Streamers of primal vowels, full of meaning yet unfathomable. Forest Hymn; Sweet Lullaby. The tracks of that summer. We lay on the grass, my friend and I. We closed our eyes. We held hands. Someone stepped behind us. I heard her say: God isn't this lovely? Matthew said: Amen to that.

Then: silence. We must have drowsed for a time. I awoke with clover stuck to my mouth. I was lying in the shade of a dim cloud, a slow one. I sat up. I gazed around. I caught the tail-end of a wailing siren. I drank some water. From a bottleneck of barriers, people seemed to be pouring into the park – probably demonstrators from the march. A popular volume was on the rise, but the sun was in decline. The sense was of an interval, of a pause between two acts. I stood up. Pale searchlights heralded the oncoming dark. Matthew said: Ouch, give me a hand. I yanked him by the arm. He stretched a **lallie***. We decided to return to the action, but a gentler way round, along a proper

lallie (noun): a leg (Parlare) e.g. *Vada the bona lallies.*

path. We ambled past a cross-legged beard with a hookah. Matthew said: How Cairo. I said: Vada, darling: drag-queens. He said: I was starting to wonder. As we made a bee-line for their nylon glamour, we strolled along some municipal flowerbeds. Matthew mentioned, en passant, how he hated floral mish-mash, jumbled varieties. I made a mental note – don't quite know why. And he, as if he had – don't quite know why – access to my mind, further said that he only liked blocks of solid colour. Save him from botanical Pointillism. He was wearing his dark glasses. The flowers were, as it happened, a perfectly balanced amalgam of pastel; but I got the gist. No tonal fancy.

Dotted about the crowd, I began to spot errata: nurses from the hospital, pecking at a bag of popcorn; Nilson in the distance, with what I took to be his wife; a sloe-eyed mistake of Kelly's; two separate ones of mine – since introduced, and now introducing tongues. I tried to chivvy Matthew toward the concert platform, away from potential embarrassment, but he told me not to worry. He'd had a gorgeous time; why stick around for an anticlimax? Besides, he wasn't keen to drive at night. The car? Of course he knew where it was parked. We headed for the exit, arm-in-arm. Near the gate, a nunnish woman with a mawkish smile and dangling crucifix and purple cardigan crept up in stockinged sandals – up to *me*, actually. There was something meant in her advance. Perhaps I looked like a soft touch. I asked her what she wanted – money? She didn't answer: she just handed me some circular, patted her satchel, and continued on her round. Matthew said: Let's get away while we still can. I glanced at the leaflet. My eyes fell on its title: BEREAVEMENT COUNSELLING. I thought: Fuck You Cunt. The leaflet fluttered to the ground.

Matthew didn't drive me back. He was in a hurry to get on with his Ganciclovir, so he dropped me off where our directions parted – at a busy roundabout. I felt slightly frazzled, but thought that I would go out clubbing. When, eventually, I reached my flat, I switched off the phone and had a lie-down. Later, as I headed to the kitchen for a glass of courage, I discovered a message flashing. I played it back. Matthew's voice sounded worn out: Pick up the phone; you must be home by now; I should never have taken that stuff; where the hell are you?

He took an age to answer. He'd been injecting his line. I asked what had happened. He said: Get this, I'm driving along and suddenly, as I'm waiting to turn from a main road into a sidestreet, I start to feel sick, but of course I'm stuck in the middle of bloody traffic, so I can't very well pull over, and anyway, I mean, I didn't even have time to wind the window down. (And?) And I threw up all over the car. Dashboard, windscreen, upholstery, the whole production. He felt shattered; he hadn't even cleaned up; it would just have to wait; he'd chucked his clothes into the washer, but that was as much as he could manage.

I said: Give me half an hour. I hung up. I raced across town. He let me in. He looked drained, but his infusion was done. He was wearing a dressing-gown, and tidying up. I didn't mention the tab. I felt ambivalent about it: guilty about its adverse side-effect, but glad that it had served to enhance our time at Pride. I told him to stay put and watch the tel for a while. He asked what I was doing. I told him to stop worrying. I filled a bowl with soapy water and went off to scrub the car. The street was quiet. I got down to my task. I surprised myself. I found that Matthew's vomit did not cause me revulsion. I suppose it's like the vomit of your child: (not nice, but) natural. I went back. I said: All done. He said: You're a star. I said: Don't talk rubbish; any food in the house? He said: Only Humble Pie. I said: I'm allergic to that; let's order pizza. He said: How lovely, Captain; memories of Napoli.

After supper, Matthew told me to take his car. He didn't need it until Monday. I had come to him by taxi, and the expense both ways seemed mad. OK – if he didn't mind. As I stood to go, he said: And listen, you should probably have a key to this place, in case anything should happen. I said: Great; now

I can sneak round and jump you. He said: You should be so lucky. I kissed my friend. Try to rest now. I left him for the night. The car still smelt of acid. I would give it another go when I got back. But as I drove in winding silence through the lengthening shadows, I felt a fear, a pang, a fearful pang that this afternoon's Pride might have been Matthew's last.

Next morning, I rang. No answer. Must be asleep. I browsed through the paper. I had a shower. Again I rang. Still no answer. Not like Matthew. I wasn't going to panic. I got dressed. I made some coffee. I told myself to stop worrying. I disobeyed my own commandment. I gave up. I went down to the car, and – windows open – drove to his flat. Air-freshener: I would have to get some. Pine. I parked too fast. I bumped the car behind. Calm down: that's the whole point of bumpers. I got out. I glanced across the street. And there he was: Matthew: quietly seated in a wing-chair. My insides fluttered. I felt lighter. The room looked darkish. I could see the flicker of his television, shards of light along a wall behind him. I rang the bell and, after a struggle with the key, let myself in. I heard him shout: Which of my captains be that? I felt choked up. I said: Why aren't you answering the phone? He said: Didn't know you'd rung. I said: Where've you been? He said: To breakfast – is that a crime? I said: Christ almighty, Matthew. He said: Just simmer down, I'm not in the mood for aggro.

I went into the kitchen. His medication was all set out. So why hadn't he started his Ganciclovir? Because he had better things to do. Such as? International rugger, darling. Come and look at these arses. Aren't they fabulous? Makes you want to give those beefy shorts a whack. I walked into the sitting room. He was holding his magnifying glass up, up to the screen, and moving it around, as if he were chasing the scrum, as if those widespread buttocks were butterflies. I asked when he was going to do his line. When he damn well felt like it. I said: What the hell's got into you? He told me to get off his back. He'd hardly slept a wink. He was tired. (I paused. I heard the explosion of a crowd. A try.) I went into the bedroom. His sheets were on the floor, dumped in a bundle. I sniffed the reason why: he'd been sick in the night. I stood by the window and looked out across the garden. Chaos. The chaos had begun.

At the beginning, I would not have it. I would have to do something. I yelled at Matthew that his place looked like a pigsty. He was deaf to my affront. He told me, with a chilly sort of grandeur, that perhaps I'd like to call a taxi. I was stung. I sat down. And for a while we festered thus: he, wedded to the rugger; I, steeped in adulterated silence. Then, I got up. He didn't ask. I went for a slash. I washed my hands. The basin was caked with scum; the lavatory − never mind. I went into action: I scrubbed the bathroom, changed the bed, put the dirty sheets in a bin-liner, folded the clothes that had been left in the dryer, stowed away the junk for his Ganciclovir, changed my mind, put enough supplies for three infusions in a bag, grabbed the yellow bin for Sharps, and packed fresh jeans, socks, pants, shirt, jumper − all with ostentatious crashing about. As I staggered to the hall in search of a vacuum, we bumped into each other. He asked why I was being so dramatic. Because the state of his flat was so disgusting − whatever had happened to standards? He told me that I sounded like a schoolmarm. I told him that he sometimes made me want to punch his lights out. He told me that he didn't doubt it.

One of the things about Matthew, one of his gifts, was that he could go to the heart of me. He said: Don't punish me for feeling lousy. It stopped me in my tracks. I said: I'm not, but you'd be making my life easier if you came back to my flat. He said: Fine. He turned off the match. I picked up our bags. He led the way out. He said: Don't forget to double-lock, Captain. We got into the car. He said: God, it smells foul in here. I didn't reply. He said: Sorry, darling. We wound our way back. Slow traffic. We joined a convoy of limping cars, a caravan. He switched on the wireless. A ballad from his prime. I didn't know the words. He took off his glasses. For the world was slowly turning and the lights of love were burning in his eyes . . . He wished he had the wisdom to find some simple words to make me see that the things that meant a lot to me didn't always seem to mean a lot to him. He needed to breathe. He needed to leave. When the sands of time went drifting by, he might be on his own, but he'd be free.

Nilson was in finest fettle – genial, cordial, jovial. Grand, thanks. Yeah, he and the wife had really enjoyed themselves at Pride; nice to see so many people having a good time. But down to business: how were things with Matthew? Bad, I blurted out. Matthew told me not to exaggerate. I said: He's been throwing up, and trying to skip his line. Nilson wondered why. I wondered whether it mightn't be to do with that half-tab. Matthew told me to belt up. Nilson doubted it. In which case, I asked, how would one account for the current setback? The doctor pulled a calculated face, calculated to suggest that he was talking theorems, not practice: Matthew had probably developed a resistance to Ganciclovir. So what was to be done? Nilson looked at me diagonally, as if to indicate that I shouldn't be bothering him – a busy man – with straightforward questions to which he knew that I knew the answer. I co-operated; I proposed the obvious: Switch to Foscarnet? Nilson didn't say: Clever Florence Nightingale. He said that the choice was down to Matthew. The patient could either persevere with his current drug in the hope that the nausea would subside, or reduce his present dosage for a while, or take a holiday from intravenous medication for – let's say – a fortnight, or, if he felt like being proactive, sure, give Foscarnet a try. Matthew was nearly sulking. He made me feel as if I'd outed him and got him into trouble. The trouble was that Nilson wouldn't stick his neck out. I didn't like to corner the man, but nor did his non-committal attitude make me like him. Who needs counsel from a coward? Still: Any other problems? Yes, I said: Cramp. Only to be expected – intramuscular. This resolved nothing. Anything else? Yes, sore throat and furry tongue – might Matthew have thrush? Nilson advanced some unlikely-sounding answer: Fluke-Honour-Soul. I beg your pardon? Flu-con-a-zole; antibiotic; anti-fungal; most effective on the market. He wrote it down. He stared at his pad. He asked if we were done. Not quite. Matthew mentioned inflamed glands. Nilson said: Classic – as if illness were a style. Matthew admitted to a herpes attack. Front or back? The patient spelt it out: Just inside the entrance – exit, rather. Nilson didn't seem to find this funny, but I made up for it. Matthew declined the offer of a poke-about. See you in a week's time. We took the lift down to Pharmacy. We collected more supplies. We went off for a coffee and a fag. I gave Matthew a light. He took a deep drag. He rubbed his eyes and said that he should probably switch to Foscarnet. No use procrastinating. I said that I was sure that he was right. But my only real conviction was that we were treading on thin ice. You could almost hear it cracking.

Then came the cracks – minor ones at first, no graver than the irks which routinely affect the rest of us: a cough, a rash, a headache, the runs. Importunate suitors; common or garden; nothing to worry about. Yet as this cluster of annoyances began to multiply, annoyances which Matthew was advised to swat like flies, one by one, with pills for this, and ointments for that, and inhalations for the other, so they conspired to undermine him; for it seemed as if, every few hours, he was being reminded (not that he was vanquishing some bug, but) that his defences were being worn down. If his lunch-plate was a planet, brightly-coloured capsules had become its satellites. It amazed me that such cheery-looking capsules could contain such toxic granules. Meals turned into ordeals. His moods became erratic. His temperature, likewise. He was sweating in the night. His dreams were largely bad. One morning, at my flat, he announced that he was sick of taking tablets, sick of gagging. I struggled to persuade him that it was a question of mind over matter. He struggled to persuade me to leave my clichés out of it. What, he

argued, was the point of forcing all those pills down, only to
chuck them back up? The effort seemed futile. And yet – it soon
enough transpired – his difficulty lay not with some psycho-
somatic constriction of the gullet, but with the fact that, almost
overnight, his red cells had plummeted. He was borderline
anaemic; his blood lacked iron; a transfusion was on the cards.
So: what had provoked this sudden downturn? Sod's law: his
system wouldn't tolerate Foscarnet – a reversal which *was* a
graver matter, for without intravenous treatment of some type,
administered twice-daily through his Portacath, his eyes were
bound to give up. At our next appointment, and with fantastic
tact, Nilson told me – while Matthew was being sick in an adjacent lavatory – that the patient was too strong, that his weight
was too high, that people with Retinitis were normally dead
before they went completely blind. But let's not get wound up:
Nilson's wisdom was but one in a brooch of priceless pearls to
which I was treated around this time. And besides, my purpose
was not to bridle at gaffes: it was to encourage Matthew. Perhaps
that's why the nurses called me a life-enhancer. Later they would
call me all kinds of other stuff – more or less behind my back.
But, by then, I'd grown adept at not hearing offensive sounds,
such as Matthew's coughs and burps and farts.

I would describe the next instalment of my friend's decline as
bewilderingly prepositional, by which I mean that it became
unclear to me whether his medication was being prescribed
properly *for* him – for his specific benefit – or merely *to* him,
gesturally, in order to show willing; or, even, *at* him, in the
aggressive statistical abstract; or, indeed, *despite* him, mechan-
ically, without the fiction of his future in scientific mind. For I
could no longer tell exactly where, or when, a name lost its
identity and became a number, or a number became a case, or a
case became a syndrome, or a syndrome a sign, or a sign a probability, or a (regular) exception, or, more bluntly, an unwelcome

drain on some depleted medical budget. I couldn't figure it out. It has taken me a decade to decipher the muddle, but now, at last, I have; and what I have discovered is that a preposition eclipses a conjunction; and, furthermore, that the most powerful preposition – the most vivid, the most binding – is With. Would I walk with him beyond the road's turning? Would I walk with him all through his journey? I would. With all my heart.

But it wasn't as romantic as it sounds. Matthew was taken off Foscarnet, and, in a matter of days, seemed to be floundering. He was vomiting beyond the extreme of bile. He was forever on the pan. He said that his arse was on fire. He was shitting (not diarrhoea, but) blood. He couldn't bear to have a bath. Even water stung. His piss was brown. His piss was pungent. His piss went all over the tiles. His eyes weren't up to much. I suggested stronger glasses. He told me not to be crass, not to treat him like a child – didn't I think he knew that his retinas were buggered? He said: Give me a brandy and sod the time. I obliged. But I also rang the clinic. I said: Put-me-through-to-Doc-tor-Nil-son-please. Nilson volunteered the stock Uhuh-uhuh-uhuh, and said, oh well, better take the poor lad round. Something – he supposed – ought to be done. And something was: Matthew was hospitalized.

The Hivvy ward was full: so, once again, luck – if luck it could be called – had smiled. At the nurses' station, Matthew tried to smile back. We were advised to sit and wait while a room was made up. I attempted not to envisage some previous incumbent. I tried to dispel an image of departure. Right, said some Sister, we can settle you in now. Perfunctorily she gathered the patient up. He grunted. As he let himself be led along the lino, shuffling like some geriatric, I saw, for the first ghastly time, the tell-tale crevice of that whole ghastly malady, the sunken nape, the wastage of the pillar which, once, had held the head of my friend so high. We arrived. Room 5. It smelt of – what? – damp blankets? Dank humanity? Your guess is as good as mine. I thanked the nurse and told her not to worry: I could put my friend to bed myself. She said: We can do with an extra pair of hands round here. But her mouth was tight. Her name doesn't matter. She was in Charge — that's the bit that counts: her title. She didn't care to close the door behind her. I cared on her behalf. Silly cow. Matthew said: Please don't start. I need to be top of the class.

And then, the tests began. Never mind Matthew's sight. It was the professionals who were now fumbling in the dark — which presumably explains why, of a sudden, the patient was being suspected of everything under the sun, a whole panoply of coded crimes — some real, some imagined: CMV, MAI, PCP; Potential This, Most Likely That; you name it, Matthew could not be presumed not to have it. We must leave no stone unturned, they said; must cover all eventualities; nothing can be ruled out. And although, admittedly, the charges were announced protractedly, with a creepy diurnal regularity, the conclusion, to me, had been apparent from Day One. No-one had a clue as to what should be done. No-one had an answer. The hospital opened a second file. The first had grown too cumbersome.

I would never have believed it — not beforehand — but, in the event, Matthew was incarcerated for the 'best' part of a month. I won't bother you with details of the torments to which he was subjected — renal, rectal, lumbar, hepatic, bronchial, cerebral, ocular, cardiac — because, though those procedures took a heavy toll on his morale, they proved — as they disproved — nothing. But this, I would say, is when my proper education began. I learned to **try** (in both senses of the verb, transitive and intransitive). I learned to recite reams of complaints and reams of drugs. I learned Matthew's dosages by heart. I learned about relinquishing control of someone whom you love to those for whom one patient means the same as any other. I learned to seek advantage. I sought Sukie's number. I rang Paris. I explained what was happening. I said that the French were more advanced than us. I dictated the list of medicines currently being prescribed to

Matthew, which promised little more than yet more suffering. I told her to pull every string in her social archery. I told her to talk to her (remaining) friends in Fashion. I told her to phone the Institut Pasteur. I told her to call the American Hospital. I told her to track down someone with clout – an expert, not some bloody charlatan. I told her to get hold of the latest trial-results. I told her that there *had* to be an answer. I told her to run. I told her, I told her, I told her. She told me that she would call back. She told me to calm down. She told me to give Matthew her love. I had to hang up. I was starting to choke up.

I went out to a predictable club, and wandered about the habitual scenic fug. Same old faces; same old subculture. A drag-show was tonight's attraction. The attraction was rising to full flutter. Cock in a frock. Man dressed as dowager, miming about sending in the clowns. I lurched toward the bar. I propped it up. My eyes met with a distant empty glass, set further down the counter. A fist was clenched alongside – emphatically. While I waited to be served, I scanned its owner's rising forearm-elbow-biceps, but my gaze was distracted. It must have frozen at his shoulder-line. I was thinking about Matthew. I was thinking about irony: about richness, about queerness, about the loss of timing, about late careers, about bliss and disapproval, about tearing around while others can't move, about fuss, about fault, about wanting and not wanting, about sorrow and bother, about not being here, about maybe next year . . . when suddenly the fist had opened into a hand and waved. It pointed at me. What did I fancy – a pint? No, thanks. (I wasn't in the mood for gratitude. I was in the mood for action.) I acted dully. Dully I ordered something. But the man – whom, though unknown to me, I vaguely recognized – grabbed his drink and came across to where I was standing. Hi.

His name, he said, was Dom. He wore black leather chaps, weathered by the storms of darkrooms. His demeanour was blunt. He shook my hand, as if shaking were contractual. His grip was hotly tough. His hand was large. I grabbed my glass. He fondled his endowment with an indolent smugness. I held my sights above the salience of his pride. How was I? Fine. And he? Just back from Amsterdam. If a smile was ever trafficked, my memory recalls none. My memory only recalls the deepness of his voice – resonantly gruff – and his mien of boredom, which was bloodshot. Did he live in Holland? Kinda – ran a business out there, but was really based in London. Penthouse round the corner, he nudged. Handy, I replied – failing to make it sound sarcastic. So he threw in, threw down, the words With Dungeon – as if a gambit were a gauntlet. There was something cynical about the man – jaded and narcotic and corrupt, all of which I liked – but I allowed the banter to lapse. I had better things to think about, or worse perhaps. Yet he, notwithstanding what I left to be desired, stood his ground and stood it studiedly. The suggestion seemed to be that I merely needed time to size him up and succumb; time to believe my luck. But as he lingered at my flank, musing over his lager, a bunch of vested sycophants crept up to yak with him; and while I eavesdropped on their stilted repertoire, which bore a conspiratorial slant, full of sloping letters that I recognized, the carefully constructed mystery of this unlikely suitor was dismantled. Dom had been around for years, at last I realized; but he had hunted harder after Kelly's gang – smiling beauties on the cusp – than after scowlers such as I, who were trickier to fathom and toilsome to entrap. His confidence, which wasn't mild, stemmed from two factors: his wealth – allegedly industrial, and allegedly substantial – and his anabolic outline, which the likes of Kelly found horny to die for. Dom was not a tall man, but he was criminally handsome, and his build was massive – i.e. massively enhanced. Still; I wasn't going to let a little thing like a syringe dishearten me. Why? Because Dom, you see, was more than merely attractive. He was that most attractive thing of all: a benefactor, a contributor of funds to research hospitals. He sat on pharmacological boards.

He dined with top virologists. He rubbed shoulders with red-ribbonned royals. He stood closer to the miracle than most ordinary mortals. He might have been a pervert and a user and an arsehole, but, beyond such nouns, he was generous to a fault. He aided the cause. He infected you with hope. My personal suspicion was that his manifold philanthropies were more than merely honourable – that they were fuelled by some contracted hopelessness. But, let's be honest: was that my problem?

We began to talk. I alluded to my friend, not *boy*friend – a distinction which I made treacherously obvious. I mentioned the local hospital, and how you couldn't seem to get any sense out of those doctors. He described my predicament as not uncommon. It made me want to whack his gob. He told me that you had to go to the top, to the people in the know. I told him not to state the obvious. He wondered, with a leery curiosity, whether the obvious bored me. I ignored this lubricious detour, and said that the kindness of strangers interested me more – I didn't have an entrée to the hallowed échelons of which he spoke. He boasted that he did. I boasted that I knew. He took a lengthy swill, then said: So what's the story? I told him to tell *me*. He told me that he wasn't into mixing business with boys, but seeing – I cut him short. I said: I think I'm past my boyhood; come to the cottage. He scoffed at my proposal: cottages were grotty. Did he object to grot? Put it this way: he preferred to spice it up with toys. Such as? Butt-plugs? Handcuffs? Dildos? Ropes? He frowned. He'd thought me more 'advanced' than that. I said that he would have to be the judge of my depravity. He went quiet; thought about it; asked what I 'wanted'. I said: An introduction to the best consultant in the land. No problem. One slight snag, though: Dom's address-book was back at his flat. So? So he might have to break his rule about not being good and bad at the same time, and take me home – just this once, you understand. I said: Done. He clucked his tongue, and slowly impressed an index on the pipe above my Adam's apple. Masterly. I was getting hard. It was easy. For, with every throb of my increase, fate was pointing me closer to the grail of Harley Street.

Dom had been right. His place was a stone's throw from the club. I wouldn't myself have called it a penthouse, but I did call it large. It spanned the entire top floor of a block of Victorian mansion-flats. And yet, once the rickety lift had ferried you up there, and delivered you to a door with many mortises, you entered a world apart – reminiscent, more than anything contemporary, of Seventies Stuttgart. The flat had been 'done' (doubtless by some quintessential, quintessentially tight, pair of moleskin trousers) in the sheeny, tinty, glassy, wall-to-wall aesthetic which queers of Dom's variety then considered smart. Self-consciously monochromatic. 'Greige' was, I think, the reproachable name of the irreproachable colour. Despite carefully recessed lighting (which did – I granted him – help dissimulate the ceiling's wanting height), the overall effect was slightly naff, slightly charmless, certainly old-fashioned. A hip Manhattanite would have given it the instant thumbs-down; but Matthew would have been mesmerized, because the sinister neutrality of this environment, its deliberate avoidance of a single painting or sculpture or, even, empty vase, would have rendered the victim of some crime – grievous bodily harm, for example – incapable of describing in any forensic detail the scene of the drama. I tried to imagine the sprawling layout in its original plan, before its partition-walls had been sledge-hammered. I envisaged, as inhabitants, a middle-class family at the start of the nineteen hundreds. Father, a clerk at some bank, off to work in his bowler hat; mother imparloured, a captive bird, swishing with frustration in her pleated bustle; a lap-dog, Pomeranian perhaps; a couple of daughters, bolshie flappers with painted mouths, mouthing off about Mrs Pankhurst; an only son, bursting with young life but gone, gone to some great war, never to be back . . . I stopped in my tracks. The door was being locked – from inside. By the time that I'd turned round, all trace of a key had vanished. Dom blew me a kiss, placatory in character; then, chased it with a spittled sound. I swallowed hard. He said: Don't look so jumpy; it's gonna be fine; come to my study. He led the way. I felt like a child. But he seemed calm, almost kind, kind of wonderful. Trusty. Seductive.

The study, in keeping with the expanse which had led up to it, was a decorative blank. Everything was concealed behind flat panels. He parted the wings of a cupboard, to reveal a desk, functionally flip-down. He pulled a stool from beneath a flap. He sat. I stood behind. He wrote a name and an address along an envelope – but I couldn't read his words with accuracy. His handwriting, in paling black, was slapdash, not unlike the hurried hand of a consultant. His ink was running out. He grabbed another biro, which his fleshy grip rendered tiny. Now he began to scrawl across a letter-headed card. He paused. He half-looked up. What was my name again? George, I lied. (Admit to Quintus? Pull the other.) And surname? I divulged it. I had to. I thought of Kelly; I thought of our parents; further thoughts of them evaporated. Dom was sliding his written introduction into its cover. With the most protracted lick in the history of power, he sealed the pointed back. Big deal: I could read the contents afterwards. He handed me the note. Put it away carefully, he advised; don't want you forgetting it. I thanked him. He said: That's *my* side of the bargain – gentleman, aren't I? Now let me show you to the dungeon, where the fun starts.

This is how it started. Never in my recollection had I felt like fairer game, never readier for a gamble. Certainly my stance – complaisant yet compromised – held me fast in a moral vice; but looking back, back at the looking-glass which wrapped itself around the wall outside his dungeon, it is also true that my reflection – physically pliable while sexually stuck-up – must have seemed perfect to this man, picture-perfect for the part in which, to judge by his shifty eyes, he already had me cast: a light-weight cameo, no doubt; but not, despite its levity, a laughing matter. Sadomasochism, like the making of true love, offers limited scope for hilarity. You meet; you might converse; you might (think you) understand each other; adjectives such as Synchronous and Godsent might even come to mind as gradually you rise toward a plane beyond reality and yes, of course you hope to fly, to be lifted up where you belong, to where the eagles cry, far from the world below, high toward some burning neverending sun in the belief that you live only for your ardour. But listen: some people die of it. They combust. Icarus was one.

The chamber of Dom's pleasures seemed like a further variant on the subject of neutrality; and yet, unlike the rest of his flat, which was plain unremarkable, this room turned out to be a triumph both in and of disguise. For, far from hinting at esoteric sexual functions (by means of the customary hides and straps and assorted links of ironmongery), it evoked a modest kitchen for a modest bachelor. Breakfast-table to one side; white-enamelled mod-cons to the other; storage units spaced about. The floor, which felt spongy as you advanced, had been sensibly over-rubbered in some sensible, indeterminate colour. I fantasized that, in its day, the boards underlying might have been trodden by (not masters, but) staff; that this place might have served, for instance, as scullery. A scullery felt apt. Dom produced his vanished keys, which writhed and grated in a leather pouch, and laid them, with a muffled thud, down on the counter. He peered at a barometer which hung at a slight slant. He moved toward the window and fiddled with a thermostat. He turned the heating up. The blind had already been rolled down. Its thick plastic lining – silver if you spied from the side – screened you from prying eyes. I noticed, as he walked about, that the walls, before being coated in pale vinyl, had been cork-lined – perchance for soundlessness. All that you could hear was the progress of a clock devoid of numbers, marking time. He went toward the fridge, but passed beyond, to an elongated perspex splashback, laboratorial in character. The sink, in pristine aluminium, bore surgical taps, of the type that you can govern with an elbow – when your hands are full, or tied, or bloodied.

He retraced his steps toward the door. Smoothly he closed it, and, just as smoothly, slid a bolt. This move did not unnerve me: it reassured me. It struck me, perversely, as loyal. It made me feel as if his sole determination were to stop the world from stopping us. And my surmise cannot entirely have been wrong, for, next, he dimmed the track of overhead spots to the delicate tenor of romance and bathed us in the honeyed sort of haze which heralds sunrise. You have to understand something: despite his (extr)overt muscularity – those jutting pecs and bulbous arms and henchman's thighs – there was an inner sadness, a deeper softness, an interesting, sentimental gentleness to the man. A certain shyness. He mumbled a couple of syllables. I didn't quite catch them. What? Strip down, he instructed. I wasn't affronted. I wasn't, really, surprised. I merely thought: I'll take off my clothes when I want to. And even as I heard the warning – Do as you're told unless you want a wallop – in my bones I knew that no real malice was aforethought. I wasn't in danger. He wasn't in earnest. His command had only been a false imperative; (im)purely rhetorical. It amounted to code – code established by 'convention' for the fetishist who wants to claim the role of (not Bottom, but) Top. The (not Sub, but) Dom. The Sorter. But I'd been around. Blocks and blocks. I knew what was what. The tougher they want to seem, the harder they want to be broken. Same with horses. And so, dismissing pudour and precaution, I resolved to (not really obey, but) yes, indulge his words. I started to disrobe. He told me to take off my watch. I stuffed it in a pocket. I folded my clothes. I put them on the floor. With a well-aimed boot, he slid them toward a corner. Not even surreptitiously did he glance at my exposure. Perhaps my nakedness was not the object. Perhaps he wanted me to step into some other, more specific uniform, righter and more fitting for the moment. But no. He wanted me (in good times, in bad times, in good-and-bad-at-the-same-time times) just the way I was: up against a wall, buttocks touching painted cork. Silently he came toward me. He stopped. He groaned that I was hot. I reciprocated the compliment. He stroked me warmly yet abnormally, nostalgically almost, as if he were stroking some private loss. His eyes had closed. He put his mouth – open – to my shoulder. A kiss was not bestowed. Slow breath was. He said: I haven't done this for so long, God, not since my ex was – never mind – you've got the thighs of a young boy, ectomorph, slender bones. Steroids would transform you, really make you strong. You're not supposed to have a hard-on. Undo my flies, but leave my cock alone. That's good, churn my balls. Tighter, harder man . . . And then, just when I thought that I had heard it all, he asked if I had ever heard of Sounds.

Not in his sense I hadn't. Never mind; all I had to do was trust him. He turned toward the laminated counter. The storage units were – uniquely in my experience of Formica – all subject to safeguard. All locked up. With a master-key he unclicked, first, the cupboard on the far right; then, its neighbour, then a further, taller one – tall enough to house, say, a domestic ladder. The doors to those cabinets, which hung on unexpected pivot-hinges, seemed to swivel inwards, and slickly disappear from view. Inner lights came on, as if dark habits deserved luxury wardrobes. To reveal? No dildos, no handcuffs, no whips or coils of rope, no paddles, no butt-plugs, none of the obvious props. No sign, even, of uniforms. Instead: white shelves and white drawers-upon-drawers, each labelled with meticulous exacti-tude, punctiliously, like the trophies of a collector's trove. There was an unexpected, academic rigour to the tableau. Spiritual almost. I wondered about alcohol, but: No, said Dom; can't be getting sloshed; this is all about control; mine and yours; lose our heads, and the whole thing might go wrong; don't suppose you fancy a trip to your local hospital. (I must have looked fucked off, because) next he said: That was stupid of me; sorry; try to relax; just hand over; let me do the honours; I can give you pleasure like you've never dreamed of. His tone was kind but authoritative. Professorial. Certainly superior to that of a mere doctor.

Sounds, he explained, had nothing to do with hearing. The

term was exploratory – marine, if anything. When a sailor lowered a weighted line into the sea, to measure the water's depth, we said that he was sounding it, didn't we? Right. Now, Sounds – in medical speak – were urological instruments. They were used both on men and on women, but their respective lengths and shapes differed. People sometimes tried to flog you the wrong thing, so you weren't to be fooled – otherwise you could wind up in difficulty. And no, Sounds were not like catheters. Catheters were tubes, whereas Sounds were rods of steel. The point of Sounds was to stretch the urethra. Surgically speaking, their aim was to unblock internal scar-tissue and ease the flow of urine. The diameters of Sounds varied by tiny degrees, less than half a millimetre. The urethra became dilated as you upped the size of rod being introduced. In a more specialist context (by which he meant theatres of power-exchange), Sounds could provide great stimulation – both for the giver and the receiver. Of the two types of Sounds then available to men, Dom, who had done his research, favoured the J-shaped Van Buren, which was designed to accommodate the curve in the male plumbing-system. The Sound was slipped – never pushed – into the penis, and allowed to drop to the bladder of its own volition. The only hitch, he stressed, was if the Bottom got a hard-on during the proceedings. Then the Top must stop immediately, because, at that point, a Sound should neither be inserted nor removed. Risk of injury. Flaccidity was crucial. I was riveted, I admit. Fortunately, I was also shrivelled.

He leaned into a low drawer and, from it, took a rolled-up mat of foam – quilted in white plastic, and squishy to hold. He spread it along the surface of the table, which was embossed with a ridged metallic geometry. From a further drawer, he pulled a neatly folded square of terry-cloth, like a nappy of yore. This he laid over the mat, and patted flat. He told me to climb up – no, not like that – legs over the narrow side. Inevitably, Kelly came to mind, Kelly during his trials with Kindergarten-meister. I thought of the happy-snaps that I had burned in

Bedsitland. How Kelly would have laughed now, an eternity down the line, at the ludicrous sight of me, hunched in the artificial light, turning my moronic neck this way and that in an attempt to follow Dom's determined steps of preparation for our understanding. From the taller cupboard, he produced a modernistic version of a butler's tray, with a perspex lid and folded perspex legs. He assembled them. He said: There. He deposited the arrangement near my nakedness. He pulled a stool from underneath the table. He tested it. With the assistance of a lever, he arrived at the right level. He stood back up. He paced about. One of his boots emitted syncopated creaks of straining rubber, unintentional reminders of other trysts with other men on other nights. Other sounds.

But, as he laboured, so he kept me primed. I wanted teaching; I wanted learning; I was wanting in instruction. He told me that these Sounds, after last having been used (and he couldn't quite remember when that might have been, but don't let his dodgy memory affect the importance of the principle), would have been washed in detergent and soaked for half an hour in watered bleach – 1:10 was a good dilution – then, wrapped in a clean hand-towel and loosely bound with string, after which the bundle would have been pressure-cooked, on high, for thirty minutes. Sterility was imperative. Danger of transmission. You know what I mean. Now he brought a serving-dish of porcelain – reminiscent of Oriental settings – and gingerly lowered it onto the perspex tray. From a plastic tub – originally of ice-cream, I would imagine – he took (what I took to be) his set of Sounds, swaddled in white towelling and suitably bound. He placed the package with slow care down on the china, but left the contents covered up. He returned to the cupboards. I crossed my ankles. I hung around. He carried back twin cardboard boxes: the first, sprouting the beginnings of a soft tissue flower; the second, laden with disposable latex gloves – a couple of pale fingers hung limply from an ovate orifice. He spread a single tissue out; then, precisely above it, a partner; and over these, at an angle, he positioned a syringe, of standard plastic, of the type that adults use to medicate the very young. Proximate to the syringe, he laid a virgin tube of lubricant, and advocated, while he was about it, the avoidance of gels which had been stabilized. Stabilized how? With Monoxynol Nine. Why? Because it was an irritant – to the urethra. Ah. He fetched a bottle of pharmaceutical alcohol, which he said that we'd be needing once we had got started. I'm almost certain that the label's warning about flammability was in Dutch, but I wouldn't stake my life on it.

Dom took off his leather waistcoat and disclosed his upper half. Corpulent chest, symmetrically feathered outward. Nipples: not bullets, but undoubtedly powered. Ribs protuberant, hard-shadowed, and, below these, the intimation of a gut. He fiddled with the cross-laced waistband of his leather chaps. He directed his right hand toward the denim of his open flies. He crouched for purchase. Out – but matter-of-factly – came his tackle. His cock was soft but fat; his balls, low-slung and dark. Balls of a grown man. I tried to think of other matters. It mattered that I not get hard. He said that we were nearly there – just needed his special gadget. He rummaged in a drawer . . . and found it. He arranged a clip-on strap around the equator of his skull. He aligned a further strap along the domed meridian running from his forehead to the bump that houses grey matter. He adjusted some contraption at the front; centred it upon his brow. State-of-the-art, he remarked. Halogen bulb. Got it in Amsterdam. Now: make-or-break time. The spot came alive. A beam shot out. He trained it on my eyes. He fixed me with a smile. I winced, then said: Clever, that. He said: Very leading-man, don't you find? – the sole (surprising) note of camp to be struck during our bargain. Still, as Matthew used to advise: never trust a man without it.

At the sink, Dom filled a basin with warm water, into which he plopped a bar of soap. Back-turned to the room, he said: No scented rubbish, always stick to anti-bacterial. He came toward the side from where I watched, and propped the basin on the stool. Fleetingly his light flooded my groin; then, flitted off. He asked me to lie back. It didn't seem too much to ask. I rendered myself supine. I wondered where to put my arms. I left them by my sides. I forgot about them. He slipped something under my rump. I raised myself a fraction. The thing felt like a tea-towel, or perhaps another of those nappies. He sat himself down. I closed my eyes. He began to lather up. I could hear the slither-squelch of suds racing through his hands. He settled to my parts. He cupped me. He washed me with a ritualistic calm. I did not feel undermined. I felt anything but. I worried that I was becoming hard. Two, three seconds ticked by. He said: Nuh-uh: think of something boring, like a party-political broadcast. He sloshed the water round. He rinsed me thoroughly. He towelled me dry. He concluded this first stage of my induction with an audible satisfaction. One might even have hazarded the haphaz-ardous adverb Lovingly. Stranger things have happened.

And thus to the release of Sounds. As Dom begins to unravel the sterilized towel, which he leaves – more open than a secret – on the china, I hear the clank of instruments colliding. I try to sit up. He asks me to relax, to lie flat, to close my eyes. There's nothing to worry about; he will talk me through every step of the action. Perfunctorily, he reassures me that we could stop at any time. Less perfunctorily, he confides his hope that we won't have to. He tells me that he's going to arrange the Sounds – a set of eight – in order of size, so as later not to have to fumble around one-handed. Incidentally, he points out, only ever touch a rod by its handle. I wonder what a handle looks like. Unto the rising stillness he must have raised a sample, a lofty example, because next he says: You can look now. A glacial shaft of halo-gen travels through the Sound. The Sound silences me: it's a gleaming skewer of steel, long as a knitting needle, but thicker, with a heavy curve at one extreme. His fingertips, like pincers, demonstrate the touchable end of the exhibit. I try not to grimace, but – frankly – how does he think he's going to get that thing into my dick? He says that I shall see. I ask: Don't doctors use anaesthetic – spray or something? He replies that anaesthetic would defeat the object here. It would deaden my sensitivity; would diminish the whole experience; would feel like cheating – believe him. Now he's trying to draw some lubricant into the syringe, but he needs to go easy – to prevent bubbles from getting in. Easily he succeeds. He taps the result. He sets it down. He alludes to gloves. I hear a pair being extricated: yank-yank. Then I hear a harsh dry crackling, followed by consecutive elasticated twangs as he tugs distended latex past his wrists, on to his forearms. Next he's going to scrub each Sound with alcohol, to kill any lingering bacteria or fungi. Hang on, I interrupt, I thought that the Sounds had already been sterilized. That's right, but you can't be too careful. Air particles, inadvertent touching, that kind of stuff. He's taking no chances – largely for my sake, he might add. I say that this is getting a bit heavy for my liking; I'm not sure I've got the – What? – the gumption. He tries to soothe my doubt. How can he convince me that we're in this thing Together? Good question. Matthew might have had an answer.

He seems to be inspecting my glans. I think that he's spreading the aperture. He's trying to figure out the largest size of Sound with which to start. Bigger the better, apparently: less sharp, less uncomfortable. I feel a coldness on my tip. I ask what that is. Just a blob of lube – to prepare the way for the syringe. He puts the plastic nozzle in the slit of my urethra. His thumb, poised on the plunger, applies pressure to the jellied juice; then, begins to push. It's the strangest feeling: neither pleasant nor unpleasant; just weird – like a worm worming into you. He tells me that you need a good amount of lube. He explains that if this were toothpaste, you'd be injecting about an inch. He holds the syringe in position, but massages my shaft – to discourage the gel from shooting out. He tells me to ignore any stinging. Textbook symptom. It will pass in a minute. I hear his fingers flexing and contracting, as if working up to something. Now he holds my limp penis upward, perpendicularly to my trunk. With his

other hand – his right – he presents the initial Sound. French
size eighteen, whatever that means. I try not to breathe. He alerts
me to the fact that he's beginning to go in. Any pain? Not really.
See? – a properly managed Sound should slide naturally, by gravity. Dom's job is merely to guide the rod toward my underside.
Next, for no apparent reason, the rod gets stuck. I can do nothing. But *he* can: he teases at my penis, tugs at loose skin – an
expedient which . . . yes, does seem to have rectified my urethra.
The rod proceeds. How does it feel? Kind of buzzy. Told you,
he tells me. We're doing just fine. He attunes me finely. The
Sound, he says, has slipped right in; right inside me. He tilts my
cock down, lowers it to meet my scrotal sac. A latexed knuckle
presses my thigh. Next he brings my cock back up. He wiggles
the rod by its handle. What's he doing now? Engineering the
curve in the plumbing, so that the Sound can enter the bladder.
Instantaneously my sense is heightened. What's it like? Bizarre;
throbbing from inside; almost like some kind of orgasm. He says:
Exactly. That's because he's working on my prostate in a way no
other sexual contact can. And suddenly I hear myself gasp. For,
as he begins to withdraw the Sound, which he does with a
rhythmic art, by means of very gradual fluctuations – forth and
slowly back and forth and slowly back – I find myself subjected
to the longest-drawn-out climax. I suggest that perhaps this is
what a woman means by rapture. But Dom won't have it. Leave
women out of it. This is about Us. More lubricant. He's going
up in Sound. Size nineteen. Size counts.

I can't recount the rest with accuracy. I seem to be tongue-
tied, but he tells me to lie quietly. I must be more than
lubricated, but he prescribes a further top-up. He intensifies my
treatment before I can recover from the last; yet, even as my fever
mounts, my desire is to protract and protract. Time no longer
matters. Nothing does. With how many rods does he finally fuck
me? Three? Four? Five? Don't even know; I don't bother to ask,
for I have grown (not erect, but) reliant – until he, ever-reliable,
announces that that's that. We've reached my max. My what?

Optimum size. Larger would be asking for trouble. How come? Because when the tip of the cock starts to stick to the Sound, and the tissue begins to form a slight funnel – as it just has – it's a sign to stop the fun. My practitioner informs me, while robbing me of my ultimate orgasm, that the urethra possesses fine capillaries which, when stretched, will sometimes yield blood-cells; but even if these cells should leak into the lubricant, they're no cause for alarm. Deftly he extrudes the final Sound – in one. No shilly-shallying. He squeezes my cock to force any surplus jelly out. With a cloth he wipes the upshot. He brings into my focus some vaguely pinkish gunk. I try to remain sanguine. He repeats: No cause for alarm. He simulates a weary yawn. He yawns the weary platitude about how all good things must – but I'm on the way back from bad punchlines. I sit up. I look about. His cock is priapic and angry; yet his indifference to his own arousal could not seem blither. He peels off his gloves. He forces himself back into his flies, and buttons up – as if ejaculation were anathema to this whole transaction, or, perhaps, as if he preferred to save his essence for some other. For some other, more deserving, departed counterpart.

As I dress, he fusses to restore the dungeon, and, while fussing, dispenses advice. He advises that I drink plenty of fluids – in order to flush out unwanted microbes. He advises that I not be surprised if, to begin with, I pass only small amounts of urine: it just means that I've stimulated the nerves which signal the urge to piss. He further advises that I not worry about a burning sensation – at least not within the next twelve hours. But if the feeling should persist beyond, say, tomorrow night, then I'd be wise to get myself checked out. What's he talking about? In case of an infection. What infection? Of the bladder. I want to say: You stupid motherfucker. But I hold my tongue – luckily, because he conceives a contigency plan. Just as I can do without embarrassment, so, it seems, he can do without comebacks. He opens a narrow drawer, rattles about, and hands me a small bottle of tablets. Here's some antibiotics, he announces, puffed up by his prescience of mind. I squint at the label. It's one of those Mycins. Makes me think of Matthew. I say: (not How kind, but) Let's hope the need doesn't arise. He struts past my ingratitude and ushers me out. He tells me to take it easy now; to mind how I go. Yet, as I step into the lift, his toe-cap interrupts the door and jams it open. One last thing, he adds – an afterthought. Only ever play with Sounds inside a caring and supportive partnership. He smiles. He flabbergah – the door slides shut. I fumble for my watch. Five in the morning. Matthew expects me at nine. Never mind. At least I've got the note for the consultant. A Mr Farquhar.

Despite the exertions of the night, I made it to the hospital on time: I must have drawn fresh energy from the hope of a visit to Harley Street. Yet Matthew, who, for the last three weeks, had lain slumped in passive resignation on his waterproof mattress, now seemed actively riled. I found him stumbling around the bathroom, struggling to shove things back in his sponge-bag, but, often as not, misjudging; dropping stuff. His jaw was grinding. He hissed that he'd had just about enough. I ascribed his irritation to the torment of encroaching blindness; but when he mentioned that some orderly had recited him a notice tacked to his bedside cabinet, I learned the more immediate reason for his conduct.

THE SINGLE ROOMS ON THIS WARD ARE NOT 'PRIVATE' AND ARE OFTEN REQUIRED AT SHORT NOTICE FOR PATIENTS WITH SPECIAL NEEDS. OCCASIONALLY PATIENTS WILL HAVE TO MOVE TO THE MAIN WARD IN ORDER TO ACCOMMADATE THESE REQUIREMENTS. IN THESE CIRCUMSTANCES WE WOULD RESPECTFULLY REQUEST THAT PATIENTS WHO HAVE TO MOVE TO THE

WARD DO NOT QUESTION THE MEDICAL
AND NURSING EXPERTISE UPON WHICH
THESE DECISIONS ARE MADE.

You mean they're chucking you out? Looks like it, doesn't it. Why the hell? Someone else needs the room, apparently. *Who* else? Don't care; too tired to argue. He shuffled back to bed and collapsed. Right, I said. I flew out. I flew to the main desk and asked for the Sister in Charge. Not due for another hour. A face glued to a computer-screen wondered if anyone else could help. I said: *You* might. The face said: Try me. I said: Why does Matthew have to be the one to be transferred to the main ward? The face looked not the brightest. I said: Listen, Matthew needs that room. The face said: Listen, I don't make the rules round here. I said: When the Charge Nurse gets in, please tell her that I'd like a word with her. The face said: Will do. The face, of course, did no such thing. Too busy clicketty-clicking. You've met the ilk. But I find this whole episode tricky, so I'll cut through the frills.

The reason why Matthew was being ejected from his room was (not because anyone else enjoyed a higher entitlement to it – by dint, say, of private medical insurance; nor on account of some infectious new admission – 'openly' tubercular, for instance, but) – simply – because the other patient happened to be female. I hope that in the past I've managed to convey my high opinion of women. I wish that I could claim a similar esteem for decisions which, however aggrandized by adjectives such as 'medical' and 'nursing', have nothing to do with expertise and everything to do with whimsy. Still; the established regulation at this singular institution was that females should only suffer the ward in the plural: in triplicate – a trinity of the gender being the requisite minimum. But, given that the casualties of this epidemic were so predominantly male, it didn't take a doctorate to glean that the probability of three women coinciding at a single stroke was next to nil. And since the pretender to Matthew's privacy was, predictably, the only female in that midst, well, rules is rules. I was told to try to see the situation from the woman's point of view. Instead, I just saw red, bright as hell, but futile, because – let's face it – bulls are colour-blind. Yet I would say that if the occasion when everyone kept bashing into Matthew was enough to turn one into a homophobe, this current altercation fed me with a foretaste of the tangy noun Misogyny.

Matthew already knew that his rival was a woman, and that her condition wasn't critical. He also knew that she wasn't British; wasn't even European. But none of those particulars (which would have rankled with me) seemed to bother him. Something else did. Although it used to be said that the vicious thing about this disease was the accuracy with which it struck at the part of you that you most prized – in Matthew's case, his eyes – it struck me as a covert mercy that his mounting blindness should prevent him from witnessing his own decline. And yet, when this whole argument about expulsion flared up, I discovered that his principal anxiety concerned (not relegation from the top of the class, but) being clocked by a wardful of faces that he couldn't clock back. My own anxieties, though arguably minor, touched on the minor luxuries which I had hitherto been able to provide – luxuries which, in a public ward, I feared might inspire public spite: regular flowers, pedicures, manicures, Reiki massage, haircuts, treats to tempt his palate – smoked chicken, white asparagus, gravadlax. But, treats aside, I also worried about how he would adjust to yet another baffling environment; whether he would manage to steer himself to the night-lavatory without crashing into a stranger's bed, or, worse, having an accident. Would he be able to find the bell for assistance? Would assistance be forthcoming in time? I couldn't risk finding out. I must do everything in my power to impede a transfer. Frightfully sorry. Matthew wasn't budging. Try some other sucker. Get me the Sister in Charge.

We went into some office, she and I. Did I want a cup of tea?

I didn't, thanks – but I wouldn't mind a little sympathy. She liked my sense of irony – bit of a comedian, wasn't I? (Muted laughter – dignified.) We sat apart. We sized each other up. I tried to (pretend to) be thankful for her time. She apologized for her late arrival, and blamed it on the Underground. I asked if she'd had far to travel. Not as bad as some, but still – from Highgate. I said: Northern Line's a nightmare. She said: Tell me about it – and rolled her eyes. My eyes rolled likewise – to unite with her front. Still (she reckoned), no good moaning; lots to be done. Now, was something the matter? Not the matter with me personally: I was here on Matthew's behalf. Of course; Matthew. Matthew (she must say) was jolly lucky to have me. Matthew (I must say) was jolly unlucky to be dying. She passed on that, but wondered what in particular I wanted to discuss. I particularly wanted to discuss this business of a transfer. Might she know why? Because a transfer would be harmful to Matthew: if anyone's needs were special, they were *his* – he was, to all intents and purposes, blind. She pulled me up: Unsighted. I said: Quite. She presumed that I had read the notice on his bedside cabinet. I nodded that I had. Including the clause about not questioning professional decisions? I resorted to the myth With Respect, and stipulated that to downgrade a patient after *weeks* of inconclusive tests, especially when that patient had lost his sight, struck me less as professionally decisive than as unkind, and prejudicial, and – to be perfectly frank – prejudiced. What on earth did I mean by that? I meant that it was sexist. She feigned incomprehension. I specified: my impression was that Matthew was being shifted to the ward not because somebody else was iller than he, but merely because that somebody was a woman. The Charge Nurse assumed the charitable sort of sneer that one assumes for half-wits. She said that there was nothing 'mere' about being a woman: it was especially difficult for female patients to live with this illness – there were so few directives for them, they were in such a minority, they were often made to feel like second-class citizens. I said: Which is precisely how Matthew has been made to feel, notwithstanding his British citizenship. She called my little coda: Uncalled-for. I called it: Ironic. She told me to call it what I liked, but she was standing for none of that racist nonsense. I apologized. And thus, thus emboldened by my (false) retraction, she proceeded with her take on our discussion. The thing, George – you-don't-mind-if-I-call-you-George – the thing is this: for a woman to find herself alone in a male ward can be extremely inhibiting; women are by nature shy. I said: Funny that. Funny why? Because so is Matthew – shy, I mean; Sister, I don't think that gender dictates personality; I'm sure we've both met battle-axes in our time, and you don't have to be a lesbian to be that. She glowered at my obnoxious mouth, then looked away – shyly. She thought that we were veering off the subject. I conceded that she might be right. (But the woman was brilliant; she was wearing me out.) I changed tack. Leaving the other patient aside, what did Sister imagine would be the actual benefits of a transfer for Matthew? She said: More intensive supervision, and – I interrupted. Matthew didn't need more intensive supervision; what he needed was more conclusive test results. She repeated: More intensive supervision, and social interaction. I said that I could safely be relied on to provide him with whatever social interaction was required; it wasn't very taxing; cocktail-party chit-chat didn't exactly figure highly on the priorities of a blind man who was on his uppers. She told me not to bank on it. I assured her that I banked on nothing, but I also assured her that, in his present circumstances, Matthew wasn't the life-and-soul of awfully much. She told me that I would be surprised: the nurses apparently found him charming. So why should he be penalized for *that*? He was not being penalized, George; no one was being penalized; but I must appreciate that a Charge Nurse wasn't a nanny: this was the National Health, you know, not some private hospital where greater resources allowed staff to cater for individual foibles. I told her that the NHS was not being asked to cater for Matthew's foibles-as-she-called-them. I was perfectly capable of seeing to those myself. Up to a point. What point? Well, from the standpoint of a layman. I confessed – mere layman that I was – that I hadn't been too impressed by the findings of the professionals. She couldn't possibly comment; she wasn't familiar with Matthew's notes. I said: Precisely – had Dr Nilson been consulted about the plan to move Matthew? The Charge Nurse said that Dr Nilson was entitled to his say-so at the day-clinic, but she had Total Jurisdiction over the running of her floor. Let yourself be bossed about by a bunch of doctors and – well, it was a recipe for disaster. I reiterated that the real disaster was moving Matthew out: I'd struggled all this time to keep his spirits up, and now, in one fell swoop, the hospital was going to crush his morale. He was bound to fall apart. Did she have no feelings about that? Did I have to let my friend disintegrate in order to be proved right? Did emotions not come into this somewhere? Emotions, unfortunately, were not a luxury which a Charge Nurse could afford: it wasn't always easy, but someone in her position couldn't allow herself to be subjective. Well, her attitude to her own gender didn't exactly strike me as *ob*jective. Any more (she said) than my attitude to Matthew struck her as relevant. How *did* it strike her then? As well-intentioned, certainly, but defensive and – if she might say so – a tad hysterical. I wasn't hysterical (or so I claimed), but I did feel angered by a decision which, as well as being reversible, smacked of unfairness. The Charge Nurse smiled with passionless compassion. She could see what a redoubtable – *redoubtable* – champion Matthew had in me. I waited for the But, but none was forthcoming. Anyway, to return to the patient for whom Matthew was being ousted: the woman supposedly needed a couple of lengthy transfusions – after which, all things being equal, she should be released. So perhaps (said Sister) we could come to a sort of gentleman's agreement: if I undertook not to get Matthew's hopes up, she undertook to do her best to ensure that Matthew was returned to his old room once the lady had been discharged. We would play it by ear, Sister decided. Couldn't say fairer than that. And then she said: If you'll excuse me, I have a great many things to sort out. The bitch had won. Actually, both bitches had.

My nerves were in an uproar. I was frantic for a smoke. I took myself down to the lobby; bought a paper at the stall. I leaned against an outside wall of glass and tried to ignore the screech of cabs – late arrivals, swift departures; the happy, the lucky, the done-for. With blurred incuriousness I drifted over seas of printed news, until I landed at the obituaries, whose waves of valediction seemed daily to wash up known corpses from the flood. Named Hivvy casualties. And yet, too often, the cause of their demise was left untold by their families, for I suppose that, just as the bereaved prefer to have their Loss portrayed in a flattering light – beaming from a college summer, strumming on a hippy guitar – so they're entitled to the seemly weeds of dis(semblance), the seamless veils of social opacity. 'Debilitating illness' was a favoured euphemism; 'pulmonary infection', another. But let's not carp about decorous half-lies: at least the dates cranked up your maths. You couldn't help but calculate how young the dead had been when they had died.

I killed my cigarette and binned the hopeless *Times*. I went off to the lavatory. I stood, swaying with fatigue and puzzlement, at the pissoir, where I noticed, far below, an errant pube squirming on the lip of the gutter. I wondered whence it could have come, from whom it could have jumped. A shuddering relative? An aimless lover? A chaplain? An optimist now witnessing the birth of his first son? It defied understanding. My head was scrambled. I scrambled up the fire escape. I ran up countless flights. I raced to Matthew's side. I braked outside Room 9. I opened the door a fraction. His bed was bare, stripped down. An overall was scouring the bath. My boy had been moved out. I prowled the gallery. I found him. They had plonked him on the lousiest bed of all – between two slack-jawed write-offs: conclusions foregone. I said: There you are. He said: Neither use nor bloody ornament. I said: Don't talk nonsense. He said: What's the point of struggling on? I said: The point is to be patient. He

330 ~ Paul Golding

said: Patient for what – the obvious? For results from the laboratory; it's worth it, I promise you, and I promise you another
thing: give me three days, and I'll have you out of this here, three
days only; now listen, I've got to get back to the flat, I'm desperate for a lie-down. Nurse Bitch has worn me out. I'll tell you
about it when I get back. Around fourish, all right? He said: So
what do I do now? I said: Nothing, just pretend this isn't happening. He said: Easier said than done. I said: Be fair; I *am* trying;
give me a chance to sort things out. He said: Kiss me, Captain.
I said: You smooth-talking harlot. I kissed my boy, drew his curtain closed, and pissed off. The reek of the ward was beyond. It
clung to your nostrils. All the way home.

I found a couple of messages: one from Sukie; one from
some unknown. Sukie's was not good, not bad, nor yet indifferent. It just wasn't helpful. She said that she'd approached a
stylist-friend who was pretty *au courant* – he'd lost a string of
people in the last few months – and, thanks to that friend, managed to secure a *rendez-vous* with some well-known specialist on
the Pasteur staff. The specialist, after double-checking Sukie's list
of English drugs and cross-referencing occasional doubts, had
confirmed that the medicines available in Paris were – in practice, if not brand-name – no different from the ones being
prescribed to Matthew in London. France *had* recently begun
some aggressive new trials to arrest Retinitis – involving (Sukie
sighed) injections in the eye-ball – but if Matthew was already
as advanced as I'd made out, this course of action seemed not
really advisable. Kind of a waste of his time. Sorry to be such a
downer. Ring me when you can. *Je t'embrasse* – and, of course,
Matthew.

The second call was different: (not just dispiriting, but)
actively sinister, its creepiness enhanced by interference from
some anonymous public background, presumably a bar. Rever-
berating music; peripheral laughter; yabbering passers-by. I
had to play back the message several times in order to distil its
substance. The voice, a man's – an American's – sounded

bunged-up, sinusy. Its drawl seemed drunken, and kept slurring, with tuneless sarcasm, an infantile rhyme – a sing-song which, though still popular in nurseries, harks back to Bubonic London: Ring a ring o'roses/Pocket full of posies/A-tishoo, a-tishoo/We all fall down. Twice-and-a-half the voice went round, and then, after a drawn-out cackle, appeared to lose its way, or lose heart, until, bored or tired or sad, it hung up. (Who the fuck?) Hunter. Bound to be Hunter, Kelly's Yankee paramour. I rang Holland Park to find out what he was playing at. But, just as he picked up, I put my receiver down, for, at that instant, I clicked that the prankster was not he. It was Kelly, having his sick idea of fun. Well, Kelly could call back when he had sobered up.

I stared at the letter to Farquhar. I wondered what to do about it. I must keep my wits about me. My wits told me to look inside. I took a knife, and sliced. I brought the mystery to light. The note was fine. The note was harmless. The note would get me to where I wanted. It informed its addressee (whom it called Farks) that this young man (full 'name' supplied) had a couple of questions about the dreaded lurgy, which the sender (who signed himself Dominick) would be grateful if Farquhar could answer. I put the note in a fresh envelope, and tucked the flap. No saliva. No licks of power.

I ran a bath and, while it ran, dialled Paris. I told Sukie not to worry, thanked her for having gone to all that trouble, and apologized for not being able to chat. I had to run. I made myself a quick sandwich. I rushed, still munching, back to the bathroom. I turned off the taps. I washed and shaved and dressed – like a good chap. No siesta. No time. None like the present. I set off for Mayfair. I drove through the park. The Serpentine that afternoon was fit to move the quills of seasoned sonneteers, who, having of autumnal waters writ, wrote to dispel a fearful queen's worst fears. I rode over the bridge, and headed down a leafy carriageway to Marble Arch. I circled round its round-about. I drew closer to the medical parish; arrived; found a space in which to park; got out; walked along Harley Street; crossed to the other side; found the designated house. Stucco façade. Double-fronted. Numerous bells of polished brass. I rang the second down. A woman answered: Please come up. The stairs were carpeted. I stepped into a large office, and produced my introduction. From its envelope – as if contents mattered more than confidentiality – I extracted Dom's handwriting. I said: This is probably self-explanatory. I surrendered the card. The secretary peered through her half-moons, and asked me to take a seat next door. The waiting-room was empty, empty and grand. Handsome cornices; handsome fireplace; handsome bookcase – glass-fronted. I began to count the panes of dia-monds. Next, the secretary was back. Mr Farquhar was sorry to be busy right now, but he could see me in the morning, at eight forty-five, before his first appointment showed up; would that be all right? I said: Absolutely, I'll be here just beforehand. She said: See you tomorrow then. I thanked her – and added: Please thank Mr Farquhar on my behalf.

I went back to Matthew, who had followed my advice – done nothing, pretended that this wasn't happening. He hadn't touched his lunch. He hadn't touched his tablets. All that he had done was close his eyes. Gently I rocked his arm. Gently does it. He said: *There* you be at last; what the hell have you been up to? I said: Cruise to Buenos Aires. He said: Very funny, tell me about the Charge Nurse. Bugger-all to tell, I lied. He said: Come *on*, you were in there long enough – *something* must have happened. I said: Well, we didn't exactly get to shag, but I did discover that the woman who's nicked your room should only be needing it for forty-eight hours, so, with any luck, we'll have you back there straight after. Matthew said: Insh'Allah. And then he whis-pered: Listen, am I imagining things, or does this whole place stink? I admitted that it did. He said: Bring me some room-spray next time you come in, would you. And then he said: The noise of these people is unbelievable, coughing and retching the whole time. Bet I don't sleep tonight. I said: Try to sleep *now*, while it's relatively quiet. He said: Fat chance, tea-trolley's about to come round. I said: Well, what about some music? All right, but you'll have to fix me up.

I rummaged in his holdall; fumbled about; found his Walkman and fished it out, along with a knot of wires from a couple of headsets: one, recently rejected – because its metal ear-pieces hurt when he lay down – and a replacement pair, snazzier, with foam-backed speakers and a connecting headband. I untangled them. Into the machine I plugged the set that Matthew liked. I asked what tape he fancied. He wasn't really fussed. I chose a singer whom we both admired – madly continental, madly camp, madly lachrymose and overblown and fabulous. I own that tape now. But anyhow, this woman, who was just the wrong side of ravishing and sang in every language under the sun (except Polari), had covered the gamut of the torch-song repertoire, and always – or so it seemed to us – improved upon the originals, poured into them an exotic, individual disenchantment. Most of her numbers were, admittedly, schmaltzy gripes about atrocious love, but that's precisely what appealed to us. We weren't homosexual for nothing. And though I've bitched about those people who, from false propriety, used to refrain from publishing too many facts about how a charisma became a cadaver, now – now that my turn has come – I find myself unable to divulge even the title of the tape which I clicked on for Matthew. It feels too private. Indulge me while I deal with practicalities. I checked that the volume wasn't too high, and handed him his headband. He donned the gadget; slid it back toward his crown. I placed the Walkman in his palm. He clutched it. He said: Diadem and evening bag – what more could one ask for? I said: My thoughts entirely. I watched him lie back. I watched him close his eyes. I heard him sigh. I heard him say: Voice is divine. I stroked his (waxy) brow. I stroked his (skinny) arm. I kissed his (hollow) cheek. I kissed it twice. His hair smelt of soap. His skin smelt of powder. My diminishing beloved. Beloved regardless.

But exhaustion had caught up with me. The stillness of the

ward, its overheated dullness, had finally flattened me. I decided, while Matthew was distracted, to try to steal a nap – even sitting down. Better than nothing. I hung up my jacket. I drew the patterned curtain safely round. I wanted safety from the gawping public. Matthew opened his eyes. They didn't quite meet mine. They missed their target. He gestured me to lie beside him. He shouted: There's those other headphones somewhere. I plugged myself into his Walkman. He made space for me on the mattress. I lay down. He held me in his arms. I held him in mine. We entwined our heads like twins from Siam, twins united by a single heart. From this heart there flowed into our minds – minds independent yet at one – old ballads which, not so far back, had been – oh – lifeblood to us. And yet, those soppy lyrics, so full of soaring dreams and corny charm and swooping great downers which, in their very excess, had earlier made us weep with laughter, no longer felt so funny. There was a kink in their spool, a warp to their sound – mild but undeniable – as if those rhapsodies which, once, had underscored our romance, had been rewound too many times; as if those tracks which, over and over, we had claimed as ours, were, though undiminished, somehow running out. How can I convey to you the sense without betraying the manner? Let's just say that they were songs of summers past, of winters coming, of seaside villas shuttered, of crosswords left undone, of red wine drunk, of candles snuffed, of mandolins abandoned, of lovers parted and departed, of heavy hearts and vanished time and sand. It made you nostalgic. It made you sad. But at least our breathing was in harmony. Matthew's closeness lent me calm. I felt myself relax and float and vanish; and I must have slept awhile, because, when I came round – on the wings of a crescendo to the crest of some sublimely vocalized catastrophe – I knew, instinctively, that something was not right. Matthew was shivering slightly. Had his temperature gone up? I felt a trickle on my neck – of sweat, no doubt. His defences must be trying to beat a fever down. But next, as the shivers became shudders and his shoulders became racked, I understood from where, and why, this stream was coming. For the first and only time that I knew Matthew – Christ – he was crying. I was aghast. I tried to move back, tried to snatch the Walkman from his hand, tried to stop the songs that had undone him – songs for which I, who had depressed the Start button, now felt culpable. But he wouldn't have it. He hugged me harder. I froze in his embrace for as long as I could stand it, until, like a cretin, like a jackass, like any fool who ever loved, I – my throat just cracked and sobs broke out. Would not stop coming. It was beyond embarrassment, but it must have been of comfort, because we held in this embrace for a good while, weeping both together and apart, weeping for our separate selves and for each other, dissolved by an admission greater, yet uglier, than the sum of us – the one admission which could not (then, yet), be overtly made between us: the admission of Finality. And while our tears were coursing thus, I became aware of an outside voice gathering loudness, and of the curtain being parted, and of a presence intruding upon our sanctum: the trolley on its round. I waved across behind me, to indicate: No tea, thanks. But a finger tap-tapped at my calf and forced me up – to witness some (not well-meaning volunteer, but) faggy nurse exclaim how Oooh they couldn't have that kind of thing going on in 'ere! I said: Why don't you just get the fuck out? Nursey reeled with taken-abackedness, but rallied soon enough, to broadcast: Only jokin', dear, don't get yer knickers in a twist. Someone snickered. Matthew whispered: I don't believe this. I'm going to sleep.

Despite Mr Farquhar's straight-laced apparel, he wore ankle-socks of scarlet – a fad then espoused by quite a lot of chinless types. In the case of Farquhar, it might have been designed to imply that, established as he stood upon the plateau of consultancy, yet he remained, notwithstanding, a bit of a maverick; for, despite his trademark Athenaeum tie, and his crisply doubled cuffs, and his links proclaiming him a fisher of (not men, but) trout, he also seemed, well, not entirely unlike the sort of chap who might, over Christmas, spare himself the bore of picking up his shaving brush, or, on Easter Sunday, step into boxer-shorts jollified with Bunny girls, or, at midsummer bashes for the young, not say no to a little token hash, or even, at quieter times, quietly say yes to an advertised enticement from the dearest Russian doll come to Soho since Glasnost – Katya – to whom, at the point of introductions, he might introduce his penis as Ivan.

These things I worked out while Farquhar sat to scan Dom's card, which had been tucked by some helping hand into a blotter with corners the colour of saddle. Once reminded as to how, and why, I came to be consulting him, the consultant cast me a glance of roundabout befuddlement. Then, he took me by surprise. He didn't ask how he could help. He said that I looked fit-as-the-next-man. I explained that it wasn't about myself that I had come, but about a friend of mine. Farquhar did beg my pardon, and put his pen down. He leaned back. I cleared my throat, and suddenly – I seemed to have begun. It felt like an exam. I raced through Matthew's hurdles from the moment when his cells had first, formally, been counted. Farquhar nodded as I exercised my mouth, yet I could tell that his intelligence was absolutely focused on the facts. (You're aware of all the steps which had led to the current pass – this medical impasse – so I'll spare you a recap; but) when I reached, breathless and parched, the end of my marathon, Farquhar had become uncomfortable. He stood up, clasped his hands behind his back, and started to pace about. May he be completely candid? I replied that less would seem impractical. Yes, indeed, in which case, well, he might as well confess that his impression, based, of course, on what I'd said, was that my chum wasn't long for this world. I asked about time – time left – could he hazard a guess? Wouldn't dream of it, he said; not a fortune-teller. Yet nor could I allow Matthew's misfortune to rest. Surely *something* could be done which hadn't been? Farquhar didn't think that he was altogether with me. I wondered whether, for instance, there wasn't some experimental drug which, even if not yet official, my friend could be pro-cured. Farquhar said that, had this been the States, he might *just* have been tempted to agree: perhaps I was aware of some recent anti-retroviral trials where protease inhibitors, used in combination with standard nucleosides, were giving cause for encouragement. But Farquhar was afraid that here, in Britain, this type of therapy was only being suggested to patients at the incipient stages of the disease – asymptomatics mainly. His guess would be that, were my friend to request, say, a cocktail containing Saquinavir, his application would be refused. On what grounds? On the grounds that, given the high cost of these new drugs and the importance of long-term monitoring, chemical companies didn't consider 'advanced' applicants to be – how could he put it? – as effective an investment as basically healthy ones. I told him that this mercenary line of argument struck me as scandalous: a basically healthy applicant had a stronger resistance to the virus, and a greater chance of hanging about for science to come up with something more than merely encouraging. Farquhar said: That's as may be. But the sheer discrepancy between demand and supply had made it necessary for *some* sort of selection process to be established. I said: That *still* strikes me as scandalous. What was so wrong with merit based on gravity? He said: In principle nothing. But really the business of who was, or wasn't, chosen for those research-studies lay with the pharmaceutical companies, not the medical establishment. Doctors provided patients' data, but it was the laboratories who did the deciding. Hospitals had no effective say in the matter. (I effectively said nothing, but) I did say: So who *can* help Matthew?

Farquhar thought about it. He said: I think *you* can. How was that? By easing Matthew on the way out. I asked if we were talking euthanasia. We most absolutely weren't. He was dead against that kind of thing, and besides, it was a criminal offence in

England; go to Holland for your – what's the expression? – mercy killing. He trusted that he'd made his position clear. Now he sat down. He rubbed his brow. He looked at me directly, as if there were nothing left to hide. His manner grew milder, humbler. His voice dropped to the voice of a man whose dark task it had become to tell the same dark truth a thousand times. Death comes to all of us, he began, and your friend's seems to have come to him sooner than one might have liked. I said: You bet it has. He said: I understand. I said: Forgive me, but how can you? He paused, then muttered: Lost my own daughter last summer. (*That* shut me up.) He continued: What I'm trying to get at is the difficulty of predicting when one's number might be up; there are no pat answers, but one thing which I've discovered, less from personal experience, as it happens, than from my years in practice, is that there often comes a point when a patient decides that enough is enough, that it isn't worth the trouble, and *that's* the point at which one must learn to switch gears. How did he mean? He meant: Senseless to keep fighting on behalf of someone who's already face-to-face with Thanatos. Although he said that it went almost without saying, nonetheless he said: Thou-shalt-not-kill-but-need'st-not-strive-*officiously*-to-keep-alive. It sounded like a reprimand. He recommended that I concentrate on providing Matthew with the things which he wanted and *could* have, as opposed to those which he couldn't and probably didn't even want. I should follow my friend's initiative, not the other way round. Belligerence achieved nothing. No use getting into snarl-ups with hospital staff. Better to take Matthew home if I – or rather he – thought this would make him happier. Farquhar had no doubt that Matthew's doctor would respect such a plan. But first I should try to discover Matthew's own final wish, his dying one. For all that Farquhar knew, it might be a short break somewhere. Sometimes patients got a last-minute reprieve, an unexpected breather. They called it the honeymoon period. One should grab it while one could. One definitely should.

Farquhar pulled his chair back, and summed up: That's my best advice. I thanked him. Together we walked out. At the door I asked – don't ask me why – how his daughter had died. Silly motor-scooter accident; great shock to us, but there you are.

I may not have come away with anything miraculous, such as a miraculous new potion of new drugs; and yet, for once in this journey taken toward ghastliness but undertaken in the name of love, I felt myself to have been granted proper guidance, by which I mean precisely the right guidance at precisely the right hour. I shall always be grateful to Mr Farquhar; for, even if I failed, at our brief hearing, fully to grasp the power of his advice, I have since had plentiful occasion to appreciate its impact. After all: I had applied to a stranger for help over my friend – help which, for reasons already given, that stranger could not give; yet Farquhar, instead of dismissing me with a sniff of upper-lip indifference, effected a shift in me as subtle as it proved pivotal. He swivelled my attention from the sloping lowlands of incurability toward a field where change, indeed improvement, *could* be expected – namely in myself.

I would say that I had spent the previous year living in anything but the present, dwelling in a sort of tenseless tension. Because my life had grown so closely yoked – so conjugated – to the life of someone else, my days felt like the pages of another's journal: related, but not my own. I did, sporadically, pursue separate engagements, yet even those escapes – those escapades to Hades – had grown linked, of late, to my soon-to-be late friend. In my dreams, of course, he remained healthy and glossy and independent, but those visions were deception – teases from the fates. Not that I was in a state to make head or tail of anything. I was like a spinning coin upon a table, whirling with adrenaline, though never too far from losing my balance, or toppling over the edge. I seemed to veer from moments of anticipation (of trying to overtake the inevitable) to moments of reversal, of retrospection – but retrospection before the event. The gulf between reason and emotion is estimable, and though my head was perfectly able to accept, even articulate, the fact that Matthew was dying, my heart would not beat to the drum of his departure, could not bear to roll the ceremonial timpani of his demise. Which is why, if ever I considered, I mistakenly considered inward, and prematurely backward, as if planning a biography, or plotting an obituary, despite having no clue as to its concluding paragraph. Farquhar changed all that. Changed me profoundly.

Farquhar was a master, but his stroke proved more inspired than just a lesson in the palliative. For it was he who — whether inadvertently or otherwise — made me see that if my life, then, seemed to me (by dint of its vicariousness) to lack a sense of actuality, the blame for such a lack lay not with adverse circumstance, still less with Matthew. The blame was mine, because I, rather than contemplate the prevailing climate, which was thunderous, had scrambled up a spire of self-indulgence and turned myself into the very weathervane of denial. Thus had I swung from moods of looking in advance, far beyond the future, to moods of looking back so fast, so furiously, that the future hadn't even had a chance to *become* the past. And it was Farquhar who, oddly enough, set me aright, who led me to realize that I'd been labouring in a vanity, a temporal fallacy. The future — whatever grammarians may argue — can never be perfect. When we tell ourselves that by such-and-such a date we *will have* done something, we are not being accurate. We're being wilful and presumptuous, for — death aside — life guarantees us nothing. The most that we can ever do is hope, hope to meet our target, even if that target should boil down to the piteous provision of dignity and laughter. Certainly I had said, long before my best became required, that I would try to do my best for Matthew; and certainly I would say, now that the question no longer matters, that my best is the extent to which I tried. But tell me something: when was one's best ever good enough?

There are two types of future: the real and the imagined. The real, being by definition (de)finite, is finite. Its days, although mysterious as the windows of an Advent calendar, are numbered. Yet the imagined future, being in(de)finite, is *in*finite in its abstraction, immoderately fanciful; it amounts to a mental flight without horizons. And when Farquhar turned my head to confront the Forthcoming, what he was doing was stilling me, grounding me, stopping me from spinning about – in order to focus my attention on the only real reality: the imminence of Matthew's final paragraph. By 'switching gears', Farquhar had not meant clutching: he had meant relinquishing control entirely, swapping right round, back to the original (im)balance. The moment had come for me to revert to my natural position, which was the (dis)position of an aimless passenger, and allow Matthew, the more directed traveller, to begin his voyage – unaccompanied – toward departure. The task, for me, would prove taxing, because it demanded separation *in life*, severance *in advance*, almost a betrayal of the twinship which, with the growth of our alliance, had grown to entwine us. Yet my withdrawal was, I admit, a necessary part of easing him into the arms of Thanatos – a duty which, heavy as it felt, harshly as it fell, fell within the province of my vows.

Needless to say, I hadn't, at that juncture, figured out a fraction of what goes above, but I *had* grasped that my role must modulate from the chronologically muddled to the temporarily sharp, from the actively chaotic to the passively organized. This prospect, though daunting, struck me, strangely, as manageable, for boundaries encompass; limits lend an unexpected comfort; deadlines do not kill: they energize. The very notion of a countdown makes you want to count. Every second becomes magnified; every twitch, every sigh, every gasp is heightened. Which is why Farquhar, despite having restricted my perspective, despite having affixed me to the foreground, despite having advocated soft acceptance over hardened anger, did not cast me down.

Returning to the Hivvy ward, I noticed that – for once – Dr

Nilson was doing the round. I caught a glimpse of him, mumbling over some huddled blanket. I hurried past. Matthew was lying on his side, curled into a state of blind indifference. He patted my arm. I asked about last night. Average. He'd woken up with cramp and tried to walk about, but felt so stoned (because of his sleeping tablets) that he'd been forced to ring for help. Fat chance. The nurse had been busy chatting on the phone about some backpacking trip somewhere. Not that Matthew blamed the girl. I mean: who'd want to be stuck *here*? Talk about thankless tasks.

Nilson pretended to knock on Matthew's curtain – a charade which got no laugh – then introduced himself into the atmosphere. He said: Hello chaps – which, coming from him, was sarcastic. Matthew replied: Good morrow squire, which served Nilson right. The doctor wondered how things were. Matthew didn't pull his punches: Pretty shitey, since you ask. Nilson faked a frown, and enquired, as if mystified, why. Because Matthew was feeling lousy, and his patience was running out. Hadn't they done enough tests? Hadn't they taken enough blood? . . . So, why couldn't *some*one come up with *some* sort of result? Nilson purported to be expecting feedback any day now. I pointed out that Matthew had been hearing about Any Day Now for nearly a month. Nilson sympathized: he was really sorry that the business should be proving so protracted. Matthew twisted his neck away from Nilson's verbiage. I told Nilson that the regulations at this place were baffling, and Nilson did appear – just for a moment – baffled; but no sooner had I launched into my gripe about the woman who had supplanted Matthew than the doctor interrupted. He was up-to-date on all of that. (How? Had the Charge Nurse blabbed?) He was up-to-date because the patient in the single room happened, it so happened, to be his patient too. I suspect that this, this bitch-of-a-coincidence, marked the instant when my attitude to Dr Nilson congealed – from an initial, wobbly uncertainty into a firmer, chillier, though still gelatinous, antipathy. I asked if I was right in thinking that the Woman was about to be discharged. Nilson didn't think it likely. Well, the Charge Nurse had done – a couple of transfusions, apparently, and out. Nilson whispered that the Charge Nurse had perhaps been over-zealous in this instance. So – in this instance – I treated Nilson to a piece of my mind: I told him that I simply could not fathom how he could have let someone in Matthew's circumstances be ousted for some – some vaguely anaemic new arrival. Could it *really* be because that other patient was a female? Was clinical rationale *really* that crass? Nilson said that his hands were tied, but managed to hold them up – as if wishing, despite the lie, to feign that they were bloodless. I said: Allow me to be *straight* with you: I find this situation disgusting; I mean, can't you *see* that Matthew can't cope with ward life, that, given his eyesight, he can't be expected to stagger a hundred yards every time he needs to go to the lavatory? Nilson, faced by Matthew, whose stony silence must have hammered with injustice, yielded a tiny fraction. He admitted that the set-up might seem a bit tough, but – I pounced: it didn't *seem*; there was no doubt about it. (Suddenly I remembered Farquhar: No use getting into snarl-ups.) I said: I'm sorry; I'm getting too worked up. Then I turned to Matthew, and asked, relatively calmly: Darling, what would you say if Dr Nilson were to agree to let me take you home till some results came back? Matthew didn't hesitate. Matthew said that he would say: Get Packing, Captain.

I looked to Nilson, who seemed to need to look away before being able to concede that yes, or rather no, he didn't see the harm: Home Care had its own advantages. But nor could he capitulate outright; no hope of that; he just *had* to impose a condition before consenting to sign Matthew's Letter of Discharge. The patient's system ought by now, Nilson surmised, to have regained some measure of tolerance to intravenous drugs; so – even feeding the medication more slowly into the Portacath – he must go back to his infusions of Ganciclovir. Nilson demanded my formal assurance that Matthew would follow this instruction; and although, to me, the directive sounded as inspired as pumping petrol into a car that is already beyond salvage (or – to invoke Farquhar – as enlightened as officiously keeping alive), I gave my word. I agreed to the pact.

Outside – never mind the racket and the squalor and the drizzle and the stink of fries – outside was paradise. Matthew's mobility, because he'd been laid-up so long, was, admittedly, on the dodgy side – shuffly; and his breathing sounded tired; and his eyes weren't up to much. But I had an arm, and he had a smile, and we were off (come hell or high water, Captain) to my flat – where, within forty-eight hours, things looked, even if not all beautiful, brighter. His appetite was on the mend (he was wanting special milkshakes, packed with vitamins and calories); his energy was on the rise (he was forcing himself to move about); he was back to his usual whims and usual gags (time for my bath – and no peeping, Captain); he was sleeping without tablets, or sweats, or nightmares; even his sight seemed to have improved marginally. Over breakfast, he would tilt his head enquiringly, and conclude that Yup, peripheral flashes had to be better than total darkness – in the light of which I wasn't about to wonder whether this unforeseen revival resulted from Matthew's resumption of Ganciclovir or his rupture with Hospitality. But I did slightly wonder, as we fell back into our old routine, whether what I was witnessing mightn't be something new, something more akin to what Farquhar had described as the honeymoon period.

One of those mornings, the postbag brought a change-of-address card – effective from mid-December – sent by Douglas. It prompted an odd response in me; a regressive, sentimental sort of pang. I suppose that I missed him; I suppose that I rued the distance which had grown between us. Matthew said: For heaven's sake, he's practically your oldest friend, just ring him. So – later that evening, after Matthew had gone to sleep – I did. Douglas had just walked in from some work-related shindig, and sounded surprised to hear from me, but I'd like to think that he was pleased. How, I asked, were tricks? Not bad: he was about to move – hadn't I received his card? Yes, but I hadn't had a chance to check the street-map; I couldn't quite picture the beat. Bloomsbury, he said; easy for the City; house was Georgian, Grade II listed, retaining most of the original features; it had once belonged to some personage who meant zilch to me. But structurally, said Douglas, the place was in atrocious nick; he was going to have to gut all four floors of it, plus re-roof and underpin. And where would he go in the interim? There escaped from Douglas an embarrassed, almost nubile, giggle, as if some part of him had been tickled pink. He confessed that he'd met Someone recently, and that they'd been dating for the past few weeks, and it all looked quite promising, so, while the house was being fixed, he'd be staying with this other guy, over in Ealing. And once the work was finished? After that, he and the guy – whose name was Stan – would most likely set up home together. In? In Bloomsbury. I asked: What does Stan do? Douglas said: How d'you mean? I said: For a wage-packet. Douglas said: He works for a removals company. I said: In what capacity? Douglas, trying to sound all democratic, admitted: As a driver – which made me scream with laughter. But the hilarity backfired. Douglas snapped: What's-so-funny-I-mean-the-man-happens-to-*love*-me. I said: Sorry, you're right, it's just that, I don't know, somehow I'd never have imagined you married to a man-with-a-van. (Nowt so queer as fags.) Then I asked: So where does this leave Jack? Douglas said that it left Jack where Jack deserved: consigned to the past. I asked whether Douglas was *sure* about Stan, but Douglas didn't exactly reply. He claimed to be fed up with airy-fairy notions of romance. He would rather commit to someone who was ready to commit back than spend the rest of his life stuck alone in cuckoo-land. Douglas was ready to settle down, to settle for compatibility, for companionship – did that seem like such a cop-out? I replied that certain people might consider it a compromise. Douglas said that he would tell those certain people to grow up: just because he and Stan didn't share the same background (by which Douglas meant the same class), didn't mean they didn't share plenty of other stuff. Such as? Christ, George, maybe not a fetish for Fabergé cuff-links, but . . . they were both into jazz, and sailing-boats, and motorbikes, and country walks, and gardening. Stan had an amazing patio. And besides: Stan was kind, and he was loyal, and thought the world (as well he might) of Douglas. Sex? I asked. What about it? Sex all right? No complaints on that score either. Douglas didn't expect fireworks. He was *through* with one-night stands. He was *over* all that rubbish. He had wasted his best years waiting for Jack – a waste with which no-one, at least no-one who'd known Douglas for as long as I had done, could argue. But enough, he said, about his life. How was mine?

(Mine.) I explained about Matthew: how, after a reaction to his drugs, he'd had a bit of a rough ride; how he'd been stranded in hospital for a month; how his doctor was a prat; how no-one seemed to have the foggiest about what ought to be done; how, after some cuntish nurse had ousted him from a private room into the public ward, he'd decided to come to my flat and let me look after him . . . Douglas wondered when Matthew would be well enough to return to his own pad. I admitted the unutterable – that the possibility didn't strike me as likely. Douglas hadn't realized that things had got so bad. I said: Main problem's his eyesight, but he *has* been feeling better since he was discharged. Douglas reiterated: So what about *your* life, duck? I said: You know, on standby. He said: Fancy dinner one night? I heard myself (I who had fancied so little in such a long time) reply: I would adore that. Douglas wondered whether Wednesday suited. Down to the ground. And thus we agreed that he'd come round, have a quick drink, say hello to Matthew, and take me somewhere suitably chic. Douglas knew how prickly I could be. He thanked me for ringing. I thanked him for being sweet. Then I went to sleep – on the sofa, under a duvet.

So it must have been around this time (after my visit to

Farquhar) that I made a hard decision: to remove myself from the bed, the many beds which, here and there, over the years, I had shared with Matthew. The reason which I gave to him was that he must sleep undisturbed. The reason which I gave to myself was that it didn't matter how I slept. Soon enough I'd have unreasonable opportunity to catch up on lost rest. Now and then, however (but further down his slide toward the sea of death, by when his darkness, being all-round, no longer distinguished between night and day), Matthew would, if he felt scared, ask me to lie next to him; yet such measures were only temporary, only meant until the latest shot of analgesic had dulled him from a state of fretfulness toward a state of somnolence. Then I would creep away. It always made me feel redundant, this separation; redundant and lonely; but I knew – I know – that it was necessary. The dying, even when they can no longer tell you, need breathing-space. No-one dies together. Alone must be alone. But I'm jumping the gun, as it were.

Matthew was feeling surprisingly better. And yet, along with his betterment, there came another alteration; for, though his outward vigour had been raised, his spirits had grown graver. This is not to say that his humour had deserted him – it would only properly do so in his ultimate three words – but a certain seriousness now attached to his behaviour. Take music, for instance. As ever, he wanted it played, yet his interest seemed to have shifted from our schmaltzy songs of yesteryear toward more sober classical works, mostly choral, often sacred. Sometimes, as I pottered round the flat, he would call me to wherever he was lying, and ask me to rewind that last track; and occasionally, when the piece had reached its closing bar and the room had been returned to silence, he would say: Make a note of that, darling, you might want to have it. And in this gradual way, through his gentle guidance, I was able to compile a musical programme for his final mass. Once in a while, without warning, I would play something which, earlier, he had claimed to like – just to test him, just to double-check that he hadn't changed his mind

– but invariably he would remind me that I should already have that down. And yet, even as I followed his instructions, and made a list of what would be required, it never really occurred to me that there would come a day when I would have to hear all this without him. Unaccompanied.

Other times, we would just chat, chat largely about the past; and he would tell me – oh – about his various dalliances when he had first come out, and about his subsequent full-on lovers, and whose fault it had been and why it hadn't worked out, and about the kind of boy that he had been as he grew up, and about his travels when at art school, and about his most successful drag outfit, and . . . It was as if he wanted me to know everything about him, to be in possession of a full and accurate account – not some false impression based upon the narrowness of his more recent life. But sometimes he would digress – to dwell on mine, on my life. I remember how, one afternoon, he told me that although – agreed – he could never have coped without me, he worried about how *I* would cope once he was no longer around. He wanted me to promise that I'd get back on track, that I'd try to be productive, because our time, you know, was over in a flash. But, to me, such advice merely sounded like the advice of someone who was planning on being absent for a while. It didn't have the ring of death about it. It sounded too casual, too light.

And yet this very casual lightness is, I realize now, what lent relief to the pressure of Matthew's decline. When, for example, I prepared our supper (a procedure which, by then, had swelled into a production – both time-consuming and elaborate), he would always come and keep me company, so that while I went about the tedium of my tasks, I might have the compensation of his banter. Every night, irrespective of that day's trials, I would force myself to lay a proper table for us: flowers in a jug, candle in a stick, salt-cellar, pepper mill, linen napkins, the whole civilized bit – my logic being that, so long as Matthew felt strong enough to sit, nothing should diminish the quality of his sitting, nothing undermine the provision of his dignity. But, although I tried to make his meals nutritious, the challenge of appealing to his palate did grow trickier as his tooth, to counteract the bitterness of pills, grew sweeter. Yet, beyond such issues, the important thing was that his food should be easy to eat, because knives and forks had a habit of going flying, and I was frightened lest he cut himself; so fingers, wherever possible, seemed like the safest answer. For the purposes of drinking – drinking without spilling – I now produced a straw; but, as I guided his hand toward it, I would whisper, in order to make light of the motion: We don't want you smudging your lippy, doll. And he would reply: Quite so, once a model, always a model. Not even when I pinned a napkin, bib-style, round his neck, did he tell me not to patronize him. Instead, he'd say: Well vibed, no point staining my peignoir. So his humour, you see, remained, against the mounting odds, what it had always been: sharp and ironic and courageous and – in the best sense of the word – homosexual. And then, after pudding, while I did the washing up, he would treat himself to a goodnight cigarette, which he entrusted me to light, and supervise, and eventually stub out.

That evening, over supper, Matthew said that he'd been wondering. I asked him what about. Briefly he stalled, and told me that he wouldn't mind some wine – but not to pour it into a stemmed glass; a tumbler was fine. I repeated: What about? He couldn't help thinking that his energy was running out. It was hard to explain, he said, but his intuition kept telling him that while he still had the chance, he ought to – you know – do something, go somewhere. I told him that I'd take him anywhere he wanted. (Secretly, however, I was dreading the mention of some iconic destination, such as Philadelphia, where foreign Hivvies were – let's say – not welcomed by Immigration.) But fortunately he said: Italy, how about Venice? Hadn't he already been? He had. In which case: why go back? Because, considering his Retinitis, it seemed pointless to visit a place for the first time: at least in Venice he would have *seen* the sights. All I would need to do would be to remind him; help him imagine. Matthew said that I could be his eyes. Plus, in December, there'd be hardly any tourists about, and the canals wouldn't smell foul, and – think of it, darling – all those *gondolieri* just for us.

And thus, thus simply, was the plan hatched. The following day, I began to phone around. The fact that so few obstacles cropped up made me think that this jaunt was, in some subliminal manner, meant to happen. It made me think of Farquhar. We found airline tickets in no time. The hotel recommended by Cara (the very room, actually) was swiftly confirmed by fax. Even Nilson, whom – to be on the safe side – I had rung, reckoned: Yeah, go for it guys. But Matthew didn't want to be gone too long; didn't want to push his luck. So we decided to fly out in a week's time, for just two nights – which suited me fine: two nights at a five-star joint had to be better than five at some two-star one.

We went over to Matthew's flat, to fetch some decent clothes and grab his passport. He hadn't been back for a while, and mentioned, as we drew up, that it felt sort of weird, sort of unreal, but it was probably as well to check that some pipe hadn't burst or something. I remember how, when we arrived, he led me inside – though doubtfully. It was as if some part of him had already forgotten, or sought to forget, the finer details of his old surroundings. I remember, too, the weariness with which he dropped onto his wing-chair, and the sniffy way in which he claimed that there was a peculiar whiff about the place. The place didn't smell of anything. At most, it smelt of room-spray. I pulled down a suitcase and asked what he wanted to take. No jeans – that was for certain: his denim days were over. Trousers, shirts, jumper, dark jacket, proper handkerchieves, cashmere scarf – the big one . . . oh, and his pony-skin gloves. I couldn't find them. I said that I would get some in town. I laid everything out. I looked around. The answer-phone machine was flashing. Five-six-seven messages had been left in Matthew's absence; so, while I packed (and pinched a photo album), he listened to his calls being played back. But his reaction was: Can't deal with that now, my address-book's at your flat. And then he said: You might as well switch off the whole machine. I said: Won't you want to bleep in? He didn't think so. He told me to pull out all the plugs. Fire: he'd developed a thing about it. And as we departed, while I safety-locked, he summarized: Done there, been that.

Dinner with Douglas. Matthew was fine about it; told me to go off and have a good time; but because I felt uneasy about leaving him stuck inside the flat, I asked whether he wouldn't like a friend to come and be with him while I was out. He told me not to fuss; he didn't need a minder: so long as he'd eaten beforehand, and finished infusing his line, he was perfectly happy just to listen to the radio for a couple of hours. He could always take himself to bed if he got tired. I didn't argue. I understood his argument: visitors might be a hassle. When Douglas arrived, I met him on the landing. Something about that boy (for 'boy' – despite his thicker waist and thinning hair – is what he would always remain to me) always made me feel wrapped up, in safe hands. Perhaps it was his largeness, the hugeness of his hug. At any rate, we embraced and wandered back inside – he, I recall, superbly tailored in dark flannel. I told him, while I went in search of drinks (gin, as ever, for Douglas), to go to the sitting room and keep Matthew company; and, while I busied myself in the background, I could hear the rise and fall and ebb and flow and wax and wane of their easy laughter. You would never have suspected that anything might be the matter. It almost made you want to stay outside. To prolong the fantasy.

Only at the restaurant did Douglas admit to me his shock at Matthew's reduction – to which I, on a defensive reflex, replied that this must go to show how long it had been since Douglas had dropped round. When people remarked – as increasingly they did – upon my friend's appearance, their comments struck me less as sympathetic than as critical; made me want to say: Do you think that he'd be looking better if *you* were dealing with him? Or: How do you *expect* him to look, considering? Or even:

Are you trying to frighten me? But it was my own perception, not theirs, that had gone askew. This is peculiar. Matthew, despite his blindness, retained a perfect visual memory; photographic. When he pictured something, he did so, still, with unsparing accuracy. Yet I, in spite of my sight, refused to accept the truth which lay in front of me. I deceived my own eyes. Perhaps it stands to reason that (because our lives, by then, had grown superimposed) Matthew's day-to-day diminishment should have eluded my focus; but even when I did stand back, to observe, as he slept, his hollowed sockets and hollowed anatomy, my reaction fell short of the rational. My response – whether coloured by emotion, or in an attempt to blur emotion out – was aesthetically channelled. I didn't scrutinize him: I admired him. To me, his limbs had grown not leaner; they had grown longer; his face had grown not gaunter; it had grown finer. The more drawn became his outline, the more beautiful I found it, the graver and more spiritual and monklike. There was something of an El Greco about him. Indeed, my astigmatic attitude, my distorted judgement, seemed to extend even beyond Matthew – toward others of his type, toward further visible casualties, whose delicacy, whose urgency, whose tenebrous smiles I found nearly seductive.

I smiled across our dinner-table, and told Douglas that he looked – which he did – fantastic. Yet he, whilst not denying his dashing aspect, elected not to ascribe it to the obvious factors, namely the cut of his attire and his fair Celtic ancestry. He ascribed it to Stan. I said: Tell me about him. Not much to tell, he replied. But he added that he hoped that when I met the guy (as was bound eventually to happen) I wouldn't give him a hard time. I said: Why should I? Douglas, whom 'compatibility' and 'companionship' had rendered just a trifle smug, rose above a class-connected answer. Instead, he asserted that Stan was a Good Thing in his life. I claimed to be delighted; but my cop-out cannot have sufficed, because Douglas made a point of pointing out that Stan made him feel *alive*. I said that there was something to be said for that, and took a gulp of wine. Douglas did likewise. There ensued a brief embarrassment, and then our food arrived.

I asked whether Stan made Douglas laugh. Sure, he could be quite gassy, but Douglas didn't need to share his bed with a comedian. I thought of Kenneth Williams. I asked whether Stan was camp. Douglas said: Not as in *Vada* the **Eek***, thank Christ. I spied an irony: I spied that Douglas might be turning into old Jack. I enquired as to which of the couple – Douglas or Stan – did the fucking. Douglas, pretending to be impassive, but betrayed by a hot blush, said: Does it matter? I told him that it might. I think that Douglas thought I was being crass. I think I thought that Douglas might have been an arsehole. And yet, no doubt about it: Douglas was happy. His best interest had, at conjugal last, found an interested heart. I should be glad. I *should* be glad. I said: What does Stan look like? Douglas, all chuffed, described his man, who, if the account was anything to go by, could really have been anyone. I feigned captivation, but I found the profile dull. Sub-standard. Practically childish. I was missing Matthew. I tried to swerve the conversation away from matrimonial prospects toward more platonic climes. I mentioned my visit to Farquhar; I mentioned the trip which Matthew and I had planned; I mentioned that our hotel had once been a doge's palace; I mentioned the Grand Canal; I mentioned St Mark's; I mentioned bellinis at Harry's Bar; I mentioned this; I mentioned that; I mentioned that I could hear myself babbling. And then I heard Douglas ask whether I thought that Matthew was dying. I replied: How can you ask me that?

Douglas said: You seem rather stressed out, duck, are you sure you're going to manage? I said: Just have to, won't I? But alcohol had led me to that tenuous pass where the faintest inference of kindness can push one to cry. I pulled myself back. I questioned

*eek abbreviation of Ecaf (backslang for Face). Hence: *Vada* the *Eek:* Get that face (Polari).

Douglas about his new house. The deal, he said, was as good as done; completion was this Friday; the moment he had the keys, he'd like to take me round; surely I could spare an hour; he wanted to pick my brain before plans were drawn up. I asked about the architect. (Name meant nothing to me. Some 'contact' of Stan's.) I said: Matthew could have advised you, he's good on Listed stuff. Douglas switched subjects – to my brother. He asked if Kelly had been in touch. I replied that Kelly took too many drugs: he'd left some stupid message on my machine the other night, totally out of his skull, singing some moronic nursery rhyme. Which? Ring o'roses, American style. Douglas grinned; called Kelly a Mad Queen. I said: Glad you find it funny – Bubonic ditties aren't really my thing. Douglas said to lighten up; Kelly'd probably just been smashed. I said: Too right. Douglas paid the bill, and dropped me off in a cab. We kissed in the special way of friends who, whatever happens, whatever life's vicissitudes, are friends for life. Can never fall out.

I lurched into the lift, and pressed the – whoops – right button. I checked the time. Gone midnight. I wondered what to do. Should I sneak in quietly, so as not to disturb Matthew, or make a deliberate racket, in order not to startle him? But the flat looked so bright inside, and the radio sounded so loud, that he must still, I presumed, be up. In the hall, I turned off a table-lamp; then, with jaunty casualness, announced that I was back. No answer. No matter. I went into the kitchen, and opened a can of fizzy something. I pretended not to burp. I continued on my round. Matthew wasn't in the sitting room. Only his imprint, like some ghostly reminder, lingered on the sofa. I drifted to the hi-fi. I killed the late-night drone of some funky jazzman. Peculiar smell about. Muddled. Acrid. Distinctive but elusive; similar yet other – like some lurking old embarrassment, somewhere in the register of acid. Best forgotten. Left behind. I dismissed olfactory asides. I wandered to the bedroom. The comfort of an alabaster lamp bathed the atmosphere in amber. Again I said: I'm back, darling.

Matthew lay slumped on his front, prone on the bedcover. Now I recognized the smell: the smell of alarm. I said: What's happened? He groaned: Been sick all over the bathroom. My chest started up. I said: Don't worry. I hurried to the cupboard; hurried back; told him: You take the duvet, let me grab your top-sheet and blankets. I turned him over like a sack of spuds. It was easy. I was surprised. I wrapped him up. I said: Try to get some sleep now. He sighed; he shrugged. He was breathing through his mouth. I said: I'm sorry, I should never have gone out. I put my palm over his brow. His temperature was in the hundreds. I thought: Where's the sodding justice? I tiptoed to the bathroom. I fumbled for the light-switch; found it; clicked, and – *voilà* – vomit all over the lino, over the tiles, over the pan, in the basin, in the bath, on the way out, along the rush-matting; excerpts of vomit, even, near the sofa. I fetched a bucket. I filled it with suds. I got down. I cleaned up. It's a doddle when you're drunk. I can't describe the mess (not because it wasn't copious and colourful and pungent, but) because I was absorbed by other matters, such as the realization that Matthew's system had, yet again, reared up against the poison of Ganciclovir. So: what now? What about our travels? What about those *gondolieri* just for us? Suddenly the phone rang. Grab it fast. Don't wake Matthew. Please not Kelly. It was Douglas.

Douglas was a brick, but he wasn't going to crack me. Bad time? he asked. (Quarter to one.) It's fine, I made out. Where was I – in the kitchen? Uh-huh. Alone? Uh-huh. Well, look: he was only ringing to remind me that if at any stage I needed a hand, all I had to do was call him, understand? I said: Thanks. He meant it, George. I said: I realize, Douglas. He said: You promise? I said: I promise. He said: You promise what? That-if-I-get-into-a-jam-I'll-give-you-a-shout. I thanked him for supper. He said: Pleasure, duck, see you soon. I said: Very; good night. Mine unravelled into a sleepless one, unstrung, strung-out. I fretted in the dark; groped for uncertain answers. Would Matthew be better in time for our flight? Would it be wiser to postpone for a while? Should I assume a more realistic attitude – in other words, a fatalistic one – and cancel outright? Was I justified? On what grounds? Moral? Medical? Practical? Ought I to check with Farquhar? Would Nilson backtrack? I was getting into a panic. I didn't want to be held accountable. What I needed was permission from somewhere. Then I told myself to do the obvious: let myself be led by *him*, by Matthew. Suddenly, he called out. I leapt up. By the time I'd made it to the bedroom, he was heaving like a dog preparing to bring up its dinner. I raced for a bucket, and back. A new wave of vomiting – if you could call it that – now started; but its sole, unsatisfactory outcome was a frothy substitute, meagre and colourless. Matthew spat, and spat again. Futile. There ensued another baulking cycle. And another. His neck hung over the edge of the mattress. My hand held his head as he convulsed. On and on it went. Retching without results. Round after round. It made you impatient. It made you want to say: Be sick or be quiet. Stop dramatizing. But the drama hadn't yet begun.

Next morning, he awoke in a mood of unprecedented truculence. He rejected all directives – breakfast, bath, Ganciclovir. I said: We're going to the clinic to have you checked out. He refused point-blank. Wouldn't even react. I argued across his silence, argued in defence of anti-emetic tablets, but he gritted all the harder; lay there in a stubborn lump. I said: What the fuck's all this about? I waited for an answer. Finally he said that Nilson wasn't going to wreck our travel plans. I pointed out that we were booked to leave in three days' time: how did Matthew expect to get on a plane when he wouldn't even get out of bed? He claimed that he just needed rest. I said: Nonsense, what you need is help. Matthew sighed; then said: So now you're going to let me down, right? (I don't know why, but this side-swipe made me really angry.) I said: I'm going for a fag. He said: Can I have one? I said: No you bloody can't.

And then I stalked off for a shower. I needed sanctuary. I needed to be apart. I felt bad. I felt badly. I felt baffled. I washed. I shaved. I after-shaved. I moisturized, deodorized, and brushed. I told myself to brace myself for the looming showdown; but, on emerging from the bathroom, I saw – to my chastisement – that Matthew was already up. He'd migrated to the sofa, and was perching on its arm, wearing only a vest and underpants, like an early-morning child who can't remember something. I paused at the doorway. He was trying to force a smile, yet his countenance lacked lustre. He apologized. I pretended not to know what he was on about. He beckoned me beside him. I sat. He took my hand, and, at a stroke, cut through my silly little, selfish little scruples and anxieties. He said: Captain, won't you help me travel one last time?

I rang for an appointment to see Nilson. The receptionist said: Another patient has just cancelled; be here in half an hour. I dressed, changed the bed, and left Matthew face-down – within grabbing distance of a bucket. He had an empty stomach; nothing too dreadful could happen. He was the first to admit as much. He wished me luck, which seemed bizarre, and off I drove, slightly lost, slightly vacant in his car, trying to make a mental note of pony-skin gloves. When I arrived, Nilson looked surprised to find me without Matthew, but you wouldn't have described his look as worried; it came closer to lively. Spirit was apparent in his eyebrows, which jumped. I may, admittedly, be wrong in my assumption, but my feeling, looking back, is that the thing which had enlivened Nilson wasn't medical in character. It was more exact than that. It was the chance to settle a small score; a debt which, by dint of being outstanding, had also mounted. Let us not imagine, after all, that – one way and another – I hadn't become a formal thorn in the casual doctor's side.

I explained that Matthew was feeling under par, and apologized for his failure to show up. Nilson deemed this failure fair enough, and told me to fire. I asked whether I could I have a prescription for anti-emetic tablets. Nilson took it that Our Matt (as he dared to call the centre of my life) had been Puking Up. I conceded that yes, Matthew had been sick in the night. How many times? Countless; I'd lost track. Nilson had to smile: it didn't look to him like oral medication was going to do the trick then somehow. (How come?) Because *obviously* Matthew wouldn't be able to keep the tablets down. To Nilson, a jab sounded like a likelier answer. Mind you, Matthew *would* have to be brought in for that. The nurses upstairs would sort him out (the nurses who, once upon a time, had called my boy a sweet-heart). I asked, perhaps in an attempt to mask my earlier gaffe, whether anti-emetic jabs were intravenous or subcutaneous. Neither: they were intramuscular (you dum-dum). I asked, still determined not to appear cowed, whether they went into the arm or into the buttock. Neither: they were injected in the thigh. I persevered. I had to. I asked whether, given Matthew's problematic sight, and the nausea which prevented him from getting up – let alone into a car – there was any chance that somebody might inject him at my flat. I'd be happy to do the driving; the round-trip would take no more than half an hour. Could someone lend a hand? Nilson gazed at me with unmis-takable amazement. The gaze translated, beyond possible con-fusion, as: Who do you think you are, the Queen of Sheba?

My principal concern, I informed Nilson, was that Matthew should be allowed to rest, so that once the nausea had abated we could build his strength back up in time for Venice. The doctor pulled one of those faces, meant to mean: Hang-On-A-Second-Let-Me-Get-This-Straight. He couldn't *believe* we were still thinking in terms of travelling, and, worse, to another country. With a flat sort of courage – courage freshly instilled in me by Matthew – I said that a couple of nights abroad remained Matthew's target. My simple obligation, this far down the line, was to honour the plan. (I was sure that, put this way, Nilson would show some understanding.) He showed nothing of the kind. He showed his teeth. He said: You're off your trolley, you.

With maximum pomposity, I disabused him. I said: I'm very firmly upon it, I assure you. And thus, at last, we came to the point, to the crux of the problem, a problem which – just as poor Matthew could no longer regard – no longer regarded Matthew.

Nilson stretched an arm behind himself, and slid his fist into the pocket of a nylon bomber-jacket. Diligently he rummaged, until he found, amid a litter of rustles, a piece of gum. Blowing away some foreign fluff, he popped the pellet in his mouth. He chewed the cud with squelching gusto. He bent to scratch a calf. His wrinkled socks were ever-brown. He wondered what it was about me. In what particular? He couldn't wait to enlighten me. He said: Why're you such a little prick? (My pomposity skipped a beat.) I said: How would you prefer me – meek? He said: Reasonable would do. I said: Reasonable is what I strive to be. He said: Got a funny way of showing it. I said: Really? He scoffed and said: Come *off* it; first you give Sister an earful when all she's done is follow procedure; then you encourage Matthew to leave the ward when any fool can tell that he should still be in there; and now you per*sist* with this insane trip to Italy. I wouldn't call any of that reasonable. The patient is Terminal, in case you hadn't realized; your job isn't to spin him irresponsible ideas, it's to help us to help him. I said: I don't think it's your job to tell me what my job is; I'm not answerable to you; I'm only concerned about him. Nilson said: So are we. I said: *You're* interested in a whole Bunch of people. Nilson said: Yeah, Matthew included. I said: Which presumably explains why you can't come up with a single conclusive test-result. He said: Of course we can, you smart-arse; it's just that his results are all lousy, and what's the good of telling a patient *that*, huh? I said: Doctor, my friend may be dying, but he isn't a retard; had you known him in his prime, you wouldn't dream of being so patronizing; you'd be up-front and let him make up his own mind about whether or not to travel. Nilson said: You're talking like some hysterical wife. I said: Believe me, if I *were* his wife, it is *you* who wouldn't be talking to me in the manner which you are. He said: Bollocks to that, you've come for my advice, and I'm letting you have it. I said: I happen to've come for anti-emetic tablets. He said: Well, you know the score on that front, but what *I'd* like to know is what makes you think you've got the right to go against all sensible medical advice. I said: I'm doing no such thing. He said: You could have fooled me. I said: More fool you. *Pardon*?

Reference to Farquhar halted Nilson in his tracks: As in *Peregrine* Farquhar? That's right, it's on his advice that I'm acting. (Sorry to gloat, but the resultant pause was just rapturous; you could almost hear the clapping. The sense was tantamount to telling your Lieutenant that you – you piffling Private, you piddly gob-shite – happened to be fucking a Field Marshal.) Nilson appeared wounded by this sudden bullet to his pride, this unexpected obstacle to his dreams of advancement, but he made a brave attempt to camouflage the fact. He slowed himself right down, and lowered his tone toward the rumble of gravitas. And yet, to me, he sounded rebuffed; his voice echoed with the grievances of cuckoldry. He muttered something about all-the-bloody-same and nepotism-typical – but did so as a half-aside. For, just as it was more than I could risk to admit how little my acquaintanceship with Farquhar *really* owed to old school ties, so it was, for Nilson, too high a gamble openly to criticize the judgement of a man who, in every respect imaginable, towered above him. I stood up. I said: I'll see you when Matthew and I get back. Nilson said: I'm sure you're better off with your buddy Perry Farquhar; I bet *he* can save Matthew . . . And as I left, I couldn't but reflect on the irony that mention of the consultant should have brought about the very thing against which Farquhar himself had advised: namely a snarl-up. But I was unnerved by this whole débacle. I won't deny it.

Nor will I deny that since I sported neither of the norms – ill health nor a white coat – I suddenly felt awkward trespassing alone into the day-clinic on the first floor. I bumped into a nurse at the door: Alison. We knew her of old. She said: How's

Matthew? I said: Back at the flat; it's all got a bit dicey. She said: You want to talk about it? I said: Nilson's being a nightmare. She told me to sit myself down; she was just finishing someone's flush; we could have a chat; it was her lunch-hour. Earlier on, I had often sat with Matthew in this suavely textured room, which, thanks to a particular bequest from a particularly grateful, if departed, decorator, was more swishy than the rest of the Centre. Devised along the lines of a lobby in a small hotel, the day-clinic was furnished with boxy armchairs and sofas, these arranged, wherever possible, back-to-back for optimum discretion, with modern standard-lamps posted here and there, and coffee-tables spread with magazines-of-the-moment, and towering great plants, potted in various strategic locations designed to promote a quality which people sometimes define as 'space'. This was the place where, in less pressing days, Matthew and I had waited for his blood to be taken, or waited for him to be weighed, or waited for him to be handed fresh supplies of medication, or waited for him to be primed on how to infuse himself unaided. But, while observing the norms of patience, we had preferred, rather than bury our heads in double-spreads or pretend to be captivated by thin air, to observe other patients, who, for the most part, came alone; and, week after week, we would embroider mythologies around these strangers. I specifically recall a man of privileged Indian flavour, a creature of unbelievable good looks and unbelievable grace who, whenever he appeared, always appeared composed, and always – which further abetted his cachet – accompanied by an elegant woman who strongly resembled him, and who, like him, never spoke. To us, he could have been (therefore became) the Maharajah; and she, by extension, the Maharajah's sister, who cared for him. But we also presumed her, despite the careful chic of her public bouclé, privately to float about some endless suite of silver rooms in a magnificent apartment high over Belgravia, trailing yards of smoky sari in her wake, and being trailed, in turn, by a retinue of barefoot retainers who showed nothing to their keepers but the silent devotion of servile generations. We took the Maharajah, because his vein was so supremely sybaritic, so languorously élite, so absolutely above erotic shrillness, to have been blighted by some more exotic dint, involving, for instance, the use of a platinum syringe; and certainly his tale, embellished in this way, felt, to us, more aptly spiritual, truer to his image, which was of purest decadence. At any rate, with the passage of the months, the Maharajah and his sister warmed enough to nod in our direction; so that when, one chilly autumn Sunday, at a fashionable restaurant, we caught sight of them, looking exquisitely serious on another table, we acknowledged the pair. It was a strangely noisy place, this, for such soundless exchanges, but as places went, it could have been worse. Anyway, the two proceeded with their lunch, while Matthew and I, turning to our menus, returned to our own concerns. Yet, when coffee came, we noticed the mysterious siblings rise without a word, move off toward the coat-check, and drift away – he, wrapped in wolf; she, swathed in a sable cape. We were never to see them again. And yet, ages later, once the confidence was considered 'safe', a counsellor who had kept up with them – or rather, with *her* – let me into their (not tale, but) real end. It transpired that the couple had been (not siblings at all, of course, but) married; that he, a haemophiliac, had, shortly after their nuptials, been contaminated by transfused blood; that he had unwittingly infected his wife, whom he had preceded to the pyre; that, on his death, his parents had accused the bride of having killed their only son, and promptly despatched her; whereupon she had run for cover to her own (humbler) caste, who, having no great interest in a widowed pariah, snubbed her – and the upshot was that, cut-off and ostracized, she had perished in some hopeless hospice somewhere hopeless like Calcutta. Death: such a democrat. But back to the quest for anti-emetic jabs. I sat myself down.

Alison had always liked Matthew, not least because Matthew had always had liked her lip-liner. As I stared beyond some tinted sky, it all came back to me: how, at the first of their encounters, he had openly admired the artful contours of Alison's mouth, and how she, despite herself, had smiled. It was typical of Matthew's luck, in the days when luck still figured on the cards, that the more mischievously he'd bent the rules of 'appropriateness', the greater the favour he had found. The cheek of his charm had made people succumb. And so, when Alison, having seen me just now, had asked after Matthew, I knew her enquiry to have been more than a mere, gratuitous, platitude. It had been an interested enquiry – to which, perhaps, one would rather not have given, or indeed received, an interesting answer. But, granted the circumstances, how could I have pretended that everything was fine, thanks? I heard somebody say: Sorry about that. It was she; back; dressed in mufti. She sat. She said: So what's up? I said: Where do you want me to start? She said: Just tell me what's been happening.

I told it in a jumble, but she didn't seem to mind: the fact that Nilson was opposed to letting Matthew travel; the fact that Farquhar (whose name, whose fame, rang bells even with the likes of Alison) had said that I should do whatever Matthew wanted; the fact that Matthew was determined to get on a plane in three days' time; the fact that everything was booked; the fact that I was getting panicky. Alison said: Why, exactly? I had omitted the snag – the nausea which, unless harnessed, could scupper our plan. Alison guessed: He's rejected his Ganciclovir. I said: Exactly, but listen, there's no way he's switching back to Foscarnet, not now. Alison said: Has anyone said he has to? (Nobody had.) She told me to relax. I relaxed enough to stretch the facts. I claimed that Nilson had called me a prick for wanting anti-emetic tablets. I called Nilson a prick for wanting me to drag Matthew all the way to the clinic just for a jab. Alison said: You got a car? I said: Matthew's. She said: Then let's whip round and sort him out; I can grab a bite afterwards.

During the drive, Alison lit up. I shall always be grateful for that surprise. It raised her from the hospitalic to the fallible. As I fiddled with the gear-stick, I glimpsed that she was wearing heels. She crossed her legs. Her navy coat parted round the rock of her knees. I said: You got a man? She laughed. She *had* done – until last month. I asked what had happened. He hadn't liked her working-hours. I said: Well, start preparing for your next romance, I mean you're hardly shelf-material, Alison. She said: Nothing's guaranteed. I said: Trust me, I'm a psychic. She said: Trust me, I'm a cynic. We arrived. We went up. Where was the kitchen? She wanted to dump her things. She slipped off her coat. She put down her implements. The flat was horribly still.

It was she who called out to him. Matthew sounded puzzled: Who's that? Alison-from-the-day-clinic. He said: What are *you* doing here? Come to see you, sweetheart; gather you've not been too brilliant. He said: Understatement of the decade, dear. She stroked his head. She looked at him. Her mouth was melancholy. She explained why pills weren't any good for this, but said that she could give him an injection to stop the sense of sickness. Matthew told her to get on with it. I led her back into the kitchen, and, while she loaded the syringe, she told me to watch carefully, just in case – in case of what? – in case I ever had to do it. Practise on an orange, was her tip; not that difficult. We returned to the bedroom. She swabbed Matthew's skin. The needle pierced him. He hissed. The juice flowed in. His thigh seemed so enfeebled. It defied belief. Believe in Dreams.

On the way back to the hospital, Alison told me to get real. If Matthew and I were still wedded to this trip, we were going to have our work cut out. Whatever it took, I replied; I couldn't let Matthew down; surely Alison understood that. Of course she did, but no amount of understanding was going to make things easier. (Hers, in fact, made all the difference.) I repeated that we'd do whatever needed doing. She told me to keep my eyes on the windscreen. She said: Matthew's very weak now – but her tone was not accusatory. She reckoned that he looked anaemic; he could probably do with a transfusion; she would square the paperwork with Will – Will who? – Will Nilson. Relief: anything to avoid another of those scenes. Alison ignored me. She wasn't getting into it. I got down to business. When did she want Matthew? First thing tomorrow, just after nine. How long for? Two large bags, so say five hours. He would also need to go on steroids. Steroids? Yes, by blasting him with anti-inflammatories you were likelier to stave off a crisis. A crisis of what kind? Renal failure, liver malfunction, bronchial hassles. You wouldn't want him landing up in some Italian hospital, would you now. Tell me about it – but didn't steroids involve jabs? No, just tablets. Once this shot of anti-emetic had done its stuff, he ought to be stable for a while. He should also be given some Dexamphetamine. Speed? Yes, to boost his energy. But she warned me to remember that these were only short-term meas-ures, artificial, designed to mask his symptoms. Still, with a clean supply of blood, and strong steroids and amphetamines, he ought to be fit for the trip. And *feed* him, for God's sake – protein drinks, soup, biscuits, anything, and *water*, he's completely dehy-drated; pester him, fluids are absolutely vital. She sent me home to explain the score to Matthew, and told me to bring him to the clinic in the morning, at nine. She'd have everything set up. Action. At last. I felt so blessed by the miracle of Alison, that, as I dropped her off outside the hospital, I tried to shove a bank-note in her bag; but she pushed away my hand and told me to leave it out. Rightly. This wasn't about *me*. This was about Matthew, the boy who once had loved her lip-liner. Alison: a sweetheart if ever there was one.

As the afternoon wore on, so, gradually, Matthew's nausea wore off. He was able to sit up. We were over the hump. It was all going to be fine. I told him that Alison was taking charge – but she was sticking her neck out on our behalf, so she wasn't to be messed around. Matthew nodded like a docile child. The most important thing, I stressed, was that he force himself to eat, and that he drink like mad, more than he actually wanted. Dehydration was the bummer. Matthew promised to try. I said: So, what do you fancy? Tea and soldiers would be nice, with Marmite. And for supper? He asked what I was having. Chicken soup and shepherd's pie. Would do him fine. I explained that in the morning I'd be driving him into the clinic – for a transfusion. He looked fractionally worried: he'd never had one. He said: What's a transfusion meant to do? It raises your blood-count, it stimulates your appetite, it completely revitalizes you. In which case, he supposed, transfusion here we come. I said: And while you're in there being pepped up, I can race out. Out where? You're going to need a hat, and I haven't replaced your gloves. Matthew smiled: You spoil me, Captain. I returned to Alison's stratagem, but didn't mention steroids. I didn't have the heart. I'd rather slip them to him on the quiet, amid the battery of his other tablets, than expose him to a cruel irony: the irony of all those dedicated muscle-faggots messing up their innards for the mere sake of their vanity, while Matthew, forsaken, was having steroids foisted on him in a last-ditch medical farce, to dupe his own mortality. But I did allude to speed. I couldn't see the harm. Matthew said: Very art-school, darling; I'll thank you not to dip into my stash.

At supper-time, he asked to eat in bed, but acquitted himself handsomely: double-helpings of shepherd's pie. Plus he downed more fluid than he had done in months – lime cordial, heavy on the lime. His palate had grown dull; his buds seemed to crave tartness. He even managed a slice of pineapple – with his hands. We shared a packet of wine-gums. We nattered for a while. I tucked him up. I said: Lights out now; busy day coming up; I'm next door if you want me. I made sure that the door was ajar. Aside from one brief foray to the lavatory, he slept uninterruptedly; and so did I. Next, the alarm had rung. Day was still dark. Rise and shine. I took him breakfast on a tray: vanilla milkshake and a quartered pear. I handed him, one by dreary one, his usual tablets: antibacterial, antifungal, anti-tubercular, antiviral, anti-the-world-and-its-mother. He swallowed them without a fuss. He finished his tea. He gave me his mug. He would rather skip his bath, he said. Too early, too tired. I decided not to be a bore about it. We could deal with baths tonight. I'd heard of patients who came out of their transfusions practically dancing the rumba. I washed up. I had a shower. And then, as I was stepping into my trousers, I heard him mumble that he felt completely knackered. I told him not to start — we *had* to get ourselves to Alison by nine. He said: I don't think I can hack it. I said: Matthew, if you want to go to Italy, you're simply going to have to, so make up your mind. He said: Give me a bit more time. I said: There *is* no time. I tore off his bed-covers. I said: Get *up*. I hauled him to the brink of the mattress; but he just sat there, head bowed, shoulders hunched, hands redundant in his lap. It made me angry. I said: Let's get you dressed. He said OK — but in a wimpish sort of way; complainingly. I told him to spare me the sound-effects. I said: Come *on* now. He told me not to shout at him. The whole performance took for ever. How could some-one — suddenly — have *no* strength? I knelt. I straightened his socks. I dealt with his shoelaces. I got to my feet again. I said: One-two-three-hup, and yanked him by the armpits. He stood. I said: Well done. He nearly lost his balance. I propped him up. I wangled him into his coat. I wound him in a scarf. He wrapped an arm around my neck. I wrapped an arm around his ribcage, but I practically had to drag him from the lift out to the pave-ment. A neighbour offered to help. I was sweating. I said: If we can get him into the car, that would be great. Matthew said: Don't talk about me as if I wasn't here. I said: I wouldn't need to if you made more of an effort. He said: You're not being fair. I said: Look, it's *you* who wants to go to Venice, so don't give me that shit about fairness. We didn't reach the clinic until ten. I left him seated at the entrance. I raced upstairs. Alison was waiting, but she didn't look fazed. She looked like the best sort of nurse: unflappable, forbearing. She bleeped down to reception. Recep-tion found me help; and, between us, the helper and I helped Matthew — half-zonked — into the day-centre.

Alison had everything prepared. Drips and bags and stands, variously arranged around an armchair. We lowered him into place. We minded his legs. She raised his feet onto some further chair. She tucked a pillow behind his head; propped a couple more beneath his elbows. She unfolded a blanket, shook it open, and spread it over him. She patted his shoulder. There, she said. Matthew apologized for being so late; thought he'd never make it. She said: Better late than never, sweetheart, that's what *I* always tell them. He moaned. He sounded not there. She said: You warm enough? He shrugged. She said: Right, let's get you started. He closed his eyes. She wired him up. She worked the gadgets fast. She fiddled with some plastic taps. Graphs along a monitor danced. Electronic numbers flashed. Transparent tubes began to fill with blood – (not red, but) clotted brown. I wanted to scarper. I said: I'm off to the shops, Matthew. No reply. Out for the count.

Alison said: Hold on, George, let me fetch you Matthew's stuff. I followed her to the storage cupboard. While she was rooting around, she admitted: Got to be honest, this is looking touch-and-go. I said: Fingers crossed, just have to hope. She said: Here's his bag. She looked inside, pulled out various packets, and set them on a counter. Dexamphetamine, she began: two milligrammes per tablet, to be taken as required, whenever he feels breathless, or if you think he's flagging. Prednisolone – What's that? – his steroid, twenty-five milligrammes, normally to be given at breakfast-time, but start him off tonight; no point hanging about. And whatever you do, *don't let up.* You run into trouble, you *increase* his dose. By half a tab. Now, this is important, his official Steroid card. Best to keep it with your passports, in case you get searched by Customs. It's been known to happen. Xylocaine ointment, for his herpes. I know it's not his regular cream, but there's an anaesthetic agent in this. More effective. Go in as far as your finger will allow, and work right round. Don't forget gloves. Grab a handful on the way out, and make sure you don't take the wrong size. Other sundries: saline, swabs, sticking plaster, bandage, and – best be on the safe side – half a dozen anti-emetic ampoules. No, they don't need to be kept in a fridge. Six syringes and, here's six needles, green. Watch how you dispose of all these bits. You got one of those boxes for Sharps? Good. Easiest thing is take it with you and bring it back. Have you practised on an orange yet? Then *find* one; don't get caught out. More sleeping tablets? I'll have some here by the time you come to pick him up, but you might have to remind me. Alison returned the medication to its bag, and clipped it shut. She emphasized: To be packed with your hand-luggage. And then she pointed out: With these new drugs, it's difficult to tell quite how his bowels will react, especially during a flight. My advice, though you'll obviously have to have a private chat with him, is that you persuade him to wear incontinence pants. Hospital ones aren't that reliable, they seem to leak half the time. I don't think they're designed for people who're still active. Go to – that's the place, on Wigmore Street, they do good ones – and while you're at it, I should also get myself a rubber sheet. You never know, things *might* get tricky. I said: You're starting to freak me. She said: I'm not here to beat about the bush.

I beat a swift retreat. I took myself to Wigmore Street. The shop, with its stock-in-trade insignia of a snake seducing a stick, advertised itself as an Apothecary; but so archaic a banner smacked, by post-modernistic standards, of quaintness rather than accuracy. Come on: the place was a cutting-edge marvel, a testament to surgical advance – slick, sharp, state-of-the-art. Gruesomely fabulous. A hypochondriac's paradise. Admittedly, its windows (to dampen the prurience of passers-by, or perhaps to protect the dignity of punters) limited themselves to decorous still-lives: salutary arrangements of nail-brushes and combs and shaving-stands, crafted from semblances of outlawed luxuries – bone and tortoiseshell and ivory; and marine installations of loofahs and sponges and pumice, sprouting the surprise of an occasional, promotional, sunflower. But once you had ventured within this medical sanctum, you came to, yet seemed to gravitate beyond, a screen of perspex shelves, laden with multivitamins and ali-

370 ~ Paul Golding

mentary supplements; and behind these, like a further barrier –
but like a further magnet – rack-upon-rack of homeopathic
unguents, and remedial drops to be pipetted on the tongue, and
stacks of optimistic, holistic pamphlets, which, though intent on
teaching you the way to self-enhancement, seemed instead to
lead you, as if you had learned nothing, further away from the
street outside – from real life – until you found yourself in
another sphere entirely, more softly lit; more twilit.

This other realm which, three leisurely steps down, seemed
to stretch forever backward, glinted with a steely, almost chilling, instrumental glamour, the glamour of stethoscopes and
forceps and pace-makers and scalpels – but plonked, by this
stage, without regard for the squeamishly inclined; rather, with a
surgical bluntness better suited to the brutally sanguine. These
implements were spread along articulated aluminium cabinets,
redolent of abattoirs, amid livid anatomical sculptures of Homo
Sapiens, skinned, rent asunder, and supervised from on high by
a gargantuan, open-hinged eyeball. A resinous great half-sob,
jocularly frozen for all time, hung suspended from a dissected
duct. And look: a hoist, just like in a club; and high-tech chairs,
devised to sit in bathtubs; and over to the left, for the sake of balance, custom-leathered asymmetric harnesses; and disembodied
callipers, collapsed; and miraculous prosthetic limbs, all set to
perform a Lazarus; and meticulously crafted mastectomy pads,
begging to be touched. Fleetingly this whole department, with
its dizzying mercantile abundance, might have made you wonder whether hither wasn't where you might have come had the
coming summer's fashion-must turned out to be, perchance, a
simple straitjacket; or indeed if, one wintry eve not quite like
any other, your spirits should have felt quietly inclined toward a
recreational set of Sounds – always, of course, within the boundaries of a caring and supportive travesty.

But listen: the assistants were stars. They had customer relations down to an art. They understood that lots of us were – er
– embarrassed. They were experts at exploding (not myths, but)

shyness. Here came one of their number, in personality-jumper and slacks, and sporting the reassurance of an identity badge. Did I need help? I described my requirement as incontinence pants. He described it as diapers; but no matter, because not once, not for an instant, did his well-trained manner train itself beneath the demarcation of my waistband. What size was I after? What sizes did they have? He was sure that they had *mine*. Stroke of luck. Did I favour a particular brand? I was something of a novice, I admitted – could he advise? He peered afar, until: German, he adjudged; American diapers were cut for the fuller buttock. I said: I'm in your hands. He said: Large packet? I said: I wonder. He said: More economical in the long run. Anything else I'd like? Yes, a rubber sheet. He flinched: the world had moved *on* since such punitive antiquities. Textiles had undergone a revolution. Thankfully these days you could enjoy the confidence of impermeability without any of the corollaries that had once made life a misery – poor absorbency, excess humidity, irritation to the skin, general creaking. So what was the answer? His face broke into a smile: their waterproof sheets came faced with towelling. I said: Marvellous. He said: Quantity? Just one, thanks. Flat or Fitted? Flat. Single or double or king-size? Single should be fine. In which case, he concluded: one flat-single-sheet-coming-up. But then he added: Incidentally, if you should ever want to restock, we do deliver to our clients. I said: Now *that's* what I call service. He looked elated. Home-delivery had been his brain-wave. His retail baby.

I locked the nappies in the boot of the car, then thought: Pony-skin gloves. I drove through a stretch of green and pleasant parklands, until I reached a sign: Knightsbridge. I found a space in which to park. I hurried to the shop. A snarling uniform marred the varnished door. Grudgingly he swung it open. I breezed down to the basement. 'Fraid not, said some hand-on-hipster. Right out of *noirs*; only got choc; but I can check with our other branch if you like. I told him not to worry. Brown gloves would do me fine. I didn't imagine that Matthew would be too colour-fussed. The feel, the feeling, was what counted. Did I want them gift-wrapped? No, thanks; I was slightly pushed for time. Next: Matthew's hat. What was his head-circumference? Never mind. I plumped for a knitted cashmere number, a sort of mugger's job without the eyes – not exactly the greatest flatterer, but still: one size fitted all, Matthew's ears would be kept warm, and I knew that I could always sell the notion to him as a cloche. I also picked myself a beret – at ten times what you would have paid in, say, Provence; but my warped sartorial sense somehow dictated that I Go with Matthew. On a further impulse, I bought a navy mohair rug – not so much to combat the chill inside an aeroplane as to stifle the smell of awkwardness in the event of an accident. I whacked the blanket on a charge-card, and kept on running. But, at a swanky emporium near the bay where I was parked, I was suddenly struck. In for a penny, in for a pounding. I splurged on an overnight bag – black suede body, black leather straps. It's still around somewhere. I raced back to the flat, dragged my spoils up to the hall, and, on the way to make myself some toast, felt, suddenly, outnumbered. Alone. Frightened. I stared at a wall. I thought: Am I going to cope? I picked up the phone. I rang Douglas at the office. Not at his desk, said some colleague. (Lunch-time, I supposed.) Any chance that I could leave a message for him? Not really much point. Douglas had taken a few days off. Middle of moving. Of course. I had forgotten. I would try him at home. I got him. His tremendous answer echoed round the hollows of an empty room. I said: It's me. He said: What's wrong? I said: Oh just. And then I lost it.

Douglas was a brick, but self-pity was what cracked me. He gave me an interim in which to gather myself, before repeating: What's wrong, duck? I rattled off a list of facts. Then, I rattled off a list of potential setbacks. He said: Let me grab a cigarette; we need to think about this calmly. He set down the receiver. He wandered off toward some background. He was treading on (not ice, but) hardboard. I heard him mumbling, deep within a space which I could no longer visualize. He was bringing to a conclusion one of his own chapters. He might be feeling harassed. Preoccupied. He wandered back. And then, as if his own concerns were balls of fluff, Douglas proved to me his friendship, proved it *for* me, proved it beyond argument. He explained that Stan, who was dealing with the storage depot anyhow, would be happy to finish packing, and that he, Douglas, could, if I liked, come to Venice with me and Matthew. The lonely blankness of my wall lit up. I can't describe it. I said: God, that would be fantastic. But whereas Douglas, being a gentleman, wouldn't allow me to pay for his flight, I, who fell short of the mark, failed to pay for him to have a room overlooking the Grand Canal. His shutters, I was told, would give onto a potted yard. And yet, Douglas: wherever you may be, and despite the distance which has grown between us, know, know that when I think of you, I do so still with fondest love.

My thoughts returned to Matthew. A transfusion guaranteed nothing. This whole business might yet have to be cancelled. Still; hardly a reason not to pamper him. Preparatory luxuries could always be converted into consolation prizes. I fixed a series of appointments – scheduled for tomorrow, for the final run-up. I begged Matthew's usual hairdresser to come and give him a trim. I bullied a further girl into administering a Reiki treatment. And a beautician, who proved trickier about having her depilated arm twisted, finally consented to granting Matthew the benefit of her (not doubt, but) manicure and pedicure. Not that Matthew had ever demanded such epicene queeneries; it's just that I found clipping his nails difficult. But anyway, once those people had all been booked, I went down to the shops in search of milk and bread and fruit; came back, tidied up, fiddled about, and, when I could stand the suspense no longer, rang the clinic for news. They wouldn't let me speak to him – the phone-wire wasn't long enough – but I was told that he was starting to rally, that he was nearing the end of his second bag, and that he should be ready to be collected within the hour.

Even as I climbed the steps up to the day-centre, I knew that the transfusion had worked its magic: I could hear Matthew camping around with Alison. The two seemed to be wrecking a rendition of something. I caught a snatch of the words I Shouldn't – or perhaps it was I Wouldn't – followed by peals of laughter. The feeling reeled me back, back to happier times, healthier times. I ventured inside. Few patients about. A cleaner, cursing a vacuum. The medical day must be done. Alison appeared from somewhere. I reminded her about those sleeping tablets. Then I asked: Where's he hiding? Over there, round the corner to the right. She went off to the storage cupboard. But Matthew must have known that I'd arrived, because next I heard him, from behind some plant or screen or something, assume a Dietrich accent and, returning to the climax of his earlier cabaret, (en)chant: And you know that it's not 'cos I couldn't / It's simply because. . . . I'm the layyyyyyyziest gal in town.

My first reaction was to think: Thank God Douglas is coming. My second was to say: Good thinking, darling. But my praise may have lacked verve, because the sight which now confronted me, round the corner to the right, filled me with dismay – the sudden sight of Matthew sitting in a wheelchair. I'd never envisaged such a state; such a stage. I'd been a dunce. And then, to cap my sense of idiocy, I realized that of all the wheelchair-hostile cities, Venice, with its rickety little steps and rickety little bridges, must surely take the pizza. But as soon as we were back on the street, Matthew told me not to be ridiculous – to bung that wheelchair in the boot, and let him use his pins. It had all been Alison's idea – of a nifty travel gimmick. Mind you, he said, it might get us upgraded, dear. You never knew. And thus began our lead-up to the honeymoon. The final countdown. Thirty-six hours.

I helped him with his bath, gave him supper, slipped him his first steroid, and suggested an early night. Briefly I let him fiddle with his cloche and gloves – but there ended my indulgence. As I drew the bedroom curtains closed, I raised the subject of

Douglas. My version made it look as if it had been *he* who had jumped on our bandwagon, but Matthew didn't seem to mind. Always handy to have a hulk around, he said. Matthew gathered that in Italy you couldn't find a porter for love nor money. But I was distracted. I wanted to start packing. I told him to go to sleep now. His cheeks were flushed – flushed even before I'd mustered the guts to mention incontinence pants.

He awoke feeling quite perky; but, no sooner had he taken a few steps than he warned: Uh-uh, dodgy tummy. I took him straight to the bathroom, and, once that minor drama was done, decided to broach the question of unwanted airborne accidents. Surprisingly, his reaction wasn't one of affront. It came closer to nonplussed. I don't think that he'd had a proper chance to think in advance, because he simply said: Let me think about it once I've got my pills down. I said: Speed's on the special menu. He said: Godspeed, how divine. I loved him for those gags. I reiterated his appointments for the day: haircut at noon; feet and hands after his siesta; Reiki session at five thirty. Matthew *yes*sed. Of all the therapies attempted over the years, Reiki remained his favourite. He used to claim that even without the practitioner's fingers touching him, the heat from her palms made his blood whoosh up. Made him almost high.

Anyway, back to that morning at the flat. I remember the moment precisely. I'd been on the point of shaving Matthew, and had just made a mental note about buying fresh batteries, when the telephone rang. A woman asked if she could speak to me. Speaking, I replied. But she took me by surprise. She was putting me through now. A click, a soundlessness, and then: Hello Sir, said a man. It was Chortle-Buffer, the Buddha from the bank. I'm not going to make a big defensive song-and-dance about this, because, in a peculiar sort of way, I'd always known I had it coming. Ever since I'd flounced out of his sanctum with my elevated head whistling in hubristic clouds, managerial retribution had been logged into my karma. It would be easy to make out that homophobia, for example, lay at the core of our little fracas, but no: Chortle-Buffer, despite his hateful timing, was just an old-time dullard. He wondered if I'd taken leave of my senses. I didn't bother with denials. I could picture my latest statement, spread like unbrookable evidence, before his weskitted gut. Facts were facts, and the facts were plain enough: I'd ignored his countless warnings about unauthorized overdrafts, and taken, one too many times, his goodwill for granted. Well, his patience had run out. I said: I understand. He asked what I was going to do about it. (What could I do?) I said: Try harder? 'Fraid not; too late for that. He ordered me to return my cards to the bank – safely cut in half, as was my legal bind. Forthwith, he added. I said: As you like – and left matters at that. Considering my usual stridency, he might have been surprised to hear me go so quietly, but somehow Chortle-Buffer no longer seemed to signify, no longer seemed to frighten me. I had bigger ogres to confront. And yet, nor was I about to implore Kelly for charity. No chance of that. Douglas would have to bail me out. Hadn't he just sold his flat? Exactly: he must be rolling in money.

But Matthew, sitting just behind me, had gathered what had happened. *How* many times had he told me not to live beyond my means? I told him to spare me the preachery. Actually, I called him a prig. He told me not to be a fool – he'd been on the point of suggesting a ploy to save my skin. Oh? . . . This is how he worked it. He told me to dial his bank. He enquired of some automaton the state of his account; then, asked to be put through to the branch manager. While the automaton was twiddling with extension numbers, Matthew placed his hand over the mouthpiece, and whispered: I seem to be quite flush, darling. I said: How flush is flush? (Lordy Laud, never mind your regular financial black. Matthew was in the fullest financial pink.) I said: Parsimonia has been thrifty. He said: I'd watch my tongue if I were – yes, I wonder if you could help me. The man at the other end couldn't very well refuse. Matthew let him know that he was sending me over to Victoria Street, with a letter of authorization by way of proof, and that he'd be grateful if I could be given, in cash, the entire contents of his account. He was moving. Overseas. Unexpectedly. To Italy.

I looked at my watch. The race was on. I had to be back in just over an hour. The hairdresser would need to be let into the flat. I set up my typewriter, and bashed out a letter for Matthew. I typed it twice – not because the first attempt was wrong, but because his signature looked as if I'd tried to forge it. The phone rang. It was Alison, wanting to know whether Matthew had slept all right. I said: I'm rushing to the bank, but I really need to talk to you. She told me to call her back at – Let's see – three forty-five. Okay-bye. I had a quick shower, threw on some clothes, and skedaddled. At Victoria Street, they complied with Matthew's demand, but surrendered his great wodges with an exaggerated, almost begrudging, calm. I took the dosh directly back to the flat. I plonked it on Matthew's lap. Here, I said; your dowry. He said: Not much use to me now, you'd better have it, but remember, that's my Lot, so I trust you to be responsible about it. I felt both ecstatic and chastised. I said: Oh darling.

Next, he forced me to ring Chortle-Buffer, who, against my expectations – but not against Matthew's – condescended to pick up his handset. I said: If I were to clear all my debts within the hour, in ready cash, would you be prepared to reconsider the position about my cards? Chortle-Buffer practically farted. He was minded, he said, to stick to his guns; but considering the long years of this-and-that, and given my commendable whatever-it-was – probably entrepreneurial drive – he conceded: Very well – though this was *absolutely* my last chance. And so, while Matthew was having his hair cut, I hared across to Mayfair and delivered the stash. That's how it works in stories such as ours; accounts of love.

There was, however, a subsequent proviso, stipulated during the lull between lunch and Matthew's manicure. He proposed a deal. The deal was simple: He would say nothing about the shaming state of my affairs on the understanding that I not tell Douglas about Special Underwear. (Should I have confessed that

I'd already blabbed? I didn't; I just couldn't. Instead) I asked why Matthew was getting so worked up. Because if he was consenting to those pants at all, he said, it was only as a precaution – to stop me, should something *happen* to go wrong, from getting all told-you-so. He was not, repeat *not*, incontinent. *I* of all people knew that. As indeed I did. But the knowledge only served to increase my sense of cheapness; it fuelled my guilt.

The beautician arrived. I took her into the sitting room, left her with Matthew, and crept off to the kitchen to ring Alison, whose first concern was: His tummy all right? Not earlier on, I admitted; but it seemed more settled now. Incontinence pants? Yes, he'd agreed to wear them on the flight. Stamina? Improving by the hour. And how was *I*? A bit less panicked: I'd managed to persuade a friend to come along with us. That's great, she laughed. Listen, I said; about this wheelchair, I'm tempted to leave it behind; Matthew reckons that he doesn't need it, and in Venice, with all those steps and bridges everywhere, it's going to make life even harder. Alison said: If you're asking my opinion, I think that you'd be silly not to take it, just as a back-up; you can always travel with it folded, like a buggy. I said: What a pain. She said: Less of a pain than having to carry him. And by the way, she added, if you've got someone else coming, you should probably get a baby-alarm. Why? Because, say Matthew needs to rest, you and your friend could be in another room but still be able to hear him; stop flapping; you can buy one in the departures lounge. The main thing is that Matthew has a good time. Keep cool, and good luck, and I'll see you both when you get back.

As soon as I'd hung up, the phone rang. It was Douglas, wanting to know about tomorrow morning. When did we want to be picked up? What did he reckon – six forty-five? Seemed about right. He'd be round in a cab. Wonderful. The beautician was done. Matthew pronounced himself delighted. Grooming, he said; nothing like it – except, of course, Reiki massage. I wasn't in a position to judge, Reiki having always been *his* thing, not mine. Those secret séances which, veiled in whispers about heightened intuition and transference of energy and the power of holistic healing, sounded almost mystical in spirit, supposedly required, for maximum benefit, an atmosphere of hermetic peacefulness. My job was simply to set the scene: lay a duvet on the floor, leave a couple of pillows on top, provide a large towel – for the retention of warmth in case of sudden temperature-drops – and close the door. I'd heard it claimed that the procedure could be so powerful, so cathartic to the subject, that, in certain circumstances, it could impel you to cry. I suspect this to have been one of the reasons why I myself never tried it. Another was the fact that, given all the unfairness to which Matthew had been treated in his recent life, it seemed only fair that certain treats should be exclusively his to profit by. At any rate, the woman who, for some time now, had regularly come to the flat, used, after an hour of crouching over Matthew, to emerge from those sessions looking shattered, crimson-faced and bleary-eyed. She would always knock back, en route to her next client, two inches of neat vodka – to constrict her blood-vessels, was, I think, her argument. But today, as she staggered into sight, her countenance was not just red; it was redder. I asked if something were the matter. She said that things didn't feel right. I poured into her glass. She glugged. I suggested that perhaps Matthew's amphetamines had worked against his calm. She wiped her mouth. No, it was more serious than that. I said: More serious how? Her eyes were wild. She said: I'm really sorry, but I don't think there's any more I can do for him now. She might as well have slapped me. I wanted to say: You poxy fucking drunken liar. Instead I said: Don't worry about it. (Matthew certainly hadn't. He had adored his Reiki.)

The rest was straightforward enough. We ate supper; then, adjourned to the sitting room to discuss what I had packed, and who'd be wearing what, and stuff. Passports and tickets? In the hall. Lolly? Getting some at Heathrow. Taxi? Douglas was picking us up. Matthew agreed that I could take the wheelchair folded. He also agreed that I could buy a baby-alarm. He further agreed that it was probably best if I gave him a shave tonight. And then, because we had such an early start, he agreed to have a bath – a lengthy, steamy soak reminiscent of the glory-days of Blanche DuBois. He said: Prithee play some music, Captain. Meanwhile, I changed his sheets, cleared the kitchen, arranged our clothes, and that – more or less – was that. But I say 'more or less' because, as he was climbing into bed, he suddenly moaned about his stomach. Did he need to go back to the lav? No, he didn't have the squits; he was just feeling slightly sick. I stopped. I said: In which case, I'd better give you an anti-emetic jab. Matthew said: You can't, you don't know how. I said: I do, Alison showed me when she came round; it's no big deal, the needle's tiny. I opened the overnight bag and rummaged through his supplies. I *had*, believe it or not, managed to practise on an orange; but oranges don't count. They've already fallen from the tree of life. Dead. Can't shout. Matthew yelled the house down. And what did *I* do? I just kept on pushing the plunger. Done. I swabbed his thigh, stuck a plaster, and apologized. Matthew said: That was bloody agony. And yet, despite the agony, nothing was getting in the way of his honeymoon.

The journey out. I remember not much. We weren't upgraded, but it scarcely mattered. The plane was half-empty. We were treated like Class. We could sit wherever we liked. Douglas took a window-seat. I grabbed an aisle. Matthew looked sensational in ivory. He drank champagne. I couldn't believe it. He took my hand. He whispered: Thank you, darling. I said: I'm the one who should be doing the thanking. He said: Silly queen. Now the plane seemed to be landing. I depicted the view, the Lagoon in the distance. It was all, Matthew said, coming back to him.

Venice was misty. Chilly. The calendar was close to Christmas. Our hotel had sent a motorboat to fetch us. The boat bobbed up and down, a yard away from the quay. Douglas went ahead, and leapt in. I handed him our luggage, followed by the folded wheelchair. Matthew stood and waited, smiling at the breeze. A windy tear rolled down his cheek. Next: a hitch. I thought: How do I get him in? But the boat just kept on bobbing. Up and down and up and down and up. I tried to talk him through it. I said: You're going to have to let me lift you. He said Right. I said: Just put your arms around my neck and we can do this. I counted: One. I counted: Two. I counted: Three. And then, as I stood betwixt and between, with one foot on the concrete of the dock, which was the past, and another on the decking of the boat, which belonged to the future, and a whole cold ocean in the middle, waiting darkly beneath us, well, my boy just flew, *flew* like an hyperbole through the Venetian clouds, and landed softly on the other side. It ain't that I'd been strong enough to carry him. It ain't even that, if I was laden at all, I was laden with sadness. It's just that Matthew wasn't heavy. Matthew wasn't my brother. Matthew was properly mine. While he lasted.

At last we arrived. The hotel had a ramp, which was lowered toward our boat, and hooked up. I walked the gangplank backwards, so that he, gripping my outstretched arms, could shuffle up the rubber path, and – gently now – alight. The staff were miraculous. Not a hint of Hello Ducks. Not a single tell-tale eyebrow. If anything, they gave the impression of being accustomed to guests whose dream it was to travel one last time. Our luggage vanished. I settled Matthew upon a magisterial sofa, and sat myself beside him. He ran his fingers along one of the carved arms, as if those wooden curlicues were sensuous puzzles. Douglas went off to the reception counter, to fill in forms and surrender passports. I thought about us. I viewed us as if from above. I would say that if, in this strange ménage, in this wandering party of ours, Matthew represented the dependent infant, and I, the fretful mother, Douglas, who had once been Jack's mere cub, had grown and grown from strength to strength until, now, he embodied the archetypal paterfamilias. He was so

authoritative; so substantial. I don't think that he can have
known how much I admired him.

I looked around. At the entrance to the lobby, amid an array
of decorative marvels – torch-bearing blackamoors, fanned by
hot-house palms; gilded consoles, over Ottoman rugs; wall-
hangings of Chinese-yellow damask; urns of tumbling roses set
against panels of streaked marble – stood a central, massive
Christmas tree, the deckings of which were (not red, not green,
not gold, not silver, not white, not even transparent, but) black.
Black baubles, black bows, black candles. Call it Venetian chic. I
called it macabre – but kept off the subject. Matthew said: I can
smell pine. I said: You can smell Yuletide. Douglas came back,
dangling a pair of keys with histrionic tassels. He said: Let's go
upstairs and unpack before lunch. Matthew said: I want to take
my pills in private. I said: You can take them wherever you like.

Caged into a lift with gilded grilles and velvet padding we
were ferried up. Our rooms were opposite each other – mine
and Matthew's being the one recommended by Cara; Douglas's
giving onto an inner courtyard. Douglas dispensed tips.
Matthew dispensed smiles. I dispensed with formalities. I pushed
ahead and said: You're going to bloody love this. Matthew said:
Describe. I said: Give me a chance. A bellboy with a pill-box hat
said: Welcome Gentle Mans. Douglas said: I'll come back when
I'm done. Our luggage had already arrived. A pair of French
windows had been left ajar. We had a corner balcony. There was
a breeze from the Canal. The bellboy unfolded the wheelchair.
He asked where he should park it. Anywhere was fine. Matthew
was standing beside me. He said: What's he on about? I said: Your
chariot – then looked outward, downstream. Matthew said: We
facing water? I said: That's right. He said: I thought I could hear
lapping. The bellboy asked if there was anything else we wanted.
I asked the name of some amazing, huge-domed church across
the way. Santa Maria della Salute, came the answer. Kindly trans-
late, said Matthew. I said (I had to say): Our Lady of Good
Health. He rose above the irony. He said: In which case, Captain,

we shall drink to her at luncheon; but first let's have a go on my chariot.

All things considered, he found it quite comfortable. I, on the other hand, found it cumbersome; awkward to command. The wheels seemed to prefer to rotate backwards, as if turning against time. And yet, perversely, this reverse motion struck me as natural; I could almost understand it; sympathize. So thus it was that I manoeuvred Matthew, slowly back and counterclockwise, in unconscious emulation of our progress, that whole other lifetime past, round the French museum of tapestries. Since those days, of course, necessity had cast me in the role of guide; whereas Matthew, who had once rebuked me for my childishness, was now reduced to dado-height, like a child – albeit a child encouraged to touch. He ran his fingertips along the fluting of our bedsteads, and along the gilded wicker at their base, and along the linen of our sheets, which he decreed the finest that he'd ever felt. And all the while he would be asking: What colour's this? What fabric's that? What shape's this lamp? Are these handles bronze or brass? Do these curtains have a pattern? Let me check that tie-back – is it silk or be this *nylon*? . . . Odd as it may sound, our circuit round that chamber felt productive. Certainly not tragic. There was pleasure attached. And didactic value. It taught me how the failure of Matthew's sight had refined his other senses to such a pitch that, backward though he went, his compensatory faculties had overtaken mine. Surpassed them.

When Douglas showed up, I still hadn't dealt with our luggage. He said: If you don't get a move-on, we're not going to make lunch. I said: OK, but while I unpack, why don't you tell Matthew about those pictures, and the coffered ceiling, and the chandelier and stuff. Douglas began. As I busied myself with hangers, and darted in and out of the bathroom, I eavesdropped on his account. It awakened me to a paradox, namely that descriptions given by two different sets of eyes can differ so dramatically as to make one observer appear blind, or the other look like a liar. Take the coffered ceiling, which struck me as too dark, and too bluntly carved, and too sombre for domestic comfort. Douglas sold it to Matthew as lavish, with a focal, central starburst, and crafted beams evocative of ancient galleons. Ditto the paintings, which, to me, seemed over-varnished and over-coloured and practically kitsch, like cinquecento parodies. Interpreted by Douglas, their palette became brilliant, and their treatment exquisite, Titianesque even, with broadly textured skies and luscious mythical subjects reclining. The chandelier, blown from recent local glass, was a complete eyesore, like an octopus, wired-up to sparkle. Yet, from Douglas's vantage, it appeared opalescent and translucent and fragile, and, if anything, conceived along botanical lines. He called it fern-like. I said: Enough bloody rhapsodizing. Here are your tablets, Matthew.

He chose to walk to lunch; it wasn't far. He took my arm; I couldn't have felt prouder. When we reached the dining room, he told me – reasonably enough – to seat him with his back to the action. Not so reasonable, perhaps, was his reaction to the maître d', who'd just asked Douglas which menu Matthew might like – English or Italian. I was on the point of signalling to the effect that neither, when Matthew demanded, good and loud, that we find out from that waiter how to say I'm-Not-Sodding-Deaf in Venetian patois. Still, aside from this minor contretemps, the rest passed without mishap. I can't remember what we ate, but I do recall that Matthew abstained from drinking wine. Instead, he ordered a Virgin Mary, which I called a Bloody Shame; but he defended his good sense by citing a senseless lyric from our heyday: there was a twist in his sobriety, he said. Douglas looked stumped. I told Matthew as much. Matthew grinned. He was saving himself for this evening. He fancied a sally to Harry's Bar – always assuming that Douglas was up for it. Whereupon Douglas, as if to demonstrate his solidarity, rose from his chair and said that he was off to explore the town. He wanted to investigate the simplest route for us. He told us to go for a lie-down. He wanted us, he said, on tip-top form for the cocktail-hour. He winked at me with that faultless blend of truth and lies. And then he left, guide-book in hand, determination in his swagger, strength in his herringboned back.

I took Matthew up. As we ambled along the carpet, he said: Isn't this place lovely? I said: Utter luxury. We reached our room. The chambermaid had been. I moved some lilies away, because their scent, said Matthew, was bound to keep him awake. He brushed his teeth. I turned down our beds. I helped him into his pyjamas – the ones with crimson piping, first worn after his retinal detachment. I left the curtains as they were – to flutter. He didn't mind. He found the sound of water tranquillizing. I asked if he was sure that he didn't want to use the lav. No need, he said. He was fine. Talk about mind over matter: Matthew had constipated himself to the point of defiance. Indeed, his bowels would remain frozen throughout the time that we were gone from London. But, because he worried that I worried, he nonetheless put up with those punishing plastic pants. It wasn't such a deal, he said. His bony arse could take the bulk. Didn't you know? Big was back, darling.

He snoozed without apparent trouble; but I, for all of my exhaustion, could never have closed my eyes. Too watchful. Too anxious. So instead, while lugubrious gondolas went by, off-season, disappointed, dipping at the prow, I sat about, wrapped in a towelling-robe and smoking at the ghastly chandelier above, and wondering. But my thoughts kept with the abstract: the Red Heart at the very start; how far, since that beginning, we had come; things yet to be done; Matthew's garden, left abandoned; the wisdom of Farquhar; the meaning of honeymoons; the kindness of Douglas; the fullness of surprises; the peculiar pleasure of my provisional life; the conditional; the pluperfect; sunshine at Gay Pride; Amen to that; old tangos man-to-man; haymaking at night; walks arm-in-arm; the here-and-now; small mercies; giving thanks; great sunsets; oceans at wintertime; tides rising; palazzi holding up; hotels with five stars; dreamers; canals;

safe passages; *safe passages*; death-traps; departures. It makes me so fucking angry.

He stirred after an hour. He told me to remind him to send Alison a card, then asked why he *still* felt so whacked. I answered that the sea-breeze always knocked one out, but not to worry: we had speed to hand – did he want some? He yawned; he stretched; he rubbed his eyes. Actually, what he'd really like was a good old cup of char. I was on the point of dialling down when Douglas buzzed. Had he woken us up? No, we were about to order tea – did he want to join us? Sure; he'd be over in a minute. I rang the kitchen. Could we possibly have some tea, for three people? Ees possible, yes, with pastry or sandwichy? We'd better have both, please. (Douglas had an appetite.) Matthew dragged himself to the edge of the mattress. As his heels met with the rug, he said: My feet are killing me. I went over to his side. His ankles looked puffy. I said: That's probably from the flight; you should put your lallies up. He said: Help me into my dressing-gown, I need to look the part for when the trolley-boy comes round. Someone knocked; knocked twice. It was Douglas. Matthew said: What tidings from yon canal? Douglas replied: Piece of cake getting to Harry's Bar – mind you, brass-monkey weather out. Matthew, quick as a flash, said: Fear not, my liege, we come availed of robes and furred gowns. Douglas said: Very wise. Room Service materialized. I said: That's perfect, thank you. I saw to the niceties. Matthew took most of his pills. Douglas took most of our sweetmeats. I took stock of the tranquil scene. I thought: Don't let me forget this. This brief intimacy. This family unit. This peculiar Nativity.

The task of dressing Matthew had latterly grown into a trial, for my role had multiplied, or rather, divided, and the division caused me discomfort. My obvious function was to help him in and out of whatever he wanted, which, since he knew the contents of his wardrobe backwards, was hardly problematic. But less unproblematic was the fact that while, in his mind's eye, he held a clear idea of all his clothes, he could no longer behold his reflection dressed in what it wore. After blindness had enfolded him, Matthew's image of himself – that fixed, fuller portrait of his faultless recall – had become outdated, outmoded; and he, though admittedly spared the spectacle of his own emaciation, was nevertheless stripped of the power to discern which item flattered him and which betrayed, which remained his friend, and which – which turncoat – had turned into his covert foe. I considered, perhaps mistakenly, the question of his appearance to be my business, to fall within the remit of my commitment to his dignity; so I did, at times, attempt to exert some influence. But at others, well, I just gave in. It seemed vicious to point out that a red jumper, for instance, rendered his yellowish complexion green; or that a collar which, in former days, had proudly harboured the great column of his neck, now swam around the eroded pillar of his wastage. As if to further complicate affairs, Matthew was given to a sartorial quirk – one that I myself never shared: his choice of clothes was frequently dictated by (not fashion, not even mood, but) theme. And yet, once a notion, however loony, had come to him, no degree of entreaty could make him change his tune. Which is precisely what happened on that evening. Unaware of its treacherous hue, and seemingly indifferent to its surplus collar-inches, he resolved to sport a brushed, peach cotton shirt for our expedition. His reason: to match the bellinis which we were about to drink. I turned a blind eye to it. I'm glad that I did.

But when it came to footwear, I couldn't disregard reality: his feet had become too swollen to tolerate lace-ups. I suggested that his velvet slippers might be worth a try. We tried the left; we tried the right. He stood and reckoned that he could just about stand it – but then sat down. He heaved an exasperated sigh; he said that he gave up; he supposed that he had better be wheeled around. I wasn't wholly surprised: push had come to shove. I said: No point giving yourself a hard time. And then I said: OK, let's style you up. By the end of our session – and slightly to my own surprise – Matthew looked fantastic, soberly distinguished,

388 ~ Paul Golding

starkly handsome. Black trousers, charcoal jacket, charcoal scarf. Over these, he wore his coat – but loosely slung over his shoulders, in the manner of a cloak. I didn't want him being subjected to some wriggling divestment once we'd reached our watering hole. I combed his hair; I gave him a parting; I handed him his woollen hat. He fumbled for the label, found it, and began to mould the knitted dome onto his skull. Yet his fingers, as they sculpted, must have noticed something – his sunken sockets, his hollowed temples – because he said that he must look like death warmed up. I said: Bollocks, you look like a total star. He said: Such fervent blandishments, Captain, really, too kind. But his smile was downcast. He switched subjects: Any lipsalve about? I told him never to trust a man without it. He applied the balm with rolling gusto, and concluded that his mouth – mmm – did not need chaps. I handed him his gloves. He waved them around, as if acknowledging some crowd. I said: Put them on properly; it's cold outside. He couldn't tell which one went on which hand. I showed him how: Pony-skin side up. Then, I told him to close his eyes. He scrunched his face, like a child for a surprise. I sprayed him with a wreath of Creed – still, after all this time, his all-time best. I telephoned Douglas, who suggested that Matthew and I go ahead; he would meet us downstairs; he had a quick call to make. (To Stan, I guessed.) But as I crossed the room, I was moved by a further reflection. A revelation.

Matthew, waiting calmly in the darkened foreground, was like a sitter seated sideways. His back, though gently hunched, remained unbowed. His shaded profile, enigmatic yet sharp, seemed to gaze out toward dominions beyond encompassment. His high revers, jutting like black sails about him, breathed slowly with the failing tide; and his jaw, clenched from the struggle in a cause that was all but lost, rested, philosophically, upon gloved knuckles. Even his stately head, clad in its ribbed cupola, seemed to allude to the great cupola across the canal. It was uncanny. Viewed against this backdrop of misty, mauvy, rooftop violet, there was an air to him which, though it hurt you, made you marvel. For, at that split instant, he looked (not terminal, but) timeless. Like a doge immortalized in the grand manner, captured for everafter. Like a man who had outgrown the vagaries of human circumstance. Like a paragon. Like a champion. But he also looked, with brutal suddenness, a hundred and one. I saw, for the first real time, the approaching last. The future past. The future stuffed. And although later I would tell my ghouls to cut it out and take me back, right to the start, I have found it hard to dismiss this particular cameo. It has, admittedly, faded with writing. But it isn't always easy to forget the things which we have learned by heart.

Snap out of it. I reminded him to hang onto his coat-cuffs: we didn't want stray sleeves getting tangled in the wheels of the chariot. I warned: I'm releasing the brakes now. But Matthew, never one to be cowed, replied: Step on it, Gianni, and don't spare the camels. I locked the door behind us. We took the velvet elevator down. Tucked within an alcove next to the reception-counter, I discovered a boutique – stacked with much the sort of merchandise that you'd imagine: lace from Burano, glass from Murano, and the usual goofery by Ferragamo. But it also peddled prints and city-guides and maps and – Great, I said – postcards. Matthew told me to grab a handful, but nothing tacky – no carnival drag, or *gondolieri* scratching their tackle. I told him to grant me *some* discernment – what about St Mark's? Fine, so long as there wasn't any scaffolding. By day or by night? Whichever seemed less crowded. Douglas arrived, looking fresh and dapper and a little bit in love. I gave him Matthew's blanket for the journey back. He draped it over his arm. He wore, I recall, a marvellous alpaca coat. Double-breasted indigo. Very long.

And yet, of that first perambulation, I only recollect my panic at hearing Douglas announce that we'd already arrived. I mean: no banner, no awning, no notice, nothing. I felt socially undermined by the bar's implicit social smugness – which is how the whole conceit of open-secrecy struck me – but I tried to rise above it. I needed to suss out the simplest stratagem of access.

My blood began to thump. First, there was a step – of exactly the wrong height; then, a pair of swing-doors – of such narrowness that *both* would have to be held open for the wheelchair to pass; and finally, slap-bang in front, a circular screen – so tightly curved that it felt designed to hinder your tracks, as if to deter the likes of Matthew from upsetting the *serenissimi* with unsightly intimations of mortality. Part of me wanted to get lost rather than have his expectations dashed; but then again, you know how it goes: needs must, best shots, chin up, all of that. I decided that the most promising way forward was probably backwards, so I told Matthew about the block of stone to be surmounted – lest, taken unawares, he go toppling to the ground. Then I asked Douglas to keep the double-doors apart with his hands stretched high, so that I could introduce myself beneath the archway of his arm. I could tell that the bright interior was packed. The beautiful laughter made me blush. Just as I was on the point of starting to turn Matthew, a man with argent hair rushed out. He didn't seem like a mere manager. He wore the sweeping confidence of a proprietor. I somehow *knew* that he was going to say No Room At The Inn in Italian – instead of which, in faultless English and with a faultless smile, he wished us a good evening, and, begging me to pardon him, assumed control of the chariot. There was an art to the business, apparently. A trick, to do with quick lifts. He showed me. I could never have done it, I admit. Still, once Matthew was within, and as he was being steered toward the arena, the owner leaned down to reassure him: You know, Sir, many of our guests have come in wheelchairs; the old Aga Khan often did, so you're in pretty good company, and very welcome. To which Matthew replied: I'm very grateful to be here, thank you.

The owner, thanking a few diehards at the bar to budge, steered us past the screen to a corner behind the entrance. As he whipped some obstacle out of the way, he told us that the table he was giving us had been his father's favourite. From here (he winked) you could see Everything. I zoomed in on Matthew, lest this inadvertent gaffe had altered his countenance, but it hadn't: he was taken up with taking off his gloves. Meanwhile Douglas, relinquishing his coat, volunteered a cursory Wonderful; and at last, after a quick shuffle-round, we were parked. The room was tiny for a place so widespreadly renowned – scarcely seven metres by five. Its low-ceilinged beams were painted white, and its clubby, shiny furniture, though conceived in the fascistic style, was maritime in character. The smoky, thoughtful atmosphere, suffused with wafts of Shalimar, brought to mind a Thirties' sepia photograph – a touch overexposed, perhaps, but no less finely-framed for that. The assembled clients, irrespective of their sundry nationalities, exuded a globally untroubled calm. Their leisured gestures made it seem as if time were nothing very much, like another present to be passed. Not a luxury.

We were asked what we would like – bellinis, by any chance? – which made me feel transparent. I would have killed to answer: What I'm dying for is an absinthe; but of course I had to say: That would be lovely. Douglas agreed: Yes, for all of us. The owner, having signalled to the barman and been signalled back, awarded us a half-bow, then continued on his cordial round, which was his talent. Matthew, turning to me, now asked: So, what's the décor like? I said: Darling, you're never going to believe this, but exactly like the décor on that liner bound for Buenos Aires. How div*ine*, he laughed; give us a rundown. I sketched a general impression of the colour-scheme and ambiance, and mentioned a blown-up snap, prominently hung, of old man Hemingway, awash in a sea of pathos despite his flippant wrist and fancy sombrero, and looking, for all the world, like the very thing which he detested: an effeminate. I mentioned the electric wall-brackets (too Edwardian for comfort); I attempted to describe the logo on our ashtray (an impeccable Deco graphic), and then, catching sight of the marble ground, I launched into a breathless spiel about how the floor-tiles were absolutely ideal for a swishy tango wearing silver lamé spikes and a gossamer chiffon gown draped on the bias in eau-de-nil or aqua. It must have been this campy flurry that prompted Douglas (who, friendly as he was, was no longer a friend of camp), to shoot me a pointed look – meaning: Do you really have to? – so I made a point of looking as if I'd never heard of anyone called Stan. Matthew, unaware of visual daggers, cut in to ask: Can we deal with Alison's card? Douglas began to squirm, like a martyr to worms. I asked what on earth was the trouble. He uhmmed; he ahrred; he didn't think that writing postcards in a place like this was Done. There followed a suspenseful silence, as if someone were consulting an etiquette bible, but Matthew soon settled the matter: Don't get posh with *me*, girl; I was fucking around these palazzos long before the flood. Douglas sat corrected. Matthew didn't pay the blindest. Instead, peeling off his hat, he enquired: Does my scribe have a quill to hand? I produced a biro. Right, he said, now let me see . . . OK, put down: Greetings to Nurse Alison from a fervent admirer with love and thanks. No need to sign . . . Too right. For, by the time those thirteen words had been committed to the mail, and been winged across the air, and been delivered to the day-centre, Matthew would be dead.

What the hell. Our drinks descended. A waiter with a dicky-bow proclaimed: *Ecco*. Matthew said: Perfect; Douglas said: Splendid; and I, secretly wishing that I didn't have to say it, asked if a straw could be fetched. Whether this request was met with censure, I shall never know, for any sign of disapproval was obliterated. Good service aims to give but pleasure. The straw was brought in seconds. Now Matthew, who claimed to be sweltering, began to shed his top layer, and to loosen his scarf, and to unbutton his jacket. And, as the frontage of his shirt came to light, I saw, with a mixture of shame at my earlier qualm and vicarious pride in his judgement, that the pastel tone which he had chosen looked peerless in these sepia surroundings. Just ravishing. Next, raising his glass with a tremulous hand, and turning to either side, and smiling almost shyly, he suggested: Here's to friendship, boys. But there was a poignancy to that toast, for our eyes, at the moment of truth, were prevented from making true contact.

Never mind. To avoid the risk of irking of Douglas, I skirted round the shame of exuberant adjectives such as Nectareous and Ambrosian and Mirifical; but Matthew, having sipped from the bar's speciality, adjudged his peach-pulp & *prosecco* Sublime. Douglas called it Yum – but let's not carp. We were all, in our separate ways, of one mind. And so, thus united, we drank, savouring the privilege without saying much, quietly smiling about us, and briefly basking in a glow which, I would say, approximated happiness. Of course, it couldn't last. All too soon (but probably no sooner than Douglas' thoughts had erred to Stan) my head was wondering: What happens now? Matthew, with redemptive timing, enquired: Another drink, anyone? Douglas was on the verge of replying along the lines of Rather, when I asked Matthew if he himself was game for a further round. No, no; any more would be too much, but we weren't to let his temperance deter us. I turned the offer down; it seemed unfair to do otherwise; and Douglas, to be fair to him, instantly followed my suit. Actually, he overtook it. He called for the bill. Matthew was furious: he'd wanted our cocktails to be *his* treat. But Douglas wouldn't hear of it. Yet, when the damage was delivered, on a simple plate of plated silver, Douglas's frown betrayed bewilderment. Problem? Not really; he just couldn't make out why only two bellinis had been charged. He apprised the waiter of this accidental oversight, and the waiter scurried off to consult; but when he returned, it was to inform us that there had been no accident: the gentleman's drink (he nodded at Matthew) had been a small attention offered with the compliments of the house. Matthew beamed: That's incredibly kind. And then, to me, from the wicked side of his mouth, he mumbled: It seems you have a rival, Captain.

We prepared for the journey back. I could tell through a grilled window that darkness had already come. It was bound to be freezing outside. I wrapped Matthew up, and further enwrapped him in his dark mohair blanket. The result wasn't bad; it was Grand. Douglas, leading our procession, now cleared a path through some babble of table-hopping internationals – *Mais quel plaisir de vous revoir! ¡Pero qué sorpresa, vaya!* – so that I could wheel Matthew behind. I braced myself to eyeball any sideglancer, but, almost disappointingly, none obliged. At the door, while Douglas and I were waiting for our coats, I suddenly became aware that, on the street, it was bucketing down. Just our sodding luck. Yet luck had not (not quite) deserted us. The owner asked where we were staying, and Douglas – urbanity personified – proffered the answer, whereupon he was handed an umbrella and told absolutely not to worry; just to leave it with one of the commissionaires at our hotel; there was always traffic between the two places; but perhaps we would call in again before we left Venezia, yes? *Arrivederci!*

Supper was special – special in two senses. Matthew, despite his birdlike appetite, wanted nothing but the best tonight, the fine local luxuries: risotto with white truffles; veal, baked with artichokes – simple food, but sumptuous. I kept tempting him to have a sip of this, and a spoonful of that, and a bite of the other. Liquorice ice-cream, I raved; you *have* to try some. And vino santo, darling; each and every grape crushed by the feet of monks. And cantuccini biscuits – *who* says dunking's not allowed? I dunked. I said: Open wide for the body of Christ. Matthew feigned aghastness: Prithee curb thy forkèd tongue lest we be barred from paradise. (Munch.) And the second sense in which that supper was so special is because, as it turned out, it would be Matthew's last – but what's the big rush. After coffee, we all went up, and, once I'd put my boy to bed, Douglas, in his navy paisley dressing-gown, sneaked across for a nightcap. We chatted about the day to come: breakfast in our rooms, we agreed; foray to St Mark's; then, best just wait and see how things panned out. Douglas drained his glass, dragged himself up, and, stifling a yawn, said that he was off to Bedfordshire. He hugged me in that tremendous way that he had. He wished me a good night, duck. Matthew was, by then, already asleep – soundly. His countenance was calm. Not even his lashes were fluttering. I remember thinking: But he looks so tiny. I also remember trying to pray in the dark. So I must have been frightened.

The dawn was reluctant. It took for ever coming. Its stubborn dullness stultified you. A sulky mist just hung there, heavy, humid, idling over the canal, blurring the façades of those crumbling, discoloured houses; clogging the light. A pair of motorboats sped past, at a brash diagonal. Their racket made you want to tell them to shut up. When Matthew told me to describe the day, I had to lie. I freshened the atmosphere, crisped it, starched it, made it sound bright. I asked him how he felt. *Yeurgh*. He turned to his side. Like an idiot I said: Give yourself a bit of time. He said nothing. Still, toward noon, we finally set off for the piazza, accompanied by the clang of discordant bells from disparate towers, tuneless ministers of plangency. And yet Matthew – all these years since that honeyed student summer when the warmth of his hair had brushed the softness of his clavicle, and the future had been strewn with nothing worse than foolish flowers – seemed glad of the chance to return to St Mark's. Was it a Sunday? I doubt it. I recall an eerie absence of crowds, and a slimy ground, and a chilly gloom about my back. Douglas offered to steer Matthew, but I glared at him, affronted. Sure, Douglas was my friend, and my good fortune, and all the rest of the blarney – but the chariot was mine.

Souvenirs, anyone? My memory inclines me down, stoops me over Matthew's handlebars, has me hunched to catch his words from the wind which swept and whirled around the vastness of that piazza. He asked where we were now. At the far end of the square, I said; facing the basilica. He nodded. He smiled. He could picture it exactly. And then, as if to match that exact picture from his past, he told me to take him along the central aisle, between the rows of patterned paving which decorated the ground. Istrian stone, he remarked. I said: You Anthony Blunt or something? Less cheek, he wagged, and you might learn something –

any pigeons about? Not for a while. Well, he instructed: make sure they don't come near us – flying rats. Douglas said: Pity I didn't bring m'shotgun. Matthew said: So butch, our Douglas.

As I swivelled the wheelchair sideways, to align us for our advance, Matthew must have heard his tyres go splashering through some puddle, because he said that Venice currently stood two feet lower than it had done in the seventeen hundreds. I said: Can a sea-level rise? He said: It's probably as much to do with subsidence, but if you compare a postcard of St Mark's photographed from the Canal with a Canaletto of the same site, you'll notice a giveaway bridge somewhere. He also claimed that Napoleon had once described this sprawling great trapezoid as the finest drawing-room in Europe. I said: Where d'you get *that* from? He couldn't say for sure – probably Jan Morris before she had the snip. We proceeded. I wasn't concentrating on the view. Too busy listening. I didn't want to miss an aural trick. I recall feeling frustrated by the simultaneous roles of driver and pupil, yet simultaneously wishing to relinquish neither. We pressed on; it was cold. Matthew pointed to the right and asked about some *caffè* – what was it called again, the Florian? I thought that he was getting muddled up with Paris – Le Flore – but no. Douglas spotted the relevant awning, and said: Over there, still going strong. Matthew told us: First place in town to serve Turkish coffee; favoured cruising-haunt of Casanova's; we might pay our respects on the way home. Now he waved toward the left, toward the longest of the arcades. He asked if I could see a clock-tower anywhere. I vaguely could, but my sight was blurred; we were still miles away. He said: Poor guys who built it, a couple of brothers, had their eyes gouged out for their trouble; story goes that the officials of the time hadn't wanted anyone copying the wonder. And thus we went, in fits and starts, in dribs and drabs, switching between anecdote and history of art, until the sound of chants from the great basilica began, in waves, to reach us. Matthew said: The model for this place was in Constantinople

– some fabulous old church, long since demolished, of course; I think they've plonked a mosque on top – but it explains the whole Byzantine flavour of the cathedral, and the exotic domes, and the ground-plan in the shape of a Greek Cross. We stopped for a moment. The front of the basilica was half-enshrouded in the meshes of repair – black – but I chose not to betray this fact. I wanted to protect the glittering palette of Matthew's blindness, the vivid mosaics of his hindsight. He asked if I could see two pairs of bronzy-greeny horses over the entrance-arch. Without thinking, I said: Only just. Not to worry, he replied. The originals were apparently inside. But the best bit, he added, was the altar-piece coming up – torrents of precious gemstones, and heaps of enamel icons, and lashings of ancient gold: the *Pala D'Oro*. Dead beautiful, he called it. But next, I heard him laugh. I asked what was so funny. Oh, just remembering stuff. He'd been reminiscing about his first trip here, back in the hippy era. One of the girls in his group had got herself chucked out for looking too skimpy. I said: And you, my dear? He said: Captain, I was always demure.

But when we reached the threshold of those glories which Matthew had promised, the gateway to those introductions which he couldn't wait to effect – introductions which (now that time – not gold – was precious) felt like my rightful, urgent legacy, we discovered that the basilica lacked access for people in wheelchairs. Insufficient ramps; too many steps; too much flooding; wrong time of day – I really don't care. What I care about is this: one moment Matthew was joking; the next, he was broken. Douglas and I offered to carry him into the nave, but he said: Forget it, I'm enough of a spectacle; let's go. The carnival was over.

During our trundle back to the hotel, none of us spoke, but my innards were frenzied. I felt, on the one hand, to blame – as if, by having failed to avert this shameful turn of events, I had soured the honeymoon which Matthew had so passionately wanted and so patently deserved; yet I also felt incensed by the church's failure to cater for the poor and the maimed and the halt and the blind. Typical of those bloody padres. Talk about no room at the inn; talk about being barred from paradise; talk about irony. The guys who turfed you out for looking too skimpy had turned out to be the very cunts who wouldn't let you in when you were dressed up to the eyeballs. Wild.

God knows how I killed the next few hours – probably began to pack, and did what I do best, idle about, while Douglas, as it transpired, sneaked off to the basilica for a private eyeful. I can't say that I blame him; I might, in his position, have done likewise. But Matthew flopped into bed, rejected any further food or drink, refused to take his medicines, and just lay there, neither properly asleep nor yet awake, moaning to himself, and occasionally exhaling the languid wheezes of surrender. Yet I do remember how, standing on our balcony, I vowed never in my days to return to the city of nostalgia. Nor have I done. As promises go, the observance of this particular one has not been hard.

In the evening, Douglas and I, furnished with the baby-alarm which Alison had so prudently advised, ate dinner at the restaurant. I felt half-deaf as I strained, between clanks of crockery and clinks of cutlery and jolly soundbites from other diners, to listen out for any sign that Matthew might be in trouble. It further troubled me – being fretful to the last – that the monitor might be a two-way, not one; but Douglas dismissed my worry as irrational, and tried to keep me calm. He succeeded for a while. Yet when he insinuated that the person who had *really* been short-changed was I (since he and Matthew both, albeit at separate times, had witnessed the interior of St Mark's), I realized that there were certain things which Douglas, clever as he was, would never understand. My simple wish had been to view that fucking church *through* Matthew, *with* him, in the unity of the Holy frigging Spirit. Does that sound so unrealistic – or so blasphemous?

But by the following morning, Douglas was back on track –

sharp and reliable. He rang to wake us up. We had an early start. I couldn't wait to get us out. I went downstairs to deal with money matters. As I browsed through our list of printed items, I was awarded, first, the cheap thrill of discovering, on Douglas's account, a number dialled some dozen times (Stan's, no doubt); and then, a twinge of irritation that such extendedly sweet nothings should, in unfair reality, have to be bankrolled by Matthew. Still; the score was swiftly settled with a clean swipe of my debit card, and we were done. I returned to our room, to double-check that I'd left nothing unpacked, and to collect Matthew, who, even swaddled in his chariot, now looked grim and dismantled – beyond styling. I grabbed my coat. I closed the wardrobe. I heard an approaching commotion – Douglas, with a bellboy in tow. Our bags were taken down; our boat drew up; and next, quicker than you could say *grazie*, we were airport-bound. At last.

The departures lounge was pandemonic: foxy coats swinging about, and well-heeled stallions sporting winter sunglasses, and kids skateboarding on granite, and fulsome mouths going *Ciao! Noi andiamo a Miami!* To spare Matthew the ordeal of being trapped among such over-ebullient passengers, I asked Douglas to grab the luggage-trolley, and take himself, on our collective behalf, to the designated check-in counter. I handed him our tickets and passports, and – hang on – Matthew's steroid card. I said: When the moment comes, just point us out to the woman at the desk; we'll be waiting over there, that's right, by the Bureau de Change. Douglas joined the Latin version of a queue, which is a scrum, and I led my boy away, toward a solitary place where we might be more tranquil. His face, buried beneath his hat, looked like a mask. I couldn't understand how such an alteration could have come about so fast. I sat myself beside him. I peered toward the runway, and up to the mawkish skies. And then, some sudden dreadful thing welled up inside me, and burst beyond my gullet, and began to course from my eyes. I let the salty liquid trickle to my jowls, but I didn't make a sound. Yet

Matthew, holding out his gentle hand, told me not to worry, darling. It was all right.

Not much left to chat about. I just wanted to have this next stage done; the homeward journey, behind us. In my mind, we'd already been restored to my flat — everything clean, everything calm; no-one in the domestic frame but Matthew and I. Peering across the crowd, I kept catching glimpses of Douglas's ramrod back, inching its stalwart way toward the counter. Why couldn't those airline reps just *hurry*? Our boarding gate might be miles away. I needed time; I couldn't rush. I should have told Douglas to march straight to the front and say that he was flying with a disabled passenger. Too late now. Abide with Matthew. I cast my boy a glance. His eyelids were shut. His lungs were rasping. His jaw seemed to have slackened into the jaw of a geriatric. The process of departure had begun. Ages seemed to pass. By now, Douglas had conquered the head of the crocodile. He had taken command; he was taking care of us; he would find us the best seats to be found. Perhaps he was even upgrading us. Douglas could be given to flashes of great style. His authoritative elbows were set upon a vinyl slab; his massive shoulders were standing proud; his head was looming over the crown of some official hat, and moving up and down, and up and down, and then, from left to right. One of his hands now rose with a tremendous gradualness and — as the woman at the desk craned up — his powerful wrist emerged from its alpaca cuff; and next, his upper body seemed to be twisting in search of us. I waved. I waved hard. *Here*, Douglas, over *here* — as if here were some gorgeous seaside. He turned back to the woman, and then back toward us, and again he pointed in our direction, once, twice, jabbing his forefinger into the dense atmosphere. Had you not happened to know his business, you might have thought that he was angry. Or that he was aiming a pistol at us, as if Matthew's chariot were some target.

The woman, all of a squirm, skirted round our luggage, which was already on the weighing-stand, and jumped from her version of a pinnacle down to the lowly ground. The people parted, miming bafflement. Next the woman, furiously red and blue and white, stomped ahead of Douglas, and began to stride with bold determination toward the place where Matthew and I were parked – but Douglas caught up with her. He skidded round her, and blocked her path. She held her clip-board high. She fanned herself with hot bravado. Douglas stood his ground, absolutely mammothly, but she, undaunted by this foreign Goliath, kept nodding emphatically, as if there were no Italian doubt about something. Now, for no reason that I could fathom, she turned on her booted heel and trotted back to the security of her platform. She picked up a phone. Her air was flustered. I noticed the rest of the queue, the last few laggers, being moved to an adjacent check-in counter. You could practically hear the tutting and the whining and the grumbles of *Ma che cazzo?*

A man with a dark cap, worn at a dodgy angle, now joined Douglas and his adversary. The three kept peering toward us, briefly locking horns, then pulling back. Douglas seemed to be repeating and repeating the same reply to the same boring argument. I began to think: What's everyone so worked up about? Maybe I should go and give Douglas a hand – his languages were never up to much. But then I thought: No, keep Matthew safely apart, away from prying eyes – until suddenly, the answer to this whole conundrum (which Douglas, on the plane, confirmed to me by means of a note scrawled on a sick-bag) struck me. They'd been afraid that Matthew was too unwell to travel. They'd been afraid that he might not make it in one piece to London. They'd been afraid that the airline couldn't risk an unscheduled landing – not fair on the rest of the passengers. But, just as I began to steel myself for a showdown, Douglas snatched our boarding-passes from the woman's talons, and was already racing toward us, sweating and panting. All he said was: Sorry about that. Our gate was closing in five minutes' time. Gate sixty-nine, I ask you.

We were the last to board that flight. The cabin was crammed to fullest capacity. The rest of the passengers had already belted up – which doesn't mean that they kept quiet. Some prat behind me broadcast: Wheelchairs are meant to come on first, so as not to keep the rest of us hanging about. I told Matthew: Big deal, we're taking as long as we like. He grunted. Douglas couldn't sit alongside us: he'd been put in the row in front. I had to wheel Matthew backwards, pushing the arms of the chariot. The task felt uphill, but the public looked downward, you might even say disgusted. You might even say that you could read that they could read the signs.

I pulled off my coat, and reached for the overhead compartment. Our rack – who would have guessed? – was already stuffed. I recall a pair of bulging *Panettoni di Natale*. I said: Douglas, can you put my coat somewhere? He took my bundle, stowed it away, and sat down. I flipped Matthew's foot-rests up, for the moment when he'd have to stand. I decided that – despite the likelihood of his being bashed about – he was going to have to be seated by the aisle. I didn't have the strength to heave him across to the window – not in front of all these poor, put-upon passengers who were in such a mortal hurry. As I was preparing to lift him, I noticed that the chariot had begun to slide. I grabbed it. I tried to stretch over Matthew, round him, but I couldn't get at the brakes; my arms weren't long enough. Then, from some distant shady grotto near the ladies' lavatory, the welcome apparition of a sylphid Trolley Dolly sashayed up. About time. He stopped behind Matthew, but smiled roundabout. Now he took me by complete surprise: he struck a mannequin's pose from the days of the New Look – hand clamped on bony hip; other hand, upturned, pointing toward some unlikely future – in his case, the cockpit. His orange face sought to appear precisely what it was – indifferent. He was sporting a gilded earring with a dangly crucifix, and a high-street opal on his pinky. How were we doin'? I said: *Must* you stand there like a pillock? He said: Excuse *me*. I said: Just hang on to that wheelchair.

I hoiked Matthew by the armpits, and, after a god-awful struggle, managed to shift him onto his seat. I put his blanket on his lap, secured his safety-belt — clack — and slid a small pillow behind the small of his back. There; that's more like it. But as I tried to clamber over him, I realized that I hadn't dealt with the wretched chariot, and lost my balance, and stumbled. The Trolley Dolly advised: Take it easy now. I wiped the heat from my brow. But suddenly, with all the speed that a whip cracks, my tongue lashed out. And for once in my poxy life, I can tell you exactly what I told that henna-haired arsehole — I don't have to make it up — because the good Lord happened, as it happens, to give me the rant in rhyme: Just fold that bloody wheelchair, put it away somewhere, and bring it back at the end of the flight; and in the meantime, Miss Take It Easy Now, be a good girl and stay out of my sight.

I leapt over Matthew, and strapped myself up. He muttered: Nice one, Captain. But, pleased as I was to note that he had rallied, I just couldn't get into the banter. I felt too angry. I mean, how *dare* that stupid brat carry on like some drag-queen when he knew precisely what this was about? He should have been bending over backwards for someone like Matthew, and thanking his lucky stars that this wasn't a few years back. Hadn't anybody told him that his forerunners in cabin-crew — those earlier Cart Tarts from the Moonlight, once so happy-go-lucky, not least in their erotic habits — were now dropping like flies? If, at the time of which I write, you had cared to place a tell-tale pair of wings over every hospital-bed in London claimed by a former member of an airline, you would have thought that the Hivvy wards at Thomas' and Mary's and Guy's had been transferred to Heathrow and Stansted and Gatwick.

But next, we were up and rising, our engine rumbling through a blizzard of clouds. Of course, in the wake of my tantrum, the attendants chose to ignore us entirely; and we, for our part, chose to ignore the mealy temptation of a delicious plastic lunch. Matthew, in any case, dozed undisturbed —

notwithstanding turbulent patches. I had to nudge him awake as the plane began to lose height. We landed on a gleaming, rainy tarmac; waited for the rest of the crowd to disembark; and then, wended our way along a series of moving carpets until we reached the place where arrivals produce their passports. A bloke with a rubber stamp looked shocked to note what had become of Matthew's photograph, but – come on – at least we were back on home ground. Tomorrow I could call Alison.

We found the right carousel, reclaimed our baggage, and – having nothing to declare that was ingenious – proceeded through the green channel. As we advanced toward the taxi-rank, Douglas seemed to whip himself into a bit of an amorous hurry, but I made a point of waiting until one of those new cabs, fangled with a special ramp, had rolled up. It took seven Sorry Guv'nors before my prayer was answered. Anyhow, once Matthew was securely installed, we were ferried through the drizzling winter dark to Little Ealing, where Douglas, as we approached some fairy-lit dump, announced: Driver, here will be fine! He pat-patted Matthew's glove, gave me an (awkward) hug, and leapt out. He unloaded his Gladstone from the front; then, knocked on our window, proposed that we speak anon, and scrammed. But as our car turned on a sixpence, I clocked – tacked to the frilly, front-room window of the shrine whither Douglas was bound – a ruby-glitter constellation of pretend poinsettias, beneath which, a mechanized Santa Bear, decked in red bobbly hat and black biker-jacket, was gaily waving at passers-by. Happy Christmas from Stan.

And so, swiftly back to the flat. Home at last. While the driver dealt with extricating Matthew, I rushed upstairs to dump our bags, rushed back out, paid the man, thanked him, but didn't hang around to watch him vanish. I didn't want the neighbours smelling rats. I tilted Matthew over the front step, and wheeled him into the house – only to discover that the lift door (God all fucking *mighty*) was too narrow for the chariot. I hauled him to his feet. I forced him into the cage. He howled. How did I manage to keep him upright all the way to our landing? With some considerable trouble. I'd rather not describe it. But I do remember wondering how someone so diminished could still weigh so much.

Early in the morning, I telephoned Alison. I claimed that the trip had gone fine, which, in its way, it had; after all, the honeymoon had been accomplished and Matthew was still alive – but I admitted that, toward the end, he'd begun to flag, and now, seemed to be failing fast. Nor did I make any bones about how his acute deterioration had started to frighten me. He was in a weird sort of daze, like a drug-head, and kept letting out terse huffs which I couldn't fathom – Tough, or Rough, or perhaps Enough. Sometimes he complained about his back, which made me think that his kidneys might be packing up. Yes, I could turn him on the bed – to change his sheets and all of that – but I couldn't get him to the bathroom: he just wouldn't budge, and I didn't have the strength to take him single-handedly. So, she asked, how *was* I coping with the toilet-side of things? Well, I checked him regularly, and, if necessary, changed his incontinence pants. But that was the least of my worries. He'd been refusing food for forty-eight hours.

Alison reckoned that I was going to need supplies. I wondered how I was expected to bunk off to Pharmacy when Matthew's condition had grown so dire. Perhaps I should enlist someone – Cara, for instance – to come and supervise. But Alison must have guessed that I was in a bind, because she suggested: Tell you what, just try to keep him washed and watered, and I'll be over at lunch-time. She would bring a urine-bottle and a baby-mug. We could have a (not drink, but) chat.

When she arrived, Matthew brightened enough to mutter: I sent you a card. Oh, thank you, sweetheart, that's really nice. But then he nodded off, as fast as he had woken up. Alison made sure that he didn't have a rash, went to the kitchen, washed her hands, and sat me down. She wanted to order stuff – to make him More Comfortable. What she meant, of course, was: more comfortable in the circumstances – circumstances where nothing in the realm of hope was to be done.

This may be a presumption on my part, but I suspect that Alison was properly moved by Matthew's collapse – moved beyond the limits recommended by professional guidelines. She couldn't very well admit to so unprofessional a lapse, but her look spoke from her heart, and her heart-shaped mouth certainly looked crushed. Certainly, too, at this critical juncture, she put into motion more practical wheels than can possibly have been my theoretical entitlement, especially given my recalcitrance about consulting Nilson, to say nothing of rehospitalizing Matthew.

She told me which pills to discontinue, and which to keep up. But, above all, she told me to let Matthew dictate the pace now: we were entering a new phase in my vocabulary, the one which they call Palliative. She picked up her cell-phone, began to ring around, and, within minutes, had mobilized Care, with a capital C – there was nothing small about it – for the (un)qualified remainder of Matthew's life. A succession of district nurses would be dropping in twice-daily, to assist with the routine stuff – bed-baths, bed-sores, bed-pans – and report back. But then she dialled a further number, and asked if someone in particular was available – someone whose name I didn't catch, but whom she described as really lovely, a boy, Irish – in order to come to the flat at night. She thanked her chum at Social Services, dictated my details down the line, gave me the thumbs-up, and flicked her mobile shut. No, he wouldn't be needing a bed. An armchair was fine. But finer still is this: of the random group which was to embrace me after Matthew had vanished, that young male nurse would turn out to be one – the one with varnished hands. You, of course, were always there, right from the start; so we can file that passing piece of copy, just as you file your nails, without fuss.

The evening before the action started – by which I mean the nursing action – I was uncomfortable. I had become so used to bossing Matthew about, that, when Alison, reinforcing the advice of Farquhar, told me to adopt a passive stance, I felt as if, in some peculiar way, I were now being bossed back. It had been so much easier to nag, even to fight, than to obey this new instruction, which amounted to sitting back and letting Matthew die before my eyes. I found it hard to allow. I kept thinking: But surely I ought to be *doing* something?

I did – got drunk over a solitary supper. My marbles were so addled that I found myself laying a place for Matthew; but I suppose that his striated straw, grey and white, and beaten-silver napkin-ring, provided me with a morbid sort of company. I opened a bottle of wine; and, while I chewed on something – taken from the freezer, committed to the oven – I tried to make a list of tasks. I didn't get far. My perspectives, I realized, had all come crashing down. Thoughts of here-and-now-and-then-again-but-hold-it-best-to-take-things-one-step-at-a-time seemed to obstruct my mental path; they marred my horizons. I was stuck. I did the washing up. I lit a fag; and then, between gulps of cooking brandy, I downed a sleeping tablet. Shortly before ten, after looking in on Matthew, I extinguished all the lights. The flat was deathly quiet. Still, the first of the day-nurses was due in eleven hours' time.

But at 11:25 on that same night, I was startled out of my slumbers by sounds of screaming and shouting. They weren't coming from Matthew. I couldn't figure it out. An ambulance wailed past; then, screeched to a standstill. An ululating siren mourned, subsided, and died. I leapt up in the dark, to peer through the slats: an accident. Someone was being treated to a red blanket; someone else, to a breathalyser. Witnesses, their prurient faces muffled, were loitering about. I decided to ring Cara. She had always been a night-owl; she never turned in before midnight; I could do with bending someone's ear about my recent travels. I turned on a lamp, and tried her number. She didn't pick up. She must be out – romancing with her new, old husband. I didn't leave a message. I took a second tablet. But then, as I crawled back into bed, the luminous dial of my watch alerted me to the fact that the time at which I'd called had been (not 11:25 at all, but) five to five. No wonder she hadn't answered. Please God I hadn't disturbed her – and damn: I'd never be compos by nine. I set the alarm.

A matter of seconds later, the phone rang. Cara sounded croakier than of custom, but not angry. How'd she known I'd rung? By informed deduction. She had one-four-seven-oned (a very a modern thing to do in those days, very un-Cara), and, given that I was the only person whom she knew both to withhold his number *and* conceivably to be up at this hour, she'd decided to act on her hunch. I said: I'm really sorry – I got the time muddled up. She said: It doesn't matter – everything all right, love? It must have been this last endearment that rocked my barriers, because, even as I blushed, I heard myself reply: Not exactly. Why? I whispered that I couldn't really talk about it. Right, she said. She was coming straight round. And before I could even consider arguing, she'd hung up.

By the time that I had dressed, and redressed the sofa to a semblance of balance, she had arrived. I watched her mass of hair float out of a cab. I tiptoed to the hall and hung about, squinting through a flickering screen of intercom shadows. As she drifted into camera, I buzzed the door ajar. She pushed, disappeared inside, but seemed to forgo the lift in honour of silence. Her steps, as they rose, were light but controlled, measured in their mildness. We met on the landing. We kissed, but said nothing. I led her in. She closed the door behind us – quietly. She wore a girlish coat of speckled tweed: bottle green. I said: Drink? She said: Much rather have tea. While the kettle hotted up, I poured myself some brandy. She said: Where is he? I said: Asleep. She asked whether he could be seen. By all means. (What did she think – that I'd killed him?) We tiptoed to his room. She stood at the end of the gloom. She waited for her eyes to adjust to the shade. Now she approached the place where he lay, and drew closer, as if to inspect him. She stroked his shoulder. She said: He seems quite sedate. I told her to shush, and beckoned her out. That was to be the last time that Cara would see Matthew. Matthew, of course, hadn't been able to see anyone for months.

I carried her mug into the sitting room, and settled it beside her. She was on the hardest chair of all – punitively wooden, Shaker, upright. She rummaged in her bag, found a scrunch of velveted elastic, and began to tie her hair back. Something about the swept-up result reminded me of Kelly's party in Bedsitland, when, seeing Cara's nape exposed for the first time, I had interpreted it as an indication – dismal but lovely – of her having grown up, of time having passed. Time *had* passed. Her auburn temples, now, were shot with strands of white. She cupped her tea in her hands, and adopted a strange sort of quiet, perhaps waiting for me to start – but I was trying to fight the effects of the second sleeping-tablet. I could feel my eyelids weighing me down. I went toward the window, and peered out. Still dark. I knocked back some brandy. Only as I turned inwards did I realize that Cara was wearing glasses – rimless ovals, delicately old-fashioned, like her handwriting, like the marriage upon which she had recently embarked. I said: I didn't know you wore specs, Cara. She replied that she hadn't wanted to waste time fidgeting with contacts. Should I have apologized? I dropped the subject, but continued to hover around, feeling as tetchy as I did tired, unable to unwind – unwilling, perhaps – and peevishly half-wishing that she had never come. I longed to play music, but couldn't – in deference to Matthew. I sat in the place where I should rather have been sprawled out; then, pulled myself up. I told myself to be grateful for the blessing of Cara.

And thus, prompted by gratitude, I began. I would have slurred and rambled; I couldn't *but* have done. I suppose that I would have mentioned our room over the Grand Canal, which Cara had originally advised. I suppose that I would have mentioned Harry's Bar, which had been such a goal for Matthew, and, in the event, such a triumph – down to his special bellini on the house. I do not doubt that I would have mentioned my stickier moments with Douglas, such as the one regarding what was, and wasn't, Done. Douglas had never quite been Cara's type, but all she said was: Tell me about Matthew. I know that I related, in drawn-out detail, our noonday *passeggiata* to St Mark's, and the eventual shock of finding no proper wheelchair access into the basilica, and how this unexpected mishap had suddenly sunk Matthew. I bet that I bitched about the phone-bill which Douglas had run up; but I also bet that I withheld the fact that the whole jaunt had been financed by Matthew. I would certainly have described how the check-in officials had tried, at the eleventh hour, to prevent us from boarding our flight, and how the dick-head on the plane had behaved like a total prat, and the fairy-lit pit where Douglas couldn't wait to be dumped, and the ordeal of getting Matthew into the flat, and my dread of what still lay to come, and how Alison had said that I must step back, and my anger at the prospect of endless nurses pitching up, and the feeling of invasion, of strangers running my life, and the prospect of Matthew's friends wanting to come round, sniffing like animals, and the rest of the nightmare. I gave myself a light. Cara, whom I had never known to smoke, now wondered if she might have a gasper. I couldn't have been more delighted. And while she inhaled, she sat suspended for a thoughtful while, until, as the remnants of her smoke began to rise in rings from her unpainted mouth, she uttered, almost muttered: Death is hard.

Not for nothing was Cara a respected analyst. Later I would come to realize that, with those three key words – rather like the three which Matthew would bequeath me, between wheezes, at the last – she both assuaged and toughened me. For by having mentioned death (as opposed to dying), she had projected me into a future where whatever might lie between the present and

Matthew's final breath, seemed, in some manner, already behind me. It was merely a case of waiting for life to catch up with its own sluggish design. I derived a perverse comfort from the abstraction of death; it distanced me from reality. And although, of course, the palpable, visible, audible, bitter, foetid fact of dying was something else entirely, it was something above which, already, I could feel myself rising.

I got up to show Cara out, but recall little else of that ill-timed, yet invaluable, séance. She went off to work — plenty to be done before her first patient arrived — and I settled down to flick through the paper, which had just landed on the doormat. The sky, glimpsed through the kitchen window, had at last grown lighter; lilac. I shaved and showered and went in to see Matthew, to find out what he'd like; but the diluted apple-juice for which he asked was doomed to remain untouched. I aired the rooms, scrubbed the bath, sprayed about, tidied. Whatever Matthew's nurses might choose to imagine, I didn't want them imagining that Matthew had fallen into the wrong hands.

The first of those nurses, like the second and the rest, was much as you'd expect: efficient, polite, and stressed. Always running late; too many cases; not enough hours in the day. Those poor women seemed to rush from place to place, never quite being able to make more than the most fleeting connection with the patient to whom they were tending. I don't blame them, but nor do I feel any great obligation to dwell on them. They were all as good as interchangeable — all similarly overstretched by an underfunded health service.

But at seven o'clock that evening, the story changed. When the night-nurse pressed the bell, I remember feeling a jolt of apprehension, for, despite Alison's recommendation, I remained unpersuaded by the virtues of male nurses — specifically gay ones, which is all that in my (in)experience I had met. They struck me as flirtatious rather than dedicated; they grated on my nerves; they felt like scenic relatives of Trolley Dollies and florists and usherets. Nice enough, you might say, but not exactly what one might have chosen by way of company for unrelieved nocturnal stretches in the confines of one's own flat. Let's be frank.

And yet, when he appeared, I was stunned. As our friendship evolved (which it did with an intense velocity, like a friendship between actors cast together for a brief theatrical run – of a passion play, for example), I would come to learn that we were of comparable ages – he, in his mid-twenties; I, not too far past them. But, paradoxically, when Alison had described him as a boy, she had not been dramatizing: he looked, at first glance, as if he hadn't long outgrown short trousers, as if he were arrested in some uncanny, but unblemished, pubertal past; and the fact that he was small of stature – five feet or thereabouts – with an adolescent waist and the narrowest hips in the history of depravity, did little to quell that fancy. But, irrespective of his build, which was a jockey's, I would say that his mien of extreme youth derived mainly from his face, a face so fresh that it appeared not yet corrupted by a razor. His countenance was of a kind which takes a certain kind of breath away – the breath of suckers for innocence. His head, which tumbled with curls of very shiny, thick black hair – ringlets, in other words – was less modish than bucolic; but, by very dint of its unfashionableness, all the more memorable. Classical. And that classical head of his, which was over-scaled for the body on which it had been set, served – as if Caravaggio had portrayed it – to magnify his childlike air. His eyes, while not excessively large, were ludicrously turquoise, but attentive rather than lively; less probing than candid. They made him seem suggestible, trusting – even, in given lights, a trifle gullible. A man drawn to the pull of under-agers would have drooled at the marvel, and ripped open his (not flies, but) lap-top, and logged on to some favourite website, to share, with equally pseudonymous chatters, the confidence: MET A CHERUB WITH LIPS LIKE A CHERRY RIPE 4 THE PLUCKING; and then, in reply to a quick enquiry from viceheadboy@hotmail.com, have tapped: SORRY PICTURES ARE MINE NO ATTACHMENTS ☹.

But back to the night-nurse. His cheeks, on account of his fair skin, which was fair to the point of transparency, would flush at the merest formality. Hello, I said; thank you for being so punctual. He didn't smile; rather, he scanned me, as if wondering what I might be hiding. I remember thinking: This can't be right; I'll have to send him back. And yet, when he opened his mouth, I discovered that his voice belonged to (not the expected counter-tenor, but) a full-on basso. So sonorous was it, in fact, that, while ministering to the moribund, he tended to whisper, for fear of frightening them. His charm – or part of it – stemmed from his pure ignorance of that freakish, contradictory appeal of his, that richly-prized, if specialist, allure – so risky and yet so thrilling; like a 'hot' jewel. Instead, he wore himself mildly, with modest ease, like a comfortable pair of shoes. But, as they say in Irish pubs: Don't judge a boot by its upper. For Connor, who hailed from County Cork – that region of the Emerald Isle where both the brogue and the climate are least harsh – was no lush. He might have drunk in his spare time, and good luck to him; but, at work, he was as sober, and grounded, as they come. He would tell me: Have a bevvy for both of us; I'm fine. His upbringing was rural; his family had, for generations, farmed; his character had been forged by the rigours of foaling and lambing and whelping and calving and angling and hatching and the rituals of the slaughterhouse. But beyond his natural knowledge of the mortal harvest, he was (or would prove to be) exactly as Alison had described: lovely. Never – not even in my wildest nightmares – could I have dreamt of a better accomplice.

All that Connor had wanted at the start was to meet Matthew. All that I had wanted, first, was for Connor to realize that what he was about to meet was tantamount to a lie, to a premature carcass, stripped of the handsomeness and brightness which, in his active life, had been my friend's great attributes. I felt like a mother exposing her dying child to the scrutinies of a new nanny – at once ashamed and proud – but how could a stranger be expected to understand? And yet, as I led Connor through the silent passageway to the scene of introductions, I remember feeling a strange regret that this particular encounter should be occurring so far down the line, so close to the verge of calamity. For, had Matthew still been served by eyes that functioned, he would have been the first to approve of the sight which now approached his bedside.

I said: Darling, I've brought someone to meet you; he's called Connor, and he's come to be with us at night. I doubt that Matthew was conscious of the time. There were, to him, no longer any hours that were not dark. But he went to the courteous trouble of opening his eyes, those speckled tawny miracles which – though limited of late to staring off-beam and dull and yellowed at the whites – had once, in their sheer immoderacy, evoked the eyes of Hedy Lamar. Still; his undiminished smile sought to repair the damage. He said: Good name, Connor; you Irish? Connor laughed: That I surely am – and perched himself on the edge of the mattress. Matthew said: From the south, by the sound of you. Connor said: From the south is right; you've been to my country? Matthew said: Only to Kinsale, one summer when I was a child. Now Matthew, in a stage aside, enquired of me: Captain, be this perchance some banshee? I (embarrassed) said: Stop it, darling – but Connor can't have taken it amiss, because he uncrossed Matthew's hands, and took one up. I noticed how, despite the ghoulish levity of that last remark, Matthew's fingers gripped Connor's hard, with knuckles that bulged out, in a gesture which seemed to speak of some un-spoken pact. I said: Matthew, you'll be pleased to know that Connor here is quite the Looker. (Why must I be so crass?) But Matthew, with that special intuition which is often given to the blind, replied: I can tell as much. And next, almost avuncularly, he said: Tell me, Connor, you got a nice boy somewhere? Connor answered: No time for such trifles; I'm saving up. Matthew said: You do that.

Next, Matthew did a thing which moved me so powerfully that I could hardly bear to admire it, but Connor must have seen it coming, because he dealt with it sublimely. Matthew ran his enquiring palms along the nurse's arms, and inward from the stranger's shoulders to his clavicles, and now, the better to envisage that youthful face, began to sculpt around – thumbs under jawline, indices over eyebrows, fingers all over the puzzle. Connor bowed, to help with the charting of this facial map. But Matthew went still further: he felt up for that pastoral head of hair, roughed it, and, after dealing it a pat, mumbled: Now I can picture you in my mind. Connor said: That's to be encouraged, but don't be tiring yourself now. With which, he restored Matthew's hands to the place where he had found them, on his chest, and gently folded them across each other. And that's when I clocked that Connor's own hands, though admittedly a little blunted – not as elegant as Kelly's, for example – were in their way remarkable. Clearly varnished. They glinted in the lamp light.

Connor, despite being unaware of trends, still managed to buck them. Even when he mentioned TLC, he kicked against the dictionary, which defines the initialism as 'facetious'. But coming from Connor's lips, those innocuous consonants sounded like some balmy benediction; they resounded with a melancholy lyricism – which is what gets you about the Irish. At any rate, late one evening, while I was taking Connor through the album which I'd pinched from Matthew's flat – That's the year before we met; that would have been just after, when he still had a moustache; that must have been at some office party; that's when he came with me to Paris; that's at the house were he grew up, parents both dead now, only some ancient aunt somewhere; that's when he was still at art school, posing with a girl he dated before he came out; this looks like some Greek island, Santorini most likely; that was his favourite drag outfit, *get* those padlocked spikes – I decided to take the plunge. I asked Connor why his nails were varnished; it seemed so out of character. Matter-of-factly he replied: A fellow when he's dying deserves to be handled by hands that are immaculate.

(How non-camp was *that*?) Not once did I see Connor don protective gloves. Nilson, the Man, would have reeled like a damsel aghast, but Connor said: What those doctors care about is their steps and ladders; we're the ones who care about what matters. Connor wasn't frightened; nor, yet, was he foolhardy. He was just vigilant, and humane, and natural. Birth and death. Simple as that.

It was he who, on his second night, began to produce new supplies – sheepskin pads to protect Matthew's blistered ankles; lotions to quell the bed-sores which, like oozing bruises, had begun to sprout along his back; miniature sponges – such as are employed by make-up artists – to dab on Matthew's cracking lips and wetten his gaping mouth. It was also Connor who suggested that we dispense with incontinency pants. He would rather have Matthew bare as the day that he was born than afflicted, at the end, by nappy-rash. But the matter wasn't as simple as Connor might have liked. Matthew grew visibly distressed when he feared that something might be happening – might be coming out – because he knew himself incapable of getting to the lavatory. And although I tried to calm him, repeating that I was there and he was not to worry, his inherent modesty refused to buy my prattle. Mine was no kind of answer. Connor found one: Time to import a catheter. This was the bit which I found hardest. I couldn't bear to note how Matthew's penis had regressed, how it had shrivelled back to an infant's bud. Nor could I bear to admit that I, who had vowed to protect his dignity, was now, in my perfidy, permitting such denigrating invasions to be carried out. Connor told me that it was all for the best, that this was men's stuff; so I told Connor that the men's stuff was precisely what riled me. My boy had, in his day, been well-endowed. Now he looked reduced to (scarcely a penis at all, but) some clitoral travesty, some hormonal mishap. When the catheter arrived, I left the bedroom fast partly out of respect for Matthew, but largely because I dreaded that the nurse whose task it was to insert the line – a woman, as men's stuff would have it – might damage his urinary passage. And then, the screaming began. Lumber-punctures, eye-drops, Portacaths; forget all that; they were as nothing. I came the closest that I've ever come to passing out. Someone said: Get the man a brandy.

So, in accordance with Alison's advice, I acceded and stood back; for they – the professionals – were the ones who knew what should be done. Connor, in an attempt to comfort me, claimed that the patient's discomfort would pass. But, before such a prediction was proved right, I lost count of the times that I had to take Matthew's hand, restraining it in mine, to prevent him from ripping out that tube of bloodied plastic – as, indeed, I lost track of the occasions when, once the days began to drag, I had to tell visitors for heaven's sake to avoid the piss-bag. It was vile. And yet, as often happens – especially with vileness – I grew accustomed; grew accustomed, even, to those strangers who, having paid their last (what *was* it exactly? Respects? Regrets? Patronage?) dues, would shoot me devious glances – intended to imply that, had Matthew been entrusted to their good care, and not to the vagaries of some jobless idler like myself, a better job would have been made of this whole sorry affair. A *catheter*? At *this* stage?

His friends. Apart from Claudia and Viola, that long established lesbian couple who, when they came to his beside, stood holding hands in deathly silence, too stricken to cry, but strong enough, as they departed, to kiss him goodbye – they apart, Matthew's former cronies were a righteous pain in the arse. Of course, at the time, I could hardly tell them as much. But I can tell them now, can tell them good and loud: You, and You, and You, and most particularly *You* – the insufferable bitch who gave his cremation a miss because Judaism refutes the validity of such rituals: what he cared about was (not your lofty principles, but) being spared your sighs while he lay in misery. Yet it was *I* who, to my lifelong shame, allowed those creatures to bring their creeping stoops around his death-bed, *I* who permitted them to inflict their self-pitying snivels upon his piteous wretchedness –

until, that is, I ceased answering the phone. The rest of Matthew's time was mine, mine entirely, mine in which to learn whatever there remained to be learned about the unholy mystery of dying.

Once I'd closed the door to all but Matthew's nurses, who, when they appeared in the day, now began to appear in pairs, I entered a new phase – one of preparation. I wanted everything in readiness. While Matthew was being washed and shaved, and having his wounds dressed and his bag changed, I would make brief escapades in search of cleaning stuff, and flowers, and food – and drink, needless to say. But during those interludes when we were left alone, I would either – if he'd grown agitated – lie next to him, or, otherwise, drift about, double-checking details: scented candles round the clock; sleepy music all day long; volume of the phone turned down to nought. The washing-machine (though safely out of earshot) seemed seldom to be off. Matthew's nurses plainly found it odd that I should still be bothering to iron his bedclothes with so starchy an obduracy; but I proceeded under my own steam. I suspect that they suspected my fastidiousness to be – you know – therapeutic. It was, in fact, a far simpler thing: a matter of vanity. I wanted *my* best for Matthew. He could no longer sit; he could no longer eat; the least that he could do – or so it seemed to me – was rest, if not exactly in peace, at least on well-pressed linen. Besides, hadn't I nagged him to death about standards? Well now it was my turn to practise what I'd preached.

When Connor pitched up in the evenings, which he did with on-the-dot precision, I generally felt able to breathe with greater ease; for, beyond his basic nursing skills, there was some further, special quality intrinsic to him; some greater gift. Certainly, all things considered, he felt good to be with. And certainly, too, he led me to believe that looking after Matthew, felt, all things considered, good. He once went so far as to call this bleak interim a blessed relief, which struck me as pushing it; but I came to appreciate his point of view. Connor was frequently despatched to certain districts (by which I don't necessarily mean the less salubrious) where, no sooner had he entered some new palliative picture than he found himself embroiled in the most surreal domestic scenes: siblings and half-siblings and step-siblings, pitted like terriers and baring their eye-teeth, growling about prehistoric grievances and snarling about recent wills, and feuding over the pate of some old pater, who, however close to the point of snuffing it, had no earthly hope of extinguishing his candle until those kinsfolk had been coaxed out of the house − once, Connor confided, staggering from the effects of (not liquor, but) an unruly carving-knife. So for Connor to care for Matthew at my flat − which he called home − amounted, perversely, to a sort of treat. Home, to him, was not about bricks and mortar and deeds, nor, indeed, automatically about family; it was about where one felt wanted, and protected, and loved. And Matthew, Connor assured me, was all of those participles here: wanted, protected, and loved. I know that it smacks of some condom advert, but I also know that I was grateful for such wisdom, however homespun.

I liked to rope Connor into supper (not because I was concerned about his skimpy figure, but) because I disliked being left alone in the kitchen. From the first of his visits, a comfortable armchair had been moved into the bedroom, and there, unless he and I happened to be trading histories, was where he preferred to sit − reading into the early hours (since Matthew wasn't bothered by lamplight), or catnapping. I would sometimes wake up in the middle of the night, to shuffles next door, and unintelligible mumbles; so, while Connor did whatever needed doing, I would sneak across to ensure that nothing untoward had happened. But he would systematically shoo me out, telling me to stop fussing and get some rest now. This is irrational, but his very dependability conspired to make me feel shunned; I

420 ~ Paul Golding

became, despite the undoubted boon of his company, subject to odd twinges of something – jealousy, most likely – because even when, for instance, he referred to Matthew as (not He, but) We, the appropriation of that pronoun raised my brow. And equally, when Matthew's speech began to suffer, and his words became trickier to understand, but Connor continued to make out that he could perfectly interpret each and every syllable that issued from Matthew's mouth, I – though able to fathom less and less, and though increasingly panicked (lest anything of vital import should have passed me by) – would force myself to feign, as if my honour were being challenged, that I was absolutely au fait with Matthew's garblings. It was, in a peculiar way, like the reverse of what can happen in the nursery. Instead of being made to regret that I'd missed out on my boy's first word, it felt as if I were being made to suspect that I'd missed out on his last. Later, however, I would come to appreciate the workings of Matthew's mind, which, despite his body's weariness, remained bright: he was saving himself for the moments that really mattered. When regular chores were being carried out, such as bed-baths, he would merely let out grunts, which translated as agony. But when he wanted properly to convey something, then, his careful diction, however sparsely delivered and however softly announced, left no room for doubt. You have to believe me on that.

Yet the question which now began to worry me was not so much what Matthew had or hadn't said, as what – even if he seemed a million miles away – he might have heard. I couldn't quell the suspicion that, of his various faculties, his hearing would be the last to subside. Nor could I dispel those accounts which people sometimes gave about how, while laid out on an operating table, impotent and numbed, they could nevertheless grasp the double-entendres of theatre-staff. I asked Connor when a patient's hearing could safely be assumed to have given up; but the evasiveness of his reply – to do with wariness of generalities – only served to strengthen my hunch. Hearing: *that* was the one to watch out for. Ready, Maestro? Let's face the music and die.

Orchestration; fine tuning. *Rubato*. Of the advances made in modern times, the one for which the medical profession merits most thanks is its ability to suppress physical suffering. And, once it became clear that Matthew's pain had grown too great for any modern man, Connor took me, once again, aside. He told me that tomorrow he would speak to Alison and arrange for the delivery of a diamorphine pump. The thought of morphia – its very sound – felt dramatic, glamorous; like absinthe. Better surely to have Matthew borne along the woozy waters of some analgesic current than thrashing to get out. But then, Connor added that, with an opiate of this calibre, there was always a chance that the patient's mind might become compromised. Let's not beat about the bush: Diamorphine meant Smack. Cheap at the price, I replied; quashing pain couldn't be a crime. Connor didn't argue, but he did suggest that I might want to call a priest round. *What* priest? I knew none. Connor had a ready supply – jotted at the back of his diary. He hadn't dealt with these guys *personally*, he emphasized; but when, in the course of his care-work, a clergyman had happened to impress him, he always tried to extract a contact-number. It sometimes came in handy. Connor's varnished nail slid down the alphabet for addresses, until his index came to rest at the underpopulated letter X. He half-opened the page, but hesitated. He seemed to be considering which of those various entries would best suit our purpose. At length he suggested a pair of contenders – the first, older-fashioned; the second, trendier – but anyway: Catholics both. And both, as Connor put it, cool about Express Cases. I could do worse than give my choice a bell. But I wasn't to prevaricate: it was important to try to get the priest and pump to dovetail. Priest and Pump. A duet if ever there was one. Or an Irish pub.

In fact, the pump came first – unannounced. It may have been assumed that I wouldn't be out gallivanting. Although it was Nilson – as I later learned from an initialled copy stuffed inside the package – who had prescribed the poisoned chalice, a chirpy van-driver delivered the parts, in a brown paper bag. The she-nurse who, later that morning, set up the gadgetry, was a stranger to the flat, which made the procedure more impersonal, less hard. The nurse looked grave, so I tried not to look glad – but the truth is that my insides were jumping. At last something constructive was about to be done, something to help Matthew rise above his body and become abstract.

The nurse asked whether Matthew could rate his pain on a scale of one to ten. Matthew raised his hands, but only tucked one thumb away. The nurse asked whether Matthew would like that pain brought down. Matthew's moan was emphatic. The nurse asked whether Matthew felt able to sign a form of consent. Matthew paused, as if to harness his strength; and then, incontrovertibly, said: Yes. The nurse produced a ball-point pen – leaky red. We propped him up and helped him scrawl his name along some dotted line. It came out at a mad slant, but no matter. The nurse was satisfied that the patient was of sound mind. The assemblage of the syringe-driver and the rest of the paraphernalia now began. The nurse kept consulting some fact-sheet – Pain Management in Palliative Care – which, when she left, she left behind. Somebody had highlighted the reminder: IF IN DOUBT SEEK SPECIALIST ADVICE, but the facts were indubitable: the pump was run on a battery; the solution came in 50cc bags; I could order refills from my local pharmacy; the needle in Matthew's hand was called a Butterfly; the tubing was standard; the dose was to be administered every 3–4 hours; if the pain went through the roof, this feat was called a Breakthrough; relief from such eventualities came in the form of a Rescue dose. And it was to that – to the word Rescue – that I pinned my hopes.

The priest, when he took my call, sounded, though suitably sacerdotal, nevertheless cordial – traditionally-voiced, of course, yet without the stuffiness too frequently espoused by men of the cloth. He couldn't quite put his finger on any nurse called

Connor; mind you, his memory was no longer what it was. Sieve-like, he called it. But let's not quibble about utensile comparisons, because we lived in forgiving times: there was a chance that the Reverend might be able to come round. He checked his itinerary: How did five o'clock sound? Fantastic, I replied (and then): Thank you, Father – which reduced me to childhood. But one had to be grown-up. And the grown-up way in which I sold the scam to Matthew was by pretending that I'd rung a priest for my own peace of mind; in order to have an ally lined up. Matthew said: Quite the party planner, aren't we? But he was in less distress now – equanimous, as opposed to spaced out. Indeed, when our visitor arrived, my reaction was (not *Deo gratias*, but) Crikey. Matthew seemed to have perked up.

Fr Frank, for his part, seemed the lusty type: ruddy and rotund, port-and-cigarish; possibly a trifle clammy about the thighs. I wouldn't – to be honest – have put Connor past him; so it struck me as a felicity that this pastoral descent should have been fated to precede the nightshift. His apparel, while distinctively clerical, was less archaic than classic: no swishing soutanes. I recall, beneath his black worsted lounge-suit, a halterneck of tailored grosgrain, and a blush of episcopal damson about his coat-lining. His Homburg, which he handed me the moment we had shaken hands, had been blocked, according to its inner band, by the best hatter in town; and his gold-ringed brolly had been assembled by that time-honoured firm where the management, if so instructed – though obviously for hush-hush cash – will fit a trigger-blade inside the spike. Can't be too careful about muggers. His solid briefcase, boxier than the nine-to-five average, was well-worn; it had acquired the seasoned patina of vintage luggage; it made you think of jewellers after the war, smuggling parures of yellow diamonds – purportedly Tsarist – from Geneva to Paris; but anyhow. His socks – I saw once he'd sat down – were of black knee-length lisle, identical to mine, which made me think (not Snap, but) twice; and his highly-polished shoes, one of which seemed keen to tap, gleamed with rakish side-buckles. It heartened me to imagine that the Lord might not entirely revile a dandy. But when the padre and I settled to our preliminary chat, and he wondered whether he might be availed of some facts, I realized that, beyond sartorial trivia and hospitalic tittle-tattle, I knew nothing. I *presumed* that Matthew had been baptized; I *presumed* that he had been confirmed; I presumed, even, that he was in a state of (not mortal peril, but) grace. Yet all that I could confidently assert was that, when filling in pre-operative questionnaires, he had always put himself down as RC, and that his wish had been expressly for a Requiem. The priest said: You had better take me to him then. But into this veiled imperative I suddenly read Danger; for, if old Frank got it into his head to be cussed, and demanded that Matthew repent of his homosexuality, I'd be buggered. I'd have to go back to square one – in other words, give Father Trendy my best smarm – and *still* risk missing the sodding (not bus, but) hearse. Yet something in the glinty eye of Fr Frank told me that there was no need for any of us be vulgar.

Darling, I began (so that there be no need for lies): here's Father Frank. Matthew said: Morning, Father; thank you for coming. The priest ignored the fact that the sun was already down, and simply replied: That's quite all right. I went off to find a chair, so that our guest could perch near Matthew, but when I returned, he was already seated on the bed, though safely away from tubes and drips and other medical sundries. The man was obviously familiar with palliative tableaux. He was vaguely enquiring about Matthew's past – his schools, his jobs, his general background – and although Matthew was gradual about yielding answers, his powers of recall remained intact. Dates were cited, addresses, even the name of the church where he had been baptized. I would say that Matthew was slightly on best behaviour, but he was also slightly high: his voice had risen in pitch, grown flutier in timbre, become purer, lighter, as if lifted from quotidian dullness by the consolation of some prize. Next, Fr Frank, firmly but politely, asked whether I awfully minded leaving them alone for a while. Of course I bloody minded; I minded wildly; but the Church – Lord love it – must always out. I retreated backwards. And yet, in truth, I should have been grateful to Fr Frank, for, during my absence, he succeeded in resolving those enigmas which, earlier, had stumped me – the sacramental niceties. Baptism, tick; First Holy Communion, tick; Confirmation, tick; Chosen Name: Daniel. Last Confession? Question-mark.

Exiled to the sitting room, I played the latest wave of messages from callers whose enquiries I no longer bothered to answer. Only one surprise: Sukie. Sukie was in town, hoping that we could meet up; she had a new man; it might be love; he was something in fashion-publishing; *plus ça change*; she'd been thinking about Matthew; how were things on that front? As ever, she rang off with *Je t'embrasse*. I rewound the tape, made a note of her number, and prepared to dial the nest of her lover. But just as I picked up my handset, I heard the creaking footsteps of Fr Frank. Was everything all right?, I asked. He popped his head round, and smiled: Yes, fine; such a nice chap. I said: Glad you like him – but thought: Spare me the blather. The priest went to the hall, fetched his case, and retraced his path to Matthew. This time, however, he closed the door behind them. It was out of my hands now. I remember thinking: I'll never forgive this fucker if he freezes me out.

A few minutes into the silence, Fr Frank called me back. The room had been turned into a chapel. Along my chest-of-drawers had been spread a runner of white cambric, with lace scallops. On this cloth there stood a crucifix – ebony cross, ivory body – and, alongside, a votive candle, already aflame and speaking in shady tongues along the wall. There lurked the mystical aroma of a match that had been struck, and burned, and blown. I recall a small, circular object of oxblood morocco, not unlike the case for a pocket-watch, and a tiny, cylindrical, mother-of-pearl bibelot – exotic. On the armchair where Connor liked to read, now lay a liturgical volume, spread open, with a black silk ribbon running away from the centrefold. Fr Frank had slung over his neck a ceremonial accessory which those conversant with ecclesiastical modes imagine is a Stole. But let's not joke, because two serious factors now came to the fore: first, the undeniable beauty of that stole – white silk brocade, white floral embroidery, fringing of threaded gold; and second, yet equally undeniably, Matthew's countenance, which had altered. It was aglow. During the time that he and the priest had been alone, something beyond the ordinary must have gone on. Fr Frank, as it transpired, had heard Matthew's confession. If any penance was inflicted, I never heard of it. Nor did I hear how the Lord's representative, in virtue of the faculty given to him by the Apostolic See, had granted Matthew full remission for all his sins. But I can perfectly envisage the magnificent, cruciform gesture that would have ensued. I hate to admit this, but Fr Frank was chic. Let's hear it for the priest.

He hadn't asked me in because he needed a witness. He'd done so because Matthew had asked it of him. Matthew urged me to come and sit here, but Fr Frank intervened. He instructed me – I who had bridled at the mere suggestion from a tango teacher – to kneel. I did as I was bid, but I can tell you: I could have done with a Protestant cushion, because, when it comes to adopting postures of humility, rush-matting ain't the thing. Still; thus began what we call the Last Rites – but which Fr Frank, without the faintest whiff of irony, introduced as Extreme Unction. I rather admired his reactionism; its camp insouciance. Matthew was practically smiling, probably with relief that the slate of his sins should, with such plenary speed, have been wiped clean. I stroked his cheek, but the priest felt it best for Matthew not to be distracted. What he meant, of course, was that the Lord's proximity, not mine, was what mattered. At any rate, Fr Frank, with the help of a small brush, such as cooks might use for glazing pies, now began to flick holy water about, hither and thither and lavishly; then announced: Peace be upon this house. There followed a pause which flummoxed me – I couldn't think of what to reply – but the priest replied on my behalf, declaiming: And upon all who dwell herein. Matthew began to chuckle. I couldn't imagine why – at least not until he'd straightened his face and apologized: it was just that he'd thought that Fr Frank had said: All who deal in heroin. I thought: Please don't let this count as a brand new sin; but it didn't; it can't have done, because Fr Frank, after sucking his cheek, proceeded with the ritual. Yet Matthew, from this point in, remained absolutely serious. A new serenity came over him.

I'm glad that the priest should have resisted the temptation to conduct himself in Latin, which, to us, would have been double-Dutch; yet I remain glad that he should have adhered to the old vernacular – for the perfectly irreligious reason that I preferred its formality. In any event, following an introductory litany, which was rattled off at a fair lick, we got down to the nitty-gritty: The Anointing of the Sick. Fr Frank fetched his mother-of-pearl cylinder, and, by means of a deft twist, removed its inlaid lid. He dipped his middle-finger into a balm of oils, which he decreed ancient and holy and from Rome, but which, for all I knew, might have hailed from some souk in Agadir. Now he began to ask the Angels, Archangels, Patriarchs, Prophets, Apostles, Martyrs, Confessors, Virgins, and all the Saints together (talk about a party) to intercede on Matthew's behalf; and he called upon the Almighty to forgive whatever sins Matthew may have committed through his sense of Sight. Fr Frank bore down, and, with a small sign of the cross, anointed my boy's eyelids. Next, he called upon the Almighty to forgive any sins that Matthew may have committed through his sense of Hearing – and similarly anointed his lobes. And in this method-ical way he worked through the remaining senses: Smell (a cross on the bridge of Matthew's nose); Taste (over his Cupid's bow); and, finally, Touch (on the hand without a Butterfly). But then, just when I presumed that we were all sensed-out, Fr Frank began to beg forgiveness for any further sins that Matthew might have incurred through his ability to walk. I could only think of modelling. I let out a snort, which I converted into a fit of nervous coughing. Yet, by the time that Fr Frank had anointed Matthew's feet at the place where stigmata usually go, I had regained a semblance of composure. The priest launched into an invocation about the Lord hearing Matthew's prayer and letting his cry come to Him, and about grace being a healing remedy. He beseeched the Lord to bind Matthew's wounds, and to rid him of all anguish of mind and body. And all appeared to be going smoothly until Fr Frank decided to suggest that Matthew, with God's help, might be able to take up his work again and – Hang on a sec: Deliver Thy servant from his sickness? Give him health anew? Stretch out Thy hand and set him on his feet? Oughtn't Fr Frank to have skipped those bits? But what's religion without a little optimism? Amen.

The celebrant approached his improvised altar, set down the oils, and, with consummate care, took up the circle of morocco, which, perhaps because I looked so bewildered, he explained was called a Pyx – from the Greek for box. It was, in point of fact, a portable tabernacle, the vessel in which the Eucharist is ferried from pillar to post and back. Now Fr Frank returned to Matthew, and knelt down. I caught him wriggling on the matting. I thought: Join the club. Dextrously he opened the Pyx – rather as one might open a powder-compact – and extracted a single, consecrated host, which, between index and thumb, he held up. He showed the host to Matthew, who could see nothing. He showed it to me, who must have been scowling, and said: Viaticum – which my pidgin Latin took to mean: Be Gone With You. So I got up. But now, with placatory kindness, Fr Frank set me aright. Viaticum: Provisions for a Voyage. Matthew's Last Communion; coming up.

I began to feel divided, split between the safety of scepticism and a perilous sudden urge to vanquish it, until Fr Frank, with gentle gravity, announced: This is the Lamb of God who takes away the sins of the world; happy are those who are called to his supper. Matthew's eyelids were shut. I wondered whether to nudge him, but, next – slowly, almost inaudibly – he had begun: Lord I am not worthy . . . Then: a gap. He seemed to be ransacking his brain for the rest of the right answer. Fr Frank prompted Matthew; gave the cue: To receive you. But Matthew sighed, and arched his neck back. Something was too much; I must do something; I must speak on his behalf. I said: But only say the word. Yet next, without warning – God – my throat had seized up. I was on the brink of crying. Get me through this nightmare; just this once. And then, Fr Frank, with godsent timing, took over and concluded: And I shall be healed.

He glanced at the supplicant's mouth, which he must have judged too parched to accommodate a host in its entirety; so he snapped the wafer into two equal parts. The Body of Christ, he whispered, and offered a half-moon to Matthew, who received it on a whitish, trembling tongue. I presumed that Fr Frank was going to wolf the other half – you know what priests can be like, with their waste-not-want-not mentality. But instead, he did a thing which, perhaps because it took me by such complete surprise, filled me with an overwhelming, humbling sort of gratitude. He leaned across the bed, and, nodding with encouragement, granted me the second, sacred segment of Matthew's Viaticum. Communion. Mutual Participation. Sharing in the Blessed Sacrament. It felt – with all the naïveté that this may imply – like my very first time. And you can scoff if you like; but here, now, disbelief be damned, because next, Fr Frank bent down and gave God's blessing to Matthew. And then, unbelievably, he kissed my darling's brow.

And that, pretty much, was that. The priest packed away his stuff, wished me luck, told me to keep in touch, and – brolly hooked over arm, head splendidly hatted – vanished into the night. Not long after, Connor arrived. He asked what had happened. I told him that Fr Frank – the old-fashioned padre – had been round to perform the Last Rites, and what a relief it was to have that whole business behind us, not least for

Matthew, who, just as I'd grown energized, had grown more tranquil, more resigned, better poised to go forth upon his journey, to go from this world, to go in the name of the Omnipotent, to go on his course; to go. It's all there – and not just for the old – in *The Dream of Gerontius*.

I'd forgotten to return Sukie's call; I ought to let her know that I couldn't escape at the moment. Connor asked why not. I pointed to the bedroom, and said: Isn't it obvious? Look, he replied; nothing was going to go wrong; not just like *that*; these things took time. Besides, in the unlikely instance that something *did* crop up, he promised to ring and get me to come back. I wasn't to fret; I must have faith. What I needed was a break, he said; a change of air. I took Connor at his word, and dialled Sukie's love-nest. Her paramour was working late, putting some edition to bed, so she was free as a bird. Where, she wondered, did I suggest that we went? I suggested the (no-longer-quite-so) fashionable restaurant from which – God, over a year ago – the beautiful Maharajah and his beautiful Maharani had walked away for ever. Sukie fetched a pen, jotted down the address, and said: Eight thirty then; *à tout à l'heure*. When I arrived, she was already at our table, looking like the personification of composure. She wore (not her usual trucker-ballerina drag, but) the perfect nothing-dress, in the latest, most sophisticated shade of Comme des Garçons black. Her hair had been shorn to a boy's cut. She had dispensed with her glasses. She was blindly in love; she bore that luminous expression – at once sated and startled, and (like Douglas) vaguely smug. Ah! she laughed.

Sukie was a whole mélange of Francamerican attributes, but, despite this mix, not garrulous. Ever since our first encounter at that laboratory in Paris, I'd been struck by her capacity to draw one out – a quality which she shared with Cara; but anyhow. Now that I held her attention undivided, I didn't really feel inclined to dwell on Matthew's plight. I wanted to put him out of (not his misery, but) my mind. Yes, he was at home; and yes, he was dying; but his night-nurse, who was fantastic, knew where to find me. Sukie found me (she paused for the *mot juste*) Fatigued. Yet, beauteously as this adjective sat upon her lips, I could have done without the sympathy. I said: Thanks a million. She took my point, but didn't try to fix it. We decided to decide what we should eat. She recommended protein. I ordered beef. Blue.

But what of *her* news? Oof, she replied, with a self-effacing *moue*: her guy worked for Condé Nast; she described him as Recently Unmarried; no children, luckily; she wasn't *en principe* against a move to London, but the proposal would have to come from him – Mark – who yes, she smiled, was plenty tall enough, one metre ninety-five, and dark, and certainly handsome – which, coming from Sukie, must mean that he was a total fuck-ing knock-out. I said as much. Her lashes fluttered with concupiscent pride. But now, as if in a bid to negotiate some delicate further passage, she laid her hand upon her breastbone, and added that Mark was cool with (I thought she said Come on, dear – but what she'd said was *Comment dire*. And then, she said): You know, queers. Sometimes, the boys in the office got the hots for him, apparently, but he was never unkind about it. I told her, with unnegotiable unkindness, that it amazed me how so many straight men seemed to assume that every queer they ever met was desperate to jump them; and although I'm not sure that she understood what I was on about, I'm certain that she hadn't meant to rile me. It's just that nothing which took place that evening – particularly as I grew drunker – could have been right; not even the discreet elegance with which she managed, as she slunk off to the lavatory, to slip the management a credit card. I was too distracted, too irritable – dare I say: too fatigued. I should never have gone out. She offered to see me home, but I declined. My rule about no visitors stuck. I put her in a taxi, leapt into another, and, as I drew up to the flat, felt oddly elated to be back.

Connor was in the kitchen, making himself a mug of something. Had I had a good time? Kind of; how was Matthew? Seemed quite calm. The place was like an oven. I pulled off my coat and went through to the bedroom, which was bathed in amber light. The air was laced with notes of cinnamon and lavender. Motets lined the background – Byrd, I think, or Tallis. A heady peacefulness filled the atmosphere. Swathes of Matthew's linen were shot with heavy shadows, like biblical sand-dunes at dusk. There was something ancient about the tableau, and oddly monastic, as if depicted by the brush of Zurbarán. Darling, I said; I'm back. Matthew shifted a fraction. His mouth was puckered. I dabbed his lips with water from a sponge. I lay beside him, and surveyed his ascetic profile: his jaw, tilted to the heights; his nose, aquiline and magnified. I whispered: Are you awake, sweetheart? He half-opened his eyes, but I could only see their whites. I stroked his hair, which felt damp. And then, because my drunken courage told me that I must – while I still had the chance, before Connor showed up – I said: Darling, you know that you don't have to keep on fighting; everything is done; there's no need for you to worry; you don't have to hang about; you can let go whenever you want; you're surrounded by love . . . He gave no sign of a reaction, so I backed away, and sat up. But now he began to wheeze and pant; and, as I put my ear close to his mouth, I caught those three stark monosyllables which – had I known that they were doomed to be his lucid last – would have cut me more effectively than any stab: No More Love.

By the following morning, he was talking rubbish – but rubbish which, however irrational, sounded visually precise. It struck me as a morbid irony that, blind though his eyes were to reality, his imagination should still be able, and with such clarity, to envisage its drug-fuelled phantoms. I would sometimes interrupt his babble, as much to check that his hearing remained active as in an attempt to banish those visions that seemed to frighten him. But no, he would insist, he could see water-bearers on the right, above the door, and warriors on horseback, and his mother somewhere. Yet if I tried to enter into those figments, and pressed him for further details, he would lapse into silence – not as if he hadn't heard, but as if nothing, no-one could save him from the place where he now found himself. This hallu-cinatory new realm conspired to bring me renewed anxiety, for it made plain that the medical result of having suppressed Matthew's bodily agony had been to render his mind (not merely 'compromised', but) doolally.

Still; the day-nurses were reassuring about it. They told me that the prattle was just a nervous reaction; it happened to every-one; I wasn't to get myself worked up. They also told me that the pump needed re-charging. I should go to the chemist for a fresh supply, so that they could get the juice up and running after Matthew's bed-bath. They made a point of making me write down the exact driver model-type, for, only the previous week, some lad on the local estate had got into a muddle and given his mum a twenty-four hour dose in 2.4 hours. It made you won-der. After I'd got back and surrendered the toxic bag, the nurses did their technical stuff, and left Matthew in as settled a state as could be mustered. Clean and well-tended, I don't deny; but undeniably agitated. So I pressed the trigger and gave him a (not bonus, but) bolus. I came to the rescue. You could hear the poi-son zooming into his bloodstream, up to his brain. Zoom, it went; zoom-zoom. And, with those zooms, came relief. Repose returned to his features; tension left his limbs. That's how I knew that I hadn't been mistaken. They call it Discretion.

There followed an awful lot of hours, during which I veered between wanting to be with Matthew and wanting to be any-where but, between feeling frightened and feeling angry, between wandering about the flat as if nothing on earth were happening, and wondering how long this nothing-on-earth could be mustered to last. But accurate estimates can't be given; you can only play it by ear. So I just kept repeating the same sacred music, over and over, fearing that a break in continuity might be disconcerting to him. And yet, even when there'd been no aural change, he would start moaning again, and I would break through my (not pain, but) patience, and return to the rescue. They call it Caring.

After lunch, another pair of nurses descended. And then I had a siesta. And then I fed myself. And then I had a bath. And then I went to check on Matthew. And then I changed his candle. And then I walked back out. And then I thought: This vegetative state has nothing to do with life – nothing to do with dominion over the fish of the sea, and over the fowl of the air, and over the cattle, and over every creeping thing that creepeth upon the earth. And then I realized that today, the sixth since our return from Venice, augured no good: tomorrow was Connor's sabbath. He wouldn't be coming round. A new bloody night-nurse, some total stranger to the fiasco, would be bursting in, brimming with life-experience, just as Matthew died. Justice, don't make me laugh.

When Connor arrived, he made no bones about the fact that he found Matthew discernibly weaker than even twelve hours back. I myself was no longer able to tell – possibly because I lacked the requisite detachment, or perhaps because I'd gained too much. But certainly when Connor failed to earn any hint of recognition from Matthew, I failed to be surprised; for, to me, it felt as if – despite his pulse – Matthew's essence had already departed. I suppose that the split, the brutal moment of truth, had come with his plea for no more love. But if earlier I had taken trouble to make Connor realize Matthew's former loveliness, now, I realized, it was *I* who was having trouble associating the wreck before us with the smiling, laughing, shining, strolling, dancing boy whom I had loved.

While we were still in the bedroom, I told Connor that I was worried about who would be covering for him on the next night; but Connor frowned, meaning that I shouldn't be discussing such trivia within earshot of Matthew. Instead, he addressed Matthew directly, and explained that we were going into the kitchen for a quick bite, all right? Matthew, predictably, gave no indication either of approval or objection – he was too far gone for reactions. So, on our way out, I dealt him an extra boost of intravenous palliative. Connor didn't turn a hair. What he turned was a blind eye. And then my accomplice told me to plug in the baby-alarm.

In the kitchen, even as I installed the listening part of the device, I asked what was the point of a monitor this far down the line. Connor said: To keep an ear out while I talk to you in private. Ear out for what? The rattle. I was staggered; I'd thought that such effects belonged with melodrama. I said: Is that seriously on the cards? Connor said that it was only natural; integral to the process of dying. Anyway, the worst was apparently over – for Matthew, for me, for everyone. Death, in cases such as this, tended to come calmly. Connor thought that Matthew was unlikely to live beyond sunrise. I thought: Please God let him be right.

I told him that I was getting panicky – I'd never seen anyone die – but he told me that my panic wasn't any use to anyone. Besides, once you had confronted death, particularly in someone you loved, you realized that there was nothing of which to be frightened. You just took the business step by step, and, before you knew it, everything was done – the present had become the past. He would show me how it happened. In a way, he reckoned, I was lucky to be spared the hassle of some meddlesome family. And then he said a very sweet thing: Come on, you're coping brilliantly, now have your supper. I asked about *him*. He'd long since eaten. Well, at least have a cup of tea.

Supper, for me, amounted to a banana and a walloping brandy, but I prevailed upon Connor to linger in my company. And it must have been while I was smoking, and waffling ad infinitum about anything but mortality, that, suddenly, down the baby-alarm, the dreaded rattle announced itself. Had Connor not been there, I don't know what I should have done. He held my arm. He said: Relax, it's not as bad as it sounds. But I think that Matthew must have been as shocked as I, because, when I got into the bedroom, I noticed that his eyes were staring out.

The noise seemed to rise from some resonant profundity, to spiral from a source seemingly stronger and darker than the enfeebled, desiccated gullet of a dying man – and it was the sheer volume of this unearthly vibrato which I think most alarmed me. It sounded, if anything, death-defying. I didn't voice this thought to Connor – not because I didn't want his guidance, but because I didn't want Matthew to hear my anxiety. Instead, I pointed to Matthew's own mouth; but Connor, with a gesture which sliced through the quivering candlelight, conveyed that, by this late stage, it was futile to worry about sponges. Just leave the man be, seemed to be the advice. Leave him to rattle.

And yet, as with all questions of habit, even deadly ones, one swiftly grows accustomed. The death-rattle, I discovered, is a prelude, not a fugue; it heralds, rather than accompanies, eventual flight. And the fact that the current, guttural rasp sounded so rhythmic and percussive and grandiose, only served to confirm – perversely – that we were still some aural way from a finale. I went in search of a top-up, lurching as I advanced. Connor followed me toward the brightness. Listen, he whispered: this is going to go on for a while, so you may as well get some kip while you can; no point both of us staying up; I'll let you know when the end looks like it's coming. There came a stage, he explained, when the rattle itself faded away, and the patient's breathing began to subside, and it was then that I would want to be with Matthew. And thus, when he offered me the chance of an interval, I grabbed it. If this rattle wasn't *it*, then I didn't need to stand it. The noise was insufferable. It made you want to grab Matthew, and shake him by the scruff, and tell him: Stop that racket at once, you're going to wake the neighbours up; by all means snuff it, but cut out the theatricals.

I shut the door behind me, and, against all likelihood, managed to nod off. I recall that when Connor came to fetch me, I'd been dreaming about Matthew, Matthew in an earlier life, right at the start. He'd been walking down a busy street, just one head among a crowd, but I could pick him out, and he was trying to reach me, and he was waving from afar, and then the people seemed to vanish and now he was running and running toward me, as if he, or I, were late for something. Connor whispered: It's time.

Four forty-five. The dead of night. Matthew's music had run out. His rattle had modulated into a gentler, less dramatic sound, of extended sighs, of universal tiredness. Connor stood beside me, as I – reluctant to move closer – perched on the edge of the armchair. From the low place where I sat, Matthew's head, cast upward, resembled an incipient skull, mottled with black cavities – sockets, temples, nostrils, mouth – abstract holes agape with shadow. I thought: This isn't Matthew; this is just matter. And yet his inhalations were so vast, so cavernous, that I was struck by the enduring potency of his lungs. The lengths for which he seemed to hold his air were so protracted as to make you realize just how hard a man will fight for every single precious breath of poxy life. You felt that, underwater, he could have gone – oh – for miles and miles, all the way to edge of the horizon.

Connor moved from my side. I didn't dare look round, in case I missed something, but I heard his footsteps drift away from the background – so delicately, so generously – and leave me, for whatever brevity fate might allow, to keep sole vigil over my cadaverous charge, singly to witness the moment, the crucial split-second, the definitive, life-altering occurrence. The mortal miracle. I watched and watched and watched and watched, forcing my eyes not to blink, absolutely focused on Matthew's breathing – which, the harder I gawped, the more tenuous it seemed to become. I counted dozens of seconds between gasps, and then over a minute before the next one, and then the ticking in my brain got muddled, and I gave in, gave up, and simply stared, lost to time, until, after – I don't know, some while –

Connor came back, and moved toward the bed, and felt for Matthew's pulse. And then he said: It's over – and closed Matthew's eyes. The vital instant had passed me by. Death had been an anti-climax, but it doesn't matter. Only I was there. Only I. And for that, to this day, I remain glad, and grateful, and proud. The sun was rising.

Connor must have thought that I was going to throw some kind wobbly because he told me not to be upsetting myself now. I told him that I was fine: what came next? It depended on what I wanted. I could go and make myself a coffee while Connor lay Matthew out, or – I said: Sod that, and switched on a tape of ancient songs from ages back, Motown anthems from before Matthew and I had even heard of one another, and I told Connor: Help me do this fabulously. And then – fabulously – Connor helped me finish the brandy, and we made a toast to Matthew, and we flung the windows wide.

Can't tell you the relief of seeing those surgical tubes being taken out. Connor did it fast; you couldn't hang about. But his voice sounded too loud. I asked: You sure he can't hear us? Connor said: Don't be so daft. I pointed out that even when a lizard's tail is chopped, it keeps on dancing. Connor grinned – he'd heard it all now. We got down to our task. Connor washed Matthew; I towelled and powdered him. Next, Connor asked: How d'you want him dressed? I said: I've got to change the bed first. Connor plainly thought this notion crazed – because of the delay involved in turning a dead weight – but I was not to be deterred. In some inexplicable way, I just knew that Matthew, whose joints were still compliant, would not have had it otherwise. I remember whispering to my boy, explaining what I was doing, as if he were merely half-asleep and I didn't want to wake him; weird, but anyhow. Connor and I managed to spread a sheet beneath the exhausted body, and stretch the linen across the mattress; and, once that was done, we put Matthew into his best pyjamas – you know the ones. And then, over his lifelessness, we spread a matching shroud, a virginal partner. Those sheets – sheets for which Cara would one day chide me – were the finest in my cupboard; they were sheets which I had saved for the day when I met my true love. And then a particular song came on, and I turned it up, and it was the peculiarest sensation, as I cologned my boy's head and gave his hair a final brush. Because, although the voice came from a woman, it felt as if it were coming from Matthew, but Matthew impersonating a drag-queen, romantic, ironic, powerful. And, through this song-of-songs, I knew beyond human doubt that he was wishing me goodbye, and telling me to take good care of myself, and not to shed a tear, and to remember him as a sunny day that I once had, and as a clown who made me laugh, and as a big balloon at a carnival that ended too soon, and as a breath of spring, as a good thing, and to remember, when I came to drink the wine of sweet success, that he had given me his best. And then, at everlasting last, I saw that my dead friend – who, more than any lover, had been my beloved – lay in the state which I had vowed, a state of dignity; and my head became filled with the gorgeous echoes of his unforgettable laughter and laughter and laughter.

Taste

There's no accounting for it. Mine, once Matthew's body and soul had parted company, was for dispatch. I'd never seen the point of lingering over a carcass, snivelling into black-edged handkerchieves while word spread among the flies. But I've since come to suspect that my eagerness to rid myself of his physical aftermath must, in part, have been a trick to force my memory back, back to a time when Matthew had been as healthy and as handsome and as active as in my dream as he lay dying. And yet, hard as I tried to re-shuffle those preterite cards, I found myself messing up my grammar, confusing tenses, clinging to the present, when, already, I should have moved on to the past. Connor reckoned that these things took time. We should deal with more immediate matters.

I rang the nearest medical practice, so that someone could be sent to confirm that the deceased was indeed defunct – a bureaucratic nicety without which the corpse could not be budged; and, while I waited for a doctor to pitch up, I phoned a firm of undertakers from the back of Connor's diary – not a firm in my locality, but one which, whatever it may have lacked by way of proximity, it more than possessed in terms of Papist cachet, boasting as it did long links with lengthy branches of recusant Catholic families – which snobbery I trusted might enhance my prospects when it came to vying for Matthew's final mass. A suitably formal woman answered, heard my enquiry, and, after a muffle with her mouthpiece, undertook to send some men round. I should expect them within the hour. As for the doctor, I only recall two things about him: his fatuously woebegone manner, and the manner in which he was slapdash. For, when, fifteen minutes after his visit, I went over to his surgery to collect the requisite, hand-completed scrap, I discovered that, among the causes of Matthew's death, he had entered, not just a lie, but a misspelled one – *Pnumonia*, for fuck's sake. Yet I refrained from mentioning the missing vowel. He would have taken my correction to mean that I was (not just pedantic, but) traumatized. So I doctored the error myself, back at the flat.

The undertakers, by contrast, were wondrous. First came the Conductor, a badger-haired ghoul of most fantastic height and most lugubrious countenance, clad in stripy trousers and the clunkiest, shiniest hobnail boots that you've ever encountered. Fantastically Dickensian. Really played the part. His job, he explained after half-crushing my hand, was to cast a careful eye around – in case of awkward turns and narrow angles and what he called Suchlike. But once he'd satisfied himself as to the smoothest 'modus operandi', he crept off to some van and mobilized a couple of underlings, who, when they appeared, looked felonious and cowed, as if labouring in moral manacles. You sensed that shady deeds hung, like skeletons, in their biographical cupboards, and that the Conductor, by some sinister accident, now held the master-key to those crimes. One of the men sported an impressive facial scar, carved in the shape of a scythe; the other, a sovereign knuckle-duster on a hand which carried what I took to be a suitcase, but turned out to be a stretcher, collapsed. The pair, after swerving past Connor, headed for the bedroom, but advised me to stay out. I didn't argue. My concern was for Matthew, not for the disposal of flesh and bone and a half-rusted Portacath.

Now Connor hit me with his departure, but made it as painless as the situation allowed. We embraced; we mutually thanked. He gave me his home-number, and made me promise to let him know as soon as the funeral was organized. He wanted to be there. Whatever happened. Briefly we argued as to which of us had derived the greater pleasure from this week of ghastliness, and next, he was off down the stairs, racing to his well-earned day of rest, his nursing sabbath. I sequestered myself in the sitting-room, and switched on some music – grave enough not to seem dancy, but loud enough to deaden any external sound. And yet, despite such devices, I couldn't fail to hear the noise of bumps against the wall, and heaves and humps and groans, as the undertakers bore away the breathless weight of a blighted life. Eventually, the Conductor knocked at my door. All done, Sir. We would speak in due course. Yet, as I led him out, he added: May I say what a lovely flat you have.

I'm afraid to say that, as soon as the trio was gone, I scuttled back to the bedroom, to check that no magpie had made off with any glinting fancy. But everything was fine; even the sheets had been left tidy. And then, in a dazed sort of frenzy, I rid myself of Matthew's rubbish – pills, tubes, specs, straws, gauzes, nappies, slippers, sponges, build-up drinks, the whole shebang. Actually, that's a lie. I kept the speed. Might come in handy. But later in the story, when amphetamines could indeed have lent some vigour to my lassitude, I found myself lacking in heart.

I grabbed Matthew's address-book, and rang a succession of names, just to let them know the worst, which they, among themselves, would have deemed for the best. Mercifully, however, most of those people were out at work, which simplified the exercise – seldom had answer-phones felt more welcome. At any rate, amid Matthew's connections, I found an Auntie Iris, who, when at last she managed to untangle her handset, sounded a bit ga-ga – didn't even bother to enquire in what circumstances her sister's only son had died. But, as I prepared to hang up, her wits seemed suddenly to sharpen: He leave a will then? I told her that he had done, and that, if need be, his solicitor would write to her. Did I know that Matthew'd had a sister in Ottawa? I did, I said – a half.

Of my own contacts, I rang not just the ones who'd known Matthew, but also the ones whom I'd neglected in recent months. Perhaps I wanted them back, or perhaps, a little cheaply, I wanted to mitigate for my absence. And then – how could I not have done? – I rang Kelly, to whom, let's face it, I owed my whole bond with Matthew. Yet it was not Kelly's commiseration that I sought; what I sought was to unburden myself of my loaded tidings. And since, in New York, it would still be office hours, I reasoned that I could safely leave a message at his apartment and be done. But, peculiarly, Kelly was at home, and answered: Thanks a bunch for waking me up, what's wrong now? I told him that Matthew had died. To which, after a yawn, he replied: So another one bites the dust; deal with it, that's life, you'd better tell Hunter, he's in London. I rang Cara, and Douglas, and Sukie, who hadn't yet returned to Paris, and I rang you, of course, and then I rang Charlotte, the solicitor, at her office in Lincoln's Inn. I repeated my spiel about Matthew, and, while I was at it, referred to the beady aunt. Charlotte told me that she saw no harm in telling me that Matthew had named me his sole beneficiary. We could meet to discuss Estate and Probate after the funeral. In the interim, she would fax me a copy of the will, so that I could wield it in my dealings with the cathedral.

I'd intended to send a quick note to Alison, and another to Farquhar, both of whom deserved, beyond notification, formal acknowledgement of my gratitude; but tiredness had caught up with me. I unplugged the phone, and began to drift about the flat, closing windows and switching off lights. On my way to the bedroom, my eye fell on twin blotches of blood retreating along the rush-matting, blotches which – as the tilted corpse had been driven round a corner – must have escaped from Matthew's nostrils. I know that this posthumous mishap was of no vital consequence, yet, emotionally, it rankled. Those brownish stains felt recriminatory to me, begrudging, like reminders of no more love. I struggled to clear them up, to wipe them out, to expunge the evidence that nothing can ever be as clean or clear-cut as one might like; and then I took three sleeping tablets. I climbed onto the four-poster, and, without a trace of squeamishness, slipped between the sheets which had been laid for Matthew.

By the time that I came round – around the time when shops would have been shutting – Charlotte's fax had arrived. I told myself to ring the cathedral – to try and slot Matthew into their Yuletide calendar. But first I played a string of messages which had been left while I'd been 'out'. The most interesting came from a woman with a phoney accent, calling herself Sammy – Matthew's half-sister, Samantha – whom Matthew had called a dreary cow. Sammy had apparently heard the sad news from her (step) aunt, but didn't sound too sad about it; didn't even sound surprised; what she sounded was dead keen that I should call her back. And so: Right, I decided; let's get this done. I could swear that she picked up before a ringing tone had even sounded. No pussying around. So when was the funeral? In about a week's time – a week being the British standard. She didn't wish to seem indelicate, but shouldn't she be speaking to Matthew's lawyers or something? I didn't wish to seem indelicate, but I didn't imagine that such a move would be productive. And why was that? Well, I could fax her a copy of the will, if she liked, so that she could verify that it made no mention of anyone called Samantha – nor Iris, for that matter. Now Sammy *did* sound surprised: she and her aunt were the sole remaining members of Matthew's family. Stupidly I replied: That depends on how you define family. She told me – all sassy – to cut to the quick here: did I mean that the whole estate was coming to *me*? Listen, I said; I don't know how well you knew your half-brother, but I don't think that we need to pretend that he was Croesus. In which case, she countered, nor did we need to pretend that she could afford to schlep over to England for just some funeral. And without *her*, of course, no way would her aunt wanna come. I mean, poor Iris didn't even know . . . *you* guys. I said: That's absolutely right, goodbye. I'd got shot of the cow in under three minutes. Off-peak.

I rang the cathedral. My call was answered by some time-dishonoured minion, gormless and hard-of-hearing, whose deaf-aid squealed and hissed. He told me to hang on, pottered away, took an age, eventually pottered back, and wordlessly now transferred me to a voice whose clacky dentures seemed to be playing up, but who managed to put me through to some further, pompous prannock – one of the padres. No, the duty-priest was not about. Nor was the Choirmaster. Really, was this an emergency? It was coming up to supper-time. Very well then. Be here tomorrow. Quarter past nine. Clergy House. Ask for Father Dudley. And kindly be punctual.

There's a secret to dealing with officers of Christ: you have to make them think that if they, in their munificence, will see their way to lending you a hand, you, in your eternal syco-phancy, will see your way to greasing their palm. I know of few subjects more guaranteed to give a priest the horn than (not chastity, but) money. So, when, next morning, I materialized at the cathedral's annexe, I made a point of looking as rich as it is possible to look without actually looking like a friend of Faust. I was ushered into a gothic side-room, where, while I waited for a dog-collar to show up, I checked that I hadn't forgotten my diary, and double-checked my papers, including the music-al programme. Next, Fr Dudley arrived, wreathed in that special clerical blend of incense and stale armpit; but no sooner he had appraised me with a glance than I knew that something beyond fragrance was awry; for, beneath his velveteen suaveness, there lurked the ferrous fist of a queer-basher. I thought: Christ, Matthew, lend me a hand or I'm stuffed. I explained the busi-ness that had brought me to this house – my need to book the Lady Chapel for a sung requiem mass. The questions which emerged from Fr Dudley were not so much questions as objec-tions in disguise, softly-delivered but stubborn, like leafy logs across a road, designed to test my stamina, as if I were some lowly seminarian bent on a vocation, but he, the high priest, was judge. Naturally, Fr Dudley appreciated this, and he appreciated that; he even appreciated the name of the funeral parlour; but *I* must appreciate that the deceased was regrettably not a pa-*rish*-nah. Not in the strict sense of the word, I granted; though Matthew, who had worked for years across the street, *had* frequently attended the cathedral's midday mass – a claim which the cleric could no more deny than I could have helped making up. Now Fr Dudley, never having been acquainted with 'the applicant', felt he ought to mention that he himself would not, alas, be available to officiate; so, in my desperation, I plucked from the fetid air the name of Fr Frank. Yes, of course, splendid man, always scooting about, supposed to be terrific with the dying. Perhaps, if Fr Frank agreed to take charge, something could, after all, be worked out. Incidentally, the cathedral's fee was . . . Large. But – wake up, Dudders – I hadn't been widowed by Croesus for nothing.

And thence, down a manky corridor to the door marked Choirmaster. My knock elicited only the most faraway reaction, as if I'd tapped into some absent-minded pastime. But, once inveigled in the fustiness, I discovered a nervy little layman scurrying about, busily shifting, with the sort of stealth that tends to be reserved for porn-mags, a pile of parish rags from a chair beside him. He entreated me, by means of a nod and wince, to park my arse. Youngish as he was – in his mid-forties at most – he seemed to have sought succour in the staple trappings of the doddery don: cavalry twills which could have shuffled of their own accord; grubby cardie, the colour of donkey, with peeling patches of suede at the elbows; checked woolly shirt, with buttonless cuffs and a shredded collar; two-tone knitted tie, heather and bracken. Corrugated hair, reminiscent of dry flax, and a parting which practically fell off the side. He was puffing at the gnawed end of a pipe. A ridge of spittle had congealed around its spout. He wiped the corners of his mouth. There was something at once wet and dry about the man, like a soap that would not sud. He said: Father Dudley mentioned that you might be dropping round. So I started from scratch. While he accompanied my rendition with *sotto voce* murmurs of Ahum Ahum Ahum, I produced my musical programme, to which he lent a critical scan; but he didn't even call the selection catholic. He called it Rum. Well, he could call it what he liked: *my* concern was that Matthew's will be done. I whipped out the fax sent by Charlotte, yet this flimsy sheet seemed not to cut the thinnest ice. He returned to the prospective programme, and stabbed at a couple of items, the first of which he described as Out. Could I ask why? A love-duet by Monteverdi didn't count as sacred, simple as that. I let the veto pass. (We could have it at the Crem and no harm done.) But then he pointed to a further number – a Credo. What was so profane about that? His bushy brows spake parables. Credos didn't constitute a part of the funeral rite; liturgically not done. He must have noticed that I was getting frazzled, because *personally*, he said, he had no objection; the piece was perfectly nice, if a bit, well, lush. No, it was the powers that be who were likely to take a dim view. (Personally, I couldn't have cared a Judas kiss. I mean: who had called for the piper? Who would pay for the tune?) I asked: Couldn't the choir just sing it instead of an Offertory hymn? His nose wrinkled. He said that this was all mighty peculiar, but he supposed that he could see what he could do. I said: That's really kind of you. We proceeded – to dates. Here was my chance to be conciliatory. I said that any day next week was fine by me. Next *week*? Forgive him; we should get a few things clear. His choristers were up to their ears in rehearsals for the Carol Service, and a Boxing Day concert at St John's Smith Square, beyond which, they were off until next year. I said: Can't they be bribed to come in – pocket-money sort of thing? The Choirmaster looked aggrieved. One didn't work like that here. So what was the solution? The solution was simple. If I really wanted such a picky programme to be performed by his choir, and conducted by him, I would have to wait until — let's see — the twelfth January. Practically three weeks. And if I waited until then, did he think that the Credo might be included? I was pushing him, but — all right, so long as the authorities didn't get wind of it. We wheeled our deal. I wrote a trio of cheques: one for the institution, one for the choir-school, and the last-but-not-least for him, in his capacity as Senior Organist. And then I left, thinking: Come off it, Matthew, you can see what pricks I'm dealing with. Besides, a fridge is a fridge is a fridge.

Or is it? Fr Frank put my mind at ease. Much better to do these things properly than amateurishly. And then, to my relief, he agreed to conduct the obsequies. He would let me have a copy of the order of service, to be forwarded to the printers, and meanwhile I should give some thought to readings. Me? Absolutely. He told me to come up with a few suggestions, then run them past him for approval. As for the looming Christmas, he wished me a (not happy, but) good one. Whether it was bad, I have no idea. I spent most of it hammered. But I do recall going out to various clubs and dancing, alone yet partnered, and staring into the lights rather than crying, and wishing that he and he were dead and *he* were still alive; and I remember catching flashes of features which reminded me of Matthew — napes, hands, smiles; and flashes of Matthew as he might have looked had he survived; and even, once, near a bar, a flash of the man whom he might have become, had he been given the chance to become a veteran.

Old habits. I fretted and fussed. I riffled through the Bible, until, at last, between its myriad fiddly tissues, I came across a couple of pronouncements that didn't seem too damning — one in Apostles, another in Romans. The first, I thought, could be read by Cara, because, though more my friend than Matthew's, she was reliable; the second (as a doff to Matthew's side) could be read by one of the Sapphists who had loved him — the less retiring of the couple. And then I told myself that I, too, should force myself to do something, lest, merely through fear of embarrassment, I fell short of my avowals. After all, I had promised to take Matthew to the final curtain, and the final curtain wasn't yet in sight. But since he'd never been a *mea maxima* culprit, I felt it only meet and right to redress, in however small a way, the steep religious imbalance of this production to commemorate his life. I needed to include something which spoke of (not sanctity, but) humanity, of messy death in messy times, of relief and loss and love and sadness. Of friendship and romance. I noticed a book of poems, and pulled it down. And, in the providential way that these things happen, its dusty pages fell open at an ode in memory of Baudelaire, composed by Swinburne. Those verses, let me tell you, must have been godsent – not only because they perfectly articulated what I could not myself articulate, but also because Swinburne had been an inspiration both to Aesthetes and to Decadents, as well as a drunk and a pervert and a self-professed flagellant. There's a gamey little tale – about him having sodomized a marmoset before feasting on its flesh – which made me think: Perfect, Matthew would adore the irony. Or rather, would have done.

I faxed the sacred readings to Fr Frank, along with the relevant stanzas from *Ave atque Vale* (*Hail & Farewell*), taking care to omit the identity of the degenerate who had penned them. You never knew quite who knew what in ecclesiastical circles. Next day, Fr Frank rang back, to say that all seemed fine; but he stipulated that the verses, by dint of their secular genre, should wait until after Communion, right at the end of the mass – which meant that I was sentenced to spend the entire ceremony in a needless state of anxiety. But I got my own back. I told Fr Frank that a homily wouldn't be required; it seemed superfluous somehow. Nor did the priest deny it. Difficult to be personal when one had scarcely known the person who had died. A musical interlude, during which the congregation could pray quietly, seemed to Fr Frank a better course of action. (What –

to the booming *Credo* from the St Cecilia Mass? Not a hope, darling.)

The Funeral Conductor rang, wondering: Coffin or casket? Search *me*, I replied. He gave a naughty, snorty sort of laugh, the sort of laugh, you somehow knew, which didn't often get an airing in his funerary patter. Well, he explained, a casket wasn't coffin-shaped; it was more like a chest, rectangular, and the top-half of the lid came up. Not a good look, I didn't imagine. He said that the more conservative among his customers tended to favour this style, though he himself wasn't awfully partial. I enquired which style he had picked for when *he* kicked the bucket. He chuckled, and called himself a simple man. But perhaps (he said), since we weren't in any desperate hurry, the best thing was for him to post me a catalogue. That way, I could make a decision in my own good time. I told him that flicking for a coffin wasn't exactly my idea of a good time. He gave another mischievous chuckle. I asked him to take me through the options while I had him on the line – finishes, prices, all of that. Delighted. Caskets came in wood or steel, or otherwise – I interrupted: I thought that we'd agreed about no caskets. Silly him; so we had. Coffins came in a wider variety: willow, oak, mahogany – although this last, he should point out, was actually mahogan-ized. I ruled it out: Matthew had never been an *izer*. Nor, it would appear, had the Conductor, who, working further through the brochure, next explained that I could also have bamboo, or basket-weave, or reclaimed pine, or – I said: Let's go straight to the back, shall we; Matthew wouldn't have approved of extravagance over this kind of stuff. In which case, what about recycled chipboard, or, even, eco-friendly cardboard? But, before I could decide, the Conductor contributed the revelation that, for a really colourful send-off, people sometimes liked to decorate the coffin themselves, with topical subjects and memorable backgrounds and jolly bits of whatnot. I said:

You're joking. He wasn't, but he could tell that I wasn't about to try my hand at aping Hockney. I reminded him that the corpse wasn't being buried, it was being burned. Indeed, Sir. So what was the point of squandering a bundle on something that was headed for the oven? His thoughts entirely. Besides, could one ever be completely sure that the coffin actually went *into* the fire, as opposed to being set aside and flogged to some other, unsuspecting punter? *There* he had to stop me, Sir. He gave me his firmest assurance that no such thing ever happened. I asked whether people ever went backstage to dispel any niggling doubts. Simply not practical — there was generally a queue to contend with; the process of cremation not being, you understand, instantaneous. So, instantaneously, I gave the Conductor to understand that Matthew was to have the simplest, cheapest coffin to be had. The Conductor said that the decision was, it went without saying, mine, though he couldn't help but wonder whether a plain cardboard box mightn't look a bit out of place at a place like The Lady Chapel. I'd need to think about it. He understood entirely. Anyway, next week he'd be bringing me a rough set of proofs, and some sample programmes — for me to compare styles of script and weights of paper etcetera — so any final decisions could be made at that juncture. Wasn't it a bore for him to drag himself over? Not in the least, Sir; all part of the service. So we made a date for the following Wednesday, at ten. The Conductor led me to believe that he was much looking forward to it, and I, from my end, led him to believe that I was already shaking coffee-beans.

I took myself to the Town Hall and registered the death. New Year's Day came and went. I tracked down a seamstress, who, labouring under the impression that I was after a counterpane, agreed to run up a ceremonial pall with scalloped edges, in dark green velvet. Meanwhile, the news of Matthew's death seemed to spread. People kept ringing for details, and not just people whom I'd phoned; strangers; people fond of euphemisms such as 'passed away'; people from his former place

of work, arseholes who now claimed to have 'suspected something'; women from his student days, including Anna, his old
girlfriend; a married couple who, summers ago, had apparently
run some seaside Greek taverna; some man without explicable
connection, who seemed less upset than in terror – Roving
Willy, for all that I cared. Should they send flowers or make a
donation? Flowers without question, to the funeral directors, on
the morning of the twelfth. The mass was scheduled for 2 p.m.
Did I have any suggestions? Yes. Matthew had always hated
floral mish-mash; they should order wreaths of a single colour,
preferably in a single variety of flower. And then I said: No
carnations, no crysanths, nothing naff, no measly bunches, no
cellophaned rubbish; make it classy or leave it out. I'm amazed,
in retrospect, that those callers should have proved so acquies-
cent in the teeth of my demands, but perhaps the tone of my
intransigence led them to clock that, had they opted for some
paltry token, it would have landed in the sacristy.

I drove to see the florist whom I'd originally visited with
Matthew, the one who'd been commissioned to make a circlet
of wheat – modelled on the woodcut by Eric Gill, the cathedral's (in)famous sculptor-in-chief. When I told the florist that
Matthew had died, he looked (not taken aback, but) impressed.
He'd never known anyone order a funeral wreath for themselves. He called it a first; and then he called it brave. I said: My
friend was a rare bird. And then, while I was there, I ordered a
further wreath, for my friend from myself, to be made entirely
of dark roses, darker than blood, darker than wine, darker than
a butcher's heart, dark as the darkness of an Arabian night. No
need for a card. Matthew had been right. One day, he had fore-
told, I would understand. I understood now. For, when you
took into account the headaches which people sometimes had
to endure in the wake of losses such as mine, my lot felt – despite
the cocksuckers at Clergy House – untroubled. No squabbles
over money. No legal wrangles. No meddlesome family.

Everything according to plan. Everything nearly done. But I still had time on my hands.

Claudia, the less reserved of Matthew's Sapphists, contrived to keep me occupied. We'd been discussing the funeral, and the protraction imposed by the Choirmaster, and her allotted reading – which, far from describing as dull, she described as flattering – when I mentioned that the Swinburne was starting to panic me. I'd never been any good at reciting; I must have been mad to imagine that I could deliver those lines without fluffing. Claudia wondered whether perhaps I should go to be coached by her father. Give the old man a distraction from his crossword and Third Programme. He'd been as good as bedridden for some while. She was sure that she could wangle it.

Claudia's father had, in his distant prime, been an actor of the first British magnitude, one of the finest verse-speakers around, up there with Gielguds and Scofields and Burtons, the great theatrical giants. Later, when the kitchen-sink brigade irrupted, and classical declamation became unfashionable, his health – but not his passion – went into decline; and thus, rather than toil against the loveless public tide, he took to writing books on drama, and to tutoring the young – boys and girls who, in turn, went on to flourish. At Christmas time, their cards would arrive from distant climes, as if those former students, those current stars, could never quite forget, nor repay, their early debt to their master. Which explains why, though the idea of elocution had initially struck me as a clever means of doing Matthew proud, now, as I drew up to the house in Barnes, I felt less clever than callow.

I was let in by some housekeeper, and remember noticing, on my way up, a flashbulb portrait of a young man, looking virile and chiselled and handsome – not unlike Claudia now, in fact. But I also recall being unable to reconcile this image with the sight of the fragile character who, as I reached the first-floor landing, greeted me from an armchair – wrapped in a paisley dressing-gown, with a tartan rug over his lap. You could see the tips of his bedroom-slippers peeping out. His hair was snowy white, and parted like the hair of an Edwardian child; and his specs seemed to have grown too large. But he was bright as a button, and all set to start, with pencil and notepad to hand. It struck me as a gesture of moving kindness that this infirm old gentleman, from whom the spectre of death could never be too far, should have agreed to help a stranger recite a poem in such morbid circumstances. What is more, he had the charm to call the piece that I had chosen: Divine, my dear, divine.

Mind you, he pointed out, I hadn't set myself an easy task by kicking off with just about the trickiest word in the English language – O – but never fear, we would get there somehow. He must have made me repeat that wretched O two dozen times. I admitted how reading to him alone felt more inhibiting than the thought of reading to a whole crowd. *Reading*? No, no, the piece must be learned by heart. We wanted it word perfect; none of that glancing up and down. You fixed your sights on the far end of the church, and forgot everything in front. As for the crucial O, you pitched it upward, almost as if by accident, and did not hurry. You invested the weighty syllable with a converse tonal lightness, delivered it, then let it float away and die. Needless to say, the old boy, even sitting hunched, could do it just like that. O, he intoned; and O again, rising and subsiding. I could hear exactly how the word should sound, but my vocal chords wouldn't oblige. He sent me to the corner, made me face the wall, and told me to try now. I tried. Tremulous as a bubble, my O gently bounced back. That was more like it. Next, he made me do it from the landing outside. He made me raise my chin and take the deepest breath, but hold it in my lungs; then, he said, just let the vowel glide from above – like a cloud over the sky. He taught me about pace. He taught me about variety. He taught me about playing to the emotions of the (not congregation, but) public. What emotion were we after? I mulled it; I supposed nostalgia. Well, nostalgia wasn't a thing that one could demand; one could only hope to inspire it. One's voice was instrumental, certainly; but without those god-given verses, there was nothing. Oh, I said. *Exactly*! Well done. He slapped his thigh.

The rest of the piece wasn't so hard – apart, that is, from an adjective which, for reasons of scansion, had to be stressed against the grain of custom. Obscure, was the adjective, but *Obs*-cure was how it ought to be pronounced. I kept mucking it up. In the end, I had to visit the old boy three times: he wouldn't give me leave until he was fully persuaded that those verses were perfectly memorized, satisfactorily enunciated, and entirely to his exacting standards. But I admit that, by the time the stickler and I had parted company, I did feel closer to the possibility of doing credit to Matthew.

Wednesday. My date with the Conductor had come round. He pressed the bell before the appointed hour, but, far from seeming apologetic, he seemed glad – the Underground hadn't played up for once. As he took off his coat – a task performed by means of sprightly little shudders – I asked whether he'd ever had to deal with anyone who'd thrown themselves onto the tracks. Mercifully not, he replied, widening his eyes. Messy job, he would imagine. He rubbed his hands. Nippy outside. Coffee? Gosh, that would be lovely. How did he like it? Black as your hat. Cup or mug? The Conductor was a bit of a cup man. And yet, despite his penchant for the formality of bone china, his manner was discernibly more relaxed than at our first encounter – you might even say expansive. I was relieved, actually; relieved to be spared superfluous displays of professional gravity.

After a gulp, he asserted: Really can't beat proper coffee, can one. He rummaged in a briefcase, extracted a bundle of sample programmes, and, after fiddling in his breast-pocket, donned a pair of bifocals. His taste in lettering turned out to be more ornate than mine, and his feeling for card, too textured for my liking; but on weight of paper we saw eye to eye, as, indeed, we did on colour – off-white rather than ivory. Human error taken into account, his proofs contained remarkably few typos, but the Conductor seemed nonetheless disgruntled. Those printers had been given plenty of time; he would have to kick their backsides. He winked a wink that told me to look down. His toe-caps were viciously shined. I thought: I wouldn't like to be at the receiving end of *those* mothers. We moved on to other matters. When I told him that I'd decided to go for straightfor-ward chipboard, he looked a bit mahoganized. But his spirits rallied at the news that a green velvet pall would conceal the unsightliness. He described my ruse as Canny, and promised to keep the cloth rolled up. If necessary, it could be steamed at the last moment – they had all sorts of useful gadgetry down in the morgue, for dressing bodies and so forth. He also agreed, because of the unusual choreography, to deliver the coffin to the cathedral half an hour beforehand, so that the scene could be set before 'guests' started arriving. How many cars to the crematorium did I think that we'd be wanting? Three, I said, though I couldn't think who'd want to come. Not to worry, said the Conductor – in the instance of a change in plan, I knew where to find him. He couldn't have been more obliging. I tempted him with another cup. He mustn't, but thanked me. We were done. We stood, and strolled out. I helped him don his coat. Now we faced each other. His smile was faintly anxious. And then, as he was on the point of leaving and I was on the point of sticking out my hand, he did an unexpected thing: bore down, and kissed me on the smacker. I tried not to reel back – but in my head I could only hear Matthew screaming with laughter. Undertake *that*.

I left for the cathedral, alone and before time. I wanted to get there in advance of the others. The nave looked deserted, but I genuflected – not taking any chances. I walked along an aisle, past a line of closed confessionals, and headed for the Lady Chapel. No sign even of a sacristan. As I stepped through the half-darkness onto a patterned, marble platform, I was struck by how this place evoked the Byzantine flavour of St Mark's. From arches lined with mottled slabs, the chapel rose to a barrel-vaulted height, with a dome at the far back, the length of its ceiling decorated with gilded mosaic, shimmering and subdued at once. On came a light. A skinny cassock, seminarian perhaps, crept out, and began to fuss around the sanctuary, lighting candles and shifting props from some earlier mass. He nodded in the abstract. Tarnished chandeliers, Orthodox in character, hung at intervals along the colonnades, while, also overhead, ornamental cherubim and etiolated bits of botany added to the splendour. I noticed that some winter foliage, which I'd ordered in advance, had been arranged, in tall bronze amphorae, along the sides of the chapel. (I'd made a peevish point of not buying proper flowers, because I knew that, as soon as the funeral was done, they'd be transferred to the main altar for the greater benefit of the parish, about which I didn't give a duchess.) I mooched around the ranks of chairs which had been set out, wondering who should sit where, and whether sixty pro-grammes would be enough. More lights came on now, with loud clacks. People, out of sight but mumbling, began to scuttle about — singers, I imagined, on their way to the choir. The Choirmaster appeared, ever-fusty but begowned, with a batch of scores under his arm. He muttered something about a last minute run-through, and vanished. I went back outside.

The cortège of cars, when it drew up, made me feel lonely, because I had no-one with whom to share my pride: Matthew's hearse was heaped with wreaths — some of them, large as tyres. High-buttoned drivers were stepping out, and opening limousine-doors wide; and, while they loitered about the piazza, I caught glimpses, on the leather seats, of further rings-upon-rings of colour. The Conductor, in ceremonial tails and top hat, was issuing orders to his flunkies — the underlings unmistakably among them. Mist was streaming from his mouth. I was longing to light up, but decided to return inside rather than witness the box being dismounted. While I hung about the chapel, waiting to receive the body of (not Christ, but) Matthew, the central doors of the Cathedral creaked apart, and the procession, after a minor jostle-round, began. Miles away, I could make out the dull-coloured coffin, wobbling on black shoulders, being swivelled round a font, and, with a stately gradualness, now advancing along the south aisle. Hobnails clanked against the flagstones, then grew duller as they drifted onto an interlude of herring-boned parquet; and now, as they approached the place where I was standing, resumed their earlier loudness. The Conductor, topperless, paced at the head of the party, with the green velvet pall draped over his arm. Matthew's coffin had arrived – but he wasn't inside. He was in my head, telling me not to worry, telling me that it was all going to be fine, telling me that the kiss of shame guaranteed as much. I winked at the Conductor, and straightened my tie – an old one of Matthew's: black stars and black moons set against a black sky. As the men hoiked the coffin onto the marble platform, the Conductor stood aside and shook my hand. He asked whether I was all right. I said: Just about. He squeezed my arm, and told me to leave it to them, Sir. And then he whispered that the wreaths were absolutely stunning. I asked his men to leave them on the step; I preferred to arrange them myself. If someone could put a programme on each chair, that would be great.

I draped the cloth over the chipboard coffin, which felt unnaturally cold, and let the scalloped edges trail along the ground, its corners fanning out. The first wreath that I picked was Matthew's, the simplest, humblest, in its way the most lovely: a circlet of wheat, greyish green. I laid it on the coffin, singly. Then I found my own, dark-rosed offering, and propped it vertically, facing the empty seats. The rest of the tributes I organized by shade and type and size: hyacinths, camellias, ranunculi, lilac, snowdrops, lilies, a burst of imported sunflowers – from Claudia and her friend Viola. I couldn't resist peering at the names that accompanied these offerings in memory of

Matthew. Cara – ever true to type – had sent a ring of hothouse orchids, of a delicately greying pink; Douglas, black parrot tulips, stylishly funereal; Sukie sent the model's favourite – white narcissi; even Connor went to the trouble of ordering a small ring of crimson freesias, with a brief, but true, inscription: Matthew, I cared for you. And you, of course – wicked though you were to circumvent my floral rules – sent a stroke of genius: a crown of laurel leaves.

Fr Frank came in, grinning, and said: what a delight, all these wreaths. I said: I slightly bullied people. He said: The end justifies the means. I thought: In a manner of speaking. He glanced at his watch; he'd better be off to get his gear on. I asked if we might have more candles. He didn't see why not; he would tell the sacristan to raid the store. The Choirmaster was back at the organ, twiddling with his stops; improvising. The underlings, with their trolley, had returned outside. Only the Conductor remained, dutifully planted next to a pillar at the back. My peculiar ally. But I felt uncomfortable – less like a mourner than an usher. Now I heard footsteps advancing. Here came Cara, wearing a grey velvet coat, military in style, with a matching astrakhan hat – her going-away outfit, as it happened. I asked her to sit at the front, on my right. Did she have a copy of her reading? She patted her bag. And then, others began to pitch up: some, looking solemn; some, looking calm; but all, I could tell, impressed by the display before their eyes. It made me think: Yes, this is going to be all right. A pair of altar-boys walked onto the sanctuary, bearing candelabra with brass branches, which they placed on pedestals of alabaster, and which, with long wax tapers, they now ignited. Sukie, when she appeared, set tongues wagging – the glamorous woman with short-cropped hair and long, Japanese garments. Connor, who kissed me without embarrassment, came toggled in a duffel-coat which made him look like a school-child. Douglas, who wore the same coat as he had done to Harry's Bar, came with a man swaddled in one of those pneumatic puffa jackets –

whom I took to be Stan. They sat toward the back. You, in your smoky mohair cloak and wide-brimmed hat, wore, I recall, a veil over your eyes. Then, unexpected people started to swell the numbers: Charlotte, the solicitor; Alison, the sweetheart; Anna, Matthew's one-time girlfriend, who introduced herself along with her husband; a few sulkers – notably the creeps whom I'd allowed to gawp at Matthew as he lay dying; a further bunch, whom I couldn't identify – former colleagues of his, most likely. And, last of all, came Claudia and Viola – polo-necked and jacketed and trousered. I asked them to join Cara at the front. And then the organ paused, and the chandeliers burst into light; and the introductory anthem started up, and the congregation rose as one, and Father Frank, preceded by his acolytes, made his entrance, clad in vestments of gold-embroidered black. And thus began, one dismal afternoon in January, the mass for the repose of the soul of Matthew. I felt numb.

But at least the scene looked glamorous. I can vouch for that. And yet, as Father Frank worked his way through the rite, and the musical interludes began to crop up, I recall thinking how much better those numbers had sounded on tape, when I'd listened to them with Matthew – how much more real than in this vacant version of reality, where he, though hypothetically present, was absent. The Choirmaster, sequestered in a loft behind us, *would* take the tempi too fast, and his singers, though their disembodied voices reverberated like mad, sounded sharp half the time. I worried that the Credo, which, back at the flat, had flown by, would seem, in this doleful atmosphere, too lengthy by half. When Cara went up for her reading, I couldn't see her mouth. All I noticed was the hem of her coat quivering beneath the stand. When Claudia stepped onto the platform, it was another matter, gruffer, her delivery more dramatic. But I could hear programmes rustling, and late arrivals, and people stepping over one another, and hacking coughers in the background – uncontrollable factors, like the trail of blood which, as Matthew's stretcher had been taken from the flat, had appeared along the rush-matting. It brought a bad taste to the mouth. People were tittering behind me, but I didn't dare turn round; I felt sure that they were bitching about this neverending religious travesty. Congregation stands, congregation sits, congre-gation kneels, congregation yawns, congregation stands, congregation kneels, congregation must be groaning to get out. Relax. Won't be long now. Communion coming up. My heart begins to thump. How many (supposed) Catholics figure among us? Maybe the others are waiting for me to lead the charade. Father Frank shoots me a glance, so I go to receive the host, return to my seat, and bury my face in my hands. But I can't be giving thanks. I peer out. Others are walking up – Connor, Viola, Charlotte, one of the sulkers – clutching a sodden hankie; then, a few stragglers. The queue trickles down to nothing. My reading is next on the programme. The chapel sinks into silence. Father Frank, assisted by his acolytes, descends onto his throne of damask. Time. As I approach the lectern, I can picture Claudia's father telling me to hold my chin high. But, for an age, I cannot seem to start. And then, as I inhale and gaze over the coffin, to the far back, towards a dot above the head of the Conductor, my lines – like a cloud over a sky – float out:

> *O sleepless heart and sombre soul unsleeping,*
> > *That were athirst for sleep and no more life*
> > *And no more love, for peace and no more strife!*
> *Now the dim gods of death have in their keeping*
> > *Spirit and body and all the springs of song,*
> > *Is it well now where love can do no wrong,*
> *Where stingless pleasure has no foam or fang*
> > *Behind the unopening closure of her lips?*
> > *Is it not well where soul from body slips*
> *And flesh from bone divides without a pang*
> > *As dew from flower-bell drips?*

> *It is enough; the end and the beginning*
> *Are one thing to thee, who art past the end.*
> *O hand unclasped of unbeholden friend,*
> *For thee no fruits to pluck, no palms for winning,*
> *No triumph and no labour and no lust,*
> *Only dead yew-leaves and a little dust.*
> *O quiet eyes wherein the light saith nought,*
> *Whereto the day is dumb, nor any night*
> *With <u>obscure</u> finger silences your sight,*
> *Nor in your speech the sudden soul speaks thought,*
> *Sleep, and have sleep for light.*

A few more prayers, a triple-blessing, and a booming hymn to see us out. While the congregation, amid exhilarated descants, does its best to bring the house down, the Conductor and his flunkies convey the coffin back to the piazza. The celebrant and his acolytes return to the sacristy. And that, I would say, was the moment when my confusion began; was the beginning of my descending spiral.

It felt like a bad party. People were sniggering about how some drunk had appeared in the middle of the mass and plonked himself beside someone and asked: Some prince being buried or something? I could hear myself being thanked. I could hear myself thanking people for having come, as if this whole thing *had* been a party. I could hear people of whom I'd never heard, speaking about Matthew as if they'd known him better than I. Where was his family? Didn't have one, I replied. Too sad, the saddo piped up. Here came Father Frank, relieved of his skirts and ready to be ferried to the next frill of the saga. I asked Cara to take him in the second car. I couldn't face having to affect an air of piety. I honestly can't recall who came in mine – not Douglas. He went with Stan, in the third and last.

The crematorium was foul, so I'll skip a song-and-dance. We were ushered into a room with a municipal reek about it. The coffin, now stripped of its pall, was plonked on a conveyor-belt of rubber. Fr Frank read a few excerpts of holy guff. When the Monteverdi love-duet began, one of the loud-speakers turned out to be bust. Worse: long before the piece had reached a climax, some jerk behind the scenes had pressed some button, and, next, to my horror and my everlasting anger, the coffin, with its piteous wreath on top, was trundling off toward a viscose drape, and he was gone. Grotty, no? Well, that's how it was. Outside, darkness had fallen. In some cold back-yard, the remaining wreaths had been deposited on a gravel path. While people loped about, lighting up and muttering about stark contrasts, I crouched to collect cards, and to make a note, on the back of each one, of who had sent which flowers. I came across a pretty shabby effort (tiger-lilies, of a rusty salmon) signed: Love Kelly – but in Douglas's handwrit-ing – the result, presumably, of some transatlantic confab. And then, when, at long last, I reached the end of the long line, I realized that – despite my request to the crematorium staff – the circlet of wheat had not been burned along with Matthew. I grabbed it, slung it under my arm, and said: We're out of this dump. Our convoy was driven back through a mire of infernal traffic. Outside the Cathedral, I bid goodbye to the Conduc-tor, thanked him, and told him that I was donating the pall to his parlour. I bid goodbye to Fr Frank, who, as I slipped him an envelope of ready cash, reckoned that the mass, at least, had been a triumph. I bid goodbye to Douglas, who was afraid that he and Stan had to rush; but I agreed that, sometime soon, I would go round to Their new house. And thus, in a blur, people began to disband, until – I don't know – five, perhaps six of us were left standing in the drizzle on the piazza. So we went out, at an absurdly early hour, for a drunken supper at a little Italian restaurant which, years ago, Matthew and I had frequented – less for its gloopy fare than for its name: Il Convento.

I hung the circlet of wheat over my front door, and discovered, as I dragged myself through the motions of acceptance, that the greenish ring, floating on the greenish wall, lent me a strange sort of remembrance – not of Matthew's cremation, but of his enduring presence. Before the impetus deserted me, I wrote to those who had sent wreaths – at least, to those for whom I had addresses. Simultaneously, letters of condolence began to arrive, mostly expressing the deep and heartfelt platitudes that often result from social embarrassment, but some, for which I was more thankful, designed to make me smile even as my eyes welled up, letters sprinkled with anecdotes about Matthew during the sunny days to which I was struggling to get back. Perhaps a week after my battens had come down and my sadness had begun to look more like ill manners, I received a letter from Alison – in reply to the postcard from Venice which had been delivered too late for anybody's comfort – and her words, so measured yet so powerful, so completely outside the realm of professional formality, left me in little doubt that the nurse who, more than any other, had called my boy a sweetheart, had not done so for nothing. Sukie sent a card, which simply said: Come to Paris. Have my apartment. *Je t'embrasse.* Douglas wrote, on posh new stationery, trying to arrange a dinner-date for me with him and Stan, who was looking forward to meeting me at long last. Cara wrote; Connor wrote; both, urging me to get in touch as soon as I felt up to it. But, of all the communications which sought to bring me comfort, the most bizarre (and only typewritten one) came from Kelly, who, though he failed directly to mention Matthew, wrote to say that he'd heard that the funeral had been great – from Hunter. From Hunter? I hadn't even clocked him at The Lady Chapel. Might Kelly blame me for the oversight? Later, he might have blamed me for greater ones.

Not long thereafter, I drove to South London, to pick up the vestiges of Matthew's carcass. Mortlake, would you believe, was name of the dump. The urn, if you could call it that, was the cheapest to be had – a snip at £3: a purple plastic container with a screw-on lid, reminiscent of an old-fashioned sweet-jar. At the counter, a peroxide bombshell in a kittenish jumper explained that, inside the jar, I'd find a sealed bag containing the 'cremulated' ashes. Cremulated? Yes – it meant ground to a fine powder. I asked what human ashes looked like – flour? More like flakes, really; greyish-white in colour; similar to Ready Brek – a healthy cereal for all the family. I gawped. She struggled not to crack, but it didn't last. You had to laugh. The sweet-jar travelled in the boot of the car, and, once home, went into a cupboard stacked with luggage – for a less rainy day, when I felt readier to Brek the back of the task. One of those days, I heard a debate over the airwaves about the relative merits of euthanasia. Some Dutch proponent was arguing that a killer-needle was the kindest answer. The cruellest option, he claimed, was the one favoured by reactionary countries such as ours, where patients were pumped full of morphine, only to perish delirious – a circumstance which apparently made for bad karma. Christ above. Put a *kum-kum* in your hair, paint a *tilak* on your brow, open like a lotus flower, *Hare Rama, Hare Krishna, Hare Hare Hare*. In Dutch.

Charlotte spared me the hassle of having to go to Lincoln's Inn. Instead, over drinks, she took me through the business of the will. Everything was mine, so probate shouldn't take long to be granted – another couple of months or thereabouts. There was no death-duty to pay, because Matthew's estate fell within the tax-exemption threshold, so all I needed do was transfer his household bills into my name, and deal with his mail – her firm, as executors, could see to its redirection. She asked what I thought I'd want to do with Matthew's flat – let it, perhaps? Flog it. Fine: she could help with the conveyancing side. But long before the place was allowed to be put on the market, I went round one final time. I hadn't been back since – God – not since I'd driven Matthew to pick up clothes for his travels. When I walked in, I found everything orderly but dusty; tidily defunct. I kept his music, which explains why my collection has so many duplicates; and I also kept his books, which still fill me with sadness — because they made me realize, as I boxed them up, how broad had been his knowledge on subjects now too late for discussion. The old Chinese vase which had belonged to his mother's mother, I sent, labelled 'Fragile', to his beady aunt — along with the ancient photo-album of Matthew's 'Darwinian' ancestors. Who knew? One day, those ugly bastards might even fetch up in Canada. The rest of the stuff I distributed at random: occasional bits went to people who were happy of a reminder; most of the clothes went to charity; and furniture went off in a truck. The property would look bigger unoccupied. The garden could go wild — or hang.

Which must have been around the time when this whole chronicle began — the stage when, grateful though I should have been to find myself alive, I allowed my plight to grow overcast; when, instead of making sense of what I'd learned from Matthew, I let apathy undermine me, squalor engulf me, and all that in my self-absorption I could do, between leafing through the dictionary for a hint of guidance, was stagger past the table of my useless past, to collect inanimate packages — cartons delivered from take-away restaurants, books sent with fondest love — and thence, back to the four-poster which now lay lopsided — for another sleeping tablet. On the morning when, after my repeated failures to get up or get out or get anything done, Cara's orchid was brought round, I remembered the letter from Douglas which I still hadn't answered; so, feeling that a visit to his house would be no worse than accusations of sulky self-indulgence, I rang him and agreed to go to Bloomsbury for supper the following Saturday. But I wasn't to expect perfection, warned Douglas. The builders weren't quite done. I recall thinking: Well, are you ready to entertain or aren't you? What I hadn't entertained, of course, was the thought of Stan.

Douglas, who, with his baggy tweeds and bobbly jumpers, seemed earlier to have chanced on Faggotland by accident, had now passed into man-drag. Both he and his new lover, beneath paunchy T-shirts with porno-graphics, were wearing combat-pants. I was wearing flannels. They had shorn their heads to a No. 1. Mine could have done with a cut. I felt like a fish out of amyl. And yet – appearances notwithstanding – so must they have done; for, despite the hefty clomp of army boots on oaken planks, their struts were belied by nervy laughter, as if my approval in some way mattered, which, to Douglas, then, it might still have done. Once I'd been poured a drink, and Stan, amid gags about the new Aga and Fanny Craddock and God knows what other claptrap, had vanished to the bowels of the house, Douglas said: Let me show you round. The place, I have to say, was fabulous: sparsely furnished, but to a high standard, with a few Georgian pieces about, a scattering of old Persian rugs, and, in the public rooms, good panelling. Any touches of naffness – such as a bunch of *faux*-peonies in a waterless crystal jug, their wiry stems bent double – I ascribed to the murky region of marital compromise, a region which Douglas, in his youthful prime, would never have considered inhabiting. But still, the colours of his walls were beguiling – those aqueous greys and eau-de-nils and misty blues which are to be found on Gainsborough canvases. Only the main bedroom jarred; seemed to be trying too hard. The bed itself was so large as to swamp the confines, with the result that, while it seemed to be strain-ing to prove something, such as vigorous passion, it proved, to me, something quite other: that its incumbents didn't like to sleep too close for comfort. Nor did the walls of that room seem altogether right, for whilst Douglas had chosen a red that sought to cut a modern dash, it was, in reality, a far older red than any of us, older, indeed, than the very house. It was that edgy, almost perilous vermilion which used to be favoured by Renaissance artists when depicting the cap of a child. Yet the snags for which Douglas had told me to make allowance were trifles: a section of banister that had yet to be rubbed down; a floor in need of sanding; a window without catches; an unpaved yard. We were down in the basement by now. The scene of our supper. Stan was over-partial to candles. The dining room looked like a shrine. We sat – to finickily garnished salads of artichoke heart.

They conducted themselves much in the fashion of a newlywed couple, by which I mean that they fussed in the manner of people who haven't lived together long enough to have devised, when entertaining, a polished double-act. Too often, both seemed to escape to the kitchen at once – as if their need to ensure their gastronomic excellence were greater than my need for company. Not that I minded: it gave me a chance to think about things, such as what Matthew would have made of this whole set-up. Nor, indeed, did I mind that the pair, once returned to the table, should chatter to each other despite me – about, for instance, whether the burgundy which their local merchant had talked up passed muster. Douglas must have forgotten that I preferred not to drink red; but perhaps the tartness of white disagreed with Stan. At any rate, Stan raised his glass from the base of its stem, as if savouring some memorably sunny Alsace, and pronounced his first, dark swig: Fab. Meanwhile Douglas, with a new-found panache that did not thereby escape vulgarity, performed that tiresome, connoisseurish, sniff-and-swill-and-swallow act – Douglas who, only a few months back, had doubted the Doneness of writing postcards at a cocktail bar. When his chunky, high-tech watch began to bleep a state of alarm, thereby heralding the moment for a bird to come out of the oven, it elicited Kentuckian chuckles from Stan about how they didn't make Chicken like they used to, nudge-nudge. It pained me to grin at such half-baked *double-entendres*; and although Douglas also made, on his way out, a lame attempt to laugh, I could tell that he was – and not just vicariously – embarrassed. But Stan, unembarrassed, rushed off to lend his lover a loving hand, and I was left to twiddle while they shared and shared alike. I could picture them trading *jus* over the Aga, mouth to mouth. Anyhow, when they came back, it was with plates already piled – so high as to suggest that the remainder of Bloomsbury had been blighted by famine. Stan, it transpired, had been mother. As my mound landed in front of me, Douglas, the wittiest, sharpest conversationalist that I'd ever encountered, asked my opinion of their place-mats. My eye darted about, and – just before a gravy-boat could obscure the last mat from sight – alighted on a bog-standard disc of laminated cork with a stuck-on reproduction of some corny galleon; the kind of article that unimaginative brides place on unimaginative lists for their parents' guests to buy. I thought: How low must one stoop for love? But I said: Lovely.

We waded on through the repast: chicken, spuds, beans, and sprouts. Stan ate like a savage, so I asked about his life. He said: Good with Douglas. I said: Aside from that. He mused with brief discomfort, then peered toward his lover, as if for permission to divulge something. But Douglas was playing dumb. So Stan explained, through a skewy mouth, that he'd just been made redundant. Not too sorry, mind. Looked like a friend of his – an Ex, in fact – was interested in renting his old pad. I asked whether Stan had considered selling up. Well, the place actually belonged to the council – but still, a bit of cash on the side was always handy. Besides, busting your guts for a removals company wasn't exactly Stan's idea of fun. Too bloody tiring, for one thing. And diabolical hours. Douglas, reading my mind, reassured me that there was no need for Stan to worry.

But on to happier subjects. Stan rubbed his hands. Tomorrow, he declared, they were off riding – in Richmond Park. I really should try it sometime. I asked: Are you a keen horseman, Stan? He belched, begged pardon, and replied: You bet, though not as good as Doug. (The closest I'd ever known Douglas come to a saddle was when carving lamb; but love can be full of surprises.) I asked whether Stan wore the whole kit – jodhpurs, hacking jacket and all that. No, he said, wellies and jeans did the job just as fine; the poncy gear was for your yuppie-types. I said: You mean like Douglas? Douglas laughed like a madman. It reminded me of old times. Stan looked (not just perplexed, but) put out, so I may have found it hard not to appear delighted. When Douglas stood to uncork another bottle, Stan, also itching to get up, enquired: Extras anyone? Not for me, thanks. More for the rest of us, he replied – as if moderate appetites were an affront – and loped back to the Aga. Douglas told me: I know what you're thinking, but it isn't like that. I said: It's *you* I'm concerned about; I don't even know the man.

I'm sure that – had we ever properly discussed the subject – Douglas would have justified his choice of companion on emotional grounds. He would have claimed – this cynical length down the line – that it was ultimately more rewarding to be loved than ever to be the lover; because Douglas, I believe, honestly believed that Stan loved him. Yet what counts in these matters is (not belief, but) grittier stuff, such as the security which Stan, like a ravenous animal, had scented in Douglas; for Douglas, though a dolt in some regards, remained, as he had always been, a thorough gentleman. So where, then, lay Stan's real allure? Perhaps, at the start, it lay in the sack – but you don't need me to tell you how long *that* lasts, at least in Faggotland. Soon enough, Douglas would be coming home from some City bash, to find Stan slumped in front of a porno vid, with a vacupump clamped to his genitals and a dildo up his arse. And yet my reservations weren't to do with sexual manners. They weren't even to do with class – not now that I had learned the lessons which I had done. Take Matthew, who though hardly from the most patrician stratum, was blessed with such innate intelligence and nobility of character as to shame my own highfalutin family. No; with Stan it was something other: it was his failure to provide Douglas with even the most basic benefits of a humble background: honesty and pride. But Douglas couldn't see it, precisely because he stood so close to the lie, and because he was so desperate to cobble together a semblance of harmony, however shoddily constructed. And yet, despite the warm vulnerability which underscored his almost stolid aspect, something – perhaps the ludicrous scale of the matrimonial couch – told me that already a physical chill had descended between the unequal couple, a tacit but ugly hesitancy had been visited on the beautifully proportioned Georgian house.

While my co-hosts cleared away the plates, in advance of cheese and bread, I stole a glance at Douglas, and noticed that – although he'd always sweated too much – his face tonight was somehow *too* shiny, too flushed: it was disgruntled. As I sat there, forbidden from making myself useful, I couldn't quite determine whether the source of his vexation lay with me, for not having made a greater effort with Stan, or with Stan himself, for having, however inadvertently, shown up Douglas, or, indeed, with Douglas's own realization that Stan and I were no likelier ever to appreciate each other than, at base, Douglas had ever appreciated, say, Cara. I didn't know how much Stan knew about my history with Douglas – our forays, in the days of Bedsitland, to those orgies in the underskirts of town; the time when Douglas, driven to despair by Jack, had tried to top himself but bungled – yet I suspect that, beyond the barest of facts, Douglas would have spared his lover too many details about our shared past, partly lest Stan should feel that he could never quite catch up – that, in terms of knowing Douglas, I would always have the upper hand, but partly, too, because, regardless of our positions now, Douglas's and my beginnings in London had been so scuzzy. Douglas would have hated to disappoint Stan, whose sights were trained determinedly upward; for, however craven in his former dealings with Jack, Douglas was now assuming a different – indeed converse – persona: that of the dependable, staunch provider. And yet, for all that Stan was aspirant, I regretted his grasp on Douglas's desperate kindness; for Stan, anyone could see, was taking Douglas for a ride – not just emotionally, not just financially, and not just in Richmond Park. He was doing so in a more pernicious manner. And yet the die, I realize now, had already been cast – the die which would forever sever me from Douglas.

While he prepared coffee, his consort and I hung about the dining room. Stan, animated by his wine – but not so animated as to express the faintest interest in my regard – began to ramble about subjects that, after a while, I could no longer make out, for I'd become transfixed by the features of his countenance, a countenance which – betrayed by candlelight – now infected me with panic. I blurted out: Tell me, Stan, does Douglas know everything about you? Stan smiled and replied: Sure he does – why? I said: I don't mean just the fun side. Stan knocked back a few more glugs, then let his hackles rise: What the fuck are you on about? I said: I think I've been precise enough. He narrowed his eyes, as if to imply that I was a bilious cunt; but his umbrage no longer signified. My mind had reeled back to the evening when Douglas had taken me out and elaborated about his burgeoning romance with Stan, and I, then struggling to come to terms with Matthew's closing tragedy, had asked which of the two – Douglas or Stan – did the fucking. And Douglas had replied: Does it matter? Now, I could tell, it mattered badly. Because, from my brutal experience of sunken cheeks and gaping eyes and slackened mouths, I understood, beyond question, the truth about Stan – a truth which, I could tell, had been withheld from Douglas. But before I could inform Stan that his deception of my friend amounted to a mortal crime, he had thrown down the gauntlet of his napkin, and stormed out in search of Douglas.

If earlier, unable to overhear the lovers' culinary antics, I had been reduced to conjuring mouth-to-mouth scenarios, this time I was spared any such need to fantasize, for Stan was suddenly yelling: Get that vicious queen out of the house! A plate went crashing to the ground. But next, Douglas, shadowed by Stan, was walking back into the dining room, carrying coffee upon a tray; and absolutely silent. There are moments which, when we recall them, we recall slowed down. This was one such. Douglas poured from a shaky spout; then, with unswerving good manners, handed me my cup. Now he went round the table and handed a further cup to Stan. Yet as he sat to pour his own, he asked, almost sadly, whether Stan would mind leaving us for a while. To which Stan replied: Be my guest, love.

Up to that night, despite the differences which, in our passage toward manhood, had cropped up between us, Douglas, I am certain, had prized our friendship as much as I had done. I remain equally certain that – because he wasn't combative at heart – his aim had been to defuse the possibility of a rift between us. Yet when he attempted to rebuke me for having meddled in affairs solely of concern to him and Stan, I lost my calm. I told him that such affairs concerned me utterly; I told him that Stan was a liar of the wickedest kind. Douglas said: What makes you say that? I said: You haven't had him tested, have you? Douglas said: I see no need; I trust him. I said: You trust him with your *life*? He said: Why shouldn't I? I said: Are you a moron or something? Douglas said: Look George, I appreciate your concern, but I'm a big boy now; I'm sorry you don't like my lover, but my choice is made, and regardless of what the future may hold, Stan stays; we're committed to each other. And then he added: Just because Matthew's dead doesn't mean you have to drag the rest of us down.

And that was the split-second at which my anger swung away from Stan for the sake of Douglas, toward Douglas for the sake of Matthew. How Douglas could have taken so little heed of the hell which had befallen Matthew; indeed, how Douglas, in his deluded arrogance, could have imagined that – simply by dint of believing himself loved – he was in some regard exempt from the dangers that glared at the rest of us, well, it was farcical. Of course, I didn't give a bugger if Stan were to peg out; but if it turned out that he'd contaminated Douglas, that was another matter entirely. And yet – who knew? – maybe this was just a further manifestation of Douglas's suicidal side, a precursor to what, since those days, has become known as Barebacking. Or maybe it was a reflection of my own bitter, grieving hardness, which would not make allowance. But it no longer matters. Because next, I walked from that house into the windswept dark; since which time, neither Douglas nor I has made any attempt to rekindle contact. Yet, a few months after the fracas, I did hear, third hand, that Douglas had been spotted at a jazz concert in Hammersmith, looking well enough himself, but flanked by some character who looked like a cadaver.

Looking back to our rupture, I would say that, in its dismal wake, came the phase when – adrift between gloomy certainties about the future and gloomy doubts about the past – I floated without present for a while, then sank to such a trough of mindlessness as to suspect that I was running out of words to define my plight. Old friends, by then, were acting strange, and shaking their heads, and telling me that I had changed. And I would say to them: Well, something's lost, but something's gained. Because, though I'd looked at life from both sides now, from win and lose, from up and down, still, somehow, it was only life's illusions that I recalled. And those friends, so patient, so forbearing, so full of bounty (yet secretly so full of their own romances), would sigh profoundly, as if resigned to mourn the loss of me – even before the rocks of disaster had properly been dashed.

I fondly imagined, when probate was granted and Matthew's flat was snapped up, that I might travel. But, in the event, I travelled no further than the cupboard where I kept luggage; for, no sooner had I clambered up a ladder than my gaze fell on the jar containing ashes. I remembered the blonde bombshell in the kittenish jumper, and thought: Who needs to hang on to cremulated junk? But nor could I quite bring myself just to chuck it out. I lacked – as with the posthumous perk of Matthew's amphetamines – the heart. So I tried to think back to the last occasion when, it seemed to me, we had been happy. Venice had come too late for that. Paris had been dampened by my own diagnostic drama. Had we ever been happy dancing at some

London club? Never entirely; not if I'm frank. And then, amid
the recollective jumble, I realized that the best last time that we
had had, had been – shamingly enough – at the last Gay Pride.
Knowing what I knew now, *that* would have been the point at
which I should have liked for Matthew to have died – on the
crest of the noxious wave, before drowning into blindness. And
so, after an early April shower, I ventured in his car toward that
vaguely verdant land, that former scene of gnarled historical
romances which, though forbidden, hunted down and bludgeoned, remained old and strong and beautiful for all of that.
No bars, no stands, no ice-cream vans; no balloons nor bunting;
no unholy drag-queens; not even a crucifixed harbinger of
bereavement-counselling. Just trees in bud, and a hillock of
grass. I unscrewed the plastic jar, loosened the mouth of the bag
inside, and poured the flakes to the ground – neither glad nor
sadly, just automatically, as if carrying out the motions of a task
that should have been effected ages back. But then, once I was
done, my head grew oddly lighter, briefly brighter, and my
hands, at last relieved of the full stop of Matthew, dumped the
container in some borough-council dustbin. Let's not get too
heavy about it. Plenty of urns, still weighing five pounds, end
up consigned to a fate of suspensive dots on the Circle Line.
Ask the Lost & Found. Remains by the ton-load. So remember: any time you fancy a little harmless scattering of (not seed,
but) ash, I'm your man.

I was back where I'd begun – pissing away the hours in grotty
clubs, and feeling no more optimistic about my chances of a
new personal start than I felt condemned to the same old
impersonal scenic drudgery. And yet, an alteration of significance *had* occurred during my sabbatical; for, not long after I'd
disposed of Matthew's ashes – indeed, if I'm honest, a bit too
soon thereafter for my selfish liking – the very drugs which I
had failed to obtain on his behalf became, to widespread

hallelujahs and hosannas, available in this country. But the god-sent medical advance which, in America, was already being hailed as the beginning of the end of our collective downfall, gave rise, in the dungeons where I then wandered, to various ironies – the most perceptible being how certain exemplars of the pink miasma, men formerly as fantastic as they had been unattractive, who, with the collapse of their blood-counts and the collapse of their vanities, had grown altogether gentler and humbler, now, as fast as they reviewed their likely lifespans, also began to pat their blossoming guts and fondle their biceps and revert to their erstwhile attitudes: Sod you, mate, I'm back. A second irony was that, as Western advocacy-groups began to chart a drop in infection-rates within the queer faction, and the compass-needle of the scourge veered from the more developed colours of the map toward third-world ones, such as Africa, and the searchlight of concern became directed at the broader het-erosexual landscape – though never at the murky boundary of heterosexual buggery – the overview became that queers, against the tragic odds, but with tragicomic élan, had bounced back to the vanguard of fashion. And while I personally derived scant comfort from such tabloid theorizing, I did derive prac-tical relief from the thought that, if this trend really *were* on the downturn, it was as well that Kelly should find himself at the heart of the Big Apple, where tabulations were most advanced, and prognoses most to be trusted, and the malediction of our age most likely, in the first instance, to be vanquished. That was my thought at the time. But I was thinking in a capsule – because Kelly, as it happened, was already back in London. Banged up in a lunatic asylum.

These are the facts which – later, gradually – I was able to glean from Hunter: Kelly's outset in New York could not have been more promisingly aspected. Within weeks of his arrival, he had buckled down to a series of high-powered financial exams, which, despite his apprehension, he passed with flying colours; so, when his salary, already substantial, more than doubled, and

480 ~ Paul Golding

the further glitter of incentive-bonuses began to pour into his account, he decided to relinquish the modest sub-let in TriBeCa to some high-school friend of Hunter's, and remove, instead, to less modest surroundings: a parlour-floor apartment in a brownstone on Gramercy Park, complete with personal gym and Puerto Rican housemaid. But before taking possession of this glamour-pad, Kelly had the place remodelled by one of the most desirable decorators about town: an erstwhile porn-star with hot entrées to the former husbands of the ladies who then lunched. The photos which eventually I saw of the finished product made plain that Kelly's taste had reached a sort of landmark; he had landed at his terrestrial version of paradise – the fantastically slick type of environment for which porn-stars can (not whistle, but) wank – arrayed with multi-mood lighting, and all the latest techno-funk, and remote-control blinds, and a marble urinal, hand-carved in Carrara, and sprauncy great sofas, creamy with the textures of luxury, and expensive investments in contemporary art, such as a monumental platinum portrait, presiding over the fireplace, of Kelly sitting on the deck of some bay, shot naked from behind. And yet, those testaments to his new affluence were always unpeopled, barren, like sets awaiting action, or scenes from some architectural digest – evidence of a lifestyle that had not got off the ground; as if Kelly, trapped in some inchoate hinterland, had been documenting a potential as yet unrealized, rather than what he had already achieved, which, by most people's standards – certainly mine – was triumphal.

Anyway, when Hunter had visited – frequently, at the start – the pair had lived it up, dining without reservation at the most happening restaurants, and breezing with other A-Listers past the cordons of the hippest clubs, and dressing like precisely what they were – a head-turning couple – or, in high summer, like lovers bare-chested on the ferry to Fire Island for parties at the Pines, where they hedonized under the stars and scored all the right powders. Kelly had by now – and who could blame him in the circumstances? – outgrown the attractions of Holland Park, and preferred to have Hunter fly out, frequently and Club Class, to the splendours of Gramercy. Yet, with the passage of the months, Hunter proved less inclined to cross the Atlantic than Kelly might have liked – not because, as Kelly supposed, he was reluctant to have air-tickets constantly bought on his behalf, but because, being a model-turned-actor with hopes of magnifying his profile, he was determined – even at the price of doing tedious voice-overs for British radio and performing bit-parts in urban pubs – to earn an Equity card. That, I would say, was the initial obstacle to arise between Kelly and Hunter – the fact that Hunter's professional agenda, and his ancillary refusal invariably to indulge his lover, made Kelly feel not wanted enough; which, when one thought about it, had been Kelly's problem from the start – since even before those infantile indignities endured at the behest of Kindergartenmeister.

This is why, when Kelly became withdrawn, and turned inward for comfort, Hunter ascribed no great significance to the silence; merely took Kelly's apparent sulks in his pragmatic stride, and accepted them as part-and-parcel of being involved with a man who, though tremendously adult in many regards, remained – at some level that Hunter trusted would correct itself as Kelly grew in trust – a bit of a baby-diddums. But those slumps, for which Hunter advised Kelly to seek uppers, were sometimes countered by flights of such activity as to soar into the manic, episodes during which Kelly would take himself on euphoric shopping sprees – splurging, for instance, on seven identical pairs of shoes at a single swipe, so as 'never to run out' – or racing in the middle of the insomniac wild to faggy hotels where faggy rooms were provided on an hourly basis to strangers in pursuit of anonymous night-time succour. But Kelly did not, I do not think, partake of the luscious fruits on offer to punters of his desirable type. Rather, in a bid to while away his panicky blackness, he would telephone Hunter with what must have felt like promiscuous malice, and wake him, and berate him for always being absent, and taunt him with the gargoyle of adultery – ruses which, apparently, Hunter found less worrying than tiresome, for, being stalwartly attached to my brother, he believed Kelly to be lacking in insight rather than dishonourable of character. And yet, after a while, and despite the ties that bound them, Hunter grew weary of those harangues at unreasonable hours, desisted from picking up his handset, and instead would leave Kelly to blather down the answering device – a strategy which brought no benefit to either party; for, while it still prevented Hunter from achieving his main goal – to sleep uninterrupted – it led Kelly to the conviction that Hunter must be out on the tiles. Later, as I tried to pull together the pieces of that fractured puzzle, I came to realize that it would have been during this phase, during those forays into deranged nocturnal havoc, that Kelly, deprived of any conversational comeback by Hunter, would have left messages on my machine – reciting, for instance, that creepy nursery rhyme: A-tishoo, A-tishoo, we all fall down.

But then Kelly would enter a phantasm of respite, an abnormally calm normality, during which he would beg, across weeping continents, forgiveness from Hunter, making out – with the guileful sort of dissemblance which I have since discovered to be 'syndromatic' – that he didn't know what had got into him, that it must have been a clash between his uppers and his downers, that he was just being childish; and he would confabulate all manner of further plausibilities in order to dissimulate what was *actually* the trouble. So Hunter would forgive, and try to be understanding, and almost relax – for a while – until the calls resumed (from Wall Street sometimes, so that Hunter couldn't play the 'sleepy' card); and those calls would come with a tyrannical new stubbornness, during which Kelly would deny having phoned only a few minutes back, and flip, from a humour which Hunter described as loving, to sudden, irrational, choleric outbursts, threatening, at one point, to go back to his apartment, and – unless Hunter promised to get his arse to New York *now* – neck a bottle of sleeping tablets.

Which is exactly what happened. Hunter refused to be bullied into submission, and Kelly submitted to the downers. Yet when, twenty-four hours down the line, he awoke to find himself (not flanked by a contrite Hunter, but) caked in vomit and blood and convulsed by stomach cramps, he further sabotaged his position by resorting to the very person whom he should not have done – his boss at the bank – who came to the quick rescue, had Kelly efficiently hospitalized, sat outside Intensive Care until being told that, despite the hepatic damage wrought by the barbiturates, a liver transplant wouldn't be required, and then, while Kelly convalesced, found a means – professional burnout, no doubt – to terminate the whizzkid's contract. Yet Kelly, once apprised (by fax), could not have been more delighted, not just because he'd lost any further interest in the world of finance, but because, now that he found himself without profession, he could devote himself wholeheartedly to professions of love. Hunter could tell that my brother was suffering a nervous crisis, but the truth of Kelly's nerves was more critical than anyone – save Kelly, perhaps – could have imagined. His brain had become neurologically compromised. He was going barmy. But not to worry, he baited Hunter: he still had a good stash of tablets up his batwing. So, at last, Hunter, worn down, made Kelly promise to stay put in Gramercy Park, and boarded a flight to JFK – on stand-by. But by the time that, delayed and jet-lagged, he let himself into the spectacular apartment, Kelly, with spectacular ill-timing, had jetted back to London. He had forgotten his promise to Hunter. Hunter put down his bag and rang Holland Park, where Kelly began to fulminate down the line, refusing to believe a word of Hunter's argument, insisting that Hunter must be round the corner with some shag, and claiming that nothing mattered any more, that their relationship was beyond salvage, that he would show Hunter. But instead, Kelly showed up –

faking an American accent – at a psychiatric clinic in W1, where staff, unaware of the patient's pathological reality, kept him under drugged surveillance for forty-eight hours in the hope that the 'psychotic' glitch would pass. Meanwhile Hunter, finding, on his return to London, the deserted studio looking like a bomb-site, tidied up and vainly waited, until – having no better means of tracing his absconded lover without resorting to gossip-mongers – he resorted to the police for guidance. And it was while the police were failing to make headway with their enquiry that he rang my number, and, in a state of understandably slurred anxiety, relayed a few of the details which go above.

Kelly was never, in fact, tracked down, because, just as he'd taken himself to Bedlam of his own volition, so his doctors (once the medication had returned him to a mirage of balance – in other words: a British accent) were powerless to prevent him from taking himself, just as voluntarily, out. And thus he staggered, bewildered and dishevelled, back to Holland Park, where, after six weeks' separation, Hunter was shocked by the fragile state to which his lover had sunk. Kelly, however, wasn't feeling in the least bit fragile; he was feeling horny as fuck. But Hunter resisted such puerile come-ons, and instead seduced my brother in an altogether subtler, kinder manner: by assuming the role of the one persona whom, in truth, Kelly had always craved more desperately than any blue-eyed answer – a mother who loved him. Hunter fed the boy, reassured him that everything was going to be all right, helped him into the bath, put him to bed, told him to shush now, and tucked him up. Only once the grown-up child was safely asleep did Hunter dare sneak off in search of food supplies, leaving a note by Kelly's bedside, explaining that he'd just nipped down to the local supermarket. But during the ensuing quarter of an hour, Kelly woke up, took the note to amount to yet another fucking lie, and soared into a paranoid panic. When Hunter got home, he found Kelly naked in the kitchen, squatted over the counter, trying to wrench open a window in order to throw himself out.

Now it was Hunter who panicked: dragged his lover back inside, wrapped him in a dressing-gown and blanket, bundled him into the car, strapped him up, and raced through a battery of amber lights to the very hospital where, as luck would have it, Matthew had languished but a few months back. By some further stroke of lucklessness, Dr Nilson happened to be on duty at the time; but, surmising from the admittance form that Kelly must be my brother, and having extracted confirmation of this hunch from Hunter, he pretended not to be chuffed at having been granted the last laugh.

If anything, the deal proved even more unfunny for Kelly than it had done for Matthew, because, though admittedly the virus hadn't ravaged his sight, it had so undermined his co-ordination, and blighted his grey matter, as to render him a liability both to himself and to others. He had reached that fearful pass where – never mind not trusting Hunter – he could no longer trust his own mind. I think that the flashes of lucidity, because they were so painfully stark, pained him more than the stretches of insanity, which, at inopportune moments, could prove quite enlivening. When a priest took it upon himself to steal into Kelly's cubicle for an introductory chat, Kelly had apparently shouted: Get your hands off my arse – which sent the chaplain scarpering and the rest of the ward into paroxysms. But, black humour notwithstanding, the tone of the production was not exactly enhanced by Nilson's assumption that I must be lurking in the background, too cowed, after our clash over Matthew, visibly to include myself in this new cast, yet doubtless still indulging in my favourite brand of skulduggery, such as running for direction to the likes of Farquhar. But Nilson was mistaken. It was Hunter who – though dismissed by the medics as an expendable front-man, and a Yank at that – bore, single-handedly, the brunt of that scenario. I was not a witness to Kelly's dénouement; I was merely kept abreast of his unravelling by Hunter, who, knowing that relations had, for quite a time, been strained between us brothers, preferred to proceed gradually – by which he rightly meant at whatever pace Kelly might want. For, just as, years ago, I had opted not to involve myself in Kelly's finale, so Kelly had opted, at the last, for the proximity of an emotionally-inclined lover over the proxy of any blood-tie. Nevertheless, he knew that Hunter and I had been in touch, and was made aware that I would go to him whenever he asked – which, ironically, may explain why my offer wasn't taken up at once. For, the longer I could be kept away – seemed to be the loopy rationale – the better Kelly could feign to himself that he was faring in the futile struggle against encephalitis. Pride was ever better than a fall. We all know that.

But medically, of course, he stood no chance of feeling proud. All the requisite tests were carried out, with predictably crushing results, and the patient was given six weeks on the outside – less (said Nilson) if Kelly was lucky. Dementia was a bummer. But because – despite our fraternal disparities – I understood the inner workings of my brother, I advised Hunter not to divulge to him this long-awaited blow from Damocles, which would have been greeted with (neither dignity nor stoicism, but) mythical outrage. Acceptance had never figured in Kelly's vocabulary. Defiance was what, for such an improbable surf of time, had kept him afloat the deathly tide. Indeed, he had managed to survive for so long since his 'assault' at the hands of the Knife, that no impartial party – such as Nilson, for want of a more impartial example – could have pretended that Kelly hadn't had his statistical share of time. I mean, it wasn't as if he were seventeen and starting out. He'd *had* a life – and, by all accounts, a not half bad one. But I knew otherwise: Kelly's life, ever since that criminal first diagnosis half his lifetime back – and whatever the advantages of his beauty and his resilience and his money – had been wrecked by the perpetual spectre of this looming nightmare. And now, just to exacerbate matters, he managed, with symptomatically lucid cunning, to buttonhole some earnest young neurologist and wrest from this well-intentioned imbecile the brutal truth, which instantly – and dementedly – Kelly dismissed as a brutal lie: he had *always* been asymptomatic; were those doctors *retarded*? And thus, quaking with ire, he rang Hunter and ordered him to take him back to Holland Park. And Hunter – who was sick of being treated joylessly where, in any case, there was no joy to be had – pressed Nilson for six weeks' supplies, ran down to Pharmacy, raced up to his lover, and obliged. But still Kelly claimed that there was no need for me to go round. Our parents were another matter.

Everything with those two bastions had occurred one step after it should have done. Kelly had come out to them when he should have been apprising them that he was viral. And now that he was on the way out, he merely wanted them alerted to the possibility that that his immune system might be down – as if to warm them up; as if he were too frightened of (not dying, but) betraying a love which he had never really had; as if he felt to blame for that cruel reversal whereby a natural begetter is pre-deceased by an unnatural son. I myself suspected that our parents must, in their creeping bones, have feared that something might be awry, because, on the occasions when they rang my flat, never once did either of them make so much as the most vague allusion to an epidemic which, by then, was loudly acknowledged worldwide; a plague which, horror most horrible, had even claimed casualties around the social edges of their highly respectable branches.

At any rate, a couple of evenings after Kelly had been returned to Holland Park, Hunter called me – from the bathroom, with a tap running – to say that Kelly was fretting about our parents, and to ask what I thought should be done. After all, they would doubtless still be labouring under the impression that Kelly was thriving in the Americas, amassing credit for himself and bringing, by extension, credit to the family. And yet, perhaps because Matthew's death had been so blessedly unencumbered by genetic third parties, my instinctive reaction was to advise Hunter to leave our parents out of it: given their hopeless values, they were bound only to aggravate matters. But

Hunter's grunt made plain to me that mine had not at all been the sort of answer for which he had been holding out. What he had been hoping was that I might have offered to pave the dolorous way on Kelly's behalf. Yet, before I could plead a chance to think about it, Hunter had to go. Kelly was calling out.

Precisely because I disliked my father more than I did my mother, I was relieved that it should have been he who was fetched to the phone by the butler. When I told my mother's husband that I wasn't ringing for a chat, he presumed, with a scoff, that, for a change, I must be angling for money. But I advised him to pay careful attention, because this wasn't the moment for sarcasm. I didn't have the patience to rewind to the chronological start – to the Knife and McManus and the rest of the antediluvian backlog – so, skipping the hernia which had turned into a time-bomb, I fast-forwarded to Gramercy Park, and, with it, to Kelly's first attempted suicide. Must-say-all-sounds-most-unlike-him, said my father – which went to show how well he knew his elder son. I added that, as a result of the overdose fiasco, Kelly had been sacked by his bank. Now my father clammed up; yet I could tell that, in his shallow version of profundity, he had imagined this profound irrelevance to have boiled down to the crunch. So I set him aright: I said that Kelly had been ill for a considerable while, but – my father broke in to demand why, then, was this the first that he'd heard on the matter. Because, until quite recently, Kelly had been a . . . symp . . . to . . . ma . . . tic. I really spelt it out. Fair enough, but asymptomatic of what, exactly – depression, work-worries? I made it clear that Kelly was rather beyond work-worries: he was riddled with the virus. Did I mean cancer? No, I did not mean cancer – nor yet did I cite the (ob)noxious acronym: my father could do his own mathematics. After a pause, he asked how ill, then, *was* the lad? My understanding was that he was dying. Good heavens; this was all a bit sudden. Quite. Anyway, my father couldn't think of how on earth he was going to tell my mother. I said: That's for you to decide, but I shouldn't be too long about it. He said that it was hard to take in everything that I was telling him at once. Harder for Kelly, I replied – who'd lost his marbles. His marvels? His *marbles* – as in mind. So presumably, at least, he wasn't suffering. On the contrary: he was suffering madly. Where, at Mount Sinai? No, back at his flat in London. Then *surely* the situation couldn't be *so* bad. Look, it was as bad as was imaginable: Kelly was at home for the simple reason that, bar stuffing him with tablets, there was nothing left to be done. Dear-oh-dear. And was I managing to look after him? He was being looked after by Hunter. Hunter-some-nurse-or something? Hunter, I established, was Kelly's lover. My father's snort was mucous with revulsion. He instructed me that I relieve forthwith this Hunter chap, and do my Christian duty by my brother. I told him that I'd go to Kelly when Kelly asked. A fine state of affairs, observed my father. And now he wondered whether I reckoned that *they* should fly to London. I suggested that, to start with, he might break the news to his wife; then, find out how Kelly felt about the prospect of their coming – and *try*, while he was at it, to be half-pleasant to Hunter, who, besides fielding calls, was acting in **loco** *parentis*. My father didn't find this comment in the least bit funny. I told him that it had merely been a statement of fact. But Lord only knew, he repeated, how he was going to tell my mother – brain tumour'd probably be the kindest way round. And then he left me in little doubt that I'd be sorry if it turned out that I'd been dramatizing. So I told him that any further questions on this drama should be put directly to Holland Park. *O tempora! O mores! In nomine patris.*

Our parents took the most part of a week to clamber down from their scandalized altitude – during which scandalous protraction I was able to inform Hunter that, despite their buttoned silence, they were in full-blown possession of the facts. I also warned him that my father, the likelier party to make initial contact, was your archetypal club-house prat – the kind of twerp who didn't drive a car, but 'ran' one – so Hunter would be well-advised to spare himself all but the most rudimentary civilities in his dealings with the man. The safest thing to do, I said, would simply be to hand the phone over to Kelly, and let *him* decide how to deal with the whole hassle. After all, when the moment came, Kelly might welcome the chance of a rapprochement; or then again (and Hunter's guess was probably better than mine), he might turn out not to give a monkey's. Next, more driven by guilt than moved by humanity, I asked whether Hunter was coping all right, or whether – on the quiet, if need be – he needed any errands done. That was real kind, he said, but he was coping just fine. Apparently, my brother's London buddies had devised, between themselves, a rota of times to drop round, because, since Kelly couldn't be left unsupervised, day or night, someone had to stand guard while Hunter cooked and cleaned and rushed about. And who, I asked, *were* these friends? (Perhaps Douglas figured among them. But no.) They were Craig and Lee and Gary and Shane and Kevin and Darren and – no need for Hunter to elaborate. I understood with clarity: those names pertained to long-enlisted agitators from the viral subculture. I myself had only ever known such characters by sight, and would most likely have failed to recognize them now. But I did briefly wonder – because Kelly pointed so dismally in the downward direction whither they too were bound – whether keeping vigil over my brother mightn't represent for them a mental trial, or whether, alternatively, such vigils might present them with a perverse satisfaction – because they, at least, were bearing up. Who knew? Perhaps Kelly's foul-weather friends, once so bellicose and strident, were now – thanks to the medication that Matthew had been denied – quietly thriving. Perhaps they'd been prescribed a wealth of fresh new hopes for their formerly impoverished lives. I was never to find out.

When Kelly found out that his father was on the line, he took hold of the receiver and slammed it down. Within seconds, our mother had jabbed an imperious index into the dial, yet fared no better than her husband: Kelly told the woman to get stuffed. So my father phoned a further time, and now did toil to inveigle Hunter. But Hunter, either primed by Kelly or heedful of my earlier advice, informed my father that he wasn't about to act as middle-man, and that if Kelly didn't want to talk, that seemed fair enough. Yet my father, importunate to the last, persisted with some explanation about concern being only natural, especially in Kelly's mother; to which Hunter replied: Not our problem, Sir – and hung up.

But whereas, on hearing of his dismissal by the bank, Kelly could not have been more delighted, now, hearing his lover dismiss my father, he flew off the handle. The (ill)logic of it all was beyond fathoming. It had become impossible to comprehend quite *what* Kelly wanted: whether to honour or deride, whether to live or die. And so, for the first time since the couple's asynchronous return to London, there ensued an argument – presumably because Kelly's furious reaction to his lover's use of the term 'sir' had exasperated Hunter, who, despite his phoney self-abasement, had been doing his genuine best to stand up to my father. But when Kelly hurled an alarm clock at Hunter's crotch, and scored a bull's-eye, the dispute erupted into a slanging match; for Kelly, raging beyond acrimony now, and scarcely in control of his insults, would not have seen reason if it had hit him between the eyes. Hunter, concerned about the rising volume, attempted to settle his lover, and slipped him, in the context of some yoghurt, a tranquillizer – which Kelly spat out. Now Kelly spat at Hunter. But next, the adversaries were silenced by a neighbour, hammering at the door outside, telling them that it was half past bloody midnight, that upstairs he had a newborn child – wide awake, thanks very much – and that unless Kelly and Hunter stopped their racket, he was calling the environmental health people round, did You Stupid Dipsticks understand? So Kelly, who understood entirely, yelled back:

Who gives a toss about your stupid fucking brat, you stupid cunt?

And thus, inevitably, the noise-pollution brigade rolled up – a couple of pubescent eco-fascists who threw the rule-book at Hunter, and whose sympathies were soon revealed to lie (not with Kelly, whom – never mind Care in the Community – they said should have been hospitalized, but) with a reasonable couple who, reasonably enough, were trying to nurse a babe in arms. And so it came to pass that, after another, equally unproductive battery of calls from my parents, Hunter grew too anxious to continue looking after Kelly at Holland Park; and yet, proportionately wary of returning him to the snare of Nilson's clutches, he sought assistance from some Hivvy helpline, which pulled its finger out and organized to have the patient transferred by silent ambulance to a hospice for the terminally ill, on the verges of north London.

And that's when I received the crucial call from Hunter. Although – since Kelly hadn't strictly asked for me – Hunter wasn't strictly calling on Kelly's behalf, he nevertheless felt that I should have an update. My brother's condition had apparently worsened overnight, and he was no longer very articulate; but he'd been moved to a private room, where he seemed calmer. Hunter's personal opinion was that if I wanted to see my brother before he had faded too far, now would be the time. I said that I would try to get myself to the hospice tonight. Visiting hours were flexible; you could come and go much as you liked. But I went at once.

I remember thinking, as I inched my way through some gridlock at Marylebone, what a covert mercy it was that this meeting should be occurring neither at the local hospital nor at the studio in Holland Park – both of which places reminded me, more than of Kelly, of Matthew. The roads, as I drove northward, seemed to grow quieter and narrower and lusher; became almost countrified. You could glimpse snatches of field flashing by, between red-bricked houses. The season was autumnal; but the weather, sunny. Leaves were curling to chestnut; trees, not yet skeletal. When the district grew Conservative – residentially chuffed – I presumed that I had gone too far. So I drew up beside a headscarved Barbour-jacket with a lollopy basset, and asked if I had overshot the mark. No, the woman barked, I was headed the right way: little further up the hill, then do a sharp right; signpost outside. I resumed my rise, and suddenly had arrived. Death-homes can never be nice, but Kelly's hospice, with its ivy-clad façade and gravel drive and spacious car-park, seemed, when all was said and done, preferable to the hospital in which Matthew hadn't had to die – and where Kelly, now, wouldn't have to either. I parked, got out, and, as I scrunched toward the entrance, tried to order my mind. Had I come to apologize? I told myself that I had come to say goodbye.

All these establishments – once inside – seem much of a muchness: it's about the general feeling of entrapment rather than about individual trappings. And yet, I was so accustomed to nurses by now, and so adept at masking the apprehension that invariably led me to their antiseptic environs, that I cranked up a smile akin to the smile which one would sport if one had come to see some girlfriend who had spawned a bouncing nine-pound son. The only difference was that I wasn't carrying flowers. Still: I was pointed in the direction where I could find my brother. Straight down the corridor. Room 9. The door was shut. I took a breath, and rapped.

When my knock was answered, I was greeted by a blinding burst of light from some midday garden. The silhouette which let me in, though a mystery to me, must have belonged to one of those zealots from the subculture, because it instantly stepped back, turned toward the company, and – as if announcing some tardy messiah – proclaimed: Never gonna believe it Kelly, but your brother's come at last. I heard a further visitor hasten to stand in the background; and then, as I stepped into the room, clocked him looking daggers at me. I can't suppose that I smiled, but I did manage to say: Hi, Kelly – to which Kelly, after a couple of splutters, replied: Couldn't have chosen a worse time. He mumbled something about Hunter. Dagger-Looks couldn't resist informing us that Hunter had gone for a crap, but Kelly, deaf to such refinements, ordered: Getimback – which prompted Silhouette to raise an eyebrow, designed to signify: *See* what *we've* been putting up with? And then, after a sneer-of-sorts, both those censorious marvels waggled off in squeaky jackboots. I closed the door behind them, and sat myself on Kelly's bed. Wondering.

Kelly, despite Hunter's daunting forecast, didn't strike me as on the brink of dying – not compared with Matthew. For a start, he was sitting up; and, though admittedly thin, nonetheless looked robust. He was tanned rather than sallow. His chest and shoulders were still defined. He was sporting a white singlet, dreamboat-style; and his hair, which hadn't been cut for a while, further abetted this salutary aspect. There was no sign of drips or tubes or the usual surgical artefacts. He smelt, as I approached his smoothly shaven face, of almonds. Now he twisted to rummage for something – a cigarette packet – which only served to corroborate my suspicion that Hunter had jumped the valedictory gun. I noticed that my brother's dextral biceps had been blazoned with an indigo tattoo – of our coat-of-arms. How typical, I reflected, that, in his inability fully to embrace either of his ruling cultures – the highly homosexual or the highly bourgeois – but in his enduring struggle to effect a truce between those two inimical factions, Kelly should have hit upon a compromise that so deftly resolved the dichotomy of his snobbishly yobbish requirements; a solution which, while remaining élitist, could yet appeal to the masses; an emblem which, combining as it did modernity and tradition, could alternatively be adjudged either hip or grand – and sexy into the bargain. I said: That tattoo's fantastic. He said: Province. And then he said: Town. But his words were frustrating to understand; for, though his speech was loud enough, his diction had been robbed of consonants. His tongue was lolling about, seemed to be giving him trouble; perhaps it was ulcerous. His mouth hung out of joint, as if the hinges of his jaw were coming apart. Those gleaming caps, whose smiles had earned him so much favour in the past, had, since, receded at the gums. He handed me his cigarette, and said: Light – but not in the manner of a baronial brat; rather, like a close accomplice. His hands, which I had long admired, were now more elegant than ever: delicate and tremulous and fine, like the hands of an ailing heir who hadn't lifted a phalanx in his life. Not a liver-spot in sight. I gave him his cigarette – duly ignited – but asked: Are you sure this is all right? He didn't even dignify my qualm with a reply; and I, despite myself, could not but admire the hauteur (born of foreign primogeniture) which had resurfaced at the last – as if to erase his (even more foreign) flirtation with passing guttersnipes. After he'd inhaled, I heard his chest begin to rasp; but he didn't seem to notice, or perhaps had grown inured to the sound. I said: Here's your ashtray – and propped it on his lap. But then, after a gradual exhalation, he reverted for a moment to the language of our childhood, and whispered – as if wanting to impart a secret which no grown-up could understand: *Quiero morirme.* He wanted to die. And tell me – all you palliative luminaries out there – what do you say to *that*?

Someone knocked at the door; and next, without waiting for an answer, appeared in a black fisherman's jumper. Despite the flickering nature of our first encounter, high on a nightclub balcony in another life, I took this someone to be Hunter – an assumption which, no sooner had he addressed my brother, was confirmed by his accent, which I'd forgotten was attractive. Now he approached to shake my hand, and, after the briefest hesitation, gave me a kiss – an initiative which, elsewhere, I might have considered a bit of a cheek. But here, the cheek felt fitting; for, though Hunter and I had only dealt in telephonic snatches, yet we had dealt with more than platitudes. And besides, I was indebted to the man, not just for having taken the burden of Kelly off my back, but also for not having stirred further trouble between us already troubled brothers. Kelly said: This is Hunter – to which I replied: Yes, you introduced us years back. Hunter smiled. Now Kelly mumbled something which I failed to catch, but which Hunter interpreted as: He wants us to be friends and help each other. Kelly nodded like a sage, then added: Afterwards. I said nothing; but, inwardly, I promised to myself that I would try. Hunter said that he was leaving us guys to chat for a while, we were bound to have lots to catch up on; and as I watched him quietly close the door behind him, I reflected that it might not be so hard to observe this tacit vow.

No sooner were we left in private than Kelly began to cry, spilling tears onto his vest and ash onto his blanket. I took away his cigarette, stole a drag, and crushed the stub. He dropped his head into his hands, and apologized. I'm sorry, he sobbed – really sorry, really am. I stared at him perplexed, but, although he stared back, I couldn't really tell how clearly he could make me out, for his eyeballs were darting in manic spasms. I handed him a handkerchief, and, while he blotted at his sadness, I looked down. The blanket on his bed – baby-blue plaid – I recognized from way back. On the far side of the mattress, I caught sight of a fluffy bunny-rabbit – doubtless a regressive totem from some friend oblivious of the irony. I asked: Where did that rabbit come from? Kelly didn't answer, but picked it up; and, as he coddled the toy, began to suck his thumb. It was a sorry sight; but – reverting to his earlier remark – I reassured him that there was nothing to be sorry about. He looked, at length, away, toward the sky. The moment had passed. I told myself that I had come to say goodbye. And yet – before I came to that – I needed to make my peace with my brother, to atone for this relationship which, though hardly helped by the viral chasm, had never exactly amounted to an idyll of fraternal love. I didn't want to blame our parents, because, even as pretexts, they felt too trite. Nor did I want to blame myself, because, in truth, the onus didn't feel entirely mine. So instead, I gathered my brother's slender hands, and held them up at a formal height, and acknowledged something which, occasionally (such as when he'd brought me that platter of glass), he'd told me in the past – a thing that I had never had the courage to say back, but which, at this moment, I meant with all my heart: that I loved him. He smiled in tranquil silence – as if the fact had scarcely needed utterance – yet I could tell that he was gratified; pacified. I was suddenly choked up. I got to my feet and pretended that I had to rush, that I was badly parked. He asked when I'd be back. I said: As soon as I can. And then, I kissed him like a man and scarpered like a coward – having omitted to say goodbye.

Throughout that fitful night, I struggled to persuade myself that the omission hadn't much mattered; that, beyond my declaration of love, Kelly wouldn't have cared one way or the other. And yet, when I awoke, turning and sweating and long before sunrise, I also knew that the scene could not be left untidy. So I resolved to head back to north London at once, in advance of the early-morning rush-hour, and hopefully before any other visitors showed up. I drove under a flock of dove-grey clouds.

Except for a hazy crimson light, the section of the hospice where Kelly was harboured still lay in shadow; but, as I crept unseen by nursing eyes through the lugubrious gallery, I recognized that the woeful, incoherent moans which conspired to upset the fatalistic calm were issuing from my brother. I reached the lintel of his tragedy. He was supine in the dark, and, despite the senselessness of his senescent vowels, clutching at his bunny-rabbit. I sat on a chair beside him, switched on a lamp, and whispered his name in order to determine whether he were compos or absent. Something, some mishap, had occurred during the night – a seizure, perhaps – for he'd since become embroiled in tubes and monitors and bags. I noticed evidence of a catheter; its accumulated urine, tannin-brown. Kelly must have known that I'd arrived, because he struggled to stir, but I tried – on account of the apparatus – to discourage him. His hand endeavoured to convey that he'd forgotten about the gadgetry. But then his hand confirmed that his neck was in the vice of some paralysis. As he sucked his thumb for the meagre sustenance of saliva, he appeared indifferent to – beyond – my company: I could have been anyone. And yet my very superfluity felt welcome; for it seemed – despite machinery which declared him to be alive – to declare that he was already beyond those confines, already headed outward, already de- livered to the mental flight which heralds eternal inaction. But next he grew fretful, and seemed to want to hold my hand, which he grabbed with pressing hardness. He mentioned Hunter. I had the feeling that Kelly wanted to direct me down- ward, beneath the baby blanket. I dreaded the possibility of some hitch with the catheter – what if a nurse couldn't be found? His other hand released the rabbit, let it tumble over the cot-side, and now began to fidget frantically, as if his pyjama- cord were too tight. And then, as he unveiled the bedcovers to lead me to the root of the crisis, I realized that what he wanted, despite the presence of the catheter, was a hand-job. His erection was absolute, but I was absolutely not Hunter. I couldn't recall ever having seen my brother's genitals – still less in a state of arousal. I said: You'll have to wait till Hunter comes. Kelly gave a shudder, as if he'd suddenly understood the extent of his blunder. So then I said what I had come to say – that I had come to say goodbye. There ensued a burning blank, during which he appeared to need to concentrate on some- thing vital. And then he nodded with slow, heraldic gravity, as if in understanding, as if in benediction, as if in acknowledgement of the farewell that was our last.

I fled, covered in guilt and pity and relief and thanks; jumped into the car, raced to the gates, turned a sharp left, and went smack into a van. Nobody was hurt, but my car was a write-off. And that's when I realized that this – this prang, not the ashes – represented the real, full stop of Matthew. I took the

Underground home and scribbled a note to Hunter, which I delivered through his letter-box by hand, telling him that I'd been to see Kelly but wouldn't be going back, and that I'd be grateful if he could let me know when my brother had died. Two days later, he rang, to say that Kelly had been given the last rites just in time – in time to tell the Reverend to make it snappy – and that the coma had only lasted a few hours. There had been no struggle. I didn't bother with the morgue: I hadn't bothered for Matthew, and I wasn't about to do so now.

Kelly's funeral was held at a convent in Kensington, run by nuns whose Spanish counterparts were meant to have educated my mother. But both she and her consort elected – despite the intervening week's grace – not to attend their firstborn's final Mass. When I rang to let them know that Kelly had died, my father, after a pensive humph, replied that there was really nothing, beyond announcing the death in the local paper and, of course, praying for the poor lad, that he and his wife could do now. My mother would be too distraught to cope with the flight, and my father's foremost responsibility was, as it had always been, to her. Besides, they felt sure that they could count on me to represent the family; and then, perhaps come home for a while. But since that brief exchange, I've had no further dealings with either of my parents – the owners of the house which, though never really home, presumably remains the place where Kelly and I were so stupendously brought up.

The ceremony, in accordance with Kelly's lifelong vacillation, was conducted in two languages; but perhaps this bilingual eccentricity had been intended as a (futile) gesture to our meretricious mother, whose English – among various other things – left something to be desired. Yet it was Hunter – not I – who with impressive savvy managed to dig out a Spanish priest from some lacklustre suburban parish, a cleric less moved to directing the spiritual steps of well-shod heels than to guiding the faith of trampled espadrilles – Hispanic immigrants who lived by their (not legal status, but) menial wits. In almost every way that

I can think of – including his crumpled tunic – that cleric was the antithesis of the lofty frankincensual rule; a man of (not godly raiments, but) the people. He made you think. And perhaps because I wasn't as personally involved – or numbed – as I had been at Matthew's funeral, I was able to view Kelly's obsequies with a greater acuity. Yet, for all of my detachment, this ritual, too, proved a paradoxical experience – akin to consulting a medium; where, while not wholly believing, you need wholly to believe.

Though Kelly's friends had taken pains to adorn the church with their conception of panache – petals scattered round the sanctuary; rainbow-coloured bows tied around the candles – it would be unjust to pretend that either their embellishments or the quality of attendance was on a par with Matthew's requiem at The Lady Chapel. And yet, despite the linguistic mish-mash, and the musical efforts made by some corralled herd of *a cappella* nuns, the verbal substance of Kelly's hybrid mass may, on balance, have won out. There is a force peculiar to foreign accents: their very oddness – like a note that jars – seems to compel one to listen the harder. And no sooner had Kelly's priest begun to declaim in his Castillian version of the English tongue than the congregation became rapt. His words were delivered with a courteous, almost courtly formality, as if he were addressing the lace mantillas of some antiquated hamlet on the hills above Soria, rather than the gathered scalps of a desultory homosexual smattering.

Hunter, as chief mourner, chose the first reading – a passage from Ecclesiastes. But, because I was overly engrossed by his timbre, which seemed to carry in its wake faint traces of the Deep South, I only recall the punchline: Consider the work of God; *who* can make straight that which He hath made crooked? I remember thinking: Lordy, *you're* no arsehole. But next, a bolshy-looking Brummie, trying to make some kind of virtue out of a red biker-jacket (left epaulette decked with cock-strap), trundled up to the lectern, thrust his thumbs inside his waistband, and delivered an excerpt which his aggravated diction rendered markedly less comprehensible than that of the Spanish padre – who was next to take the stand. Unlike Fr Frank (whom I'd discouraged from sermonizing), Kelly's priest chose to direct a few brief words to the gallery. For even though – as he readily confessed – he had never met the deceased, whom he called Michael, he was aware (presumably from Hunter) of various factors pertaining to Kelly's life. He didn't waste words with paeans extrapolated from glamorous photographs, nor with testimonials from people who had never fully known my brother. Instead – doubtless inspired by our parents' absence, which, even by *his* kind standards, must have epitomized the kind of Catholic conduct for which he had least time – the cleric chose to dwell on (not the Fifth commandment, Thou shalt honour thy father and thy mother, but) on the true definition of the word Family – as exemplified by (neither biology nor nuclear advance, but) *us* – those who had come together for this mass. Next, he made some passing reference to the Apostles at the Last Supper, which, given my dubious role in Kelly's all-male tableau, flushed me to a self-conscious shade of embarrassment – an embarrassment only heightened when the lengthy Eucharistic prayer began; for, given that it was recited in Spanish, and given my mother's conspicuous cop-out, it suddenly felt directed at *my* blushes. But I pretended otherwise. Kneeling at an isolated side-pew, I sneaked a few glances at the rest of the kneelers around. I caught heartfelt sight of Douglas, who, by the final blessing, had evaporated – presumably in a bid to make plain that, gone as Kelly was, and unforgotten as he might remain, yet I myself stood unforgiven for my unforgivable stand against Stan. The only other person whom I recognized was the Fluke, Kelly's first employer from the days of the Square Mile, who, though smitten by my brother from the start, had never once given vent to his desires. Of all the mourners apparent, he, the Fluke, looked, I would say, the worst stricken by this lousy upshot, this unconsoling prize for his undeclared passion. I had, of course, been looking forward to a quick glimpse of old Kindergartenmeister; but it turned out that the dedicated nappy-enthusiast, with whom my soft-hearted brother never quite lost touch, had visited the hospice (armed – *of course* – with that iconic bunny-rabbit), and, after being granted licence by Hunter, taken off on some long-scheduled trip to (where else but) Thailand.

On my way out, while the coffin was being hoiked onto a hearse, I clocked Hunter being cultivated by three disgraces, munching goatees whose condolences seemed, more than to hearten, to leave him cold. As I tried to circumvent them, Hunter grabbed me by the shoulder. About the crematorium, he asked: did I want a lift in his car? I told him (not that the crem was a dump, but) that it was where I'd taken Matthew, so, if he didn't mind, I'd prefer to give the place a miss this time. Hunter let me off with merciful lightness: the important bit, he said, had already kinda happened. So this is how we left matters: he was flying to New York in a couple of days' time, to jettison Kelly's ashes on the beaches of Fire Island and deal with the contents of the apartment, which he was hoping either to flog to the landlord or off-load through some auction house. The stuff was too cumbersome for London, and too laden with emotional baggage – which is when I understood why Kelly, from his deathbed, had wanted to apologize: he'd left everything to Hunter. But Hunter promised to give me a call as soon as he got back. We could get together; have supper; something.

After my brother died, people thought it in poor taste that I should have taken up with his former lover. But it made perfect sense to me, and it made equal sense to Hunter. Yet, when the latter rang on his return to Holland Park, I can't have had the faintest notion of where I was headed, which was dizzyingly skyward, sunward, toward the ultimate.

If, for our first date, I suggested Claridge's, this was not from a desire to dazzle. My choice had more to do with the fact that, given the complications which had sullied my relations with my brother, I hoped, now that he was beyond sullying, to amend the record by paying tribute to his past, and convey to Hunter – in suitable surroundings – how, for all the cracks in Kelly's emotional structure, he had, at heart, been a man of quality, a man of class, and a good one. Given (as I still maintain) that I knew my brother better than anyone who – whatever the colour of their eyes – ever chanced to cross his path, I felt compelled to explain that when, in later life, Kelly had elected to feign the obverse of what he'd really meant, this had not been from anything so pat as duplicity of character. Kelly's rationale had worked in a subtler, more contrary manner. His obfuscations had been devised to suss you out, almost to hoist you with your own petard – the implication being that, if you couldn't take the trouble to read between his lines, well, that was your – not his – lookout. But so exigent a stratagem was, predictably, bound to backfire, for most people (and why should they not have done?) simply took Kelly at face value, just as he, in his youth, had taken plenty of others – including Kindergartenmeister. And yet the consequences of pretending, for example, to be a lout, were invariably disastrous, because, with depressing regularity, Kelly would find himself sussed by the genuine article – a real lout – and jilted back into the same old scenic sludge, ever-reduced to dangling the bait of his attractiveness in the hope of hooking some fresh, but ever-unlikelier, catch – at least until Hunter showed up. With Hunter, I would say that Kelly did succeed in his quest for being intimately valued; and certainly he achieved a state of real emotional balance, based on precepts worthier than the common homosexual standards of youth and cock-size. And I therefore wanted, not just to thank Hunter for his conjugal kindness to my brother, but also to acknowledge that such unstinting devotion had not been for nothing; for, beyond the obvious advantages of having inherited Kelly's money, Hunter's greater benefit lay with the good fortune of having brushed hearts with a man who, whatever his pretences to being a bog-standard faggot, had been anything but. Kelly had always shone out, had always gleamed with a high calibre.

When Hunter appeared at the restaurant, he was wearing a dark velvet suit which I recognized as having once been made for my brother – though worn with a T-shirt rather than a tie, and too tightly, which I liked, for it lent him a perversely touching sartorial provenance. I also recall, secured to his broad wrist, a dress-watch which Kelly had been given when he'd turned twenty-one – a memento that only seldom had he sported, not so much because its bracelet slopped around, as because the timepiece had never been fashionable enough for his fashion-conscious liking. It was the kind of flashy accoutrement which he'd only really donned to show those whom, despite appearances, he had reviled, such as homo-medics at red-ribboned galas. And yet, those outward links with my brother's past, combined with gestures and expressions that Hunter, being a suggestible actor, had absorbed along the osmotic line, now seemed to endow him with an intriguing air of Kelly – a presence beyond his own presence – which struck me as doubly striking. And Hunter, despite the numerous discrepancies that had always existed between us siblings, nonetheless chose, sitting across the candlelight, to invest those enduring resemblances which I had long ago dismissed as mere genetic *faux-amis* with a fateful significance; auspicious. It was as if, being together, we were somehow drawn closer to Kelly's substance, for we reminded one another, in a manner less sinister than nostalgic, of that departed third party whose spirit seemed to hover about us. And yet I suspect that Hunter and I, while lent solace by this mysterious triangular circumstance, were also, in our separate ways, trying to make reparation for some niggling, former inadequacy; because, at a bleak, unspoken depth, we both seemed to regret that, in our respective bonds with my brother – whether fraternal or amorous – Kelly should always have regarded himself as the disappointed party. But Kelly's emotional hunger had been devouring. Impossible to satisfy. And since, secreted amid my dusty historical archives, I still kept a working key to the rusted gates of the panorama which had nourished that voracity, I was able to lead Hunter back to the distant era when Kelly and I had been children on our plenteously negligent island; feed him details which answered questions hitherto unanswered; untie the ravel of influences which had conspired to bring about the fabulously exotic but ultimately faulted creature that had been my brother. And Hunter, from his side, was able to provide me with clues as to the crucial but elusive piece for which, in order to complete the puzzle of Kelly's life, I still hankered: that amorphous enigma pertaining to his final chapter.

Hunter, by this stage, hardly matched my reminiscence of him at the nightclub of our first encounter, when he and Kelly had been smoking spliffs over a balustrade. He'd grown bulkier since that time, and greyer, and wiser about the eyes – alterations which only ennobled him in my own sight. He may conceivably have been on steroids, but I refrained from asking – not so much because I didn't want him to turn out to be like every other über-faggot, but because, just as my relationship with Matthew had been founded on the potency of words, so my connection with Hunter was forged on the back of another, less definable, power: an unspoken, unspeakable, erotic attraction. For the first time in my life, I can honestly say that the symbiosis of this sexual tide was a mutual one, because Hunter (it soon enough transpired) had become as captivated by me as I was captured by Hunter – captivated beyond the literal constraints of any dictionary, in any edition or language. And I, over and above the bounds of brotherhood and chocolate and the charms of the outdoor life, quickly came to recognize in Hunter my perfect counterpart – my canopy, my trunk, my buttress. For, when we were banished to the desert of our exile, he became the snow on my Sahara; and if ever my burning hopes

threatened to scatter like dust across my track, he became the
moon that shone upon my path. He – and he alone – is what
made a man of me. Hunter took me to regions which – oh –
never in my dreams would I have dreamed of charting. Regions
proximate, perhaps even integral, to Paradise. But that, as yet,
was all to come.

At our first dinner, after I'd told him the things which I had
planned to do, and further reassured him that I no more
resented his having been named Kelly's beneficiary than I
minded having been made Matthew's, Hunter, in return, told
me things which I had always doubted. He told me that Kelly
(whatever his public disclosures about my Negativity to those
who, for his pains, came to call him a public-school wanker)
had privately loved and admired me, and been grateful that,
despite the 'corrective' parental backlash, I should have cajoled
him into coming out to our mother and father; and that he had
been grateful for my backstage spat with the Knife (an anecdote
relayed to him by Douglas, Douglas in better times); and that he
had been grateful for my company when we'd been to see
McManus, and for my efforts to provide him with a friendly
dentist in the days when dental friendliness had become like
gold-dust. But, above all, said Hunter, Kelly had been grateful
that, despite our many fall-outs, I should have desisted – at least
until Hunter compelled me to act – from letting the cat of his
condition out of the bag of confidentiality to roam unchecked
along the branches of our native but complicated socio-
religious jungle. It further transpired that my brother had
defended me in the teeth of those who had bitched about my
idleness and stand-offish attitude, telling them that they understood nothing, that I was just a late starter – but that they
should watch out, because my time, he predicted, would come.
In relating these particulars, of course, Hunter made evident
not only that he knew considerably more about me than I
might have imagined, but also (by having abstained from
betraying whatever vicious truths about me Kelly must also

have divulged) further made plain that, on the occasions when he spoke, he did so sparingly, tactfully, and – unlike many an American – quietly.

Right from the start, which felt less heady than profound (for, perhaps thanks to Kelly's peculiar intervention, we were, peculiarly, spared the shrillness of infatuation in favour of the low-pitched certitude that underscores the big-time), Hunter and I travelled hand in hand. But, aside from that shared and shining clasp, we wandered unaccompanied, for no member of our former circles would have countenanced, even by dint of their incidental presence, condoning what we recognized to be perceived as a most unpalatable twist on the sweet theme of romance. Yet the collective chill which descended on our shoulders neither came as a great surprise, nor, indeed, did it feel like grave punishment; for, by the time that this socially inclement season had come round, Hunter and I were lucratively furred against any Siberian blizzard. We could do as we liked; and, while we did precisely that, we flourished without those who didn't like it.

Whatever the conjecture surrounding our respective pasts – Hunter's with Kelly, and mine with Matthew – our adjudicators were misguided. For, just as my friendship with Matthew had never, despite its transcendent emotional power, overstepped the platonic mark, so Hunter's bond with Kelly (I was later given to understand) had not, beyond the initial throbbing fortnight, been erotically manifest. It had been brotherly. *That* (and not his encephalitis) is what had caused the fear of infidelity so to erode Kelly's inner landscape. But why hadn't the physical side of Kelly's bond with Hunter worked out? I never cared enough to enquire. I was keener, if I'm honest, to banish the memory of my brother from a kingdom that I now considered mine, and return him, for eternal safekeeping, to the innocent gardens of our childhood. But perhaps he and Hunter had been too similarly cast; or perhaps some kind of kibosh had been put on the proceedings by Kelly's medical crux – about which, I happen to know, he was always up-front. And yet, whichever the answer, it hardly mattered now. Hunter and I made sure of that – Hunter, by imparting to me lessons which never in a million years would he have taught to my brother; and I, by teaching Hunter lessons only ever imparted to me by the secret voices of my mind, the hornèd demons of my underworld.

Notwithstanding the distorted theorems of outsiders, there did exist practical parallels between the positions in which Hunter and I found ourselves, not least the fact that both of us had cared for young men who had died. But, precisely because we both understood the worth and the waste of all of that, we never really bothered to discuss the (dead) matter. We simply – and wordlessly – dwelt in the conviction that we'd acquitted ourselves to the best of our separate abilities in our separate trials. After all, Hunter had only known of Matthew through Kelly's sketchy outline – a portrayal which, this late in the day, I felt no more inclined to paint by chronological numbers than such an effort would have interested Hunter. As for Hunter, well, I was soon enough to know more about *him* than even Kelly might have liked. Besides, had we ever laboured to swap forensic accounts, I suspect that the essentials of our exchange would have overlapped; for, various as are the strains of that inhuman virus, the manner in which it mortifies humanity never varies much. Flesh is flesh; ashes are ashes; over and out. And yet – whatever else we may have done – Hunter and I did succeed in bringing to fruition Kelly's wish that we should help each other. Afterwards.

Although Hunter would never have been so crass as to regale me with the verdicts of Kelly's subcultural buddies, I did myself fall prey to a few surprises – surprises delivered by the likes of Connor, who immediately took my 'nasty affair' to amount to an offence against (not just my brother, but) Matthew; and Sukie, who, despite her claims to erotic worldli-ness, small-mindedly proposed that the incestuous under-currents of my *ménage* would enthral an analyst; and Cara, who, when I sought to describe the miracle which had been visited upon my life, did nothing so revealing as overtly to react – but nor did she express the remotest curiosity in meeting Hunter. As for Douglas, I can't suppose that he ever found out. Nevertheless, the consequences of this new ostracism did pay dividends which I would call constructive. For now that, thanks to my prominence on Hunter's horizon, his intention to settle in London had mounted from the resolute to the absolute, he was propelled to pursue the grail of an Equity ticket with still greater passion – but without further need to fret about whether a particular job happened to pay badly. Meanwhile, from my own perspective, his professional absences allowed me to seek to honour Matthew's request that, after he were gone, I try to be productive – because life was over in a flash, darling. So it must have been around this time that, in order to clear my biographical decks before making a fresh (and final) start, I began to think about attempting to exorcise – through my own base words, and for my own base sake – the spectres of my past.

Beyond the parallels which I've tried to describe, it further seemed as if Hunter, by sharing his proceeds with me, which he did lavishly, was in some unwitting manner making good what I'd interpreted as the cause of Kelly's lachrymose sadness: namely his repentance at having snubbed me financially. And equally, it felt as if, by dividing my own legacy with Hunter, I were coddling Matthew's nest-egg within the warmest, closest nucleus of our unnatural brand of family. So, although the symmetry wasn't absolutely Mozartian (insofar as Matthew and Hunter had not themselves been brothers), yet there remained an orderliness about our set-up, a balance to the design, a rightness that led me to reproach myself for nothing. Besides, given Hunter's life-saving advent, who *needed* psychobabble about roads less travelled, or pamphlets about SAD, or mystical spookery by Teresa of Avila? No; this time there would be no Maybe about it. Nor regrets. Nor goodbyes. Just a shapely design. Shapely as fuck.

And thus, on to the big-time. Hunter and I continued living apart, but because – given the fates of both Kelly and Matthew – the studio had become afflicted in my mind with undercurrents of fatality, we tended to sleep at my flat. I would, of course, occasionally go over to Holland Park; yet, on the occasions that I did, this was less from a polite desire to show reciprocity (since Hunter and I were reciprocal in all the impolite ways that mattered) than for reasons of straightforward practicality – such as when, owing to some work-assignment, he had to be up at an ungodly hour. For, unless one of us happened to be out of London, never in our idyll did we spend a night apart.

Dreamily, sporadically, we discussed the possibility of joining domestic forces in a manner which, while befitting our mutual dependence, would equally suit our independent styles. We even considered buying a couple of flats – adjacent, so that neither of us would need to feel hampered, but with an internal layout whose very unorthodoxy matched our outward standing. My personal preference was for a sole, interconnecting door (a secret panel, inserted, say, in a bookcase somewhere) through which we could conduct our forbidden passion without recourse to the public landing. And yet, in such romantic scenarios, it tended to be I who did the conjuring, while Hunter just nodded and mulled and smiled in that adorable way that I can picture even now; for I suspect that his pleasure at humouring my fancy, and at hearing about the lure of objects which I considered covetable, was greater than the real appeal of my elaborately gilded plans. Hunter was, in essence, spartan; he could happily have dossed on a haystack, and therefore shared more common ground with Cara than Cara herself might have liked – she of the high seas and mountain peaks and tropical rainforests and indifference to objects inanimate. But I'd been raised by people whose conviction it had always been that one couldn't call oneself discerning, still less a gentleman, unless one had tasted privilege from the start, unless one had soiled one's infant romper-suit while crawling across the silken archipelagos of a Persian carpet; so perhaps this coursing desire for luxury was, to some extent, endemic in my blood. And yet, it cannot have been entirely, for, no sooner had Kelly been able make his own decorative mark than he rejected our parents' faith in old-fashioned artifice, opting for more artful, more modern, more brute surroundings. No matter: regardless of whether Hunter was more attuned to Kelly's aesthetic than to mine, one issue remains beyond doubt: on the erotic front, I won hands down.

As if to indulge another of my fantasies, we toyed with the notion of adopting a (not child – since having been one felt like quite enough – but) pair of dogs; perhaps even litter brothers. Yet, despite the broad terrain of our concurrence, we approached the canine prospect from diametrical angles. Hunter favoured the bigger breeds, not from anything so glib as the fact that they're considered more 'masculine', but because he objected to the principle of species being 'bred down'. He liked his dogs to run wild, to run and run in spirals ever wilder, so that he could admire their bounding grace from afar – as if their hearts beat closer to the course of nature than to the whimsy of man. One afternoon, while browsing through the Kennel Club bible, he mooted the possibility of deerhounds; yet I – while entirely appreciating the elegance of their snouts, and the sweeping purity of their ancient line, and easily envisaging them cutting an Arthurian swathe around the Serpentine – nevertheless preferred the idea of pets better suited to city life, such as dachshunds, not least because I didn't think that I could handle clearing up after large animals – an incidental which would never have bothered Hunter.

But while we mused about such abstractions as moving flats and rearing dogs and embarking on a lifestyle which, while drawing us closer, would nonetheless keep us tantalizingly apart, we proceeded with our actual lives: his acting, my writing; our disparate days and nights united. In our twilit leisure hours, we would take ourselves beyond the stringent social perils of my erstwhile companions, and out, into an altogether broader, safer, more unsocial type of playground: lowly clubs where not even the lowliest of Kelly's former cronies seemed to venture; or, if ever they did, merely cut us — which suited us nicely. For, irrespective of whether our stigma had been inspired by financial spleen or moral bile, the matter that inspired *us* regarded neither finance nor morality. Our complicity was, as you know, based on — nourished by — quite another value: true lust, by which I mean a lust not incompatible with love. What is more, we recognized this nourishment to be finer than the finest cream, which, even as it tempts the palate, quietly threatens to go rancid. We valued it for what it was: a substance both unfathomable and everlasting — ambrosially rank, aphrodisiac, like truffles — designed by the fates to serve our debauches ad infinitum.

We would generally phone one another from our separate hideouts, and, depending on our mood, either agree to meet somewhere for supper, or, more usually — since food, however scrumptious, was never at the true source of our hunger — convene in one of those dank Gomorran caverns which, like fungal hybrids, had lately sprouted along the seamier parts of town, in derelict wharves and obsolete factories and under abandoned railway arches. And yet, when we did make a date to converge at some restaurant, Hunter tended to arrive in advance of the proposed hour, for he was fastidious about tables, and liked to claim for himself an illicit sort of vantage, the better to command a widespread view without widely being seen back — except, that is, by my feasting eyes. And, at these feasts of ours, he would order food which, though considered fine, I considered 'charged' (admittedly not asparagus, which would have rendered his urine over-pungent, but still): oysters, preferably of the fleshy, Portuguese variety; or king prawns, whose brownish offal was his favoured part; or brains, or tripe, or trotters, or tongue, or, on summer eves, nasturtium salad, the blooms of which he would push into my mouth. It was the most romantic thing imaginable. But even more romantic is the manner in which he sometimes chose to surprise me. One of his tricks was casually to unfasten a couple of buttons of his frightfully conventional shirt – to reveal, underneath, the steel-ringed cleavage of a leather harness, or his hairy torso punitively bound in twine, or his nipples being bitten by tit-clamps. The very glimpse of such obscenities used to make me hard; but he, as if wishing to verify that his effect had been desired, would further press a foot against my crotch. Once, at a solemn Russian restaurant where the rest of the diners looked like executive cardsters (i.e. bored out of their skulls), Hunter leaned back, and, vaguely wondering what I thought of his new belt-buckle, encouraged me to peer across and down – to discover that, inside his baggy jeans, which were already undone, he was wearing (not underpants, but) leather chaps, so that the exhibit of his genitals doubled as reward and punishment for my erotic gluttony. I don't recall much in the way of conversation passing between us at such visual banquets. Our best, most meaningful exchanges took place during our private acts; but those dialogues were never strictly verbal: they were expressions in another idiom, on another register, and with quite another end in mind. They were onomatopoeic declarations between our open body-parts; devoid of inhibition, yet almost chivalric in their balance. You begin to see why Hunter was my perfect counterpart, the answer to my prayers, the late but long-awaited prince of my desperate imaginings.

Clubs; caverns; catacombs. Various of those cellars met our base requirements, but the one which I recall with basest gratitude is Skum, particularly on Friday nights, when the dive was pungent with depravity and the weekend spread before the throng like some mud-spattered bacchanal. Hunter and I preferred to kick off around midnight, to give the field a chance to fill out; but, in contrast with our fixtures at restaurants, here it was always I who first pitched up, for he was never late by less than half an hour. It was a point of dishonour between us – a point that used to drive me frantic: the pulsing wait, the surging desire, the need to keep my rising damp under wraps. But the feeling was fantastic. A fantastic preamble to the constant affirmations – over and over and over and over – of our love.

Having got myself a drink, I would weave through the gathered morass, round leather slings hanging from rusted rafters, and past sooted arches leading to anonymous depths of carnality, eventually to settle for a niche beneath some glaring shaft of light, partly because Skum was a place where vampires thrived, but mainly so that Hunter could clock me once he'd arrived. When, in slow due course, he had, it was always the same, weird thing: those assorted voluptuaries whom, but seconds back, I had almost admired – hookers who hooked at no charge, and groomers in guerilla-drag, and waders with masks, and slaves with collared masters, and peacocks without fans, and turkeys without stuffing, and bears with the souls of mice, and mice with the hearts of giants, and giants with dreams of reduction, and whipping boys without endowment, and bootlickers with purple tongues, and voyeurs, and poseurs, and dreamers without hope except in darkrooms – all seemed to blur into an irrelevant mass as my sight became filled with my lover at last, my lover glowing like a moonlit warrior above the swarming multitude. I would watch him wander through the abyss and amble, unglancing, toward one of the bars, from which he wouldn't budge until he'd downed a slammer and grabbed a bottle of something. Only then might he resolve to embark upon his voyage toward the cove where I happened to be harboured, but never would he sail straight up. Not just like that; not likely. He would hold back, take his taunting time about it, for there was a quality at once predatory and tame about Hunter, as if he could never quite decide whether to drop, or weigh, anchor. And I couldn't help but notice, while he navigated through the vacillations of this ambivalent charade, how people used to drool over his weatherbeaten handsomeness, people whose drools seemed invariably to announce: Not fucking bad. But I know – just as he knew – that his appeal, however massive, was in no small part indebted to our love, for a primal confidence had been poured into our alliance, a confidence which, naturally, all those marauding primates wanted to savage and devour. Anyway, Hunter would always loiter in the distance at the start – against a facing wall, for example – from which he would gaze at me askance, until I, in my turn, felt disposed to let him catch my eye. And then he would nod, but only very casually, like a stranger in the night, merely exchanging glances, merely wond'ring what were the chances before the night was out. My lover. My accomplice. The selfsame new one every single different time.

I would never bother to nod back, nor yet would I, beyond this simulated gamble which was really a foregone triumph, allow my eye to rove from his wide-thighed stance. Rather, I would gloat over every part of him, meanwhile goading – and having him gloat at – my own parts. I recall how, once, while he was rummaging in his trousers, some fool mistook his craving for a craving of another type, and next, was up there brandishing a cigarette at Hunter – an offer that struck me as funny, because Hunter didn't smoke tobacco. Yet, rather than politely decline, Hunter politely accepted this enticement, and further accepted a light, and then – to my unutterable satisfaction – wandered over, planted the filter in my mouth, and coolly returned to the base where he'd been anchored. Such were the steps, the moves, the preambles to our seductions.

Other times, he would jostle round the edges of the mire, and I would do likewise, in a courtly overture which always rendered onlookers baffled, for, by this stage, they could no longer tell whether Hunter and I were trying to avoid, or approach, each other. Finally, of course, one of us would have to cross the shadows, and the one to cross would generally be I – not because Hunter was too self-possessed to take a plunge which (seem though it might like the first) might well have been our thousandth, but because it gave me the greater satisfaction to confound the leering public. And then I would go up, right up to him, and he, without a word of introduction, would engage his sordid tongue with mine – often as not, presenting me with a pill in the transaction. And then, everything would change, because we would just stand there, in the middle of oblivion, making contact only with our mouths.

Hunter's mouth was never dry – not when I was around. His upper lip, though full in profile, had no actual bow, which I loved. His eyes: they weren't just blue: they were blue-black; but, caught in the violet rays which sporadically lurched about the haze of that unreal environment, they would glow a milky white, nacreous, astral. His eyebrows had of late arrived at that beautifully poignant pass where there had sprouted, through his fair lushness, nostalgic hints of ash. And his skin, which on my bed was honey, would turn, bathed in this lunar light, a rich mahogany brown. Everything became exaggerated. And once the pill had done its stuff: imagine. Imagine how we stood together on those nights, swaying against the storm, as if shipwrecked on some godforsaken island. Sometimes he would squeeze me round the ribs so hard that he would raise me off the sand. And then, putting me down with a shrug intended to convey that I was just too much – when really what he meant was that I was never enough – he would peel away my top and stuff it somewhere; and I would unbutton his shirt, and tuck it in my waistband. And then he would kneel in front of me, and I would close my eyes, because I wanted to forget those creeps whose glares made plain (not that they liked to see my conquest conquered thus, but) that I'd made a mockery of their submissive fantasies. Hunter was the best cock-sucker in America – which is saying something. He knew exactly when to pause, exactly how to save you from the precipice of orgasm – and without cheating with his hands. These he would cross behind his back, like a supplicant. But then the supplicant might choose to stand. And next the supplicant might elect to assume command and drag me to the bar with my cock hanging out. Which suited me fine; because, as far as *I* was concerned, we hadn't even begun to be disgusting.

We would drift, woozy with lust, around the seeping flagstones of that club, feeling like two bodies which had only just discovered one another, like lost souls found, with everything to gain in a single sleazy night. Now he might decide to halt at some darkened, unexplored new cove, some inlet yet to be corrupted, where we might resume our advances. And that's when I might start to work his arse, and knead it with a spittle-coated hand; because my lover, who had the arse of arses, was man enough to let me fuck him whenever he, or I, desired. And thus, if it took my fancy, I could get myself behind him, hold him tight, and piss into his bowel, void into his innards my whole hot bladder, wash him with my shower. And he, once I was done, could, with an expertly gradual contraction, let me withdraw while still withholding my golden gallon. People, as they watched and delved into their flies, would sometimes nudge each other – people who can't have had the faintest notion of what we were actually up to. But then Hunter would strut off to the bog and spill my contents out, and come back, and, of his own profane volition, ruck his jeans down, so that yet again I might do as I liked. And I could crouch; and – since abasement before my idol brought me nothing but pride – make a virtue of my vice, and suck on his cock as it hardened, and slide, the while, a couple of fingers up his arse, and press them in my direction, toward his front, until I could feel his prostate pulsing. And then he might decide to piss into my gob – one controlled shot at a time – so that I could imbibe his copious waters gradually. And once he thought that he'd run dry, I could rise and return the last wave of his stream into his mouth. And while he lapped himself up, I could always feel his tightened hole expand, which meant, if I wanted, or he needed cooling down, that I could grab his chilly bottle from his hand

and serve it up his arse, easy as that, right in front of all my rivals, his admirers, who, by now, would be crowding round us in a bid to steal a scrap of what they could not in their lives have had – our rapture. For when, earlier, I credited Hunter with having made a man of me, I mean that he banished from my consciousness any lingering uptightness. My original shame was vanquished; it vanished in the safety of his company – to the degree that, had my lover felt so inclined, he could have turned me inside out and no harm done. I may have had all those stellar drugs to thank, but *you* have to believe me when I thank my lucky stars that – at long fucking last – I'd found a better-fitting fist than any glove.

I remember how, on one occasion, as we staggered out of Skum, gleaming with sweat and parched by some upper, a stranger stopped us at the coat-check to confess how horny he had found the way we two made out – a blandishment to which Hunter, with rare, possessive umbrage, replied: We don't *make out*; we're lovers. The stranger, whose brow shot into a primmish arch, seemed surprised that we, an established item, should choose to exhibit, and thereby cheapen, our love in such a dump; but how could he have been expected to realize that, lacking as we did the acknowledgement of society, some part of us felt reduced to soliciting the next worst thing – the acknow-ledgement of the subculture?

Our cab-rides to my flat were always chaste. We would collapse at the back like playmates who had swum too hard, chests panting, shoulders touching, as if gathering strength for the next race to the waves before the sun went down. We never talked during those intervals toward the coming paragraph, never questioned where we might be headed, never asked who might have what in mind – less because, ostensibly, Hunter and I spoke different languages (his faucet being my tap, and his tub being my bath, and my autumn being his fall, and all of that) than because, profoundly, we understood our mutual needs without the need to verbalize. And yet there did, by anybody's definition, exist a word which he was incapable of grasping – although, given its Tongan root, I suppose he can be excused. And the word was: Taboo.

Back home, we might choose to do nothing – flop into bed and crash out – but, more likely, we would pour ourselves another drink, or take another pill, or snort another line, or drop another tab and drift from room to room in virtual silence, as had become our virtual habit. Sometimes Hunter would roll himself a joint, and I would go for a shower. But sometimes, as I headed for the bathroom, he would mumble not to do that; and I, with a sigh, would bask in the relief of having found a lover who could make a command sound like a comfort. Hunter was as good a judge as you could hope to find of music which was good for fucking; but his taste – not his tact – is what steered him away from songs that I had shared with Matthew. Lyrics never did much for Hunter; he didn't care for lovelorn ballads. What moved him were hypnotic tracks, and the lull of whooshing tides, and the drums of tribal anthems, and the wails of incoherent sirens. *On Earth As It Is In Heaven* – remember that? – the kind of stuff that ravers used to play for coming down; the kind of stuff that we preferred to raise us to the next act – however unpalatable – while our clothes lay strewn like afterthoughts about.

Once we outcasts had secured ourselves within the prison of our naked paradise, we would tear our pleasures with rough strife, and, in our haste to race beyond the spurts of missionary custom, leave no deed undone: we enacted every tangle to be enacted by entangled bodies such as ours – so that our garden might never dry out, so that our realm might ever be fertile, so that our scope might grow richer than the very galaxies; because, when we two rolled into one, it was like dying and flying at the same time. And if, this late in the day, this near to the sunrise, our flesh felt too weary to live up to the violence at our hearts, we could repair that age-old paradox in a modern trice. Forget Viagra, which doesn't take effect for a whole hour.

We could sneak into the kitchen, raid the fridge, and award ourselves a cocktail of Papaverine, Alprostadil and Rogitine – injected to the base of the penis. Hunter always did himself, because it drove me wild to see him, and then he would do me, because to see him drove me wild. And next, before we'd even had a chance to laud the marvels of medical advance, we would yet again be hard, and – as if the clock had been rewound – be set, for the countless time, to return to the start.

But let me take you further back. Long before the fall of man (indeed, before the co[s]mic accident whereby he found himself delivered to this earthly planet), the ground had already been strewn with mud, and every living creature that roamed upon God's pastures, His swine and sheep and cattle, enriched the soil with dung; and lo, it was beheld that it was good to bless the fields with fertilizer. But, following the advent of Adam – whom I reckon must have looked not unlike Hunter – it was further discovered that the best manure of all, the richest of the bunch, the one which bore the fullest and most fragrant blooms in the whole Bible, was the produce of humanity. This may help explain why, in the fullness of time, Greek alchemists should have conjured solid lumps of gold from human faecal matter, and the physicians of classical Rome have cured infirmity *cum stercore humano*, and the perfumers of the Mughal have processed – from the scybala of virginal clerics – salves designed to purify, and St Marie Allacoque have ingested the stools of her ailing charges, and noblewomen of the French Renaissance have retained in their palatial households an athletic young male expressly for the task of answering nature's call in a basin of tin-plated copper, so that, once the vapours of his issuance had condensed along the vessel's lid, the stercorary elixir, which is said to have evoked the sweet musk of the civet, could be decanted into a cut-glass flask, and ferried by a deaf-mute maid to the Purple boudoir, so that Madame, in the course of her toilette, might bathe her hands and face in the precious fluid, and, thanks to its properties, which were decreed miraculous, remain beautiful for life.

And thus it was with us, Hunter and I: beautiful for life. But let's not get too recondite lest we fall between two cultural stools. You don't need to have ploughed through du Bellay's *Deffence* in order to understand what he meant by his contention that if language, once so scabrous and impolite, were to be rendered elegant, not only should it be expurgated of excess muck: verbal waste itself must be transformed into a novel form of loveliness. Nor need you be au fait with the notes accompanying the Odes of Ronsard in order to sniff what the poet was about when he described the burdensome load of his work as having been discharged. Nor need you have dipped into the moral sewage of de Sade, whose style could not have been more marquesally decorous if it had tried, to glean the significance – both phallic and phallicistic – of excreta. And nor need you be devout, or indeed a coprophage, in order to believe that Eat Shit is what the church exhorts its flock to do from birth to kingdom come. And nor need you loiter within museum lavatories in order to admire how the Messrs Gilbert and George transformed Naked Shit into most desirable art. And nor need you hail from Catalonia to know that its natives traditionally include, in their Nativity cribs, the folkloric figure of El Caganer, a shepherd who, though always discreetly consigned to the pastoral background, may nonetheless be glimpsed, breeches round ankles, in the process of fertilizing his motherland for the year to come. But should you perchance decide to venture in pursuit of what offends the faint of heart, you might, somewhere near Figueras, the village made famous by that other, painterly scatologist, Salvador Dalí, come across an even choicer Yuletide idol – a blushing nun, habit hoiked over hips, engaged in this b(anal) old pastime. So don't get arsy with me now. Too late for that.

Hunter and I had already indulged in tastelessness a million times. That's what raised us above the *mobile vulgus*. For, between

allies such as us, there was no gulf too great to straddle, no
obstacle too high to overcome, no shame too dark to exhume
and bring to light, no guilt too profound to dredge up and hold
like a pearl in need of filth for survival. So, you see, it wasn't
merely a regressive matter, this exchange of physical profanities.
It stemmed from something more enquiring: an overwhelming,
and reciprocal, emotional audacity, which rendered us at once
passive and active, convicts and judges, lackeys and masters,
martyrs and tyrants, potent friends and potent foes in one.
There was no disgust between us, no distinction between our
roles, no billing between our parts – our elbows, our arses, our
balls, our eyes, our cocks, our tongues, our fronts, our backs, our
upside-downs. Just as Hunter's waste was my gain, so my loss
was Hunter's prize. Nothing was squandered between us – no
practice, no substance, no wrong nor right. But why did we go
so extremely far? Because we must do every thing for one
another, create our unnatural product and nurture its defile-
ment. And yet our depravity never took us to a depth from
which we could not dive – even within the shallow waters of a
bath.

I recall it in slow motion, like all important things in life:
Hunter lying there like a burnished emperor, his idle beauty
framed by votive candles. I recall some soundtrack, repeating
and repeating in the background, and drops, like tears, dripping
from his lashes, and his hands crossed over his chest as I raised
a knee to step inside. I recall the sway of waves as I entered the
warm pool, the steaming font of our foetid baptism, the pit of
our cess – which is how we liked it. I would crouch over my
lover's shins and extend my hand to inveigle my knuckles in his
arse, and he, to grant me access, would arch his willing back,
and cease to breathe as my hand rose through his innards to test
the quiver of his bowel, until finally it reached the heart of his
matter, and then, either I would coax, or he would yield, the
offal of our love, while we stared at one another. And he would
gradually relinquish this ghastly shame which was my triumph,

that I might make from the indignity of his reduction a symbol worthy of the unspeakable magnificence to which we were driven by desire – an honour to which I acceded with passion. Hunter's odour was indistinguishable from mine, even before I had submerged it in the waters of our vileness. It was the soil on which we sowed the fruits of our garden, an oily soil which I would daub along my chest and thighs and face, like a savage, before kissing his mouth and rubbing the warmth of his own grit against his stubble. And then, amid the steam that rose from the muddied ripples of our Nile, I would squat over his genitals, and relieve myself over his rigid phallus. And I would lubricate him with my foulness, and writhe over my acrid fudge, and let him push his fingers under my arse, which sat splayed apart, so that he could tamper about the morass and drag my basest secret like manna to his mouth; and I would do likewise; and the taste was as it should be, the taste of elemental nothingness, the taste of mud, the taste of the place from which we came and whither all of us are bound. And then we would fuck with our foul tongues, and the fuck would be like none other, as we lay together in that bath, bound by our natural crime, the crime of animals. And then, once all had been traded between us, once we had trafficked every sense that lurks in the vernacular, we would go ahead and spunk. And then, after wiping ourselves down, we would take a sleeping draft.

We were at our apogee. We had reached the time of our lives. My words had begun to pour onto the page; Hunter's roles, to grow in stature. We were ready to merge at last, to meet the dreams which we had feared would never come, to spend our passion and our promise and our money without care or glance or doubt. It was summer. It was Monday. That night, I took a cab to Holland Park, because a crate had been delivered from Manhattan, and we needed to sort out what should be kept and what chucked out. I had my own key by then, the very key, I now suppose, which once would have been Matthew's. When I walked in, Hunter was covered in boxes and tissue and bubble-wrap, and wiping sweat from his brow, and looking disconcerted by the sight of objects which he thought should have been sold, and the absence of others that he thought ought to have come. I remember the adorable disorder which had erupted about him, the papers and the lists and the priceless junk. And I remember, propped behind some cartons, half-hidden from sight, a large picture which must have been the platinum portrait of Kelly, shot naked from behind. I could only see the reverse of the frame, and the hooks from which it would have hung at Gramercy Park, and I remember thinking how, since Kelly's invisible back was up against the wall, his invisible front was what would have faced me in another life, had I taken the shot myself, had I been there to immortalize the fact, had there never been trouble between us. And then I went to get myself a drink and have a slash, and I remember Hunter telling me to get him one, and I remember thinking that I should have pissed into a glass, and I remember flushing and not washing my hands, and I remember uncorking some wine, and shoving the neck of the bottle to my mouth, and wanting to save the mouthful until I got to Hunter, and trying not to laugh, and hurrying through the hall to reach my lover, and noticing, on the way, a note taped to the door, a memo from Hunter to Hunter: Check-up 10.45. And I remember swallowing, then asking: What check-up? And I remember Hunter looking surprised – not by my question, but by my ignorance. And I remember him, he who had never said much, saying: Check-up, you know, blood-count. And I remember whispering: Blood-count? And I remember Hunter sitting down to say: You know I caught it from your brother.

And that's when I realized why Kelly had cried at the last: because in some premonitory way – the way that is given to the dying – he'd been able to foretell that I was headed for a para-dise which, had there been any justice, should have been his in which to thrive. Kelly, the snake in my grass. And I, I who thought that I knew it all, I who knew that peanuts are a constituent of dynamite, I who knew that Screeched is the longest monosyllable in the English language, I who knew that the term Gay has become synonymous with Tacky, I who knew that to download has nothing to do with dumping, I who knew every neologistic conflation under the sun, from Scandiwegian to blaxpoitation, from mockumentary to célébutante, I who had touched the best, and seen the worst, and heard the lot, and tasted that which no-one else would taste, was left with one closing intimation:

Smell

the indescribable scent of my own death.

PAUL GOLDING

The Abomination

PICADOR

The Abomination chronicles the life of Santiago Moore Zamora, a young man born to a beautiful, emotionally distant Spanish mother and an austere English father. Adrift in a world of nameless one-night stands, living in a London of suffocating hedonism, he remembers his early years in Spain and sudden exile to boarding school in England where two proscribed love affairs set him on a course apart . . .

'A man's memory of boyhood . . .
one of the best novels of the year'
Andrew O'Hagan, *Daily Telegraph*

'An astonishing, heart-rending tour de force'
Pat Barker

'Paul Golding writes like an angel
who has recently fallen from grace'
Observer

'An accomplished first novel.
It is stylish, clever, experimental, ambitious, urbane'
Times Literary Supplement

JULIAN BARNES

The Lemon Table

PICADOR

The characters in Julian Barnes' new collection of stories are growing old and facing the end of their lives – some with bitter regret, some with resignation and others still with raging defiance. The settings range from nineteenth-century Sweden and Russia to a suburban 'Barnet Shop', where the narrator measures out his life in haircuts. In a collection that is wise, funny, clever and moving, Julian Barnes has created characters whose passions and longings are strengthened by the knowledge that, for them, time is almost at an end.

'These gracefully constructed stories are subtle, erudite, and wise; they elevate us because there are few such generous observers of humanity . . . *The Lemon Table* is Barnes at his profound, dexterous best'
Esquire

'Barnes is a top-flight precisionist, [with] the steady, pleasing wit of English comic realism, in which sheer intelligence and acute observation carry the whole production, line after line, page after page . . . *The Lemon Table*, in ways both modest and grand, helps sustain a reader's faith in literature as the truest form of assisted living'
New York Times Book Review

JULIAN BARNES

Metroland

PICADOR

Paris, spring 1969. Christopher is fully occupied revelling in first lust. Just a short Métro ride away from *les énévements*, as Toni never ceases to remind him.

The adolescent Christopher and his soulmate Toni had sneered at the stifling ennui of Metroland, their cosy patch of suburbia on the Metropolitan line. They had longed for Life to begin – meaning Sex and Freedom – to travel and choose their own clothes. Then Chris, at thirty, starts to settle comfortably into bourgeois contentment himself. Luckily, Toni is still around to challenge such backsliding.

'If all first works of fiction were as thoughtful, as subtle, as well-constructed, and as funny as *Metroland* there would be no more talk of the death of the novel'
New Statesman

'I cannot remember when I enjoyed a first novel more'
Daily Telegraph

JULIAN BARNES

Flaubert's Parrot

PICADOR

Flaubert's Parrot is a massive lumber room of detail about the great man: in it we learn an enormous amount about his life, family, lovers, thought processes, health and obsession. But the voice that tells us all this is gradually revealed to be itself in the grip of an obsession. The voice is that of Geoffrey Braithwaite, a retired doctor with a nagging need to rationalize his wife's suicide, and a more obscure compulsion to anatomize the processes of human identity.

Flaubert's Parrot was shortlisted for the Booker McConnell Prize in 1984 and won the 1985 Geoffrey Faber Memorial Prize.

'Julian Barnes' wry and graceful book, part novel, part stealthy literary criticism, traces the marks Flaubert made on a forgetting world. The writing is unfailingly sharp and often very funny, and among the best prose I have read in years'
Sunday Times

JULIAN BARNES

Talking It Over

PICADOR

Look, I just don't particularly think it's anyone's business. I really don't. I'm an ordinary, private person. I haven't got anything to say.

Introducing Stuart, Gillian and Oliver. Each takes their turn to speak straight out to the camera – and give their side of a contemporary love triangle. What begins as a comedy of misunderstanding slowly darkens and deepens into a compelling exploration of the quagmires of the heart.

'Few writers think and talk so beguilingly. This is wonderfully funny. And intelligent. And moving'
Independent on Sunday

'Quicksilver clever and allusive'
The Times

'Scintillating . . . It's funny, quick on the draw, and knows when to soften its gaze. It reads so smoothly, the pages seem to flip themselves'
Observer

'A writer of rare intelligence. He catches the detail of contemporary life with an uncanny forensic skill . . . He is, as always, a superb ironist, a connoisseur of middling, muddling, modern England'
London Review of Books

JULIAN BARNES

Letters from London

PICADOR

Since 1990 Julian Barnes has written a regular 'Letter from London' for the *New Yorker* magazine. These already celebrated pieces cover subjects as diverse as the Lloyd's insurance disaster, the rise and fall of Margaret Thatcher, the troubles of the Royal Family and the hapless Nigel Short in his final battle with Gary Kasparov in the 1993 World Chess Finals. With an incisive assessment of Salman Rushdie's plight and an analysis of the implications of being linked to the Continent via the Channel Tunnel, *Letters from London* provides a vivid and telling portrait of Britain in the nineties.

'Barnes is a rare writer . . . A fine collection of journalism – far greater than the sum of its fifteen parts'
Sunday Telegraph

'You won't find a more entertaining picture of contemporary Britain'
Sunday Times

OTHER PICADOR BOOKS
AVAILABLE FROM PAN MACMILLAN

PAUL GOLDING

THE ABOMINATION	0 330 39267 0	£7.99

JULIAN BARNES

THE LEMON TABLE	0 330 42692 3	£7.99
ENGLAND, ENGLAND	0 330 37344 7	£7.99
METROLAND	0 330 31381 9	£7.99
FLAUBERT'S PARROT	0 330 28976 4	£6.99
THE PORCUPINE	0 330 32828 X	£5.99
TALKING IT OVER	0 330 32567 1	£6.99
BEFORE SHE MET ME	0 330 30005 9	£6.99

All Pan Macmillan titles can be ordered from our website,
www.panmacmillan.com, or from your local bookshop
and are also available by post from:

Bookpost, PO Box 29, Douglas, Isle of Man IM99 1BQ
Credit cards accepted. For details:
Telephone: +44 (0)1624 677237
Fax: +44 (0)1624 670923
E-mail: bookshop@enterprise.net
www.bookpost.co.uk

Free postage and packing in the United Kingdom

Prices shown above were correct at the time of going to press.
Pan Macmillan reserve the right to show new retail prices on covers
which may differ from those previously advertised in the text
or elsewhere.